"A SUBSTANTIAL ACHIEVEMENT . . . DAZZLINGLY GOOD . . . HEARTBREAKINGLY TRUE . . .

Reading stretches of EARLY FROM THE DANCE is like attending a play in which every line is a curtain line. . . . Payne has the deepest human sympathy for his characters and knowledge of the heart; everyone in this book comes alive. . . .[Payne is] extraordinarily gifted."
The Boston Globe

"Brilliant . . . David Payne, may I say, is no longer a promising young novelist. He has proved his mettle. I've put a candle in the window for EARLY FROM THE DANCE, a witty and provocative tale of the latest Lost Generation groping for direction."
The Dallas Morning News

"A love triangle—inadvertent, inevitable, painfully bittersweet—is what concerns novelist David Payne in EARLY FROM THE DANCE. . . . A tale about the kind of passion that transforms lives."
Self

"One of those big, sumptuous novels you can sink into like a big, plush sofa. Set in the steamy, atmospheric South, it reinvents the classic plot of two best friends in love with the same woman."
New Woman

"A SYMPHONY OF A NOVEL . . .

Payne keeps us mesmerized. . . . No one has more vividly and accurately captured the *dolce vita* that young Carolinians of recent decades flocked to the Outer Banks to find."

Newsday

"There is a beautiful sustained intensity to EARLY FROM THE DANCE that carries readers along like a deep river, drawing us down into its story. Thomas Wolfe had the great talent of anatomizing the heart on the page with such sympathetic imagination that we could feel again dreams we might have forgotten, loves we might have lost. David Payne, another gift from North Carolina to American fiction, has that talent too. He makes us feel again the way we were, when we were young."

Michael Malone

"For as long as there are Southern boys who prep up North, their childhood 'buds' who stay behind to pump gas (or the equivalent) and the brassy (but inwardly sweet) girls who complicate their summers, there will be a place in out hearts for such novels as David Payne's EARLY FROM THE DANCE."

Glamour

Also by David Payne
Published by Ballantine Books:

CONFESSIONS OF A TAOIST ON WALL STREET

EARLY FROM THE DANCE

David Payne

BALLANTINE BOOKS · NEW YORK

Library of Congress Catalog Card Number: 89-32786

ISBN 0-345-36871-1

This edition published by arrangement with Doubleday, a division of Bantam Doubleday Dell Publishing Group, Inc.

Manufactured in the United States of America

First Ballantine Books Edition: March 1991

Note of Thanks

I'd like to thank the following: my friend and agent, Ned Leavitt, for his insight, his doggedness and his belief; my editor, David Gernert, another prince; Tom Robbins, Michael Malone and Larry Kessenich, who helped me see a hard thing; Randy Lombardo, for his constant fineness; my brothers, George A. and Bennett; my mother and father; and Stacy, most of all.

Also, for gifts of information, perspective and support: Lawrence Luhring and Leslie Alexander; çiğdem Önat and Arthur Housman; Letty and Bill Payne, my grandparents; Cissy Patton; Alison Brantley; Keith Nunnery; Tracy Lupton; Betsy Glenn; Kim Beaty; Nick Spinelli; Selwyn Rose; and Nedim Göknil and Ömer Borovali, who showed me the beast in a forest on the edge of the Black Sea.

This book is dedicated to the memory of
Brent Sherwin Nunnery,
1955–1976;

and to S.H.H.—
"Comme la vie est lente
Et comme l'Espérance est violente"

Contents

PART I
Stormy Monday   *1*

PART II
The Lost Colony   *169*

PART III
The Deep, Deep Sea   *469*

"For the wages of sin is death . . ."
—Romans 6:23

But "the wages of dying is love . . ."

—Galway Kinnell,
The Book of Nightmares

PART I

Stormy Monday

Adam and Jane

What might have been and what has been
Point to one end, which is always present.
        Footfalls echo in the memory
Down the passage which we did not take
Towards the door we never opened . . .

—T. S. Eliot, "Burnt Norton"

One

ADAM

Sometimes I still dreamed of him, but in my daily life I rarely thought of Cary anymore. The same was largely true of Jane, though sometimes in a restaurant or on a crowded bus I'd catch a trace of her perfume and hold the ache until it passed. But that had been another life. The old world of Killdeer had vanished thirteen years before when I'd left the South and come to New York City. I'd been eighteen then. Now I was almost thirty-two. A lot had happened. Doors had opened, I'd gone through them. I'd been almost rich and almost famous for a time. I'd watched it all go wrong. Then one day the phone rang, and across that time and distance the past reached out for me like the long arm of some ghostly truant officer collaring a wayward boy, drawing me home to an accounting I'd hoped I'd never have to make.

When I heard the phone that day I groaned and rolled to the far side of the bed, knowing that, whoever it might be, it could portend no good. The clock read noon. I noted, without surprise, that I still had my clothes on from the night before. I couldn't remember coming home—that did not surprise me either. Then I saw it, planted on my bureau mirror, a full-lipped kiss with a phone number below it and the name "Monique." It was violet lipstick. I closed my eyes as the memory of the evening came roaring back.

I remembered being at Barocco having a few drinks with Jason, my old prep school friend from Keane and the owner of the gallery that showed my work. I remembered Robert Finch-Hatton, high priest and critic for *A.R.T.* magazine, walking in, resembling a smug Charles Laughton, only bald and wearing clear-framed glasses, his portly body absurd in an Armani couture suit. I'd met him eight years before at my first show at P.S. 1 when he still had hair and his tweed coat from Princeton and I'd still been wearing black high-top Converse sneakers and a spike and spent my evenings spelunking in the clubs, following James Chance's trail of burning aerosol. Finch-Hatton had championed my early abstract work while he was still writing at the *Voice* and, later, at *Art Forum*, and even, in some measure, helped establish my career. We'd come up together, but a lot had changed since then. Now suits cost twelve hundred dollars and maitre d's greeted you by name, Finch-Hatton had his own rag and packed more wallop as a critic than Robert Hughes at *Time*, and we were enemies. Two years before, when I'd begun to feel like I was suffocating in that bloodless mental world of lines and dots and turned away from it toward realistic image, Finch-Hatton had seemed to take it as a personal affront. Then when my most recent show at Jason's had further developed the trend, he'd thrown away all pretense at restraint or objectivity and attacked me in some blind fit of inexplicable distemper. Thanks largely to him, the show had flopped. Collectors who'd once begged and suffered waiting lists to buy my work had started to regard me with plague-fear in their eyes, as though maybe what I'd contracted was contagious.

And suddenly there he was, at the bar, sipping absinthe, or perhaps chartreuse. There I was, drinking bourbon on the rocks. "Don't do it, Adam," Jason was saying, giving me a warning look, "don't give him the satisfaction." Satisfaction was the last thing on my mind. I stood up.

I remembered Finch-Hatton's eyes widening with almost comical alarm when he saw me moving through the crowd in his direction. I remembered the sparkle of ice cubes flying through the dusky lights, the amber stream of fluid elongating like pulled taffy as I threw my glass of bourbon in his face. I remembered being jeered and applauded by different factions in the crowd. I remembered how my heart was beating. I remembered the flushed face of the young blond maitre d', his chic haircut, the trace of distaste in his eyes together with the trace of fear. "You'll have to leave," he told me, none too confidently, and I just stared at him on a hair trigger, ready to go all the way, till his glance flickered, when I shoved through the door into a cold spring rain.

"That was smart, Adam," Jason said, throwing my raincoat at me hard as he burst through the door, "that was just fucking brilliant," and I said, "don't start with me, Jason, don't even bother. I should have kicked his motherfucking ass." "Fuck Finch-Hatton, Adam," Jason said behind me, "I'm not saying he didn't deserve it, but just fuck him and forget him. Let's talk about you—what the hell is wrong with you?" I laughed and spun to face him. "Do I really have to spell it out for you, Jase?" I asked, "I mean, Jesus Christ, I only spent two years of my life on those paintings." Jason said, more softly, "okay, he did a hatchet job on you, but, wake up, Adam, he's a trasher— everybody knows it. That still doesn't mean you can go around throwing drinks, pulling this cowboy shit," and I said, "what do you suggest then, Jase? Maybe I should just bend over, drop my pants and take it with a manly smile? No, man, somebody needed to make it real for Robert," and Jason said, "then let me make it real for you. That review hurt me, too, it hurt the gallery. But the stunt you pulled in there just now made matters worse—not just for you, Adam, but everybody. Now Finch-Hatton's going to go out of his way to bash every show I hang."

Jason stared at me from somber eyes made older than his face by cares I hadn't known, cares I feared and also sometimes envied—marriage, fatherhood, the responsibility of running his own business—and the simple justice of his point cut like a knife. Digging down through my hurt pride toward an apology, I tried to find the words, but he spoke first. "Plus now I have to pay to have his suit dry-cleaned," he said, and if I hadn't known him like I did I might have missed the joke—his deadpan never wavered. His generosity touched the root of my affection for him, and I said, "I'm sorry, Jason, you're right, man—I'm a selfish asshole." I meant it, too, though I suppose I also hoped he'd contradict me. He didn't. He just said, "tell me something I don't know," and only then did his lips betray the fraction of a smile.

He reached out and cuffed me lightly as he said, "come on, let's get some food." I shook my head. "I don't think so, man," I told him, "I'm going to take a walk." He frowned and said, "go home, Adam, make it an early night for once," and I said, "I'm not sure my circadian rhythm could adjust," trying to be funny, but Jason didn't smile. Narrowing his eyes at me, he said, "What is it, Adam—really? It's not the show, it's not Finch-Hatton—there are still a lot of people out there who believe in you—why are you so unhappy?" I just stared at him and didn't answer—I didn't have an answer—then started to turn away. He grabbed my sleeve. "Get over it, Adam, I'm not kidding," he told me, "get back to work. The further you slide the further you're going to have to climb to get back where you started," and I said, "you want to know something, Jase?" and he said, "what?" and I said, "where I started wasn't all that great," then walked away from him into the hissing shiny darkness of the street.

After that all I could remember was getting drunk and loud at a dive downtown on Avenue C and hitting on some black-garbed East Village waif girl, who, yes—it was coming back to me—wore violet lipstick and whose name, I now deduced as I lay in bed and the phone kept ringing, had been Monique. Clearly she'd come home with me, and, after all, considering the state of the world, it was a deep relief to discover I had not disrobed during the festivities. The only evidence of what Monique and I had embarked on together was a highball glass on the floor brimming with some eight ounces of straight George Dickel—bourbon being one of the last vestiges of my southern heritage—and the mirror on my bedside table flecked with grains of spit-glued coke and the snail-tracks of our licked fingers. Yes, I knew as well as anyone that blow was desperately passé. I'd given it up when it went out and bought a treadmill along with all my saner friends, but, a traditionalist at heart, I'd gone back to it under pressure like a dog to an old piss-trace, and Finch-Hatton's review the month before had provided the excuse. This, more or less, is how things had gone with me since then, from bad to worse. You might say my life had started going south on me, figuratively speaking, even before the phone call sparked my actual trip.

The answering machine, on delay, finally picked up. "I'm sure you know the drill by now," a hip snide stranger said, "wait for the tone and give it your best shot."

It was my own voice.

A single word, a single letter, changed it all.

"A.?" the caller said, and I felt the small hairs lift all over my body like kelp stirred by a cold deep current, "A. Jenrette?" It was an older man. I didn't recognize his voice, but the use of the initial, the thick patrician southern accent, sent me instantly reeling down a darkened corridor into the past. No one had called me A. in years. "A., this is Stuart Littlejohn, your Aunt Zoe's attorney, down in Killdeer. I'm sorry to have to let you know this way, son, but Miss Zoe passed away last night." Littlejohn paused respectfully. "We're going to bury her day after tomorrow, Tuesday. Wednesday morning we'll be reading the will in my offices on Commerce Street. If there's any way possible, I think you ought to try and get on down here. . . . Look forward to hearing from you, son, hope you're all right."

He recited the number and I heard the click.

I sat there in a trance, touched off not so much by the specific message—I'd only seen my great-aunt once since the ninth grade when we moved from Killdeer to Winston-Salem—as by where the message came from, the fact that it had come at all. The whoosh of traffic on Columbus Avenue rose through my open window like the breaking of a distant surf. My gaze drifted to the seashell paperweight on my desk—a gray lightning whelk—lingering there a moment before moving to the stack of unpaid bills beneath it.

The spell broke, and I suddenly found myself wondering if Aunt Zoe had left me any money. I tried to push away the ghoulish thought, but thanks to Finch-Hatton and the failure of the show, for the first time in several years I could foresee the coming of a day, not so distant, when I was going to be in trouble. Trying to derail that train of thought, I took a swallow of the previous night's bourbon and suddenly caught an image of a silver-haired old lady with a gravelly cigarette-ruined voice drifting through an enormous house which had a chandelier I'd once been quite convinced was made of diamonds. The recollection of my aunt brought a mist to my eyes and made me smile. She'd also owned a ukelele which she'd let me play and a Chinese ginger jar filled with Mary Janes from which I'd stuffed my pockets. Perhaps because Aunt Zoe had no children of her own, she and Mama had been very close. The thought of Aunt Zoe's childlessness brought back the mercenary thought, but when I looked squarely at it, it struck me as unlikely that she would have left me anything of substance—probably some bad family portrait. There were closer relatives, and, besides, there'd been trouble, bad trouble, between Aunt Zoe's brother, my great-uncle Herbert, and my father over Daddy's novel, *Rubber Man*, and I'd been too young at the time to get a sense of whom my great aunt had sided with.

Rubber Man had caused a terrible scandal. The heart of it was money, family money. Zoe and Herbert were two of the three heirs of Dixie Bag. Their father, Price Kincannon—my great-grandfather—had started the mill in Killdeer back before the First World War. The third heir was my maternal grandmother, Rebecca, whom I'd called Nana. Nana married a close friend of Herbert's, a man named Ian Trefethen. Trefethen was an English colonial whom my Uncle Herbert had met in the East, traveling the jute market circuit as a young buyer for Dixie Bag. Trefethen had come home to Killdeer with Herbert for a summer holiday, and he and Nana had fallen in love. They were married and returned to Trefethen's native Malaya where Nana's inheritance was used to buy a rubber plantation. Mama was born there, on the banks of the Slim River, and lived there till she was seven when Trefethen sent his wife and daughter back to Killdeer on the eve of World War II, staying on himself to try and sell the property. When the Japanese invaded the country, Trefethen had fled to Singapore. Nana had received a letter from him sent from there, dated just a few days before the Japanese overran the city. He was never heard from again.

After the war it was discovered that the plantation had been sold to a Chinese merchant. This man was interviewed and claimed to have paid in gold. There was no reason to doubt his story—the deed transferring title was in order. The natural assumption was that this money had been confiscated by the Japanese, who'd either killed Trefethen immediately or impounded him in a labor camp where he'd later died. There was one incongruous detail, however. A former overseer on the plantation, a Tamil from Ceylon, wrote Nana a letter shortly after the war claiming to have seen Trefethen, or a man he thought was Trefethen, entering a hotel in Singaradja on the island of Bali. He'd followed and made inquiries, but the desk clerk had informed him that no one by the name Trefethen was registered there. Yet he'd been convinced enough to write the letter. This report was investigated and ultimately dismissed by the detectives. But it was this one detail that had captured Daddy's imagination in his fictional retelling of the story, and in the last scene of his novel we glimpse a "tall stalwart Englishman," fitting Trefethen's general description, "with a dark-skinned mistress," sitting in a deck chair under a palm tree in a snow-white Panama hat drinking gin tonics, "in the English fashion, without ice," on some remote Pacific island which he'd purchased with his wife's money. Hence the title. *Rubber Man.*

The critic for the *Boston Globe* called Daddy's book "the most promising work of fiction by a young southern writer since Erskine Caldwell burst over the literary horizon," helping to nudge it onto the *New York Times* bestseller list late in the spring of my eighth grade year where it remained all that summer of 1967. What Aunt Zoe had thought of it I never knew. My uncle Herbert was another matter. No longer a young jute buyer, he'd become the reigning patriarch of Dixie Bag by then and was known as Big Herbert, not just by the extended family but by everyone in town, and undeterred by what the critics wrote, he made his opinion known.

As I took another wincing sip, the perfume of the whiskey conjured the scene from my eighth grade year that still sometimes woke me in the middle of the night. In my mind's eye I saw my father, in the proud flush of recent publication, standing on the lawn of the Episcopal Church in Killdeer, shyly receiving the congratulations of a crowd. I stood on the steps in my acolyte's robes admiring Shelley Fielding's bosoms and discussing whether *succor*, from the sermon, might not be a dirty word. Glancing across her shoulder from time to time at Daddy, I felt the tug of my heart's pride. I remembered seeing Big Herbert moving through the crowd, the swiftness and purpose in his stride somehow out of keeping with the languor of a summer Sunday morning. He was tapping his walking stick—a silver-headed one made of black Malayan ebony, a gift from Ian Trefethen—on the slate flags of the rectory walk. I remembered how my casual interest had turned to horror as Big Herbert stopped and raised that stick above his head. The lacquered shaft flashed in the sunlight, and suddenly things began unfolding with the ponderous and irresistible quality of slow motion. The stick came down across the broad of Daddy's unsuspecting shoulders, he stumbled forward and went down on his knees, all conversation stopped—there was no sound except the wind through the leaves of the old oaks high overhead—and everyone, all the assembled hosts of Killdeer, stopped what they were doing and turned to stare, including Shelley Fielding. Having taken Daddy in, she turned to me with two wide frightened

eyes, regarding me like she had never seen me till that instant, regarding me like I had just been born.

As I remembered this, the day seemed to grow suddenly
darker outside my brownstone window. Knowing this memory led to even darker ones, I tried to resist its gravitational
pull. Thinking maybe it would help, I snorted a quick line.
But the first domino had fallen, and when I lifted my face
from the magic mirror I found myself staring at my mother's
portrait on the bedside table in its tarnished silver frame. I
saw a young bride, bare-shouldered in a satin dress, a spray
of lace across her bosom, and a natural wave in her dark
pretty hair. The photographer had caught her laughing naturally, and there was a shine of happiness in Mama's eyes. But
back behind that I could see—I, who'd had eighteen years to
study and to search—a cultivated tameness that trusted life
too easily and had no response to hurt except forgiveness. As
the cocaine hit, I closed my eyes and saw another picture, a
photograph that existed only in my mind. This one showed a
different woman, one with grizzled short-cropped hair just
starting to grow back after her second round of chemotherapy. This, too, was Mama. Her eyes were closed in an expression of peace that seemed somehow angry—or had, at
least, to her fifteen-year-old son—like someone putting an
unpleasant scene behind her, her seventy-five pounds lost in
the silken vastness of the coffin, and one of her frail tiny
hands twisted like a claw.

Two years had separated my father's humiliation and my
mother's death. We'd moved to Winston-Salem in the meantime. I'd gone away to Keane. But the curtain had closed on
the tragedy, as it had opened, at the Episcopal Church in
Killdeer as six pallbearers, one of them myself, carried Mama's coffin down the granite steps toward the waiting hearse
for the short drive to Laurel Ridge Cemetery, in fulfillment
of Mama's wish that she be buried in the family plot.

I hadn't seen my Aunt Zoe since that day—it was my one
adult memory of her. She'd stood at graveside gazing at the
bier covered with a sea of lavender tulips, Mama's favorite
flower. I'd seen Aunt Zoe whispering inaudibly, perhaps
praying, before pressing two black-gloved fingers to her lips
and touching them to the metal surface of the coffin. Then
she'd turned to me. Aunt Zoe's eyes hadn't shifted and apologized like so many of the others' had, but gazed directly

into mine. She'd reached out and laid her hand against my cheek, holding it there for perhaps three seconds before she spoke. "That isn't her, honey," she'd whispered in that husky voice of hers, "that's not your mama—you know that, don't you?" and though I didn't answer she'd nodded as though I had.

Cary had been at Laurel Ridge that day. I hadn't known if he'd show up, but when the service ended and I saw him there I remembered feeling like a castaway who's spied a ship on the horizon, a brave white ship. He stood beside the new VW his father had just bought him for his sixteenth birthday with his hands in his pockets like he didn't know what else to do with them and with his dark handsome eyes full of pain—not his, but mine. He was all I had. Because by then it had gone bad with Daddy, too. I left the cemetery with Cary and the limousine drove on ahead.

Cary took me out a country road, and eventually we pulled up at his family's trailer at the lake. Inside, he picked the flimsy lock of T.O.'s liquor cabinet, taking out a fifth of Seagram's 7. The two of us sat out on the picnic table passing the bottle in silence as the earlier rain changed to drizzle then a fine scudding mist like atomizer spray. We didn't talk at first, but I could sense him studying me, and waiting. There was an uncharacteristic deference in his eyes that day, as though my suffering conferred some perverse celebrity on me. "I don't think I'm going back to Keane," I told him finally, as the liquor started working. I wiped my mouth and passed the bottle to him, and he placed it between his knees without sipping. "What are you going to do?" he asked, and I said, "I don't know. Maybe I'll go down to the beach and stay at the cottage. I could get work on a fishing boat." And Cary, who'd worked since he was ten years old in his father's cafeteria, who hadn't been insulated by early privilege as I had been and knew so much better how the real world worked, didn't challenge the impracticality of my project. He gave me permission to express my sense, so clear in the devastation of that moment, that life could not go on as it had before, understanding that I needed to express it more than live it. Cary simply took a swallow from the bottle and said, "you can stay here if you want," passing it back to me, and I said, "thanks, spud," feeling my eyes brim, but having expected no less of him. And it had seemed possible that I might take him up on it, possible that I might step out of my life and hide out at the Kinlaw's trailer at the lake like Tom Sawyer in Huck Finn's secret world. I didn't consider what I'd do there, perhaps simply wander through the woods searching for roots and berries, a crazed saint muttering to the birds. But after two days the charm of crazy sainthood had worn off and Cary had driven me back to my father's house in Winston-Salem, and the following day I'd caught a plane to Keane.

It had been during those two days following my mother's funeral that I'd first heard Cary mention Jane McCrae. They'd just met at Jefferson Davis Private Day School at the beginning of the year, and Cary wasn't dating her then—Jane was still with Deacon Griggs—but I remembered how his eyes had glowed and deepened when he talked of her.

At the thought of Jane my gaze returned to the whelk shell on my desk and my mind leaped forward from my mother's funeral to the summer after graduation. I suddenly caught the clearest flash of Jane walking far out ahead of me on the beach in Kill Devil Hills, lifting her long skirts as she waded into the tidal pool the storm had left. Something had captured her attention and, as I'd watched, she leaned over and reached into the water, turning back to me and shouting, "look!" as she waved something overhead. Her green eyes had shone like sunlit churchglass as she turned the whelk in her lean brown hand, proudly demonstrating its perfection, saying, "listen," in an excited whisper as she held it to my ear. The shell had seemed silver then, fresh from the pool in the morning light, with an orange blaze along the inner rim where the living meat had left its signature. Now, on my desk, it looked gray and dead. It still implied a debt, unpaid and unforgiven. But it was too late now. That had been another life.

Gazing at the falling level of the bourbon in my glass, I realized I was getting drunk and didn't care—the day was trashed already, better just to write it off. Tomorrow I'd turn over a new leaf. Or maybe not. The lines of a couple favorite old songs floated through my brain—Lou Reed, the Grateful Dead—and I wondered for the first time in months, or even years, what had become of Sweet Jane, if, like me, she'd lost her sparkle and wasn't the same. Maybe she'd had kids and gotten fat. I didn't know, and it seemed better not to. I knew where Cary was though—back home in Killdeer underneath the sod in Laurel Ridge where the grass would just be starting to turn green again as the tenth spring swung around.

And as the shadows lengthened outside my brownstone window in my long day's journey into night, at some point I got up and rifled the bottom drawer of my desk. I took out several years of correspondence—each fat brick held together by a rubber band—and finally, toward the bottom, I found the Polaroid snapshot of the three of us from that same summer after graduation, all eighteen, standing on the gazebo at the beach with a dark ocean behind us, Jane in the middle, Cary and I on either side, our arms linked around each other's waists. Jane and I, who'd been at the beach all summer, were both deeply tanned, but Cary, who'd only come down for the weekend, was lobsterish with a fresh burn. His slightly crooked grin, the left side turning upward higher than the right, seemed simple and heartfelt, while there was trouble in both our faces, Jane's and mine, something grave and lost.

At the very bottom of the drawer was a folding Barlow pocket knife with a handle of polished yellow bone, the first present Cary had ever given me and the last thing I still had of his. For years I'd carried it in my pocket like a southern boy, even after I came to Columbia where there were no more ropes to cut and no trees and picnic tables to initial. At almost thirty-two I could still make out the tiny scar where he and I had used that knife to knick our veins that day by Ruin Creek where we had fused our wrists, rapt with the blood ceremony we had read about in books, passing a cigarette afterwards like Indian braves as we sat on the crumbly limestone banks, our eyes shining but avoiding one another's in the shyness of our boyhood crush.

We'd been in sixth grade then and I'd carried that knife till I was twenty-one and time had turned the stainless metal dark, carried it until the day the phone rang with awful insistence at six a.m. and I crawled out of bed with Lisa Daniels—we were at the beach house over break—and I picked up the receiver and heard my father's voice. "I've got bad news, son," he said, "it's Cary," and then words failed the author. He paused before he said, "I'm sorry, A., he's gone." I sat in stunned silence, thinking of a car wreck, some drunken wasteful accident on the highway late at night coming home from Durham in the rain, and

Daddy said, "he took his own life, son." Deep inside myself I felt something pop like a bad spring as the mechanism went awry—the clock stopped ticking there and something froze in me forever. I didn't weep, I just hung up the phone and walked past Lisa, climbing up the dune toward the gazebo, and then I started running. I ran and ran, north toward Corolla, twelve or fifteen miles, out to where the line of houses ended and the dunes grew wild, feeling it breathing on my neck, only that and the desire to run and not to let it catch me. It never had, not till those ten years had passed and I took out that knife, which I'd put away after Lisa and I had returned to Columbia and not taken out again till that cocaine afternoon when an unexpected phone call brought it all back again and made the past more real than anything in the desert of my present life.

It didn't seem like a major psychological initiative, putting that knife back in my pocket, just a wistful sentimental gesture from an old contender, washed up at almost thirty-two. I couldn't be cool anymore—a southern boy at heart, the long effort had just messed me up, so I abandoned it along with all the rest and slipped that Barlow in my jeans, aware that I was reclaiming something, but not what.

I passed out that day knowing I would never go to Killdeer— not in a million years, not for love and not for money. If Aunt Zoe had left me anything, they could send it to me COD, or they could keep it.

Some hours later when I woke up, my mind had changed. I hadn't changed it—it had changed all by itself. I saw that I didn't really have a choice. More accurately, I had a choice, but it was unacceptable. My choice was to stay there in my apartment doing coke and getting sloshed, screening my calls, ordering-in Chinese, till I reached enlightenment or slit my wrists. Even Killdeer seemed preferable.

Two days later, at high noon, Louis Bascom, my aunt's aged black chauffeur and general factotum, met me at the Raleigh-Durham airport in her Bentley, having made it there by sheer miracle alone, half blind and so stooped and shrunken he had to sit on a stack of phone books to see across the wheel. Louis grinned when he saw me and tried to take my bag, but I held on to it, afraid that it might topple him. As we climbed in the car Louis turned to me with red teary eyes and said, "she gone, Mist'A., ain't no mo' like her neither—that mol' is broke," and realizing his sorrow was deeper and far more intimate than mine could ever be, I said, "you were very close, weren't you, Louis," and he sniffed and said, "yes suh, loved her better'n my own wife—either one of'm," and then he gunned it, laying down an unintentional line of rubber across the speed bumps at the terminal.

On the drive he tuned in a black R & B station and the music was so good and I enjoyed his company so much I almost forgot where we were going. But when we pulled up on the shoulder beside the low stone wall of the Episcopal Church in Killdeer, I remembered. The old darkness fell over me again, and it grew even darker as the funeral cortege passed through the grassless dusty yards and sagging tin-roofed shacks of Killdeer's black section on the way to the cemetery at Laurel Ridge, where I watched them lower my great-aunt into the ground. I sat beside Big Herbert in his wheelchair, realizing I still hated him, and threw the second spade of soil into the grave after his, then stood there accepting the commiseration of people I hadn't seen in fifteen years or even longer, many of them relatives whose faces were familiar but whose names and exact connections I could not recall. Yet they all knew me perfectly and greeted me like I had never left, and in the strangeness of that moment as my eye drifted across the crowd, somewhere toward the back, holding off as though diffident of her right to be there, I saw Sadie Kinlaw, Cary's mother, bareheaded and pale in a black dress which had seen too much use for one lifetime. In that sudden rush of feeling I felt almost brave enough to go and speak to her, but the tide of the event swept me another way, toward the limousine and a long afternoon of calls and reacquaintances in Zoe's big house which my great-grandfather had built with the fortune he'd made at Dixie Bag, and which I was to learn the following day, I'd just inherited.

Taking her brother Vince's arm, Sadie turned away and the two of them walked uphill over the green sward toward a solitary oak. My last image through the window as we pulled away was of her standing on that rise with a line of greening forest behind her, looking on as Vince knelt down to straighten a vase of immortelle which had toppled over in the winter wind and throw away the twigs and acorns that had scattered over Cary's grave. Stuart Littlejohn, who sat beside me in the hearse, a man twice my age, patted my arm and looked away, respectful of my grief, thinking my tears were

for my aunt. But it was more than that. I cried for all of it—
for my mother whom death had stolen, for my father whom
I'd lost to something even worse, for Sadie up there on the
ridge and for Cary under it, wondering if I'd made a big
mistake by coming home.

Though I didn't see her in the sea of faces, Jane McCrae was
in the crowd that day as well, turned out with her mother who'd
played contract bridge with my Aunt Zoe every Tuesday afternoon for fifteen years. I don't know why Jane came. Maybe she
had nothing else to do that day, or maybe it was just to catch a
glimpse of me and see if it stirred anything. I didn't learn she'd
been there till a few nights later at Miss Misha DeWitt's annual
cocktail dance, the Azalea Fête, so-called, which always kicked
off Easter week. Miss Misha had been my aunt's best friend,
and through her good offices Killdeer society opened its arms
to me like the prodigal son returned. I was standing in the DeWitt
drawing room under a lead-crystal chandelier that would have
snuffed out three generations of the town's social life as cleanly
as the Civil War if it had fallen, sipping neat George Dickel and
trying hard not to think about the coke in the side pocket of my
jacket, when I looked up and saw Jane's reflection in the gilded
mirror in the foyer, taking off her wrap and handing it to Charles
with a big dazzling smile, knowing her effect and doubting it so
beautifully.

She was wearing a black velvet sheath and a string of pearls
instead of cut-offs, which changed the tone a bit, and her hair
was dyed, but her body hadn't changed—I noticed that right
off—she wasn't fat, not fat at all, and her eyes were still the
same green I remembered, like broken bottle glass with milky
light pearling on the edges. I'd heard somewhere that she was
married and living in Atlanta, and her name had showed up in
the guest book at the gallery after one of my shows—her maiden
name, which had seemed a little odd—but aside from that and
the letter she'd written me after Cary's suicide, I hadn't seen or
heard from her since that summer at the beach when we were
eighteen years old, the day she climbed into her mother's Olds-
mobile and drove away, following Cary after everything had
come to grief, and the last thing I was expecting that night at
the dance was for her to be in Killdeer and to meet her face to
face after all that time. I guess that's why I lost my head and
tried to slip out the side door to the patio. Not that I was planning
to leave exactly—I didn't have a plan—just get a handle on my-

self is all, take a deep breath, maybe do another pinch of blow off the tip of my new housekey. I didn't think Jane had seen me, but I guess I was wrong, because the certain truth is I never made it to that door.

"Hello, A.," she said, "I see you're still practicing your exit."

Thirteen years, and those were her first words to me.

Two

JANE

I wasn't nervous about seeing A. again—not much. I was only about to pee on my leg, is all, not that I was going to let him know it. The way I remember it he spoke first and what he said was, "I see you dyed your hair." I came right straight back at him with, "and I see you're still practicing your exit." A. looked like he was calculating a comeback, and I said, "don't bother to say something clever," and he said, "I won't, but I think you got that story backwards . . . seems to me a certain other party made the exit," and I said, "I don't think so, but you may be right, it was a long time ago." As though maybe I'd forgotten. I wasn't going to give him any satisfaction if I could help it. That was the hypothesis I was using to explain what I was doing there talking to him—not giving him any satisfaction. *Paging Dr. Rosenkrantz . . .*

And A. said, "what was wrong with it the way it was?" and I said, "wrong with what?" and he said, "your hair," and I gave him a hard squint and said, "you haven't improved much with age, have you?" and he said, "shit, Jane, you know damn well you could have dyed it blue and it wouldn't make a difference," which sent my pulse rate up a notch or two, but all I said was, "all these years and you still haven't learned to make a compliment, except out of your rear end," and he smiled at that and said, "you haven't changed much either," and I said, "you'd be surprised, honey," and he raised his eyebrows in that mocking way of his and said, "would I?" and I said with complete

18

sincerity, "you really would," and he said, "you want to give me a for instance?" and I said, dropping back down to his level, "not really, but for one thing I've changed my taste in men," and he said, "really now? from what to what?" and I said, "I gave up the mean shitty kind," and he laughed, but I could tell it stung him. He took a swallow of his drink, jiggled the cubes around a little bit, then looked me straight in the eyes and said, "good for you, Jane," not mean, but like he really meant it, and that made me remember what I'd liked in him, though I also knew A. Jenrette well enough to know he wouldn't be including himself in the category I'd alluded to, namely mean and shitty, and to be fair, he never had been mean.

But the pace was getting a little fast and furious then in a way I hadn't foreseen and certainly hadn't intended—at least not consciously, though I'm sure Dr. Rosenkrantz, my therapist, would have made hay out of my "unconscious motives." But Dr. Rosenkrantz was back in Atlanta and never came to parties anyway, at least not mine. Nevertheless, I did rein it in and change the subject. "I read about your pictures in a magazine a while ago," I told him, "sounds like to me you're doing pretty well . . . I guess you made it, A., I'm glad to know somebody did." He laughed and said, "how long ago did you read that?" and I said, "oh, a year or two," and he said, "well, it's a whole 'nother can of worms today, as the expression goes." I didn't take it up because I thought maybe he was just being modest—miracles do happen—and anyway I was wondering if I should tell him that I'd been to his gallery on a trip to New York City and seen his paintings hanging on the walls and hated how smart and cynical they were until I turned that corner and saw myself like a reflection in a magic mirror from the past. That young girl didn't really look like me, not quite, yet it told me how I'd looked to A. back then, standing in the bathhouse of the Lost Colony Hotel beside the running shower, stepping out of my suit and looking back over my shoulder as a shaft of sunlight broke through the door, which was just parting open. And who would be behind it? Bingo, Mr. A. Jenrette. I went back to the Sherry Netherland Hotel and wept just like the pouring rain, but I was pretty fragile then anyway because that was the worst time with Robert, my ex, also known as Shit-for-Brains.

And breaking in on my thoughts, A. said, "I heard you got married, Jane," and I said, "did you hear I got divorced?" flaunting it at him, waving my naked finger which still looked strange to me after six years on the trail of tears, and A. said, "no, I didn't hear that . . . I'm sorry, I guess . . . how was it?" and I said, "which? the marriage turned out to be a big mistake, but this divorce feels like the real thing," and he said, "you sound bitter," and I said, "*moi? pardonnez-vous, monsieur*, just jaded is all—how about you?" A. stared at me for a month or so and then just shrugged it off and said, "things could be better," and I said, "I thought I heard you just inherited a million dollars," and he gave me a grim smile and said, "well, you heard wrong," and feeling my toe begin to tap I said, "well, this conversation's about as much fun as dental surgery," which was Robert's chosen calling and a line I used a lot those days, adding, "without the anesthetic . . . now tell me something fun," and A. said, "how about I've got some anesthesia, if you're into it." He tapped the pocket of his Italian zoot suit and I widened my eyes and said, "I hope you don't mean what I think you mean," and A. grinned like a red Indian who's been in the firewater again and said, "sorry, I'm afraid I do," and made a pointed sniff, and for a moment it was like those thirteen years had never passed at all, like we were right back at the Lost Colony in Kill Devil Hills, only A. had grown up to be Cleanth Faison, his former mentor.

We stood there a minute, hesitating at the gate of Memory Lane. It would have been the ideal point to break it up, and I considered it. I'd just wanted to stick my little toe in and see how the water felt, and now I had, and I'd satisfied myself it was still warm, and that was all I'd been after—or so my original hypothesis had run, the one I'd used while dressing to explain why I was going to Miss Misha's party knowing A. Jenrette was going to be there, who "I really didn't care to see." He'd been in town for a week, and with the exception of the funeral—which I'd attended solely out of respect for his Aunt Zoe—I'd avoided him like a venereal disease. Dr. Rosenkrantz was back there cheering me on to make an exit of my own, but the cold truth is I didn't really want to break it up quite yet, and even if I had I wouldn't have gotten the chance.

About that time A.'s eyes took on a sharp distant focus over my shoulder like someone he knew had just walked through the door. I almost turned to look, but he said, "I saw Sadie Kinlaw out at Laurel Ridge," and I knew what he was seeing wasn't in that present room with us and wasn't Sadie in the graveyard either. "Did you?" I asked, not wanting it to go that way, and he said, "she looks just the same," and I said, "only to you, honey, that's how you wanted her to look," and he said, "have you seen her?" and I said, "not for a while, not to talk to anyhow, but I was out there, too," and he said, "at the funeral?" I nodded, and he said, "I didn't see you," and I said, "well, I saw you and Sadie both . . . and by the way, I was awfully sorry to hear about your Aunt Zoe, and so was Mama"—some little voice just added that—"she was a special lady," and A. said, "I hardly even knew her," and I said, "that's your loss," and he said, "I suppose you're right," and we took another pause.

Then, changing tracks himself, A. said, "it's good to see you, Jane," and gave me that nice clear smile of his which had become a little smoother and more practiced over time, and I knew that was my cue to say, "it's good to see you, too, A.," but I just passed, fighting down my breeding, and he said, "I'd like to think we're still friends," holding out his hand for me to take, and I considered saying, "were we ever?" because, whatever it had been, friendship didn't seem like the main theme now—but instead a little flash came back and I glanced down at his hand and said, "I'll let you know in writing within thirty days." He smiled remembering that joke and said, "I don't expect I'll be here thirty days from now," and I didn't bat an eyelash, I just said, "I'm leaving in a week myself," and he said, "oh, where to?" and I said, "I'm helping Mama move her things to Windy Gap for the season."

A. surprised me then. I saw him suck it in and push himself. "What about tonight?" he said. My heart was pounding ninety miles an hour then, but I said, "what about it?" just as coolly as you please, and he said, "you want to go someplace and have a drink?" and I said, "you've already got one," and he drained his glass and said, "so much for that objection," and I said, "the music hasn't even started yet, A., and besides, there's enough whiskey right here to sink a battleship, and Tolly over there in a nice white jacket and a bowtie just dying to refill your glass," and A. grinned and said, "wouldn't the expression be to *float* a battleship? considering the context, I mean," and I said, "either way you want it," not giving him an inch, and A. said, "I was thinking just the two of us," and I said, "oh, I see . . . well, what did you have in mind?" having a grand time putting him through his paces, and he said, "I'm not sure yet," with that boyish grin of his which was also devilish, and I gave him a hard squint and he backed down and said, "I just feel like talking, Jane, that's all," and I said, "what's the topic?" and he said, "how about old times?" and I said, "too general, besides I've pretty much covered that with Dr. Rosenkrantz—why get it for free when you can pay for it?" which was my friend Suzanna Dixon's line, though I thought I could use it outside the Atlanta city limits, and he said, "you're seeing a shrink?" and I said, " 'therapist' is the preferred expression, I believe," and he said, "why?" and I said, "you know what they say about a divorcée's best friend," and he said, "are you sleeping with him?" and I didn't miss a beat, I said, "not at present, though I wanted to at first . . . he turned me down," and A. said, "there's a first time for everything—is he gay?" and I said, "no, he's seventy for one thing, and for another he's a decent human being," and he said, "oh, I see, the kindly daddy type . . . and since when is seventy too old?" and I said, "you are such a toad, A., do you know that?" and he said, "sorry, I guess you're right . . . actually I considered getting into therapy myself, once upon a time," and I said, "why didn't you?" A. shrugged. "Judging by my New York friends, it doesn't seem to help a lot," he said, and I said, "maybe the problem is your New York friends," and he said, "friendship, there's a theme—a good friend is hard to find, and hard to lose, but if you work hard enough at it you can accomplish anything," and I said, "what's that from, the *The Rubáiyát of Omar Khayyám*?" and we just held each other's eyes a minute over that with Cary hanging in the air between us—I knew his next line before he even thought it up.

"Speaking of which, how about old friends as a topic?" he said, and, looking hard, I caught a flash of real unhappiness which told me it was still alive for A., far more than it was for me. "It's a little late in the day for that one, honey, don't you think?" I said, and he said, "you're probably right," and stuck his hands down in his pockets, looking kind of miserable and lost and restless in a way that brought things back, so I went on more gently, "it was a long time ago, A., I put all that behind me," and he said, "so did I . . . at least I thought I did, but I've been thinking about him since I got home," and I said, "why don't you go see Sadie, A., it might do you good," and he looked at me like *I* was doing drugs, and I said, "I sat down with her a few years back, A. Sadie doesn't blame you, or me, or anybody. She's just living her life like we all have to do, and I know for a fact that she'd be glad to see you." And sensing

sympathy like a shark will blood, A. flashed me this shy imploring look, which was also sly, and said, "come on, Jane,
one drink," and giving him the sternest look in my whole rep-
ertoire, knowing damn well I was going to regret it like the day
I was born, I put Dr. Rosenkrantz on hold and told him, "one."

I told the Templetons I wouldn't need a ride back out to Mama's,
and then A. took my arm and led me out of there with everybody
at Miss Misha's—the whole town of Killdeer, in other words,
plus the band who came from out of town—staring at us with
their eyebrows somewhere up around their hairlines or looking
sadly disapproving as I pretended not to notice. We got in his
aunt's old Bentley, which he'd inherited along with the four-car
garage to park it in and the twelve-bedroom house attached to
the garage and sweet little old black Louis who was older than
God and who Miss Zoe had taken more care of than he had of
her till she got sick, though, bless his heart, you know he tried.
It took about five minutes for A. to turn the engine over, and I
sat there mad at him for talking me into it but even madder at
myself for letting him.
    Finally the motor coughed and wheezed and we pulled out of
Miss Misha's driveway and drove up Woodlawn to the Killdeer
Country Club, which was only a matter of a hundred yards or
so, but of course the Club was closed, it being Monday night—
one reason Miss Misha always liked to give her annual dances
then, no competition—which I'd only known since I was nine.
I told A. but he didn't believe me and got out anyway, trotting
up the steps and shaking the door. He came back with a sheepish
look and said, "time to try plan B," but of course A. didn't
have a plan B—that could have been the motto for the boy's
whole life. I doubt he'd ever even been in Killdeer long enough
to have a drink since he'd been grown. His only suggestion was
to go back to his aunt's, but I quickly vetoed that idea, and we
ended up at the Red Velvet Lounge at the Holiday Inn at the east
end of town next to the Roller Rink, which had been boarded
up for years, and some old corrugated aluminum tobacco ware-
houses. I'd never personally been to the Red Velvet Lounge, as
I informed A., adding that I wasn't all that keen to spoil my
streak, but it was the best I could come up with on the rusty
spur of a dull moment.
    We took a little table in the corner off the dance floor, which
neither one of us so much as looked at once, and to add insult

to injury the waitress, this saucy bleached-blond little country thing with a wad of gum in her cheek and black net stockings and a skirt that came up somewhere near her neckline, wagged her plump behind up to us and stood there smacking her gum and tapping her pencil on her pad looking me over like I was some captive alien in a circus freakshow. But the minute A. turned up those baby blues of his she was all smiles and started batting her false eyelashes at him like migratory birds on the homeward route, as if A. was a traveling soap opera star or a TV evangelist or whatever the stuff her dreams were made of. Of course, A. lapped it up, flirting back and giving the poor thing a thrill.

Actually, A. was very nice, and I guess the reason I was being such a pad about the whole affair was because I was so nervous and confused about being there with him in the first place. Dr. Rosenkrantz would have made it into something nice like that if he were there, though it's also possible I'm just a natural bitch, a theory that had been proposed widely among a certain other group of males when I was younger and still in circulation. But even if I was a bitch back then—and I'm admitting nothing—it was only because I had to protect myself against my own native sweetness. Actually, I have a very sensitive giving nature, too much so, which all goes back to Daddy, who sort of cultivated that in me—yes, I was his special precious baby girl—only he didn't give me any defenses. That was Rosenkrantz's hypothesis, and he got ninety bucks an hour, so who was I to argue? And with your father you don't need defenses, or God help you if you do, but around age fifteen or thereabouts—that's when it was for me—you move up to a tougher league, and on top of everything, that's when Daddy died, about six months before I fell in with Deacon Griggs, which was before I ever knew A., or even Cary. But Deacon is another tale. And the reason I even mention the existence of this closet and the skeleton in it—my own—is because this hypothesis of "hidden sweetness" had become a major "motif" in my current explorations with Dr. Rosenkrantz back home, who had led me to discover and acknowledge my own natural sensitivity—which had been abused by certain unscrupulous persons, beginning with Deacon, but not ending there by any means—and this whole sensitivity business was something you could miss, you see, unless you knew me pretty well.

A. did know me pretty well, at least once upon a time he'd

known me, in any sense of the word you care to apply, Biblical or otherwise. But sitting there across that table from him in the Red Velvet Lounge after all those years, I wasn't sure A. had ever really got that part—about my sensitivity, I mean—or had wanted to, or could have done it if he tried, and that was what mattered to me now, sensitivity and care and a little r-e-s-p-e-c-t. Yet A. had come so close at times—the two of us had—as close in some ways as I'd come with Robert. I'd trusted A. and surrendered something very precious to him—precious to *me*, at least—and the end was just so miserable and I took it so badly, though it wasn't totally A.'s fault. What happened to us wasn't anyone's fault, it ran way past blame. But generosity aside, A. still funked it. Yes, he was only eighteen at the time, but then so was I, and I didn't funk it—not in the way that mattered, not with Cary, not with A. But A. just shit on both of us and did the cakewalk out of town. And even realizing men are weaker when it comes to love, which was a secret I'd always suspected but never wanted to believe until that day when, thinking I was being awful, I finally said it to Dr. Rosenkrantz—he looked up from his notes with his sad gentle smile and said, "yes, dear Jane, that truth is hard, but there's no escape from it"—even taking all that into consideration, I had never really forgiven A. Jenrette for it, and that's why I was having second thoughts about being there with him at the R.V. Lounge, as it's known to its habitués, and probably why I was ragging on the poor cocktail waitress who I'm sure had boy problems just like mine and maybe worse. Maybe she had daddy problems, too. But that secret about love, Dr. Rosenkrantz's and mine, was probably the reason I *was* there with A., though if I'd seen that then I would have turned around and run like hell.

When the drinks came, A. started talking. He didn't go straight into the heavy golden oldies like I'd expected, which was a relief. I guess he was leery of it, too, however bravely he might have threatened it. Instead he started telling me about the estate and how all Miss Zoe's cash and stocks and whatever else there was had gone to Herbert Jr.'s children, as if they needed it with their grandfather, Big Herbert, five minutes ahead of the hearse with a bank account about the size of the Atlanta airport. "A. Jenrette, the poor little rich boy"—A. said it, not me—and it was pretty humorous except I knew that was always more or less how it had been for him and his whole side of the family since A.'s grandmother, Miss Rebecca, lost her money out there in

Malaya, which I knew about along with everybody else in Kill-deer or Lawford Corner or practically the whole state, because I'd read *Rubber Man*, which was Mr. Clay Jenrette's "fictional" novel about the whole episode, the one that got him into such trouble with Big Herbert Kincannon, A.'s great-uncle, who horsewhipped Mr. Jenrette on the lawn of the Episcopal Church. That story had two sides like most stories do—family loyalty on the one hand, artistic license on the other—but, since Big Herbert had become the head of Dixie Bag, the chief employer in Killdeer and environs, at the time when *Rubber Man* came out, most everybody saw it from Big Herbert's point of view. My Daddy—who was also from a foreign land, namely Virginia, and had a little money of his own which he'd sunk into catfish aquaculture on the farm and a few acres of tobacco—was one of the exceptions. He said it was "a damn good book, and the whole thing was a crying shame."

Any way you stacked the load, it was a killing thing to A., who was only thirteen when it happened, and even worse for his mama, Miss Allison, who developed cancer—you know it had to be related—and was dead within two years at thirty-six. Mama, who was three years ahead of her at Highlands, said Allison Kincannon was the most beautiful girl who ever came from Killdeer. A. kept a picture of his mama on his bedside table at the cottage at the beach all that summer, and he never talked about her, not even once, not even any little thing, but you could tell he thought about her. I guess considering the way things had worked out with his father, she was really about the only thing that A. had left in the way of family. And she was dead. That's what just tore you up, and made you understand why A. was like he was sometimes, which is something Cary and I had talked about, because Cary was the only one who ever really understood A. deep down—that's what A. thought any-way. And even Cary didn't get it all.

And now A. had that old white elephant of a house on his hands, the Kincannon homeplace, which you just knew Miss Zoe had given A. to spite Big Herbert, a house which was big enough for fourteen armies and which A. didn't want and couldn't sell because nobody could afford to buy it. Nobody with good sense would have wanted to live there anyway. The place probably hadn't even been repainted since the Eisenhower administration. A. told me how he was coming down the front staircase after his first night in the place when one of the steps caved in and he got stuck and started yelling until old Louis finally rescued him a half an hour later. They went back to the scrap pile behind the gatehouse, A. said, and found some old piece of board more rotten than the one that broke and nailed it in, which was how A. said he planned to approach the restorations, "one board at a time, as they go." You had to appreciate the way A. was taking it, and I noticed he'd picked up a sense of humor even about himself, which was not a trait that sprang instantly to mind when you remembered how A. was before. And there I was, and everybody else in town, thinking A.'s worries were over. But they were only starting, let me tell you. I felt sorry for him, and I didn't even grudge it all that much.

Every half an hour or so A. would get up from the table and go to the men's room and come back sniffing and looking reinvigorated in a wild-eyed sort of way. He was getting on a tear with this life story he was telling me, and I didn't try to rein him in because it was entertaining, and I was interested anyway, and I hadn't been around that kind of energy in a while, though you knew three-fourths of it was toot. But the other fourth was A., and I'd always liked him when he was like that, till he wore you out with it. That was a subtheme of my aforementioned "boy problem"—I liked exciting ones. So tell me why, dear Dr. Rosenkrantz, they generally turn out to be the mean shitty no-count kind, which brings up the further theme of self-destructive pleasure and why it's so much fun. In other words, for about a half an hour there when A. was at the high point of his roll, I was having a strong impulse to visit the powder room with him, but Dr. Rosenkrantz got through and put his foot down, and I remembered I was thirty-one and divorced and starting a new life, not eighteen at the Lost Colony Hotel, where A. and I had done some lines in our own time. And remembering my better self I guess made me remember a better one in A., which I knew was down there under the blue crackles of cocaine voltage, and I think that's what finally made me say to him, not meaning to be self-righteous, but from the bottom of my heart, "what on earth has happened to you, honey?"

That took him back a little, though not all the way by any means, and that's when he went off about his show and how he'd done this major piece which he'd called "Parable of Fish and Loathing," which he felt was a real breakthrough in the history of art, a sort of take-off on the Last Supper and the miracle of fish and loaves combined. He'd painted a group of his New York friends, he said, around the table in the disciples' places and himself from the back in Judas's seat. He'd considered being Christ, he said to shock me, knowing I was religious—though not Born Again, thank you very much—but I wasn't fazed in the least. In the end A. had glued a small mirror to the canvas in the place where Christ would have been so that the viewer could see himself. The crowning touch though, according to A., had been his inspiration of wiring a real platter to the canvas so it appeared to be sitting in the middle of the painted table and putting a fish on it, a real one—"a catfish," he said, without apparent reference to me or Daddy—and leaving it there to rot through the whole show, forcing the audience to deal with the "real, uncomfortable facts of mortality and decay," which sounded real uncomfortable indeed and from what I gathered simply forced the audience to stay at home.

A. looked at me then with this big manic grin like he was waiting for applause, and I had to ask him, "what happened then?" and he said that Jason, his old friend from Keane who owned the gallery, had asked him to take the sacred catfish down after the review appeared and replace it with a stuffed trout from an antique shop, which A. seemed to regard as some big compromise as though he'd sold his soul and his integrity as an artist by giving in to it, "because decay is part of life," he said, "it's a lie and cowardice to deny it . . . and isn't that what art is supposed to be about, to make us face the truth?" He was all worked up and righteous by that point, though he had so far avoided using "crucifixion" in reference to himself and the review, and though I felt bad for him, I also felt like he needed to hear it from somebody, and if his New York friends weren't going to tell him, then I guess it fell to me, because who else was there? So I said to him straight out, not mincing my words, "it sounds to me like you asked for it, A., and you got it right straight on back."

He looked like I'd kicked him in the balls, his last remaining source of pride, and then he brought his fist down on the table. "Goddamn it, Jane," he said, "I'm an artist not an interior decorator," and I said, "try again," and he said, "I'm not the fucking feel-good man," and I said, "amen to that, brother, truer words were never spoken," which almost got a smile from him, but then I let him have it with the second barrel, I said, "and wasn't that the same excuse your daddy used?" referring, of course, to *Rubber Man* and the "integrity of art," which was

Mr. Clay's excuse for the havoc he'd wreaked on his family, an excuse A. had long since ceased to buy from his daddy, though it now seemed to me A. was trying to sell it for himself. I was also trading on the fact that A. had admitted to me once that the reaction to the book had been the real reason they'd moved away from Killdeer to Winston-Salem, not his mother's chemotherapy as had been alleged, and which I further suspected was why A. had never come back home.

"You just aren't going to cut me any slack at all tonight, are you, Jane?" he said, and I said, very softly, "no, honey, not tonight, though maybe on another day . . . and anyway I'm not sure slack is what you need, the A. Jenrette I used to know didn't ask for it." I knew I was taking a big chance making myself all vulnerable like that, and, yes, Dr. Rosenkrantz, it did misfire. I guess A. was just too wired to hear the little note of tenderness I was trying to throw out, because he said, "well, I'm fucking sorry, I guess I didn't reach perfection like some people." So I sighed and let go with impunity. "Nobody ever asked you for perfection, A. Jenrette, that was your own problem, but whatever else there was or wasn't between you and me, you were the most talented boy, or man, or whatever the hell you were, I ever knew," I said, "and whatever has happened to you since I don't know and I'm not sure I want to know, but I'll tell you the first thing Cary Kinlaw ever said to me about you, 'Jane, he's just like a retriever going for a stick, he'll break his heart before he stops, sometimes you've got to hold back the stick on A.,' and the second thing he said was, 'but he's a royal pain in the butt sometimes,' which was the gospel truth if it was ever uttered . . . your butt was evident in the first five minutes after I met you, A., but it took me a long time to see the heart and I'm squinting hard right now trying to see it. And you want to know when it finally dawned on me what you were made of? It was the day you walked in through that bathhouse door just giving up and letting yourself be weak enough to need somebody else, that's when I finally knew what Cary meant when he said you had heart . . . and while I'm on the subject, how come you left yourself out of that bathhouse picture? which I saw by the way . . . I'm no artist and no damn critic either, but I would have thought that was the most important part, what was happening to *you* . . . or were you supposed to be the ray of sunshine breaking in that young girl's life?"

At that point I was all flushed and flustered and about to cry.

I hadn't meant to make a speech, and I'd lost my train of thought anyway, so I just stopped. A. was sitting there staring at me with this soft glow of surprise on his face, and he said, "I know you saw it, I saw your name in the guest register," and I said, patting my eyes with the cocktail napkin, "I don't remember signing it," and he said, "well, someone did, and whoever it was used your maiden name, as though maybe I wouldn't know her married one and she wanted me to know she'd been there . . . unless it was another Jane McCrae," and I said, "wipe that smug grin off your face, A.," though it wasn't really smug, "I always sign my name McCrae since my divorce," and he said, "but you weren't divorced then, were you?" and I said, "no, but I might as well have been, Shit-for-Brains was already off with Bimbolina, his hygienist, in Grand Rapids or wherever that 'convention' was," and he said, "I'm sorry, Jane," which was pretty human of him actually.

But then he simply couldn't help himself, he had to spoil it, so he added, "I thought you said you'd changed your taste in men," which was the first time he'd been truly mean, but by then I had regained my poise and took it right in stride. "*Touché*, darling," I said just as suavely as you please, "the change was since," and he said, "so the mean shitty kind no longer stand a chance?" and I said, "none at all," and A. just said, "I see," and mulled on that until his battery was charged, and then, "if an old dog like you can learn new tricks, why not others?" and I said, "I don't appreciate the canine reference, A., but yes I'm trying," and he said, "then there must be hope for me as well," and I said, "I'm sure I wouldn't know, but I wouldn't hold my breath if I were you," back to the hypothesis of denying him all satisfaction. And thinking I was simply flirting and playing hard to get with him, A. got so smooth and mellow and manly and in control and understanding of my needs and games and little foibles, he just said, "Sweet Jane," with a whole symphony orchestra in those two little words, and reached across the table for my hand, which I would have rather seen withered by St. Anthony's fire or cut off at the wrist than playing magic fingers with Mr. A. Jenrette right then—men are such devious shits, they go right for your soft spots, the very best that's in you, so that you feel like holding back is cutting off your life. They're just like tigers going for the neck, and the worst thing is they don't even know it, they think they're being good, it's pure instinct.

But I was wise to Mr. A. Jenrette—after all I'd seen him work before. So I just breezed my little hand out from under his great big one, smiled and batted my eyes and let him have it with the cannon I was packing, a girl's last refuge—sex, in other words, and the subtle variation known as *you can't have it.* "Listen, A.," I said, "let me tell you something, buddyroe, don't you dare come on to me, don't even think about it, because speaking of dogs, that one won't hunt, boy." "You always did sound southern when you were mad," he said, and I said, "I *am* southern, A., I always was and always will be and I'm proud of what I come from, not like you, you're the one who traipsed off to New York City and became a Yankee and acquired a Yankee accent—not that I have anything against Yankees or their accents in their place, only you aren't one, honey, that's another thing that doesn't change, your blood . . . you've got the same stuff running through your veins as I do, only you don't want it, you went off and took transfusion treatments to purify yourself of all provincial content and shit on everything you came from in the process, which was a lot, and if you want to know what happened to you that would be a damn good place to start the search, in my opinion," and I guess that must have finally knocked the wind out of the boy, because his face went really solemn and he held my gaze a minute—he was absolutely pale—and then he said, quietly, and even with a certain dignity, "humbly submitted, humbly received," which was the closest he could come to admitting I was right. However he put it, it hurt my heart to hear, for him to have to say it to himself much less to me, but at least he took it like a man and that gave me the first real hope I'd felt for him all night, and I said, "now let's change the subject, honey, or call it even, dial the ambulance and go on home."

Another pause ensued then, which was heavy, but also had some sweetness in it and so wasn't as uncomfortable as many that had preceded it, like maybe we had finally cut down to some heartmeat and might end up as friends after all, if nothing else, and he said, "I take it you didn't like it then," and I said, "what?" and he said, "the bathhouse painting," and I said, "she didn't look a thing like me, except her body, which is all you would get right." Ignoring me, A.'s eyes took on that concentrated abstract look they'd always had when he was drawing me before he made a stroke, and studying my face, he said, "you're right, I missed it, it's hard to work from memory . . . and I wasn't aiming for realism anyway," and I said, "what were you aiming for?" and he said, "just a feeling," with a hangdog look, and I said, "what feeling, honey?" and he wasn't catching my undertone at all, he said, "either you got it or you didn't, you don't have to rub my nose in it," and I said, "seriously, A., I'm interested," because I wanted to hear what he would say, and spearing me with those blue eyes of his he said, "the feeling of when something new comes into your life and breaks the thing wide open," and I said—my voice was positively trembling—"what about the feeling of when something old comes back and you're afraid it's going to shatter it in little bits—that would be a subject, wouldn't it, A.?" "Did you really hate it that much?" he said sadly, and I said, "it broke my heart, A., it just broke my heart, exactly like the man who made it," and we both sat there staring at each other, bleeding right out in the open and not afraid to let it show. But something else was coming through—maybe it was hope. I just know A.'s eyes were moist and shining, and I let myself appreciate his handsomeness again for the first time. As for myself, I probably looked like I'd been dragged behind a tow truck down a five-mile stretch of gravel road—that's about how I felt, at any rate, and I said, "you've plumb wore me out, A., I think you better take me home now before Mama has a fit on my head."

Only he didn't take me home, at least not straight. He took a little detour first, driving out Route 319 into the country. "Mama's is the other way," I told him, "in case you'd forgotten." He gave me this funny mellow sort of look and said, "this'll only take a few minutes." I thought it was way past midnight, which would have made it Tuesday morning, but the DJ in Soul City disagreed. When A. turned on the radio, tuned to Louis's listening choice, it was T. Bone Walker singing "Stormy Monday"—that's what A. said it was, at any rate, the Temptations being about as far as I go back that way—and when I checked my watch, sure enough, it was just a quarter past eleven, though it had been known to stop before and leave a lady stranded in places that weren't like fairy tales. "I'm not going parking with you, A.," I said, "if that's what you have in mind, it isn't seemly at my age and in my social position as a divorcée." I was only teasing him, of course, and making fun of Mama. If I'd thought that was what he was really up to I wouldn't have made the joke, but I sensed it wasn't, and after all those drinks I was at the point where a little flirting seemed okay, though nothing more.

And then for some reason I remembered that newspaper clipping from the *Killdeer Sentinel* that Mama had mailed me a while back, and I said, "you aren't going to jump my bones and leave me out here like that poor girl they found last summer buried in that tobacco field, are you?" and A. looked at me like I had put the lampshade on my head and said, "now tell the truth, Jane, where does that stack up on your current list of worries?" and I said, "I had a dream about that girl," and he said, "what did Dr. Rosenthal have to say about that?" "Rosen*krantz*," I told him, "and I don't remember if we talked about that one in particular, but he says everybody in the dream is you, or at least some part of you," and A. said, "that sounds wise to me—what part of you is she?" and I said, "I don't know, I never have, but I know she's down there," and he was quiet over that, which made me think he respected what I felt and maybe even understood a little, and then he said, "I've had dreams like that," and I felt we were getting close, but just a little bit too solemn then, which was something I was still afraid of, and then that little voice came up inside me which said, "maybe he'll be bored and not like you anymore," which went back to Daddy, who was often bored, or seemed that way to me, though it was just his gentlemanly "reserve," I know. I think I also knew A. wasn't bored, but something made me change the subject anyway, something made me turn to him and say, "you mean you aren't even going to *try* to jump my bones?" and my laugh sounded false and social in my own two ears.

A. looked at me like my cookies had finally crumbled, which made me feel like a damn fool for opening my big mouth, and his face got all wise and tolerant and gentle, and he said, "we've both had a lot to drink," which was exactly what a gentleman would say in the circumstances, administering the rebuff, but mildly, and including himself, but I felt petulant because he looked so much like . . . well, just like Daddy—not his face, but his "reserve"—and because I knew exactly what my motives were in running the whole routine, as though Dr. Rosenkrantz had got inside me and become a part of me and was never going to go away, and things were never going to be so simple as they used to be when I just did things without thinking what they meant, not even when I'd had too much to drink like now, and that seemed like such a sad, sad thought, like I had to stand in the corner for the rest of eternity and couldn't have any more fun. And maybe it was that girl buried down in that tobacco field inside me who didn't want to grow up, who resisted every step I took, and who said to A. right then, "Well, I can at least be insulted with you for not wanting to, can't I?" A. didn't even take it up. I sat there feeling sorry for myself the whole rest of the way out there, wanting to be with A. very much wherever he was going, more than was reasonable, but reminding myself that I was tight and it would look different in the morning.

I wasn't paying that much attention to the road but it seemed to me that maybe A. didn't know his way around those twisty roads too well and got lost and drove around in a big circle before we came out on Lake Drive and started coming up on Jefferson Davis Private Day School, where they'd put up a new brick building two years before. When I went there it was just two trailers parked out in the middle of a pasture.

A. had never been there at all. They'd moved to Winston-Salem just before Jeff Davis was set up to ward off the "black plague" the year the schools were integrated. A. had no memories associated with the place, which is why I couldn't figure out why he would want to take me there that night—Jeff Davis was Cary's place, and mine, not A.'s. That's what I was thinking when A. kept going right on past the school, which is when it finally dawned on me where he was headed.

"Turn this car around right now, A. Jenrette," I told him, "I don't want to go out there," and he said, "just for a minute, Jane, we're almost there, you don't even have to get out of the car," and I said, "and you don't have to either, *spud*"—it just slipped out. A. didn't even look at me, but I saw that little band of muscle flicking in his jaw, not a good sign, ever, in a man. "A team of wild horses couldn't get me out of this car, A.," I said, "and you're not going either except over my dead body"—another slip—and A. just drove right on.

Then I begged him more or less because I really didn't want to go. I hadn't been there in ten years and if I never saw the place again it would have been too soon for me. I said, "honey, if you just feel like you've got to do it, do it in the daylight when you're sober, and if you don't want to go by yourself take Louis with you, or call me, I'll go, but not at night," and he said, "I'm sober now, as sober as you are." He gave me a hard look and I said, "I hate to be the one to break the news to you, A., but you're about as sober as the worm in a tequila bottle, not to mention the fact that you've been dizzying up your brain with toot . . . take a look in the rearview mirror if you don't believe me, your eyes look like two flying saucers," and he got this grim little smile on his face and said, "that's exactly what I'm doing," and I said, "come again?" and he said, "looking in the rearview mirror," and I said, "come on, A., let's go home and you can write a poem about it," and he laughed out loud at that, though it was not a happy laugh, and turned to me and said, "you think you've got my number, don't you, Jane?" and I said, "I know so, honey, I always did and always will . . . now, please, it's pitch-black darkness out there and you could slip and fall if nothing else." A. gave me this accusing look on that and said, "people don't just slip and fall off two-hundred-foot drop-offs, Jane, not drunk, not sober—haven't you and Dr. Rosenkrantz got that far? It never happens, they make up their minds to it and then they go, which is what Cary did, and whatever you may think of it you don't dishonor that decision by pretending that he slipped," and I said, "honey, please, you're scaring me, and besides I wasn't saying that about Cary, nobody ever believed that anyway, but if you think you can't slip you're a fool, that's just the cocaine talking, and if I'd known you were that wired I wouldn't have even got in the car with you or let you get in either, now just pull over, A., and let me drive," and he said, "you can drive on the way home," and I said, "somehow I think you missed my drift, A.," and just gave up, because by that point we were pulling into the parking lot of the Little Wabash Dam and it was too late anyway.

I could already hear the soft roar of the water coming up from the Killdeer River way below, and the air got cooler and had that fresh smell to it which was the only thing I'd ever liked about the place. A. parked sideways in the Handicap space, which just seemed like one more thing, and sat there with the engine idling and both hands on the wheel and this expression on his face that made my heart turn over, like maybe it wasn't just a nostalgia visit he was contemplating. Then he eased and said, "I'm sorry, Jane, it's just something I've got to do," and I said, "that phrase has sunk a lot of noble ships, A.," which was something Daddy used to say. He turned and looked at me and said, "you're actually a fairly remarkable woman—did anybody ever tell you that?" and I said, "not near enough, so why don't you just stay right here and make up for the past," but he smiled like he'd already made his mind up, so I said, "just what exactly is it that you've 'got to do,' A.?" I think he might have even felt a little foolish by that time, though not enough to back down, of course. "Just go out there and stand and look at it and see what it feels like, that's all," he said, and I said, "then go on, you obstinate butt, get yourself killed and see if I care, just leave me the keys." He smiled at that and said, "I'll be back in a minute."

The overhead light came on and he got out and I threw myself back in the seat with my arms across my stomach like a pouting twelve-year-old, which is what I felt like, just about that help-less, and he walked out of the headlight beams. "Girl," I said, "just let him go, there's not a damn thing you can do about it," which made me remember something Sadie Kinlaw told me the time we had that talk about how you can't ever stop being a mother to them, and wondering every time your little boy walks out that door with his football pads and cleats if he's ever going to come back through it, and how you can't stop even when they don't—that's what she said to me with those pretty mild brown eyes of hers all hot and full of tears, which was a feeling I knew, too, from the perspective of a wife who loved her husband for two years at least, and tried the best I could another two, and then gave up and suffered through the rest till he walked out the door, the same damn thing. They just don't know what life is, men don't, they don't know how to value it and love it, always chasing after something that's not here, and I thought, damn it all, if A. is going to be dramatic, I will, too, since I'm drunk anyway and don't have to be accountable—that would have been the tobacco girl—so I threw the door open and shouted at him, "A., if you do anything, I swear I'll kill you." I couldn't even see him then, but I heard his smoky laugh out of the dark, and I said, "I mean it, A., I can't live through it twice, I won't be responsible again," and he said back, "you weren't responsible the first time, I was," and that right there is when I felt the fear of the living God run through me, "no, honey, no," I said, "you didn't put a gun to Cary's head, it was three whole years later, A., you weren't responsible, and neither was I." But I guess those three years just seemed like a blink in time to A., because he didn't answer.

I saw his long figure appear against the pale whiteness of the concrete rim—there wasn't any moon—walking out toward the middle. When he got there, he stopped a minute and then he

went down on his haunches and dropped his head over—I
couldn't tell if he was looking down, or just hanging his head—
and it struck me as an odd gesture for A. Jenrette to make,
squatting down like a farmer or some old country man to draw
you a picture in the dirt, getting close to what he knows. Maybe
A. was praying, I know I was, I said, "please, Jesus, if he wants
to die don't let it be tonight," because I knew people could want
it, which is something a lot of folks don't believe, but when
you've seen it once you know better, life is just the vapor in a
perfume bottle and when you take the stopper out it goes, and
anything can take it out, that's not the hard part, the hard part
is keeping it inside. I guess I knew because there'd been a time
when I wanted it myself, an hour down in Oakdale when it just
seemed easier to go than stay, to dissolve into the smell of something that's gone and not coming back, a smell in someone else's
nostrils who can mourn for what they did to you and maybe love
you then.

And remembering that hour I caught Cary's scent all around
us out there on the dam in the freshness of roiled water, which
brought him back for me again. And when you got right down
to it, having known them both in every sense, and loved them
equally, though differently, A. had always struck me as a better
candidate for it than Cary, and Cary wasn't here, only the heartsick smell of him. So my little prayer was not a joke, though
A.'s going out there might have been, a joke or a test, it's all the
same to me, I don't like either one. And having always been
religious, though "haphazardly," as Mama put it, I'd like to
think my prayer had something to do with A.'s getting up and
coming back the same way he went out.

We climbed back in the Bentley then and sat there for a minute. I didn't look at him because I knew it was something personal for A. that he might not want to share with me, or anyone,
but I could sense his mood. "I could feel him out there, Jane,"
he finally said, which is exactly what I would have said to A. if
he had asked, and then, invited, I did look. A. wasn't crying,
or even near it, his face looked grave, serene and innocent, he
seemed refreshed and younger, like he was eighteen again, the
way I always remembered him in love, that handsome boy buried out there in a sand dune somewhere on the Outer Banks,
who loved the girl in the tobacco field and did her wrong, and
maybe that's what I was seeing, a memory, my old love which
never died but just got twisted up and sick. "Out there you can

almost understand what he was feeling when he went,'' A. said,
''not something bad, but just going down to the water, no more
thoughts, just that whisper, listen . . . it's so soothing . . . it's
not a bad place like I always thought it would be, there's something good here, it's Cary, I can feel him like he's sitting right
here with us.'' Big tears were rolling down my cheeks by then
and I put my hand out on his coatsleeve and A. leaned his head
down against it and we both had that quiet cry we never got to
have before, and when I lifted my head, for just a second, A.
looked almost like Cary had that awful day in the cottage in Kill
Devil Hills when things came out. But when A. raised his face
it was shining where Cary's had been so dark and troubled and
locked rigid in a kind of terror I don't think it's possible to
comprehend, not even when you've been there and come back,
because the human mind won't hold it. It just can't. That was
the darkest well I've ever looked into or ever will, and I'd wanted
to run away from it, but I didn't, not that anything I'd done had
helped. But it was way past helping then, yet you've still got to
try. I think you do. A. was the one who funked it.

And sitting there in the front seat of the Bentley, I was not
forgetting that, and I knew I'd never forgiven him for it and that,
despite the little tingles running through me, I probably never
would. There was no point in even getting started. So I said,
''I'd like to go home now,'' and A. looked up wiping his hand
across his eyes and said, ''do you want to drive?'' in this tone
that would have broken an unconverted woman's heart, but I just
said, ''no, I'd probably put us in a ditch and never hear the end
of it, and if it's going to happen I'd just as soon blame you,''
and he said, ''I can drive okay, I think,'' and I said, ''convince
the road, not me.''

We didn't say a word the whole way to the farm—we'd said
enough for one night anyway—and when he stopped the car I
turned to him and said, ''well, A., it's been grand—don't be a
stranger,'' and he said, ''can I call you?'' and though some little
voice in me wanted to say yes, I told him, ''I'd appreciate it if
you wouldn't,'' feeling psychologically grown up and rather sad.
''You don't want to see me?'' he asked with this look of woebegone astonishment like such a possibility was not admissible
in a rational world, and I said, ''I'm not sure it's such a good
idea,'' pausing before I opened the door, I'm not sure why—
maybe to give him one last chance to talk me out of it. A. just

stared off through the windshield and said, ''okay, Jane, if that's the way you want it.''

I got out and ran up the steps, sensing his eyes following me, and remembering a younger girl coming in from dances and giving her date one last opportunity to see her legs. But I wasn't that young girl anymore, and A. wasn't a young boy, and whatever we had just come back from, it wasn't a dance—A. had never been a dancer anyway, though once upon a time I'd tried to teach him. Or maybe in a way it was—our dance, a private number. A. pulled off with a little spray of gravel, getting the last laugh of the evening, which is what a southern boy would do, a country boy, a native son. He did have some neglected talent.

Before I went in the house, I stood there on the porch and watched him going up the road, his headlight beams jouncing off the line of oaks on either side along the drive, and I had a premonition he was heading into something, though what it was I didn't know. That's when the song came back, ''they call it Stormy Monday,'' which by my watch it still was, though only by a minute. Some part of me wanted to go with him into Tuesday—I felt her stirring deep inside—but knowing it was just that girl in the tobacco field who liked the lonesome whistle of a freight train for a lullaby, the one who always got me into trouble, I hushed her and went in to bed.

Three

ADAM

After dropping Jane off I turned out of her mother's drive, went a hundred yards, and had to pull over on the shoulder. I was too high, shivering and sweating ice water, but the cold felt good, and it struck me that another line might make things even cooler. Better not, I decided. Glancing at my watch, I noticed that it was five minutes after midnight. *The Honeymooners*, my favorite show, had just ended in New York. For that matter, it had ended everywhere. Why was I thinking this? Suddenly I heard Ralph's voice: "You're a riot, Alice, a regular riot . . . bang! zoom! to the moon!" I started to laugh—I was *way* too high—and suddenly my eyes were wet.

I sank my head against the steering wheel and slowly banged it. Jane didn't want to see me. It was her one obvious response, yet I couldn't believe it. For a few brief moments at the dam I'd seen her eyes deepen and her glow come out. I'd seen the girl I used to know peer shyly at me from behind the wall of clever repartee and bitter charm the woman had erected, and, for that moment, reflected in her eyes, I'd been different, too, I'd been someone I remembered being proud of, a lean strong clear-eyed boy who could look himself in the mirror without revulsion, a boy whose name was A.

I decided I would have that line now after all. I snorted off my key and punched the radio button. As the toot kicked in, the music from the Bentley's Blaupunkt started coming out

40

in color and 3-D. "One too many," I said aloud, regretfully, and closed my eyes, settling in for a big blow. The music filled me like a sail and carried me away at impossible speed over a dark blue ocean with whitecaps breaking over it. "Whoa," I said, catching spray in my face, and suddenly shooting stars were running through my arms and legs leaving glittery cold tracks along my nerves. Suddenly the floor had dropped away and I was free-falling through dark air filled with the honking of geese—Snows—the rush of wings, the whisper of a vanished ocean in the volutes of a lightning whelk.

I opened my eyes in Cocaine Never-Never Land. I was aware of music blaring loudly, but it was Way Up There. Down here, where I was, it was still and silent and things happened in slow motion. I suddenly realized the amazing fact that I was home. *Home.* Thirteen years had passed. Everything had changed, but nothing was different—Jane was close but out of reach, Cary should have been here but wasn't, I still missed him, and I still didn't know my way. I'd run fast and hard and far, but running hadn't helped. My life had turned full circle and brought me back to the same place where I'd started—home, the good right place where everything went wrong. I still needed something here. I didn't know its name, but as I gazed through the windshield of the Bentley I could sense it out there in the landscape, a sinister and heartbreaking magnetism rising from the turned earth of the fields, and I knew it had drawn me home for a reason.

I put the car in gear and pulled out on the road, not knowing where I was going, letting it drive me.

On the outskirts of town I entered a lighted world again and turned down Depot Street, instinctively looking for the time on the handsome German clock inset in the gable of the old railroad station under the blue slate roof. I remembered looking at that clock and wondering what it said, a very little boy, carefully dressed, holding Nana's hand on the platform as Mama tipped the liveried black porter, waiting for the whistle of the Southern Star which would carry us to Richmond. There was no clock now. Not even any station. Just a paved lot where the wind pushed a few scraps of litter. I drove past blinking my eyes in disbelief, feeling strangely frightened.

On Main, still greater changes greeted me. A great death

had occurred. The dime store was the only business that remained from my childhood. Many of the storefront windows
were soaped or boarded over. Those that weren't had grills.
I stared at the noble old post office, like a Greek temple with
its fluted granite columns from the local quarry. The door
was padlocked now. There were broken windows in the fa-
cade, graffiti on the walls—not the stylish tags of the hip-hop
New York street kids, but a crude skull and "Megadeath,"
the name of the Heavy Metal rock band, sprayed in dripping
red block letters. The green swath of lawn which had once
separated the bottom steps from the sidewalk had turned to
yellow dust. Under the oak, on a bench where I remembered
spinster secretaries eating their lunches with birdlike hands,
a man lay stretched out with a sheet of newspaper across his
face. Further on, a few marginal black businesses had moved
in—a pawn shop, something called Lucilles Super Thrift, and
a third establishment, One $ Shoppe, which advertised, on a
pathetic hand-painted sign, "All Item Guaranteed 1$ Very
Nice." A sad urine-colored cloud had settled over everything. And yet, as in a double-exposed photograph, I saw the
ghostly image of the past town, the one I remembered, looming up from underneath the present one. I remembered a
clean inviting middle-class boulevard lined with solid two-
and three-story brick buildings where respectable merchants
kept their shops in the storefronts. That had been D. W.
Edwards & Son, where, in seventh grade, I'd contemplated
the mystery of a pair of saddle shoes and had no problem in
my life except how to get them. That had been the drugstore,
the jeweler, the stationer, those, the two banks to whom one's
allegiance was set at birth, like one's religion.

The only thing that hadn't changed was the burlap smell of
jute. I looked up and saw the great twin stacks of Dixie Bag
dominating the skyline from five blocks behind, belching clouds
of white smoke into the cool spring night. The graveyard shift
had just come on.

As I stopped at the red light I heard the heavy chugging of
an unmuffled V-8, like a diesel inboard. A jacked-up Camaro
sidled up on my right, with oversize tires, a spoiler, and mat
patches of hand-sprayed primer on the fender. Pinching his
cigarette, the driver sucked it to the filter and dropped it on
the pavement, flicking a quick glance at me. He was a sullen-
looking kid with dead angry eyes, long greasy hair and a

silver cap on his front tooth. "Scode"—the ugly pejorative popped into my mind from some deep forgotten place. I knew him. He was from the north end and his daddy worked at the mill and beat the shit out of him on Friday nights when he got drunk. I knew him from the corridors at Spaulding Elementary, the bathroom, the parking lot and playground. I knew him from the football field. Mostly I knew him through Cary, who felt a strange attraction toward that murky violent underworld and the vicious losers in it, though he came from a different one himself. I think it was their pain that spoke to Cary—perhaps he saw his father in such boys. For me, it was the staggering purity of their rebellion. For Cary, who introduced me to that world and was my surety in it, was never more than an observer there—I got involved, going through a period of delinquency that started roughly with the publication of Daddy's book and lasted into high school.

Listening to the Camaro idle, I caught a sudden flash of myself and Cary standing in the crossed headlight beams of two running cars out on Braswell Road, passing a bottle of Southern Comfort in a group of North Killdeer boys. It was the summer after Mama's death, and I'd driven down from Winston to show off my new black Jeep. Cary didn't want to go to Braswell Road—he'd pretty much outgrown the bad-ass phase by then— but I wanted to check out my new machine. We stood there drinking, among the taunts and ugly laughter, gazing down the gravel straightaway which ran for three hundred yards then turned left almost perpendicularly. If you kept straight you left the road where there was a narrow path between two walls of trees, issuing into a grassy field. Two cars blazing down that stretch, side by side, blowing dust, toward a path only big enough for one. The other had to stop, or turn, or crash. We'd already won twice and I felt pumped up and invincible. The third time Cary said no, but when I climbed behind the wheel anyway he followed.

The Trans Am jumped out half a length at the start and halfway down the stretch Cary said, "slow down." But I thought I could nerve the other driver out of it and make him turn. "Goddamn it, A., hit the brakes!" he shouted, and I did, but it was too late to stop. I jerked the wheel into the turn and felt a rollercoaster vertigo as the Jeep tilted up on two wheels and poised there for one long sickening moment before coming back. We fishtailed through the gravel, pine branches whipping the windshield, till I finally got control. I sat there with my heart pounding, then started laughing and held out my hand for him to slap. The look of dark sober anger on Cary's face caught me up. "What's the matter, spud?" I asked, and he said, "what the fuck do you think, A.? what are you trying to prove?" and I said, "take it easy, man, nothing happened." I started to turn around, meaning to rejoin the group, but Cary held the wheel. I stared at him, surprised, and he said, "keep going," and I said, "but . . ." starting to object, and he said, "drive the fucking car, A." I pushed his arm away, acting pissed, but I obeyed him. I'd always counted on Cary for that—to tell me when to stop. Because I never knew. I never gave that authority to anybody else.

The light turned green and I looked at the homeboy in the Camaro unconsciously tensed for a challenge, expecting him to leer and shoot the finger as he scratched out. He just stared at me like a dog so beaten he didn't even resent it anymore, envying the Bentley, the sadness of a dirt-poor kid from nothing in his face. It shocked me like a slap. I was The Man in the Big Shiny Car to him, an enemy too high and powerful even to defy. It shocked me deeply—because somewhere deep inside I was still lost in that same angry world with him. And Cary, Cary was gone.

I drove on, turning down Advance Avenue, then into the Hills section, down dark roads where the big houses were set back from the road, the litany of the families that had lived in them playing like a sad chant through my mind. The faces of my grade school friends flashed past, all still twelve years old. I went around a wooded curve and suddenly the golf course opened on my left, Number Three fairway coming down to water where I'd held my breath, scooping through bottom muck searching for lost balls. I pulled over to the side, my heart beating hard, a weird twisting in my gut, feeling suddenly like I was going to cry, feeling suddenly like I was not all right. I looked across the grassy field I'd cut every week for pocket money to where it rose into a stand of poplars, and in the gray shingled house on the top of the hill there was a light on in the window.

As I gazed at my old house, for a moment it was like we were still up there. The light was Daddy's study. He was up there typing late, already working on his second book. Mama's window was dark. She hadn't felt well at dinner, though she was getting better. The chemotherapy had got all the cancer. I was packing in my room, putting a few last things into the black steamer trunk I'd take to Keane. We were leaving in the morning, Daddy and I—Mama wasn't up to it. But it wouldn't be long till Christmas—that's what she'd said when I said good night to her in her bedroom. She was staying in the guest room now. Till she felt better. "I'm so proud of you, darling," she'd said, regarding me with her beautiful kind dark eyes I had no secrets from. "So proud," she whispered, drawing me close, and I stood enduring her embrace, as a fourteen-year-old boy about to start high school must, feeling awkward and embarrassed and more moved than I cared to show. The tide had already turned against us then, but it would be okay. Things were still reclaimable.

The next day I flew to New York with Daddy, and we had dinner with Eleanor Rosenberg, his editor, the first time I'd ever been to the Four Seasons. I'd never seen a restaurant like that before. It seemed like a promise of what my life would one day be, what I would be embarking on at Keane, something magnificent. We drank champagne and Eleanor toasted the success of *Rubber Man*, completely unaware, as far as I could tell, of the ambiguous feelings it stirred in Daddy and me, all that it had cost. Yet we celebrated bravely, though I could see a deep restless agony in Daddy's eyes, becoming habitual then. He drank too much at dinner, and we took a cab back to the hotel, where I said good night to them in the lobby. They had business to discuss and were going to the bar.

I went up to my room and watched television for a while before taking a shower. As the water ran I thought about the morning and all that lay ahead, wondering if I was up to Keane and the boys I'd meet who came from this glittering city, so much better prepared. It was for him, for Daddy, part of it, a challenge he had posed me, to be the best that I could be, because he'd never had that chance. I felt I had to honor his hope in me and prove myself, but there was cold fear, terror really, at the thought that I might fail, not just myself, but him.

I thought about Daddy and all the things he'd given me. I remembered a cold September morning standing with him in a stubble field in rural Warren County, drinking coffee and waiting for the sun to rise, how he'd stood behind me and showed

me how to settle the stock to my shoulder, and the way my heart
fluttered as the first doves flew, so high and fast, and his arms
around me and his calm voice as he said, "elbow up, both eyes
open, son, don't look at anything except the bird—not the sky
behind it, not the clouds—just the bird, lead it, feel its motion
and its speed and don't shoot where it is but where it's going
. . . now," and I felt his big cold hand close my small one in it
as I squeezed the trigger.

The bird stopped its frantic motion as though it had fallen
asleep in mid-flight, as though it was a kindness we had
done it to allow it to stop. It spread its wings out in a gesture
like prayer and then began to drop, end over end, down into
the stubble corn, and I shouted with pride and ran for it. I
picked it up and it was so small and helpless, its body soft
as a kid glove filled with water, still warm—not warm, but
hot—though it was dead. Tears welled in my eyes and I
looked up in Daddy's face, and he reached out and drew me
to his leg. I could smell the canvas and the oiled leather of
his boots and the lingering trace of powder in the air. I
closed my eyes and cried, and he said, "that's all right, son,
go on and cry," and then he knelt beside me and held me
at arms' length and said, "it's good to care, A., that's part
of hunting, you have to care and do it anyway, only the
strong can hunt," and I wiped my sleeve across my eyes,
and he said, "now you know," and I accepted it, I felt the
mystery of life and death rise up from the stubble corn,
something old and true, and I never doubted him, not ever,
he was the only one who ever taught me anything worth
learning, that the good things are never fully clear and simple, never easy, always a dark thread running through them.

And that night at the Sherry Netherland after I'd showered,
I went to brush my teeth and found I'd left my dop-kit in
Daddy's room. I put on my shirt and pants and went down
barefoot to the desk and got a key. There was a "Do Not
Disturb" sign on the door, but I didn't think anything of it.
I put the key in, turned the lock and entered. It took a moment for my eyes to adjust, and then I saw Eleanor lying
propped up on the pillows against the headboard with her
eyes closed and her face turned toward the ceiling. She was
naked, I felt a terrible swimming confusion like maybe I'd
entered the wrong room. Because I didn't see him, not at
first. Then she moved her hand and the silver bracelet on her

wrist caught the light coming from the hallway—I still see it sparkle—and I saw her hand was resting on the draped form of his head between her legs beneath the bedsheet.

Eleanor opened her eyes then and stared at me. First there was shock and then a desperate pleading apology together with the certain knowledge of its futility, that it could never be undone, what was passing in that moment, and she said, "Adam," just that—she began the trend that continued on at Keane and, later, in New York, my new identity—and then her hand tensed and she said, "Clay." From beneath a great flurry and commotion in the covers he popped up like a jack-in-the-box, or the buffoon adulterer in some comic silent movie short, and my life changed forever. "Son," he said, and I didn't answer, and he said, "bud," more anxiously, and I simply stared as understanding dawned, seeing so clearly who he was and trying to remember another man, one I'd thought I'd known, my father.

This man who'd popped up from the sheets was someone else, someone who resembled my father in all the outward ways but lacked the thing inside, the thing I'd felt that morning as we stood over the dead dove, the thing that always made my soul hum like a tuning fork and my eyes burn at the mention of the word *honor*. This was not the same man who'd taught me how to shake hands with just the proper degree of pressure and to meet the other man's eyes with a steady level gaze, who'd taught me what it was to give your word and keep it, and what it meant to honor a debt. Everything my father had given me, every sacredness implied in the word *gentleman*, and, beyond sacredness, the mere decencies, all of it went up in flames that instant in the Sherry Netherland Hotel—that he could do this to Mama, who'd never reproached him for the book, who was back home fighting for her life against the cancer other people whispered *Rubber Man* had caused. I hadn't believed that accusation, but from that moment forward the affliction that had fallen on us—social disgrace, Mama's illness—no longer seemed occult. It had been his doing, this careless man who was once my father, whom I'd loved and defended against all comers, even against myself and my own doubts. I stopped defending him there and swore never to be like him. Something had gone wrong in me that instant and never come back fully right, not in all the years since.

That was the last I saw of my father, Clay Jenrette. He dis-

appeared on that September night in 1969 between Eleanor Rosenberg's svelte thighs. Not long afterward I lost Mama, too.
From there on out Cary was the only thing I had left from the
old world of Killdeer and childhood, the last right true thing
that wasn't spoiled or broken. Cary was the ground to me. I
could stand on it and walk around and know where the fuck I
was.

Part of what joined us was the shared perception that everything, or almost everything, was full of shit, though Cary
was a little sadder about it and I was a little angrier, I guess
because I still believed I had a *right* to something better, like
a decent father, and maybe Cary didn't feel that way. We
didn't talk about our fathers often—there was no need. It was
understood.

I remembered one night watching TV at Cary's house, eating
popcorn and drinking Cokes, when *Cat on a Hot Tin Roof* came
on the late show. I didn't want to watch it because I had this
idea that Tennessee Williams was too intellectual and arty, and
I was so sick of that from Keane, but Cary kept it on. By the
end of it both of us were sitting there crying and trying not to
let the other see, especially that last part where Brick finds Big
Daddy in the cellar going through the million dollars' worth of
junk he brought back from Europe on his trip with Big Mama.
Somewhere among the porcelains and bibelots, Big Daddy
comes across an old suitcase with a uniform and a trooper's hat
from the Spanish-American War inside, the only things Big
Daddy's hobo father left him, and in the hour Big Daddy learns
he's going to die, he discovers that old suitcase and its contents
are the only things that matter to him, the only things worth
saving, the memory of his father's love, and over that he and
Brick are reconciled. I don't know why Cary cried, I guess the
same reason I did, because he loved T.O. in spite of everything,
just like I loved my father, though I didn't know it at the time.
I didn't know that the disappointment and the damage fathers
inflict makes no difference to the love sons bear them—if anything, they make it stronger—but maybe Cary knew.

So another part of my shared bond with Cary was in the lost
cause of our fathers, a rebellion which was also a devotion,
something we were too young to articulate to one another, or
even to ourselves. For a long time after that Cary and I went
around talking about the "stink of mendacity." Big Daddy's
catch phrase became a kind of private joke between us, like the

night we were sitting in the old Ambassador theater still talking when the lights went down and some woman behind us said, "shhh, there are other people here, too," and she was perfectly right, of course, but at sixteen you aren't going to see that, so Cary turned to me and said, "I say, Brick, you smell somp'm pow'ful and awb-noxshus in the vicinity?" and I said, "yes, sir, I sho do, I b'lieve that's the stink of mendacity, Big Daddy," and we cracked up and slapped five, and she called Mr. Boland who appeared with his periscope-type Boy Scout flashlight and made us leave, but we went holding our noses. It was totally sophomoric, but a good memory to me.

Killdeer was the cosmic mendacity landfill to both of us, but it was complicated, another rebellion which was also a devotion, because while I was away at Keane I couldn't wait to come back. I kept a calendar on my wall and every night after dinner I'd take out a Magic Marker and very slowly, savoringly, blot out the square—that was the chief satisfaction of my day, having got through it and throwing it away with joy, bringing me one step closer to home.

And at the same time Cary was out there at Jeff Davis plotting his escape from Hicksville, thinking I was off in the great world, a young lord, having my horizons broadened like some kind of plastic surgery. He listened when I told him Keane and Boston and New York City—at least what I saw of them in my friends' homes—were pretty much the same thing as Killdeer all over, only with a better interior decorator, or at least a slicker one, but it was like Cary was humoring me. Whenever the subject of my so-called "privilege" came up, which never struck me as all that great—hell, I'd have rather been out in a cut cornfield shooting doves at the beginning of September than coming into Logan Airport to catch the bus to Keane—or maybe something about my father's book, or our Kincannon ties, it was like Cary would get real quiet and his eyes would widen with little stars in them—perhaps not that extreme, but in the general ballpark. He was like a little boy listening to stories of some faraway lands with special radiant beings in them, lands and people he would never know or visit. But why not? Why couldn't Cary be anything he wanted to be and do anything he wanted to do? It was like he'd already decided he couldn't, even in the sixth grade when we first met.

With my life going to pieces, I wanted to tell him "privilege" wasn't all it was cracked up to be. I'd hated every minute of

every day I was at Keane, except, I guess, when I was running—
not the meets, but autumn training days when I was by myself
going through a stand of hemlocks back along the river, their
dead branches like broken ladder rungs climbing up the trunks
and rays of sun filtering through the canopy, and suddenly out
into full sunlight on the bank and a long view down the open
water where some boys were pulling in a scull. That, and maybe
sometimes drawing, was what I liked about Keane, the times
when I could get away from it and lose myself, which wasn't
being there at all, and always alone. Anything that I was ever
good at was something lonely.

I used to call him on the phone a lot, especially the spring
after Mama died. There wasn't anybody else. I didn't realize it
at the time, but I was so messed up it was almost like I was
living in another world. The people I passed on the paths just
flitted by like ghosts and I'd faze out in class and find the teacher
asking me a question, and then I'd have to ask him to repeat it,
but, of course, I wouldn't know the answer because I hardly
cracked a book all term. Not that I was lazy, though that was
suggested, but that I couldn't read, really. I was literally illiter-
ate. I knew the words and I could say them, but they had absolutely no meaning to me, like something in a foreign language.
And because of the way things stood with Daddy then, there
was really only Cary to hold me down. I counted on him to keep
me straight, and he was the last thing I'd ever loved. Except for
Jane.

That's what I was thinking when the red light came on in the
rearview mirror of the Bentley and the policeman shone his
flashlight in at me. His face was like a cold stone wall as he
asked me for my license and registration, and I thought there
might be serious trouble for a minute till he read my name. He
peered at me more closely, and I pointed past him toward the
gray shingle house on the hill which fell away to the far side
toward Ruin Creek. "I used to live here, officer," I told him,
and he said, "I thought I recognized you," handing back my
documents, "you're Clay Jenrette's boy, aren't you?" and I
laughed and wiped my eyes as I said, "that's right—yes, sir, I
sure am," and he said, "I played ball with your daddy, son.
You better move along. Those people up there thought you was
a burglar." He smiled apologetically, and I said, "yes, sir, I'll

do that,'' and pulled away, sensing that the night had barely started, and knowing where the next stop on the mystery tour would be.

Four

JANE

After A. left I undressed and washed my face, then put on my old flannel nightgown and sat down at my vanity thinking I would put on eye cream, but instead just staring at my sad old face. There was something haunted about that mirror. I could always see her in it, the girl, as though my previous reflection had got trapped there from long usage. Whenever I went home to Mama's I felt the change, but never more so than that night, after going to the dam with A. I tried telling myself what all my friends were telling me, that I looked better than I had in two years, but it just made me wonder who was crazy—them or me. It wasn't even physical so much—though there were a few lines under my eyes other people hadn't started to notice yet—but rather something in my expression. There were lessons there the girl had never known she'd have to learn, and which the woman wished she'd never had to. A. had been one of the hardest of them. If things had turned out differently back then, I thought, the present might be a different story, too. As it was, tonight would just be one more lesson. I didn't like it much, having never been the student type, and would have liked to put it on A.'s tab together with a lot of other things. But I couldn't blame him, really—all he'd done tonight was to be himself, and you can't blame a hound dog for howling at the moon. And, besides, I'd gone to the party, and I'd left it, too—with him. I had no one but myself to blame, but that thought depressed me just as much as usual. The worst part was, I couldn't tell whether I was upset because what I'd wanted to happen at the party hadn't, or because it had.

In either case, I was exhausted and knew I wasn't going to sleep a wink. Having had my fill of late-night TV, I decided I'd try reading for a while and went to my old bookshelf to see if some juicy novel, something with as much romance and as little real life as possible, didn't leap out at me. But my eye went straight to the line of yearbooks on the bottom shelf. I knelt down and took out the first, from tenth grade at Jeff Davis. I smiled at the name—*The Private*—remembering the old joke about the team, Jefferson Davis's Privates. I opened it and started flipping, searching for a fifteen-year-old girl with braces named Metal-Mouth McCrae, but something fell out—a sheet of yellowed notebook paper folded twice. I picked it up and read in Cary's hand:

> *Roses are red,*
> *Violets are blue.*
> *I don't know the answer,*
> *And neither do you.*

I sat down on my old bed and wept, remembering. It had been a math quiz. Cary passed it to Jean Ann Hogan and she nudged my shoulder. It was the beginning of sophomore year, right after Jeff Davis had been set up. I hadn't wanted to go there, but Mama didn't give me any choice. I'd gone to elementary school in Lawford Corner, Cary in Killdeer, so we hardly knew each other. I already had an idea Cary was interested in me though. Those first few days at Jeff Davis, standing around with my girlfriends chatting before the bell, I happened to glance up and catch him staring. There was something soulful and a little troubled in his dark brown eyes—I'd thought he was handsome—but it embarrassed me when he didn't look away. I didn't realize then that Cary knew about me and Deacon from his older brother, Cliff. As close as they were at the time, Deacon had passed along the details of his conquest to Cliff, and Cliff told Cary—that "secret" was public knowledge, known to every high school boy in Killdeer in the smart set. I suppose that knowledge of my "experience" made me seem mysterious and fascinating to Cary. Or maybe he just felt sorry for me.

The first word he ever said to me was mocking. One day he overheard me saying "gross" to someone in my crowd. Like any fifteen-year-old girl, I had a tendency to overuse that word. Over my shoulder I heard it echo back in a male voice, and when I turned to glare Cary grinned at me ironically and coolly turned his back. I thought he was mean, but he'd piqued my interest. Thus the dance began.

We chatted warily a few times at school and he began to pass me notes. I guess I knew what underlay his attentions, but I was with Deacon then and didn't encourage him. Cary wasn't the sort who needed much encouragement.

We graduated to the phone call then, which was the next threshold of intimacy and one I didn't cross willingly. Mama answered and told me who it was when she came to my room to get me. "Hi, Jane, this is Cary," he said a little nervously, and I said, "I *know* who it is," wanting to make the picture clear to him straight off—swim at your own risk. "I was just calling to say hi," he told me, preparing his retreat, and I said, "you already said that," and he said, "what are you so ticked off about?" and I said, "did I say I was ticked off?" and he said, "no, but you're sure acting like it," and I said, "is that why you called up—to criticize my personality?" and he said, "no, I just called to talk," and I said, "so talk, I'm listening," and he said, "how can I talk when you're being such a pad?" and I said, "what's a pad?" and he said, "you'll understand when you grow up," and, getting it, I said, "oh, that kind of pad—that's gross, Cary, totally gross," and he said, "well, excuse me for living," and I said, "you're excused," and he said, "thank you," and I said, "you're welcome—and FYI, I am grown up," and changing the subject quickly he asked, "so how do you like it out at Jeff's?" and I said, "Jeff's"—that was my way of acknowledging his joke—"is great"—I did a pause— "if you're a cow."

I thought my line was pretty killer, as we said back then. I guess Cary must have thought so, too, because there was a giddy note of panic in his voice as he asked, "are you a cow?" That took me back a little before I said, "you're so weird, Cary," and that was when he mooed at me—a great big belting blast of a moo like a farm boy. I lost my cool and laughed. Regarding that as a triumph, Cary cut straight to the chase and said, "you want to cut lunch sometime and go down to the lake?" and I said, "I doubt it *seriously*," not wanting to give him any more satisfaction than necessary, and he said, "but you're not absolutely positive?" teasing me. "Besides, it's too far to walk," I told him, faltering a little, and he said, "not if we drive a car, it's not," and I said contemptuously, "you don't have a license," and he said, "I will in two months, and I've got my learner's permit now," and I said, "so what are you going to do, bring your Mama to chaperone?" and he said, making it up as he went along, "if I have a car tomorrow, will you go?" and certain he could never pull it off, I said, "I might consider thinking about it, *maybe*," and he said, "see you in the pasture at twelve tomorrow," and I said, "sure, Cary," and we hung up.

How he managed it I'll never know, but the next morning before the bell he gave me this big ecstatic grin that seemed too confident to be a bluff, and I spent the whole morning with this terrible sinking feeling. We got out of Social Studies at noon and broke for lunch. I took my brown paper bag down to the big rock pile in the pasture where the girls all congregated, not far from Mr. Shafter Humphry's herd of Guernseys which grazed there. We girls were like a herd as well, the way they gather in a circle with their horns outward when they're being stalked, seeking safety in numbers. I was beginning to think I was safe when Cary sauntered from the edge of the woods at quarter past—he'd parked Cliff's VW off on a side road. He stopped across the creek from us, putting his foot up on a stump with his hands in the back pocket of his jeans, and flashed a big cocky grin across at me. All my girlfriends stopped chewing their sandwiches and looked up—exactly like cows when they stop grazing. "You ready?" Cary asked, and all the girls turned to me. I went pink, then crimson, then vermillion, and finally a brilliant scarlet red.

"Where's the car?" I finally managed to get out, and Cary pointed to the woods and said, "right over there," and I said, "where? in the trees?" as though I didn't believe him, "sure, Kinlaw, what is it, a Hot Wheel?" alluding to the toy. Ignoring my insult, Cary asked, "why don't we just take a little walk and I'll show you?", and I said, "why don't you just drive it over, Mr. Man, if your weenie's big enough?" My friends went wild on that, and Cary said, "maybe I will," and stalked off to the tune of vengeful gales of laughter ringing out above Jeff's pasture, where Mr. Humphry's Guernseys were lowing, too.

Five minutes later the VW swerved into the parking lot spewing gravel. Mrs. Stevens, our homeroom teacher, who was standing on the trailer steps, regarded him with an immense surprise. As it bucked the curb, the car went airborne for a few seconds before touching down in the grass. As Cary jounced down into the pasture Tommy Vernon and Brewer Payne, who were smoking cigarettes, both dropped their jaws and dove for their lives in opposite directions. Cary never even took his foot off the gas, not till he reached the creek, where he hit the brakes and swerved hard to the right, the car stopping dead in its tracks. Cary lit a cigarette with false casualness, putting his elbow on the window and taking a deep drag. Then he cut his eyes at me and said, "any further questions?"

My girlfriends all swung their heads around and stared at me. There was no way out—no honorable way—and after all his effort I didn't have the heart to stand him up. Trying to look casual as I got up, I tugged my shorts down, dismissing my friends, who were razzing me from behind now with jeers and knowing looks, and then sauntered over and jumped across the creek. Only I didn't quite make it. One of my sandals got sucked off in the mud and I went back for it with ruffled dignity before throwing myself in the shotgun seat of the VW, leaning back against the door as far from Cary as possible, and glaring at him as I said, "I don't have the slightest idea why I'm doing this, but if we get in trouble I'll slice your balls off and feed them to my collie, Sam." Cary blinked his eyes in stupefaction, then grinned and stepped on the gas, shooting all the girls the finger through the open window, with them shooting it right back. Pissed off by their fickleness, I joined him, and about that time we hit the curb and went flying back into the gravel. There was Mrs. Stevens with Mr. McAfee, the principal, staring at us from the steps with their hands on their hips. Cary looked at me and I said, "no!" opening my eyes wide, but he shot one at them, too, throwing everything to the winds. Blowing the horn, he wheeled out of the lot, slushing off a line of gravel, and we took off toward the lake.

Fear of punishment was probably uppermost in my mind right then, but I was also seriously impressed by Cary's stones, and flattered. But I hardly knew Cary then, and I was so distrustful. The temperature started dropping even before we reached the dam. A lot of it was Deacon. Though I was only fifteen then and Deacon was my first lover, I thought he'd taught me what men wanted from me—all of them, Cary included.

I was so in love with Deacon then I couldn't really think about another boy. I remembered looking at those magazines at the grocery store while Mama was in the check-out line, speed-

reading stories like "Ten Ways to Keep His Interest." Deacon
was off at State, but I had it all planned out how, after we were
married, I was going to cook him shepherd's pie and meet him
at the door at night when he came home from work, wrapped
in cellophane, butt naked, and holding his slippers in my mouth
like Ruff the dog. Sometimes at Jeff's, standing there outside the
classroom with my girlfriends before the bell rang, I'd listen to
them talk about going to second base and whether it was okay
to jerk your boyfriend off in the car if he was really pitiful and
begging and in pain and telling you how it would be your fault
if he got "blue balls" and had to walk around bowlegged for
the next two days, and I'd feel way above that, like a married
woman listening to a bunch of teenage pads who haven't even
found out what it's for yet. But I knew, and I'd think, standing
there, "I'm *his*," and that would give me this shivery mystical
feeling inside, which had to do with security, my lack of it and
my pathetic strategy for getting some.

Dr. Rosenkrantz and I had covered all that, and I remembered
telling him about the first time I'd gone down on Deacon, how
I'd wept on the couch. The whole idea had seemed unnatural
and disgusting to me at the time, but Deacon was five years
older and I delivered myself over to him so completely, trusting
in his gentleness and mercy—there'd been so little. Deacon
coaxed and pushed and finally I screwed up my courage and
obliged him. I'd never realized just how big it was, purplish and
shiny like the throbbing root of some big tree. Trying to be
careful with my braces and with Deacon pulling on my head
when he began to get excited to make me take the whole thing
down—like swallowing a big cucumber without chewing—I'd
had to stop several times to catch my breath and let my stomach
settle. My eyes were watering so bad I could hardly see, and
when he finally shot his wad—it tasted just like Comet cleanser,
it all does, more or less—I made myself swallow it because he'd
told me, "love is swallow, like is spit it out," and I came up off
him so proud, smiling and blushing and about to puke.

Deacon looked at me with his eyes all sleepy and sated and a
flush spreading over those plump baby cheeks of his, and I said,
"was it okay?" and he grinned and said, "outstanding—I was
kind of sweating it there about the hardware though." As though
I was going to gnaw his precious pecker off with my braces.
Then he reached out and nudged my lip up with his finger and
plucked out a crinkly blond hair that had got stuck between my

wires. He studied it a minute and then handed it to me, saying, "keep this as a souvenir," and I did. I put it between two pieces of Scotch Magic Tape to preserve it and hid it in my goddamn hope chest.

My eyes still burned remembering that, and other things, like the night before he went up north to Harvard Business School when he took me to his parents' house and showed me the diamond ring his grandmother had left to her first grandson—him. He slipped it on my finger and let me wear it while he fucked me in that funny little bed in his room with the model airplanes hanging from the ceiling on clear fishing line and the college pennants thumbtacked to the wall. When it was over he took it off my finger and put it back inside its box and said, "if you're good while I'm away, you may get to keep it." And I was so good.

I was so good I never even really gave Cary a chance, after he'd taken such a chance for me. It was my "goodness," together with my experience with Deacon, that made me turn to Cary that day after we reached the dam and say, "I guess you think you earned yourself a piece of pussy with that production number—well, you better think again." I'll never forget the look he gave me, like he was shocked, first off, at my mouth, and then disgusted—I don't know what all, except that I felt judged. Probably it was just my judgment against myself, but when Cary didn't respond, I said, "you aren't a queebo, are you?" and he said, "where'd you pick up *that* expression? as if I didn't know." His eyes mocked me, and I said, "you don't know anything, Kinlaw," and he said, "I know more than you think I do, McCrae," and I said, "oh, yeah?" and he said, "oh, yeah," and I said, "like what?" and he said, "like about you and Deacon Griggs?" and I said, "what about us?" and Cary said, "come on, Jane, it's not like it's a secret—everybody knows." I stood there thunderstruck, my jaw swinging in the wind, because it was beyond my comprehension that Deacon could have talked, much less talked the way he had—after he'd told *me* we had to keep it secret "to protect my reputation." As I cast about for some way to explain it, Cary said, "is every guy who doesn't try to get in your pants a 'queebo,' Jane? because if that's what you want you don't have to ask twice." I didn't answer him because, among other things, the sad truth is, I probably did assume that then, not knowing shit from apple butter.

Cary lit a Marlboro and strolled out on the lip of the dam where he sat dangling his legs and watching the water way below, dark with wavy white lines through it where it sluiced through the spillway gates. I tried to coin some killer line to scorch him with when he came whining back like I was sure he would. When he didn't, the tables turned and I started worrying he didn't like me, so I picked up this rock—just a little one that wouldn't hurt—and walked up to the edge. "You're no fun," I told him with a pouty smile and threw it at him. It missed, skittering along the edge before dropping over and bouncing off the lower wall.

Cary watched it the whole way down and then flicked his cigarette after it, gazing back at me like my peace offering hadn't cut it, so I said, "I'm sorry I called you a homo, I don't think you are." His expression mocked as it forgave me. "That's real big of you, Jane," he said, and then a hint of something hurt and fierce flashed in his dark eyes and he said, "lies don't mean shit, it's the truth that hurts you," in that way he had of coming out with things. I didn't know exactly what he meant by it, but something changed for me right then. I realized I'd been wrong about what I thought he was after. But I still didn't know what he *was* after. So I asked him.

"Why'd you do it then?" I said, "why'd you bring me out here if it wasn't that?" and Cary said, "because I like you, does there have to be another reason?" and I said, "I guess not," glad he liked me, but still a little mystified. It seemed too simple.

"Why don't you sit down and make yourself at home?" Cary asked with a little grin, patting the concrete beside him, and I said, "I don't think so, I don't like it out there, it makes me kind of sick to the pit of my stomach," and Cary said, "I like it here," bragging like a boy, and I said, "why?" screwing up my face like I thought he was crazy or something—the girl part of the script.

I didn't really think he was crazy though, because I had similar places, like the apple tree in the back yard I always used to climb up in when I was little. I'd sit there in the crook watching things happening in the yard, or just looking out at the ponds where some fat catfish would make a groggy thrash every once in a while. I'd think about all sorts of things up there, like about when I was even littler and Daddy had just had the ponds dug, how sometimes at twilight he'd take my hand and we'd walk along the edge listening to the pump motor droning in the tank house where we kept the fry and I could feel how happy Daddy was, which made me happy, too, and then he'd pick me up in his arms and start singing in that sweet rusty baritone of his, that Gershwin song, "Summertime," about the catfish jumping and the cotton high, and how one did, too, a big old catfish, right when he was singing the song. Daddy laughed like he'd known all along that catfish was going to jump on cue and had made it happen just for me. I guess there must have been a hundred times he sang that song—it got to be a sort of thing between us—and it only happened once that the fish obliged him, but it was that one time I'd remember sitting up there in the apple tree. Best of all, back there behind the leaves nobody could see me, I could see them but they couldn't see me, and I'd think of myself growing up and still living there on the farm, I'd see myself much bigger, Mama's size, but Daddy would be exactly the same way he was now, and Mama wouldn't be part of it at all. So I had a feeling about what Cary was doing, but it was different, too, because up there in my tree I felt safe and enclosed, but out there on the dam you were all exposed under the sky with that terrible dropoff yawning under you down to the Killdeer River. It was scary, not safe. At the time I guess I figured it was just a difference in a boy, but, looking back, I always remembered that, Cary sitting there with his head tilted forward but turned up to the side with that mocking pixie grin of his, squinting at me and saying, "I like it here," and me saying, "why?" and him shrugging and saying, "I just do." That had been the start of it for me and Cary.

After that he'd begun calling me more often. We'd talk on the phone for hours, and he'd buy me presents practically every week so that I got used to it and was disappointed when he didn't. It was records mostly, little forty-fives, whatever Motown tune was number one on the charts—"Stop in the Name of Love," or "Ain't No Mountain High Enough" by Marvin Gaye and Tammi Terrell. It was always something about love, and I guess I knew Cary was in love with me, but it seemed okay for it to stay the way it was. He took me to the State Fair in Raleigh one time and paid for me to get my ears pierced. I knew Mama was going to have a fit, but I just wanted to—I'd wanted to since I was nine—and he bought me a little pair of fourteen-carat studs, the first I ever owned. I still have them. It was such a happy day, and what made the memory bitter was that after it was over I made Cary drive me to Deacon's dorm at State and I went upstairs to say hello. Deacon talked me into bed, though, and I left Cary sitting in the car for half an hour. He didn't speak to me the whole way home.

But Cary forgave me. He was so generous, and when he loved you he loved *you*, not what you did, right or wrong. He was different from other boys that way, though like them in so many others. I remembered how he'd tried to kiss me sometimes, like once at that Halloween party after we'd been dancing. Cary had been drinking and when we went outside to cool off he pushed me back against the wall and started pawing me. I could feel his hard-on. It wasn't exciting to me, just irritating, like when Sam was a puppy and would get up on your leg, but it made me think about him.

With Deacon off at State, then Harvard, Cary and I had spent almost every free minute of our sophomore and junior years at Jeff's together till I went away to Meadows as a senior. Deacon and I had held it together pretty well all the time he was an undergraduate in Raleigh, but when he went off to Cambridge all that changed. I was supposed to visit him over Christmas junior year. I'd bought a ticket and a new dress and was all packed and ready to go when he called me the night before and told me not to come. He'd got a "special assignment" from one of his professors, due just after the holidays, and he was going to have to work through the whole vacation. It wouldn't be fair to me, he said, because we wouldn't have any time together, but if he really humped—that was his expression—he just might be able to make it home by New Year's Eve. Mama was furious, but I defended him to her—we had a big fight over it.

Deacon didn't make it home though. He didn't even call. I passed up a party and sat by the phone till midnight had come and gone. At quarter past I just couldn't wait any longer so I dialed his dorm room. A woman answered. There was music and laughter in the background, and I said, "is Deacon there?" and she said, "may I ask who's calling?" with a chilly poise that sounded definitely proprietary. Her voice was so sophisticated and mature—crisp northern syllables, like an announcer on National Public Radio—and though I got a queasy feeling right then, I said, "Jane McCrae, who's this?" giving it right back to her, and she said, "this is Jennifer Warren, Jane McCrae, nice to meet-you-over-the-phone." As I made a gag sign in the mirror, she said, "just a minute . . . Mr. Griggs, tele-

phone for you." Her tone was coy and flirtatious, and I heard
Deacon say, "who is it?" and she said, "someone named
Jane?" with a teasing rising accent as though amused by the
whole thing, and I felt like I was going to throw up for real.

"Happy New Year," Deacon said in this exaggerated upbeat way that just had guilt written all over it, and I said,
"Happy New Year," trying to suppress the tremor in my
voice, and he said, "I was going to call you," and I said,
"that's okay, I couldn't wait," which was a real wimp line if
there ever was one—I believed him though. "Where are
you?" he asked, and I said, "at home," and he said, "you
didn't go to the Club?" and I said, "I thought you might
surprise me," and he said, "sorry, I should have called,
things got too crazy up here. I just got back from the library
half an hour ago. There are a few people over here—we just
opened the champagne," and I said, "who was that girl?"
and he said, "what girl?" and I said, "the one who answered," and he said, "her? that was Jenny, Jenny Warren"—now it was "Jenny"—and I said, "she told me her
name—who is she, Deacon?" I could tell he was irritated
and settling in his stance. "She's on our project team," he
said, and I said—I didn't want to, but I couldn't help myself—
"does she have big tits?" Deacon was quiet for a second
before he laughed—it was forced—and said, "I don't know,
Jane, I haven't checked them out. I could try though, if you
think it's necessary to your peace of mind." I felt like such
a pad, but I still said, "you better not," and he said, "I've
got to go, there's someone waiting to use the phone," and I
said, "Deacon?" and he said, "what?" and I said, "I love
you," and he said, "me, too," like he was embarrassed to
say it out loud in front of all those people, and hung up.

All that winter into spring I wrote him long letters filled with
all my love, and he'd scribble something on a yellow legal pad
about how he was fine and would write later, but he never did.
When spring break came I called his house and his mother answered. She seemed very held back and reserved and when I
asked if he was home yet she hesitated a minute before she said,
"Deacon's in Vermont for the holidays, Jane, I'm sorry, I thought
you knew," and I said, "no, ma'am, I didn't," and she said,
"well, I'll certainly tell him you called," eager to get off the
phone as quickly as possible. The next thing I knew Deacon
was engaged to Jennifer Warren of Vermont. And he never called

or wrote or ended it or explained why. It was like being lashed across the face with a leather strop, just to know that such contempt was possible, that I could be the object of it, and that it could come from someone who was not my enemy, someone who was not supposed to hate me, but had loved me as intimately as it's possible to love another human being. Something had died in me.

I spent the whole spring crying and clinging to the memories. I imagined them together, investing her with unreal qualities, exalting her to my own detriment. Finally I moved to searching for the secret flaw that had defeated us, the danger signs that must have been there if only I'd known how to look. No more a student then than later, I just drew a blank.

That spring was the first time Cary and I slept together. He'd wanted me for two years, building it up in his mind so high. I wanted him, too, though, in my state, it was less passion than the need to hold someone and be held back. Cary was so tender and gentle with me—it was like a granted mercy—I thought I'd discovered something new, a different kind of love. It wasn't the same deep slaying ache I'd felt with Deacon, but I thought that would come with time as I got over Deacon's loss. I wanted that with Cary so badly, for there to be passion in our bed, to go with all the other things we'd built as friends.

Late that spring we started going steady. Cary gave me his class ring from Jeff's and I wore it on a chain around my neck. That was our time, the summer after junior year before I went away to Meadows as a senior. We spent it at the lake. I always remembered riding in the boat at dusk as the light turned blue, the wind blowing our hair and making our skin tingle with the day's new sun. I remembered drinking beer sitting back against a pine tree watching him skip flat stones across the water. After a good throw, Cary would turn back, smiling as he asked, "did you see that?" "A-*maz*-ing," I'd say, widening my eyes, and he'd laugh and say, "fuck you, McCrae," and I'd smile and sip my beer. I remembered spreading his old Boy Scout sleeping bag in the pine needles, the lightning bugs flitting among the trees, the lies I told Mama to spend the night there, the sound the rain made on the trailer roof, the soothing droning of the fan. I remembered the expression in Cary's dark handsome eyes as I came back from some great mental distance to find him lying beside me in bed, studying my face with tender pained perplexity, wanting to give me what I needed to keep me from those unhappy travels. I remembered his patience, my gratitude. I remembered my hope.

Ever since I'd known him, Cary had talked about A., but it was only toward the end of that summer that I finally met his friend. After Cary's build-up, disappointment might have seemed inevitable, but of all the adjectives that sprang to mind to describe that first meeting among the three of us, disappointing wasn't one. I was never sure how much a part, if any, that strange day played in what came later.

But the thought of A. jarred me back to the present. Remembering Cary was one thing—A. was something else. After the evening's events and my decision not to see him, getting all dewy-eyed about the past was the last thing I needed.

I reached for the Jackie Collins on my shelf, and it worked like a charm. After half a dozen pages I was out.

Five

ADAM

After my run-in with the police, I bought a six-pack at the all-night 7-Eleven on my way out of town and cracked one as I cruised down the ramp onto I-85. It was coming on toward two a.m. and the air was moist with dew, but it felt good blowing in on me through the open window of the Bentley. I followed the highway for five miles and then took the exit toward New Hope Township, heading for Blackburn Point at the lake.

I passed Ray's Bar-B-Q and caught a whiff of hickory from the pit out back. I remembered coming out of the blinding brightness of a summer afternoon into that soothing dingy darkness, sitting at the bar with Cary drinking frosty long-necked Millers and eating hush puppies and chopped pork barbecue sandwiches on steamed white buns, our lips and fingers stained and tingly with the vinegary red hot-sauce. "Up north they don't even know what barbecue is," I'd told him, and Cary's expression was so dumbfounded I had to laugh. "They think it's grilling out in the back yard, or the sauce you baste a piece of chicken with," I continued, and Cary said, "that's pitiful," and Ray, who was listening, too, had nodded in sober agreement. There was a trophy above the bar, an eight-point whitetail buck, and Ray had been telling me the story of the kill, how he'd been in cover near a creek waiting for dawn, sitting on his camp stool with his shotgun cradled. "I must have closed my eyes," he said quietly, stabbing out his cigarette, "because next thing I knew it was light, kind of blue like it gets, and right down at the stream, twenty-five, thirty yards, there he was.'' I'd felt chills creep down my spine as Ray talked. ''Had his head down, drinking,'' Ray said, holding up his forearm with the wrist bent demonstratively. ''Minute I opened my eyes, he raised it up,'' he continued, straightening his wrist, ''blinked his eyes, looked right at me.'' Ray's nostrils flared almost imperceptibly and his eyes went smoky. ''He knew,'' Ray said, ''didn't even try to run, just stood there, proud.'' ''And you shot him,'' Cary interjected with undisguised distaste. I kicked him underneath the bar as Ray calmly met his eyes and blinked. ''That's right, son,'' he said, ''I shot him.'' That had been when I'd changed the subject to barbecue. Cary had hated hunting. It was probably the thing we disagreed on most strongly.

The town had died, I thought, as the neon ''Beer'' sign diminished to a spark in my rearview mirror, but Ray's was still there. In my mind I could see the Kinlaws' trailer so clearly, I could see the dusty gravel road leading down to it, I could see the turn-off. That was where I was going, but I couldn't find it. I drove up and down that road for an hour. I came out on the lake in half a dozen places, but none of them were the right place. A weird sort of panic came over me, and I got completely lost in a terrain whose every feature was familiar to me. I passed a tobacco barn I recognized, the same weather-faded advertisement painted on its side—''Sun-Drop Cola . . . refreshing as a cup of coffee.'' A section of split-rail fence jogged my memory. The air turned cooler and I heard the gurgling of water as I crossed a small bridge I knew, and on a hillside above the road my high beams picked out luminous eyes and I heard a whinny and hooves cantering away in the darkness. It was a horse farm where I'd taken riding lessons as a boy. But I couldn't put any of it together. I took an angry swallow of my third beer and fired it out the window at a yellow ''Deer Xing'' sign, missing by a mile.

Finally, by some occult route I couldn't have reconstructed in a thousand years, I came out at the marina at Dawson's Landing. I could have cried with frustration—Cary's place, less than half a mile by water, was at least ten miles by road, and I didn't have a clue how to get there. I did a line in the car and then got out and went up on the dock, carrying my remaining beers in the plastic rings. I sat down on the bench and looked at the building, remembering Joanie and wondering if she and Chub still owned it. The same tin "Merita Bread" sign was on the screen door, the same bubble-headed gas pump on the dock. I opened a beer and stared out over the black water. A wind was coming up. The dock wallowed slightly underneath me and I could hear the lapping of small waves. I narrowed my eyes into the breeze and scanned the far shoreline, able to make out the opening in the cove only by the break in the opaque wall of trees. A single light burned there, a pinprick no bigger than a star. That was it—the yard light at the Kinlaws' trailer. A light rain fell out of a clear sky, then stopped, and at five o'clock the fingernail of the new moon rose in the east dissolving to invisibility as dawn broke.

I dozed, and when I woke, with light on the land, everything was different. The way was clear. I got back in the car and in fifteen minutes I was there. The road had been paved, I noticed—probably why I'd missed it. I felt almost pleasantly washed-out, but I was still a little wired and wide awake.

Time and neglect had changed the place. The yard was overgrown, and the trailer, which I remembered as brand spanking new, seemed old and poor-looking now. Streaks of rust ran down the sides, and as I wandered around back I found the Chris-Craft on its trailer—the tires had all gone flat—covered with a dirty canvas tarp. The whole scene made my heart ache, like a visit to a museum—only a very personal one, dedicated to my past, my youth.

What struck me most was the woods that edged the clearing in the back yard between the trailer and the lake. There were two distinct sections, one mostly hardwood with a lot of underbrush, the other pine planted in orderly unnatural rows, giving evidence of the fire that had burned there long ago, the one Cary and I had fought and beaten side by side. The Kinlaws had replanted, but as I wandered into the green scent I thought I could still catch a trace of woodsmoke, and I found the fallen trunk of an old oak that still showed evidence of charring.

I made my way down to the dock which was stranded in crusted stump-studded mud fifty yards from the lake's edge. The water had receded as the Corps of Engineers sent it down the Killdeer River to some more prosperous location via the Little Wabash Dam. I could have almost walked across the cove. Feeling desolate, I sat down on the planks, dangling my legs, and as the sun turned the east red, I caught a glimmer in the mud and reached down. My fingers fished up an old poptop, the kind the breweries had stopped making years before, and as I turned it in my hand my mind went back to the summer after my junior year at Keane.

After working as a lifeguard at the beach, I'd gone to Outward Bound in Pisgah National Forest at my father's bidding and left the program early. I called Cary from the airport in Asheville to tell him I was flying into Raleigh-Durham. It was a week before he was expecting me, but he didn't ask what had happened, and I didn't offer.

It was the first time we'd seen each other that summer. I'd asked him to come to the beach with me, but he was hot and heavy with Jane McCrae—I hadn't met her then—and didn't want to come.

Cary was at the airport when my plane touched down. He was wearing cut-offs and his red Lacoste with a leather thong around his neck with a turquoise bead I'd given him as a protection against the evil eye. His hair was short whereas mine was shoulder-length and unwashed. I hadn't had a bath in days.

On the ramp we slapped five, then hugged and clapped each other on the back. Throwing my pack in the car, we made a pit stop at a Quick Pick in Durham for beers before driving on toward Killdeer. Cary sailed his pop-top out the window, flicking it from behind his ear. It was a new trick he'd learned and I asked him to show me how, but I couldn't get the hang of it. There was a haze in the sky and it was hot. We were in his Volkswagen with the windows rolled down and the wind ripping through our hair, shouting at each other to be heard. When Cary asked me if I was happy to be home, I said, "sure," but the feeling wasn't really there yet.

On the drive I pulled two plastic bags out of my pack, one filled with marijuana, the other with magic mushrooms, which Cary had never seen before. I'd brought them from Keane and saved them all summer so we could do them together.

On the way out to the lake we stopped off at Ray's and picked up a case of beer, then drove the last mile and turned off the paved road onto the dirt one leading down to the trailer and the water's edge beyond. We changed and went out to the dock and dove. Cary pulled down his suit and mooned me in the water, and I said, "you could use a serious shave, spud," and we had a water fight, splashing and ducking. Cary held me under for a

few seconds, which surprised me and hurt my pride a little. I
started swimming out toward the opening in the cove and deep
water. Cary just watched. I guess he realized by then that I was
going through something and would tell him when I was ready.
When I came out, I found him in the back yard, smoking and
raking pinestraw into piles at the edge of the trees. "Why don't
you stop being such a pill and go get that plastic bag?" he asked,
grinning at me, and I grinned back and said, "which one?" and
he said, "the little one," and I said, "the big one's got more
fun inside," and he said, "let's just have a little fun right now
and save the best for later. Jane's coming over tomorrow. She
might want to trip with us."

Only we didn't have any rolling papers, so we went for a pack
of Tops. And coming home, as soon as we turned off the paved
road, far off from behind the trailer we could see smoke billow-
ing up through the trees.

I think Cary realized immediately it must have been his cigarette. "Shit," he said, gunning it down the dirt road. We
jumped out and ran around the back. The fire had already spread
from the pinestraw into the edge of the woods. The pines were
dry and there were flames crackling up the trunks, some of
which were splitting open with big thunder-pops bleeding out
the resin, which sizzled and made the fire burn hotter. "What
do you think?" Cary asked, "maybe we should go back to Ray's
and call the fire department," and I said, "shit, man, we can
do this—it's not that bad." It didn't seem that serious to me at
first. "Besides," I said, chugging my beer and reaching for the
rake, "by the time we call and they get out here there won't be
anything left."

Cary watched me doubtfully as I started tearing up the piles
of pinestraw and beating them down. When I came out of the
fire I felt pumped up and excited. "Don't just stand there,
you piece of shit," I told him, "put your shoes on and help
me." Cary got the bucket he used to wash the VW and found
a tin basin in the trailer. We began to fill them at the outdoor
spigot, running relays. We fought it at the leading edge where
it was spreading fastest. The wind was hurling flame in our
faces, but it wasn't really a wall of fire, though it was threatening to become that. There were lots of separate outbreaks
growing and joining with others. We'd put one out and run
down to the dock and then come back to find another someplace else. It was at least a hundred-yard trip, and we ran it

over and over for two hours. Our faces and bodies were all sooted and glistening with sweat, flaming limbs were cracking off the trees and falling all around us, but I remember feeling happy there. I think Cary was, too.

At the end we were both exhausted, moving like sleepwalkers. We were beginning to isolate the fire and drive it down toward the water, and then—I'll never forget it—it started raining. First the thunder rolling out across the lake, and then light drops. We both stopped and Cary held out his hands and gazed at me with a wondering expression. A bolt of lightning crackled down out over the middle of the lake, and suddenly the air turned thick and blue-black around us and the rain fell harder, spitting down into the flames and sending up little plumes of smoke. As it drove down in sheets around us, we stood there with water dripping off our bodies, our faces streaked with bleeding soot like war paint, and raised our chins, whooping like braves. I put my arm around him then, feeling happy and expansive, and said, "we beat it, man, we kicked the motherfucker's ass," and it was like God had challenged us and we'd defied him, and won.

At dusk, after we'd cleaned up, Cary and I took the Chris-Craft out and motored across to Dawson's Landing for dinner. There was a rinsed light in the air, everything clean and fresh, and we were high. I felt a kind of quiet happiness then like I was "home," finally, that magic place I'd been longing for. It wasn't Killdeer anymore, much less the house in Winston, but a double-wide trailer at Arrowhead Lake, and Cary was part of it, just as though he were my own brother, though in some ways we were even closer than brothers—with family there isn't any choice.

Cary treated me to a couple of cheeseburgers and Joanie's homemade onion rings, and on the trip home he let me take the wheel. It was getting dark by then and he'd turned on the running lights. I pushed the throttle up until the boat was skipping like a stone over these little waves that had come up. You couldn't even see the water underneath except the whiteness of the bow wake, just leaping up as though to get away and then smacking back down against whatever was there. The moment had faded—that feeling of home—and I was trying to get it back, I guess, and didn't know any other way to do it, really, except by pushing down the throttle.

The next thing I knew, Cary had reached around me and pulled back the stick. The bow dropped in the water. "We almost missed the cove,'' he shouted above the engine, as though that was why he'd done it.

As we passed the point we could see the floodlight through the trees up at the trailer, and there was loud music blaring down with a strangely distorted echo over the water, elongated and lugubrious-sounding. Right that moment I got a bad feeling about it, and so did Cary. ''It's probably just Cliff,'' he said, cutting the engine a good way from the dock. We coasted up on our own overtaking wake which swashed around the pylons like something thrashing from the deep. We moored the boat and started up the path—the ground was still smoking—and when we got to the edge of the lighted clearing Cary held my arm. ''If it's Daddy he's probably been drinking,'' he said, ''and we're not going in,'' and I said, ''suits the hell out of me.'' We made our way stealthily around front, and there was Cliff's VW right beside Cary's. When he saw it, Cary visibly relaxed and hit my elbow. ''Come on, spud,'' he said, and we walked in through the front door.

There was Deacon Griggs, sitting on the couch rolling a joint over the coffee table out of my stash. He looked about twenty pounds heavier than the last time I'd seen him, like he'd been lifting weights, and I felt Cary's vibration change the minute we walked through the door.

Deacon was just finishing the jay. He looked up at us and then back down, very coolly licking the paper before he acknowledged us. Then he sat back tossing that shelf of blond hair out of his eye, spreading his arms out on the sofa back like he owned the place and giving us this brazen grin like, sure, I know it's yours and you know I know, so go ahead and make something of it, but you aren't going to do that, are you, guys? so let's just forget it and sit here smiling at each other like good buddies.

''Been playing with matches again, Cary?'' he asked, and Cary said, ''what's it to you?'' and Deacon pouted and said, ''Smoky's disappointed,'' and Cary said, ''I care, too, Griggs.'' Deacon narrowed his eyes with an expression of intense ennui and shrugged dismissively. I noted this interaction with surprise and mild alarm—it was clear they hated each other, but I didn't have a clue why. Cary had never mentioned Jane's previous relationship with Deacon. ''So, Jenrette,'' Deacon said in an appreciably warmer tone, ''haven't seen you in a while—how you liking prep school?'' In spite of everything I was a little flattered at his tone, like he was surprised and glad to see me—

it meant something back then, coming from someone five years older—though when you got down to it there was no reason why Deacon should have cared, and I'm sure he didn't. So I said, "it pretty much sucks," trying to be offhandedly cool and to keep my tone close to what I was feeling from Cary. And Deacon said, "there are a lot of Keanies at Harvard. You should come down to Cambridge and visit me sometime—it's not that far," and I said, "thanks, man, but I don't get down there a whole lot," and he said, "you still running cross country?" which was one of those things about Deacon. He'd toss out some personal detail like that to make you aware of him, as though he had stock in you and was keeping tabs on his investment. "Yeah," I replied, "and two-mile in the spring," and Deacon said, "you should get this bud of yours to quit smoking butts and get off his slack ass to run with you—you heard that hack?" and Cary said, "don't put yourself out over my health, Griggs— where's Cliff?" and Deacon said, "in the head, little bruh," and Cary shot him a dark look and said, "by the way, Griggs, who invited you to help yourself to the pot?" and Deacon said, with that same provocative grin, "it was just lying here for the taking, nobody's name on it, I figured it was house supplies . . . of course, if I'd known it was yours, little bruh," and Cary said, "it's not, it's A.'s," and Deacon said, "well, hell, Cary, if it's A.'s what are you getting so bent out of shape about? I bet A. doesn't mind, do you, A.?"

It was an awkward moment because it really wasn't that big a deal to me, but on the other hand I could feel Deacon screwing his thumb down on my head, and I didn't want to undermine Cary either. When I hesitated, Deacon acted like he took offense. "Shit, man," he said, "let me pay you for it, all right?" He leaned forward and pulled out his wallet—"how much—a dollar? Five dollars? Just tell me what you want." "Take the joint, Deacon," Cary said, in a tone of disgust, which was, increasingly, my sentiment, too.

About that time we heard the toilet flush and Cliff came from the bathroom zipping the fly to his shorts. I had a strong affection for Cary's older brother, but he scared me—not physically, some other way. Cliff had that same Kinlaw generosity, like Cary—he'd shown it toward me many times. One night when I was visiting and Cary was busy doing something else, Cliff had taken me out drinking with his friends, and he'd been good to me when I got drunk and threw up in the back seat of his car.

But there was something in Cliff that could turn on you in an instant. It never happened except when he'd been drinking, but my one personal experience was enough to keep me wary around him ever after.

I'd been talking about Keane one time and saying how much I hated it, which was the line I always took, when Cliff laughed his high, languid laugh and started telling me in detail the subtle snobbery and hypocrisy of my attitude, how I used the fact to my advantage in assuming a social superiority and then pretended to disdain it "with a little backhand flick of my wrist," which was just a more advanced hypocrisy. And the thing about it was, Cliff had a point. A lot of what he said was probably true, except, really, the overall picture, which completely ignored the fact of my real, not imaginary, misery there. But that was just a little part of Cliff, and the one thing I knew was that he loved Cary. There was an almost telepathic bond between them, like two buddies who'd been to war and made it back, only each had left a little of himself on the battlefield—which, I guess, for Cliff and Cary was some part of childhood I never really saw—and each understood the other's loss and knew to exercise a watchful care for the times when it came back.

Anyway, Cliff came toward us down the hall zipping his fly and veered against one wall and bounced off and laughed, and when the light fell across his face I could see the telltale glaze in his eyes and a kind of sloppy laxity in his demeanor like a happy drunk, only not so happy, and he said, "Aeeeee," putting his arm around my shoulder and coming close up in my face, "welcome home, bud, we thought we'd roll out the Welcome Wagon," and I said, "how's it going, Cliff?" flattered and uncomfortable. Cary winced, turning his lip, and said, "uggg, you smell like puke, Cliff, it's not even eight o'clock and you're already tight, man," and Cliff let out that laugh, releasing me and taking the same hold on Cary, making every effort to breathe in his face. " 'Shit, man,' " he mocked, " 'you smell like puke, *man.*' " He turned to Deacon and they both said it—"man!"—and cracked up. "Lighten up, man," Cliff said, "it's Friday night, what difference does it make what time it is? Does it show better social tone to be drunk at midnight than at eight o'clock? Let's ask A.," and he turned to me and said, "what's your opinion on the subject, *man*?" and I said, "I wouldn't know, Cliff," and he said, "well, I thought if anyone would, it would be you, A. And besides, Cary"—he turned back—"it's only five o'clock in California and they're already drunk out there, they've got three hours on us, so we've got to hurry to catch up. Just think how drunk they'll be at midnight, and we'll already be passed out. You see, man, there isn't really any hope, and it's all relative anyway, so why not get drunk and have a party to celebrate burning down the fucking forest?"

The impact of this precision blow, coming on the heels of Cliff's intoxicated ramble, was considerable. Cary just stared at him a moment, then said, "you *know* who you remind me of," close up in his brother's face. Something darkened like a cloud over Cliff before the smile came back. "Fuck you, Cary," he breathed with that bad smile, and it was said—both exchanges—with a quiet intimacy like that of lovers. "T.O. still isn't going to be too pleased about his trees," Cliff said, and Cary pushed him off, saying, "tell him then, Cliff, okay? Just tell him." Cliff stood there staring at Cary, his face a mask of mockery with hurt eyes peering through—I knew from that look, if I hadn't before, that Cliff would never tell—and said, "you little shit." Turning his back, he walked toward the couch where Deacon was twirling that jay between his fingers, grinning not just at Cary, but at me now, too, with brazen mockery like he hadn't expected the evening to be so interesting.

"Come on, let's go," Cary said to me, and Deacon said, "hey, little bruh, don't wuss out on us. We're going to show you lads how real men party. You don't want to leave, do you, A.?" He took a deep toke, then leaned way off the couch, passing it to me in an act of preference. I don't know why, but I took the joint. "There might be some women coming over later," Deacon said, smiling, "you might actually get laid, which would be a first, wouldn't it, A. boy?" and before I could deny it, Cary said, "I thought I heard you were engaged, Griggs," and Deacon said, "yeah, well, if you can't be with the one you love—right?" winking at me as though I might sympathize with his position, or at least know the song. "Harvard's done a lot for you, Deac," Cary said, and Deacon said, "let's talk about that five years from now, okay, Cary? and by the way, where'd you hear I was getting married?" He arched his brows as though the question were somehow loaded, and Cary's face darkened as he said, dead sober, "Cliff told me." Deacon just said, "oh," with little rounded lips, "I thought maybe you got it from another mutual friend of ours," and Cary said, "shut up, Griggs, before I smack your ugly face," and Deacon said, "Mommie, Mommie, call the sheriff," laughing and alert. Cliff pushed off the wall where he was leaning, casually stepping into Cary's path as Deacon said, "and anyway, little bruh, seems like to me you tried that once already, only it wasn't my face that got smacked," and Cary said, straining over Cliff's shoulder, "you're a real bad guy, Deacon, especially when it comes to working over people younger than you."

Deacon's face darkened for the first time and he started to get up. "Sit down, bud," Cliff said with icy cheer, turning toward him, "both of you, just be cool." Deacon stared at Cliff as though weighing his options—there was this tense pause—and then he flashed that grin and said, "just stretching, Cliff," and sat back down. There was something galvanizing in that room, like pushing down the throttle. I felt the danger and ugliness of it—the thing we'd felt all the way out on the lake across the water—but something in me didn't want to leave.

"Come on, Cary," Deacon said, "let bygones be bygones. Suzanna Grissom's coming over here, and we thought A. might like to meet her." He found my eyes and said, "I mean, you don't have all that much chance to get laid up at school, do you, A.?" He said it like he was really concerned about my emotional health and welfare, and I knew where he was heading, but I just said, "not really," and Deacon said, "it's all boys, isn't it, A.?" knowing damn well it was, and I said, "yeah, it is," and Cary jumped in and said, "so what, Deacon?" and Deacon said, "so what do you do for pussy, A.?" and I said, "mostly go without," and Deacon said, "mostly? what about the partly?" and Cliff said, "his right arm looks pretty strong to me." Even Cary laughed. "As long as you don't get hard-ons in the showers, A., you're probably okay," Deacon said, "though they say you can't be absolutely sure till twenty-five at least, and it's just that I've heard some nasty rumors circulating about the two of you," and Cary said, "yeah, right, Griggs, just like the ones I've heard about you and Cliff," and Cliff said, "calm down, boys, nobody here's a homo," and Deacon said, "yeah, but you can never be too careful, Cliff," and Cary said, "you're a real asshole, Deacon, did anybody ever tell you that?" and Deacon took a wincing toke off the pinched roach and said, "at least I didn't have to wait in line for what I wanted"—he grinned, blowing out his smoke—"but I broke it in for you real good, didn't I, little bruh?" and the room erupted.

As Cliff and I reached out, Cary tore between us like a half-back through the line, going straight over the coffee table. Caught off guard, Deacon feebly tried to fend him off with the hand that held his beer, but the can went flying, hitting the floor with a sick thunk and gurgling out into the shag. As I lunged for Cary, I heard a second sound—that unmistakable smack, like someone tenderizing veal with a wood mallet—as Cary's fist connected with Deacon's face. Though Deacon outweighed Cary by probably thirty pounds and was no doubt a good deal stronger, Cary had him from above, pounding the shit out of him. I heard at least two more blows and saw Deacon's chin fly sideways into his shoulder as I struggled to pull Cary off. Deacon had his hand in Cary's face trying to find a grip as though to rip the flesh off the skull. Finally I managed to lock my arms around Cary from behind, pinning his elbows to his trunk as I pulled him away, thrashing and bucking. As Deacon started to get up Cliff tackled him again, pinning him to the sofa under his full length. "Get him the fuck out," Cliff yelled at me as I wrestled Cary backwards toward the door. "You faggot piece of shit," Deacon bellowed, pushing up from under Cliff—a line of blood dribbled from his nostril and his face was almost strangled-looking with rage—"I'm going to get you, motherfuck, I'm going to mess you up!"

When I got Cary outside on the small entry deck, he stopped straining toward Deacon and turned on me, pushing me back hard with both hands. "What? you want me now, too, you shit?" I shouted, "come on then, asswipe," and I shoved him back just as hard. Cary stood there glaring at me, then spun around and stormed down the steps toward the car. "Where the fuck are you going?" I called over the rail as he threw the door open and got in. When he didn't answer, I vaulted over into the grass. He'd already turned the engine over and shoved it in reverse. "What do you think you're doing, man?" I said leaning into his window as he backed, and as he slammed on brakes and went to first, he said, "get in or stay here," and I said, "will you just wait a goddamn minute?" but he was already rolling. I sprinted around to the passenger side and managed to fling the door open and get a foot inside as he gunned it up the road.

Cary went right through the stop sign, fishtailing onto the blacktop and mashing the accelerator to the floor until the chassis of the VW was shuddering like it was going to break apart. I just sat back against the door staring at him, pissed off and waiting for an explanation. He didn't even look at me. "What the fuck was that, Cary?" I said finally, "was he talking about Jane?" Cary shot me this dark look like he was going to say something sharp, but caught it before it came out. "Just forget it, A., all right?" he said, "it's between me and Deacon," and I said, "forget it?" laughing harshly, "like hell, Cary—what was he talking about, man?" Cary gave me an angry look and said, "figure it out, A." My jaw dropped. "What are you telling me, spud?" I asked, "him and Jane?" Softening a little, Cary said, "no, A., not now, it's over." I blinked my eyes, trying to put the pieces together. "What?" I said, "he used to date her? this is your big problem?" Cary stared at me ferociously and said, "he told her he was going to marry her while he was telling Cliff, and everybody else in town, how much stink he was getting." I was quiet for a minute, letting this sink in, and then I said, "so Deacon's a piece of shit and she's not a virgin, so what? it's not a fucking tragedy, man, it happens all the time," and Cary said with quiet intensity, "she was fifteen when he started dating her, A., he was twenty." The significance of this age differential wasn't lost on me, but I couldn't pinpoint its relevance to Cary's present situation—and, any way you cut it, it seemed to me he was making too much out of it. "A lot of fifteen-year-old girls aren't virgins, spud," I said, "and it seems to me that was about the age you got it, too—it isn't all that different," and he said, "don't give me that progressive bullshit of yours, A., it's totally different for a girl, and you know it, especially when the whole town thinks you're a whore." Getting an eye-opening crash introduction into the gritty specifics of Jane McCrae's background—till then I'd heard only glowing generalities—I said, "if she was a whore you wouldn't be going with her," choosing to emphasize my faith in Cary's judgment as Jane's stock dipped. "Goddamnit," Cary said, "she was in love with him and he fucked her over—that's what Jane did wrong, okay?"

He stared straight ahead down the road, and after a minute I said, "I still don't get it, Cary. I mean, fuck him, man, she's with you, right? what's the deal?" and he said, "it's not that simple, A.," and I said, "why not?" and he said, "can we just drop it?" and I said, "what, man? does she love you or not?" and he said, "yeah, she loves me," in a depressed tone, and I said, "but?" and he said, "there isn't any but, A., she just hasn't totally gotten over him." I stared, waiting, and I saw his whole mood crash. "It's like this spell she's under, A.," he said quietly, flashing me a pained look that tore my heart, "not that she wants to be with him—she hates his guts—but she can't get out from under it, and because of that she can't really be with me, not totally—but it hasn't even been that long." Listening to him, I felt, perhaps for the first time, the ache of helpless queasy pity one feels as a good friend spins his wheels, trying to justify a hurtful love. "I don't know, man," I said, filled with misgiving, and he said, "I'm making it sound worse than it is, A.—really. All things considered, we're doing pretty good. I guess I just want her to feel the same way about me that she felt about him—it's pretty childish really," and I said, "bull*shit*, Cary, it's not childish at all, if Jane McCrae doesn't feel that way, there are plenty of girls who will"—I shook my head— "no, man, I'm sorry, but I've got to say it, fuck her, Cary, just fuck her," and he looked at me with the softest expression, as though what I'd said amused him in some tender way, and he said, "I don't want anybody else, A."

I really felt it then, like coming up smack against a wall. I stared at him and he said, "I'm in love with her, spud," and it wasn't like a seventeen-year-old saying it, it was way outside the range of anything I knew. I'd had a few crushes then, and been pretty woebegone over a couple of them, but I'd never really been in love like he was or wanted anything so badly as he seemed to want Jane. Really, it was a new thought for me, that you could love and not be loved back in the same way.

Feeling Cary's pain and reaching down inside myself for something to give back to him, I said, "you want to know why I left Outward Bound?" He turned and stared, and I said, "we were doing this drill called 'Trust,' which wasn't anything too difficult—all you do is close your eyes and let yourself fall backward in your buddy's arms trusting him to catch you, and I don't know why I did it, Cary. I liked my partner, his name was Roger, and he was from Wadesboro, and he was really okay, but when we got to this drill—I was catching, right?—well, I guess I just freaked or something because I stood there and watched him hit the ground. It was almost like my arms were paralyzed. He didn't get hurt, he just lay there and looked up at me blinking his eyes like what the fuck was that.

"Then the instructor, Mitchell, got into it. He came over and said, 'you want to try that again, A.?' and suddenly I went from feeling ashamed to being really antagonistic, and

I said, 'no, Mitchell, I don't think I do.' He gave me this condescending look and said, 'well, I think you should give it one more try,' and he helped Roger up off the ground, and I said, 'don't do it, Roger, I'm not going to catch you,' and Roger said, 'come on, A., what the hell is wrong with you?' and I didn't know, Cary, I just felt sick, really awful, I was sweating and I felt like they were trying to humiliate me. So Roger falls again, and Mitchell has to catch him, because I couldn't do it, I just looked at Roger and said, 'I'm sorry, man, but don't ever trust anybody else, not with your life, count on yourself,' and Mitchell gave me this real grim look and tried to make me take my turn, but I just shook his arm off and picked up my pack and started heading up the trail. Mitchell came after me and pulled me around and said, 'what are you doing, A.?' and I said, 'I don't want to be here, Mitchell, I didn't want to come in the first place, it was my father's idea, and I'm leaving.' He just stared at me and I turned around and walked.

"I got about a mile up the trail and took my pack off and sat down under a tree. I felt really strange, Cary, like I was underwater or something, and suddenly I just felt like crying, only I couldn't really get it out. So I got up and hiked out to the Blue Ridge Parkway and started thumbing, and this was really weird, man, but this old white Mustang convertible just like the one Daddy used to drive came around the bend, and right up till he stopped for me and I saw his face, I thought it was Daddy. He was a really nice guy and I guess he sensed something was wrong with me, because he took me out of his way all the way to the Asheville airport, and it wasn't till I got on the plane that it hit me. Because when I was a little kid first learning how to swim—I was four or five, I guess—Daddy would take me out to the Country Club Pool sometimes at dusk after he got off work. It would just be the two of us, and we'd work a little in the shallow end and then he'd take me to the diving board and he'd tread water in the deep end trying to coax me to jump off. It took me a few times to work up to it, but after that we did it every night, it was my favorite part, I couldn't wait. But one night when I ran off he didn't catch me, I went down and caught a mouthful of water, and when I came back up I saw him standing on the side, and he said, 'swim, A., swim,' and I made it to the side. Of course, I know he would have saved me if I'd really started drowning, but I just lost it, Cary, I couldn't stop crying all the way home. And you know what Daddy told me in the car, what the whole point of it was supposed to be? Exactly what I told Roger, 'don't ever trust your life to anybody else, save yourself.'

"I'll tell you something, Cary, I may not have appreciated it at the time, but it was a good lesson, because when you get down to it, man, there's nobody else but you. So what's the point of making yourself sick about this girl? I don't care how great she is, no woman is worth that. Nobody is. I mean, it's sad that her heart is broken and it's great that you want to help her, but not if she's not giving you something back and if it's fucking with your head. I mean, who's more important, you or her? It's obvious, Cary," and I looked out the windshield at the broken yellow line on the highway flashing past like Morse code, and I didn't say anything else, because it was the only thing I knew.

I could feel Cary looking over at me, and finally he said, "your father really did that?" and I said, "yeah, he did," and Cary said, "and you think that was a good lesson?" and I said, "I think it was the truth," and he said, "really, A.? is that what you really think?" and I said, "goddamnit, Cary, read my lips, isn't that what I just said, yes, that's what I really think," and he said, "then I feel sorry for you, spud, because that's a crock of shit." I could tell by his tone he wasn't trying to be mean, but it still made me furious, because I was on the level with him and saying something that I didn't have to say, so I told him, "listen, Cary, you're the one with the problem, man, not me," and he said, "I think you've got a problem, too," and I looked at him and said, "go to hell, Kinlaw," thinking maybe he would stop the car right there and ready to get out if he did—I'd already hitched one ride that day, and I could hitch a second, or I could walk—but Cary laughed instead and chewed on it a minute and then he said, "so that's the answer, huh? yourself first, and anybody else who gets in your way or sees it differently and isn't going to give you what you want can go to hell?" I didn't answer and he went on, "that's great, A., so I just forget Jane, and maybe I forget Cliff, too, and Daddy, maybe I just say fuck you, too, A., because sometimes you're a real pain, like right now— and what do you end up with? that's my question," and I said, "you end up with yourself, Cary, and that's the only thing you can count on in the end," and he said, "you end up with nothing, spud, that's what you end up with."

I could feel his eyes on me and I didn't want to return his

look, because maybe I sensed the selfishness of what I was
saying, only I believed it was the truth and there wasn't any way
around it, though, so help me God, I would have preferred not
to believe it, but I felt like I knew where Cary was coming from
in this thing he had for Jane. Maybe I hadn't been there with a
woman yet, but I remembered lying on my bed at Keane that
winter after Mama died, crying my eyes out every night and
thinking that my life was over and that nothing good could ever
come to me again, and I told Cary, "I made it through my
mother's death, which was whole lot worse than anything you're
going through, and I'll tell you something, man—this is something I know—I can't tell you what happened, but one morning
in the spring—not the first one, but only this past year—I woke
up and something had changed. I went outside to breakfast and
the sun felt good again, I felt strong like I was going to make it,
and nobody helped me get there, I made it through myself. So,
yeah, Cary I'm sorry, but just fuck them, man, fuck everybody
else. That's exactly what I think, spud, and maybe I don't have
it all together, but I'll tell you what, I'm not crying anymore.
And I'll tell you something else, I'm never going to hurt like
that again, not if I can help it, and if that's cold, too bad, I'll
live with it. So don't piss on what I'm telling you." Neither one
of us spoke again until we reached the dam, but I could sense
Cary brooding. I knew I hadn't convinced him, but I'd made
my case, and I felt better to have got it off my chest.

It was full dark by the time we got there. The stars were
out and it was really clear. Cary took his pack of Marlboros
and two of the beers we'd bought earlier still in the plastic
six-pack rings and got out. We walked barefooted over the
cold wet grass, and I said, "hold on, man, I've got to take a
piss," and he said, "you want me to hold it for you?" and
I said, "eat shit and die, Kinlaw," and he grinned and unzipped his own fly, hitching it up with his free hand, and we
stood there side by side, intimate and separate, and I looked
up and you could see the Milky Way like a pale sparkling
wash splitting the sky in half, and I listened to the plash of
piss fusing over the low distant whoosh and rumble of the
water through the spillway running into the river below us.
Cary cracked a beer and handed it to me and then opened
his own and we just stood there taking frosty swallows and
looking up at the sky, and the last dregs of the anger I'd felt
washed out with the piss and left me feeling calm and strong

and easy in his presence, and when we finished and zipped up I said, "I didn't mean to jump on your case, spud, I'm sorry we argued," and he said, "forget it," and I said, "I hope it works out, man, I'm sure it will if she's got any sense at all." Cary didn't answer, he tapped a cigarette out of the pack and pulled out his lighter. The flame lit up his face as he leaned into it, and there was still something drawn and brooding there, and I said, "it's good to be home, man," and he flipped his lighter shut against his leg and took a deep no-hands drag, turning his face up and letting the smoke out of one side of his mouth, then he squinted over at me and said, "yeah, I'm glad you're here, even if you are an asshole I still miss you," and I said, "you're another, Kinlaw, and I feel exactly the same way," and he said, "watch it, spud, I might have to put a whupping on you," and I said, "you could try," and he said, "I did pretty good with Deacon, didn't I?" and I grinned and said, "you kicked his fat red ass," and we laughed and slapped five before Cary walked out on the lip.

I let him go and sat down on the bench, staring down at the ghostly luminescence of the water, then out at him. I could see his coal rising, glowing intensely every time he drew, then falling to his side and growing fainter. There was something soothing, almost mesmerizing, in the low rumble of the water, and I understood a little of Cary's feeling for the place. We'd been there many times, it was where he went to be alone and think, and we rarely talked out there. It was a little bit like church. But that night I felt like talking, I thought he needed me, though maybe it was me who needed him, so when I saw his coal flick over, streaking like a meteor, I followed him out there and said, "are you okay, man?" and he said, "fine," and I said, "what you thinking about?" and he said, "nothing much," and I said, "Jane?" and he said, "partly," and I said, "you seem a little down," and he said, "I was also thinking about you and Roger," and I said, "what about it?" and he said, "just thinking." I could sense something brewing, but I didn't say anything until he reached out and put his hands on my shoulders, maneuvering me so that my back was to the lake and his was toward the drop-off, and I said, "what the fuck are you doing, Cary?" because the ledge was not that wide, and he said, "I want to see how much you mean it, A.," and I said, "don't be an asshole, Cary," and he looked in my eyes with a calm measuring expression, his hands still on my shoulders, and said, "let's do it, A., " and I said, "do what?" though I knew, and he said, " 'Trust,' " and I said, "Cary," and he said, "I'm going to close my eyes and fall," and I said, "I mean it, Cary, don't fuck around," and he did, he toppled backwards and I caught him by his shirt and felt his weight tug in the cloth as I pulled him back. He opened his eyes and stared at me with a look of quiet vindication and said, "that's what I thought." I stared back at him a minute and then turned around and walked back off the dam and sat down on the bench again, feeling so humiliated—that same underwater feeling as before—and then I just went numb.

I saw Cary light another cigarette and finish it, and then he came back in and sat beside me, watching me. I didn't look at him, until finally I just turned and said, "why would you want to do that, Cary? why would you want to humiliate me like that, man?" and he said, "because I care about you, A., and you needed it," and I said, "who the fuck do you think you are, Kinlaw? who are you to teach me?" and he said, "I'm your friend, A., that's all—that's what it's for," and I said, "you're an asshole, Cary," and he said, "you already told me that, and you're probably right, but not half as big a one as you." There was no anger in his voice like there was in mine, it was almost gentle, with a trace of amusement that was affectionate, not vicious, and I guess it was that tone more than the words themselves that prevented me from saying something sharp and final back, though I felt near it. But I didn't, and Cary said, "you want to know what I was really thinking about out there, A.?" I didn't answer, and he said, "I was trying to remember if there was ever anything like what you told me about your father and the diving board that happened to me, and there was something, though it's not the same—you want to hear that story?"

"Go ahead," I said, and he said, "the first time I ever remember coming out here, Daddy brought me. It was after my twelfth birthday—you remember that party?" and I said, "no," and he said, "well, you were there. It was the year we met in Mrs. Edward's class, sixth grade." Cary waited, as though for me to respond, but I didn't, and he said, "one night after supper Daddy looked up from his plate and said, 'I'm going to ride, you want to come?' You could have knocked me over, A., but I went. It was a day or two after the party, I remember because we were eating leftover birthday cake for dessert. We'd decorated the playroom—me and Mama—with balloons and ribbons

and bought those little tin-foil party hats with silver fringe around
the outside and those little paper things you blow and they unroll. I got a black Cypress Gardens slalom ski—that one I still
use—and a pair of red Everlast boxing gloves from Daddy, only
the writing on the card was Mama's, and anyway I knew she
bought them because he never did that stuff.

"Well, about three days before the party Daddy went on a
drunk, a bad one like he'd only do once or twice a year. He'd
stay upstairs in the bedroom and come out in his robe from time
to time to go to the bathroom or the kitchen. Mama would keep
the door closed and make her bed up on the sofa and put the
sheets away every morning before we got up to try and hide it
from us, but we knew, by then we did. So this was going on
upstairs the whole time we were planning the party and deco-
rating downstairs, and I could tell Mama was worried, but she
didn't want to disappoint me because twelve is a big birthday,
sort of like sixteen, it's when you aren't a child anymore. I'm
sure she must have said something to him the day of the party,
just asking him to stay upstairs, which is probably why he didn't.
Do you remember this?"

"No, what happened?" I asked, and he said, "about halfway
through the party—I'd just blown out the candles and started
cutting the cake—Daddy came downstairs with his pint sticking
out of his bathrobe pocket. He hadn't shaved in three, four days,
I guess, and his hair was all greasy and tousled, and all the kids
got suddenly quiet—I can't believe you don't remember this,
A.," and I said, "maybe just a little, kind of vaguely," and he
said, "they all stared at Daddy with these big eyes. I guess they'd
never seen anything like that, and I was so embarrassed and
ashamed, A. Daddy said to Danny Tolbert, 'what you looking
at, boy?' because he was closest to hand, and then he came over
to the table and mumbled something about 'gittin' him some
birthday cake,' and he cut off a hunk of it and put it in his hand
and staggered back upstairs. 'Mr. Kinlaw isn't feeling well,'
Mama told the children, 'the doctor's given him some medication that makes him feel funny,' and after a while everybody
seemed to forget and have a good time, but I couldn't really
enjoy myself after that.

"And then a couple of days later, after he'd sobered up and
gone back to work, like I was saying, that night after supper he
pushed back his plate and looked at me and asked me did I want
to go to ride, and I got in the car with him and we drove out

here. And the only thing he said the whole way out here was, 'that was sure some good birthday cake your mama made, won't it, boy?' and I said, 'yes sir, Daddy,' and he said, 'I never had me none that good, I never had no birthday cake at all, just one cookie, we were poor, son,' and it wasn't like he was mad at me because of it, A., he was just telling it. After that we didn't speak at all, and it was sort of calm and peaceful, A., just the two of us in a way I can't really remember any other time, so I didn't care whether he said anything or not. When we pulled up, Daddy got out and hitched his pants up from behind and walked over to the edge of the bank—right over there—and I followed him and he said, 'you know how many gallons run through here a second, boy?' and I said, 'nuh-uh, Daddy, tell,' and he said some big number I can't remember and looked at me like it was the most amazing fact he'd ever heard and it explained the whole thing, I mean the meaning of life and everything, just some big number, and then he didn't say anything for a long time, just staring down at it. Then he reached out for me all of a sudden and grabbed me up next to his leg—almost like he was going to hit me or something, which made me flinch—and he looked straight down at me, there were tears in his eyes, A., and he said, 'I never meant to hurt my boys,' and his voice broke in the middle of it. I wanted to say something back, to tell him it was all right, but he just let go of me and walked off by himself and wiped his arm across his face and sniffed. When he'd got himself together he turned to me and said, 'come on, boy, le's us go git a ice cream cone.'

"On the way home we stopped at Jerry's and he ordered me a banana split with everything. I didn't even want it, but I ate it anyway because I knew he wanted me to, that was his way of making up to me about the party, and he sat right there and watched me and every once in a while he'd say, 'gimme some of that vanilla with the nuts, boy,' and I'd dip it up on my own spoon and put it in his mouth, and he'd say, 'that's purty good ice cream, ain't it, boy?' and I'd say, 'it's great, Daddy,' and he'd say, 'that's Pet, that ain't no Sealtest,' and it made me happy to eat it, A., the whole thing made me happy, because that was the first time I ever really knew my daddy was a good man, before then I hadn't, but that was when I knew that right down at the core of him he was, and all the rest you had to give him because he couldn't help himself. And everybody's like that, A., everybody's got something wrong and hurt about them somewhere if you just scratch a little bit beneath the surface—my daddy does, and your daddy does, too, so does Mama, and so does Cliff, Jane's got it, so do I, and so do you, A., you do, too. But you've still got to love them, spud, you've got to do it anyway."

Cary was crying by the end of it, but I wasn't. I was moved, and maybe I even knew deep down that he was right, and I felt sorry for him, but I couldn't admit that he was right, not to him, and not to myself, all I could keep thinking was, "I'm not like that, there's nothing wrong with me, I'm okay." Cary cried for a long time, and at the end of it we both got quiet and then he said to me, "you know something, A., with you there was that one really bad thing, and I'm not making light of it, but ninety-nine percent of it was good, and it's like you're throwing all the good away because of the one thing that was bad. But with me it was the exact opposite, there was one good thing and all the rest was shit, but that one good thing is what keeps me going, and for you it's the one bad thing that stops you," and I said, "it's not stopping me, Cary, not anymore, I'm over it," and he said, "no, you're not, A., it's still stopping you and you don't even see it. I'm telling you, A., you've got to love people. You've got to love something," and I said, "yeah, Cary, but first of all you've got to love yourself," and he said, "you know something?" and I said, "what?" and he said, "I think if I felt that way I'd kill myself," and I said, "bullshit, Cary, that's just total bullshit," and he said, "you think so?" and I said, "I know so," and then he stared at me, sizing me up ironically, and said, "you talk a tough line, A., but when it comes down to it you're as tender-hearted as my grandmother," and I said, "you mean the one that wears the combat boots?" and Cary laughed and said, "I've seen you wetting your hanky at the picture show," and I said, "Yeah, like when?" and he said, "like *Gone with the Wind*," and I said, "you're full of it, I don't even have a hanky," and he laughed like he'd won whether I thought so or not, which I didn't, but by then I didn't feel the need to push it any further, the feeling was restored between us and I just let it go.

I'd always remembered that, Cary saying if he'd felt like me he'd kill himself, which is what made me think that maybe I'd helped convert him to that point of view.

When I came out of my reverie the sun was a good hour above the horizon. Blinking my eyes, I found myself back on the Kinlaws' dock with the pop-top still in my hand.

On the way back to town I almost took the turn-off that led to Jane's, then didn't, realizing it would do no good. My move toward her had done no good the first time, that summer long ago, yet it had also taught me there's a time when you move away, willy-nilly, in the service of a deeper urge beside which right and wrong are merely words.

Six

JANE

The next morning around eight o'clock, which was high time for decent folks to be up and doing in Mama's view, she rapped on my door with those sharp knuckles of hers like the house was burning down and whipped on in without so much as pretending to wait for an invitation. "He's on the phone," she said, standing there in that old housecoat I was going to throw out if it was my last mortal act, with one hand akimbo on her hip and giving me the Armageddon meltdown stare.

"Who?" I said, sitting up and watching Jackie Collins hit the floor. Prying my eyelids open—they were sort of fused along the seam—I did a quick check to assess internal damage. I knew exactly who it was, of course, and I was absolutely furious with him for calling after the very last thing I said to him was not to. But Mama seemed suspiciously familiar with the whole scenario all of a sudden, which made me suspect that she'd been observing with her eagle eye through the curtain of her bedroom window last night with the light out like she was asleep—an old trick of Mama's I thought I'd outlived. And at the very thought of her spying on me I was fit to be roped and hog-tied—like I was sixteen damn years old again, which, of course, was exactly how Mama saw it. I could be down there in that big house in Oakdale by myself crying on my Cheerios or slitting my wrists, and all she could ever find to tell me on the phone was, "my marriage to your father was no bed of roses either, sugarpie, I never heard of one that was," taking utmost satisfaction in the statement because, of course, she blamed me like it was my fault that Daddy enjoyed being with me more and not hers for being like she was. But just as long as I was married it was okay, God was on his pearly throne and all was right with the world, I was safe and respectable, but now that I was divorced, God help me, the forces of evil were abroad in the land again like a team of red-eyed yard dogs panting on the lawn around a bitch in heat—yours truly—just waiting till I had to come outside to pee, which Mama wasn't going to let happen, not if she could help it. She was going to keep me under lock and key and make me hold it till I busted, she was just so afraid of her damn pussy, that woman, and, by extension, mine, and if you ask me, that was her and Daddy's problem. That was my hypothesis anyway, which I made a mental note to take up with Dr. Rosenkrantz when I got back, suspecting, on the basis of bitter past experience, that it might need a little work.

And Mama said, talking to her little problem girl again, who she was going to solve if it killed us both, "A. Jenrette, your beau," tapping the toe of her slipper on the floor. And I said, "why Maaaa-ma," like I was all surprised and tickled at the thought, "were you spying out your window last night when I came home?" determined to get the satisfaction of hearing her admit to it if nothing else, though I wouldn't have put Confederate money on my chances, and she said, "I most certainly was not, young lady, I was sound asleep in bed where any respectable married woman should be at that hour," and I said, sitting up, "Mama, I'm not married, and neither are you . . . and anyway, I was in by twelve o'clock, as you *well* know," and not about to fall for that or condescend to respond to my insinuations, she said, "you most certainly are too married, Mrs. Robert Edward Pegram, Jr.," knowing how much I hated that, "till death so do you part is what you promised, and I may be a widow, but I'm still married in the eyes of God."

I was about to point out the contradiction to her when she said, "Letty Templeton called here at the crack of dawn this morning and everybody in Killdeer and the surrounding countryside is talking about your escapades last night at Misha DeWitt's, it's probably on the front page of the *Sentinel*, I just haven't had time to look yet, what with fielding calls and attending to your social schedule," and she gave her foot a few more beats on that just building up to it before she fired. "Did he get what he was after?" she asked, and climbing out of bed,

I said, "number one, he wasn't after it, and number two, it's none of your damn business what I do," and she said, "don't you cuss . . . don't you cuss," getting all flustered and hysterical—she'd been drinking too much coffee—"don't you dare take that tone with me, not in my own house," and I said, "it's my house, too, Mama, and I didn't do anything," like a little girl who once upon a time spent her church allowance on a Milky Way and got caught eating it, giving Mama the victory, which is what she wanted anyway.

She squinted me over like she was deciding whether to give me the benefit and take my word, and then she said, "people don't know what you do, sugar, that's between you and Him, all people care about is what it *looks* like you do . . . I'd have thought you'd have that figured out by now," and I said, "I figured that out a long time ago, Mama, right before I figured out I can't run my life on what other people think of me, like you always did," and she said, "looks like to me, Jane-girl, you aren't running your life too well one way or the other," and we faced off over that with our weapons emptied, her looking hurt and fierce, and me feeling hurt and sad, and she said, "I can tell him you're indisposed," and I shook my head, "no, Mama, I'll take it," and she said, "girl, God help you, what are you getting yourself into? . . . how many times do you have to get kicked in the head by the same mule before you learn to step around him?" and I said, "drop it, Mama," and walked around her to the hall where she followed me, shaking her head and shuffling off the other way toward the kitchen for her umpteenth cup of Maxwell House.

I picked up in Daddy's office. "I've got it, Mama," I called with my hand across the mouthpiece and listened till I heard the click, and then I lit into him like forty wildcats, "Adam Clay Jenrette, *the third*," I said, "do you have any earthly notion where the little hands are on the clock I'm staring at?" and he said, "do you mean do I know what time it is?" and I said, "Don't be a smart-ass, you know exactly what I mean," and he said, "no, as a matter of fact I don't—what time is it?" and because I wasn't actually looking at a clock but merely employing a figure of speech, I turned my wrist up and squinted at my watch, which said four o'clock, and though I knew that wasn't right I said it anyway, I don't know why, just to throw him off I guess—or maybe, even then, God help me, I was playing for a laugh. Which I got, along with A.'s response, "I think you're a little slow, Jane.'' As I put my wrist up to my ear and shook it, I said, "honey, I'm not slow, I *stopped*, which still puts me way ahead of you," leaving him to draw the implication. But being a man and a butt besides, with no appreciation for the finer things in life like a hundred dollar put-down, A. just plowed on through.

"Listen, Jane," he said, "I know you asked me not to call and I apologize, I really do, but I need to talk to you," and I said, "what, A.? just what is so important that you have to call here at this hour of the morning against my explicit request when I have a Number Seven hangover directly attributable to you?" and he said, "I just got back from the lake, Jane—I was at the trailer."

At that moment I felt a curious tingle as though someone were tapping at the key of an old piano, abandoned and forgotten in the basement, something once central to the house that filled its rooms with music, now unused but still there. I almost told A., "I was out there, too," because I had been, in my thoughts, but even that concession seemed too dangerous. "You just don't get it, do you, A.?" I said instead, "it's over, honey, it's too late, Cary's gone. The time to talk was thirteen years ago, or even ten, A., after Cary died—we might have still been able to talk back then—but now? No, A. I went through those dark woods once all by myself, I won't go again—not for you. There was a time I would have, but that was then and this is now," and he said, "can't I be something in your life, Jane? just a friend? I mean, can I just mow your grass or something?" and he almost got me there. "Don't do this to me, A.," I told him quietly, and he said, "do what?" like he really didn't get it. When I didn't answer, he said, "what happened to us, Jane?" which was when I caught my second wind. "Let me sum it up for you in two brief words, sweetheart," I told him, "you split," and he said, "I know, I know I did, and I'm sorry I hurt you, but I didn't have a choice, I had to do it," and I said, "then maybe you'll understand that I have to do this, too, A.," and I quietly hung up the phone.

I was so upset I was trembling and could hardly breathe. In a state of eerie lightheadedness, I sat there in Daddy's chair staring at the phone foolishly expecting it to ring. It was silent, but deep inside that piano was playing a jangled but familiar melody. It felt so wrong to cut him off that way even if he'd done the same, and worse—much worse—to me. "Can't I be something in your

life, Jane?''—the question got me where I lived. Why couldn't
he? I was over it, wasn't I? It was in the past. Was it fair to keep
him up there on that cross forever? After several minutes in a
guilty quandary, not knowing whether it was right or wrong, I
took out the phone book and looked up Miss Zoe's number and
tried to call him back, not knowing what I was going to say—
just apologize, I guess, for hanging up on him. The line was
busy. I kept on for twenty minutes until I realized he must have
taken the phone off the hook. I dressed, faced Mama's inquisi-
torial stare as I picked up her car keys from the kitchen counter,
and drove on over there.

The old azaleas along Miss Zoe's driveway were full of big pink
blooms and the garage door was open. The Bentley was gone,
but I saw Louis's Studebaker, and there was music coming from
the house, that old black whiny hound dog kind that A. and
Louis listened to, so I figured Louis was there anyway.
   It took him about three weeks to answer my knock, but I knew
he was in there and had to come out eventually, so I just worked
that big brass knocker with one hand and the doorbell with the
other. Finally the door swung open and Louis looked around it
squinting, that bald chocolate head of his with the little white
tuft around his ears like feathers catching the sunlight. When he
recognized who it was he gave me a look like I'd come to re-
possess the furniture.
   "Why, Miss Jane," he said with surprise, and I said, "is he
here, Louis?" and keeping the door between us, Louis said,
"Mist'A. lef' here not fifteen minutes ago, ma'am, didn' say
where he's goin' or when he be back . . . will tell him you
dropped by though." He started to close the door, and I said,
"Louis," in a tone between begging and extreme exasperation,
"do you mind if I wait?"
   Possession being nine tenths of the law, Louis studied me like
he wasn't too sure he wanted to risk it, but, bless his heart, I
think he saw I was upset, so after a brief hesitation he said, "you
come right on in the house then, Miss Jane," opening the door,
"I'll fix you a cup of tea." I followed him into that big dark
foyer, which was as cold and gloomy as a tomb, took one look
at the chandelier and wanted to run straight for a stepladder and
feather duster. Instead, I just stood there as his guest in a house
that belonged more to him than it ever would to A. Jenrette,

feeling just as shy as if I'd come to pay a call on the Emperor of China.

"You like Earl Grey, Miss Jane?" he asked, starting through to the back, "we got five poun's lef' in the pantry of Miss Zoe's, 'bout all they is in there 'cept 'bout a hund'ed brandy fruitcakes from the fun'ral, cain't stan' either one myse'f, or Mist'A. neither," and I said, "don't put yourself out, Louis, I had breakfast before I came," which was a lie, but at least ladylike, and, anyway, I didn't like them either. Louis stopped and looked at me like, well what in the world do we do now, and said, "but yo' mama, she might like one," and I said, "thank you, Louis, I'm sure she would," and he said, "fine then, I go git it," and I stood there while he did and looked around and saw that pale board A. had nailed in the dark wood of the staircase, and Miss Zoe's portrait through the dining room, an old woman my age in a green satin décolleté gown with bobbed hair and a cigarette in her hand, and I started listening to Louis's music, which was some man singing in this high falsetto voice, something about going to the graveyard—I couldn't really make it out—making these little whoops and shouts, "wee!" and "haw!" and it sounded so beautiful and eerie it just reached right down inside me like somebody's hand and made me feel all cold.

Louis brought the cake back in a Christmas tin and said, "you tell yo' mama I said enjoy it in good health," and I said, "thank you, Louis, I certainly will," and he said, "fine then," and smiled at me still looking a little nervous, and I said, "what's that music, Louis?" and he said, "tha's the Rev'run Gayree Davis, Miss Jane," and I said, "where's it coming from?" and he said, "back to my room, ma'am, off the kitchen . . . got my rekit player back there, big ol' Dumont Balladier Miss Zoe give me back in sixty-three or fo', cain't 'member which, when she purchase the Zenith console . . . never did sound as good as that ol' Doo-mont though, big ol' thang, mus' weigh two-hund'ed pounds, I reckin, why it sound so nice. I listin some in the daytime when I cain't fin' no mo' wo'k to do." He laughed. "So much to do 'roun here cain't fin' where to start, though me and Mist'A. git at it 'fore long, you watch, jus' windin' up to sprang is all."

He paused and asked, "you like blues music, Miss Jane? Mist'A. sho do, he be axin' me 'bout it three, fo' times a day like I'm the bluesman from Bluesville." He laughed, and I looked at him, catching what I thought he meant, and I said, "oh, Louis, I'm sorry," and he shook his head, "tha's awright, Miss Jane, I know he don' mean nothin' by it, he jus' int'restit is all and ax 'cause he don't know . . . he almos' have a fit when I tol' 'im I knowed Brownie McGee and Sonny Tayree . . . didn' really know 'em but listened to 'em play a couple times up to Dur'm," and I said, "where, Louis?" and he said, "Dur'm, Nawth Ca'lina, Miss Jane," and I said, "oh, Durham, I'm sorry, Louis, I didn't understand you," and he said, "tha's awright, Miss Jane, I know I soun' funny to you jus' like you soun' funny to me . . . two diff'ent thangs, Miss Jane, all in the wurl' it is, but any*how* . . . like I's sayin' 'bout Tayree and McGee, didn' really know 'em jus' drank liquor with 'em one night up to Dur'm like I tol' Mist'A. But listen to me ramblin' here, plum' forgot what I was sayin'," and reminding him, I said, "I like the blues just fine, Louis, as long as somebody else has 'em, seems like I spend too much time down with it myself these days to appreciate the fine points. I do like what you're playing though." Louis laughed and said, "come on back here then and set down a minute and git off yo' feet, I'll play you some Mist'A. like in pa'tic'lar."

As we started off he said, "I swear, Miss Jane, I don' mean nothin' by it, but Miss Zoe always did say you was a fi'ecracker jus' like yo' mama, and I b'lieve she hit the nail on the haid," and I said, "Louis Bascom, she did not," and he said, still laughing as he opened the kitchen door for me, "beggin' yo' pa'don, ma'am, but she sho did," and I said, "just like my Mama?" and Louis said, "jus' like, the vurry same thang." We walked down a narrow corridor then into his little room, which looked so sad and dingy, like something from an old sepia photograph, with the little iron bedstead and a cane-bottom rocking chair—nice chintz curtains, though, on the window with a white sheer, which I knew was Miss Zoe's doing—and I said, "well, if I didn't have the blues before, Louis, I've sure got it now, after what you said." Louis took the record off and started taking out another one, and said, "don' say that, Miss Jane, you got to love yo' mama 'cause she the only one you got." I sat down on the end of his bed. "Is that what the blues is, Louis?" I asked with a little smile, and he smiled back, shaking his head, "yes, ma'am, you got yo' han' on it right there, next time I tell Mist'A. jus' ax you." He pulled the switch and sat down in his chair and started rocking while we waited for the record to drop, both feeling more relaxed, though I guess it must have seemed a little strange to him like it did to me.

"Does he seem all right to you, Louis?" I said, "A., I mean," and Louis squinted to make me out and said, "you axin' me fo' real, Miss Jane, or you jus' want a stawry? you want the truth you got to take the consequences," and I said, "the truth, Louis," and he said, "awright, ma'am, I tale you then . . . Mist'A. be doin' too much toot, or whatever y'all callin' it now, but no way fo' 'im to come but back on down." My jaw almost hit the floor. Louis wasn't squinting anymore, he was studying me with a deep down knowing look. I had an impulse to try and cover, but he was wise to me, wise in every sense. "He's just doing it right out in the open then?" I asked, and Louis shook his head, "no, ma'am, he be vurry discrut, jus' ax me did I want some when I walked in the do' on 'im," which just about sent me through the floor, "look up skeered a minute then git that big ol' grin like Mist' Clay Jenrette and say, 'wawnna catch a buzz, Lou?' " Louis wheezed with laughter, slapping his hand on the rocker arm.

"Took some, too, Miss Jane," he said, "got to tale you 'cause you axed the truth, didn' want to be impolite, 'cause me and Mist'A. be frien's, ma'am, and this be man to man, jus' like passin' a bottle, don't turn it down when yo' frien' han' it 'roun' yo' way . . . yes, ma'am, did two lines las' night, sho did, he gimme two mo' to hol' onto, did 'em both this mawnin' right 'fore you knocked on the do', why it took me so long to git there," and I said, "Louis Bascom, you're lying like a doormat!" and he shook his head, and said, "no, ma'am, Miss Jane, I be tootin' now," and he just laughed and worked that rocking chair till I thought he was going to wear a hole in the floor.

"Well, I ought to turn you both upside down across my knee and whale the stuffing out of you," I said, and Louis said, "you gotta catch yo' turkey firs', Miss Jane," still laughing, "catch 'im, chop his haid off, stick 'im in a boiling pot, pluck his feathers, *then* you stuff 'im . . . never do git used to it, leastways I never did, always make me sick on my stomick, but you gotta do it if you want yo' Sund'y dinner, yes, ma'am, and tha's what they call the Turkey Blues, Miss Jane, Lawd have mercy, yes."

I was simply speechless, which was just as well because Louis went right on like the dam had broke. "Everythang got it's own pa'tic'lar kin' of blues, Miss Jane, jus' like you with yo' mama

. . . you got yo' han' on somethin', you not sho you like it all that well, but you cain' let go 'cause it the only one they is and you hooked up with it some whichaway, tha's the only definition I know, and I be studyin' on it a lawng lawng time,'' and I said, "well, I never . . . Louis, you're higher than a kite," and he said, "yes, ma'am, jus' be comin' up right now . . . don' be mad though, Miss Jane, I be tootin' up to Hollem lawng 'fore you or Mist'A. either one was even bawn, up there six months, couldn' make a go, all I could fin' in the Promise Lan' was workin' fo' white folks jus' like I be doin' 'fore I lef' the south, so I come on home where I like it better, got my ruts here, Miss Jane . . . we call it somethin' else up there, woofin' or snuffin', somethin' like that, cain't 'member now . . .

> *no new pleasure, no new pain,*
> *same old circle toinin' roun' again,*
> *a-wee-hoo!*

you ever heard that song, Miss Jane?" and I said, "no, but I appreciate the rendition"—he sang it—and Louis nodded, acknowledging my compliment and ignoring my irony, and said, "I jus' made it up fo' you, they the Miss Jane Blues."

"Don't make fun of me, Louis," I said, and Louis said, "I ain't makin' fun, Miss Jane, jus' ridin' the train, and don't you worry 'bout Mist'A. ma'am . . . he be flyin' like a eagle now, but in a week or two he be back down in the dirt where you can git yo' han's on 'im and pluck his feathers . . . jus' let 'im go right 'haid on and hit the bottom, he come out th'other side bran' shinin' new," and I said, "I don't want to get my hands on him, Louis, much less pluck his feathers—what makes you say that?" and Louis looked straight at me and said, "you don' want to pluck 'em, ma'am, but you want 'em gone—hea' what I say?—jus' like any woman do, yes, ma'am, woman want her man on her Sund'y table lookin' clean and settin' still, but you gotta kill yo' turkey firs', Miss Jane," and I said, "well, A. Jenrette may be a turkey, Louis—you got that part right—but the last thing I want is to kill him, and the further he is from my Sunday table the safer I'll feel," making a joke of it, though Louis was probing dangerously close to a nerve. "You say, ma'am," he replied, "not to contradic', but if so you one in a million and he better grab aholt . . . jus' 'member, Miss Jane, they's many diff'ent ways of killin'."

I sat there both annoyed and [torn up?] [by?] Louis. Why did they both make th[e same scent?] [A.?] and me? It was like some scent I ca[n] [only?] [recognize?] only recognized through other people[...] [...] somethin', Miss Jane," Louis said, "[...] chlowrine bleach, but she have a black he[...] to catch my breath on that, but he was [...] dapping at his eyes—"you 'mind me of M[...] way, ma'am, sho do, and one thang she always d[...] you want a good dawg, pick the runt." He gave me a point[ed?] squint on that and went on, "not 'tendin' no offense to Mist'A., 'cause he tall and strawng jus' like his daddy, Mist'Clay . . . but in another way it fit, 'cause he a only chil', you see, that make Mist'A. the pick and the runt, too, and that right there the Mist'A. Blues."

Feeling like Louis was casting some strange spell on me—as though *I* was doing drugs—I rallied and told him, "I appreciate your advice, Louis, and next time I'm in the market for a dog I'll come see you, but you're wrong about me and A.—we were close once a long time ago, but now we aren't really even friends." Putting back on his deferential Step 'n' Fetchit face, Louis pursed his lips and said, "yes, ma'am, jus' like you say, Miss Jane." I think my jaw dropped a little. "You don't believe me, do you?" I asked, and Louis said, "all I know is what I see and what I hea', Miss Jane, and what I hea' this mawnin' is Mist' A. holdin' the telephone like it a snake done bit his han' and sayin', 'she don't want to see me, Lou,' lookin' like that broke his heart—tea's stan'in' in his blue eyes, I wud'n' lie to you. Now what I see is you over here after 'im with that same confus' 'spression on yo' face . . . but don' min' me, Miss Jane, I jus' a ol' man, cain' even 'member what it like to be young and into the condition—ain't my place nohow to be puttin' wuds in yo' mouth much less feelin's in yo' heart. Jus' the cocaine rile me up and make me ack so foolish."

I was so spooked by then I decided I'd better end the interview. "Well," I said, getting up, "I guess he's not coming back right away, I've got things to do, so if you wouldn't mind, Louis, just tell A. I dropped by," and he said, "sho will, ma'am," pushing up out of his chair, "vurry firs' thang when he git home." He escorted me to the door of his room, "Don't trouble yourself, Louis, I know the way," I said, turning back and giving him my hand, and as he took it, he said, "don't know 'bout you, Miss Jane, but I 'joyed our chat . . . hope you ain't goin'

made myself smile and told him, "I'm not
which was true. I felt more sad than anything,
aguely lost, like I was drifting in a dream world.
ore releasing my hand, Louis pressed it and his face became very gentle as he said, "he a good boy, Miss Jane . . . I
know he got some problems like anybody do, but Mist'A. true
blue undaneath . . . he fin' his pot of gol' 'ventu'ly, ma'am,
you watch and see if he don't, all he need a little he'p along the
road," and I said, "I want to be A.'s friend, Louis—you can
tell him that from me. If he'll try, I will, too," and Louis said,
"yes, ma'am, Miss Jane, you run along home now and don't
you wurry none. I 'speck you hea' from him direckly," and I
said, "thank you, Louis," and floated off toward the front door
like someone who's just seen a ghost.

Seven

JANE

I moped around the house the rest of the day waiting for the phone to ring, but A. never called. I considered trying him, but my pride rebelled. After all, it was his turn—I'd made my move. And there I was, thinking about him in those terms, like it was some sort of adolescent dating game. The current was a lot quicker than it looked from the bank. I kept telling myself, no, I wasn't going to let it happen, only it seemed so selfish, like maybe I just didn't believe in myself enough to risk tenderness with A. again, even in friendship. Yet he seemed to need a friend, and he'd been important to me—I'd loved him once upon a time. Maybe what I was afraid of was that if I opened to A. at all I wouldn't be able to stop halfway. The tobacco girl turned over out in Daddy's fields, chomping at the bit, but I just shoved her back into the ground. And Dr. Rosenkrantz, who I could have used right then, wasn't saying much, just looking sad and taking notes.

I helped Mama in the yard some, clipping back her boxwoods till she came around the side in her straw hat pushing the wheelbarrow with a load of dandelions and Queen Anne's lace which looked so pretty it just seemed a shame to kill them. She dropped it on the spot and lit off after me like a feral cat, taking those shears out of my hand like she was going to skin me alive with them. "What on earth do you think those bushes are, girl, poodle dogs?" she said, and for some reason I burst out in tears. "Lord, have mercy on us," she said, "I'm so glad I'm not

young—what did we ever think we saw in it?'' I waited up till
eleven-thirty and when A. didn't call I went to bed and woke up
in the morning with a toothache from grinding my teeth all
night.

I was making coffee the next morning when the phone rang.
I caught it in the middle of the first ring and to my surprise a
woman's voice—a sort of timid songbird trill I recognized but
couldn't place immediately—said, ''Jane?'' ''Yes?'' I said, and
she said, ''this is Sadie, Jane, Sadie Kinlaw,'' and I said, ''Miz
Kinlaw!'' feeling a mist across my eyes, ''it's good to hear your
voice,'' and she said, ''yours too, darling . . . it was so sweet
of you to come over at Miss Zoe's funeral, I'm sorry we didn't
get a chance to talk . . . I think about you all the time, Jane, I
really do,'' and I said, ''I think about you, too, Miz Kinlaw,''
and she hesitated before she said, ''dear, I wanted to tell you
I'm sorry things didn't work out for you with the Pegram boy,
it's such a shame—are you all right?'' and I said, ''yes, ma'am,
I'm getting by,'' and she said, ''that's right, honey, let your
Mama take a little care of you, we all need it, I wish I still had
mine, I'd be right over there now knocking on the door,'' and I
said, ''are you okay?'' and she said, ''one day at a time, honey,
that's all the Good Lord gives us, or the best I know anyhow.''

In the pause that followed my mental wheels began to turn—
I expect she could probably hear them. ''What is it, Miz Kinlaw?'' I asked, and I heard a sigh escape her as she said, ''oh,
Jane, I was up half the night wondering whether I should call or
not''—she took a deep breath—''A. was here, hon, he came to
see me yesterday.'' I guess it was her tone, but I found myself
quivering like a leaf and had to sit down in a chair. ''What
happened?'' I asked, ''he's okay, isn't he?'' and she said, ''I
don't know, honey . . . I mean, yes, physically he was fine, but
the way he acted . . . I was just concerned, Jane. I don't know
if I was wrong to call, but he said he'd seen you and I didn't
know who else to call.'' We both fell silent for a minute as I
tried to decide what to do, then I said, ''can I come see you,
Miz Kinlaw?'' She sighed as though relieved and said, ''yes,
hon, you come right on over, I'm not going any place.''

I threw on some jeans and headed out, up the interstate to
town, then down Advance Avenue past the Killdeer Mall. It was
still early and there was a big fat policeman in Ray Bans, a
trooper hat and a day-glo vest directing traffic out of the Mc-
Donald's drive in window. I had to stop there, and then again at

the traffic light, which hadn't been there the last time I drove through. Though I was worried, I still noticed how strange it seemed, like one day it was a quiet little residential boulevard with sprinklers going and kids playing in the yards and neat little brick houses with one great big oak tree apiece and big old boats of cars going past at twenty miles an hour, and that damn German shepherd of Mr. Hepwhite's that used to wait for your car, crouching on the wrong side of the bush right there in front of you but thinking you couldn't see him till he jumped, and the very next day it was this. In some part of me I still expected it to look that way, but it didn't. Things had changed and a part of me hadn't, the part that used to ride home with Cary in his VW after school, I guess . . .

Every time he got to that bush he'd slow down and crouch at the wheel just like that old German shepherd crouching at the bush, both waiting for the other in dire love and malice, and when the dog finally jumped Cary would stick his head out the window and bark right back at him, that German shepherd going crazy trying to get up the door . . . Cary would take off just laughing his head off . . . I always *hated* it when he did that, it wasn't even that good of a memory, but thinking about it as I drove to his mama's made me so sad, that dog was gone—I expect he finally bit someone and had to be put down—but I even missed the dog, the whole charm of the place was gone, it just seemed harsh and ugly and new, and I felt old, thirty-one years old, but somewhere inside me there was still that fifteen-year-old girl in braces, Metal-Mouth McCrae, riding down that street with Cary Kinlaw to get a Nutty-Buddy at Dell's Grocery, which was gone, too, and Cary, sweet Cary, was gone, and I knew as long as I lived Advance Avenue was never going to seem right to me, I was never going to accept it, but always see the thing it used to be and miss that, and I knew that that's what getting old is, living in a world that's gone, and I didn't like it. Normally I could have driven down that road and not felt a thing, except maybe some little queasy scratching dissatisfaction way down deep inside, but that Wednesday morning the earth just turned.

I turned right down Robin Hood and pulled Mama's car over to the curb beside the last house on the right and got out. It was just an old two-story brick house from the nineteen-fifties, strangely antique-looking now and solid, with the living space upstairs and an unfinished basement where

Cary had a dance one time while I was still with Deacon—
the first time I ever saw where he lived—and a big garage
they never used filled with boxes, with an aluminum door
painted white with two porthole windows in it. Cary's stuff
was probably down there now, I thought, with all the rest that
Sadie couldn't use and couldn't throw away. I hoped it was,
because the last time I'd visited Sadie, several years now, she
still had Cary's clothes hanging in his closet, and certain
things of his around, though not too much. She hadn't made
the house a museum, like some will, but still . . .

Sadie's driveway was covered with catkins, and so was her
Cadillac, which looked strange sitting in the driveway of that
house underneath the basketball goal which was about to fall
down. Cary's daddy, T.O., used to buy her a new one every other
year or so. He was generous that way, though, Lord knows, it
was little enough and she deserved it. But this car looked old. I
couldn't tell how old. Maybe it was the same one she was driving
when Mr. Tommy died the year before Cary. But that seemed too
long. I never had much sense with cars anyway. The whole place
looked a little sad and rundown, but Sadie was all by herself, and
I knew how hard it was to keep things up without a man around.
But her azaleas looked just as pretty as ever, and the jonquils were
opening down along that little creek they had. I looked up the
steps to the kitchen door and she was standing there behind the
glass looking down at me with her red hair in a bun up on her
head like always and a sad expression in those deep pretty liquid
brown eyes of hers, which were just like Cary's.

"Looks like an old widow woman lives here, doesn't it?" she
said, opening the door, and I said, "the sweetest one I know,"
and she studied me a second more, then suddenly, like she was
making up her mind to it—that way she had that I guess I'd
always taken for granted, but noticed now and appreciated so
much, being older—she just beamed at me and said, "come on
in this house, you purty thing, let's see if an old widow woman
can't clear off a place for you to sit and find you a cold Tab in
the refrigerator." I didn't even drink them anymore, but she
remembered. She was such a lady.

When I came in the kitchen she hugged me and pulled back
holding my elbows, just reading me for a second, like Mama
will sometimes when I first get home, with a little furrow working right between her eyebrows, that way an older woman will,

just really deep down checking to make sure you're all right. I guess Sadie thought I was, because she relaxed and smiled again and patted my arm, and went and opened the refrigerator.

"Well, sugar," she said as she put ice cubes in my glass and poured my drink, "maybe I'm making too much out of it, Lord knows I don't want to worry you . . ." She glanced at me a little doubtfully over her shoulder, and I said, "it's all right, Miz Kinlaw, I've been worried, too. I don't know if A. told you, but the other night I went out for a drink with him, and on the way home . . ." I hesitated wondering whether I should tell her, but she said, "yes, hon?" Her look heartened me, so I took a deep breath and said, "well, ma'am, the thing was—I didn't even know what he was doing, Miz Kinlaw, truly I didn't—but he drove out there to the dam." I paused and her eyes got deep and hard and misted over like the frost had touched them. "It was pitch-black dark," I said, "and he walked out there, Miz Kinlaw, right to the middle." I guess I gazed off thinking about it, because when I focused again she was staring at me with this deep deep knowing look. She reached out and gave my hand a squeeze before handing me my Tab and a paper cocktail napkin. "Come on, honey," she said, "let's sit down in the den and I'll tell you all about it."

The console TV was turned to a religious program, and Sadie's morning paper was folded over to the crosswords with her reading glasses on it and a complimentary ballpoint with somebody's advertisement, all sitting on the same plaid couch, underneath a framed reproduction of "Starry, Starry Night," which just leapt off the wall at me the way I knew it must have done for A., because before I ever met A. he'd given Cary a coffee-table book of van Gogh's prints which Cary did a book report on at Jeff Davis one time. We spent break looking at it in the car. Toward the end Cary had become almost obsessed by those paintings, not because of anything with A., I think, but because I guess that's how things looked to Cary then, all swirling and terrible.

Sadie saw me looking at it, and I reached out and took her hand as we sat down on the couch. "Well, sugar, I don't want to talk," she said, "but I think maybe A.'d been drinking when he came over here." She looked at me like maybe she wasn't so sure she meant drinking—because she'd had plenty of experience of her own with T.O. over that—but anyway, "drinking" was close enough and we could talk about it in code that way

and understand each other, and she said, "I mean, he was just
as sweet as he could be, only he seemed so overwrought, though
I know it was hard for him to come over here after all this time,
and it meant a lot to me to see A., honey, it really did . . ."
and I said, "yes, ma'am," encouraging her, and she said, "well,
it was about nine o'clock yesterday morning, I guess . . . I
heard a knock on the door and when I went to answer it there
was this big tall black-headed man standing on my stoop—my
heart turned right over, Jane—he looked just like Cary standing
there all grown up, so help me, they always did look so much
alike . . . when he saw me he got that big old hyena grin on his
face just like his daddy—that was when I realized it was A.—
and put his hand up flat against the glass . . . I let him in and
he walked right in the kitchen, Jane, nervous as a cat, and didn't
say a word . . . he looked so uncomfortable, dear, I just held
out my arms and he came right to me and gave me this big old
hug, just like he used to do when he was little, and broke down
crying—it tore my heart to see, honey—and I did, too, both of
us just bawling like two old hound dogs."

Sadie sniffed, and then her tone got quieter and more intense.
"But he just couldn't stop, Jane," she said, "he couldn't get
control of himself. I don't know how long it lasted. I pulled out
a chair for him and he just sat there, honey, sobbing into his
hands and trying to tell me something, and when he finally got
it out he just said, 'I'm sorry, Miz Kinlaw, I'm so sorry,' and
broke down again."

Sadie stopped and looked at me. "At first I thought A.
meant he was sorry because he hadn't come to see me, Jane,
and it wasn't till I thought about it later that it struck me that
he meant Cary—like in some way A. feels what happened
was his fault . . ."

We held each other's eyes on that, and Sadie sighed before
she said, "maybe I'm wrong, Jane, I hope I am, but I understand
A.'s feeling, honey, truly I do . . . not that I ever blamed A.,
or anyone, sweetie, I blamed myself most and I know every one
of us that loved Cary did in some way, it's just that after ten
years . . . that A. could still feel so . . . well, honey, it just
caught me off guard, I guess . . . he calmed down after that
though, Jane, really he did, we came in here and sat down like
you and I are now and looked at pictures . . . A. sat right there
in Cary's rocking chair and I took down all my albums and
Cary's old scrapbooks—I hadn't looked at them in two or three

years—and we went through them page by page . . . sometimes
he'd look up and tell me something he remembered, or ask me
a question, in some way it was like he didn't really remember
Cary all that well, I mean, of course, he did, A. remembered
his love, but the details were faded for him and he just wanted
to get it back as much as he could, and the only thing about it
was, Jane, that the whole time A. was here he didn't say a word
about his life now, what he was doing, nothing about his painting, the only thing he seemed interested in was Cary . . .''
Sadie paused and sighed.

"It'll be ten years tomorrow, honey," she said. "A. remembered the exact date," and I said, "oh, Miz Kinlaw, I'm so
sorry, I knew it was this month but not the day, it must be awful
for you," and she smiled unhappily and said, "I just can't enjoy
the springtime anymore, Jane, isn't that a shame? It used to be
my favorite time of the year, with the flowers and the little green
leaves . . . now just looking at my azaleas makes me heartsick,
it just seems like I don't even want to go outside till they're all
washed down," and I said, "don't tell me that, Miz Kinlaw, or
I won't want to either." She gazed at me with dewy eyes and
said, "sweetheart, you don't have to call me Miz Kinlaw anymore . . . look at you, all grown up and married with troubles
of your own, just call me Sadie," and I said, "are you doing all
right about it?" and she said, "honey, I still hurt about Cary
sometimes, of course I do, but, yes, I'm all right, and I don't
want to talk about myself anyway," and I said, "well, did A.
say anything?" and she said, "not too much, honey, mostly it
was him asking and me telling . . . he was very gentle about it,
but it was clear to me what he wanted to know—how Cary was
at the end, what he said . . . I guess A.'s real question was why
Cary did it, honey, but I couldn't answer that because I still
don't know . . .'' Her voice caught and she shook her head
before going on.

"Well, honey, I told A. about that last year after Cary dropped
out of Chapel Hill and came home . . . you know how it was,
God bless you, dear, you saw him some, but you can't know
what it was like here in this house . . . it was like there was this
dark cloud hanging over Cary raining on him everywhere he
went, we all felt it and nobody knew what to do for him, there
wasn't a one of us that wouldn't have rather died ourselves than
see it hurting Cary so, I truly mean that, I know I would have
given my life willingly if it could have helped him, and Tommy

would have done the same thing, I know, if he'd still been here, and I think it hurt Cliff most of all, but there was nothing any of us could do, or if there was we didn't know what it was, the air was just dark and thick around Cary then, I can't describe it any other way . . .

"Cliff would come home from UVA every weekend just as soon as he got out of class, all that way, and try to cheer Cary up and get him out of the house, he'd take him out to the golf course and try to make him laugh and drink a beer and just enjoy himself, but Cliff said Cary would stand there and swing at the ball as hard as he could and couldn't even hit it, or just knock up a big piece of grass and stand there staring down at it and get angry with himself because he couldn't . . . it was way down deep inside his body then, Lord knows, not just in his mind and spirit, and it just overwhelmed us, Jane, that's what it was, it just did . . . Cary went up there to the psychiatrist in Durham a few times and they gave him some medication, but then he wouldn't go back, he said it wasn't helping him, and we couldn't make him. I never thought about committing him, Jane, I just don't know how you could ever do that to your child when he's hurting so, I felt like Cary came back home to us because he needed something here, though, Lord knows, he never found it, and I never believed he'd kill himself, Jane, even when he talked about it, I never quite believed he meant it. I guess I failed in that, and I blamed myself so much for it, but it was just beyond my comprehension that he could really want to die, I still didn't believe it when I saw him in his coffin, I still didn't really know he was dead, it took me two years to get over looking for him in the afternoon when I'd come in from work, and that last day—I told A. this—I'll never forget it as long as I live . . .

"Cary was already up when I left for work, he stumbled past me in the hall coming out of the bathroom, he was so bad then, but it didn't seem worse than other days, and I kept thinking, Lord, if he can just hold on it's going to come around for him, and when I came in the kitchen he was right in there standing at the range scrambling eggs, hon, you would never think that, would you? that he'd want to get up and eat his breakfast like any other day, I kissed him good-bye and he hugged me around the neck and said, 'bye, Mama,' it wasn't any different, but I can't forget it, Jane, those were the last words he ever spoke to me, 'bye, Mama,' just like that.''

Sadie and I were both crying, and she had to pause before she went on. ''On the way down the steps I just had this feeling that maybe I shouldn't go in that day, maybe I should call in sick, but I knew it would upset Cary to see me fussing over him, and he wouldn't stay around me long anyway, so I got in the car and went downtown, and when I walked through the office door I just got this awful feeling—I remember it so clearly—I stood there and closed my eyes and said, 'Lord, I give him to you,' those words exactly . . .

''When I came in that afternoon he'd washed up his dishes and put everything away so neatly in the dish-drain and spread the cloth out on the counter, but he'd forgotten about his milk glass, he'd left that out on the table and hadn't even touched it and his pill right next to it . . . that was the first thing I saw when I walked in that door, honey, and I don't know what it was, but I just felt something come over me when I looked at it, I got this terrible fear . . . I called him and went all through the house looking for him, afraid to open every door, and it wasn't till I came back that I looked out front and saw his car was gone, I hadn't even noticed when I drove up . . .

''I sat down and waited half an hour thinking maybe he'd gone up to Dell's for a soda, and then I called my brother, Vince, and he came right over, just as worried as I was, we talked about what to do and finally he picked up the phone and called the sheriff's office . . . then we just waited and waited till it got dark, Cliff was in the middle of his exams and I didn't want to worry him till we knew something, but when it got to be nine o'clock that night I felt something just give way inside me, I think that's when I gave up hope, and it wasn't until the next morning at seven o'clock with us all sitting here—Vince, and his wife, Annie, and my mother and father—drinking coffee and not talking, listening to the birds start singing in the yard, that J. R. Blakely, Sheriff Coffey's deputy, called here and told Vince they found his car out at the Little Wabash Dam with the door open and the engine still running, which always made me think, honey, that Cary just got out of that car and ran.'' Sadie looked at me with the deep amazement and incomprehension of it in her eyes, she wasn't crying, not anymore, and neither was I. ''That was Tuesday morning, they started dragging the river then, but they didn't find Cary till Wednesday evening around supper time, four miles downstream past the rapids right up near the bank.''

Sadie's eyes had glazed as she talked like she was describing a movie running right before her that only she could see. Her face looked grave and drained and peacefully unhappy, if that's possible, though somewhere way far down in those brown eyes of hers there was a high note of despair that was engraved in her and wasn't ever going to go away. "Vince was sure it was drugs, Jane, that Cary had been doing something and went out there and slipped, I didn't know whether I wanted to believe that or not, I just didn't know, but the autopsy showed there was nothing in his system, not drugs or alcohol or anything . . . I told A. that yesterday, just like I'm telling you, and he said, 'I never would have thought there was, Miz Kinlaw.' ''

Sadie looked at me like can that help you, honey, I don't know what you're after, and then she said, "we talked about all that, Jane, and that's when I took down the albums . . . I had to go off to the beauty parlor and left A. here and when I came back an hour and a half later he was right there where I left him, still flipping through them page by page, and he just smiled up at me like I'd stepped out of the room for a phone call and come right back . . .''

Sadie broke off, and I said, "you don't think A.'s . . . ?" I faltered, not even wanting to put the thought in words, but Sadie understood me. "Like Cary was?" she asked, and I just stared. She shook her head. "I don't think so, honey," she said, "but the truth is I don't really know. All I know is that A. didn't seem himself. I wish I had more to give you, but I've told you all there is." We sat there holding one another's hands, staring at the TV screen where the preacher, standing in a wading pool with his vestments floating out around him, dipped a young girl over backwards in the water. "Maybe it was a mistake to call, Jane," Sadie said, "it's just that he seemed so alone and troubled. I didn't know who else to turn to." I shook my head. "No, ma'am," I said, "I'm glad you did, Sadie, it's just that this is all so unexpected and I don't know what to do about it.''

"How do you feel about A. now, hon?" Sadie asked me quietly, and feeling my eyes grow suddenly hot I looked away out the window at a sprinkling of dandelions in her uncut grass. "You don't have to talk about it if you aren't comfortable, dear," she said, and I said, "I don't know, Sadie—after that first night I asked him not to call, but since then I haven't thought about much else.'' She gave me that studying look of hers which was so kind and mild but so very deep, inviting but not pressing, and I said, ''maybe it's just some past thing cropping up again, Sadie, something that isn't real—I don't know how you tell the difference.'' Sadie smiled a little and shook her head like she didn't have the answer either. ''I certainly didn't think about A. during my marriage,'' I continued, ''if things had stayed the same with Robert I believe I could have spent my whole life with him and never thought about another man, but what there was between us just got killed and stomped on, Sadie, Robert's gone and I don't even want him back.'' Sadie nodded like she understood, and as I struggled toward my feelings, my eye drifted to the window again where a gust of wind was passing through the grass, and I said, ''I was working in the yard yesterday with Mama and she came around the side with a whole load of dandelions and Queen Anne's lace, and I thought, why not just let them grow? they come back every year anyway, and maybe that's what this is, Sadie''—I looked at her—''like some old plant you pull up in the yard, you look out the window and you don't see it any more, you think it's gone, and then you walk outside one day and there it is again, that same old weed, A. Jenrette''—I laughed unhappily as it occurred to me, and Sadie smiled. ''I guess I ought to pluck it up, but the truth is, I'm just not sure I want to kill it, Sadie, God help me, I guess I'm learning it myself right as I'm telling you—do you think I've lost my mind?'' and she said, ''not your mind, honey,'' with a sad smile, and then my tears came.

Sadie put her arms around me and drew me close, and I said, ''I just don't know if I can do it again, Sadie,'' and she patted me and said, ''Lord knows, honey, don't ask me, I don't have the answers—look at the one I picked,'' and we both laughed and cried at the same time. Then I pulled away from her and said, ''I just love you so much, Miz Kinlaw,'' and she said, ''I love you, too, honey, just like you were mine, I used to think . . .'' She looked at me and I understood her, there was no need to say it.

''But I understand, honey,'' Sadie went on, ''I always understood how you felt, and, sweetheart, you may not believe it coming from an old rundown widow woman, but once upon a time there was a boy who loved me just like Cary loved you and I couldn't return it either, I chose Tommy Kinlaw instead, maybe it was a mistake, I don't mean to be ungrateful, Tommy was a good provider and I've got all I need to this day, I won't ever take that away from him, it's so easy to look back and see what you did wrong, but if I'd married that boy or you had married Cary it would have just been something different, a different love with different problems, no road is paved with gold, and looking back from where I am now after it's all over—no, don't say anything, honey, because it is, for me in that one way it's over—even with what happened to my baby, I loved my husband and I wouldn't choose another life, not even if God offered it to me, I'm just thankful for the one I've had . . . that was my answer, Jane, I don't know what yours will be . . . but I do think A. could use a friend right now,'' and I said, ''I don't know what I could do for him, Sadie, but I do want him to be okay,'' and she said, ''God bless you, dear, I'll pray for you.'' I dried my eyes and stood up, taking a deep breath. ''I guess I ought to go on over there and see if I can find him,'' I said, and she said, ''let me know, Jane,'' and I said, ''yes, ma'am, I'll call you,'' and we hugged one last time before I left.

I never even touched that Tab.

Eight

JANE

I went by Miss Zoe's place right after I left Sadie's, but no one answered my knock, and both cars were gone, so I drove back by the Food Giant and bought a half-gallon of Rocky Road ice cream and a whole package of plastic picnic spoons just to get at one and sat right there in the parking lot in Mama's car, helping myself and wondering what in God's name I was getting myself into. After all that time with Dr. Rosenkrantz discussing my "boy problems" and trying to get a handle on my constant choice of hurtful men, was I going to travel down that road again with A.? Was that what I was feeling—leftover rewarmed love? Having eaten half the ice cream and feeling worse than ever, I threw the rest in the dumpster and drove home.

Back at the farm I found a note Mama had left on the refrigerator—"playing bridge, back at 3," and then, "I love you, honey," underlined three times. It was just a little thing, but I got all teary again, reading it. Having nothing else to do, I took a long walk down by the ponds. We'd given up harvesting them two years after Daddy died and I'd thought they were all empty now with the blight, but I saw an old catfish roll over out there in the water swallowing a skater bug, which made me contemplate the nature of the Skater-Bug Blues as I went on down in the fields.

Lonnie Satterwhite was out there with his son, Willie—he was leasing the acreage from Mama now—doing his transplanting,

putting down the little new green tobacco shoots off the back of
a tractor which they drove over from the seed bed up the road.
He tipped his hat to me, and Willie stared, and I smiled back
and walked on through the sparkling crumbly dirt, listening to
all the dead voices crying out of it, one of them my own.

Having opened the door to what I felt for A. with Sadie, the
memories tumbled out like keepsakes from a cluttered closet,
things that had no present use but were too dear to throw away.
My mind went back to the first time I'd met him, the summer
after junior year.

Even that first day when I was still with Cary, I'd seen A.'s
specialness and been attracted to it. Not in a personal way—it
wasn't like I wanted to jump his bones—it was just a nice charisma that made it fun and interesting to be with him and made
me want to get a little closer.

It was out at Cary's trailer at the lake the day after the
forest fire. I'd driven over around noon, and I was shocked
to see the trees all scorched and the pinestraw blackened underneath them. The place smelled like a day-old campfire.
A. wasn't up yet, and Cary and I were sitting out back on
the picnic table when A. appeared with a groggy face and a
Coca-Cola in one hand. He was wearing cut-offs with no shirt
and he had a nice body, lean and tan and well-defined, though
on the skinny side. He looked like he could use a bath, and
his cheeks were stubbly. He was good-looking, too, though
in a different way from Cary. Cary had dimples when he
smiled and a twinkle of fun mischief in his eyes, while A.
was more like something carved. There was a distance in A.'s
face and his smile was subtle, just a fraction of a thing under
eyes I liked, grayish blue and restful to look into at times,
calm like the lake. But it was like A. was gazing back from
a long way off, as though he knew something and it was all
settled for him in a certain way, and whatever it was he knew,
it was something sad.

A lot of what I felt about A. came from Cary, and another
part from what I knew about his family. What had happened
between his father and Big Herbert at the church over the book,
their flight from Killdeer, A.'s mother's death—that story was a
piece of local lore I'd heard about long before I ever knew A.,
or even Cary. That made it interesting to meet him, like a character in a book. I remembered his daddy, too, from when I was
a little girl. Mama had pointed him out to me one day when we

were in Killdeer going to D. W. Edwards's to pick out a tie for Daddy's birthday. Mr. Jenrette was walking down Commerce Street toward the *Sentinel* in white pants and a white short-sleeved shirt, bareheaded, with that coal-black hair, and all the other men on the sidewalk had on their felt hats and sober business suits. He was a head taller than anybody, and I remembered being struck by him, those blue eyes like A.'s, and a little abstracted smile like he was thinking about something interesting and not paying attention to what was going on around him. "That's Clay Jenrette, the author," Mama said, and I said, "that's the man I'm going to marry." She laughed out loud and stopped the car dead in the middle of the street—there wasn't any traffic—and rolling down the window called out, "Clay?"

Mr. Jenrette looked around and up in the air like someone in a second story, or maybe a bird had hollered at him, and Mama said, "Clay Jenrette!" and honked the horn. "Mama!" I said, and Mr. Jenrette stared at her like he didn't know her, and then that big clear grin spread across his face and he walked over. Putting his hand on the door, he leaned in and said, "hello, Sally, causing trouble like always, I see." Mama flushed and said, "you know me, Clay," with a giddy overtone in her voice, which was a side of Mama I'd never seen before. She was flat out flirting, though harmlessly. "I sure do," Mr. Jenrette said, "and I ought to make a citizen's arrest on you, stopping in the middle of the street—what brings you to the metropolis?" "It's Walter's birthday," Mama said, "we came to buy a present," and Mr. Jenrette said, "why don't you take a catfish out to the taxidermist and get it mounted for him? Everybody knows he's not raising them for money but because he can't catch one on a pole," and Mama said, "why, Clay, you're simply awful—I'm going to tell him what you said." Mr. Jenrette smiled and said, "wish him Happy Birthday for me, too."

"Clay," Mama said, "the reason I stopped you, Jane just said the cutest thing. I couldn't drive another foot unless I told you." Mr. Jenrette blinked those big clear eyes at me, and I said, "*Ma*-ma!" and she said, "hush, girl . . . Clay, I told her, 'that's Mr. Jenrette, Jane, our local author,' and she said, 'I'm going to marry him'—now isn't that the cutest thing you ever heard?" Mama laughed and I sank beneath the seat, hating her not only because she told it, but because she told it wrong, and Mr. Jenrette looked straight at me and said, "well, that's the nicest compliment I ever got—I'll look forward to it, Jane," which was the thing that always made me think he was a gentleman, whatever A. or anybody said, because he didn't tease me, but said it like he meant it, even if he didn't.

When Mama told that story over dinner, Daddy got this funny look on his face and said, "you want to know about Clay Jenrette?" more to Mama than to me, and then he took down that old dog-eared book of poetry he liked so well and read a poem named "Richard Cory," but all I could remember from it was that Richard Cory glittered when he walked and ended up shooting his brains out, which was sort of prophetic on Daddy's part, though not literally, thank heavens. But the thing about it was, you could tell Daddy liked Mr. Jenrette, even if he grudged it some, and Daddy didn't give that lightly. And all that was working somewhere in the background the day I met A. at the lake.

Cary's back was to A., so I saw him first. Tipping my dark glasses down, I peered at him across the bridge and said, "so this must be the famous A. Jenrette," firing a preemptive volley as was my way back then. Cary swung his head around and said to A., "you up?" with a big grin, proud of me for A. and of A. for me, and A. said, "morning, spud," ignoring me with an affected sullenness that underneath was shy. Cary turned his watch up on the underside of his left wrist and said, "try afternoon—it's one o'clock," and A. said, "give me a break—you know how long it's been since I've been able to sleep in?" and Cary winked at me and said, "he needs his beauty sleep, he had a tough workout yesterday putting out that fire," teasing A. and building him up to me at the same time—it was interesting to watch them. "It wasn't just me," A. said, "you were there, too, as I recall," building Cary back, and Cary said, "yeah, but I wanted to call the Fire Department," denying credit. It was like a game of tennis where the ball was a compliment of manly bravado that neither wanted for himself, sending it back across the net to the other, who fired it right straight back, and I said, "well, you should have called them. You know you were just being hotdogs—you're lucky you didn't get yourselves killed," which was also a compliment from the backhand, girl to boys. A. didn't get it. Still not addressing me, but Cary, he said, "too bad she wasn't here, huh, spud? We could have used a cruise director."

Tilting my Wayfarers down again at A.—a mannerism I'd

picked up from Audrey Hepburn in *Breakfast at Tiffany's*, my favorite movie at the time, and used too often—I said to Cary, "he's *real* nice," and Cary laughed and said, "don't take it personally, Jane, sometimes he's like that in the morning before we feed him," and I said, "well, maybe you should keep him in his cage until you do," and A. said, "you can both French-kiss my ass," which had a prep school ring. "Bare it, spud," Cary said, and I said, "boys, not in my presence, if you please," which I thought was pretty good.

Enjoying our repartee and thinking we were getting on quite famously, I didn't see that A. was flustered. His own natural tendencies combined with all that time in a boys' school had made him something of a social retard, though of an endearing sort, except when he turned dangerous, so I was caught off guard when A. turned and said, addressing me for the first time, "So, *Jane*, Cary's told me a lot about you," turning dangerous. The way he said it made it clear the remark was not intended as a compliment. I felt a touch of frost, but said, "oh, he has, has he? like how wonderful I am?" trying to make a joke of it. "Close, but not exactly," A. said, and I just turned to ice.

Cary gave A. this look like, good move, spud, and I could tell from A.'s expression he hadn't meant it to go that far. I felt my eyes stinging and was glad for my dark glasses. Nobody spoke. They both fidgeted and swallowed nervously, looking lost and worried like two little boys, but I wasn't going to save them. "Come on, Jane," Cary said, "it wasn't like you think." He tried to put his arms around me, but I nudged my shoulder up, resisting, and A. said, "what's the deal?" like he really didn't get it, or really didn't want to."

"What do you say, Jane?" Cary said, "you hungry?" and A. said, "I'm starved," and Cary said, "let's go to the marina and get a boi-gah," and his grin said, don't be mad. "What's a boi-gah?" I asked, feeling bruised, but glad to change the subject, and Cary said, "you know, like a *ham*boi-gah, or your basic subvariety, a cheese boi-gah—that's how they say it up north, right, A.?" and A. said, "right-o, spud"—it was their private joke—and I said, "I thought you were talking about something you pick out of your nose." Cary laughed and went inside to get his wallet, leaving A. and me standing in the yard. A. shuffled around a little nervously, shy of me and wary, I suppose, just like I was of him, then Cary reappeared and we all headed down the path to the dock.

"I'm going to ski," Cary said, pulling his black slalom out of the back of the boat and skating it across the water, "see you gaters later." Falling over sideways in the lake with a salute, he came up swinging his hair around to the side and blowing, a big grin on his face, waved and started swimming toward the ski. And there we were, me and A. alone together.

"You want to get that line?" A. said, indicating the stern rope, and I said, "you're going to drive?" It was clear he'd assumed he would, but to be sporting he said, "have you driven it before?" and I said, "Only about a hundred times." A. hesitated as though at a loss and then said, "okay, then, what the hell—you take it," which surprised me—it was almost sweet. "That's okay," I told him. I started to lean over, but feeling shy of giving him a broad view of my ass, I knelt facing him instead and slipped the figure eight off the dock cleat. A. wasn't watching anyway. He pulled out slowly, then idled as I tossed the rope to Cary, who was squirming his feet into the cups. The tip of the ski came up and Cary leaned back and dipped his head, letting the water slick his hair back. Then he held up his thumb and A. pushed down the stick, and I felt the bow breast up and the rope thwang tight against Cary's weight, shaking the water off in thin sheets like cellophane, and we passed through the mouth of the cove into the main body of the lake.

As soon as we cleared the point Cary leaned over and rode across the wake and then cut back and did a jump. He whooped and cut down really low fanning out a rooster tail of spray, holding the bar in one hand and dragging the other in the water. I watched intermittently, kicking off the floor and wheeling back and forth in my chair. "Check it out," A. yelled over the wind and engine roar, wanting me to see Cary and appreciate him, and I said, "he's showing off," and A. cut his eyes at me and said, "no, he's just good," as though my remark required a parry, and I said, "I've seen him ski before, A." A. blinked at me appraisingly and then made a hard turn to the left so that Cary skated almost even with us off the right side. Cary waved and whooped and A. whooped back and straightened the wheel and Cary fell away again in the wake.

A. turned on me directly and said, "don't be mad at him because of what I said, Jane," surprising me again, "Cary didn't say anything bad—he's crazy about you. It's just that Cliff and Deacon were over here last night, and Cary and Deacon got into it." A. cut his eyes at me and there was something deep and steely in them, and I asked, "what happened?" feeling suddenly a little sick and excited in a way that wasn't pleasant. "Cary kicked his ass," A. said quietly, his nostrils flaring and his eyes going smoky with some strange male emotion—pride perhaps, or vindication. He stared away over the windshield to hide it from me. "I didn't know what it was all about till later," he went on, "Cary said you used to date him and that he was pretty shitty to you. That's all he said, Jane. I should have kept my mouth shut. I didn't mean to hurt your feelings." I liked him then. "Thank you for telling me, A.," I said, and he just shrugged, downplaying it with an obtuseness I found almost touching. I smiled at him and he smiled back and said, "yeah, well Deacon's a real asshole anyway," nudging back the throttle, because by that time we were coming up on the dock at Dawson's Landing.

Cary was exhilarated from the water and really happy. "Hey, sweetheart," he said to Joanie, giving her a big smack on the cheek as we walked through the screen door with the tin "Merita Bread" sign on it. "Don't you get me wet," Joanie said, threatening him with a spatula but obviously enjoying it. "I swear to God," she said, "I just mopped my floor this morning," and Cary took the towel from around his neck and stood on it, swiggling his feet from side to side, and said, "okay?" Joanie gave him a deadpan squint and said, "y'all want something to eat, or you just dropping in to make my day?" and Cary said, "how about some boi-gahs?" and Joanie, who was in on the joke, too, said, "what kind of boi-gahs?" and Cary said, "cheese boi-gahs all the way, two apiece," raising his eyebrows at A. and me to see if that would do. "One's enough for me," I told him, and Cary said to Joanie, "Jane's got to watch her figure," giving her a wink, and I said, "I most certainly do not," and Joanie said, "you tell him, shug, looks just fine to me—if anything, I'd say you could use to eat a little more," and I said, "thank you, Joanie," sticking out my tongue at Cary, and Joanie said to me, "you watch out for that one, shug," indicating Cary, who said, "you got any Bermuda onions, Joanie?" "I got no Bermudas," Joanie told him, "but I got Vidalias," and Cary laughed and

said, "we got no Bermudas today," and I said, "no onions for
me, Joanie, thanks," and A. said, "me, either," and Cary raised
his eyebrows and said, "maybe I should reconsider," and I told
him, "don't bother on my account," and Joanie laughed and
said to Cary, "I guess she told you, smart britches," and A.
said, "don't worry about me either, spud," and everybody
laughed.

At some point over lunch the subject of 'shrooms came up
and I asked what they were. Cary stared around suspiciously
like a spy about to pass top secret information, and said,
"*drugs*," in a low evil-sounding heavy-metal growl. I felt a
creepy little tingle, half excitement, half alarm, and said, "I've
never even heard of it."

Cary turned to A., giving him the floor, and A. said, "magic
mushrooms, Jane, psilocybin," and I said, "what does it do?"
and Cary said, "it's like a six-hour orgasm—that's what A. told
me." A. blushed, and I said, "come on, really?" and Cary
nodded at me significantly, like, *really*, Jane, and I said, "but
don't they change your chromosomes or something?" and A.
said, " 'shrooms are totally organic, Jane, they grow right out
of the ground like cabbages," and I said, "so do poison toad-
stools," and he said, "these are different, they aren't poison,"
and I said, "but how do you *know*?" and he said, "how do you
know the ones you buy in grocery stores aren't poison?" and I
said, "because I've eaten them," and he said, "there you are,"
like I'd only proved his point.

Back at the trailer, A. opened the freezer compartment of the
refrigerator and took out a plastic baggie which he held up for
our perusal with this grin like the Big Bad Wolf. That was when
he started coming out a little, as though some switch had flicked
in him and he'd gone into overdrive. That was the thing about
A.—he had a kind of secret wicked charm that came out at
certain times, like that fire, or doing mushrooms, that was different from his normal reserve, something very on and upbeat,
and so quick, always two steps ahead of everybody else. I began
to get a sense of what Cary meant about him and who he was
inside. It was like we were embarking on a journey into the
wilderness, and A. was the only one who'd been there before,
and he was going to show the path to me and Cary and lead us
to the treasure, and I might have resented him for putting himself
forward in that way, only he was so excited and eager in a winning boyish way, and it was obvious he wanted us to be excited,

too. However deep his problems were, it was like there was something burning inside A., and that thing was beautiful and joyous and in love with life, and you can't resent something like that.

Inside the plastic bag were these things that looked like little skinny mummy penises—heads on them and all—and these snaky little tails. "Those look like mummy dicks," I said, just coming out with it, and A. laughed and said, "wait till you meet the mummies," and it was like already at that point before we even did anything we started to feel strange, all of us, like we were weighing anchor and leaving behind the world we knew.

A. put the mushrooms on a plate and sat them on the coffee table in front of us. "Take two apiece," he said, "they're pretty big. We'll save the rest for later, should it become necessary," and he grinned like he thought that last part was especially clever. "What do you do, just eat them?" I asked, and A. said, "there are lots of ways. You can fry them up with onions and soy sauce"—I laughed because I thought that was supposed to be a joke, but I guess it wasn't because he gave me a tolerating look—"or blend them up in smoothies, or make tea with them. If they were fresh we could do it any of those ways because they taste pretty rank, but the dried ones aren't too bad really, sort of like eating funky straw. So what do you say?—let's do it."

He looked at Cary like *this is it* and said, "you ready, spud?" and Cary shrugged and said, "what the hell," and A. said, "choose your weapons," offering him the plate. Cary turned to me and said, "ladies first," and since I'd about had it with the suspense and was ready to get the show on the road, I said, "this mummy looks like my kind of guy," taking the biggest one and putting the whole thing in my mouth at once. It tasted like old dead leaves in the yard that never got raked up with an aftertaste like maybe Sam had done his business there, but that was pretty faint and I didn't feel like I was going to barf or anything, at least not at first.

"This one's got your name on it, spud," A. said to Cary, putting one in his hand and closing his fist around it. We all sat there then like a bunch of cows chewing their cud, and I said, "this is *real* fun," and A. said, "it gets better," and I said, "I hope so," and A. said, "trust me," and winked, which was the last thing I was about to do. We each ate a second one, and I said, "what now?" and A. said, "just wait," and got up and

said, "I'm going to get a glass of water—anybody else?" and
Cary said, "to hell with water, let's crack a brew," like now
that he'd done it he was ready to go all the way.

Then Cary got up and followed A. into the kitchen and the
two of them slapped five—front, back, between the legs—and
Cary opened the refrigerator and shoved a can of beer in A.'s
hand, and they gazed at one another with an excited fondness—
I could see how much Cary looked up to A.—happy that they
were going on this adventure together, and A. said to Cary, "it's
going down, motherfucker," acting like a black boy.

It wasn't too long after that when I said, "I think I'm starting
to feel something." A. raised his eyebrows like he was interested and said, "yeah? it's kind of soon." He held his hand up
in front of his face with his studious little frown and moved it
like a mime touching the pretend glass wall. "What are you
doing, spud?" Cary asked, and A. said, "trails—sometimes
you see them, like smoke off your fingers," and I said, "that's
not what I mean, I feel kind of sick to my stomach." "That's
normal, Jane," A. said, "Don't worry about it, it'll pass," and
Cary said, "it's probably the boi-gahs anyway," and both of
them cracked up, which wasn't very sensitive at all. I was truly
uncomfortable—my forehead had started sweating—and I was
scared because I felt like the two of them weren't paying any
attention and were maybe even laughing at me, though deep
down I knew they weren't.

That's when it began. I looked out through the open door and
noticed something like a pale green fog floating above the grass
out over the field, and when I looked back at the two of them it
was like suddenly they were different. Their eyes were really
big and dark and they both had these smiles on their faces like
wild animals, happy eager animals, but dangerous, and they
were staring at me like they were going to eat me or do something terrible to me, and suddenly I wanted to stop what was
happening and go back to how I was before, but I realized I
couldn't, and I started crying. I put my face in the pillow and
curled up on the sofa and wept, hiding from them, and then I
felt a hand, icy cold, touching my shoulder, and a voice said,
very gently, "Jane, are you okay?" and I didn't want to look at
who was talking, but finally I made myself, and there was someone sitting there—it was Cary, but it didn't really look like him—
with this kind of olive-golden glow seeping off his skin, but
really coming from somewhere deeper down inside him. He was

staring at me with these eyes that were solid black, no irises at all, and he was really beautiful in a way, only very scary, and I said, "you aren't Cary," not understanding how he couldn't be but only that he wasn't, and he looked across the room at the other one—which was A.—who was also very beautiful, only his glow was more a silver color, and colder, and the two of them exchanged what seemed to me a kind of secret sign which made me ever surer it wasn't A. and Cary, and Cary said, "yes, I am, Jane, I'm Cary and everything's okay, we're not going to let anything happen to you," and he tried to touch me but I drew away and said, "no, you're not, you're trying to trick me," and Cary said, "then who do you think I am?" and I shook my head and said, "I don't know, but you're not a human being."

Cary laughed like he couldn't help it, but then he made himself be serious and got up and crossed the room to A. and the two of them started whispering in some language I couldn't understand, only I knew they were conspiring against me, and I said, "I know what you're doing, you're hatching plots," like I wasn't going to let them, and both of them came over and Cary sat beside me on the sofa and A., the silver one, sat on the coffee table and leaned up close to me and said, "listen, Jane, I'm A., and this is Cary, and we aren't 'hatching plots' against you or anything like that, we both like you, it's only that I think what happened was when we took the mushrooms I wasn't really taking into consideration that your body weight is less than ours, so you're a little further out there than we are, but it's okay and if you'll just relax and let go and trust us we won't let anything happen to you and it will be really beautiful, okay?"

A.'s voice was like a kind of music whose meaning I felt more deeply through the melody than the words. It soothed me, but I also felt myself becoming mesmerized. I drew back afraid, thinking maybe he was doing it on purpose and said, "if you're A., why did you change?" He smiled and I felt something tingly like electricity or rays come from his mouth and eyes and shiver through me. "You're just seeing who I really am, Jane," he said, "my true self, and Cary's, and we're seeing yours—you look different, too." He got up and took the mirror from the wall, laying it across the table. We all gazed into it.

At first I couldn't believe the person I was seeing was really me. She looked like someone staring in at me through a window-pane, someone I knew or used to know but couldn't place from where or remember her name. Then A. said up from the mirror, "pleased to meet you, Jane McCrae," and she smiled at me—it was my own face smiling. I touched my face and she touched hers, but it was her hands touching me. Tears of happiness streaked down my cheeks, but they were her tears, too, and suddenly I realized she was the person inside me who I'd always known was there and wanted to meet, and that moment felt like a miracle. "We don't know them, but they know us," A. said, "they don't forget," and I understood so clearly what he meant—I was the stranger, and she, the girl (the tobacco girl, though I didn't call her that till later) was who I really was and wanted to be, and could be, that however deeply buried she was, she was always there and always would be. I stared at A., amazed at his insightfulness, and he said, "I don't think we need this anymore," and rehung the mirror on the wall.

The next thing I remember is that we went outside. It took A. and Cary a long time to convince me, because I really didn't want to go. Just looking through the door was bad enough. Not that it was ugly. It wasn't. If anything, it was too beautiful, like eternity or something, and this was the door of the spaceship, and once you walked into that landscape you couldn't be sure you were ever going to make it back. And the sunlight was so bright it looked unendurable like it might turn you to ashes. Then A. said, "look, I'm going," and walked out on the porch and down the steps into the yard. "See?" he said, turning back to us with a big smile and holding out his hands, and I noticed in the distance that the light on the trees was exactly the same as the light around his shoulders and that it wasn't really cold, just silvery.

Then Cary took my hand and we followed him, and I saw that the light coming up from the ground, which was that white-yellow Carolina clay, was like Cary's light, and I tried to explain it to them. "Your light is like the trees," I said to A., and then to Cary, "yours is like the earth." Cary frowned like his feelings were hurt, like he didn't want to be the ground, and I stroked his cheek because it wasn't anything to be sad about. "It's a beautiful light," I told him, but I could see he couldn't understand that, and it explained something about him to me more clearly than I'd ever seen it before. "I think she's seeing auras," A. said to Cary, and I said, "can you? because I want to know my color." Neither one of them could tell me, though A. said, "when I close my eyes and try to see you I see lavender," which pleased me, as though we were two fairies and he'd made me a compliment in fairy language, and it was like A. understood what I was thinking because he made me a gallant little bow.

Then A. said, "let's go down to the water, that will be our destination," and we started off, only it took us a long time to get there, hours and hours, like the whole thing was a journey that lasted thousands of years and the lake was what we all wanted to reach, but we'd get caught up in something every few feet—the bark of a tree and your hand against it, like they were different but part of the same thing, and that's what made it different from before, that they were part of the same thing, whereas normally they didn't even seem related. But what was that one thing they were both a part of? You couldn't name it, or even see it really, but you could sense it there all around us. A long time would pass before we remembered where we were going, and then we'd walk another few feet and something new would distract us, only it wasn't like being distracted because everything had its own magical importance, and you'd miss something if you went too fast, and A. said, "it's all here all the time, if only we could get to it."

He was leading us, and Cary and I both knew it. It seemed natural, but long before we reached the woods I noticed something happening to Cary, which A. didn't see because he was too busy out searching and sniffing things, reconnoitering like a scout. I was sitting on the picnic table beside Cary when I began to feel his heaviness, like a pressure on my neck and shoulders, and when I looked at him he was staring down in his lap with a sad expression like he was going to cry, and his color had changed. There were blues streaking through it. I reached out and took his hand, and when I did he raised his face and asked me, "why am I like the dirt?" and I said, "not the dirt, Cary, the earth—that's what I said," and he said, "it's the same," and I said, "it isn't something sad, it's just different from the trees—your light is golden," but it was like Cary couldn't see it in himself and didn't really believe me.

Right then A., who was standing at the edge of the yard, turned back to us and put his finger to his lips and pointed. There was a rabbit crouching in the grass, trembling, and he walked toward it very carefully, smiling, and the rabbit never moved, not even when A. was standing almost over it. Then suddenly A. clapped his hands as though expecting the rabbit to leap away, but it didn't, it simply startled and trembled harder.

The smile drained away from A.'s face and he bent down for a closer look and then turned to us and said, "it's hurt."

Perhaps it happened in the fire, or maybe some farmer's dog got it, but one of its hind legs was broken, twisted and lying all wrong with the bone sticking through the fur. Cary and I went up beside A., and I said, "what should we do?" and looked at Cary and his eyes were dark and troubled, but he didn't answer, and A. said, "there's only one thing we can do," and Cary said, "no, it isn't suffering," and A. said, "how do you know?" and Cary said, "I just do." He picked it up gingerly by the scruff of its neck and tried to cradle it, but the rabbit struggled so that he had to drop it. It lay there kicking and flopping on the ground, and A. said, "look at it, it can't even run. We should just do it—that's probably why it came to us." Cary laughed, a short sharp bark, and said, "what—to die? maybe it came to us because it wanted help?" and A. said, "like what? what sort of help do we have to give?"

Cary stared at it with a troubled face and suddenly there were tears streaking down his cheeks like maybe he believed A. was right but wasn't giving in anyway. "We could take it to the vet," he said, and A. said, "number one, nobody here can drive, and number two, the vet's going to tell you the same thing I am," and Cary said, "you want to, don't you, A.? it's just like hunting." Something hurt and furious clouded A.'s eyes before he pushed it down and said, "it's not, it's different," and Cary said, "how's it different?" and A. said, "I didn't break its leg," and Cary said, "no, you didn't, but you'd be glad to kill it now, wouldn't you?" A. just stared at him and then said, "fuck it, Cary, do what you want, man," starting to turn away. But Cary grabbed his arm and said, "no, A., if you're so sure about it, do it then." A. turned back and said with an assumed off-handedness I could tell he didn't really feel, "do you have a gun?" and Cary said, "no," as his eyes ranged around, "but there's a stick—do it with that." For the first time, A. seemed unsettled, and Cary said, "go ahead A., go all the way. Use the stick, or your bare hands—hell, A., tear it apart with your teeth, we can eat the damn thing raw and drink its blood." Cary picked up the charred branch and held it out to A., and A. stared at it and took it.

I didn't know what was right. Cary was being hard on A., but it was clear it went back to something old between them, and I guess my instinct was on Cary's side. But it was hard to tell how bad the injury was and how much the rabbit was suffering—A. had his point, too. I think he was simply doing what he thought was right, taking charge like the one who has to go out to the barn and shoot the crippled horse when everybody knows it must be done and no one wants to do it. Nevertheless, I sensed that it would be a terrible thing for A. to take the stick and club it dead—leaving the rabbit out of it, terrible for A. I think A. knew it, too, because after standing there a minute, his clinched fingers white around the sooty limb, he threw it angrily into the forest and stalked off by himself.

Cary and I put the rabbit in a big cardboard box with some iceberg lettuce in the bottom of it and left it standing in the yard, following A. into the woods. Everything was burned there from the fire, the pinestraw on the ground was black and the trunks of the trees were charred. It was like a wasteland and the whole mood changed as though we'd gone through another, further door. A. was standing with his back to us studying it, deeply absorbed. When he heard our footsteps he turned around, and I could see from his expression that he'd forgotten all about the rabbit.

"You know what this place is?" he asked, and Cary said, "what?" and A. said, "the end of the world," and smiled like it was a mysterious adventure to him. Cary let go of me and walked toward him, putting his hands on A.'s shoulders, gazing earnestly in his face. "Why do you like it here?" he asked, and A. said, "because it's beautiful, just like that is," pointing back to the area we'd come from where the fire had never burned. Cary shook his head and said, "it isn't," and A. said, "you really have to look, it's not as obvious," but Cary held his ground. "I have," he said, "it isn't right to like it," and looking hurt, A. said, "why do you always question me, Cary?" and Cary said, "because there's a line and you can't see it. You see lots of things that I don't see, but I can see the line." A.'s eyes misted and he said, "I love you, man," and Cary said, "I love you, too," and then they hugged. And as they came together those two lights, the gold and silver, blended in a single perfect flame so beautiful it took my breath away.

As I watched it was like another eye opened in my head, or not so much in my head as in my heart or somewhere in my body, and I knew them—even A.—like I had always known them, as though they were both my lovers or my sons. I saw their different natures, how they were drawn together to make up a completeness—A. was height and aspiration, an untethered upward impulse, Cary was depth and foundation, the grounding force. They were like an education life had provided with the purpose of each taking something from the other, and giving something—two different things—so that those two lights could blend and burn in each of them alone. That was the beauty of their relationship, but there was something deeply tragic in it, too, I saw it as they drew apart into their separate diminished flames—how each was blind without the other and committed to his blindness pridefully, as though it were an act of loyalty and honor to need his friend to supply the thing he couldn't give himself.

I could see so clearly into them in a way I couldn't see into myself, and I wanted somehow to tell them what I saw, to do something for them. But my one clear move was to come between them, and that is what I did. The whole future course of our relationship was enacted in that single moment. I went up to A. first and hugged him. I could sense his surprise but also that he understood. His body was a little stiff, but tender underneath—that was the first time we ever touched—and then I turned to Cary and gazed into his eyes for a long time before I said, "I love you," and kissed him on the lips. He trembled in my arms and I felt something warm and wet against my neck. I drew back surprised and saw that he was crying. "Why?" he asked with something pained and desperate in his expression, and I said, "Cary, Cary," taking his hands, "why can't you understand how good you are?" and he shook his head and said, "I'm not, Jane, not like you think, and even in the ways I am it doesn't help," and I said, "your goodness helps me," and A. said, "it helps me, too," and Cary said, "they why doesn't it help me?"

He sank down cross-legged in the blackened straw and picked up a smooth white piece of cloudy quartz, turning it over and over in his hand and staring at it fixedly. A. knelt down and placed his hand on Cary's shoulder and said, "what's the matter, man?" and Cary said, "there's something wrong with me," and A. said, "bullshit, Cary," and Cary turned on him and said in a fierce accusing tone, "you don't know, A., it's not the same for you. I should never have done this, it makes me feel it more." A. gave me a worried look and I knelt down and said, "feel what, honey?" and Cary said, "I don't know, it's like there's something following me—it's been there ever since I can remember," and A. said, "what is it, man?" and Cary said, "sometimes it's a little man, like a cartoon character," and right at that moment a cloud passed across the sun. It threw a shadow in the wood and I felt chilled. Cary turned to me as though he knew exactly what I was feeling, and he said, "you see? it's out there now," and stared away into the trees. "I feel it, too," A. said, like he was awed but eager to see it, and when I looked at him there was something scary in his face like a tiger or a wolf, and it gave me more insight into how they fed each other.

"I only saw it once," Cary said, "when I was little out at Maw-maw's farm one time for Sunday dinner. I was outside playing with Cliff and my cousin Rodney, and Rodney picked up a rock—it was just like this one—and threw it at Cliff, only it hit me instead, right here." Cary touched the stone to the middle of his forehead where there was a tiny scar I'd noticed before, only it had a kind of icy whiteness coming from it now. "it knocked me over cold right there in the dirt," he said, "and when I came to there was this black thing like a panther with vertical green eyes leaning over me, sniffing. When I opened my eyes it jerked up and backed away, and then I heard the porch door slam and Mama called my name. I looked in that direction and saw her running toward me, and when I turned back it was gone. I told her I'd seen it, but she said it was just my imagination."

Cary stopped and stared back at the woods. "Sometimes it's just a black shape like a cloud," he said, "or something in the wind, other times it's like it's got inside me." He rubbed his arms, shivering like he was cold, and A. said, "shit, man, what do you think it is?" and Cary said, "I don't know, but it's evil, and there's no escape from it," and at that moment we heard a terrible noise—a snarl over a high-pitched bleating sound. We all stood up and in the clearing the box was lying over on its side. Then we saw the dog—a white hound with liver-colored spots. A. started to run after it, but Cary held his arm. The dog stopped at the edge of the far woods and looked back at us with the limp body of the rabbit in its mouth and then it shook it, almost like it was laughing, and trotted into the brush.

Suddenly the three of us were like little children huddling there in the forest, lost and afraid, and there was something much larger and older than us all around which none of us understood, something menacing, which wasn't just a dog, but the thing that sent the dog or took its form. "I think we should go after it,'' A. said, and Cary said, ''no, A., it's not a game—let's get out of here,'' and I said, ''Cary's right,'' instinctively.

I could tell A. didn't agree. He felt like he could handle it, that whatever was out there he would vanquish for Cary, or at least help Cary vanquish it for himself. There was something brave and loving in his impulse, but his eagerness frightened me. I could see that the main thing for A. was the exercise of his own power, which was what made him feel alive, and the difference was that Cary felt alive already and wanted to protect that in himself and all of us, whereas there was something in A. that could have thrown it all away so joyfully to be carried home in honor on his shield. ''It's never going to go away until you face it,'' A. said, and Cary said, ''whether you face it or not, it's always there, A.—sometimes you have to turn away.'' Moving to Cary's side, I slipped my arm around his waist and said to A., ''I don't think we should go.'' A. stared at us with deep frustration, then spun away and walked toward the lake.

I turned to Cary and said, ''are you all right?'' He glanced back in the direction where the dog had disappeared and said, ''it's gone now,'' and as he looked at me I saw the weight lift off him. Relief and ease crept across his features, then he smiled, and it was like the comfort of returning to a house I loved and knew so well, where every detail was my choice and taste. I smiled back and put my arms around him, feeling gladness in his comfort and in our deep familiarity, but also feeling—not for the first time, yet never so clearly—that something great was missing from our house. At seventeen I didn't know exactly what it was, except that I was lonely there.

Over Cary's shoulder, my glance drifted through the trees to A., and for a moment I let myself wonder, simply wonder. He was sitting on the bank staring out across the water. The sun had come out and the grass was lit up all around him, sparkling like jewels, and I thought silently, ''we're the grass, me and Cary, that's what's real, A. is just the shimmer off the grass,'' and I hugged Cary tighter as the shimmer held my eyes like an unknown promise.

Remembering that trip brought it all back to me, all that was fine and good in A.—his beautiful attack—no finer and no better than what Cary had, but different. Coming around full circle back to Mama's house, I wondered once again, as I had so many times in the past, why I'd chosen A. instead of Cary. So many things might have turned out differently, I thought, if it had gone the other way. I didn't understand the answer now any more than I had then, but as I came up from the fields I realized the question had become relevant again—not just to the past, but to the present, and maybe to the future, too.

Nine

It was after two o'clock when I heard a car turn off the road.
Thinking it was Mama, I looked out the window only to see the
Bentley rolling up the drive trailing a big cloud of dust. I went
all jittery and nervous—whether more from excitement or dread
I couldn't say—and wondered if I should go out on the porch to
meet him, whether that would seem too eager, or stay inside
and pretend I hadn't seen him till he knocked. The sheer per-
verseness of the thought decided me. I went out and leaned
against the upright at the top of the steps as the car came to a
stop.

Climbing out, A. emerged like a Bedouin from a sandstorm
as the passing dust cloud dispersed down toward the fields. Raising his dark glasses, he revealed two white lens-shaped rings of
cleanliness in what might otherwise have passed for vaudeville
blackface. Under other circumstances I might have laughed, but
I noticed then—one sharp clear flash that hit me like a physical
blow—that there was something about his shoulders, about the
thickness of his hair across his forehead, that moved me inexplicably like the lingering smell of pipesmoke in Daddy's study,
something I remembered not with my mind but in my body. It
was too serious to laugh.

Shading his eyes from the sun as he squinted up at me, A.
said, "Louis told me you stopped by," in a tone that told me
he was nervous, too. "Did he?" I replied, sounding meek, and
A. just nodded and sauntered casually to the foot of the stairs,

130

propping his foot on the bottom one and leaning across his knee.
"I knew you couldn't resist me," he said, flashing that hyena
grin, as Sadie called it, and though he said it with a shy self-
ironizing sweetness it still pissed me off. "What you know
wouldn't get you time in jail, A. Jenrette," I told him, not entirely without fondness, and his voice was softer as he said, "if
you want me to leave, I will," and I said, "when I make up my
mind, you'll be the first to know."

He was wearing the same suit he'd had on at Miss Misha's,
though the tie and jacket had disappeared somewhere along the
away—it was all so crumpled up and ruined he might as well
have bought it off the shelf at the Farm Supply. I don't think he'd
shaved since I'd last seen him, or probably even washed his face,
and his eyes were all red but shining oh so bright—too bright. I
could see how high he was, and how exhausted, just running on
something else, God knows what it was.

"So, A.," I said, sitting down on the top step, putting my
elbows on my knees and my chin in both hands, studying him
like the sad riddle of my fate, "to what do I owe the honor? or
is this just a social call?" He smiled and said, "you want to go
for a ride?" and I said, "where to?" and he said, "let it be a
surprise," and I said, "after the other night, I've about had it
with your surprises," and he said, "the beach, Jane—come with
me."

"The beach . . ." I said, and he said, "wouldn't it be great?"
grinning beneath eyes that had a vulnerable boyish eagerness in
them I remembered. "Why, A.?" I asked quietly, and he said,
"why not, Jane? what do you have to do right now that's so
important it can't wait a day or two?" and I said, "leaving me
out of it . . ." He sighed and the light in his face went out as
though someone had turned down a dimmer switch inside him.
"I don't know," he said absently, "maybe I just feel like going
for a swim," and his eyes flicked away evasively, but I saw the
troubledness in them then.

Rising slowly, I brushed off my seat and walked down the
steps. A. rose to meet me, and I took his hand, gazing deep into
his eyes. "I think it's time we had that talk, A.—I'm ready now.
I won't go to the beach with you, but I will take a ride," and he
said, "come on then, we'll go back to my aunt's," and rolled
his head toward the car.

As we started out, I watched him with sidelong glances, trying
to get a read on where he really was. He certainly didn't seem

crazy, which relieved me after what Sadie'd said, but on the other hand he didn't seem entirely right either. Of course, he hadn't been right that first night at the dam, but the change seemed more pronounced now. For one thing, he kept turning to stare at me until I finally had to tell him, "I wish you'd keep your eyes on the road, A., you're making me nervous," and he said, "I'm just glad to see you—I can't believe you're here," with a soft moistness in his eyes that stroked me just like silk.

Reaching out to touch his arm, I asked him softly, "how are you, honey?" and he said, "I'm okay, Jane," and I said, "really?" and he said, "really." Realizing I was going to have to prompt him, I said, "Sadie called me, you know." Looking like that surprised him, he said, "she did?" and I said, "she was worried, A.," and he said, "why? I thought we had a nice visit," and I said, "why do you think? she said all you talked about was Cary, like you were obsessed—what is all this Cary business anyway?" He stared away through the windshield then, clenching and unclenching his hands on the wheel, and I could see from his face that I'd touched the deep nerve of the problem.

"I don't know what it is, Jane," he said with quiet earnestness, "I really don't," and I said, "make a stab at it, honey," and he said, "ever since I've been home I can't think about anything else." He sighed and then fell quiet for a while. "It's so strange, Jane. I never think of Killdeer. My life went somewhere else a long time ago. But since I got here, practically from the moment Louis and I crossed the town limits, suddenly my life in New York, everything that's happened to me in the however many years it's been—none of it seems real. It's like the clock stopped when I left, Jane, and I'm some sort of caveman who's been frozen in the ice, and it wasn't till I got back that it began to tick again and the ice began to thaw, and now all I smell is rottenness. I smell something dead," and I said, "like your fish." A. flashed a look at me. There was a shine in his eyes like however bad it was, he was grateful someone else could understand it. "Like my fish," he said softly and looked away again.

"What is that fish to you, honey?" I asked, and he said, "I don't know, Jane, but I know where it's buried. The closer I get to it, the stronger the smell becomes, and everything's conspiring to draw me back there," and I said, "back where?" knowing, but wanting to be sure. "That summer at the beach," he said, "come with me, Jane, we could leave right now. There's hardly anybody down there now—it would be so cool—we could open up the cottage, take the grill out. We could go crabbing, Jane," and the bright charm of his manner was so thin, like a veneer. "That's why you want to go down there, isn't it, A.?" I asked, putting it together finally, "to be back in the same place where it all happened before," and he sighed, deflating, and said, "I don't know, Jane, maybe so, I just feel like I could get myself straight down there," and I said, "I think you may need some help to do that, A.," and he said, "that's why I wanted you to come," and it hurt me to have to hurt him, but I said, "professional help, honey," and he held my eyes with a directness I admired as the pain flashed through his own, then nodded and looked away.

We were pulling into the drive of Miss Zoe's house by then. A. didn't speak as he led me toward the library. "Can I get you something?" he asked and I said, "where's Louis?" as I sank into the deep cushions of the couch. "He's off today," A. said, and I said, "I'm okay right now," and he said, "I'll be right back then." The boards creaked as he trotted up the stairs, and I sat there staring up at the medallions in the plaster ceiling, nervous and a little bit excited to find myself alone with him, trying not to wonder what was going to happen, but wondering anyway. Did I want something to happen? My mind said no, no, no, but from some deeper place another voice just laughed. Except for one drunk night, I hadn't been with a man since Robert left, and I'd almost forgotten what it was like to feel excited, that sort of tingly giddy feeling like when I was a little girl and Dr. Hobgood, the dentist, still used ether. A. had always done that to me—even now, rotting fish and all.

The minute he came back I knew exactly where he'd been and my heart sank, though I wasn't surprised. "How about a drink?" he asked, going to the bar and pouring his own. "Wouldn't you rather I fixed some lunch?" I asked in a voice that sounded suspiciously like Mama's. A. gave me a mild look like he'd caught it, too, and would forgive my nagging. "If you're hungry, Louis made some great pimento cheese," he said, I shook my head, and he said, "I'm fine, Jane," and there was a deep relaxed confidence in his face, something very male which I'd always responded to, and I knew it wasn't the coke that put it there, but only allowed it to come out:

He sank down beside me, sipped his bourbon and then turned to me smiling and simply took me in for a long time with a glow of something in his eyes—pleasure, amusement, I couldn't tell, except that it was fond and made me feel a little flushed and breathless, that out-of-control feeling of the first time on skis when you begin to feel the mountain move beneath you. "So, Jane," he said, "why *did* you dye your hair?" and I said, "you hate it?" touching it impulsively, insecure as a schoolgirl, and he smiled and said, "you look good, Jane." I'm pretty sure I blushed. "I guess I just wanted to feel different," I told him, and he laughed and said, "maybe I should try it—does it work?" I smiled and shrugged. "For a week or so," I said.

A. sighed and leaned his head back on the cushions. "I miss him, Jane," he said, and I felt a surprised sob rise to my lips, but I held it back. "So do I, honey," I said, taking his hand. A. pressed mine back and said, "I still don't get it, Jane. I mean, I talked to Sadie, she told me how he was at the end, but you know what?" and I said, "what, honey?" and he said, "the whole time I was listening to her I couldn't quite make myself believe it," and I said, "believe what, A.?" and he said, "that Cary broke and just gave up at the end, that he went out that way, because in all the years I knew him, Jane, he never crapped out once, not toward me. I crapped out on Cary, but he never did, and I don't care what Sadie said, Jane, somewhere deep inside I've always believed he killed himself for a reason, and I still do," and I said, "what reason can there be for suicide, A.?" and he said, "I don't know, Jane . . . maybe Cary just got to the point where everything was simple, like an equation, and there was just one answer to the problem, and Cary had the clarity to see it and the courage to act on it," and I said, "oh, A., A., it wasn't like that, if you'd been there you'd know that," and he said, "what then, Jane?" and I said, "you know what I think?" A. blinked, inviting me, and I said, "I think Cary just had a bad day in a bad string of days and hurt so much he couldn't fight it any more. I wasn't there like Cliff and Sadie were, but I saw him some, A., and I know enough to tell you Cary wasn't making the sort of fancy computations you're talking about. Honey, he could hardly even speak English anymore, or focus his eyes on your face when you were talking to him or remember what you said two seconds after you said it. Don't make him out to be a hero, A., because he wasn't. Cary never tried to be a hero, that was always you. That's what he looked up to in you, A., and whether you realize the fact or not, that's why you loved him so much, more than you ever did love me, because he could bring you down off that cold lonely mountain-top you live on where everything's about challenge and endur-ance, and you could put it down, A., whatever it is you carry, honey, with Cary you could put that down and just relax and joke around and drink a beer and be a kid. Remember that, A., Cary's special gift for life—it's a rare thing in a man. At his best there was a kind of sunlight in him, but at the end he wasn't at his best, A., at the end he wasn't really even Cary anymore. So don't spend all your time concentrating on his death and painting pictures in your mind of Cary with the sunlight on his armor riding off to slay the dragon, because that's not how it was, honey, I don't know what was in his mind that day, nobody does, not Cliff, not Sadie, nobody knows or ever will except for Cary and he's not here to say, but whatever it was that made him go out there and throw his beautiful life away it wasn't trumpets blowing in the sky and knights in shining armor, it wasn't honor, honey, Cary was so far past that storybook b.s. it isn't even funny, I don't know what it was except that it was something sick and twisted and in pain beyond endurance, and if he'd waited one more day or one more hour it would have eased enough for him to be here with us telling us the parts that we don't know, but he's not, A., Cary's gone and he's not coming back.''

My face was wet by the time I finished. A. looked close to tears himself as he said, "that's what I don't get," and I said, "what?" as I wiped my wrist across my eyes, and he said, "why I'm here and he's not," sipping his drink and looking off again. Something in the way he said it chilled me and I turned to study him. "That's what you meant, isn't it?" I asked, as it dawned on me, "when you apologized to Sadie," and he said, "isn't it obvious?" as that mask of ugly New York cynicism flashed back across his truer face, and I said, "not really," and he said, "let's don't shit each other, Jane, Cary had his problems, but until that summer he was okay, he was making it, and I know all the reasons—it was three years later, it was T.O.'s death—I've been through every one, but they're all excuses. The bottom line is, if what happened that summer hadn't, Cary would still be here. It broke his heart and he never put it back together," The import of his words sank like an arrow to my heart. "I don't believe that, honey," I said, almost whispering, and for an instant his eyes burned fiercely before the saddest gentlest smile spread across his face. "I know you don't believe it, Jane," he said quietly, "but it doesn't matter, because I do—I *know* it," and he laid his fist over his heart.

The emotion was so heavy in the room at that moment it was almost like a drug, the whole weight of the irrecoverable past, and then I said, "even assuming you were right, A.—just for the sake of argument—what then? Don't you see, there's no place you can go with it, taking on that guilt isn't going to help you get your life straight now. You've got to get past it and go on. You need to think about the future," and he said, "you're probably right, Jane, the only problem is I don't seem to have a whole lot of choice in what I think about these days or where my life is headed." He shook his head and drained his glass— "your guess is as good as mine, Jane, but I'm pretty sure the future isn't it."

I think it was only in that moment that I fully realized how deep his trouble was. I know it was then that I first felt truly afraid for him, deeply, viscerally afraid. There was a sense of real jeopardy in the air, and A.'s casual, almost lackadaisical attitude was the most worrisome thing of all. "Listen to me, honey," I said, sitting up and taking both his hands, "I don't know completely what you're feeling or what you're into, but I do know I believe in you, A., deep down I do—I always have— even if the top few levels are a little shaky, and I want you to know it, too. But I've got to tell you, A., I'm worried for you, honey, really worried, I think you're depressed and utterly exhausted and I don't want to see you fuck it up and go throw your life away like Cary did, because I couldn't stand it, A. I want you to take care as you go now, hear?"

A. gazed down at our joined hands, nodding vehemently and struggling not to cry. When he'd regained control, he looked at me, his blue eyes shining, and said, "thank you for saying that," with a vulnerable quaver in his voice. He tried to smile, but it came out crooked and awry. Feeling my own eyes brimming up, I gazed at him, seeing an earlier A. in his troubled face, the boy I loved one summer at the beach who I thought I could have loved a whole lot more till he left one day without a word and broke my easy heart, and only came back after thirteen years, a man with so much unhappiness in his handsome face, and an ugly cynical humor just like mine, and I hadn't been sure the sweet A. I'd loved was still alive in him, but I could see him there, far down, just like the tobacco girl was still alive in me. I slipped my arm around his shoulder and laid my head against his chest, closing my eyes and breathing in his smell, like walking into my old room at Mama's after I'd been away a long time. I felt his solid weight as he pressed me to him, his warmth melting into mine, and though my heart was beating hard, it was all so easy. He dropped his face into my neck, then kissed my ear, and the touch of his breath against it made me shiver. Drawing back, I said, "I'm going to fix us lunch now, okay?" and he just nodded, looking somehow shrunken but a little eased, and I went off toward the kitchen.

Ten

After we ate, A. took a shower at my suggestion, and I sat at the kitchen table listening to the water running through the pipes upstairs. After a while I went to check on him, and found him in the master bedroom stretched out on Miss Zoe's big tester bed, his black hair gleaming from the bath and his face clarified and shining from the razor. He smiled when he saw me and patted the mattress, slipping over to make room. "No funny stuff," I said, and he drew a cross over his heart, watching as I reclined.

After a while he turned over on his side and we just gazed in one another's eyes for a long time like lovers do, the way we'd used to, only there was a sadness and a weight on both of us I hadn't felt in the past, and we weren't lovers anymore. Yet it struck me as I looked at A. that the weight had probably always been there, even if we hadn't known it or had let ourselves forget, and that maybe it always is. Yet in that moment the weight of our predicament, A.'s and mine, didn't seem so vastly different from the normal predicament I was always in, whatever it happened to be, along with everybody else I knew, which made me think that it's just life, the way it comes to you in a particular moment or hour, and this trick of gazing into someone else's eyes is the only thing that ever makes it go away, and even then the weight never really leaves, it just gets bearable, and, sometimes, even good to hold.

"Try not to worry, Jane, okay?" he said, "I'm not," and

138

then he leaned over and kissed me deeply with his clean new mouth and I kissed him back, until I felt him roll his thigh on top of mine, and then I drew back, asking the question with my eyes. Not that my answer was a straight no, I just thought his timing wasn't good—it never had been—but I think A. took it that way because he sighed and rolled away, saying up to the ceiling, "I'm sorry, Jane, it's just a goddamned reflex," laughing at himself as it came to him, and I laughed, too, at his sweet beautiful confidence in the midst of all his troubles and rolled my leg on top of his and kissed him back, and when I pulled back he said, "can I just sleep with you then? no sex, I mean, just mutual intimate unconsciousness," and I smiled and told him, "only if you be the pillow," and he smiled back and said, "you always liked that," and I said, "I still do," and lay down on his chest and gradually I felt his breathing slow and deepen.

I raised my head to check if he was sleeping and couldn't really tell, then fell into a tender study of his face. Relaxed the way he was, A. seemed younger and I felt all sorts of lights blink on inside my body, old doors opening and drafts blowing through, trembling the prisms in the chandeliers. I remembered the surprise I'd felt as that eighteen-year-old girl, having experienced that sensation with Deacon—something I thought could only happen once—to recover it again in A. It had filled me with such joyful wonder then. The wonder was still there at thirty-one, but the joy had turned bittersweet. With a troubled mind, I lay my head back down on A.'s chest and my thoughts went to Cary.

I remembered senior year at Meadows, how much I'd missed him when I first went off, the subtle drift that started with our separation and how it grew so large so soon. I tried to pinpoint where that change began and couldn't find it. I'd started making friends at school—there were parties, dances, other boys that made me feel a different tingle. That had been the core of it, the realization that what I'd felt with Deacon was something I could feel again and that it wasn't there with Cary. I'd waited for it, wished for it, but it hadn't come. I still believed it might, and there was so much else binding us together, so much history and tenderness and knowledge of each other's personalities, but that essential fire was lacking, and the reason I'd given myself for its absence—that I still wasn't over Deacon—grew harder to maintain as I felt it with other boys, some of whom I hardly even knew. I didn't act on it, but there were times I'd wanted to, and then there was a day when, hardly thinking anything about it, I began to wear Cary's ring inside my blouse. Cary felt me drifting, and I felt him feeling it, and hurt for him, and drifted further. He began to call me more frequently—from once a week, to twice, then finally almost every day. At first it simply irritated me, but then I began to dread his calls, the false upness in his tone as he said, "what's going on?" and the real downness in my own as I said, "nothing new," and, later, "the same thing as last time," deliberately cruel. Then he'd say, "what's the matter?"—it was like a script, and I'd mouth his question silently before he asked it. "Nothing's the matter, Cary," I'd tell him, and he'd say, "you seem depressed," and I'd want to tell him, "I am, it's these phone calls," but instead I'd say, "I'm not, I'm just preoccupied—there's a lot going on," and he'd say, "if you're busy I can call back later," and I'd say, "that's okay," and then there'd be a silence on the line before he said, "what is it, Jane?" with a begging tremor in his voice, and then I'd have to go to dinner, or someone else would have to use the phone, and I'd say, "there's nothing wrong, Cary," and he'd say, "you're sure?" and I'd say, "I'm sure, I've got to go now," and I'd hang up on him.

Those calls simply killed me. I hated myself for treating him that way, and hated him for making me. It was like we were two different people, not Jane and Cary, and I'd watch myself off at a distance hating the hack role I was playing but unable to do otherwise. It made me feel so ugly. Then I went up to Lucy Carlisle's one weekend outside Charlottesville and met a boy from Woodberry Forest, Edward Langley. We made out in the stables—it was no big thing, except that the whole time I felt Cary's ring pressing against my breastbone, and I felt guilty guilty guilty and knew it had to change. I had to make a decision, one way or the other. So I asked him to the Christmas Dance.

Cary arrived on Friday morning sometime. He'd driven up with George Jackson, who was dating Cissy Mayo, the only other Killdeer girl at Meadows. The boys looked really nice in their blue blazers and rep ties, kind of eager and nervous and scrubbed shiny, and I was glad to see Cary. I could tell they'd been drinking a little, but not too much. Cary tried to make out with me on the front lawn the minute he saw me, but I gave him my cheek and said, "no PDA," and he said, "PD, what?" and I said,

"Public Display of Affection"—they weren't big on that at Meadows. Then I took his hand and led him off to English class.

Miss O'Neil played us a record of T. S. Eliot reading his own poetry in this voice that sounded like the air leaking out of an old tire or a rocking chair creaking in some lonely room, very depressing and kind of pitiful, and though I thought T. S. Eliot had about as much spunk or life in him as the doormat on Mama's front porch, old Miss O'Neil sat there with that aristocratic frown of hers and her eyes half closed like she was in a trance or ecstasy or something, her eyelids trembling so that you could see the whites like two slices of hard-boiled egg. It was "The Love Song of J. Alfred Prufrock," and though I couldn't tell what on earth it had to do with love, I guess Miss O'Neil must have thought so, because when it was over she dabbed her eye with her handkerchief and said, "so very moving," as she lifted the arm off the record.

Then she emitted a tiny little sigh before gathering herself to her full formidable height and turning dead on Cary, saying in that deep voice of hers, "perhaps our young gentleman caller"— she looked at me with a gleam in that fish eye of hers—"can enlighten us concerning the dilemma of the older gentleman caller in this poem." I was sure Cary was going to melt right down in a puddle on the floor, but he didn't miss a beat. "She doesn't understand him," Cary said, and Miss O'Neil said, "who doesn't understand whom?" and Cary said, "the lady in the shawl doesn't understand the speaker," and Miss O'Neil said, "the speaker?" and Cary said, "Prufrock," like it was obvious—I was already lost. Miss O'Neil arched her eyebrows almost imperceptibly, which meant he had her interested, and said, "go on," and Cary said, "isn't it about regret?" and Miss O'Neil eyed him with her severest look and said, "regret for what, young man?" By that time Cary's brow was sweating, he looked like his life was on the line, and he said, "isn't it just for not having lived his life to the full?" like he was asking her.

Miss O'Neil simply fell in love before our eyes. If she'd had a spoon I think she would have eaten him and licked the dish. But remembering her age and dignity, she just said, "your name, young man?" and he said, "Cary," and she said, "not your Christian name—we are not so intimate—your surname," and Cary said, "Kinlaw." Miss O'Neil mulled on it before she said, "a good Saxon name, and a good father's poem to a wise son— I approve." And because we'd never heard Miss O'Neil give her unqualified approval to anything before, and because we had no idea what she was talking about, we all fell silent at the table with our mouths wide open—Cary blushed a hundred shades of red—and then we burst out cheering and applauding him, because it was the last day of class anyway and we were ready to cut loose.

When we got outside, Cary turned to me and said, "you don't think she was being sarcastic about Daddy, do you?" I laughed out loud at that. "She doesn't even know him," I said, and Cary smiled a little nervously—he was always oversensitive about T.O.—then shrugged it off and said, "good thing," making a joke of the whole deal. "Where did you come up with that bulldookey anyhow?" I asked, "or did you just make it up?" Cary leaned toward me and said confidingly, "we studied it at Jeff's two weeks ago—that stuff about regret? that was Mr. Mill's line." I opened my eyes wide and said, "why you dirty little sneak," and he grinned and said, "that's what you get for leaving me and going off to get an education."

I punched him in the arm, and he said, "ouch, that hurt," and I said, "you deserve it," and rubbing it he said, "well, the rest of it was mine," and I said, "I don't believe you, I don't believe a word you say," and he said, "you better watch it, Jane, one of these days I'm going to put you across my knee and give you what your daddy should have given you a long time ago," and I said, "promises, promises," and he said, "you think I won't" and I said, "a gentleman doesn't hit," and he said, "and a lady does?" and I said, "only under provocation," and he said, "that's a double standard, Jane," and I said, "I'm not a feminist, Cary"—that wasn't big at Meadows either—"and besides, nobody ever claimed that life was fair. All gentlemen know that and know they have to suffer for their privileges." Cary grinned and said, "okay, I've suffered, now what about my privileges?" and I punched him again and said, "don't hold your breath, son."

Of course, he started to, right there on the landing in the stairwell of Elway Hall. I just folded my arms and glared at him with my I-am-not-amused look as all these girls flocked by to class. Lucy Carlisle stopped and said, "what's the matter with him?" and I replied, in my most understated manner, "he's holding his breath in the hope that I will grant him my fay-vuhs," and she rolled her eyes like she'd experienced similar problems and walked away.

By then I was beginning to get a little nervous because Cary was turning sort of blue and the veins were puffing up in his neck and forehead. Tapping my toe, I said, "are you finished yet?" and finally the air just exploded out of him and he fell down flat on his back. I about half thought he was serious by that point, because he wasn't breathing or even conscious as far as I could tell. "Cary?" I said, kneeling down and shaking his shoulder. He didn't answer, so I said, "Cary, stop acting like a jerk and talk to me." Suddenly his eyes flew open like windowshades and he gasped, "air!" Before I realized what was happening he'd pulled me down to a wet sloppy kiss. As I drew away, he grinned sheepishly and said, "artificial respiration—that doesn't count as PDA, does it?" I tried to smile at his joke, but what I really felt was more like pity. "Don't try so hard, Cary," I told him, "you'll get a whole lot farther." I didn't mean it hurtfully, but he was hurt—I could see it in his face, all vulnerable and searching mine for the confidence I would have liked to give him, but couldn't.

He was quiet over lunch, and afterward I took him around the campus showing him what there was to see. We were polite and almost formal with each other, and things got heavier and heavier. Then I had a late-afternoon math class, and since I figured Cary wasn't interested in the quadratic formula or whatever we were studying, I told him to meet me on the lawn in front of the administration building at ten till five, which was when I got out. But Cary didn't show. I waited twenty minutes, and then I figured he and George had probably gone to town to buy whiskey like they'd talked about, so I went back to my room and started dressing for the dance.

I was sitting at my dressing table in my bra and underwear doing my hair, bobby pins between my teeth, when there was a knock on the door. I figured it was probably Lucy, who was going to borrow my Chanel camellia, so I said, "come in." The door swung back, and there was Cary. He had his jacket slung over his shoulder and his sleeves rolled up and his tie-knot down about a foot and his eyes were glazed like he'd been drinking. "You aren't supposed to be up here," I told him, and he made a sloppy shrug and said, "I don't think I was tailed," and I said, "well, come in before somebody sees you," getting up and pulling him by the hand.

The minute I closed the door he tossed his coat across my chair and said, "guess what?" with a grin I didn't like, and I said, "what?" and he said, "it's privilege time," and I said, "Cary . . .," but before I could go on he'd put his arms around my waist and pulled me tight against him, putting his face down in my neck and running his hand through my hair—all my bobby pins went spilling across the floor. I could smell the liquor on his breath, and if it hadn't been Cary I'd have been afraid. I just stood there stiff as a board in his arms and said, "let go of me right now, Cary, and go in the bathroom and close the door while I put on my dress." He did let go, but he didn't go in the bathroom. "It's not like I haven't seen it before, Jane," he said, and the minute it came out he looked really depressed like he didn't want to play that macho game. What really broke my heart was that I just knew he'd been out in some bar drinking and building up his courage to the point of coming in and sweeping me off my feet in this way he thought would be exciting to me, more like Deacon than himself. "Come on, Jane," he said, stepping toward me again, and because I didn't want it to turn into any more of a situation than it already was, I told him firmly, "Cary, you're drunk and I don't appreciate it, not at all—don't push it any further," and he said, "or what?" and I said, "just don't, okay?"

He lifted the ring on my neck, stared at it, then let it drop and said, "I haven't seen you in two months and you won't even kiss me. I shouldn't have to beg." The justice of it stabbed me, but I said in self-defense, "that wasn't begging, Cary, you didn't even ask," and he said, "okay, I'm sorry, but I shouldn't even have to ask, should I? Tell me, Jane." His eyes implored me, and I said, "please, Cary, don't start on this, it isn't the right time." He lit a Marlboro and took a drag off it, then said, "well, when's the right time going to be, Jane? I've been waiting a long time—how long do you need to make up your mind?"

I felt something wash over me like a wave then, something heavy and sad and bitter-tasting—not toward Cary, but just in general—and I said, very quietly, "I think it is made up, honey." He just stared at me with disbelief as his ash dropped on the floor, and I said, "I think maybe we should see other people, Cary, I think we've both felt it for a while," and he said, "don't tell me how I feel, Jane. Goddamnit, I happen to be in love with you, I'm not interested in anybody else." When I didn't respond, he sank down on the bed and said, "you're telling me you don't love me anymore?" I went over and knelt in front of him and took his hand, saying, "I do love you, Cary, more than

anyone—you know I do," and he said, "but not 'that way,' "
with a bitter smile. "Don't be mad at me, Cary, I can't stand
it," I told him, feeling my eyes brim, "I wanted it to work, I
don't know why it doesn't—it isn't you, honey, it's me—but
you're still my best friend in the world," and he said, "I don't
want to be your friend, Jane." I knew how he meant it on a
deeper level, but on the surface it was meant, and taken, as a
slap.

"I never did," he said, becoming earnest, "I always had this
feeling about you, from the first time I ever saw you, that you
were it for me. And if I had to wait, I waited, didn't I? I'm still
waiting, and I don't even care, Jane, because I know it's going
to happen for us one day, even if it isn't now, even if the timing
still isn't right—I just feel it in my heart, don't you?" He seemed
incredulous that it could be different for me, and his certainty
made me doubt myself again. "I don't know what I feel," I told
him, because I didn't, except an enormous ache of pity for him,
at his extravagant expenditure of hope, and confusion at myself
because I wanted to be touched by it, and wasn't.

"I still think we ought to see other people," I told him, because that alone seemed clear. I slipped his ring off and held it
to him in my fist, but he just pushed my hand away and said,
"so see other people, I don't care—you saw Deacon and I lived
through that. Hell, I'll see other people, too, but you aren't ever
going to find anyone who loves you like I do—you can't just
throw that in the trash, Jane, I won't let you," and I said, "I'm
not talking about throwing anything in the trash, Cary," and he
said, "so what are you talking about?" smiling suddenly like I
was just being female and airheaded about the whole thing.
Ignoring that, I said seriously, "don't make me say it," and he
said, "there's nothing you can say that's going to make me
change my mind, Jane," and in spite of everything I appreciated
that, however his persistence exasperated me. Feeling like we'd
taken it as far as we could, I got up off the floor and said, "let's
go to dinner," a little wearily. Cary fell back on the mattress
and said, "you go ahead, I need to take a nap," and I said,
"should I bring something back?" and he said, "don't worry
about it, I'm not hungry," and I put on my dress and left him
there.

In the dining hall all these girls asked me where my date was
and I lied and said he'd had to go to town for something, only
George and Cissy were at the table and knew it wasn't true.

Heading back across the grass, I had a premonition he wasn't going to be there—maybe it was a disguised wish—but he was.

Cary was standing in the dark looking out my window over the meadows that gave the school its name. Way in the distance you could just see the first lights blinking on in the windows of the houses in town, and then the streetlights, a whole string of them at once down West Catawba Street, and then the colored Christmas lights. "I'm sorry about the way I acted before," Cary said in a quiet voice without looking around, and I just went up behind him and slipped my arms around his waist and laid my head against his back. I guess I'd known he'd have to crash after all the voltage he'd put out before to keep his confidence from wavering. I'd crashed a little, too, just watching it.

After a few minutes like that he pulled my hands apart and turned around to me, still holding them. He seemed very gentle and sure and sad, and all of that together made his face especially handsome. "I think I'm going to head out," he said, and I wasn't too surprised. But far back in his eyes I thought I saw a spark of something asking me to tell him not to, so I said, "come on, Kinlaw, let's go show these piss-ants how to shag." Cary smiled like he appreciated me saying it, but also like he knew it was just a courtesy I was extending. He just shook his head, still smiling, then squeezed my hand and pressed it to his lips before he walked around the bed and out the door. Following him, I leaned against the jamb and watched him going down the hall. "Cary?" I said. He turned back and looked at me, and I discovered I didn't really know what I wanted to tell him, so I just said, "you call me the minute you get home, you hear?" He nodded and started off again, and I called after him, "you promise?" Without looking back, he raised his hand before he pushed the swinging door and disappeared into the stairwell. And he didn't call me either.

I didn't really have the heart to go to the dance after that. I just lay there on my bed getting my dress all crumpled and I didn't care if I got in trouble for not going. I stared off into space remembering all the things we'd done together and wondering if there wasn't something wrong with me that I couldn't feel for him what he felt for me. I asked myself if I loved him and the answer kept coming back, "no . . . but yes," but the no was stronger, yet the yes was also strong. At the bottom of it all I think I was afraid to lose him because he loved *me*, and I thought perhaps I needed that even if I didn't fully want it, or couldn't accept it. The next day Mrs. Bradford, the house mother, knocked on my door with a dozen red roses. There wasn't any card, but I knew whose they were—I was happy, too.

But in the days and weeks that followed, as my feelings settled, relief crept over me, like something heavy had been lifted off my chest. That feeling made me sad, but I could breathe again, and in that mood of freedom I felt Cary, I felt purely and simply the boy I'd known and loved.

Perhaps that's why I called him when I got home for spring break. He came out to see me and behaved with a cautious boyish shyness I found deeply touching. My heart was full to overflowing with an emotion I didn't understand then, or believe it was necessary to understand, not old or wise enough to know that there's a magic in the moonlight of every parting that can't survive the bright light of real life. Perhaps I learned it there, because later I made love to Cary at his trailer at the lake. I initiated it from first to last, and while it may have been a mistake it did not seem wrong. Afterwards we lay gazing into one another's eyes for hours. For me it had changed nothing—I think my impulse was toward comfort for the loss of one another. How Cary felt I didn't know—he was very quiet, very still throughout it all. Yet I know it was the thing that let him keep his hope alive. Perhaps that's what I wanted. Afterwards I blamed myself most for that, for my selfishness.

I didn't see him again till summer, when I came home from school before going to the beach, where events took their strange turn . . .

As dusk fell outside Miss Zoe's window that evening I still didn't understand it any better than I had that Christmas long ago when Cary went home early from the dance. Cary had helped me so much and was so good to me. He'd needed me, too, in a way I wondered if A. ever really had. I couldn't help thinking that if I'd been able to return Cary's love it might have saved him, or at least helped him save himself. My life might have been so different, too. So why couldn't I? Why A. and not Cary? I only knew there'd been—still was—something different in the taste of A.'s mouth, a different ice and fire in his touch that Cary never sparked in me. At eighteen I'd asked no questions—it had seemed enough—but at thirty-one with the benefit of hindsight I knew it hadn't been, and I did ask. I still wanted to believe innocently, as the girl had believed, that there was a deeper reason for the chemistry, but in my woman's heart, with a marriage and half a life behind me, I again asked the question, as I had so many times before, whether the chemistry weren't just God's terrible mockery of us, and I lay clinging to A., seeking comfort from the thing I feared, and wondering if I could be brave enough to try loving him again, knowing perhaps—at least sensing—that what I wanted made no difference. I was no more the pilot of my ship than A. of his, and knew no more than he where it was taking me.

How little did I know.

Eleven

ADAM

It felt so strange and so familiar, having Jane there again, lying beside me in bed snuggled up to my shoulder. There had always been that double sense of a thing that remains impossible even while it's happening. That night at Aunt Zoe's I remembered having felt the same emotions thirteen years before when I was eighteen, in bed with her that summer at the beach. Only it wasn't like remembering. At moments I slipped into the recollections as though they were presently occurring, and even when I pulled out, reminding myself where I was by fixing on the furnishings in Aunt Zoe's room, the aura of the past remained intact. I knew Cary was dead and that it was no longer appropriate to feel guilty about being there with Jane, but in some strange way his death made no difference. It wasn't just Jane and me alone together in Aunt Zoe's bed. It was as though Cary were standing there at the foot observing us with hurt somber eyes the way he always had in the past. I tried to shake it off and escape into sleep, but when I closed my eyes the pictures started up again. My mind went back to that same visit, the summer after junior year—the weekend of the fire and meeting Jane.

I'd told Cary then that my dad had promised me the beach house in Kill Devil Hills for the following summer as a graduation present and that I wanted him to go down with me. He didn't have to be coerced. We started making plans and continued talking about it all through senior year over the phone or in letters. He wanted Jane to come and I agreed, just to make him happy.

One morning just a few days before graduation I was walking through the quad on my way to the PO. The first really beautiful spring weather had finally broken at Keane around mid-May. After all that time I'd finally stopped marking the days off my calendar at night, I guess because I felt Keane ending and, after everything, I didn't really want to let it go. Part of it was knowing that the punishment, the endurance match was going to be over. There wasn't going to be another autumn trek back north, and that gave a flavor of sadness to what had seemed merely grueling before and without the sweetness of closure. All that was left was the sprint to the tape, finishing and doing it with a certain flourish. What made it best of all was that just beyond the finish line—which was graduation—there was the summer-long party at the beach to look forward to with Cary. I had my heart set on it.

I'd just finished my last exam in American History when I found two letters in my mailbox, one from Columbia and one from Yale, the two schools I'd most prized and coveted. I was already into Chapel Hill, so in any case I was safe, but this was what I'd been waiting for. Everything went out of focus for a few seconds while I went over in a corner and tore them open—first from Yale, where I didn't really think they'd take me after the C average I'd pulled sophomore year following Mama's death, then Columbia. They were both acceptances. With the opened letters in my hand I sprinted out the door into the quad. That golden spring sunlight touched my face like its sole purpose was to please me. There wasn't a cloud in the sky and the grass was so green it was almost like tripping, only what it was was just feeling happy, stroked, for the first time in so long I'd forgotten what it meant. The leaves on those old elms were starting to full up and the bells were ringing for fourth period and they sounded happy, like they were celebrating for once, whereas all that time they'd seemed so baleful, like a dirge, and I just said fuck it to my fourth period class, fuck Latin 42, fuck Virgil and Catullus and Terence and Horace, too, fuck Julius Caesar and Cicero and their horses and legions and forced marches and Gaul and all three parts of Gaul, fuck their idioms and conceits and stodgy honor, their victories and losses, just fuck the dead language, and stodgy Mr. Crenshaw with his stodgy bow tie, fuck him, too, fuck my slavery and fear, it was all over, none if it could touch me anymore, they could forward my demerits to the cottage at the beach, because I was fucking out of there.

So I cut class and sprinted up the hill to the dorm because Cary was who I really wanted to tell anyway. I went down the steps past the Butt Room to the pay phone and as I started dialing I realized something else—I wasn't going to go to either Columbia or Yale. I didn't even want to and maybe never had, only I'd had to prove to myself I could, that I was good enough—the same thing I'd wondered about that night at the Sherry Netherland, only it wasn't for my father anymore, it was just for me—and somehow those acceptance letters freed me up to do what I suppose I'd wanted to do all along, which was to go home to Chapel Hill where Cary would be going. We'd be roommates and raise hell like it had never even been attempted, and fuck the DKE House where my father and grandfather had pledged and where my cousins would be pledging, we'd make our own fraternity, a Jeffersonian meritocracy of mad poets and artists. Instead of bourbon we'd drink psychedelic potions compounded from recipes brought back from the darkest Amazon by demented anthropologists, or perhaps psychedelic potions in our bourbon, and become legends in our own time. That was the scenario that was unfolding in my mind as I dialed the number.

"Where are you, dear?" Mrs. Kinlaw said, "are you in Winston?" and I said, "no, ma'am, I'm still up at Keane, Miz Kinlaw, I haven't graduated yet, but I'll be home next week," and she said, "well, for heaven's sake, don't leave without graduating, hon," and I laughed and said, "no, ma'am, I won't," and she said, "well, I can't wait to see you," and I said, "I can't wait to see you either, Miz Kinlaw—guess what?" and she said, "what, darling?" and I said, "I got accepted to Columbia, Miz Kinlaw," and she said, "oh, A., that's wonderful news, honey," and I said, "and Yale," and she said, "well, goodness gracious, A., you're just going to be so educated you won't know what to do with yourself, will you, hon?" and I said, "I doubt that," because I'd embarrassed myself blurting it out like that, though I knew she didn't mind, so I said, "is Cary home, Miz Kinlaw?" and she said, "yes, dear, he's around here somewhere, let me see if I can find him for you," and I said, "thanks, Miz Kinlaw," and she said, "A., hon?" and I said, "ma'am?" and she said, "I don't want to worry you, dear, because everything's all right now, it truly is, but Tommy . . . Mr. Kinlaw, had a heart attack Monday night.''

I was so startled I didn't know what to say, and she said, ''I thought you ought to know before you talk to Cary, because he's been a little low,'' and I said, ''but he's okay now, isn't he?'' and Mrs. Kinlaw said, ''as well as can be expected. He's going to have to have an operation though, a bypass,'' and I said, ''is that dangerous?'' and she said, ''some, but the doctors tell me not to worry,'' and I said, ''he's pretty tough, Miz Kinlaw,'' and I could hear the smile in her changed tone as she said, ''yes, Lord, that's the truth, hon. He'll probably be laid up for a while though . . . I'll get Cary now.''

As she went off I thought my own private thoughts about the situation. In all the years I'd been around that house I couldn't remember a kind word or gesture from T.O. toward me, and not even, thinking back, toward Cary, or Cliff, or Sadie either—not that it hadn't happened, but only that I hadn't witnessed it, though I'd seen a lot—and I knew it was wrong of me, but I just couldn't help thinking that maybe Cary would be better off to just be free of all that, like I'd been freed from my own father in a different way. I believed the truth had dropped down on me like a demolished building that night at the Sherry Netherland, and it had almost killed me, but finally I'd crawled out from under the rubble, and now I knew what fathers were, not just mine, but all fathers, and that what I'd felt for mine, and what others felt, was based on some sort of lie which came from not knowing what fathers really were inside, that they weren't the wise sober benevolent judges and mentors they appeared to be, but just wild unhappy beasts an inch or two beneath the surface, who knew no more than anybody else or any better how to cope with life and trouble, and it was necessary to see that and to escape before they destroyed you with their bestiality under the guise of wisdom and benevolence. I thought probably all fathers were like that, and I knew for certain in my heart that T. O. Kinlaw certainly was, not that it was anything he could help, or my father either, but you still had to get away from them, you had to get free like I thought I was free, and if the only way for Cary to get free was through T.O.'s death then I really wouldn't have minded all that much, because, let's face it, I didn't care for T.O., I never had, but I did care for Cary.

''Hey, spud,'' Cary said as he came on the line—his voice was subdued—and I said, ''Cary, man, I'm sorry about your dad—your mom told me," and he said, "thanks, A.," and he paused before he said, "so you got into Yale, congratulations," and I said, "thanks, spud, but you know what I'm thinking?" and he said, "what?" and I said, "I don't even think I want to go," and he said, "why not?" and I said, "I think I want to come back home and go to Chapel Hill," and I let that sink in before I said, "we can be roommates," and Cary said, without hesitation, "I think you should go to Yale." I felt like he'd punched me in the stomach. "I was never going to Yale anyway, Cary," I told him, "if anything it would have been Columbia," and he said, "well, Columbia then, if it was me I'd go to Yale, but if you like Columbia better, go there," and I said, "what's wrong with Chapel Hill? it's a damn good school,"and he said, "yeah, but it's not Yale, you aren't going to get the same education," and I said, "fuck education, Cary, I'm OD'ed on education now, I want to close the books and live a little," and he said, "that's going to happen anywhere you go," and I said, "it didn't happen here," and he said, "college is different, A.," and I said, "just let me make my own decision, Cary, all right?" and he said, "you're going to anyway," and I said, "if I screw it up, I'll just have to deal with it, right?" and he said, "right," and I said, "so do you want to room with me or not?" and he said, "what do you think, spud?" and I said, "okay, o-*kay*, and forget college anyway, that's a thousand years from now—let's talk about the beach."

He didn't respond, so I continued, "are you getting psyched?" and he said, "I've been psyched all year," and I said, "all *right*! so have you talked to Jane?" and he fell silent before he said, "not too much lately." I waited for him to elaborate, and when he didn't I said, "she's still coming, isn't she?" and he said, "as far as I know—she and Lucy Carlisle put down a deposit on a cottage," and I said, "well, that's great, isn't it?" prompting him, and he said, "sure, I guess," and I was beginning to notice that he seemed more than a little down, not so much like he was sad, but listless or apathetic, and I was getting frustrated with him and with the phone call in general. I mean, okay, he didn't have to do backflips because I got into the Ivy Leagues, and he didn't even have to be all that enthusiastic over the idea of us as roommates, because I knew how Cary felt about me, he didn't have to say it all the time, and, yes, his father was sick and I wasn't being very sensitive, but T.O. was *okay*, he was going to be *all right*. That's what I wanted to say to him—hey, spud, snap out of it, people who have heart attacks get a second chance, it's the ones with cancer who go into the hospital and don't come back.

I felt a tremor of real anger pass through me on the phone, part toward Cary, but even more toward things in general. I guess what it was really about was envy that Cary still had what I'd lost—a family and a home and a father he could still care about like I couldn't care about mine. I wanted back my innocence, and Chapel Hill and Cary seemed like my best shot at it, and I just didn't think Cary knew what he was talking about, telling me to go to Yale. Cary just didn't understand that everything good was gone and there was only anger left, and if I let go of that I'd just dissolve in a poof of smoke and not even be there anymore.

It was at that point in the conversation that it finally dawned on me what was up, and I said, completely stunned, "you're still coming, aren't you, man?" and when Cary didn't immediately answer I said, "you aren't, are you?" and he said, "I don't know if I can, A.," and that was when my heart just broke. "Cary, come on, man," I said, "we've been planning this all year. I just got a letter from Mick at the Beach Service and he's counting on us to be there by Memorial Day," and Cary said, "yeah, A., I know, but Daddy's counting on me, too, he's going to be laid up for a while and somebody's got to deal with the cafeteria," and I said, "why can't somebody else do it? why can't Cliff?" and Cary said, "Cliff's going to be in summer school at UVA," and I said, "yeah, but why you, Cary? why is it always you?" and he said, "that's just the way it is, A., there's not a whole lot I can do about it—and besides, I owe it to him," and I wanted to say, for what? exactly what do you owe him, Cary?, but I held back and said instead, "yeah, but, Cary, what about you? what about what you owe yourself?" and he said, "come on, don't get philosophical on me, Jenrette, it's probably only going to be a few weeks. If things work out maybe I can come down for the last part of the summer," and I said, "well, there's no way Mick's going to hold the job for you," and Cary said, "screw the job, A., there are plenty of jobs, I don't have to be a lifeguard, I can wash dishes if I have to," and I said, "yeah, okay, but what about Jane?" and he said—there was a little joking edge in his voice by then, he was taking the whole thing extremely well, too well, in my opinion, almost like he *wanted* to stay in Killdeer and work for T.O.—"you'll just have to look after her for me, won't you?" and I said, "great, man, that's all I need," and he laughed and said, "you'll survive," and we hung up.

I stood there staring at the letters in my hand with the whole great summer we had planned in ruins, and I just balled them up and threw them as hard as I could in the trash can in the corner. That was the only satisfaction I got out of the whole episode. Then I went to lunch. But when I came back to the dorm I went downstairs and fished those letters out and took them up to my room where I carefully uncrumpled them and read them through again, like at least there was something, and wondering if maybe I wouldn't be going to Chapel Hill after all.

Feeling too upset to sleep, I slipped my shoulder carefully from beneath Jane's cheek—she was out—then reached for my coke vial in the night table drawer and headed for the bathroom.

Twelve

JANE

When I woke up A. was gone.

I sat up and rubbed my eyes, calling his name into the bathroom where the light was on. When I didn't get an answer, I felt the first twinge of fear. It was full dark outside, and when I glanced at the clock, thinking maybe it was seven, it was after ten. I'd been asleep almost four hours. My senses came to full alert, and that was when I heard, away from the depths of the house, the sound of music. Chiding myself for my worry, I went off to find it.

As I padded down the stairs, I realized the sound wasn't coming from the library, but Louis's room. I glanced out the window and saw the Studebaker, hesitating at the thought of facing him again. Gazing into my reflection in the darkened pane, I glanced my fingers through my tousled hair, only mussing it further, and then decided Louis could just think what he wanted—he would anyway.

A wedge of yellow light spread across the floorboards from the parted door, and I said, "knock, knock," peeking in. Louis almost fell out of his rocking chair. "Lawd have mercy, Miss Jane," he said, gazing at me with startled eyes, and I said, "I'm sorry, Louis, I thought A. was in here—have you seen him?" and he said, "no, ma'am, sho hadn', jus' come in from visitin' my sister, didn't think a soul was in the house." I saw the calculations flash across his shrewd old face then, together with his effort at disguise. My blush annoyed me, but I held his eyes,

admitting nothing—it was all out there in the open anyway—
as I said, "was the Bentley here when you got back?" and he
said, "no, ma'am, sho wud'n'.'"

Another wave of queasy premonition washed over me then,
and I said, "how long have you been home?" and he said,
"fifteen, twinny minutes, Miss Jane," and I said, "do you have
any idea where he could be?" and he said, "you axin' the wrong
pu'son, ma'am, if he didn' tale you, he sho didn' tale me
nothin'," and I said, "I'm worried, Louis," and he said gently,
"I 'speck he be back direckly, ma'am, you we'come to set down
with me and wait." I obeyed in a distraction and then, deciding
to be frank, I said, "I took a nap upstairs—A. was here when I
fell asleep—but that's been hours," and he said, "he prob'ly
jus' gone up to the sto' to git some beer, Miss Jane," and I said,
"but what if he didn't?" and he said, "don' go makin' thangs
up to wurry 'bout, Miss Jane, plenty 'nough as it is"—he pointed
to the clock—"tale you what, he ain't back in ha'f a hour we
rethink our position, till then we jus' set a spell and 'joy the
music—that soun' reas'nable?"

We sat there for several minutes, Louis rocking, his hands
folded in his lap, and finally I said, more out of nerves than
anything, "well, you may as well say it, Louis, you were right.
Mama knew it, too. Like always I was the last to know, but here
I am, so go ahead and gloat." Louis didn't gloat though, there
was something gentle in his face as he said, "always ha'd to see
it when yo' face right up in it, ma'am," and heaving a sigh I
said, "I must seem pitiful to you." Louis shook his head. "No,
ma'am, you ain't pitiful, all you is is young and fallin' into somethin' you ain't sho you want to be in. Don' be sad though, Miss
Jane, leastways somebody else fallin' with you—y'all meet up
at the bottom, ma'am, see if you don't," and he gave me a
consoling wink.

His kindness together with my fear and the host of other emotions I was feeling had me close to tears, but I felt suddenly so
grateful and so close to him. "You know something, Louis?" I
said, and he said, "wha's that, ma'am?" and I said, "you re-
mind me of my Daddy, he was wise like you." Louis smiled
and said, "you jus' missin' 'im, honey, is all, I an ol' man and
I still be missin' mine, jus' wishin' I could go home one mo'
time fo' Sund'y dinner"—he shook his head—"but they gone,
honey, yo's and mine both." A tear did roll down my cheek
then, and as I wiped it off I said, "I'm sorry, Louis, I don't know

what's wrong with me tonight," and he said, "nothin' in this wurl wrawng with you, Miss Jane, 'cep' you need a man to he'p you . . . what you missin', chil', is a full-growed man with full-growed man sense, jus' like yo' mama a full-growed woman with sense of her own what you gittin' now, Miss Jane, right here this evenin' over here huntin' Mist'A. Jenrette you gittin' it, jus' like he out gittin' his where he at . . . all it is, two diff'rent thangs, chil', cain't never be the same but got to be together, all in the wurl it is or ever gonna be, cain't let go, Miss Jane, jus' cain't do it . . . you hang on now, hear? give yo' own true lover boy the rope to hang hisse'f, I tale you what, he stretch it right out to the en' and bounce back in yo' lovin' arms, honey, wise as Louis or yo' daddy either one . . . got to let 'im go to grow, honey, Lawd knows, got to let 'im go to grow."

My face was wet again and I reached out for Louis's hand. As he patted mine, my eye drifted toward the clock again. Hardly ten minutes had passed, but I said, "he isn't at the store, Louis," and then I finally spoke the thought that had been flirting at the edges of my mind for several minutes, a dark insinuating whisper. "He's gone to the beach," I said, and Louis suddenly stopped rocking and said, "what make you say that, Miss Jane?" and I said, "because he talked about it this afternoon—that's exactly where he is."

I got up and paced to the window staring out anxiously, praying to see headlights turning in the drive, but knowing they wouldn't come. "But why wouldn't he have waked me up?" I asked, spinning back to Louis as though maybe he might have the answer. "Maybe he skeered you try and talk 'im out of it, Miss Jane," he suggested, "or maybe he jus' don' want to in'errup' yo' res' and wurry you," and I said, "well, what did he suppose I'd think when I woke up?" and Louis said, mildly, "he prob'ly jus' need a little time alone, Miss Jane," and I said, "but he wanted me to go, Louis, he asked me to this afternoon."

I stood there at the window trying to decide what I should do. Really, though, there was only one thing to do, and my decision was simply whether I would or not. I turned around and gazed at Louis, and he gazed back, then nodded with a sad wise smile. "Go 'haid on then, honey," he said, "if tha's the only way you can ease yo' min' I ain't goin' try to talk you out of it," and I said, "but I don't have a car," and he said, "mine settin' in the driveway, keys in the 'nition, go on after 'im." I threw my arms around his neck impulsively and said, ''thank you, Louis, I won't ever forget it,'' and he said, ''tha's awright, Miss Jane, you jus' drive careful, little fog out on the road when I come in.''

Thirteen

ADAM

The first line didn't help.

I laid out a second one on the marble countertop in Aunt Zoe's bathroom and the minute I hit I began to sweat and shiver. "One more, one more," I told myself thinking maybe it would turn the tide in my direction. It didn't happen.

I splashed my face with water and leaned across the sink, staring at my reflection in the mirror, touching my face with my hands. I didn't know this man. He was old. Years I didn't remember, years I hadn't lived, had carved lines in his face and smudged circles under eyes whose expression was unrecognizable and frightening to me. Those years had fallen like dead brittle leaves and been swept meaninglessly away by a cold wind. I didn't want to be him. I didn't want his knowledge, his unhappiness, his defeats, not even his victories. I gazed and gazed, searching for the bright carved essence of the boy in the dead stone of the man's weathered face. I couldn't find him.

The box springs creaked in the outer room as Jane rolled in her sleep and I turned toward the door, holding my breath, like a thief about to be discovered. She didn't appear. And when I looked back in the mirror my face was swollen, strangled-looking, a forked blue vein pulsed in my forehead. I started panting and pressed down on the countertop to hold myself upright as things began to spin. My vision swam and I went down on my knees, then toppled face first to the floor like a felled tree.

When I came to I felt the cold tiles pressing my cheek, and as I raised my head I became absorbed by the pattern of the floor, like a puzzle, a complex mosaic in which there was some order, but whose guiding principle eluded me. I tried to decide where I was and then remembered I was at the beach. I blinked my eyes and stared around. My actual surroundings—Aunt Zoe's bathroom—confused the impression but didn't break it. At some faint remove I was aware I was delusional, but the point seemed academic and held small interest compared to the delusion itself.

And when I went into the outer room Jane lay sleeping in my bed like an enchanted princess, still eighteen. The shimmer played around her face and body—even in the dark I could see it, like river mist—and I leaned down and inhaled the sweet breath of her skin and hair, afraid to touch her, that she might wake and it would not be real. The disbelief of having her, that she could love me, the fear of losing her, all the anxious tenderness, the depth and wonder of the changeless change of my first love, came back to me. And for that moment—perhaps an hour, perhaps a fraction of a second—Cary was still at home in Killdeer suffering for a father who would never love him, still loving Jane, still loving me, still trusting us, still knowing nothing.

Then the spell broke—Cary was dead—and suddenly Jane looked dead, too. The bed was the bier where she lay waiting for the magic kiss to wake her, but I knew it would never come, because the prince . . . the prince was the most dead of all. I remembered him though, the boy who'd once lain there quietly beside Jane, star-struck with a happiness he'd never quite believed would last, a happiness he'd known just once, hoping to the last that it would work out somehow so that no one lost, so that none of those he loved was hurt. It had been that boy's foolish hope, his innocent belief in miracles that had made the tragedy possible. But A. was gone. I knew it as I sat there staring at the vacant impression he'd left in the coverlet. Jane was still Jane—however much life had changed her, she'd kept the essential kernel of her self intact. I hadn't. I'd shattered and become another person. I was Adam now, the reflection in the bathroom mirror, in a thousand bathroom mirrors. There was a dam in my name now, a damnation, and however much Jane had led me to hope I knew it was just another lie to believe that I could go back to being A. Gone, I thought, outta here. Bang! Zoom!

I stroked Jane's hair softly and leaned down and kissed her. "Sweet dreams," I whispered and walked out to the car, dimly aware that the events of thirteen years before were repeating themselves verse and chapter. It didn't seem important. Nothing seemed important.

Outside the night air sparkled with prisms of suspended water. It smelled like rain. Random thoughts drifted through my head: *the rain in Spain falls mainly in the plain . . . the rain of pain falls mainly . . . in the brain.* I'm losing it, I thought, but it's not so bad, not like they say.

I drove slowly down the drive, mildly surprised at my coordination. "Where am I going?" I asked aloud and then I remembered—the beach. I frowned a moment, pondering whether I still wanted to go, then decided what the hey, I could use that swim, and turned toward the highway.

As I neared it, passing through a patch of ground fog, suddenly a golden shell emblazoned on a blood-red ground loomed overhead—the illuminated sign of a Shell Oil convenience mart— and I turned into the lot, thinking I wanted something there.

The young kid behind the counter regarded me with a dull expression, his face scarred by acne. He was wearing a paper hat so absurdly comical I almost laughed. "Nice hat," I said, hoping he could share the joke. He turned his eyes up to the brim, then back to me and said quietly, "I have to wear it—they make us," and suddenly I felt so sorry for him I wanted to cry. I noticed that his eyes weren't dull, just dulled. *The rain of pain,* I thought. "I'm sorry," I told him aloud, "I didn't mean to hurt your feelings," and he said, "that's okay, you didn't," studying me with shy interest, and I said, "I have to wear one, too," as the thought occurred to me, not understanding what it meant, but only that it was important to make him understand. I grinned and pointed to my head where I could feel my own hat resting like an enormous wedding cake, a baroque cathedral whorled out of confectioner's sugar. "We all wear different hats," I said, "you can't take them off, but sometimes you can change them."

Maybe that's what's happening, I thought, changing hats. The insight seemed hopeful, but the boy's look had changed to one of deep suspicion. You can change yours, too, kid. *No, I can't—* the voice came from inside him—*they don't let you change.* Who doesn't? Who are they, kid? *You know.* Suddenly I felt deflated, weary—his resistance wearied me. Yeah, kid, I know. *And, any-*

way, we need the hats. Do we? Why do we need them? *The rain*. Yeah, forgot about the rain.

"Look, mister," the boy said, "I don't want no problems, 'kay? It's fine by me if you're drunk, but maybe you just better oughta get what you come in here for and go, 'kay?" His eyes begged, and suddenly he seemed familiar, so familiar. "Sure, kid, sure," I said, trying to place the resemblance, "it's just I can't remember what it was I wanted," and he said, "the beer's in the cooler," and I said, "right, thanks," realizing that was it and wondering how he knew. I started off, and then turned back and said, "you look like someone—I don't know you, do I?" and he said, "doubt it," looking uneasy again, but his eyes said, *sure, you know me*. Where from? *A long long time ago*. Can't remember. *It was raining*. Right, met you in the pouring rain. "In the cooler," the boy reminded me, and I said, "right," and turned around, thinking, met you in the cooler, too. *A cooler rain*. That rain was cold. *So cold*.

I opened the misted door of the refrigerated case and shivered in the cold wind. The condenser drone was mesmerizing. Another world in there, I thought. A fellow could get lost inside that world, never find his way back out.

I took out a six-pack of Miller High Life and laid a bill on the counter as I walked by, not bothering to check what it was. "Your change," the boy called after me. I'd already pushed the door open, but when he said that I turned back to look at him. "Don't forget your change," he said, and for a moment he looked just like Cary, for another moment just like me. Then he just looked like everybody else. "Keep it, kid," I said.

Outside a black Jeep idled at the pumps. I stopped stock still on the curb and stared feeling a queering tingle shoot up my neck. A dark-haired boy stood with his back to me, bent over slightly to squeeze the trigger of the gas nozzle as he filled his tank. The counters in the pump head whirled round and round, blurring as the total mounted. As I watched a girl climbed down from the passenger seat, stretching and smoothing back her hair. The boy flicked on the automatic feed and stood up, circling her waist with his free arm and drawing her close. They made out deeply in the harsh glare of the fluorescent lights, and as he reached up and cupped her breast she shoved him off with testy fondness. I couldn't move from the spot or take my eyes away from them. Far away, as though at the wrong end of a telescope, in the country of the past, it was Jane and me.

Over his shoulder she saw me staring and whispered something in his ear. He turned to look, and suddenly I saw the Jeep was green. Reaching for a beer on the vinyl roof, he took a reckless swallow, wiped his hand across his mouth and called out tauntingly, "you looking at something?" and I said, "I thought I knew you," as I started to get in the car. "You don't know me, you don't know shit," he said, starting toward me. The girl reached out and held his arm. I pulled out quickly and as I turned onto the road I saw him leaning over in my rearview mirror, scooping something from the ground. A handful of gravel pelted my windshield. "Asshole!" I called out the window, then accelerated up the ramp.

I hadn't gone a mile when I heard the loud rumble of the approaching engine. My mirrors flashed with high beams. I floored it, trying to stay ahead of them, but he pulled into the passing lane, drawing up beside me, matching my speed. He honked his horn repeatedly, turning his lights on and off. I bore straight ahead, refusing to look at them, and then he swerved across the yellow line and almost ran me off the shoulder. When I glared at them, the girl laughed. Her expression was frightened and excited. He leaned over her and raised a can of beer in a toast, swigging from it before he put his thumb across the mouth and shook it, spraying it out the window. Cold suds flecked my cheek like spit. "Fuck you, pussy," he shouted, swerving again, barely missing me. I flew into a rage, and when I looked again the girl blew me a kiss off the tip of her raised middle finger. "Come on, man," the boy shouted, "let's do it," flashing a taunting canine grin at me, a grin with the absolute boyish confidence of knowing absolutely nothing. It was my grin, my face. The driver was me. The Jeep lurched forward as he floored it, and I said, "okay," not to them, but to myself—to something— "okay," I said, "let's play," and I floored it, too, chasing a phantom Jeep into the past. . . .

Fourteen

JANE

When I climbed in the car I could feel panic like some queasy drug stealing into my bloodstream on a slow IV drip. Yet there was absolutely no reason for it, I told myself, and I didn't give in.

Then, like a blocked river coursing back through a new channel, my emotion changed to anger. How could A. have left like that without even telling me? A little voice inside my head spoke up and said, "here we go again, back to the same old mud to wallow like a pig, smack dab at the heart of my boy problem." And the heart of it was me. My heart was the problem. How well I knew that little voice, how tired it made me—its ceaseless spiteful blah blah blah—deathly tired. I was so sick of the old bitterness, I wanted it behind me. Yet it was so like A. Yet it wasn't, not really. However obtuse and self-absorbed he could be, he'd never been willfully inconsiderate. He wasn't the mean shitty kind. The only thing he'd ever done that smacked of it was the way he'd left that summer, yet that was something else. He'd had his reasons, and it wasn't against me—if I hadn't known it at the time, I knew it now. But what could he have been thinking to run off and leave me at his Aunt's that way?

The bottom line was, I didn't have the slightest idea why he'd left, and thinking about it wasn't going to get me any closer to an answer, so I just wouldn't think. A five-and-a-half-hour drive along a lonely road in the middle of the night, and no thinking allowed . . .

In spite of everything, there was something soothing about being out there on the highway driving in the middle of the night, a feeling I was not accustomed to, since normally I avoided traveling after dark. It seemed more like something a man would do, just leaving everything behind and setting out on a journey— I'd never known one who didn't like it. I'd always thought it was just escape, but as I settled into the experience I realized there was a kind of freedom in it, too, which made me wonder about A., if, wherever he was now, he was feeling something similar. Though the air was chilly, I rolled down the window and let the wind blow through my hair. And it would be good, after all, I thought, to wake up tomorrow morning at the beach, with him. For a time my worries went far away, and a pleasant numbing peace stole over me.

I almost turned on the radio, but as I started to I noticed Louis had a cassette deck mounted under the dash, the only modern touch in the interior. A tape rested in the slot, and as I punched it in a black man's voice came from the speakers. The recording was scratchy and sounded old, like something from an archive. It seemed crude and primitive at first, but gradually its haunting nuance took hold of me, and before I knew it there were tears in my eyes. My mood opened to a rare expansiveness, a little like being on a mountaintop and seeing things in their totality. I listened to that high, reedy, tremulous voice singing about his mama, carrying her down to the burying ground with six white horses, so discreet and circumspect and self-effacing, just like Louis Bascom had always seemed to me, and reaching down so deep inside himself, and me, bringing something dark and shimmering up, and something grew clearer for me. The sense of weight I'd felt that afternoon gazing into A.'s eyes, still felt now—and which I knew A. felt, too—wasn't special or unique to us and our situation, not a problem or a sickness, but a general thing. It was just the pain of being alive, something so heavy, which I know Cary felt, just like the singer on the tape had once felt it, the pain of holding up the world on top of you, but there was also something strong and bracing in it, like the tang of blood in meat, and I knew Cary somehow lost that, or it became distasteful to him, because it is not a sweet taste, though there is sweetness in it, but there's a rankness in it, too. A. had tasted that rankness—that was the meaning of his rotting catfish—and I wanted to tell him what the singer on the recording was telling me, that to reclaim the sweetness you have to reach out and embrace the weight, you have to lift it, not as something that will crush you, but as something that will make you strong. Yet maybe he already knew, maybe that was exactly what, in his own way, he was trying to do.

My face was wet with tears, but it wasn't sadness. I wasn't happy either, those tears were simple understanding, and sympathy. I felt him so deeply in my heart at that moment, perhaps more deeply than I ever had. "He's just like a retriever going for a stick"—Cary's words flashed back to me—"he'll break his heart before he stops . . . sometimes you have to hold back the stick on A." The depth of Cary's love for A. seared home in the truth of that perception. I'd thought of Cary's remark so many times in college when my collie Sam was still alive. I'd had a cat then, too—the only one I ever owned—named Leaflet because I found her on a stack of them in Greenlaw Hall. The first time I took them to the beach together, Leaflet came right down with me to the water and dapped it with her paw, curious what it was. She didn't seem afraid, but once she knew she went back up and curled up in the sand in the shade of my umbrella, totally content, while the whole time Sam was down there barking and turning somersaults and drooling on his stick. He wouldn't leave me alone. Leaflet lay there enjoying the outdoors, letting the warm sand and salt air and the rhythm of the waves lull her to a contented drowsiness, but Sam could only be happy with a stick to fetch. And A. was the same way. To him the whole world was just an obstacle course to get through to the stick, but mainly to his effort in retrieving it—no ocean, no sand, no waves, no sky, no clouds, just the stick and the risk to fetch it, over and over till he was exhausted. He believed by doggy logic that one of those sticks was going to be *the* stick, the magic one that changed his life, but I could see by cat logic that wasn't ever going to happen, that whatever he brought back, however fine and brave his effort in retrieving it, it was still just going to be a stick, only that. The magic, the real change, was back up on the beach before you ever left it, and it took no effort at all, just surrender—that's why it was hard for A.

I was more like Leaflet, and so was Cary in that way. But maybe that was why I'd owned more dogs and loved them better. "Two diff'ent thangs, cain't never be the same, but got to be together"—I remembered what Louis had said, and I didn't want to change A., I didn't want to pluck his feathers or deny his stick, I just didn't want to see him break his heart in finding it. Because the stick he'd gone to fetch this time was so far out, so very far . . . But I put my fear behind me and believed. As I listened to the music, I closed my eyes and made a wish—that A. might get his full-grown man sense as I found my own full-grown womanness, and that this second chance of ours might come to fruition so that we could experience the deep heady pain of living through each other.

And sometimes wishes do come true, not just in fairy tales, but in real life, too. But lost in my own bright dream of hopefulness that night, I forgot how sometimes in the tale the wish is granted partially or turns back on the wisher with a vengeance. It wasn't till nearly four o'clock that morning as I neared the coast in the last hour of that drive that I remembered.

Rounding a hard curve through a darkened eyeblink of a town, my high beams lit up the reflectors on a small green sign—Deep Cove, it said—and as I came out of the turn I saw a wildnerness of flashing lights ahead of me—yellow, orange, blue. I saw the smashed railing of the bridge and people gazing over into still dark water where the different lights all bled together like a sickly skim of oil. I saw the ambulance, the wrecker, the dark arm of the waiting crane, the patrolman's pale strained face as it mooned in my side window. I saw glass shattered all across the roadbed, and among the glittering fragments I saw a man's black shoe. That was when it all came back to me, the way that granted wishes sometimes turn to curses, as the weight I'd been so confident and eager to embrace crashed down on me in all its dark remorseless fury.

PART II

The Lost Colony

A.

And graven with diamonds in letters plain
There is written her fair neck round about,
    Noli me tangere, for Caesar's I am,
And wild for to hold, though I seem tame.

—Sir Thomas Wyatt, "Whoso List to Hunt"

One

My black Jeep idled in the driveway of the Winston house as I said goodbye to Camellia on the kitchen steps. She was up from Killdeer for two weeks to do spring cleaning, and I'd just graduated from Keane and was leaving for the beach. She looked at me like I was a condemned man on my way to the gallows, and I guess I was feeling a little sorry for myself, too—the game plan was spoiled, Cary wasn't coming—so when she opened her arms I went right to those big black bosoms which felt just like they had when I was little, and she said, "you always goin' to be my baby, you know that?" and I nodded and said, "I love you, too, Cam," and she said, "po' little A.," and tried another hug, but I dodged it—there's only so much of that sort of thing you can take when you're eighteen.

I climbed behind the wheel still sniffing and a little teary, but once I got through Buena Vista and picked up I-40 off Hawthorne Road I started feeling better. About the time I reached Burlington it got overcast and thunder started rumbling. I could see lightning streaking down way out in the distance across some tilled fields, and it began to drizzle. I drove through it for a while until it got too grim, and then I pulled over and put the top up, shivering in my soaked shirt.

It was coming down in sheets by the time I got to Killdeer—hail was falling and all kinds of stuff. I saw the Ruin Creek exit looming up—the way to Cary's—and almost took it, then didn't, I don't know why. And just when I passed the little green town limits sign that said, "Leaving Killdeer, pop. 14,231," and the highway billboard proclaiming, "Come Back to Killdeer Soon, We'll Miss You—Fraternal Order of the Moose," the sun suddenly came out again and the road was bone-dry like it had never rained there at all. I stared back at it in my rearview mirror, a big dark stormcloud brooding over where and what I came from and I said, "fuck it, A., it's all behind you now, buddy boy."

Out there ahead of me there was sunshine and clear sailing and the two unbroken white lines on the highway running on and on and never touching. I thought of Cary and felt a backward tug. He was still my best friend and always would be. I wished he was sitting right there in the seat beside me with a cold beer in his hand and the wind blowing through his hair, happy as a dog with its head out the window, but he wasn't. Cary made a different choice, and I was angry with him for choosing a father who didn't give a shit about him over me—but his choice didn't surprise me. What would have surprised me would have been if Cary's loyalty to T.O. had wavered. Perhaps Cary was right, I didn't know. I only knew that I was there and Cary wasn't and I was going to miss him. That missing felt like something bigger than just him being a few weeks late to join me at the beach, it felt almost final. And, in a way, it was.

I got to the beach on Friday. Daddy was still there with Eleanor Rosenberg, and they were doing their little Southern-Jewish S&M routine, or whatever it was they got off on with one another. At the time it made little sense to me. I didn't have anything against Eleanor—in fact, I liked her a good bit more than Daddy then. She was generous and concerned and had no pettiness I ever saw, and she wasn't bad-looking either. I actually entertained a few modest fantasies in her regard. Eleanor was very thin and had a nice figure in a bathing suit, though her body didn't look particularly young, just sort of not-old, but she wore makeup down on the beach and her skin was extremely white and she sat under an umbrella the whole time wearing a seagrass coolie hat that tied beneath her chin, reading these big hardback books with glossy covers, like she just couldn't quite get the hang of it somehow—I mean, an ocean out there, Eleanor, and soft little waves breaking across the bar and pelicans and wet retrievers fetching sticks and people having splash fights, and sunlight, and warm sand. I guess she felt out of place, or maybe her books were just more interesting to her, but at the beach she seemed sort of pitiful in a way she hadn't in New York where she was so chic and elegant and knew just how to manage the suave maitre d' at the Four Seasons while making it look like Daddy was leading the waltz, when really he was more or less like me, solemn and subdued about the whole thing, like a little boy dressed up in his best clothes and hoping nothing really terrible would happen.

She'd tried to be nice to me, too. Eleanor gave me copies of Casteneda's Don Juan books—hardcovers, of course, first editions. "Hold on to these," she said, "they may be valuable some day," and it *was* a thoughtful gift, and I *did* like them, and I *hadn't* read them yet, though I'd been meaning to, but still and all, I just couldn't see the point, not after what happened at the Sherry Netherland. Was it some sort of commandment that we have a "relationship"? Wasn't it my privilege to just back off and say, I think I'd rather not, Eleanor, though don't take it personally because it isn't meant that way? But she kept making "gestures" and taking me apart for "quiet little asides," like when she told me that I had to try and understand that what had happened that night wasn't something done deliberately *against me, "or against your mother, Adam."* Okay, I could accept that, with my head at least. Then she told me to try not to judge my father because I probably wasn't aware how desperate he'd been at the time, that he'd been suffering and seeking some release from it. Well, I listened to that, too, though it almost made me want to spit, but that time I couldn't hold it in, I told her, "my mother was the one who was suffering, he just wrote the book, and anyway, Eleanor, what you call suffering goes, I believe, more accurately under the definition, 'cunnilingus.' "

I said it right to her face, though I wasn't shouting or ranting. My tone was pretty quiet actually. We were sitting up in the gazebo at twilight, just the two of us, drinking gin and tonics, and Eleanor turned away and looked at the ocean for a long time. I was pretty sure she was crying, but I couldn't help it—she'd brought it up. Then she turned to me and said, "you're so fierce, Adam, so very fierce, and while I admire that, I think it's part of your unhappiness," and I said, "I'm not unhappy, Eleanor," because I didn't feel unhappy, and she just stared at me with those black eyes of hers which always had a slightly pained and startled expression in them, whatever else they read, which at that moment was frustration and concern. I actually liked it when she called me fierce, it made me swell a little. I felt like Eleanor was a very nice lady whom I was sure I'd have liked under different circumstances, but, as it was, my life was my own business and I didn't choose to include her in it, especially not acting like my mother. Especially not that.

They were leaving on Sunday and my father had made reservations for Jimbo's Saturday night, which was the best place on the beach, though not the Four Seasons. I wasn't really all that keen to go, but I didn't want to make life miserable for them either, and I knew how they would take it if I didn't, so we were all dressed up and walking out the door when the phone rang. It was Jane. "What's up, spud?" she said, putting Cary right there between us from the start, and I said, "how's it going, Jane?" and Eleanor arched her eyebrows when she realized I was talking to a girl, but I ignored it, and Jane said, "well, I had a flat tire in Roduco, but two nice black men stopped and changed it for me, so I made it in one piece," and I said, "well, I'm pleased to hear that," and Jane said, "are you being sarcastic with me, A. Jenrette?" and I said, "me? sarcastic?" and Daddy smirked and I frowned at him, and Jane said, "well, I don't really know you all that well, but it sounded a little bit sarcastic to me," and Eleanor touched my arm and said, "why don't you ask her to join us?" and I started to shake my head like nix on that, but I thought, what the hell, and said, "we're getting ready to walk out the door to Jimbo's—want to come?" and Daddy said, "tell her we'll be mighty disappointed if she doesn't," and I said, "my father says to tell you he'll be mighty disappointed if you don't," and Eleanor said, "so will I," and I said, "so will Eleanor," and Jane said, "who's Eleanor?" and I cut a glance at Daddy and Eleanor and said, "an old friend of the family," and they both looked sort of grimly amused by that, and Jane said, "what should I wear?" and I said, "I'd suggest a dress," and she said, "I know a dress, butthead, I mean what *kind* of dress," and I said, "I'm wearing a sport coat if that tells you anything," and Jane said, "do I have time to take a bath?" and I said, "the reservation's for nine o'clock, that's half an hour," and Jane said, "half an hour!" and I said, "we'll wait to order," and she said, "don't," and I said, "okay, we won't—just ask for Clay Jenrette," and she said, "bye," in a tone that seemed a little miffed or rattled, and I said, "see you there," and we hung up.

Eleanor and Daddy stood there awaiting my report and when I didn't volunteer one, Eleanor said, "well, aren't you going to tell us who your date is?'' and I said, ''she's not my date, she's Cary's girlfriend, Jane McCrae,'' and Eleanor said, ''oh, I see, well in that case it was very gallant of you to invite her,'' and I said, ''it was your suggestion, Eleanor,'' and she smiled and said, ''so it was, but you may take full credit for it, Adam,'' and Daddy, also smiling, said, ''you can also pick up the tab,'' and I shot him a dark look and said, ''ha ha,'' and he said, ''I guess I'm not allowed to make a joke,'' and Eleanor said, ''now you two, we're going to enjoy ourselves this evening,'' and making a strong effort to be civilized, Daddy said, ''she's Walter McCrae's girl, isn't she?'' and I said, ''was, he's dead,'' and Daddy said, ''he's still her father,'' and I said, ''does it work that way?'' and Eleanor said, ''Adam,'' warningly, and I said, ''sorry,'' and Daddy nodded like my retraction had been wise and said, ''she was a pretty thing when she was little, and the last time I saw her she was still pretty strong.'' Eleanor looked at me for independent confirmation, and thinking not so much about Jane's looks but other things, I said, ''Jane's pretty strong all right,'' and Eleanor, teasing me, said, ''you make that sound ironic, or should I say sarcastic?'' and Daddy said, ''he makes everything sound sarcastic,'' not teasing, and the battle lines drew closer.

Jimbo came over from the bar when he saw Daddy. He was a big fat fifty-year-old country boy in a short-sleeved safari jacket and matching shorts with a bald head except for a few black strands in front which he combed down in bangs so that he looked like he had a tonsure. A sort of cheerful wicked fat medieval friar was what he reminded me of, but he was smart as shit—you could see it in those beady eyes of his sunk back there in the fat of his face measuring you all the time behind that permanent ass-kissing smile. Those eyes had a way of fixing you for a second, like somebody who plays horses handicapping you before placing his bet, and he said, ''well, damn my soul, Clay, lookahere, I haven't seen you in . . . how long is it anyway?'' and Daddy said, ''it has been a while, Jimbo, hasn't it?'' with his eyes narrowed a little warily and his posture a tad more formal than usual, like he was expecting something, and Jimbo said, ''yes, Lord, Clay, lemme see, last time I saw you in here it was with Miss Allison,'' and he looked right at Eleanor as he said it and smiled with his teeth in a way that could have been construed as obliging overpoliteness, but I didn't think it was.

''Goddamnit,'' Jimbo said, and he shook his head for emphasis, "goddamnit, Clay, I never did get to tell you how sorry I was. It just won't fair, Clay, it just damn won't,'' and Daddy said, "thank you, Jimbo, I appreciate it," and Jimbo seemed to be wiping his eyes before he turned to me with a big sniff and said, "is this here your boy, Clay? is this little A.? look at you, son, I swear one day you were in here in short britches throwing hush puppies across the room and the next day you're all grown up," and he clapped me on the shoulder and gave my muscle a couple of discreet little squeezes. Daddy always said that Jimbo was queer as a three-dollar bill, but if so you couldn't tell it from his manner. "Son, I remember like it was just this minute when your mama was down here with your grandmaw, Miss Rebecca, and Miss Zoe, and there has never been a prettier woman on the face of this green earth than Allie Trefethen, or if there was I never come across one, and I mean not in the pictures, not on the TV, not in the magazines, nowhere. There was a time, son, when about every other fella between here and Rocky Mount was in love with her. I guess I was a little bit myself," and Daddy, looking like this was getting spread a little thick, said, "I'm sure Allie would have been flattered, Jimbo," in a flat tone, and Jimbo, still sniffing and shaking his head, said, "yes, Lord, there was a time," and turned to Eleanor without transition, holding out his hand and said, "I don't believe I've had the pleasure, ma'am."

Eleanor, who'd maintained her composure admirably through all this, except that she had her clutch pinned a little forcibly to her side beneath her elbow, extended hers back and said, "Eleanor Rosenberg," and Jimbo said, "Jimbo Brown," and then, touching his big fleshy earlobe with his finger, he said, "did you say Rosen*berg*?" and Eleanor blinked her eyes with complete neutrality and said, "yes, I did," and Jimbo nodded and said, "that's what I thought," in a way so that you couldn't tell whether he simply hadn't heard the first time, or was cutting her dead, and us into the bargain.

Jimbo turned to pick up a stack of menus and I saw Eleanor put her hand on Daddy's sleeve. He was standing there, all six-foot-five of him, staring off above everybody's heads with his jaw muscle flicking like a bowstring. "Y'all coming?" Jimbo said, looking back, and when he saw the way we were he put his finger to his ear again. "You say something, Clay? I'm a little hard of hearing in my right ear—brother chucked a cherry bum right up next to it when I was little," and Eleanor, regard-

ing Daddy with imploring eyes, whispered, "I don't think he
meant anything, Clay," and I said, "I think he did," ready to
walk out the door, and Daddy seemed at a loss whether to tear
the place apart with his bare hands or just burst out in tears.
Finally he let out the breath he was holding and said, "I just
don't feel like fighting it tonight," looking at Eleanor like he
wanted her to say it was okay, and she whispered, "good for
you," whatever that meant, patting his arm, and we started off
into the dining room after Jimbo.

"How about right here next to the window, Clay?" he asked,
"best table in the house," and he pulled out Eleanor's chair for
her. "That's the Albermarle Sound out yonder, Miss Rosenberg," he said, leaning over her shoulder and pointing, "and
right over there—you see them little lights twinkling? that's Roanoke Island where the first English settlers landed. You probably heard of the Lost Colony, hadn't you? Well, that was them.
Disappeared right into thin air, never did find out what happened
to 'em." Jimbo stood upright again and said, "now if y'all need
a thing, I mean one single teensy thing, you holler, hear? And
try the soft shells amandine," he whispered confidentially, "first
this year. They're so fresh I got to keep a guard posted on the
back door to keep 'em from running off."

Jimbo finally departed and Daddy sat there gazing off in the
distance like he was carved out of stone, only there was a moist
hurt look in his eyes, and I felt sorry for him, not that it changed
anything, and finally he said, "I'm sorry, Eleanor, I wasn't
anticipating that," and she said, "I think we mistook him, Clay,
I truly do, he was perfectly nice there at the end. I think he just
didn't hear me the first time when I said my name," and Daddy
met her eyes like he was trying to assess whether she meant it
or was just being a good sport, and he said, "well, it's a little
different from New York, wouldn't you say? when we say personal service down here, we mean *personal*," and he managed
to grin. Eleanor smiled back, beautifully, I thought, though
without conviction, and I said, putting my two cents' worth in,
"well, I think he's a fat bigot fascist asshole," and Eleanor
leaned across the table with her black eyes twinkling, took my
hand, and said, "yes, but how are his soft shell crabs?" and it
took me a second to realize it was a joke, because I couldn't
remember ever hearing her make one before.

About that time the waiter brought our drinks. Daddy, who'd
had a few before we left the house, ordered a second round even

as the first was served. I noticed that with mild alarm. Then Eleanor, biting on her stirring straw, leaned toward me and said, "Adam, is that your friend?" and turning to look, I saw Jane. Actually, what I saw was a lean tall girl, very tan, in a peacock-blue jersey dress, very summery and minimal and striking on her striking body, which was lithe and angular and loose-jointed in its movements. Because, the thing was, for a split second I didn't quite recognize her. It was like the veil I'd seen her through before—which had to do with Cary—was lifted temporarily, and Jane might have been someone I didn't know standing across the room from me in a crowded bar, whom I might have walked over to after a few more looks and a second beer for courage. She was standing by the hostess's rostrum up on her tiptoes, staring around the room squinting slightly like she was near-sighted and had forgotten her glasses. She was inserting a gold earring, feeling for the hole, as she studied the crowd, and I just blinked, stunned at how beautiful she was. It almost hurt to look at her. Then the veil dropped back, I recognized her, and she became Jane McCrae, Cary's girlfriend. Maybe it was because I'd never seen Jane dressed up for the evening like that with makeup and jewelry, or maybe it was the way she'd changed over the year—she seemed older, more finished, not like a girl but a young woman, and her braces were gone, which contrib-uted to the effect—but what I always remembered about that moment was the impression of not having recognized her, or having recognized her in a different way.

Holding my napkin in my lap, I stood up and waved to her and she waved back and started walking over with this big smile full of nice new teeth. Daddy stood up, too, and Jane came up real close in my face with this expression I'd seen on other women's faces, Mama's included, in somewhat demanding so-cial situations where the difference between being excited and being tense is moot, a look of happiness that was almost insane. She might have been inhaling pure oxygen, and, come to think of it, there was this fresh smell about her, which was probably only coming in from the outdoors. I noticed it as she leaned to kiss my cheek—something she'd never done before—and she said, "oh, A., I'm sorry, I got lipstick on you," and she took the napkin from her place and dipped it in my water glass and started swabbing my cheek with it, which was something Mama used to do, though she would use a handkerchief, twisting it and wetting it between her lips, and thinking Jane really had gone crazy, or was bent on driving me to it, I caught her hand and said, "thanks, Jane, I'll get it," and about that time I felt a blush spread from my collar all the way up to my hairline. Jane stood back, her eyes opening a little wider like she was surprised, then she blushed, too, or at least colored. I might have been stark naked. Something came through—a hot flash from the front, and Jane recognized it, too—I saw it in her eyes—and wanted no more to do with it than I did. So we both let it fly on by.

I turned around and said, "Dad, Eleanor, this is Jane McCrae . . . Jane, Eleanor Rosenberg and my father, Clay Jenrette." Jane turned to them like I'd vanished in thin air and said, "I'm pleased to meet you, Miss Rosenberg"—charming schoolgirl rote—and Eleanor smiled—I could tell she approved of Jane already, and was a little fascinated, too, as though Jane were a species she hadn't encountered in New York—and then Jane said, more naturally, to Daddy, "it was so nice of you to invite me, Mr. Jenrette," and Daddy said, "please, Jane, sit down, it's our pleasure," and Jane added in a musing tone, "and you're wearing white pants, too," and Daddy looked down, embarrassed, and said, "so I am," and Eleanor arched her eyebrows like she couldn't wait to hear this one, and Jane said, "you probably don't remember, Mr. Jenrette . . ." and Daddy said, "Clay," and Jane said, "Clay . . . but once when I was little I was riding with Mama downtown in Killdeer and I saw you walking by and you had on white pants just like those and I said to Mama, 'that's the man I'm going to marry.' I had a crush on you for years," and Daddy said, "I remember perfectly," though I could tell by the vacant glitter in his eyes he didn't, and also that he was getting drunk. But he still lapped it up, and Eleanor said, "now you're blushing, Clay," and he was.

Eleanor, who looked like she was enjoying herself no end, winked at me, and though I didn't find the situation all that amusing personally, I acknowledged it, and Jane, catching it pass between us, got this distressed look on her face and said, "did I say something?" and Eleanor said, "no, dear, you're charming, but please sit down before you cause a riot," and it was true, people were staring at us from the surrounding tables, mostly men, and this one woman next to us was pinching her husband's elbow with this spiteful expression and whispering angry mincing little syllables at him.

With that, Jane plopped herself down in her chair and said,

"God," rolling her eyes and picking up her menu, starting to fan herself with it, "I thought I was never going to get here." She turned to me and said, "I thought you meant Jimmy *Bond's* over on the oceanfront. I drove all the way over there and it wasn't till I got in the parking lot and saw the sign that I remembered you said Jimbo's." She looked at Eleanor and Daddy and explained, "it wasn't A.'s fault. He told me the right place, only I haven't been down here since Daddy died and I couldn't drive then, so things seemed different, and for some reason I just thought it was Jimmy Bond's because we used to go there— would that be some kind of *déjà vu*?" She looked at all of us and no one answered, and she went on, "so I had to turn around and come all the way back up the island and cross over to the soundside, and then the road I was on didn't go through, and I was absolutely positive you were going to be in the middle of dinner when I got here, and I was so nervous I ate half my lipstick off and got the other half on A."

She batted her eyes at me and began to rummage in her purse. Finding her compact and a tube of lipstick, she pulled the cap off, screwed it up, and, watching herself in the mirror, applied it cleanly in three sure strokes, two on her upper lip, and one long slow precise one on her lower—she looked like she'd had years of practice—and then she rubbed her lips together smoothing it out, capped the tube and dropped it in her purse and looked up at all of us smiling, her lips like two cut pomegranates, as though she'd completed her entrance and was ready to move over and let someone else take the wheel for a stretch.

"Perhaps you'd like a drink, dear?" Eleanor said like she was worried that Jane had overstrained herself, and though Jane didn't seem strained in the least, she said, "yes, thank you, Eleanor, I could use one," and I said, "I'll get it at the bar," because I was dying to escape, and Daddy said, "no need, we'll call the waiter," and he raised his hand and I sat back down, and Jane said, "what are you drinking?" peering at my glass, and I said, "Dos Equis," and she said, "what's that?" and I said, "Mexican beer, want to try one?" and she said, "well, I'm not much on beer—it's so filling—but a gin and tonic would suit me right down to the ground," which sounded like something Talullah Bankhead might have said, and Eleanor said, "what an interesting expression, I don't believe I've ever heard it before," and Jane blinked and said, "it just means completely," and Eleanor said, "I see," a little tongue-in-cheek—

because it was obvious what the expression meant—and Daddy said, "from head to toe," providing further elaboration, and I said, just to get in on the action, "do you think it has anything to do with running something into the ground, like a joke?" and Eleanor, who missed my grin, said, "no, I don't think . . ." and Jane cut in and said, "no, Eleanor, excuse me, I get it. See, A. wasn't really asking a question for information, he was just setting it up so he could make a connection between me saying 'it would suit me down to the ground' and 'running the joke into the ground' as a sort of put-down of me," and I was enormously pleased and tickled that she'd caught my taunt, which I meant playfully, and Eleanor, who was catching on by then, said, "does that make sense?" and Jane shrugged and said, "to him it probably does," and Eleanor said to Jane, mock-confidentially, "do you really think he's that devious?" and Daddy said, not playfully, "you haven't even scratched the surface, either one of you," tossing off the dregs of his second drink. "That's a charming little trick A. picked up at prep school, Jane," he continued, "it takes a while to figure out, but what it is, if you like someone you try to hurt their feelings. The better the insult, the bigger compliment it implies. So, actually, you should feel quite honored, Jane."

Jane turned pale, and Eleanor shot Daddy a look. So did I. He stared straight back at me with a drunken glaze in his eyes, toeing the line he'd drawn. It hurt me just as much as if he'd leaned across the table and slapped my face. Something snapped inside me, or flared more like it, just like a sheet of paper held to flame. I wanted to shout and turn the table over, and then it was just a black curl of ash, and I said, "you should know, you wrote the book on it," and Daddy smiled, he actually smiled, his eyes staring back at me out of some smoky hellish room, and then he turned his face up to the ceiling like he was lost in space.

I stared down in my lap, feeling that old cold wind start blowing, folded my napkin with meticulous care, not knowing what I was going to do till I found myself standing up. I placed the napkin on the tablecloth, patted it, and said to Jane and Eleanor, "I don't feel very hungry," knowing I was about to cause a catastrophe but incapable of doing otherwise, and Daddy said, "suit yourself," almost sadly, and shook his head, and I said, "I plan to," and Eleanor said, "please, Adam, for heaven's sake, sit down," and I said, "what's the point in pretending,

Eleanor?'' and then, to Jane, ''I'm sorry''—I never forgot the
stunned look on her face—and then I turned around and headed
for the door. Passing through the lobby, I fished two quarters
out of my pocket—my whole fortune—and put them in the cigarette machine, pulling the lever for the pack of Marlboros,
Cary's brand, and then I stripped away the cellophane and lit
one in the door before I pushed it open and walked out into the
night.

Outside it smelled like rain and a wind had come up off the
sound. Crossing the restaurant floor, I'd felt pumped up and bad
like I was in a drama, but out there without the people and the
clink of plates and glasses and the air-conditioning and the din of
conversation, those feelings shrank to something puny and
popped like a soap bubble. Out there in nature at twilight with
a storm coming and little whitecaps beginning to break out on
the sound I got down to something more elemental, that it was
just me, that I was all alone in it and there was nobody to help
anymore if there ever had been, and it was weakness to want
help. I'd reached the point where I regarded childhood as a
dream world. Even if it had ever existed the way I'd thought,
there was no way back to it. Probably it had never been that way
at all, because, if so, why wasn't it that way now? And what
was left was a world that was a minefield and a field of battle
where you had to be strong to survive. Out in the distance above
the wooded shoreline of Roanoke Island a faint sunset blush still
lingered beneath the gray-black storm cloud, an orange kissed
with pink and silver, like the blaze along the inner rim of a
lightning whelk. That color was like a taste of something else
that might be possible if things were different, if I could change
and call the battle off. But how could I be something different
than what I was?

I stood with my foot propped on the sea wall smoking my
cigarette, staring out over the tossing waters waiting for the
downpour, not really thinking about what was going to happen
when it came—I'd just get wet. Maybe that was what I wanted,
to stand there in the pouring rain and get soaked to the skin,
drenched right down to the ground.

After a while my cigarette burned down to the filter and I
flicked it out into the water. About that time I heard footsteps
coming toward me—female by the sound of them—and I turned
around, thinking it was probably Eleanor, who'd taken on herself the role of mediator in those situations. But it wasn't Elea-

nor, it was Jane. I watched her walk up without saying anything. She stopped a few feet away and just stared. All the giddy social stuff had disappeared, her eyes were canny with some female knowingness I recognized, though I didn't know from where, and though it wasn't accusing, it shamed me. "Are you ready to go back now?" she asked, and I said, "I'm not going back," looking off over her shoulder, then out at the sound again— anywhere to avoid her eyes—and she said, "don't you think you're being a little childish?" and I said, "probably," and she said, "your father's very upset," and I said, "I doubt it, but even if he is, tough shit," and Jane said, "maybe he shouldn't have said what he did, A., but your getting up and storming off that way just makes it ten times worse. It's not exactly like you're the Good Humor Man yourself," and I said, "I never said I was, but you don't understand the situation, Jane, so I'd appreciate it if you'd just drop it."

"Well, can I at least drive you home?" she asked, and I said, " 'home,' " ironically like no such place existed, and she said, "come on, A., we could at least go someplace and have a boigah." She smiled, coaxing, as she said it, and I appreciated how hard she was trying, but I felt like she was simply taking pity on me and my pride wouldn't accept that, so I said, "I stopped eating meat, and besides I don't have any money," which was just an excuse for declining, and she said, "well, I have plenty, and we could go someplace else," and I said, "I can't let you buy me dinner after that, Jane, that would be immoral," and she said, "if it's big a deal to you, you can pay me back," which was reasonable, but I just looked away feeling strangely sad and helpless and said, "I'm really not too hungry," and Jane said, "well, just what are you going to do? stand out here all night in the rain starving and feeling sorry for yourself?" and I said, "I thought I would," trapped in my refusal and, perversely, wanting it that way, and she must have been getting pretty frustrated with my attitude by then because she said, "I didn't realize you were such a child, A.," and I said, "well, now you know, why don't you just leave?" hoping she wouldn't, but she took it at face value, sighing with exasperation as she said, "fine, suit yourself," and I said, "great," and she turned around and started walking toward the parking lot.

I watched her the whole way, feeling heartsick and ashamed, both of my behavior and of the squalid spectacle she'd witnessed inside. I wanted to be going with her, if only to the A & W for some french fries and a root beer, but I was sure she'd probably never want to see my face again and I couldn't blame her. Her headlights switched on and she pulled out of the lot and then I turned back to the sound and tried to light another cigarette but couldn't in the wind, and about that time the rain came and I just stood there feeling the big cold drops pelting my skin, soaking my clothes till they melted down in one big heavy drip. I was angry and offended by it, angry with the rain itself and with the clouds for pouring it and with the sky for having clouds. I turned my face up letting my eyelashes fill with rain, then unlaced my shoes and took my soggy socks off and threw them in the Albermarle, rolled up my pants' legs and started walking home.

I'd got about halfway to the bypass when I saw Jane's car—her mother's actually, the silver Olds—coming back. When she was up beside me she stopped and rolled the window down. "You give?" she said, grinning like she knew she had me now, and I said, "no way," grinning back, and she said, "are you always such a jerk, or are you just on a roll tonight?" and I said, "kiss my ass, McCrae," and she said, "bare it, Jenrette," and I said, "I don't think that's necessary," turning backward to her and flipping up my coattails—you could see right through—and she said, "very impressive," in her most cutting tone, and I said, "so I've been told," and she said, "how about conceited—did anybody ever mention that?" and I said, "yeah, that person is a stiff," and she narrowed her lids and said, "you're one tough asshole, A.," and I said, "sad but true." As I leaned in her window, the rain was making me blink my eyes and running along my lips and off my chin, and she said, "you look like the creature from the black lagoon," and I said, "we're related on my father's side."

Jane smiled at that and said, "tell me something, A.," and I said, "what?" and she said, "are we going to be friends?" She held out her hand obviously expecting me to take it, but I just glanced at it and said, "I'll let you know in writing within thirty days," still grinning. She took that as a yes, as it was meant, and said, "get in," tossing her head to indicate the passenger side. As I opened the door I looked in at her and said, warningly, "you're going to have the permanent imprint of one tough asshole on your upholstery," and she said, "before my patience wanes," and I piled in and closed the door, and as we pulled away I said, "how much money do you have?" and she said, "two hundred dollars," and I said, "shit, we could have a hundred boi-gahs apiece," and she said, "I thought you didn't eat them," and I said, "well, you could have a hundred boi-gahs and I could have a hundred fries. I will gladly pay you on Tuesday for a hundred fries today," and she gave me an appraising look and said, "to have been so miserable a few minutes ago you certainly seem happy now," and I shrugged and said, "insanity runs way back in our family," and we went to the drive-in and ordered and took it back to her house and ate.

Jane made me take my clothes off in the bathroom and handed me her robe around the door, and I said, "it's pink," and she said, "I've had enough of your shit, just put it on, A." I tried, but I couldn't fit my shoulders into it, so I wrapped a beach towel around my waist and when I came out I thumped my chest and said, "me Tarzan, you Jane." She gave me a funny look on that, though I didn't mean anything by it—at least I didn't think I did, though I was having a great time being with her, fucking off and acting like a four-year-old. I took her guitar out of its case and played around with it, thinking I was pretty good, and then I handed it to her and she started finger-picking "Blackbird" so that it sounded exactly like the *White Album*, so failing to impress her that way, I connected her stereo for her, and we listened to the Beatles for a while and then the Four Tops. She asked me if I liked to shag, and when I said I didn't know how, she acted surprised and said, "Cary's a great dancer," and I said, "I know," feeling a queer pang at the thought of him, but not bothering to run it down.

Finally we ended up on the couch watching an old Bette Davis movie on TV. I must have fallen asleep because I snored myself awake and found my head leaning down against her shoulder with my mouth wide open. Jane had her arms crossed over her stomach and didn't seem to mind, or else she was simply tolerating me, but it felt funny, a quick fluttering of butterfly wings inside my belly before I muttered, "sorry," and pulled away with the smell of her skin still in my nostrils, clean but personal, with a lingering trace of her perfume—Chanel 19, as I later learned.

The next thing I knew it was four-thirty in the morning. I woke up stretched out full-length on the couch with a cotton blanket over me. For a minute I didn't remember where I was and I got this awful panicked feeling like I'd done something bad or wrong. Then I saw a glass with a lipstick smear on the coffee table half full of warm flat beer and I remembered coming home with Jane and what had happened in the restaurant, and I felt sick, like now she knew everything, and I said, "fuck it, I don't care what she thinks of me," though I did care—that's why I felt sick—and to top it all off, it felt really strange to be there in that quiet house with the hum of the refrigerator and the wind outside knowing she was there, too, asleep in one of the back bedrooms. I wanted to get the hell out of there because the whole thing felt, well . . . strange, and dangerous in some way I didn't want to scrutinize too closely, so I went off to the bathroom at the end of the hall where she'd hung my clothes to dry, but on the way I passed her room and the door was open.

I started to go past, but then I stopped on the threshold and looked in. There was a cheap stained-glass panel, circular like a porthole, in the wall above the bed, which I supposed the guy who built the house—some surfer-carpenter type—had put there as a personal signature because it was a panel of a breaking wave. Moonlight was streaming through the glass, casting blue-green gleams along the sheet like underwater light, and my heart was racing like when I was in seventh grade and Cary and I and some other kids hid behind the Lewises' grape arbor on Raleigh Road at night and charged out to lob water balloons at passing cars. All I could see was Jane's bare left shoulder and her hair tossed on the pillow and the curve of her hip beneath the sheet, and I felt so excited it was almost sickening, though it wasn't sexual so much—it didn't feel that way—as the thrill of the forbidden. But I didn't want to mess with that excitement—I was afraid of it—so though I stood there for a few seconds—it couldn't have been much longer—I left pretty quickly after that.

Stepping out on Jane's front porch, I found the sky had cleared up and the wind had come around to the east, taking on a fishy smell. I dropped the towel and stepped into my underwear, which were similar to running shorts unless you really looked—I was thinking of what would happen if I was spotted by the cops—rolled up my clothes under one arm and started jogging home. It was close to five miles—I clocked it later—and I planned to take it really slow because I didn't want to screw my feet up on the asphalt, only about a mile and a half into it my feet got numb and I felt the endorphines kick in so I cut loose and hauled.

Late that night I woke up from a vivid frightening dream. When I opened my eyes I heard the door slam, and I got up and

checked the house. There was nothing, just a shutter banging in
the wind. Unable to go back to sleep, I went up to the gazebo
and watched the sun rise. I was alone on the beach except for a
single black figure silhouetted in the distance toward Camelot
pier. He was aware of me, too—I could tell because at one point
he raised his arm, waving, or perhaps beckoning me to join him.
He went down to the water and dove in, and though I waited a
long time I never saw him come back out. Shrugging it off, I
went back to bed.

Around noon there was a knock on my door. I blinked awake
and said, "come in." It was Daddy. He sat down on the other
single bed across from mine and said, "you must have come in
pretty late," and I said, "yeah," and he paused like maybe I
was going to elaborate, but I didn't figure it was any of his
business. "I waited up for you," he said, "I thought we might
have a talk, son," and I thought, oh, shit, here it comes, but he
just said, "I'm sorry about what happened," and assessing his
sincerity and finding it for real, I said, "yeah, me, too," and
he held my eyes a long time before he said, "I love you, son, I
know we've got some problems, and maybe I haven't tried hard
enough to see things from your point of view. I'd be willing to
put it on the table and talk about it if that would help, but the
main thing is, you're my son and I'm your father. We're all that's
left to one another in the way of family and that can't be changed.
I for one wouldn't want it to be, because I love you and I'm
proud of you, even if you make it a little rough on me at times."

I had to fight down the impulse to say, "I love you, too,
Dad," and it was like swallowing molten lead, but I did it. I
regarded it as a point of honor not to forget or to forgive, and
though it was a bitter discipline, I said, "what's the point of
talking? you can't change the past," and he said, "that's true,
A., but you can't live in it either. Believe me, bud, I know. I've
learned it the hard way," and I said, "is that what you think I'm
doing?" and he said, "I think there are certain things you're
holding on to that you'd be better off without," and I said, "like
what?" daring him to say it, not believing he had the guts, but
I was wrong. "I failed you as a father, A.," he said, "just once
that I'm aware of, but that once was bad enough. If you'd been
a grown man and a friend of mine, I think you could have forgiven me for it, because forgiving someone, A., doesn't nec-
essarily imply that you approve of what they've done, it just

means the person's more important to you than their acts, right or wrong. But you weren't a grown man and you weren't my friend, you were my son and you were fifteen,'' and I said, "fourteen," and he nodded and said, "fourteen then, and that makes a difference, A., I know it does. But I guess what I'm saying is that I'd like to think that now that it's behind us and we're both a little older and wiser"—he started to smile, then didn't—"we could move more in that direction, toward being friends, I mean. Do you think that's possible?"

I stared at him a long time before I said, "I don't know," because I didn't. His expression caved in slightly like a crucial timber in the underpinning had been withdrawn, but then he pushed himself and said, "well, do you think you could consider it at least?" and I said, "yeah, I probably could," and he slapped both palms down on his knees and said, "good, son, good." I think he wanted to hug me, but finding no permission in my face, he held back and said, "now let me ask you something— have you made your mind up about school?" and I said, "not totally, but I think I want to go to Carolina," and he said, "it's your choice, son, but I want you to send in a deposit to Columbia and Yale, or one of them at least, in case you change your mind," and I said, "you'll lose it if I don't go," and he said, "that's okay," and I shrugged and said, "it's your money," and he said, "that's right, it is, and it's worth it to me," and I said, "all right, Columbia would be my other choice," and he said, "I'll leave a signed check on the table when I go," and I said, "thanks," and he said, "by the way," with an almost mischievous twinkle in his eye, "I was just up on the dune and there's a school of bluefish about a hundred yards south of the cottage. They're coming our way. What say we go catch some breakfast?"

Something in me clenched tight and I said, "I don't think so, Dad, maybe another time," because I would not be tricked or coaxed into pretending things had gone back to the way they'd been before, it was not that simple, and I just felt like he wanted me to let him off the hook so he could go away with Eleanor again and not feel guilty, but when he said, "there may not be another time, A.," I became afraid that he meant something deeper than just him and Eleanor flying off that afternoon, and I was paralyzed between my fear of losing him forever and my resentment that he should issue such a warning, so when he said, "come on, bud, let's have a go at them, the poles are already rigged," I said, "okay," though I felt it was weak and wrong of me to go. I got up anyway, put on my bathing suit and followed him out on the porch.

The sun was bright but there was a fine haze in the air which you could only see in the distance near the horizon—it made the sky look white. We trotted down the steps to the front where there were two fiberglass rods with silver Daiwa reels leaning against the edge of the second-story porch. They were rigged with wire leaders and Hopkins lures, and there was a galvanized bucket with a fillet knife and a pair of pliers inside. We each picked up some of it and started up the dune, and halfway to the top Daddy looked at me and said, "I bet I can still beat you down there," and I knew it was a con, not to mention that my feet were pretty raw from the night before, but when he started running I took off, too. He had a good five yards' head start on me and was going at a pretty good clip, the rod shimmying and the bucket clanging, and I didn't catch him till the other side of the dune. Then I poured it on and passed him like he was moving in slow motion. When I reached the tide line I spun around very coolly and watched him as he staggered up. His bad knee buckled on him at the last and he went down on the other one, panting, head down, holding himself off the sand with one arm. Then he looked up at me with his face red and a sweat popping out on it and said, "I guess I was wrong, you whupped me pretty bad," and in spite of how I could see he was feeling, he grinned. "I'm just younger, Daddy," I said, feeling sorry for him, and he shook his head and said, "I was never that fast," and the pride swelled up inside me so that I had to turn away and look out at the water.

Sure enough, just in front of the house now you could see this big greasy purple stain floating on the water and the gulls going crazy over it. I made a cast, but they were pretty far offshore and my lure fell shy. As I was reeling it in, Daddy passed by me entering the water. He'd stripped his shirt off and he said, "too far out," as he waded into the trough where the shells collect, holding his pole above his head. Within two or three steps it dropped off to his waist and then his shoulders and then, just as quick, he started climbing up the near side of the bar and twenty yards out he was standing in ankle-deep water with little wavelets breaking all around like sizzling lace. "Come on," he shouted, waving back to me, and I took my rod and followed him.

The water was icy cold and the minute it touched me I felt my balls contract and my skin got that stretched-smooth brittle feeling like it was glass and if you tapped it it might break—I always loved that feeling. "You see them out there?" Daddy shouted, because it was hard to hear with the waves breaking and the gulls screeching, and he pointed and following the line of his rod I saw a small wave cross the bar lifting up the corner of the stain like a breeze lifting up a tablecloth. I moved about ten yards down from him so that we'd both have room to cast, and then I dropped the rod behind my shoulder and flicked it out, watching the lure sail twisting and glittering in the sunlight. It splashed a little to the left of where I was aiming and about that time a waist-high wave broke right smack against me from the blind side and knocked me over. I must have drifted back a half dozen yards before I caught myself against the bottom where I sat sputtering and swallowing water, trying to keep the reel above my head. When I finally made it to my feet, I started hauling back and as I did I noticed that the stain was turning in toward shore.

Then I saw something I'd never seen before. Out at the far edge of the bar the first wave of an incoming set hit shallow water and started to stand up, tottering like a drunk on roller skates, and suddenly right out of the green water wall I saw what looked like hundreds of little drops of water fling themselves outward—like when your hands are wet and you flick them at somebody—but what it was was fish, these tiny little minnows, finger mullet. They were jumping right out of the wave, hitting the trough water just as the crest toppled down on them. For a minute I thought maybe they were playing, surfing for pleasure, and I didn't know fish did that—I mean, dolphins maybe, but mullet? I cast a glance across at Daddy and he was shading his eyes with his hand staring at the same thing I was, only there was a grave set to his jaw, and then in the next wave, up along the crest, I saw the bigger fish darting like shadows.

Daddy turned to me and shouted, "they're coming in," and suddenly the water around my feet was filled with little blue and golden gleams of darting minnows, and then a big bluefish— eight or ten pounds—slammed right into my ankle. I yelled and jumped and did a sort of end-zone dance, because I'd heard stories about feeding blues, how they'll bite anything that's bright. Suddenly, I realized what was happening—those blues were driving the shoal of mullet up onto the beach.

That was when I got a strike. The line thwanged and the pole bent double and I heard the line hiss against the drag. *Zeeeeeee.* It was just instinct, because I didn't really want that fish right then, but I gave the rod a yank out to the side to lodge the hook, and then I heard Daddy calling me again. "Let's get out of here," he said, and looking over, he was pointing in toward shore for me to follow him. I raised the pole and shrugged, still reeling, like what was I supposed to do, and he started walking toward me, watching his feet and stepping really daintily, jumping several times along the way and butting the cork grip of the rod down at something in the water I couldn't see. When he got to me he said, "play out your line and follow me, once we get on shore you can bring him in." Then we both turned and stared into the deep water of the trough where all those shadowy blues were now whisking and darting. Our eyes met and he said, "come on, and move like hell."

He went first and I stood there a second building up to it before I charged, yelling and lifting my knees fast and high like in a football drill. Where it dropped off chin-deep I lost my forward momentum—it was like running through thick honey— and something glanced against my thigh. I just kept pumping my legs, hoping they were both still attached, getting no traction, and Daddy came back and shouted, "reach me your pole," and he took the end of it and pulled me closer, then grabbed my wrist and hauled me up on shore. It was incredible. In the wave swash on the sand there were what must have been hundreds, maybe thousands of those minnows twisting and wriggling and throwing themselves in the air like popping corn, or lying higher up with their sides heaving, suffocating. Remembering my fish, I gave my line a tug, but it just coiled. There was nothing on it, not even the leader or the lure, just some big bluefish out there with a silver spoon dangling from his lip like a mortal trophy.

Daddy and I sat there breathing hard, watching those minnows die, and I said, "I never saw that before," and he said, "I did . . . once," and gave me this grim significant look like it meant something. Daddy was heavy into signs, and I remembered the one time he ever visited me at Keane. It was during his worst time not long after Mama's death. He just showed up one day and I walked into his room at the Inn and found him with a screwdriver at the sink, changing the handles on the faucets. I didn't ask him what he was doing because I didn't want to know, but he told me anyway. Standing back to examine what he'd done, he pointed at the handles which had these crosslike notches on them, and he said, "they're inverted crosses, I'm turning them around." The look he gave me there on the beach was similar to that, though less intense, and he said, "I saw it with your mother once at night when we were walking on the beach in front of the old Belnord, but I was never out there in it," and trying to make light of it I said, "well, I guess fish for breakfast wasn't meant to be," and he said, "the ocean just said no," and grinned a little sheepishly, which relieved me because I saw he wasn't going to take it any farther.

We sat there a minute more than he said, "I don't know about you, but I could use a beer," and it was so complex, the way that made me feel, a manly compliment that flattered me by including me and which I wanted to accept, except for all the darker things swimming between us. Still, I said, "okay," and he said, "and maybe some blueberry pancakes?" and I said, "yeah, I could get into that," actually smiling, and he clapped me on the shoulder and said, "come on then, let's go," and we accepted our chastisement and strolled back to the house where we put the reels in a bucket of fresh water to soak out the salt.

While we were fixing pancakes—Eleanor was collaborating by that time—the phone rang and I went off to get it. It was Cary. "How's it going, spud?" he asked, and I said, "well, other than the fact that I just got attacked by a horde of rabid bluefish, not too bad," and he said, "rabid bluefish?" and I said, "don't ask," and he said, "okay, I won't," and I said, "how about yourself?" and he said, "moderate to shitty," and I said, "how's your dad?" and he said, "the bypass went okay," and I said, "I'm glad, man—when you coming down?" and he said, "soon as I can," and I said, "how soon is that?" and he said, "maybe I can get a weekend later in the month"—my heart sank—"and definitely the Fourth." "Great," I said in a dis-spirited voice, and he said, "you see Jane yet?" and for some reason I felt suddenly a little panicky like maybe I shouldn't tell him about staying at her house the night before—not that anything had happened, only I was afraid Cary might get the wrong idea. When I hesitated he said, "A.?" and I said, "yeah, spud, I'm here . . . actually she went out to dinner with us last night," which was the truth, but not all of it. "How was that?" he asked, and I said, "pretty much of a disaster . . ."

He asked what had happened, and I told him most of it, end-ing up, "she got a real crash intro to the Jenrette family circus, spud, I'm sure she thinks we're all a bunch of freaks now," and Cary said, "she doesn't think that, A.," and I said, "well, it makes no fucking difference to me because, either way, there's not a goddamn thing I can do about it now," and he said, "call her up and talk about it, A., or go see her. Don't freak out on me, spud," and I said, "believe me, spud, I'm not freaked," and he said, "acting like you don't give a shit is just another way of freaking out," and I said, "yeah, Kinlaw, tell it to the Marines," and he said, "they're too freaked out to listen," and I said, "so everybody's freaked out but you, huh, Cary?" and he laughed back and said, "no, I'm the most freaked out of all, the only difference is I'm not freaked out about it," and I said, "I'd be freaked out, too, if I was in love with somebody who looks like Jane McCrae and she was running around loose down here alone," and he hesitated briefly before he said, "she's pretty cool, isn't she?" and I said, "Jane's great, but you're a goddamn fool, Kinlaw, you should be here with her," and he said, "you think I don't want to be?" and I said, "all I know is she's here and you aren't . . . I mean, I understand about your dad, but . . ."

"That's only part of it, A.," he said, cutting me off, "I didn't go into it the last time we talked, but since Christmas things have been a little weird between me and Jane. I went up to Meadows for the dance, you know, and, well . . ."—he sighed— "she told me she wants to see other people," and I said, "shit, man, so it's over?" and he said, "no, hell no it's not over, it's just that trying to carry it on long distance this past year kind of screwed us up. Once we're in Chapel Hill it'll turn around, I know it will," and I said, "so in the meantime she's going to be seeing other people—does that mean sleeping with them?" and he said, "I suppose, we didn't spell it out," and I said, "and you can live with that?" and he said, "I guess I'll have to," and I said, "I wouldn't, I'd tell her to kiss my ass and walk," and he said, "no, you wouldn't, A., not if you really loved her," and, softening, I said, "I know you love her, spud— the question is, does she love you?" and he said, "she loves me, A., I know she does—I'm just not sure she's *in* love right now," and I said, "what's the difference?" and he laughed and said, "don't ask me, it's Jane's line, I think she read it in a magazine," and I said, "well, I think it sucks," and he said, "listen, A., I'll tell you something Mama told me—'if it's real, time and distance don't matter.' I believe that. Besides, there's too much between Jane and me just to blow her off. If I do that, I've got nothing. If I wait and let her get this thing out of her system, we've still got a chance for something really great. I don't think you get many chances like that—I can't just throw it away," and I said, "yeah, but what about your pride, man?" and he said, "screw pride, A., pride just sucks the big one. It doesn't affect my pride. So what if she sleeps around down there? It's not like I'm planning to be a monk myself, I just don't want her to fall in love," and I said, "well, I think you're weird as shit, Kinlaw, either you're a saint or a wimp, I don't know which, but I don't think you're a saint," and he laughed and said, "if I was down there right now I'd stomp your butt," and I said, "and perish in the attempt," and he said, "keep me posted, spud, okay?" and I said, "you got it, man, I gotta run now, breakfast is on the table," and we hung up.

I sat down at the table, wondering at Cary's attitude. It amazed me that he could feel the way he did about Jane sleeping with other guys. I thought that if two people loved each other then it was just settled, you didn't sleep around, and if you did, if you even wanted to, then that meant there was something wrong, something so deep there wasn't even any point in trying to fix it—maybe in a marriage, yes, but not in a relationship between kids our age—so you just had to suck it in and walk away. That was my opinion, a reflex, like when you tap your knee it jerks. My respect for Cary made me question that opinion, but looking at it, I decided he was wrong, that he was so much in love with Jane that he was willing to put up with something he shouldn't have. I guess it was thinking about all that as I sat there eating pancakes with Eleanor and Daddy that made me look up from my plate and say, "do you think it's possible to be unfaithful to someone and still love them?"

Daddy stopped with a fork of wedges halfway to his mouth and stared at me—I'd blurted it out without even thinking. He and Eleanor exchanged glances and he put his fork down on his plate and said, "do you mean did I still love your mother the night you found Eleanor and me together?" I almost croaked. Daddy reached out and squeezed Eleanor's hand, keeping his eyes fixed on mine the whole time, and he said, "if that's what you mean, the answer's yes—I loved your mother then, and I still love her now, today. I always will. I've wanted to tell you that for a long time, son, I don't know if it makes any difference, but I needed to say it," and I said, feebly, "I was thinking about

something else entirely, something Cary said over the phone."
He and Eleanor just stared at me and I said, "and you're right,
it doesn't make any difference," feeling hard even as I spoke
the words, but unable to choke them back. "I'd like to be excused," I said, getting up without waiting for permission, and
Daddy said, "where are you going?" and I said, "to take a
walk," and he looked at his watch and said, "we're leaving
soon, A.," and I said, "then I guess I'll see you later," and he
said, "son?" and I said, "what?"

He stood up and took a step toward me where I stood on the
threshold of the kitchen, plate in hand. Offering his hand with
a little smile below grave eyes, he said, "can we at least shake?"
I looked at it wanting to turn my back, but it was just too terrible.
I'd swallowed down that silver spoon a great long time ago and
it was sunk so deep inside me I felt that if I pulled against it my
heart would come up, too, and my life with it, so I took Daddy's
hand. He pulled me to him and put his arms around me and I
just stood there stiff, feeling numb, but also like I was going to
cry if it went any further. So finally I pulled away and stacked
my plate in the sink, and on my way out I stopped by Eleanor
and put my hand gingerly on her shoulder. She reached up and
covered it with her own, smiling at me out of her pretty sad dark
eyes, and I said, "bye," and walked out the screen door.

Two

A.

On Monday morning at seven forty-five I went into work and Mick gave us his annual pep talk about setting an example on and off the beach, being in by eleven and practicing sexual abstinence "to conserve our leg strength." Mick delivered that part tongue-in-cheek, though on the whole he was serious. Still, one of the new guys said, "you mean, no . . ."—he hesitated like he couldn't find the right expression, then said, "girls?" and Mick said, "you mean pussy, don't you, Parker? isn't that what you were going to say?" Parker sat there with a dumbfounded expression, and Mick said, "let me ask you something, Parker—did you come down here to save lives or to be a pussy hound?" and Parker said, "to save lives, Mick," and Mick said, "you're sure of that?" and this honor-bright look appeared on Parker's face and he said, "definitely, Mick, to save lives." Mick received that deadpan, then turned to the rest of us and said, "you guys watch out for Parker here, don't let him approach you from the rear." Everybody broke out laughing, even me, though I'd been in Parker's place the year before and felt sorry for him because I knew he'd been singled out to play class jerk to Mick for the rest of the season.

Then Mick handed out the tee shirts with the big red crosses on them and "Lifeguard" written on the back and we all got paint and brushes and piled in the pickup and Mick drove us down the beach dropping us at our stands. I'd drawn a new site, the Lost Colony Hotel, which had been the Belnord years be-

196

fore. I had a nostalgic connection to the place because my parents had often taken me there to eat. They'd danced there, too, and I remembered the ballroom with its high ceiling and crystal chandelier and bay windows overlooking the ocean. It was paneled with random widths of juniper, the same wood we had in our cottage, plentiful once, but now rare and almost priceless.

From down on the beach as I scraped my stand I could see people hanging off the side of the hotel on extension ladders, hanging shutters or slapping fresh paint on those already hung, a deep glassy green, still wet and fresh so that I could see the morning light reflected in it. The place was an old three-story hulk with cedar shakes weathered almost black and a green shingle roof hanging low over the wide verandas in the second story, like a man with a hat tipped low over his eyes. On the east porch some carpenters were working off saw horses, and I could hear the intermittent whine of the Skil saw. Mick had told me they were trying to have the place open for Memorial Day weekend, which was the upcoming one, and it looked to me like they were cutting it pretty close.

The scraping was slow tedious finger-splitting work, because the stands were eight feet tall, heavy and cumbersome with a latticework bottom filled with sneaky edges. I'd finished that part by ten-thirty and the primer coat went on in half an hour, so that by eleven, with nothing else to do until it dried, I decided to take advantage of the low tide and get in a run on the packed sand. I stripped down to my jams, suddenly regretting that I hadn't worn a jock, and set out toward Christie's pier, three miles south of the Lost Colony. I set the timer on my watch and took off, scattering a testy pack of gulls that screaked and flapped their wings and limed the beach. I hadn't realized how hot it was, not just the ambient temperature, but the sun's leering specific focus on certain body parts, particularly across the back of my shoulders and my nose and forehead. There was also the granular sharpness of the sand on unhardened feet, and occasional patches of larger shells that crackled under my soles and where I went down ankle-deep losing rhythm and momentum, not to mention the chafing of my slack swinging penis against the rough cloth of my suit. But about two miles into it, everything harmonized into the music of the run, what my running buddies and I had called "endorphine slush" at Keane, the moment when you step into the jetstream and effort ceases to be a rebuking thing, an obligation, and becomes prerogative. I was still burning, chafing, damaging my feet, but I didn't care because I didn't feel it, I just flew. Touching the creosote pylon of the pier, I cast a swift glance seaward watching an incoming wave sluice through the canted portico, and then turned back with the sun behind me and a cool light breeze in my face drying the sweat which came off my body like water off melting ice.

In the last mile I was fully stoked, my feet didn't sink in the soft places anymore—some weird effect of physics, though it felt like magic—and about five hundred yards from the finish I saw the figure of a solitary man standing in the swash directly in my line of approach. As I closed the distance, a group of others joined him. They didn't see me and I could have gone around them, but instead I held my line and cut right through them, missing the closest by no more than a foot or two. One girl squealed and jumped, placing a hand involuntarily across her cleavage, which was considerable, and I said, "sorry," behind me as I heard a male voice say, "what the *hell*?" Feeling foolishly hard-core about the whole thing I ran a hundred yards past my end point before stopping, hands on knees, to catch my breath. I looked at my watch—32:18. When I stood up and looked back they were all staring at me, so I shrugged apologetically and dove into the water, which was icy cold and consciousness-changing, exactly the effect of going from a sauna into snow.

By the time I came out, they'd gone back to their towels, which were on the hotel beach. I nodded and they all nodded back, or simply stared, except for one, an older guy—over thirty, I would have guessed, but not much—who was standing behind the others in a black Speedo, a suit you didn't see on southern men or southern beaches very often, drinking a beer, which he raised to me in an almost imperceptible toast. This guy was grinning, rather brazenly I thought, and it crossed my mind that maybe he was gay, though he didn't seem gay, despite the Speedo, yet you could have made a case for it. For one thing, he wore an earring, silver with a little hunk of turquoise in it—it looked Navaho—and there was no hair on his chest, not any, and he obviously pumped iron or did some heavy-duty workout—not that he was overbuilt or hulkish, in fact he was quite lean, but incredibly defined, like gelatin poured into a mold and allowed to harden. This guy had a great body, yet he didn't hold it effetely or self-consciously, but more like an animal would, that kind of blasé naturalness, which was the thing that made me think he wasn't gay. Maybe I didn't really pay that much attention at the time, but only found significance playing it over in light of what came later. I don't know. But that was my first glimpse of Cleanth Faison, that little toast and grin.

I sat down circling my knees with my arms and lifted my face to the sun, letting the breeze dry me, pretending to ignore the group of bathers, but hyperaware of them, and of their awareness of me. While sitting there I realized the saws had stopped singing, the activity at the hotel had subsided into noonday stillness, and it occurred to me these people might be associated with the place. I took another look. They didn't seem like workers. In addition to Cleanth there were four others, two girls and two boys in their twenties. There was a good-looking leggy brunette who hadn't gone in the water, but whose hair still looked wet somehow, as thick and lustrous as an otter's pelt. That was B.J. And on the towel beside her was a full-figured blonde—the one who'd squealed—a little plump, with one of those bombshell figures from the fifties you didn't see around much anymore—Ellen. Then there was Reese, an eastern North Carolina frat boy with a beer gut and a porky ass. He was wearing aviator glasses and his black hair was blown-dry straight back and cropped flat on top. Buzz made up their number, a surfer type, but not local, a more cosmo sort of surfer boy like you might have expected to see in Maui, or the Baja, or maybe Florida. He wore jams like mine and Wayfarers on a cord around his neck, and his hair was shagged in the style of the day, but a little hacked as though some local who understood the principle but didn't have that much experience had done it, blond hair with bleached highlights, sun or peroxide you couldn't tell. He seemed older than the others, twenty-five or -six. He was the only one you might have plausibly expected to find working as a carpenter. The rest exuded a different social tone you didn't associate with manual labor, especially the girls, who looked like former debutantes whose daddies had money, built for leisure, not for work. Maybe it was just the fact that they were older that made them seem so worldly and intimidating.

I had no plans to speak to them, but as I knelt over my paint can, stirring with a stick, the guy in the black Speedo—Cleanth—ambled over with a beer. I saw him coming, but didn't look up till he stopped in front of me. "How far did you go?" he asked, sipping from the can, and I said, "around six? I'm not exactly sure," and he said, "you looked like you were going at a pretty good clip," and I shrugged and said, "the last mile or two felt pretty decent," and he said, "how fast?" and that grin came out again. "Five and a half, five-twenty maybe," I said, "it's hard to tell in sand," and he said, "that's fast," and I said, "not that fast," and he said, "fast enough," and wondering again if he was gay, I stood up, because I didn't like being at a lower level. I brushed my hands on my shorts, prepared to shake, but not offering, and he said, "I take it you're a runner," and I said, "I run cross country at school—at least, I did. I just graduated," and he said, "from where?" and I said, "Keane?" wondering what the fuck he wanted, and he said, "I could have guessed it," and I said, "you've heard of it?" and he said, "I went there," which suddenly put the whole thing on a different footing and eased my mind, but not that much.

"You're kidding?" I said, "when?" and he said, "I graduated in '56," and I said, " '56?" running through some quick mental computations. It would have made him late thirties, and I said, "you don't look . . ." before I realized it was inappropriate, and he said, "that old?" completing my thought, and I smiled, feeling shy, and said, "well," and he said, "I stopped aging in 1967," and I said, "stopped aging," on my guard again, and he just grinned. I couldn't tell if he was joking, drunk or crazy, but that grin was beginning to get to me. It was a little fixed and disconcerting. There was something off about him, or maybe too turned on was it, and it wasn't just his body but his face as well, and his whole manner. He was so good-looking you didn't quite buy it. He might have stepped out of a fashion magazine, those same chiseled sultry features, like a blond Italian, only not pouty or sullen or loutish like your typical gigolo or model. Instead there was incredible animation in his face, the grin was just the most obvious part of it, you could see the play of emotion, or whatever it was, behind his features like sun and clouds behind stained glass, but it seemed abnormal in some way. And after a while, I noticed, a brief while, you didn't see his looks at all but only the animation, like a consuming flame. I didn't have a clue about him, but I think I knew from the first moment that I'd never met anyone quite like him. And he had eyes that were almost golden, Cleanth did, dark gold, shrewd appraising intelligent eyes that seemed to know what you were going to say before you said it, more withheld than that grin and out of keeping with it somehow.

"What's your name?" he asked, and I said, "A. Jenrette,"

and he said, "Cleanth Faison," extending his hand, which I took. "You're the lifeguard?" he asked, and I said, "yeah," and he said, "I own the place, part of it anyway—my partner's back at the hotel," and I nodded and said, "I used to come here with my parents, back when it was the Belnord," and Cleanth said, "I remember well," and because part of the protocol of lifeguarding was establishing good relations with the owners, and because the conversation obviously wasn't over from his point of view, I said, "could I get a glass of water, do you think?" and he said, "how about a beer?" and I said, "water would probably do it, since I'm working," and he said, "I don't think there's any water in the cooler, except maybe some melted ice, but come on, I'll walk you up and introduce you to Morgan. Come say hi to the others first."

As I followed him off, he looked back over his shoulder and said, "Jenrette, you said?" and I said, "right, A. Jenrette," and he said, "no relation to the author, I suppose," and I stopped, and he stopped, and I said, "he's my father," and Cleanth positively beamed, but didn't seem surprised at all, like he'd planned the whole thing, right down to the details of my paternity, and I said, "you know him?" and he said, "Clay? Only slightly. I was duck hunting at Mattamuskeet with a friend of mine one time and Clay was there with another group." He stopped, and I waited, inviting him to continue, so he said, "we met the first morning in the boat going out to the blinds and it turned out we were all staying at the same hotel. The second day it rained—not just rain but a real bad blow. Over breakfast we decided to bag it, and somebody produced a bottle and we started playing poker. Your father said he'd never played before except twice, once being strip poker with his high school girlfriend which he swore he lost. This was years ago but I remember it like it was yesterday. We were still sitting at the table the next morning when the sun came up. It must have been an eighteen, twenty hour game." He looked at me like there was more, and I said, "who won?" and he laughed and said, "come on, I'll tell you later," and then he introduced me to the others.

"People," he said, "this is A. Jenrette, lifeguard, runner, son extraordinaire of a famous father," and B.J., the brunette, said, "who's your father?" and sipped her beer, fluttering her eyelashes at me, not coyly, but with assumed ennui, and I said, "Clay Jenrette," not liking her, and also finding, on a second glance, that her looks did not hold up. I mean, she was perfect on the surface, but underneath that something didn't work, and I couldn't tell if it was physical or something deeper. "Never heard of him," B.J. said, and Cleanth said, "he wrote *Rubber Man*, it was very well received," and B.J. smiled at me with cutting languor and said, "it's a groove, I'm sure," and Cleanth said, "B.J.'s forte isn't reading, A.," and I said, "what's your forte, B.J.?" and everybody laughed, except B.J., who looked at Cleanth as though he might have an answer. She was smiling, but there was something disastrous in her eyes. And the blonde said, "you scared me half to death back there, A.," chiding me, but making it familiar with my name. "I should have run around you," I said, "sorry," and she smiled with nice gray eyes that extended me the benefit and said, "you ought to wear a bell around your neck or bring a horn or something so people can know to get out of your way." I had the impression of someone of good family who'd been exposed to opportunity and talent, but didn't have great gifts herself, and knew it, yet made the best of what she had, and she said, "I'm Ellen Davies, by the way," and I said, "nice to meet you, Ellen," smiling back.

Then Reese belched loudly and said, "damn, excuse me," and Cleanth said, "A., Reese Tyler from Ahoskie," and Reese said, "where you from, A.?" and I said, "I grew up in Kill-deer," and Reese said, "I got some cousins up there—you know Tom Fielding?" and I said, "I knew Shelley, I had a crush on her in seventh grade," and Reese said, "I bet I got further with her than you did," and I said, "that wouldn't be saying much." Reese smiled with broad hilarity, and I thought I knew the type, a budding good old boy, but with that same watchful calculating thing back there behind the gruff good humor, and Cleanth said, "and this is Buzz, who's going to tend the bar downstairs and also teach me how to surf," and Buzz said, "good to meet you, man," and shook my hand a little limply. He was handsome in an ethereal sort of way, with wide doelike eyes that seemed a little dreamy, or lost, but pure in some way, like there was just one thing for him. Then Cleanth said, "come on, A., let's get you that glass of water," and, to the others, "rest up, guys, back to work at one," and we crossed the dune to the hotel.

There was something else about Cleanth. I'd noticed it before, but became more aware of it detecting his slight limp. There was a mother scar running vertically down his left thigh, twelve or fourteen inches long and maybe two across. It was icy white against his tan and had a glassy texture like road ice which has

thawed and then refrozen and you could see the places where
the sutures had been made sticking off like railroad ties. "I was
telling you about that poker game," he said, and I said, "right,
who won?" and he said, "Clay did, your dad. I bet he took two
or three thousand dollars home with him. I lost seven or eight
hundred myself. That was a lot of money to me at the time."
He looked at me as though considering whether sons weren't
hereditarily liable for their fathers' poker sins, and I said, "it's
a lot of money to me now," wanting to make clear I hadn't seen
or profited from his cash, and he said, "true, but back then
everything cost a hundred dollars. I could buy seven or eight
things I wanted with that money then, but now everything's a
thousand. You know how that goes," and I said, "not really,"
and he said, "no, you wouldn't. It's a life change you go through
in your early thirties, if you go through it at all. Some don't
make it. I expect you will," and I said, "what makes you say
that?" and he grinned and said, "I can just tell—you're your
father's son, aren't you?" and I said, "yes, but I still don't know
what you mean," and he narrowed his lids and said, "you know
more than you let on," and it was funny, because right at that
moment I realized I did know what he meant, not from personal
experience but some other way, and also that it was critical for
me to pay attention to that deeper knowing voice and stay alert,
because this guy, Cleanth Faison, was playing poker with me,
too, some nonobvious game with stakes I didn't know, and
maybe never really did find out, or even why he picked me out,
unless he simply happened to be eager for a game that day and
I simply happened to stroll by.

"Your dad was quite an amazing poker player really, A.," he
said, "a naif, or faux naif, you couldn't tell. I still don't know
whether he got lucky or if it was the best act I ever saw. Every
time he won a hand he kept saying, 'I can't believe this, I can't
believe this, this is unbelievable, this is amazing,' acting so
happy it was almost mesmerizing so that it was worth it losing
money just to watch the act, which, after a while, you had to
suspect was an act, but you couldn't be quite sure, because he
kept swigging shots of straight George Dickel and asking about
the rules like, 'can I call now?' or 'can I raise it that much?'
His bluffs were all transparent, you could read his cards in his
face—at least at first. I still don't know, and I'm not sure I want
to. I liked him though. I liked his book, too, sort of the same
thing—naif, faux naif, style, no style, a little bit like Hemingway

with a southern accent. Where is Clay now?'' and I said, ''he just flew off to California with his editor. There's some sort of meeting about him writing a screenplay for *Rubber Man*,'' and Cleanth said, ''he sold it then?'' and I said, ''it's been optioned for a long time,'' and Cleanth said, ''which studio?'' and I said, ''just some private guy Dad met and liked. He's in advertising, I think, but he really loved the book. It took him a long time, but he finally put the financing together.'' Cleanth nodded and said, ''no second book?'' and I said, ''he wrote one, but it wasn't published,'' and he said, ''why not?'' and I said, ''I don't know. It was too weird, I guess. I didn't read it.''

''What about you?'' Cleanth asked, and I said, ''what about me?'' and he said, ''you're a lifeguard and a runner, you went to Keane—what else do I need to know about you?'' and I said, ''that's mostly it,'' and he said, ''and you like to play your cards close to your chest,'' elaborating the catalog and grinning like my reticence delighted him, and instead of saying, ''I don't know what you mean, Cleanth,'' I listened to that inner voice and said, ''I guess that depends,'' and he gazed at me with acute interest and said, ''on what?'' and I said, ''on who I'm playing poker with,'' and he said, ''excellent, excellent,'' laughing, ''and you don't know me, right?'' and I said, ''right,'' and he said, ''do you want to?'' and struggling against inbred politeness which proposed a different answer, I said, ''maybe,'' at the bidding of the little voice, and Cleanth said, ''and maybe I'll tell you,'' and at that moment our private language became established, little voice to little voice, and I felt myself slipping irrevocably into his unknown world, not unwillingly, though not so much because I wanted to or liked him either, but because the throttle was pressed down there. Something in me sensed it like a homing signal, and knowing nothing else around was likely to prove so interesting, I followed it to see where it would go. I started a strange journey there.

Three

A.

When we reached the front of the hotel facing the beach road, Cleanth led me up the wide staircase to the veranda, then through a glass door with mullioned separate panes into the ballroom. Fundamentally it hadn't changed, but the quality was different. For one thing, it was filled with greenery—filling, I should say, because men were unloading plants off a flatbed truck in the parking lot even as we walked up, huge things in terra-cotta planters that gave the room a jungle lushness, different from the resounding clarity I remembered. There were pictures on the wall, too, not the typical vapid dune and ocean landscapes you saw most places, but fine antique prints, English gaming scenes, horses and jockeys, a set of framed "Spy" caricatures from the old *Vanity Fair*, as well as Audubon's "Wild Turkey" and "Turkey Hen" from the elephant folio—I couldn't judge their value, but I knew they were good.

What drew me most, though, were the paintings—polo scenes done in oil. In one a rider leaned off his horse with his stick upraised behind him, an odd glancing sidelight casting his face in shadow and throwing a gleam along his mud-spattered arm and the tensed flank of the horse. A clod of earth stippled with accurate grass flew under the lifted hoof, a tiny jewel of precise observation. I was indifferent to the subject matter, but anatomically they were faultless, beautifully, luminously seen—more than that, they had a fine surging movement, you could almost hear the muted clopping of the hooves in the dirt and smell its black-green fragrance.

There was a portrait, too, of a young girl, perhaps eighteen, in a strapless cocktail dress, a rich mauve satin fabric with fine warm values in the cloth, below a pale slight bosom with a mole, touchingly demure, almost sad in some way, but you couldn't say why it affected you like that, which was its masterfulness. She had long dark hair done up in a chignon beneath a tiny French hat with a net veil which cast crisp lines of ink-black shadow on her skin and obscured her features. She appeared to be staring out from behind the bars of a delicate prison, and her dark eyes were the saddest I'd ever seen, the more so for the fine self-possession in them, which seemed thin and brittle somehow beside the weight of the unstated thing that she was up against. The artist had loved that girl, you knew that at a glance. It was only after studying it for several moments that I glanced down in the corner and read the artist's signature—C.F.

Deeply surprised, I turned to Cleanth, who was studying it, too, with a musing expression, as though seeing it freshly through my fresh seeing, and said, "you did this?" and he said, "a long time ago," looking not at me, but her, and I said, "it's beautiful," and extracting himself from its magnetism, he met my eyes and said, "thank you," and my whole first impression of him began to crumble into ruins, that he could have done a thing as tender and as true as this. "Who was she?" I asked, and he said, "a girl I used to know, I did it in my twenties," and, I guess, because I was moved, I said, "I paint, too," offering something of myself, and he said, "do you?" and then he nodded and said, "yes, I might have seen that in you, from the way you looked—you saw it, didn't you?" and though my surface impulse was to say, "saw what?" I knew exactly what he meant—the essence—and I said, "yes," and he said, "good, A., I'm glad you did," and I said, "I'd love to see some of your more recent work, if you don't mind showing it," and he pursed his lips and said, "there isn't any."

I stared at him and he said, "I don't paint anymore," and I was shocked that someone with such talent, who'd reached a level of real accomplishment, had stopped. I took it almost personally. "Why not?" I asked, and he said, "I lost interest," and I stared at the painting, then at him, and said, "I don't get it—how could you lose interest?" and he shrugged and said, "put it this way—life got more interesting," and his smile came back like he was toying with me now, and though I felt disposed to argue, I said, "more interesting than before? or more interesting than painting?" and he laughed and said, "both—good question though. I like your speed, A., it's not something I encounter every day," and I felt a subtle inner flush of pleasure at his flattery, which was so silken and restrained, and I was surprised at how deeply it affected me—not that it put me off my balance, but put me *on* it somehow, so that my balance seemed contingent on his stroke, or capable of becoming so.

At that moment I heard the creak of the swinging door from the kitchen—I remembered that creak—and a woman stepped out from behind the waiters' partition carrying a tray of silverware. Seeing Cleanth, she stopped and seemed about to say something, then didn't, seeing me. "Hi, baby," Cleanth said, turning his grin on her, "I've brought you someone special," and she said, "a waiter, I hope," flicking her glance at me. There was a hint of slight distrust in her expression, I thought, or maybe just a question. Cleanth shook his head and said, "much better, a surprise," and she said, "the best surprise you could possibly give me would be another waiter," checking me out again, even more distrustfully, like she was used to surprises from this man, and dealing with the fallout from them. "Morgan, I'd like you to meet A. Jenrette," Cleanth said, putting his arm around my shoulder, "A., this is Morgan Deal, my business partner and . . ." He looked at her with a hint of teasing but affectionate hilarity in his eyes and said, "well, how would you put it, M.?" and she made a wry face at him and said, "let's just leave it there, Cleanth, shall we?" and then put down the tray, walked up and took my hand. "It's a pleasure, A.," she said, "is that a nickname?" and I said, "an initial, it stands for Adam," and she said, "well, welcome to the Lost Colony, Adam," and I said, "thanks," and she smiled, making an effort to be charitable, though it was clear she had a lot on her mind. "A.'s going to be our lifeguard, M.," Cleanth explained, and she said, "I thought we already hired one," and Cleanth said, "we did," and Morgan said, "oh," and they both looked at me and I shrugged sheepishly and said, "I'm it," and Morgan laughed and said, "well, our lives can certainly use a little salvation around this place."

She was about Cleanth's age, I would have guessed, only she looked it, a woman teetering on the brink between youth and middle age. At certain moments, in certain lights, she could be

either. Actually, she was several years Cleanth's junior, but I
was surprised when I later learned that. Perhaps it was her hair,
which was prematurely gray and cropped short like a boy's, a
sort of Greek shepherd cut that gave her an impish quality her
face didn't entirely corroborate. I found her attractive, despite
the lines in her face and a general loss of tone that showed
especially in a fold of softer flesh beneath her chin. Her eyes
were large and dark and had an inky knowingness in them that
I found a little frightening, though she was not a threatening
person. In fact, there was something reassuring about Morgan,
very natural and solid, but only that, perhaps, she had not accepted all she knew. In that first moment there was an expression
of slight frustration or preoccupation in those eyes which did
not seem native there, and, looking behind it, you could just
pick out the ghostly trace of the carelessness and floating quality
of a young girl who'd been spoiled once, and wasn't anymore,
who was now a woman making her own way in the world, quite
well perhaps, but not at ease with it and fated never to be so
entirely, both mourning and resenting what she'd lost. She reminded me of someone, Morgan did, right from the start, and
it might have been my mother, the way I remembered her toward
the end, except that it felt more specific than that, and was.

Part of the impression might have been her clothes, which
were quite good, though lackadaisically worn. Yet that very
lackadaisicalness had a real style. She was wearing a pale lemon
sweater of silky cotton and a pair of beat-up but tight-fitting
riding pants with leather patches on the inside of the knees and
the stirrups riding up behind her calves, which were nice calves,
I noticed, one of those lights and moments which showed off
her youthful side. She was barefoot, too, which somehow
brought the whole thing off by throwing it all away. And it was
possible, I noticed, to catch a glimpse of skin through the loose
ribbing of the sweater, though nothing as specific as a nipple. I
must have looked, because I remember thinking she was sexy,
though in a way I couldn't quite put my finger on back then, not
having encountered it before, something a little bit corrupt, like
an overripe fruit swimming with juices that you know will squish
when you bite into it. My sexual appraisal was just a reflex, the
merest flicker of a flicker, because, for one thing, she seemed
almost ancient to me, and, for another, I assumed some connection beyond business between Cleanth and her, though it
seemed clear they weren't married.

"I like what you've done in here," I told her, and Cleanth said, "A. used to come here with his parents, M., his father's Clay Jenrette the novelist, whom I knew slightly, as I was telling A.," and Morgan said, "oh, yes, you gave me that book, remember? *Rubber Band*, wasn't it?" I laughed with genuine pleasure and Cleanth said, *"Rubber Man,"* correcting her, and I said, "I'll have to tell him that, he'll get a kick out of it," and Morgan frowned good-naturedly at her own expense and said, "well, anyway, I liked it, as I recall, especially that English fellow—he was a wonderful character," and I said, "he was based on my grandfather—all the characters were based on real people," and Morgan said, "and your father wrote it?" like she was fascinated, and I said, "yeah, he did," enjoying my brief moment of deflected celebrity once again, as I had many times in the past, and not pausing to consider that what made me fascinating to them came, not from myself, but from my father, whom I held a mortal grudge against, came, moreover, from the darkest and most painful aspect of my history, the thing I least wanted handled, but always gave away so blithely for a moment of shallow fleeting popularity.

"Was he really a crook, though—your grandfather?" Morgan asked, "did he really steal the money and run off with that Malayan woman?" and, feeling the whiplash set in, I said, "no," too sharply, and then, "I mean, nobody really knows what happened to him. Probably he was killed by the Japanese when they invaded Singapore," and Cleanth said, "so Clay just made the ending up?" and I said, "right," and they both looked at me, catching from my expression that this was not all fun and games, and Morgan said, "but your mother? how did she feel about having her father portrayed that way?" and I said, "I never asked her," wanting to run away and hide, but knowing I had to see it through to the end since I'd cracked the door to them. "Well, she must be very fine, or she must love your father very much," Morgan said, and I said, "she did." Reacting to the past tense in my voice, they both looked at me, and I said, "she's dead, she died of cancer," and Morgan said, "how terrible for you, I'm sorry," and Cleanth said, "I didn't know," and I said, "I ought to be getting back to work now," feeling I'd given away too much and angry with myself because of it, wanting to escape at any cost.

Glancing at Morgan, Cleanth said, "why don't you come by tonight, A., if you're free? we're having a small group for dinner," and Morgan said, "yes, do come, we've been running through the menu, trying to get it right before we open, and we could use a fresh perspective." They both looked at me, concerned and expectant, and I said, "well . . ." unable to think of a convenient lie, and Cleanth said, "just think about it, if you show, fine, if you don't, that's fine, too," and he put his arm around my shoulder paternally and began to lead me toward the door, and Morgan said, "and bring someone, if you like," adding, "you don't know any unemployed waiters, do you?" with a sweet smile meant to lighten things—it was clear they saw I was in some difficulties and were sympathetic—and I said, "I'll try," and Cleanth said, "fine, around eight, we'll hope to see you," and we shook hands in the doorway, and I left without my glass of water.

Four

A.

It seemed the most natural thing in the world, calling Jane to tell her about the job lead I'd unearthed for her. But when I got home I felt a little weird about it and kept putting it off. It never even occurred to me that I was nervous, much less why, but I guess if I'd thought about it it would have been because I was afraid Jane might take my calling the wrong way, like maybe I was interested in her or something, and that was one misunderstanding I definitely didn't want the two of us to have, whatever she thought of me after that business at Jimbo's.

Finally I realized I was being a wimp about the whole affair and picked up the phone and made the call. "How's the job hunt going?" I asked after a few preliminaries, and Jane said, "well, Lucy and I went over to the Double Stack today—you know that pancake house?—and the lady told us her husband needs a couple of girls and for us to come back in the morning." She sounded pretty thrilled about it, and I said, "well, I don't want to burst your bubbles or anything, but the Lost Colony is hiring waiters. I drew their stand this morning, so I'll be working there, and I can guarantee the money'll be a whole lot better at a hotel than at a pancake house," and she said, "you think we should go over there and apply?" and I said, "yeah, I do, that's why I was calling, 'cause, see, I met the owners today and they invited me to dinner and said I could bring someone, so I thought maybe you'd like to go—I mean, since you're looking for a job," and she said, "dinner?" and I said, "right," and she said,

211

"what about Lucy?" and I said, "what about her? it's a sit-down dinner, Jane," and she said, "oh," and I said, "I don't know how many people they need, but maybe if they hire you, you can get her in later," and Jane said, "well, what should I wear?" and I said, "what am I, your couturier?" and she said, "don't be a butt, I can't ever decide—would you look at a couple of things when you come over?" and I said "Jesus, Jane," though she'd posed the question ever so sweetly and with a self-doubt I found touching, and she said, "oh, all right, never mind, I'll ask Luce to help me," and I said, "can you be ready in an hour?" and she said, "no, but I will be."

So I put on my blue blazer and my Keane school tie with the gray lions rampant ramping on a burgundy ground, slapped some Grey Flannel on my cheeks, feeling self-conscious and pretty foolish about the whole thing, and I drove over to Jane's. Some sort of weather thing was happening, a front was coming in or something, trailing a warm clammy fog. It was ninety-eight degrees and so humid you could have almost swum through the air.

Jane and Lucy were both sitting out on the front steps with a big wooden salad bowl of ice cubes, sucking them and lifting up each other's hair in back and rubbing them over the napes of their necks. Lucy, who was wearing a string bikini, slouched back with her head in Jane's lap, a cold compress over her eyes and a cigarette hanging from her lip. Jane's hair was still wet from the shower, and though she had on lipstick, she was wearing what I took to be a bathrobe or a nightgown, a flowing off-white cotton thing with sky-blue silk trimming around the neck and wide sleeves, and I was miffed she wasn't ready, though seeing the two of them lounging there, both female and attractive and easy in their natural element, I felt too outnumbered to come right out with it.

Lucy was particularly intimidating, not just because I didn't know her, but something about that compress and that cigarette and, most of all, the bathing suit. I don't think I'd ever come across breasts the likes of Lucy Carlisle's, except maybe in some girlie magazines we'd passed around at Keane—just this side of obscene, or perhaps a little over. I didn't mean to be crude about it, but I guess I must have stared rather obviously, because the first thing Jane said, gazing right at me and cracking an ice cube with her teeth, was, "A.'s looking at your bosoms, Luce," and I said, "Jesus, Jane, I am not," and Lucy lifted up her compress, very coolly checking me out, and said, "are you looking at my bosoms, A.?"—that was our introduction. Actually, Lucy was top-drawer FFV, but she was in her rebellious bad-girl phase that summer, and because I was paralyzed and couldn't speak, Jane said, "aw, look how he's blushing, we're embarrassing him, Luce," and I said, "you are not," and Lucy stared at Jane upside down and said, "he's kinda cute," and put the compress back across her eyes, and Jane said to me with apparent innocence, "aren't you burning up?" and I said, "are you referring to the weather?" and Jane laughed and Lucy smiled like a wry hungover sphinx and sat up, casually hoisting her top, and said, "I've got to take a shower, Charlie's coming in an hour," and she got up and climbed the stairs, pulling her suit down over one cheek with unbelievable brazenness, then disappearing through the screen door.

I looked at Jane and she said, "isn't she the greatest? I wish we could have asked her," and I said, "if you want my opinion, she's better Double Stack material," and Jane said, "A., you're awful!" and Lucy said, from away inside the house, "I heard that," and I gritted my teeth, and Jane said, "you're blushing again," and, ignoring that, I said, "would you get ready? we're already late," and she looked confused and said, "I am ready," standing up and staring down at herself, then back at me. "You're wearing your pajamas?" I asked, and she said, "it's a kimono, *A.*," and I said, "oh," and Lucy called out, "*I* like it," and Jane said, "isn't it all right?" and I said, "it's fine, come on," and she got all serious and pleading and said, "you wouldn't let me go looking like an idiot, would you, A.?" and I said, "well, are there any alternatives?" and she clucked her tongue and sighed and said, "thanks, A., that was really subtle," and I said, "well, you asked," and she said, "can you wait two minutes?"

It was more like five, but she came back much improved, I thought, in a blue blazer like my own over a pair of madras Bermuda shorts, which though baggy and something I associated more with men, looked kind of cool and sexy and conservatively funky on her slim brown legs, and a silk scarf thrown around her collar in a way that looked extremely casual but which you knew probably wasn't. "Much better," I told her, and she said, "I'm *so* glad you approve," and I said, "come on, let's bolt," and she said, "come here a second—you want to feel something nice?" and I said, "what?" distrustfully, and she said, "close your eyes," and I said, "why?" and she said, "just do it," and I did, and then I heard the ice cubes glingle in the bowl, and her hands covered both sides of my face, still wet from where she'd dipped them. I drew back, surprised, but she held me and said, "just relax a second, A.," like I was an impossible case, and I made myself be still, though I couldn't relax entirely. For just a second though I felt what she was talking about, the delicious coolness of her chilled fingers and palms before she took them away, gazing at me with this big delighted smile. "Doesn't that feel great?" she asked, and I said, "yeah, it's all right," sort of noncommitally, and she said, "we were taking turns before," and I said, "great, now can we go?" and Jane must have found that funny for some reason, because she just laughed. The whole thing was a mystery to me.

Morgan was alone in the ballroom when we walked in, putting the last touches on the table, which was beautifully laid, set under the chandelier with a pale pink cloth and fresh camellias, white ones floating in water in a heavy crystal bowl. She regarded us uncertainly, then her eyes brightened with recognition and she said, "oh, Adam, it's you, I didn't recognize you—you're wearing clothes," and she laughed volubly, swishing toward us looking very chic in black silk, a sort of pants affair like a harem girl with a camisole top beneath a filmy short-sleeved cover that hung almost to her knees. She was still barefoot and had one of the camellias behind her ear, and in that glittery evening light her grayness seemed more silvery and appealing. High makeup had erased the mortal signs I'd previously noted and poised her in that ageless moment of attractiveness that can endure for years in certain women, but only by the light of chandeliers.

"Morgan, this is Jane McCrae," I said, and Morgan extended her hand and said, "Morgan Deal," smiling somewhat dazzlingly, though with an underlying warmth, and Jane said, "I love your flower," and Morgan smoothly shifted her grasp from shake to holding and said, "this way," leading Jane to the table where she fished a dripping bloom out of the water and tucked it behind Jane's ear. "There," Morgan said, stepping back and surveying her work with a studious frown, ignoring Jane's obvious pleasure with a charming affectation of a social soldier's duty. "One for you, Adam?" Morgan asked, and I smiled and said, "I don't think so," and Morgan said, "but it would be so nice, don't you think?'' regarding Jane for corroboration, and Jane said, ''oh, A., I think you should,'' and I gave Jane a squinty look, and Morgan said, ''you're blushing, dear,'' and Jane said, ''he does that a lot, it's so cute, A.,'' and though that last part was sarcastic, or seemed that way to me, Morgan said, ''you both are, you make a perfectly lovely couple—your sweet matching blazers.''

I thought perhaps I should demur at that point, explaining that we weren't a couple, except that at that moment Jane slipped her arm through mine, apparently not bothered in the least by Morgan's misapprehension, so I let it slide and changed the subject, saying, ''Morgan, you said you were hiring waiters,'' and Morgan blinked and said, ''yes, I did,'' and I said, ''well . . .'' and Jane protested. ''A.!'' accompanying it with an elbow to the ribs, and Morgan looked at her and said, ''are you unemployed, my dear?'' and Jane made a face and nodded, and Morgan said, ''have you ever waited tables?'' and Jane made another, different face and shook her head, and I said, ''I can vouch for her character, Morgan—she goes to church and won't steal spoons,'' and Jane said, ''thanks a lot, A.,'' and cut her eyes at me, and Morgan said, with just the proper degree of conciliation on both sides, ''yes, Adam, but can she vouch for yours?'' and Jane said, ''he's a retard in certain areas, but I think his heart's in the right place,'' and Morgan, observing all this with an amused tolerant irony like it was just a lovers' spat between two eighteen-year-old kids and not without its charm, said, ''let's give it a try then, Jane, shall we? why don't you come in at one tomorrow? we'll have a chat and go over a few basics . . . now, no more business. The others are downstairs in the bar—why don't you go have a drink? Dinner will be served in half an hour.''

As soon as we got outside I turned to Jane and said, ''how am I a retard?'' and she said, ''all men are retards, honey,'' and that word—''honey''—though I knew it was generic, even condescending, the way a southern woman will sometimes use it as though talking to a child or the equivalent, still made a different, softer warmth rise up in me through the warmth of anger.

The bar was downstairs in what must have once been the servants' quarters in the early days of the Belnord when wealthy planters used to bring their families over in private boats, or, later, on the ferry. Some walls had been knocked down to create space, but the room still gave the impression of a dark smoky hole with low ceilings, the bare joists exposed and hung with fishnet. The oak floorboards were warped and grayed from flooding, the overwash of forgotten hurricanes in seasons past, and though the bar itself was a fine piece, with beveled mirrors and soft recessed lighting behind it, the place still seemed dismal and out of keeping with the elegance of the upstairs.

Faison was sitting at a large round table at the back with B.J., Reese and Ellen—Buzz was behind the bar, shooting soda into a highball glass filled with cubes. Cleanth wore a charcoal-gray blazer, white ducks and black huaraches of soft Italian leather without socks. His shirt was a simple oxford, powder-blue, yet set off with an ascot—yellow silk with small paisley commas, red and navy, and he had a monogrammed white handkerchief in his pocket folded immaculately into points the way my father had shown me just before I went away to Keane, and I noted all this because I was trying to get a read on him. He seemed more traditional that evening, though there were little touches of other worlds beyond that good-quality rough-and-tumble preppie one implied by the blazer and the shirt—the ascot for instance. A number of wealthy men on the beach might have shown up in a get-up similar to Cleanth's, but that ascot was from somewhere else, like the earring, like Cleanth's whole style, even his accent, which had occasional exotic echoes in it. I'd noticed them that afternoon, the occasional anglicism slipping in, like the way he said, "at'chually," for "actually."

Cleanth appeared to be telling a story, but the moment we walked through the door he caught my eye and smiled and called out, "A.!" across the bar, gesturing us over and getting up himself, like he'd been waiting for that moment to begin the party. I was flattered that Jane should see me valued.

"You made it after all," he said, extending his hand and giving me his full, pleased attention as he spoke, then he cut his eyes at Jane, saying back to me, "I see why you hesitated now," and I said, "Cleanth Faison, Jane McCrae," and holding out her hand Jane said, "I'm pleased to meet you, Mr. Faison," and Cleanth laughed and took it, saying, "Mr.? Jesus Christ, am I that old?" and Jane blushed and said, "I didn't mean . . ." and Cleanth said, "no, Jane, you're absolutely right—it's terminal. Just take me out in the road and shoot me, would you?" and his eyes played with her, inviting her to play as well. I could see Cleanth's appreciation of her—it wasn't lewd, there was respect in it, and as I watched Jane bloomed under that look, almost as though against her will. A fresh color suffused her cheeks and her eyes deepened even as her discomfiture increased, and it was as though, up to that moment, with me, she had only been running at three-quarters speed, but now Cleanth had released her in some way, and I was glad when Jane demurely pulled away her hand, because Cleanth had been holding it far too long, in my opinion.

"That flower is a lovely touch," Cleanth said, and Jane said, "I like your earring, too," and he fielded all the buried implication in that statement with perfect equanimity, bending it smoothly back around like a steel rod till its tip pointed back at her. "It's a camellia, isn't it?" he asked, and Jane said, "your wife gave it to me," pointedly, not retreating—none of this was lost on her—and Cleanth said, "Morgan? she's not my wife, though I did ask her once," and he reached out and touched the petals lightly and then leaned down to sniff them, and though Jane rolled her eyes at me like this was all too much, she also shivered slightly. When Cleanth drew away he looked at me with a new regard, and his expression said now he understood me better.

Introductions were made, and B.J. said to Cleanth, "so finish the story," giving Jane a cold once-over, and Cleanth said, "I doubt it would be very interesting to A. and Jane since they missed the first part of it," and B.J. said, "A. and Jane don't mind, do you?" casting a perfunctory glance at us as though not caring in the least whether we did or didn't, and Ellen turned to me, wide-eyed, and whispered confidentially, "he knows Prince Charles," and Cleanth said, "let's don't exaggerate, Ellen, I didn't say I knew him, I said I met him, once, very briefly," and Ellen said, "they played polo," and I thought, "right, Prince Charles," and glanced at Jane who didn't seem to share my skepticism.

"Well, at'chually," Cleanth said, "what I was saying, A. and Jane, was that while I was up at Oxford, ages and ages ago"—he smiled at Jane on that—"I started playing polo. We had a club, a few of us at Magdalen, and we played teams from the other colleges. One Sunday, during such a match, we'd just scored a goal, and coming up the field, I looked and standing near their goal with his hands clasped behind him like he was reviewing a parade, was the fucking Prince of Wales. There was another fellow standing off a ways, resembling Reese in his dark glasses"—Reese grinned and belched—"who must have been his detective, and, still further, a Rolls with tinted windows.

Apparently Charles was spending the weekend in the country
and had got bored and heard about our match because, you see,
he knew this fellow, Fitzroy, on the opposing team, who was a
marquess, and, of course, we stopped and paid our respects,
and Fitzroy, who was a notorious sot, hungover and falling in
his saddle, offered Charles his place, and Charles demurred at
first because he had no clothes, but we had spares and fit him,
and he went off into a copse, guarded by his detective, and came
back and played a chukker with us on Fitzroy's freshest pony.
Charles scored a goal and so did I—it was probably the high
point of my life—but we won, you see, because we had a lead
when he came in. Halfway through it started raining though—it
had been threatening all day—so that by the time we stopped we
were all drenched and spattered. When it ended we all trooped
in line to shake his hand, and when I finally got my opportunity,
trying to be gallant, I said, 'I think, Your Highness, that the rain
put you at a disadvantage,' and Charles blinked with water bead-
ing on his lashes and said—you have to remember, he was just
a boy, even younger than we were—'oh, was it raining?' ''

Cleanth paused like he'd delivered a casual jewel into our
keeping. His confidence in his own effect was perfect, and
though I didn't think the story was all that wonderful, and
wasn't sure I believed it anyway, no one else seemed to share
my doubts. ''Oh, was it raining?'' Cleanth repeated delightedly, and B.J. said, ''what happened then?'' and Cleanth
laughed and said, ''that's all there was,'' and B.J. said, ''well,
I don't get it,'' and Cleanth said, ''it's called understatement,
dear,'' cutting her bloodlessly, without any darkening in his
expression, and B.J. said, ''fuck you, Cleanth,'' and Cleanth
pouted at her, his eyes still laughing, like that only added
sauce.

As we filed upstairs, Cleanth took Jane's arm and led her to
the head of the table, seating her at his left. I had a correspond-
ing place at the other end beside Morgan. Even before the first
course came Cleanth had engaged Jane in intense private conversation. Jane had taken off her jacket and draped it across her
chair back. She listened to him with a serious face, the fingers
of both hands interlaced and resting on the table in a composed
manner. I noticed how thin and tan her arms were, and for some
reason that seemed sad and touching.

The first course, served by Ellen, who was being prepped,
was a creamy she-crab bisque tinted palely orange with roe and

with a sprig of parsley floating atop a sprinkling of grated nutmeg. "This is great," Reese said enthusiastically, blowing on his spoon before he put it in his mouth, and Cleanth eyed Morgan and said, "what do you think?" and Morgan said, "I agree with Reese," and Cleanth nodded and said to Ellen, "ask Patrick to step out here," and Ellen brought the cook, who looked like a young fey Gregory Peck, only very thin and with a bad case of distemper, and Cleanth said, "the soup is excellent, Patrick," and wiping his hands on his apron, Patrick said, "that's good, it's from a can," smiling only with his eyes in a way that made him look very devious and very cute, and I laughed when the others did, though till then I wasn't sure it was a joke, and then Patrick said, "oh, God! my asparagus!" opening his eyes wide in mock horror, ironizing his own effeminacy, and disappeared back in the kitchen.

Cleanth engaged Ellen's eyes and nodded to his wine glass, and she said, "sorry." He'd been critiquing her performance all along, never with rancor, but relentlessly. "Don't apologize," he said, "just keep them filled, and when the bottle's empty, *assume* they'll want another. When you ask, assume that in your heart. You'll sell more and make better tips, and we'll all get fat and happy," and I could see Ellen, who was very sweet, biting her lips to keep from muttering, "sorry," again as she refilled his glass with the Sauvignon Blanc. The wine, I thought, was very good, though I knew next to nothing about wine, but this had a delightful sweetness like cold crisp apples, and the red, a Pauillac, which came with the next course, was even better.

While Ellen was clearing, Cleanth excused herself, and Morgan's conversation faltered briefly as she cast what seemed a troubled glance at him. That made me look, too, and when he came back I noticed him yawning, not as though he were tired, but through his grin. His eyes were dilated, too. I suspected he was doing something, but I didn't know what.

I didn't have much time to ponder it either, because the second course was a prime rib. I tried to be discreet about not eating it, but the rare slab cooling in its pool of *jus* became increasingly obvious as the others finished. Morgan's glance flicked to my plate as she chatted, and she was in obvious difficulty about whether it would be more impolite to mention it or not to, but finally she said, with a look of concern that seemed irritatingly exaggerated in the circumstances, "I hope nothing's wrong with your meat, Adam.'' She said it softly, but the table was not that large, and, of course, everyone stopped talking and turned to stare, and I said, ''no, no, it's fine, really,'' and Cleanth said, getting in on the act, ''is it too rare for you, A.?'' and Jane said, ''A.'s a vegetarian''—announced it, more like—attempting to come to my aid, but actually putting me more deeply on the spot.

''Are you really, A.?'' Cleanth asked as though the topic interested him, and I shrugged and said, ''I'm not a purist,'' cutting a glance at Jane. Cleanth sat back in his chair and said, ''I have a hard time seeing you in hemp sandals, scrounging underneath the boughs for fallen fruit.'' He grinned and Reese and B.J. laughed. I remained unamused, still tainted with the righteousness of all recent converts to higher causes. The incident with the rabbit while tripping with Cary and Jane the previous summer had sparked my decision, and soon after returning to Keane in the fall I'd tasted animal flesh for the last time. The initiative was connected to my father, though I didn't fully see that then—the final blossom of my rejection of him. It was as though in giving up meat I was repudiating the boyhood lesson he'd taught me that September morning in the cornfield standing over the dead dove, the blood lesson I'd accepted and sanctified as mystery, but which had degenerated, at last, into something merely squalid and obscene, another moral sleight-of-hand which Clay, the Great Pretender, had deceived me with.

''You don't look like a vegetarian, A.,'' Cleanth continued, and I said, not trying to conceal my petulance, ''what does a vegetarian look like?'' and he said, ''you know how the people look in health food stores? sort of pale and splotchy like the organic fruit they sell at triple the price? Vegetarians have mild docile eyes and they don't run five-minute miles,'' and I said, ''well, this one does,'' and he said, ''do you practice TM, too?'' and I said, ''no, why?'' and he said, ''after vegetarianism, that's actually the next step—rope shoes and Eastern religion. After that there's only death and the abyss.''

Though some of the others laughed, their laughter was becoming nervous, and Morgan, said, ''Cleanth?'' and he said, ''what?'' and she said, ''may I speak to you a moment?'' clearly meaning privately, but Cleanth said, ''go ahead, we have no secrets here.'' She made a frown and he said, ''oh, I see, ground control to Major Tom—is that it? Am I getting too intense? Am I being an asshole?'' and Morgan said, ''to put it mildly,'' and

Cleanth sat back and blinked, then smiled, saying, "thank you, M.," and to the rest of us, "Morgan is my social conscience," and to me, "I'm sorry, A., I don't mean to be vehement, but this subject just happens to interest me, because, you see, I was once a vegetarian myself."

His confession was outrageous. It almost won me over. Though he seemed dangerous, he had immense charisma. "Then what made you go back to eating it?" I asked, and he said, "you really want to know?" I shrugged, and he said, "I got hungry for a burger in a place where there weren't any, so I ate something else instead," and I said, "what was that?" and Morgan said, "I don't think we want to know—can't we change the subject now?" and ignoring her, Cleanth said, "something small and warm and furry—it wasn't pussy either." B.J. smirked and Morgan said, "nice, Cleanth," and Cleanth said, "sorry, M.," and then he pulled back in his chair and said, "come with me a minute, A.," and Morgan said, "don't overdo it, Cleanth," and as he passed her chair, Cleanth said, "there's no such thing," and before she could answer, he bent and kissed her cheek and said, "go ahead and serve dessert, we'll be back shortly," and I got up and followed him.

On the porch Cleanth leaned back against the rail and lit a cigarette, the first I'd seen him smoke. He offered one to me but I declined, and then he said, "so, A.," and raised his chin and sighed his smoke out toward the rafters, leaving that to hang there like it was some sort of statement in itself, and I said, "so," and he smiled and said, "I suppose you want to know why I asked you out here," and I said, "I assume we're going to do some drugs, correct?" and he laughed appreciatively though I hadn't really meant it as a joke, and he said, "would you like to?" and I said, "what the hey, Cleanth," and he said, "that's not the real reason though," and I said, "so what's the real reason?" and he said, "you don't know?" and I said, "listen, Cleanth, don't take this wrong, but you aren't gay, are you? Not that I mind, it's just . . ." and he cut me off and said, "no, A., that's all right, I appreciate directness, and you can set your mind at rest—I'm not," and I said, "I didn't really think you were," and he took a puff and said, "are you?" and I said, "me?" and he laughed and said, "I see, it's inconceivable for you, but not for me," and I said, "I didn't mean that," and he said, "you were just checking," and I said, "right."

"At'chually," he said, "if you want to know, I tried it once."

I didn't want to know, but he went on. "It was years ago and it didn't go very far. It was at Oxford and the attitude was somewhat different there," and I said, "when were you at Oxford?" trying to change the subject, but he said, "I got a Rhodes right out of Keane. I had a friend named Perry, who turned me on to polo. He wasn't effeminate, though most English men of his class have a preciseness that smacks of it, which is why they don't produce too many matinee idols, but Perry was openly homosexual, and it didn't bother me in the least. He talked about it sometimes, and I think it caused him anguish, but never in reference to me, and we got to be quite close. I'd been seeing a girl in London for a couple of years, the daughter of a publisher, but she fell in love with one of her father's authors, and I found out about it second-hand, so it wasn't very nice and I was pretty broken up about it.

"When Perry heard, he appeared in my rooms one night with a bottle of malt whiskey, and we proceeded to get stinking drunk and I cried and called her every foul name I could think of, and Perry let on that he'd never really liked her and had had a feeling it would turn out as it had, and at some point in the evening—I still can't remember exactly how it happened—Perry confessed he was in love with me and had been for some time, and I can't tell you how stunned I was, aside from being shitfaced, because, you see, I cared for him, and that made a difference, it wasn't an abstract thing that I could sneer at, he was my friend. And I can't tell you why, A.—the alcohol was part of it, and I suppose my male ego had taken a hard hit and was languishing, maybe I was punishing myself—but I went to bed with him. I stripped and crawled into the sheets, and so help me God, I didn't even know what we were going to do, but when Perry appeared from the bathroom, naked, with a tube of jelly and a bouncing erection, it grew clearer and I started having second thoughts. That's putting it mildly. What I at'chually felt was more akin to primal terror, and I felt this mad impulse to laugh hysterically. Thank God, I didn't, I simply said, 'I'm not sure I can go through with this, Perry,' and he said, 'let me help you,' and he crawled in bed beside me and began to knead my penis, but nothing happened. I even let him kiss me, but it was gruesome, I can't even describe it, like French-kissing a horse, which made me wonder what women see in it and speculate that their pleasure must be entirely different, geared to something larger.

"All these thoughts as I was lying there with Perry working

me with an expression that was becoming increasingly cha-
grined. Finally I took his hand and removed it from my privates
and said, 'I don't think so, Perry, I'm sorry,' and he said, 'not
at all, of course, I should have kept my mouth shut,' and I said,
'no, Perry, I'm glad you told me,' and he nodded, his chin
trembling and an expression of black despair on his face, and
then he sat up on the edge of the bed and buried his face in his
hands, and I didn't know what to do for him, so I did nothing,
and finally he got up and dressed and on the way out I said, 'no
hard feelings?' and he said, 'none whatsoever,' but he didn't
look me in the face, and I held absolutely no grudge against
him, A., nor Perry, I think, against me, we still spoke and
played together, but our friendship ended there as absolutely as
if one or both of us had died,'' and I said, "I'm sorry, Cleanth,"
and he said, "so am I," and I said, "but I'm not sure why
you're telling me all this," and he said, "number one, because
you asked if I was gay, and I wanted to allay your fears on that.
Number two, because I want you to know me—I think you're
capable of it. And, number three, to demonstrate the fact that
there's a love that sometimes happens between men who are
great friends that's very powerful and easily confused with sex,
but the moment it gets personal it's destroyed. Sex is just the
most obvious way it can get personal, but there are many others.'' He threw down his cigarette and crushed it underfoot,
then looked back up and said, "are you still with me?" and I
said, "yeah, I am—what about those drugs?" and he grinned
and said, "my thoughts exactly," and he ambled down the stairs,
pausing at the bottom for me to join him.

He turned under toward the bar, only we didn't go there. We
turned right instead on a plank walkway covering the bare sand
that ran in the open corridor beneath the porch, stopping outside
a door that said, "Gentlemen." Cleanth looked at me like I'd
appreciate the irony and pushed it open, inviting me to precede
him. The bathroom was small and smelled like ancient piss and
ancient clorinated antiseptic. A bare bulb hung from a cord
overhead and when Cleanth pulled it on I saw a rust-stained sink
with a dripping cold water tap, a small toilet and a stained green
carpet. Cleanth hooked the latch in the eye on the door-frame,
then took the mirror down and laid it across the sink. I still
didn't know what he was doing, because I hadn't learned about
cocaine and mirrors then, the way they go together, not just on
the surface, but every other way, so it was only when Cleanth

reached into the side pocket of his jacket and took out a glass vial about the size of a .410 shell with a plastic stopper in the end of it, that I finally realized what was happening.

I'd done coke only once before, bad stuff a friend of mine had copped off the street in Harvard Square, which had no discernible effect except that I'd woken up the next morning with something like dried airplane glue caked in my nostrils and got a nosebleed later in the day when I was running. Cleanth tapped a large thimbleful onto the mirror, then reached in his coat pocket and produced his wallet, slipping out a gold American Express card, which he used to chop and groom the powder before streaking it into lines, six big ones, his hands as quick and fluent as a croupier's. He rolled a crisp fifty with a dour U.S. Grant on it into a snorting tube and offered it to me, his eyebrows arched inquisitively.

"Go ahead," I told him, excited but nervous, remembering the last time, and he bent over cleanly snorting up a line. Then he stood up and raised his chin, the bill still in his nose, tapping the end of it and continuing to sniff until he'd got it all. "Have you done coke before?" he asked, and I said, "just once, it isn't really in my price range," and he said, "that's right, you're still in your hundred dollar days, aren't you?" and I said, "try ten," and he laughed and said, "don't make me remember," and I said, "or maybe even one," and he said, "now *that's* scary," and I laughed, and he said, "try this," and handed me the tube, ends reversed, and as he did he closed his eyes like he was concentrating on something, and he said, "here it comes," and when he opened them again they were filled with a confidence as crystalline and brilliant as an autumn sky, but also a liquid trace of understanding softness, and the grin opened like a flower across his white teeth, which made its etiology clearer, along with certain other things.

I was wild to try it by that time, because it was like there was an invisible glass wall separating us and Cleanth was on the other side, radiating gorgeous benefit and beckoning me to come and share it with him, so I leaned down into my own reflection and vacuumed up a line of magic dust, then stood up blinking and sniffing, imitating him, pressing first one nostril then the other, and Cleanth watched me, pleasantly interested, and after a few seconds I felt it kick into my bloodstream like the breakdown in a bluegrass tune, "The Orange Blossom Special," where the picking shifts into a higher gear. I made a clanging stroke on my own imaginary guitar, and Cleanth widened his eyes then nodded, holding up a finger like he was starting a charade. Licking an imaginary reed, he suddenly bent double, blowing an imaginary riff on an imaginary saxophone, his cheeks puffed out until the veins stood on his forehead, and I laughed so hard I almost cried, it was just too perfect. By that point I felt like I'd known him my whole life, a particular friend of mine, and I said, "you're all right, man," and he said, "a little toot does wonders," which was the first time I heard that expression, and he squinched his eyes and squealed another note, and I said, "this stuff ain't like the other stuff," and he said, "just wait, the next stuff ain't like this—do another," and I said, "oh, yeah," and did, and he said, "*oooh*, yeah," and he did, too.

"You know what you just reminded me of?" I asked, and he said, "what?" and I said, "I had this friend at Keane, a Jewish guy named Eric from New York, and he turned me on to jazz—Miles Davis, Ornette Coleman, Coltrane, Rahsaan Roland Kirk," and Cleanth said, "Rahsaan Roland Kirk?" and I said, "yeah, he plays a nose flute," and Cleanth said, "oh, yeah," and I laughed and said, "sometimes we'd smoke hash in his room and put on records, and we'd catch something together in the music and jump and shout and slap five, but occasionally I'd open my eyes and find him grinning at me, and he'd say, 'you missed one, man,' and I'd say, 'no, man, I'm just waiting for it to come back around the other side,' and he'd laugh and nod and say, 'yeah, but it slipped on by the first time,' and I'd say, 'that's because it was a slipknot,' and he'd say, 'true, but slip not is a better rule of play,' and I'd say, 'true, but play not is a rule that leads to slippage,' and we'd go on like that for twenty minutes, half an hour. Each line was like a sword thrust, and we'd be getting down to the deepest shit in each other's personalities, laughing and bleeding and panting to keep up, and the only way to parry was with effective offense, but it wasn't personal, it felt good to do it, like exercise, only mental, which is why I sort of understand what you meant before. We called it Interstellar Chess, I can't tell you why."

"You want to play a game?" Cleanth asked, and I said, "right now?" and he said, "why not?" and I said, "okay, sure—what kind of game?" and he said, "it's similar to poker," and I said, "get the cards," and he said, "it isn't played with cards," and grinned, and I said, "what's it played with?" and he said, "intelligence, cunning, stamina, bravado, heart—everything you've got," and I said, "that sounds pretty heavy, Cleanth," and he said, "it is, heavier than lead, but also lighter than a feather—it all depends on how you play," and I said, "so how does this game go?" and he said, "there aren't any rules, no formal ones, at least, but there's a code," and I said, "tell me," and he said, "first, you can't turn down an initiative, you have to respond when play is made," and I said, "okay," and he said, "second, you can lie, but you have to do it honestly; third, you have to be able to lose without defeat or failure and win without complacency; fourth, you can't leave the game until it's finished, and it's never finished; fifth, and last, and most important, you can't take it personally."

Beginning to catch on, I said, "this game sounds familiar, Cleanth," and he said, "it is—it's a lot like life, but there's a difference," and I said, "what?" and he said, "playing, A., just playing—that's the difference that makes all the difference. If you take it seriously, you're lost," and I said, "where did you come up with all this shit, man?" and he shrugged and said, "there was just a period in my life when I had a lot of time to think—a long vacation, you might say—and many things came clear, this being one of them," and because of something in his voice and eyes, I said, "what kind of long vacation?" and he said, "that's your move?" and I said, "are we playing?" and he said, "as far as I'm concerned, we've been playing since we met—before that, at'chually. This game started a long time ago. Whether we go on is up to you," and I said, "can I ask you something first?" and he said, "anything," and I said, "what do you call this game?" and he said, "it doesn't have a name, but we can give it one—what would you suggest?" and I said, "why not Interstellar Chess?" and he pursed his lips dismissively and said, "too vegetarian," and I said, "what's your suggestion then?" and he said, "we could call it Dharma Combat, but that's been used—how about Life Poker?" and I shrugged and said, "suits me," and he said, "you're in?"

"I'm in," I said, "what kind of long vacation?" and he said, "the four-year kind the government provides for free in a resort they call Fort Leavenworth—you ever heard of Leavenworth, A.?" and I said, "I thought that was a prison," and he said, "then you thought right, it's a federal pen but it's on the Army reservation out in Kansas, and that's where the Alma Mater sends you when you fuck up really bad.'' I stared at him with sudden fear as the stakes went through the roof, and Cleanth just grinned and said, ''you like this game so far?'' and, not knowing what else to ask, I just said, ''you were in the Army?'' and he said, ''don't slow down on me, A.,'' and I said, ''Vietnam?'' and he said, ''*oh*, yeah, two tours, I was a first lieutenant in a line platoon with the Americal, Alpha Company, first battalion of the 504th,'' and I said, ''why were you in prison?'' and he said, ''because I killed one of my men,'' and I said, ''Jesus Christ,'' and he said, ''no, Meyer Prosky, PFC, a Jewish guy from Brooklyn,'' and I said, ''why?'' and he said, ''because he asked me to . . . It's my turn now, correct?''

''Shouldn't we be getting back?'' I asked nervously, and Cleanth just laughed and said, ''why? if they want us they can come down here and get us. The only reason they'd miss us anyway is because they'll know we're doing something far more interesting than they are and they'll want to get their greedy fingers in it. They'll get their turns later, for now it's mine,'' and seeing he wasn't going to let me off, I said, ''okay, shoot,'' and he said, '' 'shoot'—that's good, A., if we were keeping score you'd get some points for that. So what's the real reason you stopped eating meat?'' and I said, ''it isn't all that interesting,'' and he said, ''so make it interesting,'' and I said, ''you want me to lie?'' and he said, ''only if you have to and if you think you can pull it off without my catching you. Take your time, do another line.''

About the time we hit I started getting cocaine vertigo—my first experience of it—the feeling of being on a swinging rope bridge in the dark over an abyss, too paralyzed to move, just clutching for dear life to something that won't hold still, listening to the roar below you and to the creak and groan of straining hemp. I looked at Cleanth and said, ''I feel like anything I say, man, is something you're already going to know,'' and he said, ''maybe I do, A., I probably know a whole lot more about you than you think I do, but I expect you've got a few surprises, otherwise I wouldn't be here. I like to be surprised,'' and I said, ''but it's weird, man, you're spooking me—*how* do you know?'' and he said, ''I knew you the first minute I saw you, A., when you cut through us on the beach this afternoon. It was like looking in my own reflection in a mirror, only from twenty years ago. When you ran between us, I could see that you were strong and driven, but driven not by something that you loved but something you hated and were making war against. You ran from fear, not joy, like a whipped horse, and you were so extremely isolated, so out of touch with other people, though not insensitive—that's why you cut across our space, but then said, 'sorry'—and you were proud, but of the wrong things. You held to your own line at any cost and didn't deviate, even when it made you miserable, and I think it makes you miserable a lot.'' I was staring at him, speechless, with something like awe.

"That's what I saw, A., part of it," he went on, "I also saw every mistake I've made in the last twenty years, and how you'd probably make them too, and I had knowledge but it was too late to change the past, and you had none, but all the opportunity, and I thought if the two of those could come together it might form the basis of a friendship, or at least a decent game of Life Poker,'' and I said, ''stop it, man, just cut it out, okay?'' He just grinned, and I said, ''why, Cleanth? that's what I don't get—why me? why pick me? why would you want to do it?'' and he said, "why not is a better question. That's the difference between where you are now, A., and where I am. You ask why, I ask why not, and it's the difference between living life as hard labor and living life as play. Because I'll tell you, A., while I was in the big house counting squares of light and dark through a barred window—which was my life, A., four years of it that were taken from me for a thing I still don't believe was wrong—I realized playing, the good kind, which is also sometimes evil, is the only thing that matters. The *only* thing. The rest of it is all just fear and holding on to something that, once you're in the water, doesn't float. So tell me now why you stopped eating meat.''

"Okay, man," I said, "I have this friend named Cary and we were tripping last summer—Jane was there. We found this rabbit with a broken leg and I thought we should just put it out, but Cary didn't. We got in an argument about it. See, ever since we were kids Cary and I had this disagreement about hunting— it was the only thing. But anyway, Cary handed me this stick and said, 'then go ahead, A., just go ahead,' and I started to but then I couldn't, I can't tell you why. Well, after that I just started thinking. Every time I'd eat a burger or whatever I'd think about the cow. I mean, the burger was a cow that died, and there was this long chain that started with this cow just cowing around— eating grass, having calves, giving milk, all that stuff cows do— and then went to the stockyard where somebody put it down and proceeded to the grocery store where it was just some red stuff in a Styrofoam container with Saran Wrap on the outside and finally ended on my plate, and I guess all this is obvious, but I never saw it before, I knew it in my head, but I didn't *feel* it,'' and he said, ''feel what?'' and I said, ''that I was the last link in the chain and the real reason the cow died was for *me*, so I could eat it. I was just as responsible as the guy who swung the ax—more—because to him it was just a job he got a wage for, but I got the real benefit, and I just decided other people can do what they want, but for me, no more, enough, just let the cows roam free, and you can laugh, go on, I don't care''—he was laughing—''but if you can't kill it, you don't have a right to eat it, because you kill it anyway, and if you can take responsibility for that, fine, eat away and welcome to it, but if you can't, or don't, or won't, then it's sick and evil and just plain fucking wrong.''

''You're joking, right?'' Cleanth asked, and I said, ''do I look like I'm joking, man?'' and he said, ''sorry, don't take it personally,'' and I said, ''but I do, man, it is personal to me,'' and he said, ''maybe that's your problem?'' and I said, ''so what's wrong with it, Cleanth? what's wrong with what I said?'' and he said, ''that's your second move?'' and I said, ''let's just get real here a minute and quit playing games—answer my question,'' and he said, ''that's the whole point, A., keeping it a game even after it gets real,'' and I said, ''all right then, have it your way, that's my move.''

''Okay then,'' he said, ''answer me something—you said you hunted?'' and I said, ''*used* to,'' and he said, ''a lot?'' and I shrugged and said, ''a fair amount . . . no, hell, a lot,'' and he said, ''and did you like it when you did it?'' and I said, ''I thought I did,'' and he said, ''what changed your mind?'' and I said, ''I guess I grew up or evolved—the rabbit set it off,'' and he said, ''and that one time with the rabbit outweighed all the other times before when you'd hunted and enjoyed it, or been moved by it, or felt the mystery of it, or whatever it is you feel, or anybody feels, when they go in the woods and do it?'' and I said, ''yeah, Cleanth, yeah, it really did.''

He just shook his head and said, ''you know what I think, A.,?'' and I said, ''what?'' and he said, ''I think you confused a temporary failure of nerve with a philosophical conversion, I think you trashed something that enhanced you for something that diminished you. I think you deviated from your line, A., and it puts something in perspective for me," and I said, "I think you're wrong, Cleanth." His eyes never flickered—they smiled with the confidence of perfect certainty. "Life is taking, A.," he said, "that's the natural order of things—life taking life to sustain life. Vegetarians do it, too, and you can pretend there's a difference, you can draw the line between plants and animals and pretend you're innocent and 'natural,' but no one's innocent, everything alive has got to kill to live or pay for killing to be done. That's what nature is and it's not always clean and pretty, but there's no other way, and a vegetarian is the most unnatural thing alive because the mess upsets his tummy and he doesn't want to play. The pathetic thing is he thinks he's acting for life when really he's against it. Really, what he does is an insult in the face of life.

"You gave your reasons for quitting, A., and they weren't bad as reasons go, but let me tell you the real reason, let me tell you the real reason why you quit and why I quit and why everybody quits. It's because they feel they don't *deserve* it, A., they don't feel they deserve to live at the expense of something else that has to die. A vegetarian just wants to slide by munching vegetables and lettuce and pretend it isn't happening and that he's not a part of it and keep his eyes closed till it's over, but that's not life, it's just a coma, you might as well *be* a vegetable, so why not just quit cowering and whining and stand up and take it like a man, like a fucking *human being*?

"You should have been in Vietnam, A. I saw men drop like flies, I saw them die like frightened cattle lowing at the slaughter, shitting in their pants. I saw a whole platoon wiped out in one night, fifteen minutes, my own men, eighty percent casualties, five of us walked out of there, and Meyer Prosky wasn't with us, he took the big hit from the frag. I was twenty feet away and it still almost took my leg off, it would have killed me if it hadn't hit him first. I was standing there, A., I'd just stopped, thinking, 'oh, shit, no,' when I heard the Claymore, like some weird fucking night bird, thinking, 'this is not the music to go out on,' and Jackie Esposito, a nineteen-year-old Italian kid from Astoria, Queens, who was point, just evaporated in a big pink blush. One minute he was standing there staring at his feet like he'd just found a quarter, and the next minute he was gone, no trace. That's when the frag got Meyer, and the lights came on. I went down and rounds came flying from the trees, I mean, they stirred a wind, I could feel it fluttering my fatigues, but it was funny because I couldn't feel my leg, but I could see it, split wide open, the muscles quivering and twitching, and the medic crouching over it packing it and putting on a battle dressing. I said, 'tell me the bad news,' and he said, 'it missed the femoral, don't dance on it,' and he grinned at me and said, 'you want a shot?' and I said, 'go,' but he was gone already.

"I just lay there for a second trying to decide exactly how I felt—calm, desperate, no pressure, the fear was gone. I was alive—that was enough. And it was so fucking loud, A., you couldn't hear yourself think, but it was like that loudness was somewhere way up in the trees, and underneath it, closer to the ground, I heard someone moaning. The reason I could hear it was because it was so soft. It was Prosky, and I crawled over to him. He was lying on his back and his eyes were closed. He looked so peaceful, like he was napping, or like a young boy laid out in his coffin with his hair just combed. He didn't seem that bad at first, but when I looked down one boot was smoking and the other boot was gone, his right arm was severed just below the elbow, but there was hope until I lifted up his shirt and half his guts came boiling out. I don't know how he was even conscious, but he was, he opened his eyes and watched it—he had these sad thoughtful eyes—and then he looked at me and said, 'bad chukker, LT.'

"They used to rag me about that, A., all this polo shit—bad chukker, good chukker, wot, old man? tally ho and bloody hell, they used to call each other Chuck instead of Jack, like, fuck off, Chuck, this Hershey bar is mine, and the Cong were woodchucks, and there were bad chuck woods, which is what we walked into that night. 'Bad chukker, LT,' Meyer said, 'I'm gone,' and I said, 'no, you aren't, you're going to make it—that's an order, private,' and he said, 'don't make me laugh, it hurts too much,' and I said, 'shut up then,' and he closed his eyes, and I said, 'hang tight, Meyer, there're Hueys coming in, I can hear them now,' and he pressed his lips together—it was almost prim—because he knew there were no choppers. It was solid jungle in there, wall to wall, then Meyer's eyes sprang open like a windowshade and they were just inconceivable, like ice with a black river running underneath it. He was staring up at something overhead, and he said, 'see that? see that?' and I said, 'there's nothing there,' and he said, 'oh, God, oh, God,' and I said, 'hold on, son,' and he looked right in my eyes and said, 'do me, Uncle,' and I said, 'I can't, Meyer,' and he said, 'you got to, Uncle. I don't want this, put me out, I'm begging you,' and then he started whimpering like a dog that's been run over in the road, he couldn't have lasted five more minutes, probably less, but I didn't think of that, I didn't think of anything, I just took my .45 out of my holster, put the barrel in his ear and pulled the trigger, and Meyer Prosky went away.

"That's my rabbit story, A., I told the same one to the panel in Fort Benning, the same place I went to OCS, the same place I did Airborne and went to Ranger school, four guys like me, all officers, every one of them had been in-country, they all knew, and they didn't want to do it but they didn't have a choice. The press had it by then, so I got Leavenworth, and nobody ever fucked me in the ass. The bull queers knew I was a Ranger so they stayed away. I made damn sure they knew. The only guy who ever fucked me in the ass was Duvall Lansing, a black dude from Athens, Georgia. He was my sergeant, one of the four other guys who walked out of that ambush, a twenty-year career man who could have been pushing papers in some cushy post, only Duvall liked it, but he didn't like me, and you know why?

"I'll tell you what he told me. We'd finally stumbled out into a clearing and called the Hueys in. I was sitting back against the wall finishing a cigarette, and Duvall turned to me and said, 'I saw you do it, boss man,' and I said, 'and you know why,' and he said, 'I know why—no rank?' and I said, 'no rank,' and he said, 'but I still hope they fry your motha' fockin' ass,' and I said, 'do what you have to do, Duvall, I know you never liked me,' and he said, 'it ain't you personally, boss, I just never liked that fockin' earring.' "

Cleanth pinched his earlobe and turned it toward me and said, "see this?" and I said, "yeah," and he said, "that's why I went to prison, A., because Duvall Lansing didn't like my earring," and Cleanth laughed and said, "it wasn't personal. And you want to know something funny, A.? The whole time I was in-country, nineteen months and sixteen days, I didn't touch meat once. I killed men, but my diet was strictly vegetarian, I didn't even touch an egg. Not in the hospital in Saigon, not through the court-martial at Fort Benning, but only when I got to prison.

"There was this rat, an evil fucker, who crawled up through the chase pipes every night. He'd sit there on the bowl rim on his haunches with his little paws tucked in just grinning at me. I'd throw a shoe or something else at him and he'd just duck. Finally I decided I was going to get him. I'd talk to this rat, A., I'd say,

'I'm going to eat you, fucker, I'm going to drink your blood,' and he'd just grin. I tried a dozen different traps, but nothing worked till finally I hit on this trap door. I made it from a piece of cardboard and ran it off the toilet. I'd put a gob of peanut butter on it which I brought on my finger from the mess. I just lay there on my bed and let him get it two nights running, but the third night I pulled the string and he dropped in the pillowcase. I was a happy man, A.,—it was pathetic, but that's just where I was—I felt my instincts rise, and I reached down and grabbed the pillowcase where it was struggling and thrashing, and I just squeezed, and I felt something coming through my hands, A., something clicked for me. That rat was biting me right through the cloth, my hands were bleeding and it hurt, but that wasn't it. I felt life coming into me like an electric current, the weird voltage of a dying rat. Something in my head was going, 'Cleanth, you've finally lost it, babe, this is perverse,' but that voice kept getting smaller, and it didn't feel perverse, I was calm, I didn't hate the rat, I felt no lust or wantonness, it was the thing that happens in the woods. I didn't really eat that rat, I flushed it down the toilet and then I washed my hands, but before I did, I stared down at the blood on them—some of it was mine, some wasn't—and I licked it, just to see. It didn't feel like much, but the next day I started eating meat again, and that's when things started changing. I started getting myself back and feeling like a man again.

"Life's a strange bundle, A. I shot Meyer Prosky, Duvall Lansing didn't like my earring, the Army sent me to Fort Leavenworth, I killed a rat and started the Big Change, and here I am tonight, a player, telling you the story, and the moral is, the difference between a player and a vegetarian is a player sees it clearly, there isn't any choice, it's just one way, and you can either do what life demands and like it or you can do it and despise it, but you've got to do it either way, the only choice is attitude. That's my move, A., I made it a long time ago. What's yours?"

"Listen, Cleanth," I said, "I appreciate you telling me all this, it's interesting, hell, it's amazing, I don't know if you're lying or what and I don't really care, but what's the point of it? Because you shot some guy in Vietnam and went to prison I should start eating meat again?" and he just laughed and said, "oh, man, oh, A., oh, baby, are you listening, or am I just talking to myself?" and I said, "what? just what, man?" and he said, "listen, A., I've got an idea, let's go hunting sometime, that way you can see it for yourself—you wouldn't even have to shoot," and I said, "is that it, Cleanth? is that the answer—hunting? that's going to solve my problems? right, man, sure, just grab a gun, head for the woods and shoot down everything that moves. Hell, get happy, blow the fucking world apart," and he said, "you're not paying attention, A., I told you once, it's not hunting, it's not vegetarianism, it's what they stand for, it's the things behind them. There are just two ways to live and two types of people living them. There are those who love life and accept it as it is, and there are those who are afraid of it and close their eyes and want to be off someplace else. I call the first way playing, it's the path of comedy, the second is the tragic path. And it's all so sad and boring, really, isn't it?—another angry angsted-out Timon shaking his fists at a dead sky? Does that seem great to you, A.? Is that what you want to be? I don't think so. And the thing that really gives me hope for you is Jane."

He smiled and I felt this weird thing crawling in my stomach, and I said, "Jane?" and he said, "you're very lucky, A." I didn't want to tell him, but I had to—that lie would have burned a hole inside me—and, besides, I knew he'd find out anyway, so I said, "I think you've got the wrong idea, Cleanth." He was leaning over the mirror doing one last line, but he stopped half-way through when I said that and raised his head. "Oh?" he said, and I shook my head and said, "there's nothing between me and Jane, she's Cary's girlfriend," and Cleanth blinked, then bent back down and finished it. I think maybe that was the one thing I said all night that surprised him, and, as Cleanth said, he liked surprises. He had another one in store for me.

Five

A.

We'd been down there in that bathroom for two hours and probably done two grams, and I'd gone from wondering about Cleanth, to actively distrusting him, to loving him, to hating him, and thence back all the way around again to wondering distrust, or distrustful wonder—something. Whatever it was, the game was on, and I was definitely playing. Of course, I thought I could still pull out at any time, but then I was eighteen and didn't know myself that well. Cleanth definitely extended my education.

Back in the ballroom, Reese was spinning soul tunes back behind the bar and coming out to shag with Ellen. He moved well for a big guy, and she was awkward as a cow, but pretty, flushed and working hard, obviously enjoying herself. Buzz and B.J. were in a different universe, two different universes, dancing alone together. Buzz was in some modern dance routine a little like the swim but with some surfing moves thrown in, and B.J. was just standing there, hardly moving, snapping her fingers and doing a little something in the hips and shoulders. She was looking down at her body, checking herself out, making sure the curves looked right and nothing too extreme. B.J. was very cool. B.J. was frosty.

Jane and Morgan were sitting at the cleared table chatting and watching. They looked over at our entrance, and Cleanth said, "you brought down the stereo, good idea," and Morgan said, "jolly," and Cleanth said, "were we rude?" and pouted, and

Morgan pouted back and said, "very," and Cleanth said, "it was all A.'s fault"—he looked at me—"you shouldn't be so interesting," and, despite myself, I think I beamed. Jane looked at me like, do I know you?, and Cleanth said, "you want to dance with an old guy?" and she said, "sure," and looked at me like I deserved it. That was a confusing look. There was a lot of confusion going on—that much was clear.

So I sat down with Morgan and she looked at me like, I know it's not your fault, and I'm your hostess and I shouldn't blame you, and I don't, not totally, but, well, yes . . . "I apologize, Morgan," I said, "we just got to talking," and she said, "you must have found a lot to talk about," and she reached out and smudged away a few stray grains of snow still clinging to my nose, and I started to say something, but she said, "don't bother, I know all about it," and I said, "sorry," and she said, "why? I'm not his mother, even if he acts like it at times," and she stared out at the dancers.

Cleanth had just stripped off his jacket, and she said, "God help us, the monster is abroad, you'd better leave now, A., while there's still time, and take Jane with you, or else I hope you brought your bathing suit, because I can promise you we'll all still be right here tomorrow morning when the sun comes up, and it will probably turn us into ashes," and I said, "he plays hard," and she said, "tell me," and I said, "he does this often?" and she said, "no, he rarely binges, he needs encouragement to bring out his best tricks," and underneath the coyness, underneath the surface humor, there was something else—not just concern, but hurt. "You and Cleanth aren't . . ." I said, and she said, "no, we're not—not married, not anything, not anymore," and I said, timidly, "but you were . . . something?" and Morgan turned her head toward me and said, "well, you've got stones, A., I'll give you that, I like that in a man"—her eyes emerged briefly from their inward trance and looked at me with a different quality of directness that I found disconcerting. Then it passed, and she said, "yes, there was a time."

She sighed and rolled her eyes at me, and said, "now aren't I fun?"—a coy, but sweet apology—"I'm just a barrel of laughs. He's really not that bad, A., and if he misbehaves too badly there's always the straitjacket in the attic. Come on, let's dance," and she reached out and took my hand, and I said, "I'm not much on dancing, Morgan," and she said, "oh—well, would you like to learn?" and I said, "I'm not sure I can stand up straight, much less dance,'' grinning sheepishly, and she said, ''it'll do you good to break a sweat—come on, we'll make them jealous,'' and seeing she wasn't going to take no for an answer, I reluctantly followed her onto the floor.

The music was getting increasingly beach, and prime—''with this ring I promise, I'll awwaze love ya, aww-waze luv yuh-uh.'' Taking my hands in both of hers, Morgan stepped in smiling, touching her right shoulder to mine, then back out, then in again, left to left, the basic shag step—that much I knew. Only when Morgan backed away her feet kept moving, some smooth practiced little step that looked so easy when she did it, but I couldn't follow it, I couldn't break it down, I just went back and forth and in and out, like London Bridge, and that made me remember how one time in seventh grade when I was just starting to get really interested in girls and going to little parties in the playrooms and basements of my friends' houses, I'd asked Mama to teach me how to shag. She wasn't sick then, nothing bad had happened, and she'd looked surprised when I asked her, then she smiled like oh what fun, and we put on a record, and I had felt so nervous, I don't know why.

Mama took both my hands like Morgan and she made that same little step when she went out, and I just went back and forth like London Bridge, and Mama's eyes were happy and a little teasing, she pressed her teeth down on her bottom lip and squinched her eyebrows down like she was really getting into it, and she said, ''don't march, baby, *dance*!'' and she let go one hand and stepped back still holding the other and she showed me how that step went, twisting her feet side to side and then a little outkick, but she didn't really show me, she just did it, she was dancing, having fun, and I wanted her to show me how, to break it down for me, but she didn't understand, for her it was as natural as breathing, so halfway through the song I just said, ''that's okay, Mama,'' and she looked surprised again, and I walked away and left the record playing and never learned to shag because I was ashamed to ask someone to teach me how that little step went.

At Keane nobody did the shag, they danced like Buzz and B.J., alone together, freestyle, and I was pretty good at that, but I always missed the other thing, it hurt me that I didn't know, and dance floors always brought out this tense, unhappy thing in me that made me dull and leaden when I knew I really wasn't, deep inside I wasn't. Morgan was kind and undemanding and didn't press me forward to the spins and whirls and complicated loop-the-loops the partners do still holding hands, but still, not two minutes into it, I said, "I think I better sit down, Morgan, I feel a little dizzy," and she didn't even know, she gave me an arch look and said, "too much toot," and I was glad she didn't know.

What made it worse was that Cleanth and Jane were really getting into it, they both knew that little step and all the hard stuff, too. They were spinning furiously, Cleanth was starting to sweat through his shirt and Jane was flushed and laughing. She was warming up to him, I could see it all so clearly. Jane was happy, and I sat there brooding, drinking too much beer, resenting her for it. I didn't want her to be happy, not that way, and I felt like a slug, a criminal, for grudging her her fun. But how could I blame her? I was half in love with Cleanth myself, though I didn't trust him as far as I could shotput a grizzly bear. I blamed her anyway—because of Cary. That was why—that's what I told myself. I thought about him back in Killdeer, having no fun, dealing with T.O., trying the best way he knew how to hold together a bad situation, I thought about how much he loved her, how he was probably thinking about her now, that very minute, and I felt Jane was just a fickle bitch who didn't appreciate him and wasn't worthy of him, and I felt justified in being angry. Because of Cary.

Jane and Cleanth danced for nine straight songs—I counted—and Morgan must have sensed the downturn in my mood and put her own interpretation on it. We chatted for a while, then I fell silent—I couldn't fake it, though I wanted to—and finally she got up and danced with Reese. She danced with Buzz, she danced with Ellen, she danced all by herself, leaving me alone with B.J. at the table, two brooders. "Good party, huh?" B.J. said, giving me a knowing look, and I said, "yeah, it's great," and she said, "why aren't you dancing?" and I said, "I don't feel like it," and she said, "well, excu-ooze me," and I said, "sorry," realizing it wasn't necessary to be rude to her, and she said, "so—did you and Cleanth have fun downstairs?" She sniffed pointedly, and I just stared at her, not so far gone I wanted to join her club, and she said, "don't trust him, A., don't believe a word he says, he's a liar and a snake," and I said, "what makes you say that?" and she said, "believe me, I just know, take my word for it," and she stared out at Jane like the Sultana examining a fresh young consort, hating her but taking solace from knowing how the deal would go, and she said, "you better make your move, A., you better make it soon," and she got up and left. But I didn't make a move. I didn't even know what move to make.

Then Reese put on a slow song—the Righteous Brothers, "You've Lost That Lovin' Feeling," whoa-oh—and Jane asked me to dance. My heart leapt up, and I said, "no." I had a point to make. I had my pride. My heart dropped back into the mud where it had been created. Jane looked surprised. Then she got it. "Come on, A.," she said, "it's easy." She thought she got it. "I know how to slow dance, Jane, though thanks for your concern," I said. She looked surprised again. She was so fucking innocent I hated her. This whole thing was her fault, but, of course, it would end up being mine, and I'd get to feel guilty on top of being mad and miserable—I knew the way that went— and Jane just looked at me like, what whole thing? There was a lot of subtext flying, eye to eye. I hated her. I didn't like her. The girl just had some major problems I was not sure I could afford to take on at that time, and she said, "what's the problem then?" and I glared at her like y-o-u, and she said, "quit feeling sorry for yourself and get off your lazy butt and dance with me," and she absolutely wrenched me from my chair with strength I found surprising in one so young and small. "You're such a retard, A.," she said, smiling up into my eyes before she put her arms around me and laid her head against my chest. Still I didn't move.

I looked down at her hair and smelled it—a trace of perfume, a trace of shampooed cleanness, a trace of human oils. Flocks of sleeping birds woke up inside me, ruffling their feathers, cooing, taking off into the air. Where they were going no one knew, me least of all.

Then we danced. I dissolved upward on that current of warm human-scented steam her hair exhaled, like the delightful cloud that rises from the lifted bell in some great restaurant you can afford to go to only once. My heart leapt up into the sky where it aspired to stay forever, and it might have, if it hadn't been so heavy from long saturation in the mud. When it was over we stood there a second, feeling nervous. Jane looked surprised again, but her eyes were shy—that was the first time she was ever shy with me—yet there was something in them, a spark, a melting glow, that made me think perhaps she felt it, too, a little of the same thing. But when another fast song started and Cleanth grabbed her hand and pulled her off, when she laughed and went with him, smiling back at me over her shoulder with bland apology, I knew—for Jane it was just a dance—and I hated her again. I'd lost that lovin' feeling, whoa-oh, and was no wiser when it ended than when it had begun. That was my first dance with Jane.

The night went on and on. Time slowed down to a crawl until Buzz asked me into the kitchen where we did another line with Patrick. "So, man, you surf?" Buzz asked, cutting through the bullshit and getting down to basics, and I said, "sure," and Patrick said, "I have a boogy-board," and we both stared at him, and he said, "and I'm very good—so *there*," and Buzz said, looking back at me, "there's a great break at Coquina Beach, there must be ten, twelve bars, some right, some left, it's totally amazing," and Patrick echoed, "totally," with a spiteful face, and Buzz said, "you want to go sometime?" and I said, "yeah, man, that would be real cool, I'd like that," and Patrick said, "so would I, but I know you won't take me," and Buzz said, "sure, Pat you can go, man—make sure you bring your boogy-board." He grinned and I decided I liked Buzz, and Patrick said, "oh, I will, I'll pack a picnic, too, and bring my camera. I'll throw breadcrumbs to the seagulls while you two surf, and if you're very tired when you get through, I give an excellent massage." Then he grinned, too, and Buzz and I just stared at him. It was hard to tell with Patrick just how serious to take him, or how serious he took himself. It was like he was caricaturing himself, pretending to be the pathetic lonely fag, but with a wicked intelligence and speed that weren't pathetic in the least, and through it all you got the sense that Patrick knew exactly who he was and wasn't shy about putting it out there, which I liked. So I decided he was okay, too. "Let's do it then," Buzz said, and I said, "definitely," and Patrick said, "it's a date," and simpered, and we all stood there sniffing, making chemical yawns, then Buzz and I went back into the fray, and Patrick said, "bye now, y'all behave."

By that time Cleanth had stripped his shirt off and was demonstrating all the nuances of his physique, which glowed with clean clear sweat. His hair was sopping and the top part of his pants had gone from white to a translucent gray. I noticed that his underwear were black, bikini-style—it might have been the Speedo. Even Jane had a small glow—not sweat, but puh-spuhration. The room had grown distinctly warmer. Someone had thrown the windows open, and you could hear the surf breaking, strangely muted in the fog. People were wilting and clothes were flying right and left, and finally Ellen cried, "I know, let's all go skinny-dipping!" and Cleanth said, "*oh*, yeah," and Reese said, "*hale*, yes," and ripped out a rebel yell that shook the windowpanes, and people started heading for the exits, trooping onto the east porch. I followed along to see where this might go.

Outside, garments were being peeled and little gleams of flesh, both white and tan, were starting to appear. First legs and bellies, then bosoms, asses, pubic hair. Reese's butt had pimples, or maybe it was a rash. I took off my coat and tie so as not to seem impolite and got an eyefull. Ellen had a better figure than I thought—not fat at all, just ample—and B.J. . . . well, maybe I'd been hard on her before. I was close to getting that way then, so I turned away, and Reese and Buzz, well, they were Reese and Buzz. Cleanth stood in front of Jane, stark naked, grinning, one hand on her shoulder, and she was looking down demurely, un-buckling her belt, no further along in the process than I was. Cleanth met my eyes across her shoulder and said, "and here's our lifeguard—will you save us if we drown?" I didn't mean to be a hard-ass, but everybody there was either wired on toot or sloppy drunk, or both, myself included, so I said, "I'm not sure this is such a great idea, Cleanth," and he said, "hear that people? each man for himself," and they all ran off into the wall of fog that gleamed with the floodlight from the porch, a troop of nymphs and satyrs.

I followed in the rear, and as I climbed the dune, through the moiling haze, I saw Cleanth and Jane, who'd lagged behind the others. They were on the crest, standing face to face, much as I'd seen them on the porch. Jane was looking down, and I saw him lift her chin, then bend to kiss her lips. He put his arms around her, and though she didn't actively embrace him, she didn't resist him either. "Come on," he said—his tone was ardent—and she said, "go on, I'll be there," and he ran off. I turned around and started walking back to the hotel, then I just said, "fuck it," out loud, reversed again and climbed the hill.

When I got up beside her, Jane was leaning over stepping out of her shorts, still in her shirt and underwear. "Oh," she said, startling as she stood up, "it's you." She put her hand across her breast and blinked in obvious relief—"you scared me, A." "Did I?" I said, and catching something in my tone, she blinked again and said, "aren't you going swimming?" and I told her, curtly, "no," and she said, "well, would you turn around or close your eyes or something so I can get undressed?" and I said, "are you that shy?" and she said, "I am, a little," and I said, "I wouldn't have known that, Jane," and she said, "what's the matter, A.?" in a tone of slight frustration, but also like she really cared, and I said, "you didn't seem too shy with Cleanth just now," and she said, "oh, I see, you were spying on us," and I said, "I wasn't spying, I was just going to the beach like everybody else," and she said, "and?" impatiently, and I said, "let's don't shit each other, Jane, I saw you kiss him," and she said, "I didn't kiss him, he kissed me," and I said, "what's the difference?" and she said, "a lot," and I said, "it's hard to tell," and she said, "what, A.? am I not allowed to have a good time? is that against the law?" and I said, "I was just thinking about Cary, Jane," and she said, "it has nothing to do with Cary, A., you don't understand a thing about it," and suddenly the intense strangeness of arguing so intimately with this girl I hardly knew came home to me. I felt confused, both mean and justified in pressing it, a murky doubleness I wanted to be clear and single. Trying to make it so, I said, "I guess Cary would be interested to know that," and Jane said, "then tell him, A., just tell him, I wish you would," and I said, "I'm leaving, do you want a ride?" knowing I was giving her no choice, but with a troubled softness in my mind even as I spoke hard words, and she said, "no, I don't, just go on, A., just leave, somebody else can take me," and I said, "right, I'll see you later then," but she offered me no comfort and ran off into the fog.

Six

Walking down the dune, I felt gut-shot. I missed Cary. The thought of him was like a life raft. I felt like if he'd been there things would have turned out different—I didn't know how, but different somehow, better. At least Jane wouldn't be with Cleanth, though that wasn't the main thing. But what *was* the main thing? Something else. Jane could go to hell. But Cary should have been there.

Morgan was sitting on the steps when I walked up—I hadn't noted her absence from the group until I saw her there. She was sitting in this way that women sometimes will, her thighs spread wide apart, not in a sloppy way, nor in a sexual one, but attractive for its frankness—a pose I liked a lot except that Morgan wasn't posing. She was alone and didn't even see me. Her harem pants were pulled up to her knees, exposing her slim calves, and there was a dark bottle of Dom Pérignon on the steps beside her and a flute in her left hand. Her right one held a cigarette, pinched between her thumb and index finger like she didn't smoke that often. She took a puff and blew it up into the fog, enhancing the obscurity.

She looked like she was celebrating privately, and I didn't really want to see her, or anybody, then, but it was unavoidable—my coat was on the porch rail—and when I came into the halo of the flood I saw, with surprise and some discomfiture, that her face was streaked with tears. Morgan had the loose washed-out look of someone at the end of a long evening who's released something and feels better for it, but also feels the sadness of knowing that the thing she's released was not the thing she really needed to let go.

She puffed her cigarette, observing my approach without a word, and when I stopped in front of her, she studied me and said, "my, my, we don't look very happy, do we?—you didn't like the party either?" and I said, "I'm just wrecked. I've got an early day tomorrow," and she said, "and someone stole your girl." Her expression wasn't mocking, it was calm and sorry for me, sorry for us both. "Jane's not my girl," I said, and Morgan just said, "oh," with little rounded lips, and took another sip of her champagne. Holding it on her palate, she smiled and patted the steps beside her, and I said, "I really can't stay too long," as I sat down. "Have some champagne," she said, filling her glass and handing me the bottle, "it'll clear your head," and smiling at her irony, I replied, "I haven't heard that said," and she said, "it's an old family remedy, I can vouch for it—no claims for the heart though." Frowning over her *bon mot*, which fell a little flat, she said, "oops, I must be getting drunk—excuse me, *tipsy*," and she laughed and I could see she was. "At least it beats the taste of wormwood, Adam," she said, and I shrugged and took a swig, and she said, "bravo, we don't like them anyway, do we? We'll just start over and reconvene a brand-new party, a private one, and they won't be invited," and I said, "as long as it's a short one," observing with interest the emergence of the little girl part of Morgan, the spoiled but charming princess. She ironized it, but you had the sense it came from a real place, and suddenly she seemed less forbidding, I could look at her just like a normal person, and I felt a little tingle.

"If it makes you feel any better, I don't like it any more than you do," Morgan said, "Cleanth just drank too much, along with other things—you just have to give it to him." I made a bland face, and she said, "well, you don't, but I do . . . and I'll tell you something, Adam—Cleanth likes you." I made an even blander face, and Morgan took another sip and nodded as she swallowed. "I mean it, Adam, I haven't seen him warm up to anyone like that in ages—what were you two doing down there anyway? I mean, you couldn't have just been snorting, you'd be dead," and I said, "we played a game," and she said, "not Life Poker? it usually takes him at least a week to get to that." My worst suspicions were confirmed. "He plays it a lot then?" I said, and she said, "it's Cleanth's thing—he doesn't play with just anyone though," and I said, "he pretended we were making it up as we went along," and she said, "well, don't hold that against him, if he'd told you it would steal his thunder, there'd be no surprise—you should feel complimented," and I said, "Cleanth likes surprises," and she studied my expression and said, "you had quite a match, didn't you? who won?" and I said, "I didn't think there was supposed to be a winner, but I guess he was it, because I spilled my guts to him, I told the truth, and I thought he did, too," and she said, "maybe he did, Adam."

"So why did B.J. tell me he's a liar and a snake?" I asked, and she said, "I wouldn't put much stake in anything B.J. tells you, Adam—certainly not about Cleanth. They had a fling in Hilton Head last year. We have another place down there, the Green Light. B.J. came to work for us, and I guess maybe she thought Cleanth would marry her or something. But I know Cleanth—he doesn't make those kind of promises. Oh, don't I know him. But let's face it, B.J. is a bitch and Cleanth got tired of her. He's no saint either, but he did bring her up here when she asked to come, he could have fired her and saved himself a lot of grief. But Cleanth's not that way. Underneath, he's really rather sweet, and loyal to his friends, and sad. Basically, I just think B.J. was too much for him to handle. She's a little old for him. Usually he draws the line around eighteen. That's part of why he's sad." Not exactly overwhelmed with pity, I said, "Jane's eighteen," and Morgan said, "I think Cleanth noticed," and threw her cigarette into the fog.

"But I can only assume you and Jane aren't involved," Morgan said, "otherwise she wouldn't be out there. Jane doesn't strike me as that sort of girl." She searched my face for contradiction, and I said, "well, she's involved with my best friend," and Morgan said, "oh, I see, well maybe she is," like it made no difference to her either way, and I felt the madness of a momentary impulse to defend Jane, but I squelched it like a serpent underfoot. Morgan looked at me with sympathy, which I didn't want, but also with an underlying firmness, which implied I'd made my bed and now would have to lie in it like her and everybody else—I didn't want that either. That road was closed, no point in talking about it any further.

"So what did Cleanth tell you?" she asked, and I said, "lots of things. He told me about Vietnam—was he really over there?" and Morgan blinked and said, "yes, he was," and I said, "and he shot some guy named Meyer Prosky and spent four years in Leavenworth?'' and she said, ''he told you that?'' and something crossed her face—not just incredulity—a pained shadow. She looked away and fumbled with another cigarette, and I said, ''yes, he told me that,'' and she said, ''Cleanth has led a very interesting life, Adam, interesting and checkered. I must confess, I'm totally amazed he told you about Vietnam. He never talks about that—never. Not even in Life Poker. Not even to me, and I'm the closest person to him in the world. Cleanth doesn't have that many friends. Oh, he has acquaintances, millions of them. Like your father? That happens all the time. But his intensity puts many people off. If you can handle that though, you might learn a lot from him. I think I can promise you you'll never meet anyone quite like him. I never have, which is probably why I'm here.''

She lit the cigarette she'd been holding as she spoke, and I said, ''but why did he pick me?'' and Morgan said, ''don't go heavy into reasons with Cleanth, Adam, it's an exercise in futility. He has impulses and he acts on them.'' She puffed and said, ''I have an idea though,'' and I said, ''what?'' and she said, ''I think he sensed a similar intensity in you.'' In spite of myself, I was flattered, and Morgan saw it, because she laughed and said, ''don't let it swell your head, Adam, intensity is a mixed blessing. You're also young. You haven't settled or closed down yet. Most people do. Cleanth didn't, I don't know why. Sometimes I wish he had, but that comes with the package. You either take it or leave it. That's why Cleanth prefers hanging out with people younger than himself.''

I took another swig of Dom and said, ''so how do you know him, Morgan?'' and she laughed and said, ''how do I know Cleanth . . . I'm not sure I even do, Adam, though I met him when I wasn't too much older than you are now. We lived in the same town,'' and I said, ''where was that?'' and she said, ''Fuquay Springs?'' I shook my head, never having heard of it, and she said, ''it's near Fort Bragg, twenty miles or so,'' and I said, *''North Carolina?''* completely caught off guard, and she said, ''yes, does that surprise you?'' and I said, ''you don't sound southern, Cleanth doesn't either,'' and she said, ''yes, his accent—I think he lost most of it at prep school, and then at Oxford other things crept in. I'm used to it, of course, but it is rather strange—almost like one of those Hollywood studio accents from the thirties. I'm not southern though. I'm from Florida originally, West Palm. We moved to Fuquay when I was in college. I met Cleanth during a summer vacation. His father, General Faison, had just died. Cleanth had been in New York trying to make it as a painter and he'd come home for the funeral and stayed on at his mother's. I don't think Cleanth and his father had ever really got along. I didn't know the general, but I suppose it was the artist thing—you know, not a legitimate occupation for a grown man.''

I sipped from the bottle and said, "he was good," nodding toward the ballroom where I'd seen his paintings, and Morgan said, "yes, he did those polo scenes while he was in England," and I said, "the girl, too?" and Morgan said, "no, not the girl," and sipped her wine, and I said, "who was she?" and Morgan said, "you'll have to ask Cleanth that, Adam. He doesn't tell that story the first night, not even to you." Intrigued, I pondered that, and Morgan said, "after Oxford Cleanth went to New York and started doing modern work. He was living in some awful cold-water flat off the meat district on the West Side. I don't really know what happened, except it didn't work out.

"I don't think Cleanth was cut out to suffer for art. He likes nice things too much, and I suppose he just got tired of living in an unheated room and blowing his nose in rags that smelled like turpentine. Cleanth's heart wasn't in it. He's a terrible romantic underneath it all. I suppose he was just waiting for an excuse to leave New York and the whole scene, and the General's death provided one. So Cleanth came home for the funeral and spent some months at Seven Oaks, his family place, and that's where I met him. I was not quite twenty-two, just out of Sarah Lawrence and enrolled in graduate school for the fall—my first time in Fuquay—and Cleanth was twenty-six, at loose ends, living in his mother's house.''

"And you were lovers?" I said, and Morgan blinked her eyes mildly and said, "yes, we were, Cleanth was my first—not my first lover, but my first love," and I said, "what happened?" and she said, "you're very curious, aren't you, Adam?" and I said, "I'm sorry, I don't mean to pry," and she said, "I don't mind telling you. I rather think I like you, too, Adam, I don't know why. Perhaps it's because you look so grave and handsome sitting there, and one could never believe a wicked thought had crossed your mind. I hope I'm not mistaken," and her eyes played with me, suggesting a different sort of hope entirely, frankly suggesting, and not deflecting that indefinable something that older women usually deflected when they looked at me, the look that spared even as it dismissed. Excited and alarmed, I said, "I have wicked thoughts sometimes," meaning to be bold, but sounding shy and awkward, and she said, "should I be frightened?" and I said, "I don't want you to be," and she narrowed her eyes as though gazing deeply into me, or through me, and said, "you reminded me so much of Cleanth just now— it's not your face. I don't know what it is," and she seemed struggling to find it, then closed her eyes and shook her head and said, "I *am* getting drunk," and reached out for the pack of cigarettes.

Not so much out of sudden passion, but because she seemed distressed and sad, I slipped toward her on the step and put my arm around her shoulders, and she gazed up at me with searching vulnerable eyes. "Is this a good idea?" she asked, and feeling suddenly strong and confident, I said, "I think it's a great one." She didn't seem convinced, and suddenly it seemed important, if not critical, to convince her. "Don't I seem old and horrible to you?" she asked, and I smiled, and said, "you don't at all—you look good, Morgan," and recovering, she said, "well, I guess I fished for that, but thank you anyway," and she stuck her finger in the pack and pulled one out, and I took her lighter and lit it for her, feeling the momentum ebbing subtly. "Thank you," she said, inhaling and blowing her smoke upward. She looked at me and said, "so you are wicked after all, perhaps I shouldn't tell you all my secrets," and though I knew she was teasing I froze up and couldn't think of a reply. Morgan put her hand out on my thigh almost reassuringly and said, "would you like to kiss me, Adam?" and I said, "may I?" and she said, "what if I say no? would you kiss me anyway?" and I said, "yes," and she said, "I suppose there wouldn't be any great harm in that, would there—just one? just to see?" and mad for her by then, I closed my eyes and dropped my head to meet her lips—the smell of smoke and breath soured pleasingly with wine.

Morgan's kiss wasn't coy like the girls I'd kissed before, it was a wet open splash, concealing nothing, holding back nothing, and her lips were lax and almost toneless. I went right to the bottom of it into what seemed the promise of divine corruption, and found I liked it there. When I opened my eyes again, I found Morgan's swimming slightly drunkenly nearby, watching me, and she made her breasts available in the slight camisole. I lacked the courage to take advantage, but her sexuality was like an opened door into a strange room I'd never visited before, offered lightly, without condition, so that I could visit there and know it and come away with no cost to myself, and I was wild to go.

At that moment we heard the laughter of the swimmers returning from the beach, and under that external urgency, Morgan, feeling it, too, but calmer than I was, said, ''I would ask you to come upstairs, but I know you have an early day tomorrow,'' and I said, ''forget tomorrow,'' and she smiled and said, ''yes, let's,'' and stabbing out her cigarette, she offered me her hand. ''I'll finish the story,'' she said, and I said, ''what story?'' and she laughed, and we went. I had no second thoughts, or if I did, the second thought was also, ''yes.''

Morgan had a small suite to herself on the south end of the top floor with windows facing south and east toward the ocean. They were closed and the air conditioning murmured softly. The air had a delicious chill after the outdoors. You entered a sitting room with a love seat, floral over navy, and a coffee table littered with magazines—*Vogue* and *W*, *The New Yorker*, *Architectural Digest, Gourmet*—most of which were more or less obscure to me, but piqued my sense that I was entering a realm of arcane and frivolous sensual information. This opened, through French doors, into a much larger master bedroom with an enormous mattress on a simple Hollywood frame, the sheets and coverlet pulled up but not formally made, a couch of the same fabric as the loveseat, and a dressing table with a mirrored surface strewn with cosmetic vials and brushes, cotton balls, and open jars of cream, a dirty ashtray, a china dish filled with necklaces and rings. On one wall there was a framed print which looked like a Lautrec, though not familiar to me, of an aging Parisian whore with a sad clown's face in an extravagant plumed hat, standing on a corner in the rain, her makeup running down her cheeks.

''I'm sorry the place is such a mess,'' Morgan said, ''I wasn't expecting company.'' She smiled on that and said, ''wait here,'' opening a door onto another door without a knob, which she pushed open into an adjoining suite—Cleanth's? I wondered about that. When she came back she closed both of them and handed me a mirror heaped with what must have been a quarter of an ounce of snow, a razor blade and a candy-striped plastic straw cut short. ''Help yourself, I'll be right back,'' she said, and disappeared into the bathroom. I did. The first one felt so good I just decided, what the hey, and sluiced a second. Excellent, excellent, this was totally ex'slint, man, I had a natural talent for it. I couldn't believe my luck. This woman, this *older* woman, who was worldly, rich, attractive, wanted me—it was unbelievable. In a few minutes, maybe even seconds, I'd be in the sheets with her making sweaty love.

By the time Morgan returned, in just her underwear and the camisole top, which she was starting to unbutton, I was soaring, the throttle was pressed all the way down, and I charged. I dropped her straight back, tango-style, and laid a sloppy kiss on her, full tongue. Morgan looked surprised. She looked like maybe she didn't know me that well after all, like maybe she'd got more than she bargained for. I saw that look and plummeted a thousand feet back into the vale of human life. She said, "be gentle, darling, there's no rush," and I said, "there isn't?" trying to be funny to preserve my self-respect. She laughed and said, "I have to take my makeup off," and as she pulled away I caught a flash of her full bosom awallow in black silk, a second flash of panties, also black—they had a lace panel, not going down into the crotch, but just an inch or two into her pubic hair, the merest tuft of it, French underwear they looked like, designed for just one purpose and not apologizing for it, showing you exactly what you wanted, but holding back the last, best part—a third flash of leg, a little looseness in the thighs, but who cared? Not moi, not fucking A. Catching all those flashes my hunger suddenly transformed into something more subtle and specific, and in my heart I thanked her for restraining me. I studied her as she walked away from me toward the dressing table, the muscles striking in her slim young calves, sitting down and putting on a hairband, applying cold cream to a cotton swab, taking off her base.

"May I tell you something, Adam?" Morgan said, smiling at me in the mirror as she worked, and I said, "sure, of course," and she said, "it's something you learn working in the restaurant business." She closed her eyes and wiped her lids, then she opened them again and said, "the sauce is more important than the dish, sweetheart, and the dish waits on the sauce." Then she turned over her shoulder and said, "would you mind making one of those for me?" flicking her eyes at the dessert tray. "My pleasure, ma'am," I said, separating out a line with the razor blade and running it across the mirror. I took it over and she turned on her seat and snorted it, then she looked up at me, blinking, "Have you done much of this before?" she asked, and I said, "much of what?" and she said, "cocaine," and I said, "just once before tonight," and she said, "do you like it?" and I said, "it's Alpine," grinning as the thought occurred to me, and she said, "yes, it is, isn't it? that's good," and I said, "do you?" and she said, "rarely," then her face turned serious, and she said, "I don't do the other often either, Adam," and I said, "what other?" and she said, "this," and I knew she meant us.

"I believe you," I said, and I did, though it made no difference to me, and she said, "and you're sure you think it's all right?" With her hair pulled straight back from her forehead under the green velvet hairband, the makeup gone, and the touch of vulnerable uncertainty in her expression, she looked almost like a girl, and I felt something different for her, something softer and more human than the urge to screw. That troubled me and touched me. I realized I would have preferred not to feel it, and I didn't like that in myself, but it was so. Yet the touched and troubled feeling didn't go away. "Why not?" I asked her, "it doesn't hurt anybody else," and she said, "no, but I'm afraid it may hurt you," and I said, "don't worry about me, Morgan, it won't, and even if it does, I'm not afraid of being hurt," and she said, "I am," then she faltered and said, "I'm really not too good at casual, I'd like to be," and I said, "why don't we just go for it?" and she smiled at me with affectionate study and said, "is it wonderful to be eighteen?" and I said, "you aren't old, Morgan," and she said, "no, but it's different," and I said, "how?" and she said, "I don't know if I can explain it, but something subtle begins to happen to your body in, I suppose, your late twenties, or maybe that's just when you start to feel it. It's like something leaking out of you, and you hardly even notice it, but by the time you reach my age—I'm thirty-five, Adam—the loss begins to seem immense. You make me feel it more," and I said, "I don't mean to," and she said, "I know you don't." She made a deprecating smile and said, "but I'm being very sexy, aren't I?" and I said, "incredibly," without irony, and she said, "would you do something for me?" and I said, "name it," and she said, "something I particularly like?" I raised my eyebrows, waiting, and she said, "brush my hair?" and I said, "sure, I'd like to."

She turned back toward the mirror, handing me the brush over her shoulder with her right hand while taking off the hairband with her left, glancing her fingers through her hair. I began to pull the brush straight back across her scalp and she said, "mmm, yes, that feels nice," and she closed her eyes and leaned her head back, nudging me quite intimately. It was that, but also something about the brushing and the fact that I could look straight down into her top—all of it, but mostly that gentle nudging that made the bulge appear below my zipper running down uncomfortably into the right leg of my pants. Feeling it on her back, Morgan opened her eyes and looked up at me in the mirror with that playful tease in her eyes again. "You're so tall, Adam," she said, "I like tall men," and she reached back and found my erection and began to manipulate it through my pants with a gentle, almost careless motion of her hand, closing her eyes again, and slipping her other hand into her underwear, where she began to stroke herself, making little kneading circles. I stopped brushing and reached down into her top, lifting a full breast, and she pressed my hand more deeply with her own, then looked at me and said, "just a little more?" and I said, "okay, but if I have a stroke, I'm blaming you," and she laughed and said, "you're funny," and I resumed my brushing.

"Where was I in the story?" she asked, and I said, "I can't remember, I can't even think," and she said, "did I tell you how I met him?" and I said, "I don't think so," not really all that keen to hear more of Cleanth's exploits, but willing to be martyred, a fledgling saucier, for the sake of higher knowledge, and Morgan said, "my father wanted me to have a portrait done, he'd been after me for several years. During my senior year at Sarah Lawrence Daddy retired and moved to Fuquay, where he knew some people, distant relatives of ours. He ferreted Cleanth out almost instantly, and they hit it off famously. It turned out Cleanth was doing portraits anyway, painting all the local gentry to make money while he was at home, so I sat to him right out at Seven Oaks in General Faison's library.

"I fell in love with Cleanth the first time I laid eyes on him. He was so handsome, Adam, except he had dark sleepless circles under his eyes, which were so sad and touching in his fresh face, but that made him all the more irresistible to me. He'd painted all the women in the countryside, their daughters, too, and probably seduced each one with the same face and story, but when he said he loved me, I believed him, and he probably did, after his fashion. That portrait took up the whole summer."

My erection was beginning to wilt, but not mortally, and Morgan seemed so deeply into the memory I couldn't stop her.

"But when Daddy found out it was the end. He was a terrible snob. Cleanth was well-bred, but he was twenty-six and had nothing to show. He was living at home with a widowed mother, and though Daddy liked art, and artists, too, the idea of one marrying his daughter was something else again. Cleanth begged me to go away with him, but I thought it could wait. I thought after a few weeks or months it would all settle down. In the meantime, I could see Cleanth at school, or anywhere, and Daddy wouldn't have to know.

"But three weeks after I got to school, I called Cleanth's mother's and she told me he was at Fort Benning in Officer Candidate School. The next thing I knew, he was in Vietnam. I wrote him every month for almost two years, and I only got one letter back from him the whole time. You know what it said? 'It's so much clearer over here.' One line."

Morgan stopped and met my eyes in the mirror. Her own expressed a pained perplexity that wasn't just in the past. "I'm sorry, Adam, I must be boring you," she said, "it's the toot—I don't usually talk like this." I put the brush down on the table and straddled the seat, sitting down to face her, intrigued now with the story. "But how did you get back together?" I asked, and she said, "after he was wounded I saw him in the hospital. It wasn't a happy meeting. He was heavily medicated. The nurse brought in his lunch tray after I came in, and he just stared at it and at me with the same expression, like we were equivalent and he wanted neither one. I told him I still loved him, and I could tell just by his eyes, Adam. 'I'll always love you, Morgan,' he said, 'I'll always love the thing we had. But we're not those people anymore—I'm not, and you aren't either. It's all new.' Six months later I married Brent Deal. I wanted my life settled."

Morgan sighed. "I didn't see Cleanth for, God, I don't know, several years. Then one day he showed up on our doorstep in Charleston, the same Cleanth you saw tonight—suave, fit, well-dressed, smiling, tan. He had two bottles of Dom Pérignon in one hand and a bouquet of flowers in the other, and he looked for all the world like he'd been on a world cruise instead of in an institution. There was also a young girl with him, very beautiful and charming, but very eighteen. Brent knew about Cleanth and me, but the girl made it all safe, and the two of them made out like long lost brothers. Cleanth had just received his inheritance and wanted to open a restaurant, and, you see, Brent was in real estate. By the end of the evening, another famous Cleanth evening, they'd decided Hilton Head and the two of them were going in as partners.

"It took six months to find the site. Then we started building, and in the middle of it Brent was killed in a fluke boating accident." Her voice quavered and she paused, and I said, "God, Morgan, I'm sorry," and she shook her head, struggling to hold back tears. "Thank you," she said finally, "it was a difficult time for me. Cleanth helped me through it, and . . . well, that's what brought us back together, Adam. We didn't sleep together for a long time, I wanted to be very sure he meant it. I think he did, at first. After a while though, I'd see his eyes flick to some girl like Jane—I could tell his heart just wasn't in it. So finally I just said, 'go,' and he went. We might as well have been married, we were in every way except the one important one, and we still are. We're just like family, Adam, just like family, but it's a strange family, isn't it?" and I said, "yeah, but what family isn't? and anyway, I go for strange." She smiled and said, "be careful or we might adopt you," and I said, "now there's a scary thought," and she laughed and said, "you are funny, Adam," and I said, "thanks, you're pretty funny, too," and she said, "do you think we'll laugh about this in the morning?" and I said, "let's laugh about it now and let tomorrow take care of itself," and she said, "should we do one more, for courage?" and I said, "definitely, for courage," and we hit.

I felt completely comfortable with her by then, and she said, "now that I've told you all my secrets—almost all—are you going to tell me one of yours?" and I said, "I don't have any secrets," and she said, "what, a wicked child like you?" and I just pursed my lips and shook my head, and she said, "I don't believe that for a minute," and I said, "sorry to disappoint you, but it's true," and she said, "I think I know one already," with a taunting look, and I said, "what?" and she said, "I think you have a little thing for Jane McCrae," and I said, "wrong, errr"—a game-show buzzer noise—"I told you, Morgan, she's my best friend's girlfriend," and Morgan said, "but that's a different issue, isn't it?" and feeling troubled by her persistence, I said, "what makes you say that anyway?" and she said, "oh, older women have their ways—I saw how you looked at her at dinner and how you danced," and suddenly the cocaine jetstream I was flowing in reversed and began to run against me. My mind broke into confusion, and I felt my body's tiredness like the whistle of a far-off freight train forlornly calling under the blurred rush of my unstoppable speed. The next thing I knew Morgan had slipped off the seat onto her knees. She was unzipping me and I was hard again, and the anxiety departed as quickly as it came.

Morgan stared at my erection with a musing fascination, then she gazed up in my eyes, and said, "it's beautiful," and then took it gently, her thumb beneath and four fingers above, and, closing her eyes, slipped it in her mouth, one quick lunge the way a little girl might eat a popsicle, and as she came back up she flicked her tongue along the underside where it just kills you. "Do you like being sucked?" she asked, and I said, "are you kidding?" and she smiled and went down even deeper, and I closed my eyes and listened to the wet quashing sound she made, the sound of organs touching. Then I came. Morgan took the first jet in her mouth and swallowed it, then came up and watched the second fly across her shoulder landing on the carpet. She smiled delightedly and held me as my sperm dripped down her fingers like melting candle wax, and she licked it like vanilla dribbles on a sugar cone. My body wilted, died, and my soul went someplace else—Oomba-Goomba Land where bottle caps are money—but my dick never flickered. Cocaine does that sometimes, and being eighteen does the rest. Morgan smiled at me and said, "I hope there's more," and I said, "that just topped it off," and she just laughed and laughed and I picked her up and carried her to bed.

I took the Gospel to her missionary-style the first time, heaving to with a goodwill and groaning like a sailor at the oars, and Morgan whispered, "darling." Thinking it was an endearment signaling approaching ecstasy, I went full steam ahead, until my white ass in the mirror on the wall was just an insubstantial blur of speed like the blades of a working fan. It even stirred a breeze, unless it was the a.c. that made the curtains undulate. "Adam, darling," Morgan whispered a second time, more urgently, *"Adam!"* and I checked myself with difficulty, lifting my face out of her neck to look at her. I wasn't used to conversation at that point in the process, and Morgan said, "be gentle with me, darling, you're sawing me in half," and my bottom lip dropped to my chin. That didn't sound like grateful swooning bliss to me. "Just lie still a second, feel me," she said with the tenderest face, so afraid of hurting me, and suddenly I felt like crying. I did cry, though there weren't any tears. I dropped my head back down and a few choked sobs disappeared with a muted coughing sound in the slightly tacky flesh of her warm neck. "Shh, darling," she said, stroking my hair with one hand and pressing the other gently in the small of my back.

We lay there and I felt frightened, wounded, out of my depth, realizing knowledge came at a greater price than I'd expected and had no mercy. Then I felt her thrust her hips up gently under mine, once, then a second time, and I stared at her again, surprised that she still wanted me, but her eyes said, yes, she did, and the third time I thrust back, and she locked her arms around me and whispered, "roll me over, darling," and I did. She lifted off me, pressing my shoulders to the bed and then slid slowly down my cock. I reached up and fumbled at the last button on her camisole but couldn't get it and she closed her hand over mine and tugged with a quick surprising violence and it ripped cleanly off and her breasts spilled out, heavy toward the tip like balloons filled with water and she closed her eyes and sank back down on me with a long sigh.

Then she opened them and smiled and said, "there, darling, does that feel nice to you?" and I said, "very nice," and she said, "me, too, darling, me, too, I can't tell you, it's been so long," and her eyes got moist and bright until she closed them, concentrating, feeling it, and then I saw a thought appear like sunlight through a pane of frosted glass, and she said, "you feel just like Red," and laughed like that delighted her. "Who's Red?" I asked and she said, "don't be jealous, Adam, you can't be jealous of a horse," and I said, "a horse?" and she said, "not even, Red was my first pony, he seemed so big and evil to me. I was only five or six, but I'm almost sure I used to come on him." Her expression teased me tenderly, and she said, "that's a secret about young girls and horses, Adam, and older women, too, but you mustn't ever tell."

Then her smile faltered and a trace of what looked like pain flashed across her features, and she said, "oh, Adam, I think I'm there." She gazed at me with deepened warmth and fond appreciation—there was something like forgiveness, too—and I saw the first strain in her face and a blue vein pulsing in her throat. "I'm going to come, Adam," she whispered, "can you come with me?" and I said, "I just did," and she smiled and said, "I'll see you just a little later then," and closed her eyes and suddenly stopped moving—I'd never seen a woman do that. It all seemed to unroll in slow motion from within her, a subtle wave coursing upward leaving a flush along her skin. That look of pain deepened to excruciation and then deliverance broke from it and Morgan smiled like someone blind, and, as I watched, again I felt I recognized her face from somewhere long ago, but I didn't get it that time either.

There were other times, but they were too soft to remember, which is the way it always is with knowledge—when you know you don't need to remember—Morgan taught me that. At one point in the night though, or in the early hours of that morning, I heard voices from the other room, and a girl's laugh which I knew to a dead certainty was Jane's. I remembered that, but then that knowledge came much harder and was so dear to own.

Seven

The cards were all dealt that first night—Life Poker with a vengeance. Morgan was a player, too, so was Jane. We all were, even Cary, though I didn't see that then. He played *in absentia*, by proxy—me. That blurred delicious evening which led to such pain later set the pattern for the summer, drawing Jane and me together in a way that seemed so much like sundering. That was the twist, but only a wiseman could have seen it.

When I opened my eyes the next morning the first thing I saw was that Parisian whore with the sad clown's face standing in the sooty rain. I groaned with recognition and cast a wincing glance at Morgan's face, drowned and bloated on the pillow, and groaned again. But it wasn't Morgan—the whore was me. Two things vied inside me for the upper hand—tenderness, and extreme panic. I knew I should have loved her, but I didn't, I just felt I owed her something that I couldn't pay. One voice said, stay and be a man, the other said, don't even think about it, run! I headed for the door.

I was twenty minutes late for work and had to punch in at the office. Mick was writing something at his desk and didn't so much as glance at me until I'd fed the clock. Then he looked up and when he saw my face his eyes got knowing, and he said, "looks like you caught the red-eye special in from out of town, A.," and I said, "Jesus, Mick, I'm sorry, man, what happened was . . ." and he cut me off and said, "I don't even want to know—your grandmother kicked the bucket, you had to have your tonsils out, your dog has worms—don't tell me, I've heard every one. One time, okay, two times"—he shook his head and drew a finger across his neck. "It won't happen again, Mick," I told him, and he said, "go," and as I headed out the door he said, "stop and get a BC powder and a Coca-Cola, it won't save you, but it takes the edge off," and I said, "thanks, man, really," and he pointed at the door.

Arguably the worst day of my life—a bold claim. By nine-thirty the sun had broiled away the remnants of the evening's fog and it was getting hot. My pores opened and I started sweating out a queasy mixture that smelled like Dom and cider vinegar, and my stomach, well . . . languid bubbles in a pot of road tar, bursting and sending up an acrid taste into my mouth. Making change on beach chairs and umbrellas was like doing differential calculus, and staking the latter down into the sand sent shock waves to my temples.

Around noon as I was climbing up into my stand, I happened to glance across the dune to the back porch of the hotel—I'd cast quite a few such casual glances that way already, and the place had been as quiet as a tomb all morning—but that time I saw Jane. Even at eighty yards I could see her hair was wet like she'd just come from a shower—the old postcoital ablution—and she was wearing a white terry robe too big for her, standing in profile facing the kitchen door and holding what must have been a cup of coffee with both hands, blowing into it. Something dark and horrible coursed through me, something sickening that made me want to bend right down and vomit up my heart, because, in spite of everything, I'd hoped she'd found her way back home. That robe seemed like incontrovertible evidence, and I convicted her of a capital crime—she'd let herself be fucked. Die, you bitch, I thought.

Jane didn't see me, but I saw her—oh, yeah—and as I watched Faison stepped onto the porch—at that moment he went from Cleanth to Faison. He was wearing his white ducks from the night before and no shirt, casually displaying his well-modeled hairless chest. He looked straight at me, then his eyes flicked to Jane and his lips moved as he gestured toward me with his cup. Jane turned around and seemed to hesitate just slightly before she waved. By that time I was looking somewhere else—out to sea, far out to sea—but as I turned, out of the corner of my eye, even across that distance, I could have sworn I saw the white enameled flash of Faison's teeth.

I wasn't angry—oh, no—in fact, I thanked her. Now I knew.
What I felt was disappointment. It just seemed too typical, and
I'd thought Jane was different. That night at Jimbo's I'd thought
I'd perceived a strain of fineness in her, the real article, and, yes,
what she'd done with Faison was no different, no worse, than
what I'd done with Morgan—oh, I was just—but at that hour of
the morning, hungover and disgusted, I knew the truth about
myself. What I'd done was to be expected—with a few drinks
and a little rocket fuel inside me, wherever shoddiness lurked I'd
find it with a spaniel's nose, but I'd expected more of Jane. I
didn't hold it against her—how could I?—but there had been that
hope, you know, and now I just felt cynical and jaded and confirmed in my own jaded cynicism. And there was one big difference—Cary. Jane had an obligation there, one I didn't have—my
shoddiness was merely personal, but hers was a betrayal. I started
to compose a speech. The oratory started rolling in, elaborate
and Latinate, like waves across the bar. At first it was only in
my mind, but at some point it became real to me, and I knew I
had to say those things to Jane. I owed it to Cary, didn't I? I
owed it to myself. I owed it most of all to Jane—oh, yeah, most
of all to Jane. Hadn't she said she wanted to be my friend?

The inner circle appeared through the day by ones and twos
and took their dips, showering in the weathered bathhouse. Patrick brought his boogy-board—it was a perfect day for it—and
took maniacal spills, laughing like he liked to hurt himself. I
watched it like a slapstick routine performed by a thin madman.
B.J. simply nodded at me with a trace of wary irony in her
expression. Ellen was friendly, and Buzz and I chatted about
short boards and brands of wax. It wasn't awful until Reese
walked up to me and said, "how's it going, Red?" pulling the
pop-top off a Falstaff. My soul went up in flames, and I stared
at him with my coldest face. "You gonna save me if I sink?"
Reese asked, and I said, "don't sink, Reese," and he walked
off laughing.

Faison only appeared late in the afternoon—Morgan never
showed. He was wearing the Speedo and dark glasses and held
a gin and tonic in his hand. Sipping it, he lifted his shades up
on his head and looked at me. Expecting the grin, I was surprised. His face was subdued and serious and there was a muddy
color in his eyes. "How's it going, A.?" he said, and I said,
"fucking peachy, Cleanth, I feel like I got run over by a truck,
but other than that, not too bad at all," and he blinked, regard-

ing me with solemn study, and said, "you aren't angry, are you, A.?" and I laughed and said, "why should I be angry?" and he said, "that was my next question," and sipped his drink, and I said, "no, I'm not angry," feeling undetermined, and he said, "I didn't expect you would be, but Jane seemed concerned about it when you didn't wave this morning—you did see us, didn't you?" and I said, "no, I didn't," and the lie was acknowledged and put away between us, and he said, "I asked you, A., you said you weren't involved with Jane," and I said, "and I also told you my best friend was in love with her," and he said, "I don't know him," and his eyes didn't waver. "That's not good enough, Cleanth," I told him, and he said, "I'm sorry, it's the best I have," and we faced off over that—I expected him to walk, but he didn't, he said, "I want to be your friend, A., help me out—don't you think it's just a little bit ridiculous, standing here bargaining over Jane? She's a big girl, A., she has to make her own decisions," and I said, "so do you, but if you were really my friend, you'd take my feelings into consideration," and he said, "the way I understood it you didn't have any feelings for Jane—you implied that, and so did she," and I said, "not my feelings, Cary's," and he said, "because I like you doesn't mean I owe him that," and I had to admit he had a solid point of view. I still didn't like him, but my respect went up a notch or two.

"All right, Cleanth," I said, "I see where you're coming from," and he said, "now tell me about you," and I said, "what about me?" and he said, "Morgan seemed extremely thoughtful this morning," and I said, "did she?" and he said, "I haven't seen her that way in a while—Morgan is important to me, A." His tone was serious and confidential, not admonitory, and it was clear he cared, but I said, "so you talked about it," feeling compromised because of that, and he said, "I know you slept with her and ran away, if that's what you mean," and I said, "I didn't run away," and he just stared at me waiting for an explanation, and I said, "I was late for work," knowing it was feeble and unable to believe he'd turned the tables on me. "She'll be relieved to know that," he said, and I said, "what else did she tell you?" and a cloudy version of the grin appeared as the thought occurred to him, and he said, "she said you had a nickname—Red—she told us over breakfast," and I said, "and did she tell you how I got it?" and he said, "no, she didn't mention that." I offered up a silent prayer of gratitude until Cleanth said,

"I have some ideas though. I know she had a pony by that name and how much Morgan likes to ride, but I'll take that secret with me to the grave, and so will Morgan. She spoke of you affectionately, A."

The intimacy of that moment was almost vertiginous, but it was strange, surpassing strange, because Cleanth's attitude implied, "I know, and it's okay," and though I felt a surface impulse toward offense, beneath that it was oddly comforting, oddly real to have the dirt laid out like that and judgment suspended— it was almost a relief. And there was no condescension in Cleanth's manner, his eyes were sober, even respectful, as he studied my reaction. "Morgan and I don't keep many secrets from each other, A.," he said, and I said, striking out half-heartedly, "I guess no one else gets to keep them around here either," and it sounded like whining in my ears. Cleanth shrugged and said, "hotels are built on secrets, A., but on the inside everybody knows them. Discretion is impossible and you don't need it anyway. But the secrets don't pass beyond the walls—that's the rule of good hotels. That's how it will be at the Lost Colony, too. Anyone can come here who has the money to pay for it, but they don't get to see the inside—that takes a special invitation. You got yours last night, and I thought you'd accepted it. I hope I wasn't wrong."

"I appreciate it, Cleanth, I really do," I said, "and I had a great time last night, man, but I'm not sure I'm all that big on clubs," and he said, "that's because you've never been in one and you don't know their charms and comforts. Think about it, take all the time you want—I'm going to take a dip now," and I said, "see you 'round," and as he walked away he turned back and said, "by the way—do you play tennis?" and I said, "some," though I'd beaten the number three man on the varsity at Keane that spring while I was running track—just barely, but I had—and Cleanth said, "how about tonight? the club has lights," and after a brief hesitation, I said, "sure, why not?" and he said, "seven, seven-thirty?" and I said, "fine," and he said, "I'll meet you there," and as he dove over a small breaker I anticipated with great pleasure wiping his ass across the court.

When I opened the door to my Jeep I found a flute on the driver's seat filled with warm champagne and a camellia in it. Beside it was an envelope of heavy off-white cotton fiber paper. I opened it and read:

> *This is for Red*
> *The pony boy*
> *Who worked so hard to bring me joy*
> *Who galloped through the whole night long*
> *Without a thought of being fed*
> *So Morgan's payment is this song.*

Below that was a lipstick kiss and a single word—"tonight?" I felt subtly touched, and subtly insulted. But I didn't think Morgan meant it hurtfully—if so, why the invitation? As I poured the champagne on the ground, the problem this presented glanced across my brain like an algebraic equation I didn't care that much to solve. Beneath that, I felt nothing. My thoughts were occupied with Jane. I had a speech to make.

I considered driving straight over to Jane's house from work, but instead, for some reason, I went home and showered first, slapping some Grey Flannel on my cheeks and putting on my tennis togs. That way I could go straight from her place to the match. That was the reason.

On the way over I rehearsed my speech, adding clever flourishes, and getting angrier. It felt good to be pissed off. It felt clear, and I needed to be clear. I was angry and I needed to be clear about exactly what it was that pissed me off. It was definitely Jane. It pissed me off that she was fucking over Cary, pissed me off that she was fucking up her life. I was concerned about Jane's life and future. It wasn't personal.

By the time I rapped on the glass I was all pumped up, all pissed off, nervous, sweating, excited, terrified. This was some great anger—somebody should have bottled it and sold it. Inside, I could see Jane with her back to me leaning over and staring into the refrigerator vacantly. She was wearing a tank top and a pair of pale blue underwear which were a little baggy. She looked back across her shoulder at my knock, then took out an apple and came around the bar to the door. Her hair was a little greasy—it looked rich—and her face had this clear openness like still water, and she was so fucking beautiful I could hardly stand to look at her, so fucking beautiful it pissed me off. I was pissed off that her hair was dirty, pissed off that she had that, oh, wilderness! look like she'd had her brains fucked out, pissed off that she was wearing that little tank top so that you couldn't help looking at her tits, even if you weren't all that

interested—though they were small they had a fruity rounded-
ness and jiggled when she walked—pissed off that she didn't
have a bra, pissed off that she was slouching around in her underwear, pissed off that they were a little baggy, pissed off that
when she saw it was me she came to the door without bothering
to put anything on, pissed off that she didn't even think of it,
like she wasn't even aware this wasn't cool, like I was her brother
or something when the fact was I didn't even know her all that
well, not that well at all. She just stood there behind the screen
and took a big crisp chomp out of that Granny Smith.

"Hi, A., what are you doing here?" she asked with complete
neutrality, chewing, and I glared at her with as much irony and
derision as I could muster, like, don't try to pull that shit, you
whore-bitch, you know exactly why I'm here. When I didn't
answer her question, she turned around and walked over to the
couch, plopping down in a corner of it and crossing her legs
thigh to thigh, her high foot pumping, staring at me defiantly
and impatiently, leaving it to me to open the screen, which I
did, though her lack of hospitality also pissed me off.

"Well, what?" she burst out finally, "just what have you got
to say to me that's so important?" and I said, "just tell me one
thing, Jane, okay? Just one thing . . ." I paused to build up
impact, and she said, "am I supposed to guess?" and, ignoring
that—in the speech I hadn't taken the possibility of rebuttals into
account—I said, "just what the fuck are you doing?" leaving
that to hang there in the air like the KO punch I felt it was.
"Why don't you tell me, A.," she said, "since that's obviously
what you came to do," and I said, "I'm asking you," realizing
the speech was veering off course, and she said, "no, you aren't,
you're not really interested in what I have to say, you've made
up your mind already—you just ask the question to set up your
come-back," and the pages of my speech fluttered off the lectern
and danced away across the grass. I had to admit she had a
certain point, and, of course, I realized fairness had to play
some part in her destruction—I wanted to be fair, of course—
so, ad-libbing it, feeling very fair and generous, I said, "well,
go ahead then, you tell me, I'm listening with an open mind."

Jane laughed like that was hilarious, glaring at me with
amused, ironic, woeful spite and pumping that foot harder. Taking another chomp out of her apple and chewing it like it was
the text of my lost speech, she said, "you have got one *hell* of
a nerve, boy," and I said, "me?" and she said, "yes, you,

buddyroe, you come over here like God Almighty with a thunderbolt all set for Judgment Day, and then you give me the oppor-*tu*-nity''—the word just smoked—''to defend myself, oh, thank you, thank you, like it was a foregone conclusion I did something wrong and would owe *you* some sort of explanation if I did. Well, number one, I didn't do anything I'm ashamed of, and, number two, if I did it wouldn't be any of your damn business, thank you *very* much.''

"So you didn't go to bed with Faison?" I asked as ironically as possible, and she said, "and you didn't go to bed with Morgan, *Red*?" and I said, "just leave her out of this, McCrae—what I did isn't any of your business," and she opened her eyes with an expression of hilarious amazement, saying, "and what I did is yours, Jenrette?" and I said, "I'm making it my business—because of Cary." That seemed to score a point—my first—because Jane just sat there staring at a spot in midair about a foot in front of her with her lips pursed and a brooding petulant expression on her face. Her leg was going with a life of its own. Returning to the attack while she was down, I said, "so, Jane, did you sleep with him?" in my softest voice, "I mean, I saw you there this morning drinking coffee in his robe, but I guess that doesn't prove anything, does it." Emerging from her trance, she said, "so you did see us," and it was so weak I almost pitied her—destruction first though, then, maybe, pity. "So you admit you slept with him?" I said, and she said, "I don't admit anything," rallying, "I *may* have, or I may not have. The point is, you saw me there this morning and just *assumed*, and you came over here to read me the riot act. You're just unbelievable, A., you know that?"

Feeling the momentum begin to slip away again, I decided to try a different tack. "Look, Jane," I said, "what you do is your own business . . ." and she said, "oh, thank you, A., that's really big of you," and I said, "as far as I'm concerned, I don't care what you do or who you do it with . . ." Jane snickered and said, "*right*, you don't care," and I went on, "as far as I'm concerned, you can fuck every cowboy in Dare County and their horses, too . . ." at which point Jane threw back her head and laughed out loud. "Oh, *thank* you, Red," she said, "the pony boy gives his permission, now I can just tell them all to form a line," and I said, "how do you know about that?" and she said, "Morgan showed me the poem she was writing you." I just bled and took it, returning to the text. "But you know what I thought?'' I asked her, and she said, "no, A., I have no idea—what did you think?'' and I said, "I thought we were friends.''

Jane absorbed that with an expression of amused incredulity. "You thought we were friends,'' she said, "uh-huh, I see,'' and I said, giving her my most earnest face, "yeah, Jane, I really did, man,'' and she said, "let me see if I've got this right, okay? you, my friend, were just looking out for me, right? checking up on whether I'd got home after you'd stalked off and left me there, and assuming, since I hadn't, that I was inside fucking every cowboy in Dare County and all their horses, too, and rushing over here to see if I was okay and to tell me so gently and sweetly and with such friendly concern that you were worried about me and that you were glad I was okay—is that it?'' and I said, "aw, man—why do you have to piss on it, Jane?'' and she said, "are you really that big of a hypocrite, or are you just more retarded than I thought?''

Reaching for the last shred of my dignity, I said, "you still didn't answer my question—did you sleep with him or not? If you didn't, I'm a worm and I swear I'll crawl away and never bother you again, but if you did . . .'' I paused, not sure what the consequence would be, but hoping I could think of something, and Jane said, "if I did, then what?'' forcing the issue, and I said, "then you're a stupid fucking pad who doesn't have the sense to tell piss from lemonade, which is Faison and Cary respectively. Because Cary happens to be my best friend, Jane''—I was beginning to recover traction and even getting on a roll—"in case you'd forgotten. He's my best friend and he happens to be in love with you, and I guess I just assumed you loved him, too, and maybe it's assuming too much, but I sort of thought that might mean it wouldn't be necessary to post an armed guard around your house twenty-four hours a day . . .''

Jane cut me off and said, "meaning you,'' and I said, "okay, I'm not ashamed of looking out for Cary—he'd do it for me—and it doesn't mean I'm going to go peeking in any windows or snapping Polaroids, but if you just flaunt it in my face, Jane, I mean, Jesus, what do you expect?'' and Jane said, "first it's for my welfare, now it's Cary's—what's the real reason, A.?'' She narrowed her eyes studying me like the answer to this one had her really interested, and I just shook my head and said, "that's all there is, Jane. Cary's the bottom line. I thought you loved him, and now I'm asking you, if you do, then just exactly what the fuck are you doing?''

"I'll tell you something, A.," she said, "I *do* love Cary—maybe not the way he wants me to, and definitely not the way you think, but he doesn't own me. And neither do you, buddyroe," and I said, "me? wait just a minute, Jane, hold the fucking phone. Let's leave me out of this, okay? I don't *want* to own you." Jane just stared at me like she wasn't sure she bought it, like she wasn't sure exactly what she thought, but there was just the ghost of an idea somewhere far back in her eyes. I saw it, too, and it scared the living shit out of me, but Jane didn't speak it, she just said, "then stop acting like it, A."

I nodded and threw up my hands. "Okay, Jane," I said, "I know you think I'm full of shit and I don't care about you, but I had to say it, just for the record. Cary loves you and you're going to hurt him, and I don't think Faison's worth it," and she said, "I don't know what you know or don't know about it, A., but I'm going to tell you. I've known Cary a long time and there's nobody in the whole world I care about more. Yes, last summer when I met you and we did those 'shrooms he and I were going together, but we aren't now—not since Christmas. When Cary came up to the dance I told him I was going to see other people, so whatever you may think it's not like I'm running around behind his back—and even if we did sleep together over spring break that's how it still stands between him and me. Okay? So just get that through your head—what I do down here this summer isn't Cary's business, damnit, it just isn't." She sighed and said, "I swear, sometimes I wish I could just go back to being friends with Cary the way we were before, but he won't let that happen," and I said quietly, as the true nature of her feelings became clearer, "he loves you, Jane, he thinks you're just going through some sort of phase and that the two of you'll get it back together in the fall in Chapel Hill." I left that out there as a question—like, didn't she think so, too?—and she said, "I'm not a fortune teller, A., I can't read the future—all I know is how I feel right now," and I said, "how's that?" and she said softly, almost wearily, "it's over." I just stared at her a moment before I said, "then you better tell him that, Jane, I don't think he understands," and she said, "Cary knows, A., he just doesn't want to face it." I just stood there knowing how much Cary had invested and feeling a shocked sorrow for him.

"But how can you be interested in someone like Faison and not in Cary?" I asked, and she said, "what have you got to say against Cleanth?" and I said, "well, for one thing, he's old enough to be your father," and she said, "I don't think age makes any difference, A., but mostly it's just because he's fun—can you understand that? He's fun and he's attractive and he was nice to me, unlike some people, it's that simple. I didn't say I was going to marry him, or even fall in love with him, I just like him and I want to have a little fun—is that really so incomprehensible?" and I said, "Cary's still twice the man Faison is," and Jane said, "Cary isn't down here, A. I know you're going to jump all over me for saying it, but if he really wanted to be with me, he would be. They don't need him to run that cafeteria, he *wants* to be there."

Knowing in my heart that she was right on that at least, I said, "but *Faison*? Jesus, Jane, I mean, he's interesting and nice enough, I'll give you that, but I'm telling you, there's something off about the guy," and Jane said, "I don't get it, A.—why are you so critical? Cleanth was nice to you and you distrust him for it—why? Why can't you just take it on the surface? Why can't it just be fun sometimes?"

She shook her head. "It's like you don't really like anything or trust anything and you have to analyze it all to death. I mean, I don't know you that well either, A., and maybe I'm wrong—I hope I am—but it seems like every time we're together you end up turning things into some universal tragedy where you're the hero and everybody else is wrong and it's their fault things turn out so bad. But it isn't, A. Your daddy didn't cause that scene at Jimbo's—*you* walked out—Cleanth didn't do anything to you, and neither did I. It's you, honey. You force the issue every time, and it doesn't have to be that way. Things aren't half as bad as you make out, A. You think people don't like you—you probably think I don't like you now and that's why I'm saying this, but I do like you, A. It sort of mystifies me, but I do, and maybe it's because you seem so sincere, and I know you mean to do the right thing if you only knew what it was, and I guess other people sense that, too, but this criticizing isn't the right thing, A., and I just have to ask you, from the bottom of my heart—why don't you like anything?—because I want to know so I can be your friend."

Holding myself firm, I said, "that's not true, I like lots of things—and this isn't about me anyway," and Jane said, "well, just let it be about you for a minute—name one, just one thing you like, I want to know," and I said, "I like running," and she said, "Running doesn't count," and I said, "why not?"

and she said, "because it isn't about fun, it's about testing your-self," and I said, "but it feels good," and she said, "I'm talking about something simple and lighthearted that isn't about self-improvement, something frivolous and happy, like dancing—why don't you like to dance, A.?" and I said, quietly, "I never learned, Jane," and she said, "if you'd wanted to, you could have found out. I'd be glad to teach you sometime, A." She smiled, and I said, "don't do me any favors," but my voice was trembling. "I won't, if you won't let me, A.," she said, "but it would make me really happy to see you just relax and have some fun. It's really okay to do that, you know. So do me a favor, A., make it easy for me, tell me something you like."

Sending my last ragged platoon into the fray, I said, "fuck you, Jane, just fuck you, okay? I'm not going to play your little game," and Jane actually smiled as she said, "see what I mean? That's so typical. That's classic A. Jenrette—fuck you, you're such a worm and I'm so superior I don't even deign to respond—and then you stalk off mad. And what do you do then, A.? You go back to that big old lonely cottage and stalk around those rooms, and maybe you run a few miles and read a book, or maybe you go out and get shitfaced and pick somebody up and in the morning you cut out as soon as possible so you don't have to talk to her or see her face—I mean, isn't that what you do? I don't mean to hurt your feelings or put you on the spot, but . . ." and I said, "yes, you do," and she said, "well, maybe just a little—I owe you one—but anyway, when you think of something that you really like, I want you to come over here and tell me, A., because that will make my day. We'll have a cele-bration, we'll have a big party and drink champagne and do the shag just for the frivolous hell of it, because that will really be something, the day Mr. A. Jenrette finds something that's good enough for him to like it," and because I'd spent all my am-munition and could think of nothing else to do short of breaking furniture or bursting out in tears, I just said, "well, don't hold your breath, Jane," using her own phrase, and she laughed and said, "I won't, believe me."

I turned around and started heading for the door, and just as I was pulling it open Jane said, "by the way." I stopped and turned to look "Not that it's any of your business, A.," she said, "but just because, in spite of everything, I do like you and want to be your friend—I didn't sleep with Cleanth. I mean, I slept with him, but that was all." I stood there, thunderstruck, and said, "you didn't?" feeling an amazing and incomprehensible happiness singing like a canary underneath the rubble of a toppled building, and Jane said "no, A., I didn't." She was smiling, and I said, "you swear to God?" and Jane just laughed and said, "did you bring a Bible?" and because I was too stunned to speak, a mere carcass smoking on the highway, Jane said, "I don't do it on the first date, A., whatever you may think of me," and I wanted to tell her, "I think you're a saint, a muse, a fairy princess," and I might have done it, except that Jane said, "but I have to tell you something, A., I was seriously tempted, and if he asks again, I just may take him up on it."

It was back to "die, you bitch," again—no, not quite that. I simply looked at her and thought her face was made for tragedies and sorrows, and that I would have liked to save her if I could, but, of course, it wasn't personal. And Jane said, "I don't see any reason why I shouldn't, A.," and something flickered in her beautiful green eyes—maybe I just wanted it to be there—before she said, "do you?" It was so quiet I could hear the waves lapping outside in the sound—the tide was coming in. I just said, "I guess not, Jane, if that's what you want," and Jane said, "yeah, that's what I think, too," and then she dropped her browning apple core into the ashtray on the table and said, "bye, A., come back when you're nice," and I headed out to knock balls with Cleanth Faison.

Eight

When I arrived, Cleanth was hitting off the ball machine under the lights. He was wearing black—black Polo shirt, black shorts, black leather sneakers. For one sweet fleeting second I thought perhaps he didn't play enough to know court etiquette, but that was whistling in the dark. I realized it as soon as I heard the sharp consistent *thwang* of gut and watched the luminous green balls whizzing low over the net, so hard and flat they skidded when they hit the darker green of Grass-Tex. He was bobbing in the backhand court, driving one down the line, then stepping smoothly to his forehand, sending the next one cross court, deep to the baseline, then sliding back, whacking the third ball backhand cross court, and sending the fourth one forehand down the line. It was like a dance—four shots—whap, whap, whap, whap. Bing, bing, bing, bing.

I leaned up against a pine tree, watching from the shadows, clutching my old Tad, and Cleanth went through it four times, sixteen shots, and every one was hit with that crisp sterling *thwang*, and only two of them went out. By inches. A lump formed in my throat and I fingered my strings, which suddenly felt a little woolly, but I didn't lose hope. I could also hit it hard, if not with anything like that placement, and I had a secret weapon, my first serve, which, even when I was thirteen at the Killdeer Country Club, had made grown men, strong players, blink their eyes and shake their heads as they went to pluck my aces from the chainlink fence. It was erratic though. Sometimes

271

my serve went into the fence without bothering to check in in
my opponent's service court. And my second serve was mud, I
didn't even have one, I just hit two big ones and figured, what
the hey, fifty-fifty, one of them will probably go in. I'd seen that
logic fail before. But maybe tonight the magic would be with
me. I prayed silently and walked into the light.

Cleanth had all the paraphernalia of a pro on the World Tennis
Tour—sweatbands, headband, rosin bag in pocket, three, four
rackets, towels, Gatorade icing in a thermos. He stopped when
he saw me and came over drying his face in a towel—he'd worked
up a good sweat. "A., my man," he said, holding his hand out
shoulder high, then clapping it to mine as I offered it, "how's it
going?" and I said, "I'm alive, more or less," thinking of Jane,
and Cleanth grinned into my eyes like that was good, he wanted
me alive. After shaking hands, we moved to a clear court and
started rallying. "Any time you're ready, A.," he said, and I
said, "that's okay, man, we can start," like I was doing him a
favor. Really, I just didn't want him to know too much about
my game.

I won the spin and lobbed across a couple of practice serves
to loosen up my swing. Then staring dead into the forehand
corner of his service court, deliberately telegraphing that, I
coiled back and hammered one the other way, to his backhand,
the old switcharoo. The ball hit the center line and skidded back
six inches off the ground. Cleanth bought my fake and got caught
leaning to his forehand. He still lunged for it, but his racket just
sucked wind. Inside a silent shout of glee went off like dyna-
mite, ancient and familiar—die, you fucker! read them cards
and weep—all underneath a casual, almost bored expression. I
considered yawning, but that seemed like overdoing it. I'd destroyed him, he was mine, the set was over.

Only Cleanth didn't seem all that destroyed, no attentive deferential look like a cocky dog who's just come from obedience
school. "Nice serve," he said and smiled like he hadn't expected
me to be so sly—all the better, his eyes seemed to say. No matter—I smiled right back at him. I had the fuck-wah where I wanted
him. Because I'd set up the telegraph, and the telegraph sets up
the telegraph reverse, you see, which is when you fake forehand
and go forehand. That's what I did the second time. Cleanth got
his racket on that one—no sterling *thwang* though, just a sickly
jangled sound like a guitar dropped onto concrete. The ball
bounced on his side first and skipped into the net. Thirty-love. I

began to think this might grow boring, but maybe with a little effort, I could steel myself to it.

I hit the third one straight at him, which was the variation on the variation. The ball bounced high, straight for Cleanth's head, but he stepped aside and returned it backhand. Though it was shoulder-high, he got his body into it, and I stood there with a swinging dick and watched it hit an inch in front of me and bounce away between my feet. Thirty-fifteen. Back in the ad-court, my first serve went into the net, and my second one, which I smashed just as hard, nicked the tape and landed out. We had our first rally then. Cleanth sent me cross court, cross court, down the line, making saves I considered unbelievable, while he came to net and stood there bouncing on his toes, working me like that goddamned ball machine until I knocked a home run straight over the fence. I started to go after it, but Cleanth said, "leave it, A., we'll get it later." He wasn't smiling or grinning or really even looking at me, just in a steely trance—*the* trance. I seemed to remember I was hungover, yeah, pretty wasted, not feeling too good at all. I was psyching myself out and knew it. Was I that easy? No way, man, no fucking way. I double-faulted at game point. Maybe I was that easy. It went straight downhill from there.

Switching sides, I discovered Cleanth had a big serve, too, only he also had a second one, a mean spin slice that just floated over and then went haywire. You couldn't respect a serve like that—it was a pussy serve, a Ping-Pong serve. It went funny off my racket every time. I felt disdain, and it was now two games to zip. In the third game, my serve went south on me. I threw my faithful Tad into the fence and cursed and felt my features being subtly molded into the expression of a cocky dog who's just come from obedience school. I sighed and saw my fate. It wasn't pretty. Just endure it, asshole. It ended at 6–0. The agony of defeat didn't even come close, we're talking wormhood. The only shred of dignity I preserved was managing not to suggest a second set.

Cleanth didn't either. He stood there wiping down at net, drinking icy Gatorade—I refused it when he offered—and said, "good match, A." I smiled at him ironically and he said, "no, I mean it, you played much better than your score," and I said, "actually, you were looking kind of bored there toward the end, Cleanth," and he said, "was I? I didn't feel bored at all, I always like to win," and I said, "so do I," and he said, "do you?"

with complete casualness. "Sure, who doesn't?" I asked, and he looked me dead in the eyes and said, "you'd be surprised."

I stared back at him alert for signs of insult. Had there been any, I might have bristled and challenged him, or made some cuttingly polite excuse and taken off, leaving behind any possibility of friendship together with the tennis match. But Cleanth's expression didn't taunt or mock me, it sympathized, as if to say, I understand, I've been there in that same unhappy place, now I'm here in a far better one, and I can show you how to get from where you are to where I am. The understanding in his eyes wasn't just of me personally, it seemed to extend to the mystery of self-defeat itself and to the even greater one of victory. Surprised as I was at the suggestion that I was one of those who doesn't really want to win, or can't, I bled and took it in the hope that Cleanth might tell me why, and how to change it. So when he put his arm around my shoulder and said, "come on, let's take a ride," I went.

Cleanth had a black Porsche 911—I'd seen it in the parking lot and figured it was his—and as we slipped into the leather seats, he dipped his key into the little vial and snorted off the end of it, then dipped again and I hit, too. Pulling a Miller High Life from the plastic rings, he popped the top and handed it to me. "Chin chin," he said, and turned the engine over. "What about my Jeep?" I said, not really caring all that much as it kicked in, and he said, "we'll come back for it later," and we pulled out of the lot, laying down a line of rubber on the road and spraying gravel in the bushes.

I leaned back into the perfume of the leather and listened to the engine rise into a high-pitched whine and drop back to a purr each time he shifted, incredibly powerful and incredibly precise. Within seconds we were doing eighty, and Cleanth turned to me, his towel draped around his neck and the wind flying through his hair, and said, "you like?" and I said, "normally I'm not that into cars, but this one's pretty cool." Cleanth grinned and said, "that's a double statement, A.—'normally I don't but . . .'—just like it, try being single." It was like he'd aimed a spotlight into the darkness of my brain, and I thought, whoa, *that's* what Jane meant by liking something—not a no happening inside you even as you said yes, but one clear unconflicted answer. I was getting it, a little. The cocaine seemed to help. I still had to think about it though.

Cleanth pulled over on the shoulder and said, "give it a spin," and I said, "I don't know, man," thinking how expensive that car was, and what if . . . Then I caught myself, and Cleanth caught me catching it. He grinned and I grinned back and said, "okay, why not?" and he said, "that's the question," and I said, "it's the answer, too, right?" and he said, "*oh*, yeah, you're getting it now, A., you're playing," and it was true, I was. The tennis match was forgotten, even Jane had receded to the size of a Lady Liberty on an old dime. I slipped behind the wheel and pressed the pedal to the metal. The cocaine definitely helped.

We headed south down the bypass, zipping along, passing everything in sight. I paid no attention to the yellow lines. This car wasn't made for yellow lines, there was nothing yellow about this car at all. Eight miles down we passed the Wright Brothers Memorial—a sixty-foot wing of solid granite perched on the grassy knoll of Kill Devil Hill, looking more like the fin of a Great White Shark in the floodlights that had just come on in the bluish twilight.

"Hang a right," Cleanth said, and I downshifted and started down the road to Colington Island. We hadn't gone a thousand yards when Cleanth pointed right again, and I said, "the airport?" and he nodded, and we turned onto a small winding road with a wall of pine trees on the right and an open grassy field on the left across a fence of posts connected by a strand of cable. When we pulled into the small paved lot, I stopped and said, "what's up?" and Cleanth grinned and said, "we're about to be," and leaned over, switching off the ignition and pocketing the keys. "Come on," he said.

There were half a dozen private planes lined up in a small cove built off the main runway, surrounded on three sides by trees. Above them, the squarer backside of the Memorial loomed, strangely clear and spectral in the gauzy dusk. Cleanth walked toward a white single-engine Mooney, and I said, "this is yours?" as I followed. "Just bought it," he said, "where we going?" and he said, "nowhere, just up—I want you to see the lights. Get those lines." He pointed. A length of nylon cord held each wing down to cleats sunk in the asphalt.

While I unclipped them, Cleanth slid into the cockpit where I could see him fiddling with knobs and switches. The instrument panel lit up, electronic green, and then the lights came on on the wing. "Stand clear of the prop," he called through the open door. The propeller turned once, coughed, then caught and whirred into a roaring blur, silver with the reflection from the lights. I smelled gasoline, only richer than that, and climbed into the cramped, tiny cockpit beside him. It wasn't like a Porsche, more like a sardine can with wings and a mother V-8. Turning right out of the cove onto the runway, we taxied to the north end, then reversed, idled for a second and took off across that grassy field.

Clearing a string of power lines, the stand of pines below us receded to a small clear shape like a jigsaw piece, a black kidney. As we went higher, the grid of streets clarified and you saw the streetlamps hung at measured intervals like strings of Christmas lights. I changed my mind—it was even better than a Porsche. It was my first time in a small plane, a different experience entirely from flying in a big commercial jet. The wide cockpit windows gave you the sense that you were almost out there, floating naked in it, and there was a sense of higher order you never saw below—not symmetry, but order. The cocaine probably helped, though the rush was fading then. Nothing was haphazard, and there were so many lights, millions of them, not like a city, but with intervals of darkness spacing them, making each one precious. Not just the watery greenish streetlamps, but dusky yellow ones, the red and orange glare of neon in curved shapes blinking on the hotel signs, a weird blue-purple vertical that might have been a bug light, and the softer light from peoples' windows, which seemed white below but up here was a warm yellow, a very human color. For some reason that light made me sad, though that might have been the cocaine, too, coming down from it.

"What do you see?" Cleanth asked, and I said, "I was just thinking we live in yellow light thinking all the time it's white," and he said, "does that seem sad to you?" and I said, "yeah, it does, a little," and he said, "you know what's even sadder?" and I said, "what?" and he said, "most people know it's yellow." I turned from the window to stare at him. "Do they?" I asked, "I always thought it was white," and Cleanth said, "now you're finding out it's yellow and that makes you sad because you think that's the end of it. That's what most people think, A., and it's why they fail, because when they learn it's yellow they give up. But there's another step. You can know it's yellow and believe it's white—that's what all the great players do. And you know what happens then?" and I said, "what?" and he said, "it *is* white, believing whitens it, and the more you believe the whiter it gets," and I said, earnestly, "but isn't that just pretending, Cleanth?" and he said, "the difference between believing and pretending is the difference between winning and losing, A. That's what happened out there on that court tonight. You pretended to be a tennis player, but I believed I was one. That's why I won—I didn't beat you, A., you beat yourself, and I knew you would before I ever saw you play, because I used to beat myself exactly the same way."

His perception didn't make my hackles rise that time. I listened with a strange ache of sorrow and stared away out the window remembering facing my father in similar circumstances—on a tennis court, or underneath a hoop and net—him saying, "it's no shame to lose, son, the only shame is when you beat yourself," because I always had. Daddy knew it, Cleanth knew it, Cary knew it, even Jane knew. I was the only one who didn't know. I knew though, underneath I did. Even at eighteen I was tired of it, tired of losing and being mad at everything because of it—mad at other people, mad at myself, mad at life. Feeling Cleanth's hand on my shoulder, I turned to look at him. "There's a real brightness in you, A.," he said quietly, "you're the only one who doesn't see it, and that's a shame, because if you could just release it, it would free you. When you learn to play life isn't hard anymore. The game's up here"—he tapped his temple—"and no amount of practice makes you get it, it happens in a crystal flash. You're so close, A.—I'd like to see you get there," and I said, "then tell me how, Cleanth, if you know," and he said, "you know what playing is, the real kind?" and I said, "what?" and he said, "a blood hunt, A. If you don't believe me, watch kids do it sometime—they don't take prisoners. You have that killer instinct—you wanted to destroy me and drink my blood out there tonight—but you lack the will to use it. Your mistake is thinking killing is something to descend to. It isn't A.—you have to rise to blood. We can talk forever, but the only way you're ever going to understand what I'm saying is by experiencing it yourself. You really should come hunting with me sometime, A.—it's so much clearer in the woods. I don't think you'd be bored."

"I'm not bored now, Cleanth," I said, and he took the surface compliment together with the deeper assent implied in it, which wasn't to a hunting trip, but my assent to some larger proposition whose name was never spoken aloud between us, but only in the whispers of little voices—his inner voice to mine, and mine to his.

Cleanth pressed my shoulder and we fell silent then, sharing the view from that great height. An orange blaze, the last blush of sunset, was fading in the west, and as Cleanth made a slow roll northward I caught my first glimpse of the moon, blood-red, floating just over the horizon. It was chilling. Everything else seemed small, but that moon was enormous. Below, the Atlantic undulated like a broken sheet of safety glass, glinting fractured edges grinding together over an underlying smooth-ness and fluidity. The horizon backed off to a hundred miles instead of twenty, and there was a redoubled sense of vastness there which the toylike roar the engine made only enhanced. I felt a kind of awe which came less from the outer landscape than from the curious sense that I was gazing down into an inner one which Cleanth had opened up to me.

He took us over darkening marshes and the black Albemarle with a sheen of curried moonlight in it, narrowing toward Virginia, over the vast forest wilderness of Currituck broken by occasional lakes. Far off in the distance, I could just make out the illuminated sprawl of Norfolk and Virginia Beach shimmering like a galaxy in its own fumes, and as we turned back toward the airstrip Cleanth flew low over the ocean which lay like a straightedge up against the beach, the dark water strangely brighter than the dull gleam of paler sand.

After that plane ride something was different between Cleanth and me. Till then I'd looked for reasons to distrust him—afterward I looked for reasons to believe. I never really looked back after that. Thus I acquired a master, even as a little whisper, ever fainter, said, "a monster"—both perhaps. Though I stepped reluctantly, I had to go, because no one had ever made me such an offer. No one ever did again.

Nine

A.

I wanted to go home that night. The thought of a moonlight
dip, a warm shower in the breezy outdoor stall, knocking
back a cold one, maybe two, clean sheets, falling asleep to
the sound of the ocean through my opened window, alter-
nately booming and whispering, the glassy tinkling of the
windchimes on the porch—it sounded good, just what the
doctor ordered. I was tired, wired but tired. I'd had enough
of human beings for a while, strange species. I wanted to be
alone and absolutely still.

Back at the tennis courts, as Cleanth dropped me off beside
my Jeep, he said, "I'll see you back at the hotel." One leg
outside the door, I turned back and stared at him. "Morgan's
expecting you," he said, and I said, "I don't know, Cleanth,
I'm pretty beat," and he said, "just stop in for a few minutes,
she'll appreciate it, A.," and I said, "you really think she
cares?" and he said, "she wouldn't have asked you upstairs
last night if it didn't matter to her." I hesitated, tugged in
different directions by the implied flattery, my underlying indifference, a sense of obligation, resentment of that obligation, liking Morgan, liking Cleanth, embarrassment at facing
her again, a sluggish mental titillation at the memory of the
previous night, simple weariness. It was hard being single
when you were tired. The balance tipped toward "no."
Cleanth produced a vial. We hit. The balance tipped toward
"yes."

"Can I ask you something, man?" I said, and he said, "shoot," and I said, "you and Morgan . . ." not knowing how to phrase it, and he said, "you mean *you* and Morgan, don't you?" I just stared at him, not sure exactly what I meant, and he said, "it's okay, A.," and I said, "it doesn't bother you?" and he said, "why should it?" and I said, "you know she's in love with you, right?" and he pursed his lips, becoming solemn, and said, "I know," and I said, "but you don't love her," drawing what seemed the obvious conclusion, and he said, "I love her a lot, probably more than she knows," and I said, "then what's the deal?" and he said, "there was a time I wanted to marry M., A.—it didn't work out. I had to let her go. If we'd married I doubt we'd even be speaking now, much less living together. Things change too fast, A., people do. Love changes, too. You can't hold it still—trying to is what makes the unhappiness. But, yeah, I still love her. We don't fuck—that's her decision, not mine—but I love her, more than anyone."

"What about Jane?" I asked, and he blinked and said, "what about her?" and I said, "I mean, how do you feel about her, Cleanth?" and he said, "I only met her, A.," and I said, "yeah, but it looked like it was getting pretty hot and heavy to me." He stared at me appraisingly and said, "if you don't want me to see her, A., I won't, but you'll have to give me a pretty good reason why I shouldn't. There's really just one reason," and I said, "I told you why, man, my best friend is in love with her," and Cleanth smiled beneath sober eyes and said, "that's not the right reason, A." I knew the reason he was fishing for, but I didn't even want to consider the possibility, much less speak it. Cleanth spoke it. "Are you in love with her, A.?" he asked quietly, and I said, "no, man, absolutely not, it's Cary, that's all," and he said, "I have to take you at your word," almost like a warning, and I said, "I just like her, Cleanth, I don't want to see her hurt," and he said, "hurting her wasn't what I had in mind . . . I think we understand each other, don't we?" and though I wasn't sure we did, not too sure at all, I said nothing.

"So what should I tell M.?" he asked, regarding me expectantly. I took a deep breath and said, "I've got to go home first and change." He nodded, smiling, as I climbed out of the Porsche, then rolled his window up and drove away, leaving me standing there beside the dark courts in a pool of light from the lamp, listening to the whisper of the pines. I felt confused and subtly coerced, bone tired and speeding all at once. Suddenly the thought of clean sheets didn't seem so attractive, I knew I wouldn't sleep for hours, if at all. The house would just be another loneliness, and then I saw an image of the Lost Colony lit up like an ocean liner—people, laughter, fun—was this what Jane had meant? Was this what I really wanted? Maybe not, but going home was not it either. Why not? I thought. At least the Lost Colony was something. Why the fuck not? I didn't even go back home. Those sheets stayed clean for many a night, till they got dirty by themselves.

Cleanth's car wasn't there when I arrived at the Lost Colony. I walked into the ballroom. Reese was spinning tunes. The group was there, along with some new faces. They nodded. I nodded. I went upstairs and knocked on Morgan's door. She answered in a gray silk robe, beneath which I knew there was nothing long before she let me take it off. The nipples gave it all away. I looked. She saw me look. Her eyes said, "you may look," and also, "first the sauce." "You came," she said, "I wasn't sure you would." She seemed shy and timid with me at first. I saw she'd put on makeup, fresh red lipstick. I was touched, surprised and flattered at her effort. My former hesitation began to seem unreasonable and niggardly. "Come in," she said, parting the door. I went in. It started over.

There was music playing, something classical, Chopin perhaps. At one point Morgan said, sensing my ambivalence perhaps, as we drank cognac and leaned down from time to time into an undiminished tray of virgin Alpine snow, "it doesn't have to be so heavy, you know, Adam, I really don't expect too much of you—just kindness and . . ." She smiled with a sweet coyness and I caught the rest. The record stopped and Morgan's eyes went to the window, turning somber. "You know how it should be, don't you?" she asked, looking at me above the snifter as she sipped, and I said, "how?" and she said, "him and me, and you and Jane." She held the cognac on her palate, swallowed and then shrugged with an assumed lightheartedness, becoming the spoiled princess, "but the music's stopped and we're the ones without the chairs." She got up and put another record on, a different one. I don't think it was classical, maybe blues—Sarah Vaughn perhaps. Morgan liked her. I never got the hang of it. But there was texture there, with Morgan, and richness, and her frankness was refreshing to me, a new experience, tinged with sadness but so real. That was our contract, not a great one, but not a bad one either, entirely good enough, and she was very sexy with her nipples budding in that gray silk robe.

I brushed her hair again that night, and Morgan gave me head—she seemed to like it, and I didn't mind too much myself. She did it very well. After we made love, or fucked—whatever it was that Morgan and I did together, something in between perhaps—as she lay there, pinching her cigarette between her thumb and index finger, blowing smoke rings at the ceiling and looking like a spoiled but charming princess sent away to prep school by the king, her evil father, and left till overdone, she said, not so much to me, but simply musing, "this makes it all a little clearer," and I said, "what?" and she said, "Cleanth . . . what he sees in them," and I said, "in who?" and she looked at me and said, "all those young girls," and I said, "what?" and she said, "it's being inside it"—she made a princess simper—"or having it be inside you—youth."

Her eyes turned suddenly soulful, and she said, "is that an awful thing to say?" She rolled onto my chest and searched my eyes for signs of offense. I took her cigarette, pinching it between my thumb and index finger, took a puff and blew it in her face. She laughed delightedly. I laughed, too. I wasn't offended in the least. "You're very funny, Adam," she said, and I said, "so are you . . . but Morgan?" She raised her brows inquisitively and said, "what, darling?" and I said, "since we've become so intimate, I want you to feel free to call me Mr. Jenrette." She roared. I roared, too, blushing with embarrassed pleasure. Of all the things that I'd been called, complimentary and otherwise, funny wasn't one of them. It was so easy with Morgan, so easy to be light, to speak the dangerous thought and find it wasn't dangerous at all, so easy to let go of her—because I never held her. It made me wonder if maybe Cleanth was right about love. But the wondering came later.

The second morning I didn't run away. When light came through the windows I found her bed was not a bed of torment for me any longer. There was a soiled sweetness and a comfort in the sheets we had abused so well. Morgan set her alarm for me, one of her little courtesies I grew used to. I never touched that clock. I also got used to early breakfast there, fresh-squeezed orange juice, black coffee freshly ground from sacred and expensive beans, and Patrick's scones warm from the ovens. When I appeared at breakfast there were looks, raised eyebrows, but by the third morning, or the fourth, the looks had vanished. We were quietly an item. After the first week I rarely went back home at all. My jams, my Lifeguard tee shirt, my prized Vuarnets with a cord and leather blinkers to keep out the least trace of UV rays hung on a brass hook behind her bathroom door. The gray robe occupied another. Morgan cleared a bathroom shelf for me. I invested in a second toothbrush, which rested there, along with a crumpled tube of zinc oxide, which made me think of cadmium white each morning as I smeared my nose with it. My paint box came along as well. At night I sometimes painted her, or did nude life drawings in pen and ink. In the mornings sometimes Cleanth would look at them and make technical corrections. Morgan was a willing model. They both encouraged me. It didn't seem strange at all. My previous life seemed strange. What previous life? I hadn't had one.

I began to smoke the occasional cigarette. Morgan and I would pass them back and forth in bed and elsewhere. Our greatest argument was who would take the harrowing two a.m. trip to the 7-Eleven to pick up a new pack. We took turns. Sometimes we went together. The fags seemed to help arrange the energy between lines, both drawn and snorted. I began to like wine with dinner. I tolerated white, but preferred the richness and complexity of red. I woke up sick each morning and forced myself to take a run. My lungs felt like they'd been scraped with a dull razor blade. I threw up on the beach and went in for a pleasant breakfast.

The second morning when I went down, Cleanth's Porsche wasn't in the lot. I wondered where he was and thought I knew. If I had any doubts, they vanished the third morning when I was greeted by Jane's silver Olds, her mother's car, sparkling mutedly with dew. I saw it there each morning parked beside my Jeep, two mismatched hulks comforting one another through the lonely nights. Jane and Cleanth became an item, too. B.J. fumed, made nasty comments, and fucked half the cowboys in Dare County and their horses, too. Her sheer persistence in bad will made me grow to like her finally. She had a rare talent.

The Lost Colony became my second home. My first one stood unoccupied. Inside the phone rang on and on. Sometimes when I woke up on those mornings I fancied I could almost hear it down the beach five miles away, or late at night when Morgan had passed out and I lay there with gritted teeth squinching my eyelids closed and trying to sleep through the cocaine. I knew who was calling—it was Cary. One day in my box there was a note from him. I tore open the envelope and a snapshot fluttered out onto the floor of the Kill Devil Hills PO. The Polaroid showed him standing in the cafeteria in a bloody apron, his head turned sideways over his shoulder like a flamenco dancer, his eyes squinted from the smoke of the Marlboro dangling from his lip. He held a plucked chicken to his chest, one hand around its neck, the other delicately pinching its tiny claw between thumb and forefinger as though dancing a tango. Across the bottom he'd written, "Hot Date." The note said, "call me sometime, spud." My heart ached. I didn't call, knowing he'd ask about Jane. I ran that imaginary conversation a hundred times, but none of them worked out in any fashion that seemed helpful to him, or to me. Besides, Cleanth was my friend, too, and Jane, well, I didn't know exactly what she was, but I didn't want to get into it with Cary. What good would it do him? Yet I felt guilty every time I looked at that photograph. I felt I was betraying Cary, not just by acquiescing to Jane's relationship with Cleanth, but through my relationship with Cleanth as well. It seemed against Cary somehow. But Cary was far away and receding further all the time, till he was just a black silhouetted figure in the distance like the one I'd seen on the beach.

Reese and Ellen fell in love. Reese stopped waiting tables and became a DJ. Each night at eleven the floor was cleared and he spun golden oldies. The Lost Colony became the hottest dance spot on the beach. Reese never took off his dark glasses. His theme song was "I'm a Soul Man." People shagged like mad. Grown women, fresh-faced former debutantes, after eating Patrick's subtle dishes over candlelight with their husbands and a few good friends, went back to gin and tonics after wine at dinner, tapped their jeweled fingers to the beat, and then climbed on the tables, kicking off their high heel shoes and lifting up their skirts to dance, exposing slips of sheerest silk and legs that similar maneuvers had kept young. Their husbands clapped and cheered them on, or got red-faced and apoplectic. Wondering what was going on, the crowd came upstairs from the bar. I sometimes screened the door and charged five dollars. On a good night three thousand dollars crossed my palm. I put it in a metal box and handed it to Cleanth. He dug around in it and took out five crisp twenties which I'd had to change and stuffed them in the pocket of my shirt. When I demurred, he pursed his lips and shook his finger, grinning. The bathrooms became toxic waste sites. Even if you'd had the stomach to use them, you couldn't get in. Too many people were barricaded in, hoovering the blow.

I'd never seen toot on the Outer Banks before, and I'd been in every steamy den there was the previous summer, but that year it was in. The Lost Colony was full of it. People did it on the porches where men also hung loose over the rails, sending torrents down into the sand. The women went further off and squatted, pulling down their underwear. You could see the pale gleam of their blouses in the dunes. Policemen came and lectured Cleanth. He received their lectures with profuse apology and made Reese turn the music down. The policemen were appeased. They fell deep into conversation with the master. Cleanth asked B.J. over and made introductions. Cleanth skimmed a few stray bills out of the cashbox and winked at me. That money never reappeared again. On a later evening, I saw one of those same policemen in civilian garb, dancing with B.J. and doing lines with Cleanth out on the porch. I think they played Life Poker, too.

After two weeks, the burly bearded Wanchese fishermen got word. They came over in their rusted-out trucks with engines that sounded like diesel inboards. They came up on the porch in their boots and Red Man hats and peered inside with touching cautious faces, conferred and paid me their five dollars. They went inside and leaned against the wall, packing down a case apiece. When they got loose, they tore the place apart. There were fights. The Wanchese fishermen mopped the floor. Then Cleanth got in on it. He took the biggest rabble-rouser, a fellow who resembled Haystack Calhoon, by the cheeks like he was going to kiss him. Then Cleanth turned the fellow's head to the side, not all that hard, but doing something with his fingers behind the neck, and Haystack went down like a ton of bricks, sleeping like a baby.

Cleanth grinned at all the rest of them and they blinked at him with touching cautious faces. They became fast friends. I saw them doing lines out on the porch—Cleanth treated the whole clan. When Haystack finally roused himself from infant slumber, he and Cleanth kissed each other on both cheeks, like Frenchmen. There were no more fights.

The hotel was a hit. Before eleven, the restaurant was the soul of subtle gastronomic virtue. Appellate judges brought their wives and concubines to dine. Cleanth bought a Steinway grand and hired a vagabond musician who could play Chopin or not. The high and mighty came in fleets of silver German cars. Jane became the hostess. Cleanth took her on his arm and worked the tables, graciously doling out a complimentary bottle of champagne to those whose tabs exceeded two hundred dollars. Most of them were too drunk to appreciate it, but they remembered and came back. Jimbo showed to sample the cuisine with a young girl on his arm. She may have been a beard. Cleanth introduced me to everyone—there were M.D.s and M.D.s' concubines and wives, hot young realtors in BMW's who read *New York Magazine* and *Esquire* ritually and wore the latest styles and cuts but the wrong fabrics, country squires from Edenton, their handsome faces burnished from years of careful grooming and a few burnished broken capillaries in their cheeks from years of careful alcohol abuse, and Jaycee types who regarded Cleanth with frightened eyes, teetering on the edge of disapproval, but also fascinated, like perhaps he was the Antichrist, but far more attractive than their Baptist backgrounds had led them to believe.

Cleanth made me all sorts of effusive compliments to them, mentioning my father and his book and quoting wild extravagant praise from reviews I'd never seen, and I'd seen all of them. I accepted all of it, and Cleanth and I enjoyed our little joke in subtext, eye to eye, from which the others were excluded. But it wasn't like a joke either, because the underlying compliment— which was not to Clay Jenrette, the author, but to me—was meant. That's what Cleanth's eyes said, and my eyes said back to him, "run with it, you amazing crazy bastard, I'm not going to stop you."

Sometimes Morgan and I dined alone at a quiet table in the corner, and I watched Cleanth and Jane, his arm around her waist. Snatches of his conversation floated above the general din of conversation, clanking plates and vagabond Chopin—"oh, was it raining?''—and then the laughter of the group he was amusing. Morgan's eyes were thoughtful. She studied him. I studied Jane. Cleanth gave Jane the same royal treatment he gave me, even more so, making clear that she was favored. Jane's face took on a calm and gentle glow, a stillness underneath the constant radiant smile. Her hands never touched a tray, and I thought at first—I hoped—that maybe that was all Cleanth wanted from her, all her job would be, just to stand and glow beside him, a beautiful young girl with eyes of green twelfth-century glass and poised shoulders who'd been touched by the magic wand of a man's appreciation and become a woman. By the end of the first week I knew better. She was the master's concubine and didn't even know it. For her services she got minimum wage. Something thrashed and wallowed deep inside me. I thought more than ever that her face was made from tragedies and sorrows. I tried not to dwell on it. Sometimes I succeeded.

The cocaine helped, as did red wine and Patrick's subtle *nouvelle* dinners. I tried not to look at Cleanth and Jane. Sometimes I looked anyway, and once or twice—no more than that—I thought I saw a promise of great restfulness and slaked thirst in Jane's still-shining eyes. And late at night, occasionally, I'd hear Jane's laughter from the other room, or else her choked coming cry like she was trying to be discreet and couldn't help herself. Wanting to vomit up my heart, I'd lean down and do another line, or else offer to go out alone for the new pack of smokes. Maybe Jane heard mine as well, I didn't try to mute it. In the mornings we were shy with one another, a shyness that had depths and depths, a shyness that knew everything. We were rarely alone together. I avoided it, and I think Jane did, too.

One morning we met at the breakfast buffet, not ten feet from the table where the others sat conversing. I was getting coffee, Jane, one of Patrick's scones. "Did you think of anything?" Jane asked me, and I gave my head a quizzical tilt not understanding what she meant. "Anything you liked?" she said, breaking the scone and putting butter in the steaming insides. Thinking she was taunting me, I considered leaning over Morgan's chair and giving her breasts a public squeeze to show Jane what I liked. Morgan would have laughed and chided me in her best princess tone, or told me I was funny. I just said, "I'm still working on it," and Jane said, "let me know."

I surfed with Buzz and sometimes Patrick came along and brought his boogy-board and a napkin full of buttered scone crumbs from the buffet warming tray to feed the gulls. Mostly we surfed after work, but sometimes I forewent my run and we were in the murky pitching water as the sun came up. On our first trip I tried to challenge Buzz. Catching the first wave, I wedeled down the sheer glass wall, doing quick jerk turns, whooping as I caught the old sensation, like standing upright on the roof of a car going downhill at thirty-five miles an hour, feeling more like eighty, staring down at water just as cold and hard as asphalt and knowing that I wouldn't fall. I whooped and cut back across the lip and fell down on my belly, my heart hammering against the fiberglass, two hundred beats per minute.

As I paddled out, I watched Buzz catch his ride. He'd waited for the second wave and it was better, five feet easy, maybe six. Buzz didn't do quick jerk turns. He found his feet in one smooth leap and went straight down the wall, a schuss. In the trough he did a bottom turn, almost one-eighty. His left shoulder almost touched the water, his left hand did, flaring white against the green like a struck match. His body hardly moved, just a slight torquing of the shoulders. Standing straight up, with just the slightest flexing of the knees, he shot back up the face. His board sheared through the lip and I thought for sure he was going over, but he didn't, he slewed around and crouched, riding horizontally along the wall. The wave began to break with a sound like cloth ripping in an echo chamber. Buzz stepped back on the rail and dragged his hand to slow himself. The white water roared down after him like a mine shaft flood he wasn't going to get away from and didn't want to. It overtook him, Buzz disappeared inside the tube, all except his extended leading arm with a balled fist at the end of it. That vanished, too. Buzz was gone. Buzz was underneath. He was on the inside. I started counting— one thousand one, one thousand two, one thousand three. When I hit four I was sure he'd wiped out, then I saw the nose of his Lopez appear like a lady's slipper underneath a flowing costume ball dress. Buzz was on the nose. His head sheared through the top of the tube. He shook his hair around. He didn't whoop or even grin. Buzz was in the trance. He was the best I'd ever seen. He flipped back cross the top and started paddling for a new wave. I felt like a foolish bluejay who's tried to show off aerial technique before an eagle. I began to understand Buzz better.

I'd thought him vapid, but he was simply egoless, the only one of all of us. There was just one thing for Buzz. The man was single. Totally.

We talked sometimes. Buzz told me his dad had been a surfer in Laguna Beach, California. He'd had a Woodie and a ten-foot balsa spear. He listened to the Beach Boys. He still listened to the Beach Boys, Buzz said, but the Woodie and the balsa spear were gone. I asked him what he was doing at the Lost Colony, and Buzz pinched the roach and toked, then passed it to me, saying, "it's like a wave on land, man." I grinned, thinking he was joking. Buzz didn't grin at all. He stared out at the horizon and his eyes got somber. "I used to think the ocean was my friend," he said, "when I was a kid. But I was scared of it, you know?, and I thought it was my fault for being such a wuss. When I got in high school all that changed. Then I thought the ocean was my enemy. I got a whole lot better then, I don't know why." He looked at me. "That's when I rode like you, man. Not that I mean anything by it—you're as good as almost anyone I've seen around out here, but you're still not quite there, man, you know what I mean?" "I know I'm not in your league, Buzz," I said, and he shook his head and said, "you've got it, A., you're just not quite free with it. That only happens when you figure out the ocean isn't either one, not your friend and not your enemy. The ocean doesn't give a shit, it laughs either way. What happens out there, the rides you get, isn't from the ocean being nice to you or trying to fuck you over, it's just you. When I figured that one out, that's when it got extreme. That's the difference, see? When I thought the ocean was my friend, I loved it when I got a ride and blamed myself when I wiped out. When I hated it, I blamed the waves and surfed to get revenge. That felt good, too, in a different way. Then one day about four years ago I surfed tripping and it just hit me. I realized the ocean laughs either way and doesn't care, and I laughed, too, and it got so much easier. I stopped trying too hard like you do, I stopped trying to impress the water, man, I gave up on defeating it. It got extreme, A., real extreme. Cleanth's like that, too, you know? I mean, he's like a surfer only he doesn't surf. I think that's why we get along. I don't know what he's all about, but what the fuck's a wave about? Just ride it. That's all I'm doing. That's why I'm here, I guess." Buzz was a surfer-philosopher. All surfers are philosophers, only most of them are too sad and stupid to express the reason why they give up everything to do it. They're like web-footed creatures, awkward on the land, but in the water touched by grace.

Cleanth went with us sometimes. A natural athlete, he caught on quickly, standing up on the first day. It had taken me three miserable weeks, but then I was eleven, and however great an athlete Cleanth might be, he wasn't ever going to bridge that gap, which was even greater than the gap that separated me and Buzz. Cleanth knew it, too. After taking brutal spills, going over the falls, pearling, over and over, he'd leave the water and watch us from the beach. I'd be the second out. Buzz was always last to leave.

On one of those afternoons when the light was turning dusky and there was an eight-foot swell, precision tooled, so hairy I'd had all I wanted, Cleanth turned to me and said, "why don't you quit fucking off and come to work for me, A.? how much are you making now?" "Five an hour," I said, staring at him in surprise, "plus commissions on the rentals," and he said, "so, what? three hundred, three-fifty a week?" That was above my average, but I nodded, and he said, "I'll pay you five," and I said, "Five *hundred*?" and he grinned and said, "to start." Staggered by the sum, I stared away over the water, and he said, "the Lost Colony is taking off, A. It's getting to be too much for me to tend to, even with Morgan's help. Plus, I've got other business elsewhere, like the place in Hilton Head. I need someone smart who I can trust, somebody who can take initiative and think on his feet. You'd have to travel a good bit, but there'd be lots of freedom and I doubt seriously you'd be putting in the hours you are now. I'm a good boss, A., if you don't believe me ask the others." He grinned and I said, "I don't have to ask them, man, it's tempting as hell, the only problem is I signed a contract with Mick to stay till Labor Day," and Cleanth shrugged and said, "so break it—what's he going to do, sue you?" and I said, "no, I guess he wouldn't, but he's counting on me and I did promise."

Cleanth made a dismissive pout and said, "you're worth more than you're getting, A. When I say five hundred a week, I'm just talking salary. There'd be lots of perks besides. I might even pay for you to learn to fly—in the long run it would save me money. In a year with me you'd stand to make"—he pursed his lips—"forty grand at least, maybe twice that," and I said, "a year? but I'm going to college in September," and he said, "take a year off, pay for your whole education—I can promise you you'll learn things they don't teach in any school, and college will still be there when you go back," and I said, "I don't know if I can do that, Cleanth—even if I wanted to I doubt my father'd let me," and Cleanth said, "how's Clay going to stop you, A.? don't let anybody else make up your mind for you," and I said, "I'd have to think about it, okay?" and he said, "just let me know by the Fourth. In the meantime, maybe you could take a trip for me on your day off next week. I have some papers that need to be delivered to my lawyer in Norfolk, and my car needs servicing—there's a shop in Ghent I take it to. How does two hundred dollars sound for half a day's work?" and I said, "sure, man, that sounds great," and he said, "one other thing . . ."

I raised my brows, and he said, "next weekend Morgan and I are going up to Corolla. There's an old hunting lodge up there we're considering bidding on. I thought it might be nice for you and Jane to come along. We could make a week-end of it and camp out." He grinned. "We might also get into the woods a little bit, there's lots of game up there," and I said, "you mean hunting?" and he said, "I don't mean taking nature photographs," and I said, "I wouldn't shoot," and he shrugged and said, "that's fine, do what you want, let's just have a party—can you make it?" and I said, "why not?" He grinned approvingly.

Oh, yeah, why the fuck not? That question appeared to be the answer, providing a theme song for the summer, and to that tune the days all blurred together in a slow dissolve like mushroom trails, smoke off the fingertips—cocaine leaves trails, too, if you do enough of it. I guess I must have, because things got very blurred. The intensity of life in the Lost Colony was so relentless it became, at last, monotonous, a high-pitched shrilling bore-dom. It was an amazement, looking back, to know it lasted hardly more than a month, from Memorial Day to just before the Fourth, the weekend we went to the woods. That's when the Big Bang occurred. Oh, yeah. But even before that things began to alter subtly. The sameness of those days itself became a change. Because it had started out so hopefully, so happily. It started out as so much fun, and then one day it wasn't. I was in the game, playing as hard as I knew how and trying to be single, but it hadn't made me any happier. At first I thought it was just me and felt ungrateful for all the fun and opportunity that had been handed to me on a silver platter, or in a silver spoon.

That change in me, that subtle creeping restlessness, was the first sign. The second came not from Cleanth or Jane or even Cary, but from Morgan, who realized, I think, around the same time I did, that she wasn't happy either. That's when the nights became distinct again. That's when it became extreme.

Ten

A.

One night not long after I made the trip to Norfolk for Cleanth I found Morgan alone in her room when I went up, working on her second fifth of Dom. She was wearing her gray robe from the morning and hadn't dressed all day. The ashtrays were full of butts. The sheets were roiled and twisted. The place smelled rank, and the trace of perfume lingering above the ashes made it sadder. You took one look and knew this was a room where keen disorder had descended. She was lying on the bed drinking from the bottle with the coke tray next to her. There were ashes on the mirror, ashes on the sheet, cocaine on the sheet as well, coke and ashes everywhere. "I'm losing it," she said, with an apologetic princess simper under eyes that spelled disaster, and I said, "what's the matter, Morgan?" with concern, and she said, "don't ask, let's get drunk," and I said, "you look like you've already made a pretty good start at it," and she said, "excuse you, Adam, I'm merely tipsy," and tried to laugh, then gave it up. "It's Cleanth," she said, and I said, "what?" and she said, "come to bed," patting the mattress beside her.

I sat down and stared at her waiting for an explanation, and she said, "he offered you a job, didn't he?" and I said, "yeah, he did—is *that* the problem?" and she said, "no, no, no, that's only part of it, I can't explain, it's just too complicated. I don't want you to take it though." I looked at her a little hurt, and she said, "it isn't that, Adam, you know it isn't. I love being with you and I care about you—you know that, don't you?" and

I said, "then why don't you want me to take the job?" She frowned, studying my face with affectionate concern, and said, "there are a hundred reasons I could give you, but the main one is, you're eighteen, you'll be in college soon, you'll make a life, Adam, and it will be a good one. Don't let Cleanth make one for you. You don't need to fall into his shadow here right at the start, not his, or anyone's. Don't let him take your youth, darling. It's so precious, more precious than anything he can give you to replace it with. Don't try to collapse twenty years of living into a single summer, Adam. It's not that he's a bad person, he isn't. You know how much I love him. But look at me. I'm such a mess. Cleanth does this to me. Most days I'm fine, but then today . . ." She left the rest to speak for itself.

"Did something happen?" I asked, and she said, "nothing that unusual," and I said, "like what?" not really believing her, and she said, "you really want to know?" and I said, "tell me," and she said, "you're sure?" and I said, "come on, Morgan," and she said, "okay, he made a pass at me—this morning after breakfast." I sat there feeling my male hormones stinging and my stare turning icy cold. "It wasn't all that unusual," she said, "and I *didn't* take him up on it"—her eyes italicized the negative—"but I wanted to, Adam, it hurt me to say no, but it's hurt me even more the times before when I've said yes, because I know for him it's just a temporary thing, and I can't do it that way—not with Cleanth. It makes me crazy—crazy, crazy, crazy. I just get so tired of being a mother to him, and a wife with none of the prerogatives, and a nurse and a playmate, and running around behind him with a pooper-scooper cleaning up his messes. I can't be his lay, too. You just can't know, Adam," and I said, "no, I guess not," and she said, "and I don't want you to—that's why I'd prefer it if you'd turn his offer down," and I said, "if that's what you want, Morgan," and she said, "it isn't what I want, I simply think it's best," and I said, as the thought dawned, "this isn't like, so long, farewell, adieu, Dear Joe, is it?" and Morgan smiled and said, "you're funny, Adam, no, it's not." Her eyes got somber studying me, and she said, "I suspect when that letter comes, it'll be addressed, Dear Josephine. I hope I'm wrong, and I also hope, whatever happens, we'll stay friends," and I said, "of course, why wouldn't we?"

She looked at me and didn't answer, and I said, "but this is morbid—why are we talking about all this?" and she said, "you're right," and handed me the bottle. "Let's get drunk,"

I said, toasting her, and she said, "let's." We did. We got very drunk and had our dinner brought up from the kitchen. We did blow and watched a movie on TV. I lost interest in the movie and began to fondle her. Morgan acquiesced perfunctorily and kept her eyes glued to the screen. She kept drinking, harder and harder. I began to worry. When it was over she turned off the set and said, "will you do something for me?" and I said, "brush your hair?" She shook her head. "Wait here," she said and disappeared into the bathroom.

When she came back she'd washed her face. Pausing at the makeup table, she quickly put on lipstick. Her movements had a slurred and languid quality, something thrown away, that excited me. I felt ashamed of my arousal, but also intrigued at what her acts portended. "What are you doing?" I asked, and she said, "will you play a game with me?" and I said, "as long as it's not Life Poker." Morgan didn't smile. "I had a fantasy about you, Adam," she said, "that first morning when I woke up and you were gone. It was just a single picture then, a flash, but later it fleshed out into a scene. I considered telling you, but I guess I was shy." She made a princess simper, and I thought, "oh, goody, a fantasy! corrupt knowledge!" and then the princess simper disappeared and there was a trace of something like perdition in her eyes. She didn't seem playful in the least, and it wasn't embarrassment or coyness that undermined the impulse. "No, it wasn't shyness," she said, "I was afraid. But I thought about it all day long today. It began to worry me it was so strong. I want to end it, Adam. Will you play it out with me?" Though her gravity disturbed me, I said, "I won't have to wear your underwear, will I?" Morgan pursed her lips and shook her head, and I said, "no whips or chains?" She smiled, but her heart wasn't in it, and then she said, "but it may hurt you in a different way—it may hurt both of us," and suddenly her mood infected me and I felt a creeping rush of titillated fear, like I remembered from my boyhood, knowing there were no such things as ghosts but frightened of them anyway. "Will you do this for me?" she asked, and I said, "yes," and she said, "thank you," with a shining moistness in her eyes, and took my hand and led me to the bathroom door.

"Go inside," she said, "and don't come out until I tell you." I went and stood behind the door in the dark, my heart beating very hard, and she said, "now take your clothes off—leave your shorts." I stripped away my shirt, and she said, "now knock," and I did, and she said, "come in," in a changed tone, like she truly wasn't expecting me. When I entered she was standing in the middle of the room with her back to me, looking over her shoulder with an expression of aloof curiosity. Her eyes said, I don't know you, and politely inquired my purpose there. It was extremely strange, like being double-exposed—she was Morgan, but she wasn't. I was myself, but I was also someone else whose identity I didn't know. Only Morgan knew it, but Morgan wasn't Morgan. She was perfectly, chillingly, in character, and her expression refused to acknowledge the least trace of coyness in the situation. "Morgan . . ." I said, almost appealing, not sure I liked this game, and she put her finger to her lips, emerging from the illusion, and said, "this is a small house in the country, Adam. I live here with my husband, but it's the middle of the day and he's away. I'm frustrated and unhappy in the marriage, and I don't know you. We've never seen each other till this instant. You're just a young boy running in the country. You're in training and you've gone many miles, and it's such a hot day—you didn't fully realize how hot it was when you set out—but now you're parched and you want water. Mine is the only house you've passed for miles—just a small house in a grove of poplar trees beside a stream, a house of white plaster over bricks, with a red tile roof and green shutters and a crude door of great rough planks, and windowboxes with geraniums, salmon ones. It's like a house in Provence, only somewhere else, and I'm a housewife, only not a country woman, someone who's moved here from the city. You knock on my door and I let you in, holding my robe closed across my breasts like this"—she made a fist in the cloth and opened her eyes wide inquiringly but with a slight trace of alarm—"and you say, 'excuse me, but may I have a glass of water?' " I repeated the request with a timid quaver in my voice, and she said, "yes, of course," falling back into character, obliging but suspicious.

Then she said, aside again, "you're just a young good-looking boy I've never seen before, Adam, and you burst into my morning unexpectedly by chance. It's late, toward noon, but I haven't dressed. Lately I've taken to lying in my bed all day with the blinds drawn against the sunlight. I don't rise till nearly four when I dress and put on makeup very carefully to look well for my husband. I fix his dinner, and when he comes in and asks me how my day was I tell him all the things I've done, having carefully made up the speech before. He listens with feigned interest and smiles politely at my jokes, but his eyes are remote''—Morgan's own eyes drifted and took on a resigned hopelessness.

"Wait here," she said, in character again, picking up the empty champagne bottle from the table and taking it into the bathroom. The light came on and water started splashing from the tap into the sink, and she said, through the parted door, "there's a green bottle just like this one in the refrigerator filled with water, a champagne bottle from an evening I remember. That's why I've kept it." The tap stopped running, and instead I heard a glubbing sound, as though she'd actually filled the bottle and began to pour from it. "As I fill your glass, " she said, "I remember that evening, and it seems so long ago . . ." Morgan's voice faltered and she said, "I start to cry. Because my husband loved me then, and it was a special bottle, vintage, my father gave it to us from his cellar on our wedding day. We saved it for a year and opened it on our first anniversary—we were still happy then."

Morgan paused for a long time, and the sound of her weeping wrenched my heart. "But that was years ago," she said, sniffing, "and there's nothing but the bottle left. It's filled with water now, cold clear from the stream in back that comes down through the forest, and though it's not champagne, it's cool and refreshing, and that's how this young boy seems to me—to her, this woman—cool and refreshing with his lean long body which has neither age nor memory nor sadness in it, but is beautiful and clear. Though it's not champagne, it's more beautiful than anything in her present life, and I'm so parched—she is—as parched for him as he is for the glass of water I've just poured. I realize I want him and I feel wicked and corrupt, but also frightened of him. Because I don't think he can want me. I feel I must seem old and horrible to him, a hag, and he wants only water. His request is so pure and simple it almost breaks my heart, but I want to corrupt him anyway. Even before it starts, as I put the ice cubes in his glass, I know it won't help me and may do outright harm to him, but I move anyway, and the excitement is so intense it almost nauseates me."

Morgan came out of the bathroom and her face was shocking. There was something languid, almost wanton in her drunken eyes. She handed me a hotel water glass with "The Lost Colony" in blue-letter decals, and I took it feeling deeply troubled, because I knew the story she was telling me was true, not outwardly perhaps, but inwardly, and it was terrible. She frightened me, but at the same time I grew hard and wanted her. As she moved, her robe fell open, and my eyes flicked to her nakedness—the roll of a white breast, her navel, the dark swath of her sex—and she watched me watch, then closed the robe as though its opening had been accidental, even as her eyes teasingly denied it. I raised the glass and drank, feeling its coldness streaming down my surging throat, and handed it back to her. As she took it, her glance settled musingly on my erection, then found my eyes. "Do you have to go?" she asked, and I said, "do you want me to?" and she said, "yes," still smiling, and the robe came fully open. She closed her eyes and reached down and touched herself. I saw the pink flash of her labia with a telltale glistening along the rim, like dew or nectar, and then she fell back on the bed with the robe spread out around her, one knee propped up and her forearm across her brow. She began to masturbate herself, and she seemed so self-involved and isolate I wanted her more. I stripped off my shorts and climbed on top of her, and she said, "no, I don't want you," shaking her head back and forth with her eyes closed, and I thrust inside her feeling the clingy crepiness slicken as I luged down the track. "No, you mustn't," she said, and her teasing only incited me further—if it was teasing. Her hands clasped my ass, and then I flinched, feeling her fingernails score up my back. I went mad, pressing down until our pelvis bones jarred bruisingly against each other, on and on, until I came. In the middle of my orgasm I opened my eyes through trembling lids and searched to see if she was near. She wasn't. Morgan was a thousand miles away, passed out.

Feeling suddenly perverse and sickened, still coming, I rolled off her onto my back, spilling the last of it across my belly. The tiny black comma of the orifice opened to a hollow period and ejaculated a weak spurt. I closed my eyes, not wanting to look, and felt another, my own orgasm like something external, wrenched from me by torture, not pleasure. When it was over, I looked at her. "Morgan," I said. She didn't answer. I shook her shoulder, but her head lolled slackly. The room closed down on me like a suffocating nightmare with a woman's corpse in it. I wasn't sure if I had raped her, or if she'd intended it to happen as it did. Tears rolled down my cheeks and stung my cigarette-scorched lips like poison, and inside I felt numbness like the scum across a sinister dark pool. I panicked and got up. I couldn't stay there. I went home for the first time in many nights to sheets that had got dirty by themselves.

At home, I tried to sleep but couldn't. I was too upset, too wired. Grotesque flowers, pale and fleshlike, bloomed against the screen of my closed eyelids. I took the half-drunk fifth of Dickel my father had left on the Dutch bar and went out to the hammock on the east porch. I put away six shots in fifteen minutes and waited to see if it would help. It didn't. The edges blurred but the core anxiety burned on, an electric spectral blue, like a TV set glimpsed through the window of a darkened house. I tried to understand what had happened and couldn't. I just knew Morgan had got drunk and picked the scab off some long-festering wound inside her and it had spilled all over me, over both of us. And I'd known it was wrong. From the first night I'd known she loved Cleanth, and how much, and I'd gone blithely on, deceiving myself that I could have it all, have her, for nothing. I'd thought I could visit that amusement and sample corrupt knowledge without cost, but somehow the corruption had got inside me, I'd become a part of it. Not that Morgan was corrupt, the situation was, but the situation had been part of my attraction. I'd gone for it the way I always did only to find that, having it, I didn't really like it, it didn't help the underlying thing in me that needed to be helped, which was the sole reason I'd engaged in the pursuit. What was wrong with me that nothing helped? Now I'd had Morgan, an attractive older woman who'd been kind and generous to me and taught me many things in whispers, coaxing a softness out of me that had been stunned and deadened by raised volume, and I didn't like her anymore either. I cared for her very much, but I didn't like the bargain we'd engaged in, or myself for engaging in it. I didn't want to be part of it anymore. What did I want to be part of? I didn't know, but this wasn't it. So what did I like? After a period of dormancy that felt like years, Jane's question came back to haunt me as I lay in the hammock underneath the twinkling windchimes, the bottle of bourbon forgotten on the floor below me.

I searched inside myself for something in the present, some spark of pleasure, of liking, but each time the match flared it cast shadows longer than the flame, then guttered out. I turned my vision to the past. There was Killdeer, Mama, even Daddy— I'd liked them, hadn't I? I'd liked all of it, but what was left? The hopeful brightness always brought a greater darkness in its wake, and it was all a wake, and I was lost inside the darkness, very wakeful, but wishing I could sleep. My past stretched out like a dim corridor so far back I couldn't see the end of it. There were doors on either side, but I didn't want to open those doors, knowing that behind each one of them a corpse lay rotting in the darkness, or a ghost, or worse, nothing, an empty room. It was hard to believe that there wasn't in my whole life, not just the present but in all the wide fields of memory, just one thing I'd loved or even liked that hadn't turned to ashes in my mouth. I lay there with clenched fists feeling tears begin to seep beneath my closed eyelids, and nothing came. I let go and wept just like a baby, ashamed of my self-pity, but past controlling it. I didn't even try, I just turned over on my stomach and gave up to it, banging my head over and over into the hammock ropes, and it felt good to hurt myself. And my life contracted to that gesture, the gesture was my life, banging my head against the ropes that bound me in a web I hadn't made and didn't want and didn't know how to climb out of.

I must have cried myself asleep, or knocked myself unconscious against the wooden yoke, or just passed out. When I woke up my shirt was drenched with dew, and the wind had come around to the east bringing the exhalation of the ocean, a rank fishy living smell. My head hurt, and I could feel my hangover barreling down on me like a freight train, but I was used to that—I'd been in training for a month—and in spite of everything I felt eased. Dogs were barking somewhere. Perhaps the moon, rising over the dune line then in its last quarter, had maddened them. Perhaps it maddened me, because I listened to them, fierce and hoarse and utterly compulsive, and I barked back. I raised my chin toward the moon and bayed, and then I listened. They grew silent and I could imagine them, pricking their ears and tilting their heads quizzically in the dark. Then they answered and I answered back, one of the boys, telling my sorrows in one succinct brute howl—the story of my life—and new dogs joined the chorus up and down the beach for miles.

Lights came on in the windows of nearby houses. I heard the sash weights rattling in their channels as a window was thrown open. A grown man screamed, *"shut up!"* I barked at him. "Enough!" he cried, "get counseling!" The window slammed back down. I laughed and cried and barked at the same time. I realized my mind had come unhinged, but that didn't matter. I'd found something I liked. I'd found my calling, and I didn't know what to call it, so I barked instead. I wondered if it had professional possibilities, a shaggy troubadour baying serenades at lovers' windows for a meal of doggie biscuits. I'd liked those, too, when I was little, eating them right out of the box, plain or with a little Welch's grape jelly for variety. Mama had looked skeptical, and when she refused to give them to me, I stole them out of Pete's bowl, right from under his moist nose.

And I'd forgotten about Pete, whom I'd liked, too. But that night in the hammock I remembered him, a stubby-legged mutt, mostly black but with a white patch on one eye and tweaked up perky ears. I remembered standing in the yard tossing a football with Randy Phibbs when Daddy drove up in his Mustang. Pete was standing up in the back seat with his elbows propped against the seat back, paws ear-high, pads facing outward like this was a stickup and he was giving up. His tongue was dangling and he looked like an orphan being taken for a Sunday drive. When Daddy turned into the driveway he said something across his shoulder, and Pete pulled in his tongue like, uh-oh, I think they're on to me, I knew it was one of those other dogs they wanted, maybe that Dalmatian, oh well, let justice take its course. Even after we'd had him for months, and even years, he'd get that expression and look at you like, are you going to beat me now? it's okay, I don't mind, and it always made me laugh and want to hug him. Every time we got in the car without him, he'd look forlorn like, go ahead and leave me, I'm used to it, but as soon as we started backing down the driveway he'd take off in the opposite direction through the Jenkins's yard and by the time we reached the stop sign he'd be there waiting for us with his tongue hanging out like, is one last look at fleeting happiness okay? We'd come to a stop and Pete would pull in his tongue and crouch like a runner at the starting line, then we'd take off and he'd haul out after us yapping like a maniac, good-bye! good-bye!, and making crazy little acrobatic leaps. Mama would either be laughing or, usually, muttering, or both, and stepping on the gas to get away from him, going fifty down Penfield Lane, a quiet little residential street, and the old ladies in their gardening hats out clipping back their roses would turn and stare with their hands on their hips like, Allison Trefethen, you simply ought to *know* better, and she did, but what could Mama do? Pete didn't give her any choice in the matter.

On certain issues though, Pete refused to compromise, despite his native deference. Each year as May flowers began to

peak and drop away toward high summer's greenery, Pete would
regard our exits in the station wagon with a more anxious urgency, knowing that one of these fine mornings we'd be leaving
for the beach, and though we'd never left him, he didn't seem
to trust our motives fully on that score, or maybe Pete simply
thought it wiser to supplement his faith in us with good works
of his own. In any case, from the fifteenth onward, you could
count on finding Pete camped out in the back seat of the station
wagon at 6:00 a.m. when you went out to get the paper from
the dewy lawn, having made a leap that defied the laws of gravity
through a window which had been left open to prevent third-
degree seat burn later in the day. Pete would look at you like, I
know I'm guilty, but the spirit of the law is on my side, and he'd
whine and hunker down between the seats till Daddy had to pry
him out, and even then you had to be extremely quick, slipping
through a small crack in the door and risking amputation, to
make a getaway. Then the fateful morning would arrive. A suitcase would appear in the driveway and Pete would lose his doggy
mind. We'd have to lock him in the basement while we packed,
and once Pete climbed a stack of boxes and leapt through the
inward-tilting ground-level window, hauling around the side at
forty miles an hour, doing a long skid on the concrete while we
watched with affectionate exasperation and mild awe. Pete
picked himself up gingerly, trotted off and fetched his slimy
bone-chew from the grass and then came and sat down calmly
with it in his mouth like, I'm ready, I've done my packing, too.

The other matter Pete was adamant about was crabbing.
Whenever he saw a pole net put into the car, or merely observed
Mama coming down the steps in that big floppy straw hat she
always wore when she took me, there was no denying him. Once
we'd got there, he'd stand at the edge of the dock, or with his
head sticking underneath the railing of the bridge—wherever we
were—and bark with wild demented glee as we pulled the blue
crabs from the water, clacking in the net. Once, he'd actually
got so far beside himself that he'd done a nose dive off the dock
and come up paddling and sneezing, not looking nearly so brave
but more like, help, dear God! the crabs have got me, foots
don't fail me now, and Mama had leaned over and grabbed his
front paws to try and pull him up, and she'd gone over, too, hat
first and a flash of bloomers, and I'd sat there and laughed till I
cried as Pete swam circles around her, yapping and sneezing as
he swallowed water, and then I did a cannonball right next to

them. And I'd liked all of it. I'd liked Pete, and I'd liked Mama—aside from how much I'd loved her, which was a separate issue, she'd been a particular friend of mine—and I'd liked crabbing, too, and as I lay there in the hammock in the slipstream of the memory, smitten with a strange elation that had me on the edge of tears again, I realized I hadn't been again, not even once since Mama died. I'd stopped liking crabbing along with everything else, but now it seemed critical to like something, and crabbing struck me as as good a place to start as any.

It was five a.m. A first hint of daylight showed in the east above the dunes, so pale you could still see stars sparkling in it like ice cubes in a glass of watery milk. I went downstairs to the garage and took the pole nets from the nails we'd hung them on. I found the blocks and twine right where we'd left them. Throwing all of it in the Jeep, I drove north to Camelot Pier, which opened at four a.m., and got a dozen fish heads from Billy Kerr, who still remembered me. He didn't even charge me for them. I was halfway to Colington when a thought occurred to me. Cleanth was in Charleston. Jane had probably spent the night at her place. She was responsible for this. Hadn't she said she wanted me to let her know? I laughed at the thought of her surprised face as I conscripted her into my pirate crew, and turned the Jeep around.

Eleven

Halfway up the steps at Jane's, a brilliant impulse seized me. Instead of knocking on her door, I took a pole net and went around back. Locating the stained glass panel of the breaking wave, I squatted on all fours in the grass, put the pole net on my head, honed in on her window like a dog on point and started howling. "Aoooo!" I said, "Aa-Aa-Aooo!" No answer. I cut loose again at increased volume. The stained glass rippled as though the wave were actually toppling. I thought of Memorex—another professional avenue worth exploring. The lights came on in the windows of a neighboring house. Up and down the street, dogs heard my cry and lustily supported my petition.

Finally Jane appeared like a pale moon at her darkened window. She shelved her hand against the glass and pressed her forehead to it, squinting out nearsightedly. I let out a blast that made her blink her eyes. She raised the window. "A.?" she said, "is that you?" By way of answer, I replied, "aooo!" "Have you *completely* lost your mind?" she said. I barked again, and she said, "what's that around your head?" and I said, "a crabbing net, aooo!" and she laughed and said, "oh, silly me, I thought it was for butterflies," and I said, "ha-ha-haooo!" and she said, "well, would you like to come inside, or are you more comfortable in the yard?" and I grinned and got up and went around front. Climbing the stairs, I found her waiting for me at the door.

She regarded me from a sleepy face with fond but somewhat cynical amusement and opened the door. There was a guy with a slack jaw and a prickly blondish beard sleeping on the couch under the same cotton blanket I'd waked up in that first night after Jimbo's. "Who's that?" I asked, my exaltation dampened until she said, "one of Lucy's beaus." Jane looked him over frowning, then shrugged and said, "I guess it didn't come to pass. Come on." I followed her back to her bedroom and she climbed in bed and pulled the covers over her, sitting up. "Would you like a chair?" she said, "or do you prefer the floor?" and I grinned and said, "can't I get in there with you?"

Ignoring my remark, Jane said, "so, A., how drunk are you anyway?" and I said, "moi? drunk? I'm surprised at you, Jane, you should know me better than that," and she smiled with narrowed eyes, nodding like she knew me perfectly, and said, "just don't light a match in here, okay? I don't think I'm insured against distillery fires," and she flared her nostrils, sniffing, and I said, "you can smell it?" cupping my hand over my nose and breathing in my goaf. "Ugh," I said, "I think I have bad breath," and Jane laughed and said, "it's no worse than walking down the alley past Town Hall in Chapel Hill on Sunday morning," and I said, "isn't that a bar?" and she said, "if you were being polite, you might call it that."

Then she stared at me appraisingly and said, "to what do I owe the honor, A., or is this just a social call?" and I grinned and said, "I thought of something," and she said, "you thought of something," as though the allusion had escaped her, and I said, "you told me to come over here and tell you as soon as I thought of something I liked, and I did, so here I am." I gazed at her with an expression of blatant unabashed flatulent irrepressible idiotic happiness like nothing she could say or do would deter me in the slightest, and she gazed back with an ironic smirk like she wasn't buying it that easily, and she said, "well, it certainly took you long enough," and I said, "better late than never," and she said, "true—so tell me, what?" and I said, "Pete," and she said, "Pete," in such a way that I could tell no cute maneuvers were going to pass, so I said, "listen Jane, this is amazing, it's utterly fantastic, I can't even believe it myself, but, you see, me and Morgan . . . well, we had a kind of fight, I mean, it wasn't really a fight, I don't know what it was, but it was weird, man, weird as fucking shit," and Jane said, "uh-huh, amazing," and I said, "so I went home, right? and I was feeling really miserable, I mean, *really* miserable," and she said, "really miserable," and I said, "right . . . so anyway I went home and started drinking, and for some reason I remembered how you'd asked me that, you know? why didn't I like anything? and I'll tell you, Jane, I tried to come up with something and I just drew a blank, I mean zippo, *nada, rien.*"

Suddenly I lost my train of thought, and I said, "what was I saying?" and she said, "Pete," and I said, "Pete, right . . . so anyway, I passed out or knocked myself out or something, and when I woke up there were all these dogs barking, see?" and I grinned and Jane said, "nuh-uh, not really," and I said, "I started barking, too, I barked, they barked, there was a lot of barking going on, and suddenly I felt better and that's when I thought of Pete, 'cause, see, he was this dog we used to have," and Jane said, "and he liked to bark?" and I said, "well, sometimes he did, but actually Pete was more into doggie biscuits, but anyway, barking like that made me think of him and remember how much I liked him and all the fun we used to have. So, see? I did like something, even if it was a long time ago, so I'm not a total wipeout, am I?" and Jane looked at me like I was this lost cause she had an inexplicable fondness for and said, "no, not total," and I said, "so there's some hope for me?" and she said, "a little . . . possibly," with an understated teasing smile, and I said, "aren't you happy?" and she said, "ecstatic," and I said, "come on, Jane, I just had a fucking revelation here—is a little enthusiasm too much to ask?" and she said, "I'm proud of you, A., I truly am. I didn't mean for you to take what I said so much to heart, but I'm glad you told me, even if it is"—she glanced at her alarm clock—"five-thirty in the morning, but, honey?" and I said, "what?" feeling the subtle thrill that word always gave me, and she said, "would you mind going someplace far far away now and continuing your revelation there while I get back to sleep?" and I said, "but that wasn't all," in a crestfallen tone, and she said, "yes?" and I said, "I liked crabbing, too, and I was thinking I hadn't been in a long time and maybe I'd go out to Colington this morning. That's where I'm headed now, and guess what?" I grinned at her and she said, "what?" suspiciously, and I said, "you're going with me," and she said, "I believe you're under a misapprehension, sir," and I said, "nuh-uh, *errr*"—a game-show buzzer noise—"wrong, we had a bargain, Jane, I kept my end of it, now you keep yours," and she said, "A.," and I said, "Jane," and she said, "I went to bed exactly four hours ago," glancing at the clock again, and I said, "so what? I didn't go to bed at all," and she widened her eyes and glared at me with unconvincing umbrage, pointing to the door with great authority with one hand and holding the sheet neck-high with the other as though I'd become a threat, and she said, "*go* or I'll call the police—I swear I will," and her tone was just grist to my mill.

"Go ahead," I said, moving the phone from the end table to the bed to make it easy for her. Crossing my ankle on my knee, I sat back, smiling smugly, and she said, "I'll scream," and I said, "be my guest," and she said, "that guy out on the couch is a black belt in karate," and I said, "let's see how he does against a pole net"—I'd brought it with me and I tamped the helve against her bare wood floor. "A.," Jane said again, changing tacks to let's be reasonable, and I said, "Jane," in the same tone, and she said, "I don't even like crabs," and perceiving an opening, I said, "you don't have to like them, that's not what crabbing's all about—in fact, it's better not to. You need to keep a healthy disrespect for them, Jane. You never want to trust a crab or doubt his essential scurrilousness and the evil lurking in his heart." Jane regarded me with grudging amusement and said, "I don't think crabs have hearts, A.," and I pursed my lips and said, "my point exactly. Crabs are extreme misanthropists when it comes to human beings, Jane—never doubt that, not even for a second, because that's where the crab will get you every time. He smells your weakness, and then . . ." I shook my head like it was too sad to think about.

"But all that said," I added, "crabbing is not about the crabs—they're entirely incidental to the process, you don't even have to think about them," and she said, "but you do have to touch them, I suppose," and feeling her yielding, I shook my head and said, "not at all—straight from the net into the bucket. Of course, sometimes they like to hold on with their claws and if shaking doesn't work you have to pry them off—it can get pretty bloody," and she said, "I didn't know crabs had blood either," and I said, "I wasn't thinking of the crabs," and she said, "how about a compromise?" and I said, "unlikely, but I'm listening," and she said, "how about later this afternoon? I don't go on till four-thirty—say, two o'clock?" and I said, "early morning is the premier time to crab, Jane," which wasn't strictly true, but I wasn't above lying, particularly since I knew she wouldn't know the difference, and she said, "A., please, I'm really tired," and I said, "you should lead a moral life."

That pissed her off, I think, and she said, "okay, that's it, I'm not going, now get your butt out of here," and I said, *"errr,"* and she said, "no, A., read my lips—n-o," and I stood up and contemplated her sadly, saying, "you could make this a whole lot easier on both of us, Jane," and, seeing my intentions, a look of wide-eyed alarm appeared on her face and she brought up her second hand to the protecting sheet, and I sighed and scooped her up, sheet and all, in one lightning-quick maneuver and started carrying her toward the bathroom. "A.," she said, "this isn't funny," using dignity instead of struggle in a vain effort to dissuade me, and I said, "you'll thank me later." Toeing open the frosted shower door, which was already parted, I sat her down on the tiled floor of the stall, then stood up, surveying her reproachfully as I put my hand on the cold water knob. "Don't turn that knob, A.," she said, "don't even think about it," and I said, "believe me, Jane, this is going to hurt me a whole lot more than it will you," and then her eyes hardened and she said, "go ahead, I dare you—if you do, so help me God, I'll cut your balls off and . . ." I twisted the tap and watched her hair flatten down and darken under the first blast, as she screamed and hyperventilated, sputtering, "feed—them—Sam," and I said, "your collie, right?" and closed the door.

"All right, A.," she said, coming through the bedroom door in her pink robe, looking refreshed from her cold shower and extremely unamused—a combination that suited her quite well, I noticed—"so what do I wear *crabbing*?" I looked up from the *Vogue* magazine with Morgan's name on the address label which I'd been absently flipping through, and said, "do you have a bathing suit?" and she said, mincingly, "yes, I have a bathing suit," and I said, "a bikini?" and she said, "no, it's one I inherited from my grandmother with a ruffled skirt and tights that go down to the knees." I shook my head and put down the magazine, saying, "a bikini would be better, crabs go for exposed flesh," and Jane said, "I'm sure they do, I'll wear my one-piece," and I shrugged and said, "don't blame me if you don't catch any," and she said, "I'm sure I'll be devastated. Now would you mind?" She pointed to the door and said, "I'd like to dress or do you need to supervise that, too?'' and I said, ''it might be a good idea, I wouldn't want you to commit any couturial *faux pas* or try slipping out the window or anything,'' and she said, ''before my patience wanes any further, A.,'' and I shrugged and went out to the living room where I joined Bruce Lee, still passed out from Lucy's KO punch.

Jane reappeared with a white cotton sun dress like a smock thrown over her suit and one of those two-dollar straw fishing hats with the tinted panel in the brim and tortoise-framed Wayfarers. ''I like your shades,'' I told her, and she said, ''thanks,'' and I grinned and said, ''they're almost as cool as mine,'' and she said, ''your frames are too dark for your complexion, A.,'' and I said, ''are you kidding?'' and she said, ''they make you look like a Moroccan dealer in hashish,'' and I said, ''these are *Vuarnets*, Jane,'' lifting them on the cord to look at them, ''you can't buy better glasses,'' and she tilted hers down on her nose and said, ''are you a snob, too, A.?'' and I said, ''me? no way,'' and she smiled and said, ''I think you are, a snob and a retard, too—it's a dreadful combination, honey,'' and I said, ''thanks a lot, Jane,'' and she said, ''don't mention it.''

''How long is this expedition going to take anyway?'' she asked, and I said, ''not too long,'' and she said, ''how long?'' and I said, ''oh, a few hours probably,'' and she said, ''hours?'' and I said, ''you don't just put your net down in the water and ladle them out, Jane,'' and she said, ''well, I guess I ought to make some sandwiches so we don't starve,'' and I said, ''good idea,'' and she said, ''do you like tuna?'' and Bruce Lee said, ''is it fresh?'' and Jane and I both looked at him. He gave us a bleary grin and said, ''good morning—where am I?'' and Jane said, ''does the name Lucy Carlisle ring a bell?'' and he said, ''oh, right, Lucy—are you her roommate?'' and Jane said, ''Jane McCrae,'' and he said, ''hi, I'm Roy,'' and Jane said, ''this is A.'' Roy and I nodded, and he said, ''that smells great.'' Jane had begun to mix the tuna, throwing in dill pickles and mustard and curry powder and God knows what, and she said, ''it's my mother's recipe,'' and I said, ''you ought to keep some secrets in the family,'' laughing at my own joke. Jane didn't laugh. She gave me a sharp look and Roy gave me another of a different sort, like he had me figured and wasn't that interested in pursuing it. ''Would you like a sandwich?'' Jane asked, and Roy said, ''sure,'' and Jane said, ''mayonnaise?'' and he said, ''one side,'' and then he looked at me and said, ''where's the head,

A.?'' like I was the resident expert, and I pointed down the hall and he padded off in his boxer shorts, knuckling his scalp and puttering like a horse. "Nice guy," I said, and Jane said, "see?" and I said, "what?" and she said, "you are a snob." She bagged our sandwiches, leaving Roy's on a plate on the counter with a glass of Hawaiian Punch beside it, and we left with the sound of Roy's shower rendition of "She Loves Me" ringing in our ears. Yeah, yeah, yeah.

On the way to Colington, Jane made a point of slouching in her seat with her hat down across her eyes, pretending to be asleep. She let her legs fall open and crossed her ankle over her knee with her dress tucked down between her thighs. I couldn't help looking, or maybe I could have, but I looked anyway—just once, and then a second time to confirm what I'd gathered from the first. Yes, they were legs, lean tan ones with fine sun-blonded filaments like eider that you could only see in sidelight. I thought I'd like to paint her that way, slouching with her hat down in her eyes and her legs crossed like a man, but so much not one. My interest was purely technical, and for the sake of higher knowledge that might some day translate into a great work that would make the multitudes gasp and grovel, I allowed myself a third and final glance, for anatomical purposes, which was when I noticed that there was something else about her legs that was not just legs. They had some kind of shimmer to them which wasn't leggy in the least, and on further study, I noticed that that shimmer wasn't just coming off her legs, but from her whole body, even through the dress, and there was something about that shimmer that disturbed me. It seemed to *know*, and I wondered if it was connected to that other knowingness in Jane, the one that so frequently caught me up, like perhaps they were part of the same thing, and maybe—was it possible?—it wasn't Jane's mind that knew me, but her legs, or rather the shimmer rising from them. The mystery increased when I looked down and noticed the same shimmer rising from my own, along with the vague first ticklings of an erection. I almost drove into a ditch. Oh, God, I thought, not that, it can't be *that*—did I want her? I looked a fourth time to be sure. The shimmer had departed. "Whew," I said, wiping the perspiration from my brow, and Jane tilted up her hat and said, "did you say something?" and I said, "no," and she gave me a funny look and tilted it back down, collapsing her leg till it crossed thigh to thigh and tugging down her dress. Did she know? Jane didn't know, but there was some kind of strange communication going on between us, not in words but shimmers, and it was almost like what we said and thought made no difference, it was what the shimmer said that counted. I didn't look again, afraid of what that shimmer might have to tell me. Maybe it was gone. I told myself I really ought to cut back on the toot.

I pulled over on the shoulder just before the second smaller bridge in Colington and we got out. It was six-thirty, maybe seven, and the sound lay spread out like a mirror, silvery and luminous but with a hint of blue in it there wasn't any name for, just like a broken piece of sky floating on the brownish water with a heaven feeling in it, like when you're happy and step outside on a clear day and look straight up and take a searing breath into your lungs. I was happy and didn't even know it, much less the reason why. It was sky, so sky, the way the surfers said. A few local fishermen in dories with Mercury outboards on them were coming in from checking crab or eel pots, and as I stood and watched a larger trawler, a shrimper, chugged the other way, southward, with his nets luffing. There was something so beautiful about that boat—the white paint on the planks in morning light and the grease-blacked rigging and ocher rust streaks bleeding down the sides. I would have liked to paint that, too, and save it all forever. Maybe that was why I liked to do it, to save things, the same way Mama kept her *National Geographics* in the attic, and I looked at Jane and thought I'd like to save her, too. I cared for her, and knew it—it was okay to care.

Sensing my mood—the shimmer spoke between us—she came up beside me and watched, too, slipping her arm around my waist. Though I kept my hands in the back pockets of my cut-offs, I knew it was just a friendly thing and didn't feel uncomfortable or threatened. "Would you pose for me sometime?" I asked, looking down at her, and she said, "can I keep my clothes on?" a little off the milder rhythm I'd fallen into, and I smiled and said, "you can wear exactly what you've got on now," and she studied me a moment with a trace of slight perplexity or questioning in her expression and gently withdrew her arm.

We stood there, separate but close, listening to the low putt-putt of the engine echoing off the flat sheet of the water and watching the curl of bluish smoke trail backwards from the stack and then dissolve. You could see the captain at the wheel and the mate, a boy my age, his son perhaps, standing aft with his foot up on the spreader doors drinking coffee from a Styrofoam cup as white and luminous as a beacon. Jane waved at him, and the air was so clear I saw him nod back before he turned his eyes to something else. The dignity of that nod was so fine-tuned and self-possessed I felt lifted up that he'd acknowledged us. It was like the better part of me acknowledging the lesser from off at a distance—but not out of reach. Not that morning. That morning just seemed like the touch of casual grace, though I sensed Jane was part of it—yet just a friend, a friend who, under different circumstances, might have been more, but there were no other circumstances, and it seemed okay that morning for things to be exactly what they were.

After her protests about the crabs, I was surprised at Jane's casualness toward the fish heads. She had a farm girl's lack of squeamishness, and I remembered that her father had been involved in some sort of aquaculture experiment that had won him a reputation as an eccentric. Jane's mama was eccentric, too—I had that on Daddy's authority, who, of course, had always walked the straight and narrow path of righteousness himself. Come to think of it, everybody I'd ever known or even heard of in Killdeer and the environs was eccentric, and I guessed, despite my best efforts, I was included in that bundle, too, along with Jane, whose lean brown hands I liked—the way they worked so deliberately, without superfluous gesture, different from B.J. or even Ellen, who did manual labor in a mincing way that implied they felt superior to it, a way that came off merely prim. I respected that basicness in Jane.

I showed her how to thread the twine through the mouth and out behind the gill before tying it off, meaning her to take the head I'd baited, but she watched and then prepared her own. I walked over to the line of creosote pylons that walled up the bank, propped my foot and unspooled my bait into the brown water which from above was clear but became increasingly opaque as your line-of-sight veered toward the horizontal. I summoned Jane with a head-jerk and she came over. We waited several anxious minutes—anxious for me, at least, because I felt my competence, even my virility, were tied up in success. "They're probably still asleep," Jane said, and I said, "shhh," and pointed with my free hand as the first crab sidled out of the murk. He toyed with the head, making a few discreet pinches to see if it would bite back, or maybe he was simply testing the freshness of the specimen, and then he climbed aboard and I began to draw the twine in very slowly. "Get the net," I whispered when I had him halfway to the surface. Jane did, and I said, "now slip it in behind him—not too close, go very slow," and just as I was about to give the order to attack, Jane preempted me and sprang, fishing crab and head alike out of the water, laughing and swinging it in so that I had to duck.

"Was that right?" she asked with a delighted animation in her face, and I said, glumly, "I think you got the hang of it," and she said, "this is easy," and I said, "you think so?" By way of answer, she upended him into the bucket, and then took her own net and bait out on the bridge, working off the opposite side from me. "I bet I can beat you," she said, looking back at me across her shoulder with a grin, and I said, "how much?" and she said, "how much have you got?" and I said, "you want to go for a hundred bucks?" and she laughed like a crazy woman, and I said, "what's so funny?" and she said, "you," and I said, "what?" and she said, "remember why we're out here? we're supposed to be having fun—how much fun do you think it's going to be when you have to pay me a hundred dollars?" and I said, grinning back, "oh, but you've got it backwards, don't you see, and it's going to be great fun when you pay me," and she said, "I'll bet one," and I said, "one dollar?" She nodded and I said, "that's a pussy bet, Jane," and she said, "well, maybe I'm a pussy," laughing even harder—competition definitely brought out something in the girl. We set to it furiously then. From time to time I cast an idle glance at her. She leaned over the railing like a puppeteer, with the dangling spool in one hand and the pole net in the other. I pretended not to notice when she brought one up, sauntering over to drop the clacking furious crab in the bucket. "That's one to nothing," she said, and I said, "correction—one to one, that first one was mine." She just laughed and went back for more.

Two hours passed, and by the end of it we had two dozen blue crabs moiling in the bucket, packed together like a demented Erector set, blowing bubbles and shaking their heavy orange-lipped claws at us and at each other like old men hurling impotent curses. "I don't think we can fit any more in," she said, "should we call it quits?" and I said, "you want to?" and she said, "if you do," and I shrugged and said, "may as well—you did pretty good, considering," and she said, "considering what? I caught fifteen—how many did you catch?" and I said, "I wasn't counting," and she said, "bulldookey! I was—you caught eight," and I said, "nine," and she said, "counting the first one, which was half mine," laughing gleefully. "Come on, Jane," I said, "you weren't really serious about that bet were you?" and she rubbed her thumb back and forth across her fingertips and said, "pay up, son," and I grudgingly took out my wallet and handed her a dollar. "That'll teach you next time," she said, and I said, "beginner's luck," and she said, "beginner's luck, *hell*," and I said, "well, I gave you the good side of the bridge anyway—I wasn't going to mention it, but since you're acting like such a pad," and she said, "there's not a particle of difference," and I said, "yes, there is—you had the shadow of the bridge on your side," and she said, "what difference does that make?" and I said, "that way they can't see your shadow on the water when you're leaning over," and she said, "bull, you're making all that up—besides, it makes it harder for them to see the bait," and I said, "they don't see it, Jane, they smell it," winging my tale with great abandon—it was like we were both playing, but not entirely sure the other was—and Jane said, "and anyway, you didn't *give* me that side of the bridge, you took what you wanted and I got what was left," and I said, "if that's what you think, Jane," and she widened her eyes with an amused incredulous stare and said, "A. Jenrette, I never knew you were such a liar," and I said, "it's all true, every word of it—to the best of my knowledge," adding the latter phrase for legal purposes, and she burst out laughing.

"To the best of your knowledge," she said, *"right,"* and I said, "but you still won, even with an unfair advantage, so aside from the cash doorprize you also get to keep the crabs," and she said, "what am I supposed to do with them?" and I said, "take them home and cook them up," and she said, "I don't know how," and I said, "boil a pot of water and drop them in till they turn red," and she said, "that's horrible, A., their little eyes!" and I shrugged and said, "that's the price of crabmeat, Jane," and she said, "I don't like it anyway," and I said, "you don't like lump backfin?" like she was crazy. She shook her head, and I said, "that's pitiful, Jane," and she said, "well, excuse me for living—and anyway, I thought you were a vegetarian," and I thought, "oh, no, not that again," saying, "I told you, I eat seafood," and she said. "I suppose crabs are vegetables," and I said, *"fruits de la mer,"* grinning as the thought occurred to me, and she said, "what?" and I said, "fruits of the sea—that's what the French call them," and she said, "well, why don't you take them—you can have a feast and invite all your French vegetarian friends," and I said, "gladly," and she walked over to the bucket, which was sitting on the edge, stared down at it and made a face. "They don't look very happy," she said, and I said, "happiness isn't in the crab vocabulary, Jane," and she said, "well, they looked happier out there." She mused, then looked at me and said, "I changed my mind, I'll take them after all," and she tipped the whole thing over in the sound, sticking out her tongue at me.

"Why you whore-bitch," I said, amused, but feeling like it was all out war. "Now, A.," she said, backing nervously as I started toward her, "I won, they were mine—you said so," and I grinned and put my hands on her shoulders, and she said, "you wouldn't throw me down there, would you? not with all those crabs? I've already had one bath this morning, thanks to you, and besides, I can't swim," and I said, "bulldookey, you swim just like a tuna," and she said, "but not this early in the morning," and I said, "well, I'm your friendly lifeguard, remember? I'll save you if you drown . . . maybe," and she said, "A.," in her sternest warning tone and gripped my left wrist with both hands, digging in her nails like talons. I stared down at it contemptuously and then back in her eyes and said, "you don't really think that's going to save you, do you?" and she made her saddest pouting face, which almost swayed me until she scissored me with a mean leg hook. "That did it," I said, prying off her hands, "bye bye."

I shoved her over backwards and watched as her hat came up first, floating upright like a lily pad, and Jane behind it, spluttering and blowing and holding on her glasses which had gone crooked on her nose. "You're a son-of-a-bitch, I *hate* you, A.," she shouted, dancing up on one foot, then the other, not wanting to give the crabs a target—they were all long gone by then anyway—and I just laughed and said, "the feeling's mutual, Mc-Crae," and did a flying cannonball, sending a deluge over her. When I bobbed up, her sopping dress, which she'd shucked off, hit my face with a soggy smack, and Jane laughed with wild glee and started swimming away from me, churning the water frantically and hardly moving. I caught her ankle and pulled her back and started ducking her. "Take a deep breath," I said, letting her up briefly before I plunged her back, and after the third time, or perhaps the fourth, she came up like a drowned rat in my arms looking like she was about to cry.

"You're so mean," she said, and suddenly something like a wave washed over me, a feeling of enormous tenderness and pity. "I'm sorry," I said, reaching out impulsively to curl a drenched lock back behind her ear, and that hand disappeared into the shimmer, which was suddenly everywhere, on us, on the water, the whole scene was alive with it. Suddenly I wanted to kiss her, and that thought terrified me, because I knew I couldn't. I knew that if I lived a thousand years, I'd never taste that kiss, and it made me want to cry, because that kiss seemed, in the shimmer, like the one thing that could help the underlying part of me that needed to be helped, and I knew I was never going to have it.

Jane stood there clutching my upper arms, a position of combat that changed to something else as the shimmer spoke to her, and she knew, too—her thoughts were utterly transparent to me as mine were to her. A whole conversation happened and not one word was spoken, and there was something in her eyes—I don't know what—some kind of look—not inviting, not surrendering, but like she was studying through right to the core of me, asking me the question of my intentions and even who I was. Cary was in that look, and Cleanth and Morgan, too, all of it, but also the possibility, the hope, the promise, that none of it might matter, that it might be simple and clean again, as clean and simple as just the two of us alone together out there in the middle of the sound under the second bridge in Colington with nothing but the sky above our heads to watch and know our secret. That possibility, that hope, that promise flashed across my mind like lightning, and suddenly I knew the name of the terrible thing I felt—its name was love, and I stood there knowing that and amazed, as amazed as a monk who opens his old door and finds a palace where his cell has been, and wondering if I was made to live in palaces, feeling the warmth of Jane's shoulders on my palms rising through the coolness of the water, until the moment passed and the offended shimmer went away. The whole thing didn't last five seconds. Jane's hands relaxed on my biceps, and then she shivered slightly and we both released each other and swam back to the bank.

By the time we started eating lunch, I was convinced the whole thing had been a hallucination, a product of my imagination, and only mine. Jane had felt something, but not the same thing I had felt. But that thought didn't help, because when I looked at her the change was so vast and staggering I knew she

was never going to look the same to me again. The shimmer
had transformed her like a magnifying glass so that each pore,
each follicle of hair glowed like a jewel. I quietly ate my sandwich, and even that was different. The taste was so intense it
made me never want to finish, and I sat there chewing slowly,
knowing I was in love with her and wondering why and what it
was going to mean, wishing I had a beginner's manual to explain
my next move, wishing even more that I might be spared from
making one, that I might just sit there forever chewing and
knowing and looking at her from time to time studying the ka-
leidoscopic changes the shimmer played around her, making
Jane a different person every second, but always the same.
Wanting to be cautious till I understood it better, I tried not to
look too much, almost wishing she would go away so I could
think, yet I knew that what was hard with her around would be
impossible in her absence. I don't know how I knew—perhaps
the shimmer told me. Perhaps it was also the shimmer that told
me Cary was a thousand miles away and didn't matter anyway—
not here, not in this. Or could the shimmer lie? No, it swirled
around my hands like golden smoke, and the change in Jane,
the way I saw her, was irreversible and utter, because the shimmer isn't bound by time, true love isn't human, it doesn't care
for us. True love is the joyous selfish hunger of existence for
itself, and we are just the mortal vessels for the godlike wine,
the instruments on which it plays, seeing not another, but always
and only, itself. Cleanth Faison knew that, and I learned it, too,
that summer. I started learning it that moment in the water with
Jane under the second bridge in Colington when I curled her
hair around her ear and drew my hand back trailing golden
smoke. That was also the moment when the master's lesson
began to weave itself so silkenly into the different lesson I was
to learn from Jane—not from her, but through her, as the shimmer spoke.

"The sandwiches are good," I told her, taking refuge from
that blinding light in the comfortable yellow of banality, and
Jane smiled and said, "I'm glad you like them," looking comforted, too, and grateful, and I said, edging a little closer to the
danger, "it feels a little strange to be eating lunch at ten a.m.,
doesn't it?" and she said, "everything seems strange down
here," staring back at me with a trace of pained perplexity out
of the same golden fog that I was lost in, and though we got no
closer verbally, her eyes said, "what is this? do you know, A.?"

and mine said back to her, "no, I don't—do you?" and her eyes said, "no," and kept on searching mine and questioning, until the question grew to something vast and contentless—the question was life itself, our lives, and what we were to do with them—and we swam together in that question till we started drowning, because there were no answers, and knowing we must move, against the stream perhaps, but more at any cost, I said, "I think we ought to go," and Jane said, "yes."

As we drove back past the monument and turned north on the bypass toward her house, I cast a glance at Jane and found her studying me intently, so intently that I actually startled. "What?" I said, and she said, deliberately, from beneath a furrowed brow, "I think I know what you need, A." My heart began to thunder and the steering wheel slickened in my hands— was she actually going to say it? "What?" I asked, and she said back, "I think you need a dog." I laughed like a convention of Bedlamites at Mardi Gras. "What's so funny?" she said, and I said, "a dog? you're serious, right? you think I need a *dog*?" Jane looked offended and said, "you're so weird, A.," and I laughed harder and said, "aa-aa-aooo!" and Jane's frown carved deeper channels until suddenly the spell that I'd been under broke. "You think I need a dog, and *I'm* the retard?" I said, and she blinked her eyes and made the blandest elephant face imaginable, saying, "are you finished, A.?" and I said, "If I wasn't before, that almost finished me," and she said, "you can't stay over there in that big house all by yourself—it's spooky," and beginning to grapple with the consequences of her earnestness, which struck me as virtually insane, I said, "but what would I do with one, Jane? I'm at work all day," and she said, "no, I mean a good yard dog who can take care of himself," and I said, "you mean the kind that can open his own can of food and spoon it out himself?" and she said, "exactly, one like Sam, except Sam eats rats, big ones, farm rats—it does wonders for his breath." She gave me a wry look that made me laugh and I said, "well, I wouldn't want a rat dog, especially one with halitosis," and she said, "no, you wouldn't, that would be redundant," which I thought was pretty good, though it made me wonder if I ought to brush my teeth. But Jane had eaten tuna, too, and Tuna Jane went on, "you could put a bandanna around his neck and let him sleep under your stand during the day and at night you could take him with you to the bars, or wherever you go at night," and her eyes said, as if I didn't know.

By that point it all seemed back on a friendly joking basis—for her, if not for me—and though a part of me was devastated to find itself in love alone with a beautiful monster who resembled a friendly joking Judeo–Southern Baptist mother more than a lover, another part was amused by the joke and found the idea subtly appealing. But there were practical matters to take into consideration, so I said, "but what happens after Labor Day when I leave?" and Jane shrugged and said, "take him with you," like it was the simplest thing in the world, "don't they allow dogs in Chapel Hill?" and I said, "as far as I know—there might be some sort of statute against importing rat dogs though," and ignoring my joke, Jane said, "well, it's settled then," and I said, "have you seen any yard dogs fitting the description?" and she said, "not off hand, but I know where we can probably get one cheap," and I said, "the pound?" and she said, "where else?" and I said, "the pound's in Manteo," and she said, "then turn this thing around, son."

The incarcerated mutts let off an infernal howl when we walked through the door into the outside lot where they were caged. There were sad wormy-looking puppies and a few fierce almost feral ones that lunged at us against the wire. Then Jane called me over to a cage and pointed in.

It was love, unhappy love, at first sight. I knew this dog, and he knew me—there was no question, no choice, the doggy shimmer fated us, and he seemed no happier than I. He was a mutt of medium age and build, neither small nor large, white with a black patch on his left eye—a negative of Pete, in many ways—and black ears that stood up with great fortitude and aspiration before wilting at the tips. He lay there, center cage, his head down on his paws, looking rather glum about it all, but the moment he saw me he raised his head and stared straight in my eyes, then dropped it back with a small groan. Knowing that not every dog will meet a human stare unflinchingly, only those who've lived higher incarnations and been penalized for heinous sins—this was my pet theory—I looked at Jane, and Jane looked back at me, and that glance settled it. Seeing he had us, he opened his mouth in a wide doggy grin and rolled straight over on his back and started writhing and kicking his legs, keeping his eyes fixed on us throughout it all in a shameless display of conceit, and then he started squealing in a way that was both hilarious and touchingly pathetic.

"Enough," I said. The female attendant looked at me, and I said, "we'll take him," and she said, "you're sure?"—a connoisseur of mutts. I nodded, and the dog, understanding every word, stood up and scratched himself with casual dignity and sauntered to the door, pausing while the girl unlatched it. He then trotted out and turned into the corridor, pausing only when he reached the door where he sat down and looked at us like, let's get on with it, people. Outside, he went straight to the Jeep and squirted on the tire, then leapt right through the open door and sat behind the wheel as though prepared to drive. "So what are you going to call him?" Jane asked as we drove off, and I said, "this was your idea, you name him." She frowned down at him on the floor between us, dangling his tongue contentedly, and said, "well, if it was me I'd call him Pig, because he squeals like one," and he looked up at her like however it was intended he would take it as a compliment, because, after all, pigs are intelligent and cleanly when given the opportunity to be so, and Jane said, "my other choice would be B.," and I said, "B.?" and she said, "you know, like A. and B.?" and I looked down at him and said, "B. Pig," and he squealed, accepting his anointment.

I escorted Jane up the steps to her front door, carrying her picnic basket, and Pig came, too—that was the name that stuck—to look around, and Jane said, "wait here a minute," and disappeared inside, coming back with a red bandanna which she folded over to three corners and then rolled, kneeling down to tie it around Pig's neck. "There," she said, patting his head—he softened his ears and closed his eyes, nudging upward toward her hand—"that goes very well with your complexion, Pig," and Pig seemed rather pleased with himself. Then Jane stood up and said, "thank you, A., I had a real nice time," sounding, briefly, like a country girl I'd taken on a date, and I said, "so did I," and then she said, "you're sweet," becoming something else—two different things—and raised up on her tiptoes and kissed me on the lips, just a peck, before dropping back to the floor with her hand still on my arm. She started to turn away and I said, "Jane?" not knowing what I was going to say, and she turned back and I said, "I found something else I liked today," as it occurred to me, and she smiled and said, "I did, too." My look was full of heavy subtext, but hers was just a sweet and friendly smile, which made me wonder later if I'd dreamed that other look, the one she gave me underneath the second bridge in Colington, allowing me the twisted luxury of wishing otherwise from the safety of my doubt. She went inside and I looked down at my new friend and said, "home, Pig," and he grinned up like, who's causing this delay?

Twelve

A.

There is a law that stands unaltered in the universe, that guilty action is always dogged by horrible coincidence, and thus it was that as I opened the cottage door on my return from Jane's, I opened it to a ringing telephone. Fifty-fifty, either it was Morgan, or it was Cary, I didn't know which was worse—two horns of the same dilemma with equally impaling points. I didn't know how long that phone had been ringing before I got there, but I prayed to God to stop it, counting fifteen frantic bleats, and when it didn't, I renounced my faith, said, "shit," and picked up the receiver.

"Hello?" I said, and a voice, both familiar and strangely not, a voice from another world and another life said, "where the *fuck* have you *been*, A.?" and I said, "Cary?" and he said, "A.?" as though my voice was unfamiliar, too, and I said, "oh, man, oh, Cary, oh, spud," and he said, "what the hell is going on, A.? I've been trying to reach you for *three weeks*," and I said, "oh, shit, man—have you? I'm sorry, spud, I'm really sorry, things have just gotten unbelievable down here, just fucking unbelievable—you wouldn't even believe it," and he said, "*what?* what wouldn't I believe?" and I said, "I can't even explain it, I don't know where to start," and he said, "well, start by telling me where you've been," but before I could comply his tone turned shrill again, and he said, "and where has *Jane* been? I've been trying to reach her, too. I talked to Lucy twice, but I know she was lying to me—she said she didn't know where Jane was. She's seeing someone, isn't she?''

When I hesitated, trying to pick my way through that mine-field, Cary said, ''it isn't you, A., is it? You've got to tell me, man. I'll kill you if it is,'' and I said, ''God, Cary, Jesus fucking Christ, man—how can you even ask?'' and he said, ''I'm asking, A.,'' and I said, ''no, man, *no*,'' and he said, ''you swear?'' and I said, ''I swear,'' and he said, ''on your mother's grave?'' and I got pissed off then and said, ''fuck you, Cary, will you just lighten up?'' because though I didn't feel like I was lying, technically, I was not about to bring my mother into it.

Obviously feeling he'd crossed the line, Cary backed off and said, ''but she is seeing someone, right?'' and I said, ''listen, Cary, don't you think you should talk to Jane about all this?'' and he said, ''how the fuck am I supposed to talk to her if she's never home?'' and his voice was almost pleading as he said, ''you've got to tell me, A., if you're my friend you've got to tell me.'' I sighed and said, ''okay, Cary, she's seeing someone, but I don't think she's in love with him—that's all I'm going to say,'' and he said, ''but she's sleeping with him, right?'' and I said, ''you knew that was going to happen—you told me so yourself,'' and he said, ''I meant one-night stands,'' and feeling sorry for him, I said, ''so you aren't a saint after all,'' and I heard him sigh as he said, ''I guess not, A.,'' and I said, ''I'm sorry, spud, maybe you should end it,'' and he said, ''you don't understand, A., I can't,'' and I said, ''I understand,'' because, finally, I did, and he said, ''I didn't expect her to just completely disappear out of my life, you know? or you either, A.,'' and I said, ''I'm sorry, spud, I should have called—things have just been moving so fast. You should have been here, Cary, you really should have,'' and I thought I meant it till he said, ''well, I'm coming. I'll be down for the Fourth,'' and then I knew I didn't, then I knew I wished he'd never come at all, and it was devastating, like the sound of something vast and good, the last good thing from childhood, crumbling in my ears.

''I'm going to visit Cliff in Charlottesville and then fly into Norfolk,'' he said, and I said, ''I'll pick you up,'' feeling sad and far away, and he said, ''if it's a problem, I can take a bus,'' and I said, ''no, man, I'll be there, give me your flight.'' I copied it on the back of my paycheck envelope, and he said, ''listen, A., I want to hear what's going on with you, but I've got to run right now—we'll catch up when I get there,'' and I said, "bye," and he said, "bring Jane with you to the airport if you can," and I said, "right," and we hung up.

I took Pig down on the beach, had a dip, then tried to make him fetch a stick. Pig just watched me throw it out and stared at me like, do I look that stupid? if it means that much to you, swim after it yourself. I wasn't mad or even disappointed. I understood his point of view. Pig padded down to the edge and lay down in the swash, cooling off his rocks, which was the closest he ever got to the water without coercion, and I sat down and watched that stick just float away on the outgoing tide, and I knew Pig was a wise dog, that it was wise to let it go, however much you wanted it, but I hated wisdom with every particle of my heart, I hated it so much.

Watching Pig the Wise, I thought of Pete again, who wasn't wise, whose negative Pig was in many ways, and I remembered the day, not long before we moved to Winston-Salem, when Mr. Thompson, the mailman, knocked on our front door with Pete in his arms looking like he was going to cry—not Pete, but Mr. Thompson. Pete stared at us, his tongue working as he panted, looking stupidly content but with his back legs crushed and twisted all around, a look like, it's really not that bad, a look that wasn't wise at all. Mama, who'd just been diagnosed, burst into tears and we brought him in and put him on the sofa, wrapped in Mama's special blanket, a hand-loomed Irish one with her monogram which was a wedding gift—from Nana, I believe, it came along with the trousseau—and Pete, who was never allowed on the sofa, much less on Mama's blanket, looked like his wildest dreams of bliss had finally come true. We'd granted his one wish, which was simply to be treated as a human being and loved with an inconsolable love, which I, who had no brothers, had felt for him long before that day, since the moment I espied him in the back seat of the Mustang with his paws up on the seat like he was giving up and throwing himself on our mercy—another unwise move. Mama called Daddy, who was at the *Sentinel* writing his weekly column, and I held Pete's head in my lap, patting him and trying not to cry. I didn't. I never cried for Pete.

Daddy came home and we all got in the station wagon—I carried Pete myself, nobody else could touch him—and we drove to Dr. Hayes's office, the vet. The minute we pulled into the lot Pete knew. He pulled in his tongue and looked at us like, you wouldn't, would you? not when I'm down? I wanted to go with him to the examination room, but Daddy made me wait with Mama. He took Pete in the blanket and the door opened and what sounded like a million animals let off a tortured purgatorial yowl like I'd heard at the pound with Jane, only worse, much worse, a yowl that let you know, if you'd ever doubted it, that that door was the entrance to the underworld, the gaping maw of Doggie Hell. The door whisked closed and muted it, and then it stopped. Mama held my hand and we sat in silence until Daddy reappeared.

He sat down on the table in front of me, leaning forward with his elbows on his knees, then he reached out and lifted up my chin. His eyes were wet and red, but his face was sadly gentle, and he said, "I'm sorry, bud, Dr. Hayes says there's nothing we can do. Would you like to come and say good-bye to Pete?" His voice quavered as he said Pete's name, and Mama started crying. I wanted to cry, too, but I didn't. I was too old to cry. Men don't cry. I wanted to scream, but I didn't do that either. I simply nodded, and Daddy turned to Mama and said, "Allie?" and she shook her head, no, and we left her and went back.

The dogs howled and the cats meowed thinking we had come to save them, but I knew better—I hardly heard them. We walked into the room, a cubicle with cinderblock walls painted white with a metal table in the middle of it where Pete lay on his side under a large chrome lamp. Dr. Hayes nodded at me with pursed lips, one man to another, and then he looked at Daddy, and Daddy nodded, too. I went up to Pete and stroked his ears and said, "don't be scared, boy, it isn't going to hurt," and Pete's look said, I believe you. He didn't struggle, he just flinched a little when Dr. Hayes slipped in the needle. Pete's eyes were open, the left one staring up into that big chrome lamp, and as Dr. Hayes pressed the syringe, some sticky fluid began to seep into them and they slowly clouded and turned as dull and flat as buttons, and Pete was gone. Only in death did he look wise, and even then there was a trace of that frightened expression he always got when he pulled in his tongue and became alert, like that was the last thing Pete felt. I no longer wanted to cry. I felt pretty cold about it then, cold and angry like life is just a piece of shit if things like that could happen to an innocent dog. I picked Pete up and carried him all the way home, and then I went down in the field behind the house and dug a grave for him along the banks of Ruin Creek until my hands blistered from the shovel helve and started bleeding, and I buried him in the

Irish blanket with Mama's initials on it, covering the grave with stones so no other dogs could dig it up.

Six weeks later we left Killdeer and moved to Winston-Salem. And there it was. I'd loved Pete, I'd loved Mama, I'd loved Daddy, too—maybe most of all—but since that day, or perhaps the night I walked in on him and Eleanor in the Sherry Netherland Hotel, I'd loved nothing and liked nothing either, not even myself. Cary had been the only one. Till now. Now I loved Jane, too. But I was wise, so suddenly wise, I saw that there was only one right way, just one, one just right way. Alone of everyone and everything I'd ever loved Cary had kept his promise. Pete had tried, so had Mama, maybe even Daddy tried, maybe they all tried, maybe I was the only one who hadn't tried, but now I had to, because Cary was the only one. This was one promise I had to keep.

The stick had disappeared, and I sat there on the beach feeling so cold and bitter, so bitter to have my marker called. The shimmer had departed and in my newfound wisdom I knew this world is not a place for shimmers. I loved Jane, in all those years of drought she was the only thing I'd found to love and want, but there were no promises to her. And what do you do when the wrong choice appears to be your only hope, when the right choice leaves you where you already are, a place that you can't live in anymore because you're dying there? In my wisdom the answer was so clear.

That night I went back to the Lost Colony and Morgan and I celebrated just like old times, oh, yeah, just like the times of old.

Thirteen

A.

That weekend, the last before the Fourth, we went to the woods to hunt. I traded days with Parker, agreeing to work his shift over the holiday, left the cottage keys with Reese and Ellen, who promised to feed Pig, set my alarm, and rolled into the parking lot of the Lost Colony at five a.m.—Cleanth had insisted on an early start. Through the dusty back window of Morgan's Cherokee, among the bagged tents and coolers and other gear, I made out several boxes of Winchester magnum shells and leather gun sleeves filled with heavy rigid sleeping forms. I wasn't surprised to find them there, if anything surprised me it was their number—four. That didn't surprise me so much either.

Inside I found Cleanth and Jane drinking coffee and talking quietly at a table near the kitchen, eating biscuits with raspberry jam. When he saw me Cleanth stood up and walked to meet me, smiling. He was wearing camouflage fatigues and an olive drab tee shirt with a khaki vest with shell loops unzipped over it. We shook hands before we spoke. His expression was quietly elated, eager. "All set?" he said, and I said, "yeah, I think so," and he nodded, grinning, his eyes reading me deeply out of that elation. Then he stood aside politely for Jane and me to speak. "Morning, A.," she said shyly over her cup, then dropped her eyes and blew into the steam. It was the first time I'd seen her since that day in Colington, and she was so beautiful—the shimmer was still there, my decision hadn't affected that. That didn't surprise me either. I just nodded, ate my heart out, and said to Cleanth, "where's Morgan?" "Good question," he said, looking at his watch, "would you run up and see?" and I said, "sure," and went through the lobby toward the stairs.

"I'm coming—who is it?" Morgan answered in an exasperated tone as I knocked. "It's me," I answered, and the door swung in. "Did His Majesty send you?" she asked, and I smiled, and she said, "to light a fire?" I nodded and she sighed, stepping aside for me to enter. She was wearing a khaki hunting outfit. I leaned to give her a greeting kiss, but she turned away, preoccupied, then caught herself and inclined perfunctorily in my direction. "What's the matter?" I asked and she said, "it's five in the morning and you have to ask?" I blinked and she said, "I can't find my boots—I just had the damn things," and I glanced into the inner room and saw them sitting in plain view on the bed. I pointed, and she turned to look, then smiled at me with sheepish apology and went and picked them up, dropping them with a clunk on the floor as she sat down.

Instead of putting them on, she sighed again and dropped backward on the mattress, bouncing slightly. "I'm procrastinating, Adam," she said, speaking up to the ceiling, and I said, "don't you want to go?" She laughed, then raised her head to look at me. "Are you kidding?" she said, "I'd rather be drawn and quartered," and I said, "why?" and she said, "two days up there with them humping in the next tent?" and though I hadn't thought it out in that detail and wasn't pleased by the prospect either—for reasons I couldn't share with Morgan—I said, "we'll be humping, too, though, won't we?" trying to lighten it, and Morgan, unmoved by my effort, said, "and Jane sunbathing in the raw, showing off those adorable little bosoms of hers, while mine look like two sad old balloons a week after the party?—it's my idea of hell, Adam," and I said, "you have nice bosoms, Morgan." She sat back up, gazing at me doubtfully, and said, "don't patronize me, Adam," and I said, "I'm not," and she mused a moment more before deciding to believe me. "And you," she said, "do you really want to go?" and I shrugged and said, "I think camping out will be fun."

"You know we're going hunting?" she said, and I said, "yeah, I assumed we would. I'm not going to shoot," and she said, "don't let him pressure you," and I said, "what's he going to do, put a gun to my head?" and she said, "I expect he'll be a little subtler than that," and I said, "I'm not even going to

carry,'' and she said, ''you'll have to, darling,'' and started
lacing her boots, and I said, ''why?'' and she looked up and
said, ''because we're going after boars,'' and I said, ''boars?''
and she said, ''they're very nasty, Adam, and very large. They
have these tusks—tushes''—she held her hand up, her index-
finger three inches from her thumb. ''I've never seen anyone
gored,'' she said, ''but my father did, his guide. That was in
Thrace, the European part of Turkey, near the Black Sea. They
lost a dog as well. You'll have to carry if you go, in case you're
charged. But you don't have to go,'' and I said, ''but that's pretty
rare, isn't it? for them to charge?'' and she pursed her lips and
said, ''I suppose—it happens though,'' and I said, ''I want to
see them,'' and she said, ''yes, I thought you would.'' Then she
stood up and handed me a case off the bed. ''Would you take
this for me?'' she asked, ''tell them I'll be right down.''

Cleanth, who was chomping at the bit, looking at his watch
every fifteen seconds, took Morgan's case from me and said,
''I'll put this in the car,'' and went out with it, leaving Jane and
me alone. ''Would you like some coffee?'' Jane asked, and I
said, ''thanks,'' and she went behind the screen and brought
back a cup, setting it at the table beside her place. I sat down.
''Do you take anything?'' she asked and I shook my head and
said, ''black,'' picking up the cup with both hands and blowing
into it. It gave me a subtle pleasure to have her do something
for me, but I felt nervous and distracted around her anyway and
tried not to think about it.

As I took my first sip, my eyes drifted to the portrait of the
girl in the French hat and net veil across Jane's shoulder and for
one uncanny moment she seemed alive, regarding me with solemn study from those sad eyes and about to speak. ''Isn't she
beautiful?'' Jane said, and I said, ''she looks like you,'' speaking my thought, and immediately wishing I hadn't. Jane turned
back to me with surprise, an almost wounded look, and I said,
''I don't mean her face, just something about her expression,''
trying to backtrack, and failing miserably. Still surprised, questioning, Jane studied me, resembling the portrait more than
ever—the shimmer danced across them both—and I let my eyes
slide elsewhere, taking a second sip of coffee and burning my
throat. The sudden hope I felt burned more, something in Jane's
face that said Colington wasn't just my imagination.

''Cary called,'' I said impulsively, ''he's flying in,'' and she
said quietly, ''I know, A., I talked to him,'' and I said, ''you

did?'' surprised. She dropped her eyes to her cup and nodded as she took a sip. I waited for her to say more, and when she didn't I said, ''did you tell him about Cleanth?'' and she said, ''yes, I didn't really know what to say, but I told him as well as I could.'' She looked up at me suddenly with eyes that glowed with depths of winking softness in them, and I said, ''Jane.'' ''Yes?'' she answered softly. I leaned forward, whispering, ''do you love him?'' angry at my voice for trembling, angry with my sudden breathlessness. Confusion crossed her face, then settled as she said, ''you know I love Cary, A.,'' and I shook my head and told her, ''no, not Cary—Cleanth.'' Her eyes misted like a mirror touched with steam and then she turned away as the others entered, Cleanth by the porch door, Morgan from the lobby.

''How are we going to drive?'' Morgan asked as we stood around the vehicles, and handing her a thermos, Cleanth said, ''I'll ride with A.'' He turned to me and said, ''if that's okay?'' and I shrugged and said, ''fine, whatever,'' and Morgan said, ''whatever,'' not looking thrilled with the arrangements, and then she turned to Jane and said, ''come on, dear, I'll tell you all his darkest secrets, and if that gets too dull, we'll do Tupperware.'' Jane smiled, seeing Morgan's animus wasn't directed against her personally, and Cleanth opened Morgan's door for her with an ironic courtliness. ''You'll follow us,'' he said, closing the door for her. We pulled out and I drove slowly till I found their headlights in the rearview mirror, and then I sped up and we drove north in the dark. ''Ten after,'' he said, looking at his watch, and I said, ''what's the hurry?'' and he said, ''I want to be on Penny Hill in time to see the sunrise.'' He looked back across his shoulder at the Cherokee, then leaned over and brought my paint box back with him to the front seat. ''I see you brought your weapons,'' he said, taking out a Windsor and Newton brush and thumbing it, and I said, ''I saw you brought yours, too,'' and he said, ''different strokes.''

He rubbed the bristle across my arm and said, ''you know what this is made of?'' and I said, ''squirrel, right?'' and he said, ''very good, A., *red* squirrel—this is a nice brush. How much are these running now—seventy-five, eighty bucks?'' and I said, ''it was a present from Eleanor.'' He looked at me inquisitively and I said, ''my Dad's girlfriend,'' and he said, ''she must be a woman of taste—you can tell a lot about people by the gifts they give,'' and I said, ''she is, Eleanor's very nice,'' and he said, "she isn't an artist, is she?" and I said, "no, she isn't," and he said, "then she isn't egotistical either." I looked at him, surprised again at his insightfulness, and he said, "egotistical people give gifts they'd like to own themselves—they can be the worst kind," and I said, "I know what you mean," thinking of my uncle, the philatelist, and the stamp sets I'd received each Christmas, and Cleanth said, "but they can also be the best. The highest gifts are always egotistical. And you know why selfish people give away things so valuable?" and I said, "why?" and he said, "for the selfish pleasure of experiencing their reality freshly in the appreciation of a new receiver. That's how you keep those things alive in yourself, A., by giving them away. Do you know what I'm talking about?' and I said, "I'm not sure," and he said, "I want you to give me something, A.," and I said, "what?" and he said, "I have a present for you, a very special one, and your gift to me is taking it," and I said, "what present?" and he grinned and said, "today."

"I'm looking forward to it, Cleanth," I told him, and he said, "so am I," and I said, "but I'm not going to shoot—Morgan told me about the boars, and I'll carry if I have to, but I won't shoot," and he said, "you'll use a red squirrel brush, but you won't shoot one?" and I said, "okay, you're right, and I'm probably a hypocrite. Maybe it's wrong of me to use that brush, but I still won't shoot, not unless I'm charged and there's no other way," and he said softly, "it's all a charge, A., in the woods it's all a charge."

We were quiet for a while before I said, "why did you stop painting, Cleanth? I was looking at that portrait again this morning—it's wonderful," and he said, "that was the last thing I ever did," and I said, "who was she, Cleanth?" He studied me, surprised, I think, at my forwardness, but not put off by it. "She was why I stopped," he said, "indirectly." I waited for him to continue, and he said, "would you like to know that story, A.?" and I said, "if you don't mind telling me," and he said, "I don't mind—not now though. Today is for the woods. Tonight we'll build a bonfire on the beach, and who knows what kind of stories we might tell? Perhaps you'll tell one, too," and I said, "I don't have any good ones," and he said, "if you're lucky, maybe by tonight you will."

I knew what he meant—the hunt would be my story—and I was aware of the subtle pressure Morgan had warned me to expect. But Cleanth always pushed me, and I'd grown used to it. "Just promise me one thing, A.," he said, and I said, "what?" and he said, "promise me you'll listen to your heart and not your head today," and I said, "okay, Cleanth, I can make that promise," because I knew what my heart would tell me, and that's what I wanted anyway—to be true to that. Cleanth nodded like he was satisfied.

We were coming into Duck village by then. It was still dark, though the sky was lightening to the east over the high dunes, just a paler blueness with the night above it still black and filled with stars and a waning gibbous moon in the west over the sound. It was about five-thirty then, and I was struck by the moonlight on the steeple of the little white clapboard church. We passed the quaint cedar shake cottages with their sagging porches and small bombshells in the yards like sculptures, or marking the driveway borders. The dunes had once served as a bombing range and when I was little I'd been forbidden to climb them for fear of unexploded hulks rusting underneath the sand. Some of them were brightly painted, like marker buoys, others were crumbling to rust. One yard had an old mine, probably laid by a German U-boat off the coast in World War II and later washed ashore. It was spiked and enormous with a heavy broken chain. I wondered if it had even been defused. Other yards sported anchors, or wooden channel buoys hanging from a porch eave like ears of Indian corn. There were crab pots and gill nets lying in the yards or being strung between two poles and rusted pickups in the driveways with homemade cabs—one said, "Salty Oisters" in crude hand lettering. Many of those trucks were already running, and there were bearded fishermen in billed caps on the porches drinking coffee in their bare feet, getting ready for the day, and young boys with them, nervous and alert. Sons.

We passed the ruin of the old Coast Guard station at Coffee's Inlet, once a wide sea-going thoroughfare, now completely silted up, and that was the farthest north I'd ever been along that coast. From that point on it was all new ground. The only road to Corolla was a private one, owned by the power company. Only residents, or property owners, or people with specific business were let through. We stopped at the gatehouse and an old man came out, peering in at me suspiciously. Cleanth leaned down and said, "I'm Cleanth Faison. I believe Mike Taylor at Atlantic Realty spoke to you," and the old man said, "that's right—you the one that's going up to see about the old hunting lodge, ain't you?'' and Cleanth grinned and said, ''that's me,'' and the old fellow nodded and lifted up the crossbar.

We only stayed on the road for two or three miles. ''Think we can make it over that,'' Cleanth asked, pointing to the wall of dune, and I said, ''we can try,'' and I pulled over and we both got out, locking in the axle at both wheels. I shifted into four-wheel drive and we set out up the face. The incline started gently, then it sheered up over us and I gunned the engine, two minutes straight up with the engine wound tight, whining in second gear. We stopped just shy of the crest, and Cleanth looked at me with his eyebrows raised and his lips rolled in, but I shifted into low-range and we bucked out and made the crest. The sea spread out below us like molten pewter, or perhaps the concrete floor of a dairy barn with fresh milk spilled on it, which was the whiteness of the coming sun reflected downwards from the clouds. As we watched, letting the engine cool and waiting for Jane and Morgan to catch up, the clouds began to take on tints of rose and silver, and we saw a school of porpoises, their slick dark backs rolling southward in the pale sea. The Cherokee didn't fare as well. Morgan made it halfway up and then had to back down and take a flying run at it. The second time she made it, and we drove down the windward face side by side and started racing northward up the hard-packed beach.

There was a cool breeze rising from the water, and enormous flocks of gulls—hundreds and hundreds of them—took off into the wind and then reversed, flying out ahead of us, veering and squawking. ''They're so fucking stupid,'' I said, ''why don't they just move aside and let us pass?'' and Cleanth said, ''maybe they like it,'' grinning. The tires crackled over occasional patches of shells and sizzled through the swash where Morgan edged me into it, leaving trails of steam from the hot muffler pipes. I could see Jane beside me with the window open, wearing her dark glasses and holding down her hat. Cleanth leaned over and grinned at them through my window, and Morgan grinned back and shot us both the finger, accelerating. We were doing sixty, but it felt like twice that. We were about fifty percent out of control, but I loved it, it felt like flying. Occasionally we did fly, hitting bumps and rolls you couldn't see till you were on them and crashing down until the chassis jarred against the shocks, almost bucking us out of our seats. I held the wheel and Cleanth had his feet prized against the dash. I looked over and he was doing another line. He toasted me with his key and tried to put it in his nose, but it flew out the window. He just laughed.

We passed huge stands of driftwood, smooth and grayed, tied into true love knots, and wrecks, cages of brown eroded ribs sunk in the sand, or a metal boom rising from the water offshore with a pelican squatting on it. We saw a female turtle, a loggerhead, I think, a black silhouette on the beach way out ahead of us. By the time we got there, she was already making her way through the breakers, having laid her eggs already, or perhaps prevented from doing so by our passing. It was twenty miles to the Corolla Light, but we saw it from ten miles away, a pale gleam against the coming dawn. By the time we arrived it had been turned off and the keeper was asleep—if there was a keeper. I meant to ask Cleanth that, but I forgot.

We passed the turn-off to the village, marked by rusty metal tire treads, and kept on going, past the houses on the beach— only one or two—and on to Penny Hill, which Cleanth told me the locals called Leewark Hill, like the belly of a pregnant woman lying on her back. It didn't seem that big at first, but as we neared it loomed higher and higher till the forest below receded to a dark puny scrawl. It looked like a mountain of wheat, all the wheat of America and Canada, all the wheat in the universe, spread out before us in the morning light. I felt euphoric from the drive and I said, "why the fuck not?" and gunned straight into it. I don't know how we made it, but we did. Morgan didn't even try. It was just me and Cleanth up there in a stiffer breeze, trading shots of bourbon out of the silver flask he'd brought and doing lines. "One for me," Cleanth said, taking a swallow and handing me the flask, "and one for you." I sipped and gave it back to him and he poured some in the sand and said, "and one for the spirits of the place."

The leeward face fell almost sheer down into the forests, a narrow ribbon a mile in width at most, but spreading out as far as the eye could see in both directions. Beyond the forest were the marshes, green and lush with brown estuaries snaking through them into Currituck Sound, an arm of the vast Albermarle, and the distant shoreline of the mainland, ten miles away. At great intervals in the marsh, rising from the greening cordgrass and spartina, there were hummocks, small islands of raised ground, with stands of great loblolly pines on them, a single tree, or two or three, growing straight up for sixty or eighty feet, then bifurcating into two trunks, spreading into smaller branches

that also bifurcated and reversed, woven intricately into squared
tufted tops. Some of them were as strange and delicate as bonsai
trees. There were dead ones, too, silver in the morning light,
their branches like arms with many elbows, bent with conflicted
impulse, like a ritual Egyptian dance fused into a single still
photograph. In one of them there was a nest, straggly with grayed
stalks of cattails and bamboo from previous seasons. "What's
that?" I asked, pointing, and Cleanth said, "an osprey nest,"
and I said, "osprey?" unfamiliar with the word, and he said,
"it's a kind of fish hawk, magnificent birds with a four or five
foot wingspan—the locals call them sea eagles. My guide up
here, Early Fenton—you'll meet him shortly—once told me his
father called it an ossifrage—how's your Latin?" and I said,
"*os*, like bone?" and he said, "*fragere?*" I shook my head,
and Cleanth said, "bone breaker," with a suggestive grin.

He led my eye southward toward the village, toy houses and
a road of gleaming white sand, and further off, almost to the
sound, a huge white building with a roof of blue-gray slate.
"That's the lodge," he told me, "it's been abandoned now for
years and it's for sale—the place has possibilities," and I said,
"what would you do with it? another hotel?" and he said, "an
upscale one, a whole complex really with its own built-in
amusements. We'd put in an airstrip, tennis courts, spa facilities,
perhaps, later, stables—what do you think?" and I said, "it
sounds very expensive," and he said, "it would be—very expensive, but very choice—not only a nice place to visit, but a
nice place to work as well." He looked at me. "Have you
thought any more about the job, A.?" he asked, and I said, "I
don't think Morgan's all that keen on me taking it, Cleanth." A
flash of dark surprise crossed his features and he said, "she told
you that?" and I said, "more or less," wanting to make it
appear my inference, sparing Morgan his displeasure, and he
said, "did she say why?" and I said, "something about not
falling in your shadow," and he said, "do I cast such a dark
one, A.?" and I said, "I'm just telling you what she said, man,"
and he said, "this isn't about Morgan, A., it's between you and
me. If you don't want to take the job, don't, but do it because
you don't want to, not because Morgan doesn't want you to,"
and I said, "but she's your partner, Cleanth—don't you think
you should take her feelings into consideration?" and he said,
"I always do, A., but that blade cuts both ways. You make up
your own mind and let me deal with M., okay?" and I said,

"okay, Cleanth." He nodded, then turned away as though putting it behind him.

"See that house down there?" he asked, pointing to a tin-roofed shack perched on an estuary with a dock where a small trawl boat was tied. There was smoke rising from the chimney, and a few fenced cows browsing through the rails at the edge of what appeared to be a patch of corn. "That's Early's," Cleanth said, "I thought we'd head down there and pay him a little surprise visit," and I said, "he's not expecting us?" and Cleanth said, "Early likes surprises, too," and I said, as the thought occurred to me, "what about permits, Cleanth?" and he said, "there's not a ranger within miles—besides, A., what difference does it make? you're not going to shoot anyway, right?" and I said, "right," still not liking it, and he cuffed my shoulder and said, "come on, let's go," and we went.

Fourteen

A.

The dogs started barking long before we saw the house, and then above the marsh smell, which was rank but also fresh, there was manure, not strong, but acrid with a trace of ammonia, and above that, woodsmoke. Early Fenton was standing on his porch when we emerged into the clearing of the yard, a tall wiry man with a sun-leathered face and grizzled hair cropped close to his skull, extremely thick, and a few days growth of prickly beard, uniformly gray. He had a hunk of cornbread in one hand and an enameled tin coffee cup in the other. When I stopped the Jeep he ambled out barefoot in the slick black dirt of the yard, kicking aside a chicken, which squawked and ran, then leaned in on Cleanth's side, casting a swift glance at me as he said, "well, now, I thought that might be you, Mr. Faison, when I heard the motors," only what he really said was more like, "well naow, Oi thought that moight be you, Mr. Foiz'n, when Oi hord the maoters." His accent had some low Virginia tidewater in it, the way he put an *a* sound into words like now and motor, aside from the more well-known *oi* dipthong which gave his dialect its name—Early was a "Hoi Toider."

"How's it hanging, Early?" Cleanth said, and Early replied, " 'bout a foot or two below moi knays, Mr. Foiz'n, but Oi tuck it up insoide moi shorts so Oi can walk." Cleanth grinned at me and Early took a second longer look out of permanently squinted eyes that had a glint of brusque goodwill in them, and Cleanth said, "Early, this is a friend of mine, A. Jenrette," and

337

Early said, "this your vee-hickle, son?" and I said, "yeah, it is," and he said, "what'll you toike for 'er?" winking at Cleanth, and knowing he was jacking me around good-naturedly, I said, "make me an offer," and he said, "how 'bout that old truck of moine 'n a hundred paounds of shrimp?" and I said, "that doesn't sound like a real great deal to me," and he said, "she runs good," like he was giving me a chance to re-consider, and I said, "I don't think so," and Early shook his head and said, "he's a hord one, Mr. Foiz'n," and Cleanth said, "you seen those pigs lately, Early?" and Early said, "seen a whole pack of 'em last week, 'n Oi hord 'em ever goddamn night out there in moi corn, just tarin' it to pieces," and Cleanth said, "how about we see if we can't find them, Early?" and Early dropped his head and shook it saying, "wish Oi could, Mr. Foiz'n, but Oi'm on moi way out to moi boat roight naow—gotta work, but Oi'd rather ploy."

"Goddamn, Early," Cleanth said, "it's Saturday—nobody works on Saturday," and Early said, "some works Satord'y 'n Sond'y, too, Mr. Foiz'n," and Cleanth pulled his sterling money clip out of his pocket, crisped off a hundred dollar bill and said, "that make it worth your time?" and Early grinned and said, "moight be." Cleanth stuffed it in Early's shirt pocket and said, "now quit fucking off, Early Boy, and let's go find some pigs." Early shook his head appreciatively and said, "Oi knowed it was you," and Cleanth climbed out and clapped him on the shoulder and said, "you're a psychic, Early," and Early said, "moight be that 'n a piece of shit besoides, Mr. Foiz'n, but long as Oi'm fuckin' off 'n gittin' poyed to do it, you can coil me anything you damn well plaze."

Jane and Morgan had pulled up behind us and got out. Jane stretched and turned to us with a bland contented smile. "Hello, Early," Morgan said, and he said, "good to say you, ma'am, you been keepin' this one out of trubble?" referring to Cleanth, and Morgan said, "hardly, Early, I don't even try," giving Cleanth a wry look that wasn't fully playful, and Early said, "well, what's impossible oin't worth troyin' no-how," and as Cleanth introduced Jane Early's glance flicked to their joined hands and then across Jane's shoulder. "Yoi'll come in the haouse a minute 'n let me foind moi boots," he said, "then we'll say to the daogs"—he looked at Cleanth—" 'less you want to come daown to the boat forst—something there you moight want to look at," and Cleanth said, "later,

Early," and I saw Morgan's eyes flick back and forth between
them, darkened. As Jane and I followed Early into the house,
Morgan held Cleanth back, and I heard the sounds of argument—not raised voices, but vehement whispers which I
couldn't make out.

The house was raised a foot or two on stubby pylons, and we
went through a screen door into a large low-ceilinged room
paneled with unstained yellow pine. There was a pegged oak
floor, beautifully carpentered, but badly scuffed and grayed from
lack of care. Ashes smoldered in a brick fireplace in one end
and there was a stack of fat pine kindling from the chopping
block in the front yard. Early stepped into his boots and went
back out, passing Cleanth and Morgan in the doorway. I heard
a pump motor turn on and a green garden hose coming in the
kitchen window jumped as a stream of clear water jetted into
the sink basin. When he returned, he spooned fresh coffee onto
the old grounds in a tin percolator on the range. Crumbling in
an egg shell, he filled it with water, turned on the propane, lit
the eye, then went back out and turned the pump off. I observed
this complex process with a degree of wonder.

The coffee was strong and acid-tasting, similar to espresso,
and excellent with the fresh clotted yellow cream he provided. Early brought it to the table along with a black iron
skillet of cake cornbread and a hunk of butter yellower than
any I'd ever seen, with a flower on it from the press. "This
is delicious, Early," Morgan said, and he replied with boyish
shyness, "well, it oin't fit for loidies, ma'am, but Oi don't
do much entertoinin'. Since my woife doied Oi have to do
for moiself."

"Tell A. and Jane about the pigs, Early," Cleanth said, "A.
was wondering about permits." Early looked at me, and I said,
"are they in season now?" and Early said, "for as Oi'm con-
sorned, the season storts about the toime moi corn comes up
and they git in it. Nobody ever tole me any differ'nt, 'n Oi
reckon a man's got a roight to protect his own," and Cleanth
said, "and there's some question whether they're even wild, isn't
there, Early?" and Early said, "they're woild all roight, though
whether they were woild to stort with or run woild off a form
don't know as anyone can soy. Was a feller lived up here noime
of Joimes back before Oi come, had 'im a form 'n a haouse on
it 'n lived pretty much loike me, Oi reckon. Nothin' left of 'er
now 'cept the chimbley standin' on a hummock with a big worter

oak besoide of it. The morsh took it all back, but what Oi hear, old Joimes he raised some horgs 'n fed 'em soilt hay 'n such, had 'im a smoke haouse 'n cured some soilty hams, sold 'em to the goime lodge 'n did roight well till they closed down, 'n then he doied in wintertoime 'n nobody thought to look for 'im till come spring—don't reckon it was none too pretty, but his stock run off, you say, 'n that moi be all they are, them pigs, just form stock what run woild.''

Attending all this with interest, particularly the way Early chewed and rolled his words, like a toothless man eating salt-water taffy with his gums, I said, "but aren't they different? can't you tell by looking at them?" and Early said, "well, son, at forst you can, but once they git back in the woods they choinge, it don't take 'em long, they grow hor 'n toishes—had two or thray run off on me, 'n I shot one later 'n it had a clipped ear which is how Oi mork 'em," and Cleanth said, "you ready, Early?" and Early said, "thought Oi was woitin' on you," and Cleanth said, "well, let's go find some pigs," and Early said, rising, "just let me put the daogs up in the truck 'n we can go."

They were black-and-tans in a good-sized cage of chicken wire with a slick earth floor and as we approached they set up a howl and started turning somersaults and climbing up the wire. "Reckon they knowed it was you, too, Mr. Foiz'n," Early said, grinning as he unlatched the door and entered with two rope leashes. The smaller of the pair jumped up on him, and Early clubbed it backhand with his fist and said, "git daown, you stupid bitch, you know better," and she went slinking to the corner. The male, larger and more heavily muscled, with a savage face that never deigned to look at any of the rest of us, his attention all for Early, calmly took the leash and Early brought them out and put them in the back of his truck, tying them to the rail. Early went back and knelt down by the dog house, taking out first one pup then a second. They were fairly large and awkwardly spry, and Early handed one to me and the other to Jane. "You going to hunt the little ones, Early?" Cleanth asked, and Early said, "we'll keep 'em in the cab, Oi reckon. They're eager but they're stupid 'n they'll fuck it up if they daon't kill theirself, Oi daon't want 'em runnin' yet."

Cleanth took the guns out of the Cherokee one by one, unzipping them from their sleeves. He handed me a .12-gauge Browning pump and a fist full of shells and watched as I flipped it over and inserted one into the chamber, pressing the button to send it up. I put in a second and a third, but the fourth one wouldn't go. "It's plugged?" I asked, looking at him, and Cleanth nodded, smiling, and said, "I see you know the gun," and I said, "I used to duck hunt with one just like this, only it had a longer barrel," and he said, "that's standard field length, twenty-seven inches, for ducks you were probably using a thirty-inch," and I said, "it's full choke, right?" and he nodded, and Jane said, "what's full choke?" and Cleanth said, "that means it sends the shot out in a narrow scatter at a longer distance. Modified choke makes a wider pattern, which is why it's better for smaller birds like dove and quail," and Jane said, "oh," and Cleanth said, "but those were slugs I gave you, A., not shot," and Jane said, "what's the difference?" and I said, "a slug's just like a rifle bullet only in a shotgun shell," and Cleanth said, "very good, A.," and my knowledge of the technical details was like a code-word to a special club where Cleanth manned the door.

Cleanth handed Jane a double-barreled Remington and Morgan another Browning just like mine, then took out his own gun, a beautiful double-barreled Parker, with bluish silver plating, elaborately engraved with a hunting scene. He also buckled on a leather holster with a six-shot revolver, a .44 magnum with a six-inch barrel.

I was somewhat surprised when Early asked me to ride with him. I climbed in the cab with the pups jumping all over me. I asked Early their names, but he said, "Oi don't never noime a whelp till it's been blooded, son," his manner suddenly all business. Of the older pair, the male was Turk, the female, Sal.

We pulled out of the yard, the others following in my Jeep, and started heading back the way we'd come down a sandy track with grass in the middle and high marsh on either side. Early turned to me and said, "moind if Oi ask you a question, son?" and I said, "sure, what?" and he said, "you short a gun before, oin't you?" I gave him a brief résumé of my hunting experience, and he nodded as though satisfied. "Don't toike moi askin' porsonal, son," he said, "It's just that Oi'll be comin' through the woods roight at you 'n Oi don't want to git short if Oi can help it," and I said, "I'll be careful, Early," and he said, " 'n don't shoot moi daogs neither, son, 'cause that'ud be the other thing would opset me. Oi'll be holdin' 'em onto the leash, but they've got away before 'n when they got a scent they waon't be stoppin' to ask questions. The daogs have got to trost us, son—they don't moike mistoikes, you say, 'n they don't expect us to moike none neither, you onderstand?'' and I said, ''I understand,'' and Early, having sniffed me out, said, ''roight then, we'll git along just foine,'' and turned back to the road. I sat there feeling weak and cowardly for not admitting my intention not to shoot and knowing full well why I hadn't. Vegetarianism would seem effete, or worse, to a man like Early, and strangely, as I sat there beside him, heading into his world, it briefly seemed that way to me, too.

The track rose incrementally to higher ground and the vegetation changed slightly, from uninterrupted marsh grass to a few wiry myrtle bushes with thick waxy leaves growing from dry sand. Then we climbed a ridge and turned southward down a wider road with a higher ridge above us sprinkled with dwarf pines growing at a permanent slant away from the prevailing northeast winds. We followed that for less than a mile and then turned left, eastward, toward the ocean, passing between two high banks of dune, and the terrain changed immediately. Suddenly there were tall trees overhead—live oaks with wisps of Spanish moss festooned from their limbs like feather boas, sour gums and enormous holly trees three and four feet thick with smooth silvery bark like skin over ridges of lithe muscle—they looked almost human—and there were loblolly pines as well. The ground began to pitch and roll rather steeply, and everything was covered with a tarnished copper carpet of pine needles. You could see a good distance into it except where there were stands of bamboo, and suddenly the whole quality of the day changed—we moved from full morning light into predominant shadow, though there were patches of sun along the road in places and shining slantwise down the hills. The air got cooler, almost chilly, and the smell changed, becoming fresher, losing the salt taint of the marsh. Sounds changed, too—after the rippling susurrus of the marsh things seemed much stiller, though occasionally above the engine I could pick out the twittering of birds.

As we drove on the hills grew steeper, falling away in places to deep ravines. I saw a pond, and then a second—many on both sides of the road—and they were unlike anything I'd ever seen before, small, irregularly shaped and covered with a skin of chartreuse slime that was almost incandescent where the sun fell on it. They were studded with dark decaying stumps, and in one a silvery dead tree had fallen. On its highest limbs a tremendous heron perched. Hearing the engine, it spread vast slate-blue wings, extended its long neck and took off with great oaring strokes, retracting its head close to its body as it flew so that it looked almost like a pelican. Those ponds gave the wood an almost unworldly feeling.

"I've never seen anything like those," I said to Early, pointing out the window as we passed another one, and he said, "some folks coil 'em Caroloina bayous, A. One feller tole me they was moide by fishes, said it was when the soy went back foive or ten thaousand years ago, left 'em stranded here in shaols 'n they thrashed up big haoles what feeled with roin. 'Neother feller tole me it was meetyorroights that struck, but if so, where'd they go? What I fig're is it's just worter come up from below, 'cause you stick a shuvvil in the graound hereabouts 'n you stroike worter."

As we drove on, through occasional breaks in the trees on my right I could see the sound glittering in the morning sun beyond the marshes which began a quarter mile away. Finally Early eased the truck over to the edge, cut the engine and said, "let's say if we can't foind a troice of them pigs, A. Last toime Oi seen 'em it was along in here." We got out, leaving the puppies in the cab, and Early took the bitch, Sal, from the bed and disappeared into the trees with her as the others pulled up in the Jeep. That's when I began to feel it, something I'd forgotten, the sense of quickening aloneness tinged with quivers of excitement and anxiety. I saw it in the others, too—Jane like a little girl, somber and nervous before a first recital, and Morgan quiet also. Cleanth put his hand on my arm and squeezed it, staring into my eyes with a restrained gaiety and eagerness that made him seem almost boyish.

"Step here a minute, Mr. Foiz'n," Early said, emerging from between the two parked vehicles with the dog, who seemed calmer now, though she trembled slightly and her eyes had a soft moist shine, something almost loving, except that when you really looked they reached back into an abyss. "Did you find something, Early?" Cleanth asked, following and motioning us to come. We stepped off the sandy road onto the pinestraw and walked uphill and then down into a depression. There was a large live oak there and the ground beneath it had been turned, a fair-sized crater as though a small mortar shell had exploded there. To my surprise, under the straw, instead of sand the earth

was black, wet and clotted, choked with roots. Cleanth and
Early traded looks and Cleanth said, "how old?" and Early
said, "last noight looks loike to me—oin't no crust on it"—he
nudged it with his boot toe. Cleanth turned to us and said, "they
were here," and I felt a chill pass over me. The presence of the
quarry in the woods made them different yet again—the rustling
of the leaves seemed conscious, with a trace of menace, or of
promise.

"Boars make these?" Jane asked. Cleanth nodded, and she
said, "what do they do here—sleep in them?" Cleanth glanced
at Early, giving him the floor, and Early said, "no, ma'am,
more loike they's grubbin' up some roots for sopper 'n maybe
toike a raoll in 'em, 'cause dorty's cleanness to a horg, woild or
no—either woy it's pig soign all roight. You can say where they
run off back through the trays." Early pointed to the pinestraw
and there was evidence of slight disturbance, something I would
probably have walked right over had I been out there alone.
"What we'll do is set yoi'll up on stand a little forther in. Oi'll
toike Sal 'n Tork 'n droive on up a woize, 'cause, say, the road
corves raound not for from here 'n runs up on that ridge"—he
pointed through the trees, and I could barely catch a glimpse of
it. "Once Oi git up there, Oi'll start droivin' down t'word yoi'll
'n we'll say don't we git lucky."

We went back to the vehicles, got our guns and then followed
Early deeper into the woods. Five or six hundred yards in, before we separated, Cleanth said, "one last thing, everybody—
when Early finds them, *if* he finds them, they'll probably run
toward us heading for the marsh. It's important to contain, because once they get in there the dogs can't track them, it's too
wet." He looked at me. "If they come toward you, A., even if
you don't shoot at them, fire above them and try to turn them
down toward one of us." I nodded, and Early placed us on our
stands—Morgan first, then me alone a hundred yards to her left
under a large holly, and Cleanth and Jane together another hundred yards to my left. The ground ran slightly downhill in front
of me, then dropped into a shallow ravine six or eight feet deep
with steep sides and smooth rounded stones in the bottom of it
as though a stream had run there. Cradling the shotgun in my
elbow, I leaned back against the holly trunk. Hearing a whistle,
I stepped back where I could see Cleanth a good distance to my
left on lower ground. He raised his hand, waving, then pointed

to Morgan. I looked that way and she waved, too, then we all stepped forward into cover.

I heard the engine turn over, its rumble growing fainter and fainter till it merged with the teeming stillness of the forest, and the wait began, which is what hunting mostly is. As I stood there alone with my own thoughts, I discovered I'd forgotten about that kind of waiting, which is not an idle one, but deeply charged, excitement and anxiety flirting at the edges of a vast forlorn aloneness, which is yourself, stripped clear. I remembered that same feeling from long before, standing beside my father in the corn. I'd felt it even with his arms around me as I sighted down the barrel at the flying dove, felt it, too, later, in a studio under the hum of fluorescent lights staring at the empty field of a stretched canvas, waiting for the inward thing to show its face, the thing whose blood you have to draw, the thing that is yourself. But hunting was different, I told myself, and then a voice—the little voice I'd learned to listen to with Cleanth—said, "why?" My excitement increased in pitch, and I felt the inner mooring line of my beliefs groan with the impulse of a wayward sea, which ran counter to it, but was also me. Yet the line held fast.

At first I didn't hear the forest because my own thoughts were too loud, but then they ceased and in moments I caught the faint roar of the breakers away on the beach. The twittering of the birds had stopped and I looked up and saw the leaves glittering and winking in the sunlight, going from black to incandescent, as the wind broke through the canopy like a vast slow surf. I don't know how long we waited—no more than half an hour, though it felt like days. I was beginning to wonder if something had gone wrong when I heard the first shell pop, a blank, so far off it sounded like a paper firecracker. Then I caught the hoarse mournful baying of the dogs, fading in and out on the breeze like the signal on a radio, and finally there were cries—"wee," and "ha," and "yah." It sounded so strange, not like Early's voice at all, but like a troop of minstrels approaching through the woods. I clicked off the safety and the blood paint flashed at me. I clicked it back, but moved the gun, gripping the pump in my left hand, my right one on the stock, fingering the trigger guard. The cries diminished, and thinking Early was still a long way off, I relaxed again and leaned back against the tree. A sudden loud explosion made me jump. I looked down through the trees toward Cleanth and Jane but couldn't see

them, then turned uphill toward Morgan. I never saw her
either.

In a stand of sapling pines on the far side of the ravine, shaggy
and enormous, its body like a pony's on short stubby legs, stood
a boar. It wasn't running, simply standing still, turning its head
this way and that, as though it had materialized there. I saw it
more clearly than I'd ever seen anything before. Each bristle in
its coat stood out—like rotted straw, black with dirty yellow
gleams in it. I could see the ivory gleam of tushes pushing from
the lower gum toward the snout, which was like a large sausage
chopped off with an ax, and the grim underbite of its progna-
thous jaw. I realized I'd seen this animal before—on television?—yet that hadn't prepared me for its full living size. The
TV screen was referenceless, but out there in the woods the
reference point was me, and it was so much bigger.

Suddenly it became aware of me, its eyes two slits of gleaming
mud, and I felt the hair rise on my neck. Some force shot out
of them, scalding me with hate, and as I clicked the safety off,
I saw the shimmer. It was over everything—the boar, the tree,
the ground, the blued barrel of the gun. The animal was so
beautiful—a beauty that had no trace of sweetness in it—I
couldn't take my eyes away, and as I waited for the charge,
watching, the boar's legs suddenly collapsed and it went down.
Only as it fell did I hear the shot's report. I felt something keen
and bitter, not because the animal was shot, but because I hadn't
pulled the trigger. The mooring line snapped and I got single,
very single, and only then did I notice the strange crashing sound
all around me, intensely stereophonic, a snapping and cracking
like small limbs being broken. It sounded like a steamroller
being driven through the forest, then resolved into the clear
thundering of hooves. At first I noted it only absently, haphazardly, because I couldn't take my eyes off the boar. It lay
there panting with its legs splayed around it, then rolled over
heavily on its side. Then I saw a blur of brown movement
against the brown ground of the pinestraw, as though a small
piece of the forest had become detached and started running
toward me.

It was a second boar, smaller than the first, though not by
much, already across the ravine on the same side as me. It was
barreling down the lip with heavy stubby-legged strides, and as
I stepped out from behind the holly tree it saw me and reversed
with unbelievable, graceless deftness, running twenty yards in

Morgan's direction. Beyond it, I saw other animals—I couldn't count them—streaking off into the trees, then Morgan fired a shot and the boar turned again, galloping uphill away from the ravine toward our perimeter, equidistant from us both. My heart was pounding like a hammer in a fifty-gallon oil drum, but I felt strangely calm, relaxed, almost light, like my mind had speeded up while everything around me slowed down to a crawl. I made a mental note of Morgan's position—the pig at the apex of a triangle that was rapidly collapsing as it ran, Morgan and I at the two corners of the base line. The stock had already settled itself into my shoulder. Keeping both eyes open, I sighted down the barrel just to get the feel of it. I spotted just behind the working elbow of the pig at the bottom of the chest where I knew the heart would be. There was no sense of misgiving, no doubt or question, I didn't think at all, I just felt extremely calm and speeded up at the same time, and it was like a wager whether I would shoot or not, a wager without disastrous consequence either way, merely interesting, extremely interesting.

I never knew the answer till I felt the mule-kick of the shotgun and heard the amazing ringing violence of the blast, a brutal jolt of mindless utter power. I blinked in mild surprise and watched a splotch of brilliant crimson the shape and size of a half-dollar, like a dab of pigment from a paint gun, appear in the coat, high and to the rear of where I'd aimed, a color unprecedented in the russet earth tones of the wood. The boar appeared to fly sideways with its legs still galloping straight ahead, and I watched the ejector spit the smoking cartridge at my feet as my left hand pumped another live round into the chamber. The boar recovered traction without so much as stumbling, and I aimed again, touching the cool ring of the trigger, then raised the barrel in the air as I saw Morgan in my line of fire. She held my eyes a moment with an odd expression, and then I turned and watched the boar disappear in the undergrowth toward the road.

The next thing I heard was Early's shout—"comin' through!" I clicked on the safety and watched him stumble from the woods, choking back the dogs who were beside themselves, their tongues gagging and their eyes deep and mad. Early's eyes were calm though as he stopped on the far side of the ravine. They met mine with an expression of knowingness, then dismissed me with an utterly impersonal contempt—to gut-shoot an animal and leave it to die, the one great sin of hunting. Early's look shocked me like a slap, and he started up toward Morgan's kill. Hearing crashing footsteps, I turned and saw Cleanth and Jane running toward me with anxious questioning faces.

"What happened?" Cleanth asked, and I pointed off toward Early and Morgan and said, "I think she got one." His glance homed on the red plastic shell case lying on the pinestraw, then found my eyes. "You fired," he said—not a question. I nodded, and he said, "a charge?" and I said, "not really." He nodded, smiling, but without either elation or vindication. There was something very real and almost comforting in his expression, though it offered me no sympathy—it simply understood and said, "I am the same." "Next time don't miss," he said, reaching out and giving me a sharp but friendly slap on the cheek, and I said, "I didn't, I saw blood." He arched his brows inquisitively, and I said, "it never stopped—when I aimed to take a second shot, it was between me and Morgan," and he said, "how bad was it hit?" and I said, "I'm not sure—I got it high mid-chest." I pointed to the spot on my own ribs. Cleanth's eyes took on a milder trace of the same thing I'd seen in Early's, only forgiving. "Tough luck," he said, and walked on toward the others, and the rest, the other thing, was history, the present was something else, something new. Jane stayed back a moment, regarding me with grave surprise as though seeing me for the first time—she felt it, too—and then she said, "are you okay?" touching my arm. When I nodded, she squeezed it and followed him.

I stood there feeling gentled out and limp. My hands, which had been cool before, were as warm as though I'd just drawn them from a steaming bath. I felt no remorse, just an immense surprise because I didn't. Because there hadn't even been a moment's hesitation—I'd lived in the light of a devotion for a year, not eating meat, and it had vanished without trace before a pig running in the woods, and I suddenly realized that devotion had meant nothing all along, an empty gesture. But what that emptiness meant, that I didn't know. Yet I had the sense that my not knowing in that moment was the first thing I'd ever really known at all, the only thing, both about myself and about life. It was like a bell had tolled inside me, rich and baleful and completely unexpected, and I was amazed but neither sad nor happy, only certain that I was in the presence of some truth, which was the tolling of the bell.

Cradling the Browning, I started walking up toward Morgan's stand, but stopped and knelt when I saw the blood—a few scattered drops on coppery needles in a pool of sunlight. It was dark red, much darker than human blood, clotting in droplets like quicksilver, only glutinous. I dabbed it with my finger and it clung like a soft bead, still vaguely warm. Sniffing it, I detected a faint winey scent, strong and gamey, but diluted in the surrounding air. The thought occurred to me that it was still alive, and I closed my eyes and touched it to my tongue, feeling a swarming like an anthill buzzing into angry life when it's been kicked. That swarming may have simply been my sense, but it seemed to be the blood itself, the particles of living substance in it mobilizing to resist me. Even as I knelt and sipped the blood a part of me floated off above my shoulder smiling ironically at the kneeling sipping part, and it was like a game, a drama, but more accurately a ritual. I was not the center of it, the ritual wasn't about me at all, my part was an actor's part, following the script, submitting to it, serving it. The ironic smile my floating self was wearing reminded me of that—"this isn't you," it said—and I knew that I could stop and walk away from it, resolving trial to error. But that choice seemed predictable and artificial—of the two choices available to me it was the pettier and more self-important one. To play seemed far more interesting, because it promised to lead somewhere. To stop meant staying where I was, and where I was nothing and nowhere, just a conviction based on artificial knowingness worse than any ignorance, a choice that had appeared positive and life-enhancing, but now just seemed like a refusal to know anything or to live at all. I was deeply moved, not happy, just surprised. Having participated in the darkness, I found it wasn't really dark. It was bright, exceedingly, and clear, so clear, like a sand-scoured gold doubloon from the bottom of the ocean.

I stood up and watched the others on the far side of the ravine. Early was allowing the dogs to sniff. On the first pass, they approached warily, low down on their forepaws as though prepared to spring away. When they saw the boar was dead, their manner—Turk's at least—changed to a jubilant relaxation. He urinated against one of the pine saplings, then sat down on his haunches with a dangling tongue and contented eyes. Sal continued barking wildly at the carcass, sniffing and retreating. Cleanth knelt and lifted up the head—almost as ponderous as a horse's, it took him both arms to do it—peeling back the lip to show the tushes and smiling up at Morgan, who smiled back, glancing her hand through his hair with impulsive affection. Cleanth gripped her ankle and set it on the boar, a conqueror's pose, and she laughed uncertainly. While Early tied the bitch to a tree, Jane stood at a distance from the others absently holding Turk's leash. She didn't seem a part of it at all. Finally Cleanth and Early grabbed the boar by its hind legs and dragged it down into the ravine, then up the near side, their guns in their free hands. Taking a parallel route through the woods, I started toward the road.

They posed the boar beside the Jeep with its head on its forelegs, taking pictures first of Morgan alone with it holding her gun, and then of her and Early. Sitting on the hood with the gun between my thighs pointing up, I watched the celebration with a creeping restlessness, thinking about my animal, wondering if it was over, not wanting it to be. Jane climbed up and sat beside me—we didn't speak. "Let me go git Sal," Early said, starting back into the woods, and Cleanth said, "give me a hand, A." I jumped down and helped him drag the carcass into the weeds at the edge of the road. Passing Morgan, I said, "congratulations," and she said, "thanks," but there was something tragic in her eyes as they studied me. I'd already noted some subtle difference in the way the others treated her, a hint of deference, as though the kill had conferred some magic power on her. I felt it, too, and looked away.

Straddling the boar, Cleanth unsheathed his K-bar and slit into the tough hide of the belly which parted to a white waxy fat like paraffin. He cut from the bottom of the ribcage down through the stomach to the anus, then retraced it, opening to blood. A link of intestine poked out like a fat soft finger and then the cavity opened to a wine-dark lake, a soup with organs quivering in it. A cloud of warm steam escaped with a gamey shitten rankness that almost turned my stomach. Early appeared behind Morgan, holding the two whining eager puppies, and we all watched as Cleanth reached his hand wrist-deep into that soup and pulled out the purplish liver. Shaving off a slice, he passed it on the knife to Morgan, who put it in her mouth with an unreadable expression. The second piece went to Early, and then Cleanth looked at Jane and she said, "no." I merely shook my head. Cleanth ate the third himself, then leaned back down and raked the guts out on the ground, reaching up into the chest and tugging at the heart. The intestines came out in a great smoking yellow coil, still connected at the anus. Gripping them like some tenacious root, Cleanth pulled until his face grew red—there was, briefly, something terrible in his expression, something lustfully passionate, like sex—and then they came away with a wet tearing sound and he threw them down. Tipping the carcass over so that the blood swashed on the ground, Cleanth looked at Early and said, "milk for the puppies," grinning.

Grinning back, Early set them down and they went to it, sniffing first, then scarfing down whole organs. With a rhythmic arching motion of his neck and back, the male snarled up a link of intestine, catching it lower down like a man hauling rope with a single hand. When they'd eaten, Early put them back in the truck, then brought the older dogs, giving Turk the heart while Sal took anything she could get. Jane walked away, and the rest of us fell silent over it. The only sound was the clicking of teeth, gulping swallows and the soft liquid glubbing of the organs as they tore. The sight repulsed me, but it did not seem horrible, or even strange. It had a fascinating beauty, primitive, but not obscene. It felt like something larger than watching two dogs eating the still-warm organs of a boar, it felt like standing at the table of existence and seeing how the meal is served, and what the food is—life.

Not looking at the others but at the dogs, I said, "what about the other one?" and meeting my eyes, Cleanth said, "what about it?" "It's wounded," I said, and Early said, "it's gone, son, best forgit it—she's daown there in the morshes naow," and I said, "she?" breaking Cleanth's visual hold and turning to Early with surprise. "It was a faymoile, A.," he said, "for as Oi could tell—plenty big enough to shoot though, no need to worry about that. It's just a shoime you missed," and I said, "I didn't miss, Early," and he said, "moight as well've—better if you had," and Morgan said, "don't worry about it, Adam, the same thing happened to me the last time," and I said, not addressing her but Early, "what will happen to her?" and he said, "she'll doie, son, moight be dead roight naow, or she moight live a day or two," and I said, "I think I should go after her," and Early shook his head, saying, "Oi doin't—she's out there somewhere loyin' in the grace. You won't never say 'er 'less you run up on 'er, 'n chances are she'll say you forst," and I said, "but the dogs could smell her," and Early said, "but the daogs oin't goin', A. Lost their daddy that woy, 'n he honted better'n either of these—one toime moikes a lesson, son, two toimes moikes a fool.''

Cleanth regarded me, his eyes laughing, not at me, but with surprised respect, awaiting my decision. I could tell he wanted me to go, but it wasn't because of him—I knew I had to anyway, the script was very clear, you only had to listen, and I was listening. Everything seemed new and charged with significance—even the blueness of the sky overhead seemed deeper, like it had a meaning, which was also in the script, but you had to play to find it, and suddenly I understood—for the first time, really—that this was what Cleanth had meant by playing all along, that he'd been here before me, and the laughter in his eyes both comforted and frightened me a little. "You don't have to do this, Adam," Morgan said, and I said, "I know—I want to," and Cleanth laughed out loud and said, "you want some company?" Morgan shot him a dark angry look, and I said, "if you want," and he said, "I want," wiping his knife on the boar's coat before resheathing it. "Why don't you drive Early to get his truck?" Cleanth said to Jane and Morgan, "then head out to the beach and set up camp"—he looked at his watch—"it's ten-thirty now. We'll give it two hours and then hike back to Early's and meet you there between one and two."

As they drove off, leaving us standing in the silent woods, we reloaded, filling our pockets with shells. As Cleanth locked the barrel of his Parker with a sharp crack, he met my eyes and said, "now it's just the two of us—this is where the game gets interesting." I nodded, realizing he understood the script as well as me—much better—and he reached out and laid his barrel across my shoulder, tapping it against bone. "Let's do it, man," I said, and he nodded, and we walked back down the sandy road till we found the cloven hoof prints where she'd crossed. The road fell off down a steep hill on the other side, and we scrambled down, running and breaking our speed by grabbing saplings. Near the bottom we paused over a place where the straw was turned and bloody. "She fell here," Cleanth said, nudging it with his barrel, and then we started heading west toward the marshes and the sound beyond.

We walked through woods similar to those above the road, only swampier, for perhaps half an hour. The pinestraw showed a subtle, but readable trail, and occasionally, passing through stands of bamboo, there was blood flecked on the stalks and leaves. Once we saw the pig. She was lying on the bank above a pond, panting, but she became aware of us—we were stalking downwind—and rose with a jerky labored movement, stumbling slightly and then setting off at a full run, leaving the twiggy saplings trembling behind her. I raised my gun to get a shot, but Cleanth said, "it's too far," and I lowered it. When we reached the spot, Cleanth squatted over it and I stood on the bank staring out over the pond.

There was an egret in shallow water at the far edge, perched on one foot and stiller than a decoy, white against a stand of green bamboo. As I watched, its head began to move in slow motion, then with lightning speed it speared its beak into the water and came up shaking, having missed whatever it was aiming for. Cleanth was standing beside me then, and I turned to see if he had seen. He pointed with his gun, and following that line I saw a snake, black against the vivid slime with yellow diamond markings on its back, swimming with a sidewinding motion, parting the scum to black water, which resealed itself with a silent kiss as it moved on. "It was like this in the jungle," Cleanth said softly, more to himself than to me, and I had a sense of what he meant, because there was something deadly in the surrounding stillness. Looking up again, I found the blueness of the sky had taken on a sinister edge, but it was beautiful beyond belief, so beautiful it was almost lurid. Colors were so vivid, my perceptions so keen, it reminded me of tripping, and I thought about the burned-out woods above the lake where I'd been with Jane and Cary, the charred ruin at the end of things. Now I was back in those same woods, not with Cary, but with Cleanth, and Cleanth, despite his strangeness, was clear to me in a way that Cary was the exception to—I'd loved Cary most for that. I'd wanted to become like him, and at the bottom of it all, that was the real reason I'd stopped eating meat after the lesson of the rabbit. But standing on the bank with Cleanth, watching the slime reseal as the snake swam on, it seemed a hopeful folly, a dream—I belonged where I was, a different place from Cary. The bell tolled again for me, and we moved on, Cleanth and I, completely phased and telepathic so that we didn't need to speak.

Soon after the pond we left the woods behind and entered an intermediate terrain, sandy, with laurel and house-high myrtle bushes. There was some salt grass and occasional stands of wild blackberries, so thick in places the briars were almost impassable. Cleanth walked ahead because his pants

were long and tried to hold them for me, but they tore my
bare legs, cutting and then recutting the cuts till blood ran in
twisting rills into my socks which were bunched around my
boots. We found no sign there, but when we reached the
marsh, green and vast and rustling out ahead of us, we saw
where she had entered—the grass pressed and leaning slightly
with a different shine to it. Entering, the ground turned black
again and swampy, sucking at our boots like obscene kisses.
The trail was clear for several hundred yards, and then we
reached a creek and waded it.

On the far bank Cleanth paused and stared at the slick clay
underfoot. There were no tracks and the dense wall of spartina showed no sign of passage. Cleanth studied the water
where the clouding silt from our own passage was already
sinking—if the boar had used the stream the sign had erased
itself already. He looked at me with a new intensity of concentration, not smiling, and said, "this is where we split up,
A.—I'll go upstream, you go down"—he pointed his barrel
deeper into the marsh—"if you find the spoor, fire twice,
and I'll come down to you. I'll do the same." I nodded, and
he said, "be careful now, remember what Early said—she's
wounded and she knows we're tracking her. The wind's behind us, so she knows we're here. She's dying, A., and she
may not run. Good luck," and I said, "you, too," and turned
away from him and started following the bank.

Far out ahead of me I could see a tree, silver-white and shining in the morning sunlight. I thought it was the same one
Cleanth had pointed out to me earlier from Penny Hill, because
there was a nest in it, but I wasn't sure. I used it to gauge my
distance, watching lower limbs appear above the wall of grass
like points in an emerging rack of antler. A bird circled over it,
spiraling down toward the nest, but from that distance it was
just black wings against the air, like a child's crayon drawing. I
walked the bank for fifteen minutes, elbowing my way through
stands of cattails, searching for the break where she had entered.
The ground got swampier and swampier, almost frightening.
The channel seeped out of its banks, a pooling wetness over
dark earth. I sank once to my knees and fell, but I found nothing. I kept waiting for Cleanth's shot, somehow dreading that
he'd find her first, and then I stopped, realizing I'd only been
checking the bank I was on, not the opposite one. Cursing my
stupidity, I began to backtrack and found the break a hundred

yards downstream from where I'd started. I flicked off the safety and raised the barrel in the air, but then I didn't pull the trigger. That wasn't in the script. I went in alone.

The trail led straight for eighty yards and then curved parallel with the creek for a similar distance before turning back toward the water. I came out on the bank again, sweating heavily. That's when I became afraid for the first time, confronted with the animal's intelligence—it knew what it was doing, I didn't. I was unsure which way to go, upstream or down. I'd searched both banks already, but it occurred to me she might have crossed again while I was in the marsh. I stood there a moment, thoroughly confused, then fired twice in the air and headed back downstream, without reason and without confidence. I found the break on the far bank, the one I'd searched at first after parting from Cleanth. Had I simply missed it the first time? No, this was her second pass. The fresh-pressed grass was starting to stand upright, recovering from the boar's recent passage. Shivering in a sudden gust of wind, feeling my sweat turn cold, I waded into the green salt hay.

The trace was clear for the first fifty yards, and then I saw the flattened bloody reeds where she'd lain down a second time. She wasn't there, and there was no trail leading off from it. When she'd left, she'd left walking, or staggering, but walking left no trail my eye could read, or perhaps the wind, much stronger now, had raised the stalks back up. I stood there in shoulder-high grass, drenched with chilly sweat, feeling my boots sink under me with a slow gurgling sound and knew I was in danger. I'd come to the end of what I knew, but the boar knew more and had outwitted me. I was no longer master of the dance—the gun was all the confidence I had left. The grass was high and she was out there in it, smelling me, maybe even watching me, and the odds seemed equal now, if not tilted in her favor. My fear was like a drug, sharpening my senses, but also giving me a strange fatigue. Hearing a reedy piping cry, I looked up and saw the osprey, its hawkface screaming down at me as it swooped and wheeled away, never coming close. Pumping a shell into the chamber, I freed my boots and tried to search the grass for signs of movement, but there was just the wind, and I noticed that the wind is neither smooth nor straight, the way it feels against the body, but has swirling currents in it, which I'd never seen until I watched it cross that grass—it was my fear that made me see. Then I thought I heard a sharper rustling behind me and I turned and fired blindly into the spartina. The slug disappeared without a trace. I listened and heard nothing more.

Only then did I realize the gun was empty—I'd fired three times already, counting the signal shots. Fumbling in my pocket, I took out two cartridges, squatting to reload. As I inserted the first shell, the wind swayed the grass again, and I heard something breathe, a low grunting sound. I raised my head and froze. Through a momentary parting in the wall, I saw her head, not five yards away. The second cartridge slipped from my hand— I heard it plop into the mud as I fixed the stock and swung the barrel, retracting the pump in one smooth motion. The grass exploded, bouncing and crashing as she charged. I had a clear shot to the head, straight into the dark brain behind those burning muddy eyes. My finger slipped the trigger. Her snout slammed dead into the gun, smashing it back into my shoulder, and I saw the barrel glance along her flank and pulled the trigger, knowing it was futile. As the explosion rang, I saw a single spear of grass fall as neatly as though a scythe had felled it—that seemed impossibly interesting. I watched as I fell backward in the mud, kicking out at her and bringing the gun down on her shaggy flank like a futile switch. I saw her head drop, the hair bristling in a ridge straight down into the mud. My eyes went black with it, it filled my mouth with a strange familiar taste, like food. I began to choke, but it seemed far away, a body thing that had only a minor relevance. The mud was wonderfully rich and interesting—I had the sense that just below it there was a shining world that I would enter any moment. Then my boot tore free and I flopped over on my stomach and raised my head just in time to watch her hind quarters disappearing in the grass.

I lay there for a moment, embracing the marsh, then I crawled to my knees. Wiping my face on my shirt, I looked up at the sky, noting with amazement that it was green, the same color as the grass and there were winking stars in it which faded as my vision cleared. Feeling a strange gentle wonder, I realized— that was the first time—that it would not be bad to die. But it was equal, killing her, and neither one was wrong. Nothing was. Nothing was wrong—the first, perhaps the only time in my whole life I ever felt that. My fear was gone.

I picked up the Browning and reloaded it. When I stood up, my ankle turned and I looked down and saw my boot was sliced and blood was running down it. Yet I felt no pain, no pain at all. An odd lightness filled me and I began to run. She wasn't far ahead—I could hear the grass rustling and see it parting each time my stride peaked. We were only forty yards below the osprey tree by then, and she was heading for it. The trunk loomed from the raised ground of a grassless hummock, and I saw her clear the marsh, galloping up the incline. I stopped and fired straight down on her over the grass. The slug slammed into her sacrum and her hind legs buckled. She continued dragging herself up the mound by her front legs, and I lost sight of her briefly till I cleared the grass.

When I came out, she was lying underneath the tree rolled over on her side. I slowed down and walked, knowing it was over, and when she heard me she raised her head and tried to struggle up, but came down heavily again and lay there panting. I climbed toward the tree and stood over her, four feet off, studying her head. By then she seemed oblivious to me, and I realized I wanted there to be some recognition, some acknowledgment, before I pulled the trigger. There was nothing. She was utterly absorbed in her own ending, and I wasn't even a distraction. I put the barrel just behind her ear with a perfunctory gesture, slipped my finger between the trigger and the guard, and startled as I heard my name come from the marsh—"A." I turned and watched Cleanth wade out of the grass, keeping his eyes fixed on mine until he was beside me. He stared down at the animal, and put his hand out gently on my arm. "It's finished, A.," he said, meeting my eyes, "give her the rest," and I realized he was right, that far more than putting her out of her misery, I owed her her last moment, having taken all the rest. Those words, the enormous gentleness and sensitivity of them, struck me as a rare exquisiteness, and I felt touched and humbled by them. It seemed like a lesson in some higher etiquette, the etiquette of death.

The boar raised its head and its eyes began to roll—what whites there were were flecked with blood like fertile egg yolks, the pupils two holes as large as quarters drilled into darkness. Groaning, she lay back, kicked her legs and died. "You see, it's better," Cleanth said, squatting over her and pressing her lids down with his thumbs. He stroked his right hand through her coat, a gesture less of affection than of simply feeling, then glanced at me and said, "come here." I squatted down beside him, and he showed me his hand, wet with blood from my last shot. "Close your eyes," he said, his expression deep and solemn, and I hesitated as my floating self said, "no," then I obeyed because I knew the script demanded it. Bowing my head toward him, I felt him paint the wet warm swath across my brow, four fingers wide. "You're blooded now," he said, and I opened my eyes and gazed at him, remembering Cary, the day at Ruin Creek we'd cut our wrists and fused them, another blooding that seemed suddenly childish beside the depth and power of this later one with Cleanth. I sloughed it like a used-up outgrown thing, and in some way I can't explain I left Cary there and went with Cleanth, a different way. Cleanth smiled soberly and we stood up and shook hands, sealing our contract. I felt the circuit close and something flow across the switch of our linked palms. Maybe that was it, the place I lost myself, but it felt more like discovery—it felt like finding the key to the lost door of the lost temple of a lost religion, and being greeted on the threshold by the high priest of lostness, the priest of a lost highness.

When Cleanth saw my foot he made me lie down and knelt, propping my ankle on his thigh as he unlaced my boot and pulled it off. I still felt no pain, only a slight puffy numbness like the aftereffects of anesthesia, and I stared up into the tree, realizing with surprise that it was a pine, completely stripped of bark except the lower trunk, which was what gave it its silvery hue. A blackened welt running down the trunk into the ground showed where the killing lightning had struck. The birds seemed crazed and furious—there were two of them—swooping down within ten feet of us, then veering away across the marsh. "What's wrong with them?" I asked and Cleanth said, "there are young ones in the nest," as he shucked off my sock, "they're trying to draw us off." He gently rolled my ankle in its socket and said, "does that hurt?" and I said, "not really—how bad is it?" and he said, "nothing's broken, it's just a gash," and I said, "do you think I need stitches?" and he pouted and said, "they wouldn't hurt, but it'll heal without them"—he grinned— "besides, you'll get a better scar. That'll be an asset when you tell the story."

I found his banality irritating, it ran counter to the flood of my emotion and diminished it—I didn't want to talk. Rolling his vest back off his shoulders, Cleanth pulled off his tee shirt, slit the bottom of it with his knife, then tore off a long strip, bandaging my ankle. "There," he said, gently lowering my foot to the ground, "good as new—which is more than I can say for your boots, or my tee shirt either—which was new, by the way." He grinned and said, "how do you feel?" and I said, "my foot, or me?" obliquely protesting his levity. Cleanth caught the subtext and said, "I know how you feel, A.—moved," and I said, "yeah, man, I do," and he said, "then keep moving, don't try to hold it—that part is over, A., now it's something else," and I said, "I don't want it to be over," and he grinned and said, "tell me about it—that's why you go back." He slipped my boot back on and laced it, then he stood up. "And speaking of moving," he said, offering me his hand, "we should be, too," and as he pulled me up, I said, "what about the boar?" and he said, "we've got more than we can eat already—let's leave her as an offering," and I said, "an offering to what?" and he grinned and said, "the ospreys." I stared at him a moment and then said, "no, I killed her, man—I want to eat the one I killed," and he nodded and said, "all right, A., we'll bring the boat back for her, and in the meantime the birds can get theirs." Then he rolled the carcass over on its back and slit it open as he'd done the other one, and we walked away from it.

Instead of returning through the marsh, we went out to the sound, which was only ankle-deep for at least a hundred yards from shore, and hardly more than waist-deep as far out as the channel, a quarter mile away. Turning north, we tromped through the shallows where tiny waves broke over ridged white sand, like a vast submerged desert in miniature with symmetrical dunes created not by wind but water. It was easy going and my ankle didn't hurt. There were clams and shoals of oysters, and a small trawler passed us chugging homeward, trailing a cloud of wheeling gulls. It only took half an hour to reach Early's house.

Jane and Morgan were drinking beer on the porch, and the puppies were romping in the yard. Early's back was to us. He'd tied the boar by its hind legs and hoisted it up over a stout treelimb, and as we walked into the yard he was peeling the coat down from the rump toward the head, freeing it with light knife flicks as he went. It came away as easily as a sweater, hanging off the neck like the opera cape of a sleeping vampire upside down on his bat-perch. "You going to make a coat with that?" Cleanth said. Early turned and looked at us. "A rug more loike," he said, studying our expressions, "well, boys, what's the vordict?" Cleanth grinned and tilted his head toward me, and Early nodded and said, "looks loike you faound 'er, A.," and I said, "yeah, I did," and his eyes held mine, retracting what they'd said before, and he said, "well, son, what's minnded well's as good as never broke—where's the evidence?" and Cleanth said, "we had to leave her out there, Early—can we take the boat?" and Early said, "shore 'nuff, captain, but forst yoi'll set a spell 'n' have a beer—you boys look porched."

"What happened to your face?" Jane said with a grimace, and Morgan, the first to notice, said, "what happened to your *leg*?" "A. was gored," Cleanth told them, and Jane said, "oh, God, A.—are you all right?" standing up, and Morgan said, "darling!" putting her hands on my shoulders, regarding me with shocked concern. "I'm fine," I told them, shying away uneasily, "really, it's not that bad," and Early said, "sit daown, son," pulling up a chair for me then going inside for our beers. "Do you need to see a doctor?" Morgan asked, and Cleanth said, "it's just a cut, M., he'll live," and Morgan said, "shut up, Cleanth, I didn't ask you—I knew something like this was going to happen. Give me your foot, Adam." She reached down for it, but I resisted. "Cleanth already put a bandage on it, Morgan," I said, and, undeterred, she said, "I want to see."

Sitting on the porch rail as I leaned back in the rocking chair, she held my calf across her thighs, unlacing my boot. "It's filthy," she said, and Early, who'd just handed Cleanth and me our beers, said, "Oi've got some hoidrogen peroxoide 'n' mercurochroame," and Morgan said, "get it, would you, Early?" He went for it and she said, "have you had a tetanus shot?" and I said, "yeah, this spring," enjoying the attention less than I was put off by its maternal character. The peroxide sizzled in the gash, which was about two inches long and horizontal, running straight across my ankle bone. "What about rabies?" Jane said with a frightened expression, and Cleanth said, "that boar wasn't rabid," and Morgan said, "how do you now?" Cleanth shrugged, smiling at me sympathetically and chugging his beer. "I mean it, Cleanth," Morgan persisted, "how can you be sure?" and he said, "we can take the head back if you want," and Jane said, "the head?" and Cleanth said, "that's how they tell—they dissect the brain," and Morgan said, "well, I think we should pack up and go straight back," and Jane said, "I do, too," and I said, "no, goddamnit," pulling my foot out of

Morgan's lap, "I'm fine," and Cleanth said, "it'll wait till Monday, M.," and she said, "will it?" doubting, angry, and he said, "it takes two weeks to incubate anyway," and Morgan said, "what do you want to do, Adam?" and I said, "you can go back if you want, I'm staying here," and she sighed with exasperation and gave up.

I took a long swallow of Blue Ribbon, closing my eyes to savor the briny coldness streaming down my throat, and when I opened them again they were all sitting back against the rail, facing me, regarding me with expectation. "What?" I said, dishonestly, knowing exactly what they wanted, and Jane said, "don't be a butt, A., tell us what happened," deflating me. "It wasn't that big a deal," I said, both stroked and uncomfortable with the power their eyes conferred on me, "I tracked her. I found the place where she'd lain down. She wasn't there . . ." And I told them, just the barest facts, one, two, three, blam, blam, blam. Their eyes ate it up with hungry wonder and asked for more, their eyes said, don't give us the facts, give us the feeling, but already I couldn't remember what I'd felt, or if I'd felt anything at all—only that lack of feeling hadn't been a numbness or a deadness, it had been alive and complete, something staggering that had changed me from what I was before. But there were no words for that staggering thing—I couldn't tell them that, so I gave the facts instead, and after their initial eagerness, their eyes glazed and they seem unsatisfied and even sad, but I couldn't help it, though I wanted to. The whole story took two minutes, and they asked no questions—the question was there in all their faces—why I'd done it—but no one asked, and if they had I couldn't have told them. I'd been moved, but now the movement had moved elsewhere, just like Cleanth had said—reaction set in. The tide, which had reached its full flood in the marsh, began to ebb, leaving me restless and disgruntled after the story. I went in and lay down on Early's couch. I heard them crank the engine of the boat and chug away, and then I feel asleep.

When I woke up my ankle had begun to ache, and my whole consciousness was ringing with the question—why? Looking in the mirror, I felt disgust and washed away the blood with the standing water in Early's sink. The spell was broken. I'd felt the magic in myself, and now I felt the lack of it, two real things whose reality confounded one another. Which was true—the swept-up feeling of the magic, or the abandonment that came afterward? I knew only one thing—in the magic woods the abandonment hadn't mattered, but in the abandoned aftermath the magic still did. That was what I learned in the woods. That was the master's lesson, one I never forgot and never mastered—which is maybe why it mastered me.

Fifteen

A.

By the time we reached the beach it was nearing six o'clock, and though it was still full daylight, there was a hint of something blue, and sadder, in the light, almost a premonition of autumn. Jane and Morgan had pitched the tents behind the primary dune—two of them, heavy canvas pup tents that you could stand up straight in. They'd swung a hammock between a dead tree and a living dwarf pine and collected driftwood for the fire. I put my things in with Morgan's, then climbed the dune where I saw Cleanth going toward the water with a long-handled saucepan. He waded out and I saw him lift the tenderloin he'd cut out of my pig and wash it in the sea, ducking and slicking back his hair before he returned. He set the pan on the camp table and uncorked a bottle of red wine, a St.-Estèphe from the hotel cellar, one of the most expensive on the list, and poured it liberally over the meat, crushing peppercorns in a cloth with the butt of his knife, then breaking off a sprig of bay from a bush and crumpling it in his hand, sprinkling all of it into the marinade and kneading it into the tenderloin with the heel of his palm, which he sniffed before wiping. Catching me watching, he grinned and said, "how about a swim?"

We all went. Cleanth and Morgan stripped unself-consciously and waded out together. Bringing up the rear, I saw Jane hesitate before undressing and knew my presence made her shy, so I went on ahead, leaving my clothes with the others', and dove over a small wave. The wind had come around to the west during the afternoon, blowing the Gulf Stream further offshore, and the water was bracing. I came up blowing in chest-deep water, bouncing on my toes and slicking my hair back with both hands. "Yeow," I said, feeling my cut stinging, and I stripped off the bandage and threw it out. "There's no better antiseptic made," Cleanth said, then grinned, adding, "and it's entirely local." He turned toward shore, cupped his hands around his mouth and shouted, "come on, Jane," and I saw Morgan's eyes flick to the beach. "My God, look at her," she said wistfully, "my body used to look like that." Standing in waist-deep water, she lifted her breasts in both hands, staring down at them, and Cleanth said, "don't underestimate a mature woman's charms, M.," and she said, "you mean older, don't you?" and he waded toward her and took her hands, bending down to kiss her on the lips. It wasn't obviously sexual, but it hurt me—I might not have been there. "Don't patronize me, Cleanth," Morgan said, her eyes tearing up as she drew back. Turning away, she sank to her neck and stared toward the horizon. Cleanth watched her with a frustrated tenderness, then walked toward me and said, "I think she needs some cheering up," before he started swimming in toward Jane.

Observing his crawl, my eyes drifted over to Jane as she ran out through the breakers, bobbing up through the foam of a small wave, her brows arched in a startled expression, lids pressed closed and her lips a tiny breathless o. The swash passed on and the water dropped around her, exposing first her shoulders, then her tan line, then her breasts pressed together between her elbows as she smoothed her hair back. Her nipples stood up from white flesh with no rim around them, like unopened buds dark with cold, and then her lean waist appeared glistening with wet, the second tan line and a glimpse of thin dark fur dripping brine into the golden gleam of sunlight on the water between her parted thighs. Opening her eyes directly into mine, Jane held my gaze a moment, then sank down on her knees. Aching with the chaste simplicity of that gesture, I turned and found Morgan watching me.

Her eyes met mine with an impassiveness so immense it frightened me, not pretending anymore, letting the full weight of her unhappiness rest on me. "You want her, don't you, Adam?" she said, and I said, "no, I want you," pressing off the bottom and gliding toward her through the water. Morgan didn't smile, she just said, "your lying's getting better, A., keep it up and one day you'll be as good as Cleanth," and I said, "I don't deserve that, Morgan," and she said, "I would have thought you'd take it as a compliment. Isn't that what you want—to be like him?" and I said, "as a matter of fact, I can think of worse things—he's pretty special," and she said, "he's converted you, hasn't he? and you don't even see it," and I said, "see what?" She shook her head. "Look at us—you and me, Jane and Cleanth—we're all in Never-Never Land and Cleanth is Peter Pan. He laid a glitter trail and we all followed it, and now we're lost," and I said, "I don't know what you mean, Morgan," and she said, "don't you? don't you really?" I shook my head, and she sighed. "I know, darling," she said, "to you all this seems like magic—being with an older woman, shooting boars, doing drugs and taking lessons from a guru. It used to seem like magic to me, too, but it's just sleight-of-hand, Adam, and when you finally see through it it becomes a nightmare. That's how it's begun to seem to me," and I said, "why, Morgan?" earnestly wanting to understand her, and she said, "because it isn't real, there's nothing solid underneath it. The magic only works for Cleanth and the one other person in the spell with him in the moment—today in the woods it was you, tonight it'll be Jane, but not me, not anymore. I don't even want it to be me, because it doesn't feed me, Adam, it's all just sugar candy. I want real food, and Cleanth isn't ever going to give it to me, and you can't, darling. I can't give it to you either."

She put her hands out on my shoulders. "That's why I'm not good for you, darling. I wanted to be, but I couldn't, the difference is too vast. You're still climbing toward the peak, but I've already been there and now I'm on the other side, starting down. So is Cleanth, only he doesn't acknowledge it, it terrifies him. He wants to keep climbing forever, but what he's climbing into now is just thin air, there's nothing solid under his feet. That's why he's with Jane when he should be with me and you with her, because she's climbing, too," and I said, "but what about their feelings?" and she said, "that's what makes it hopeless, Adam—I'm the only one who understands it. Perhaps you do a little, so does Jane. Cleanth is the only one who doesn't understand at all, which is what makes it truly frightening, because he's the one that's leading the dance," and I said, "what doesn't he understand? what are you saying, Morgan?" She gazed at me a long time, then shook her head. "It's cold out here," she said, "I'm going in." Deeply disturbed, I watched her swim away. A flock of pelicans passed overhead in a long V, through air that had turned even bluer and sadder. Shivering, I realized I was cold, too, and caught a wave to shore.

In camp I packed some drawing things into a day pack, took a beer out of the cooler and started hiking up the windward face of Penny Hill, my pad under my arm. After the intensity of the hunt, I felt washed-out and empty, and Morgan's words made me feel even emptier—a riddle whose meaning I sensed, deep down, but couldn't articulate. As I reached the crest, perspiring and breathing hard, the west wind broke over me like a wave, blowing back my hair and filling my unbuttoned shirt like a sail. It had been twilight in the camp, but on the far side everything was still lit with the golden light of late afternoon. I narrowed my eyes against the gust and drank in the view along with my warm beer. In the slanting light the marsh cast its own blue shadow on itself, yet the tops of the grass were still a brilliant green, and as the wind moved through a million gold and silver highlights danced, like tiny insects with fluttering transparent wings. The trees, which had been full color in the east light of the morning, had now turned solid black, like ink strokes against the enormous orange orb of the sinking sun. As I watched, a streak of pink kissed the bottom edge of a striated horizontal cloud, and the sky above it turned cerulean blue. The sound, which had been brown before, was now a glowing silver with streaks of rust in it, as were the estuaries running out to it, and over one of them a pale mist was rising which the sun turned orange-gold. Hearing lowing and the faint tinkling of a tinny bell, I looked down in the flats and saw a shadowy herd of cows moving with ponderous grace and wondered if they were Early's.

It was a scene for oils, the light had a hundred different textures that demanded building from within, yet oils would have been too slow because it was changing every second, changing drastically—watercolor or pastels might have given some suggestion, but I'd left those behind, so I sat down with pen and ink, dissatisfied before I even started, because I knew the best I could do was render out a static essence of it, what the marsh would be if there were no light and color in the world, only the shadows solid but the main thing lost.

Yet I sat down and started working furiously anyway, wasting two sheets before the hatchings of the grass seemed right. Moving out to the water, I scratched a filigree of dark lace, connected like the pieces in a jigsaw puzzle, trying to suggest the brilliant scallops of the waves outlined with their own shadows, reversing the pattern outside the sunstreak. I held it off and stared at it— it didn't seem quite right. I flipped the page and, taking a quick read into the marsh, began to draw the osprey tree, then I stopped looking and drew from memory—the two broad bottom limbs, the way they spread and changed their minds, and the shorter shattered ones branching off the central trunk, which rose at a slant from the surrounding grass, and the black nest tufted in the top of it. I jumped when I felt a hand close over my shoulder. "Hi," Jane said. I looked up and she'd put on shorts with a white polo untucked over them. Her hair was wet with the comb streaks still evident, though the wind had roiled it some. Her face had a still-gentle glow like the day had done her good. "How's your foot?" she asked, and I said, "fine—how long have you been standing there?" and she said, "not long," offering me a beer. "I brought one with me," I said, and she said, "this one's cold," and I took it.

She sat down and said, "may I look?" grasping the wire ring with her hand, not snatching it, but asking permission with her eyes. I released it with a shrug. "That's where I shot the boar," I told her as she studied it, and she said, "that's why it looks like this, isn't it?" handing back the pad, and I said, "like what?" and she said, "so old and gnarly and unhappy." "Is that a criticism, or just a comment?" I asked and Jane simply laughed. I felt the familiar troubledness return. "Why did you shoot?" she asked after a silence, keeping her eyes on the view, and I said, "you think it was wrong?" She looked at me and asked, "do you?" and I said, "I don't know—it didn't seem wrong at the time. Now I'm not sure." She turned away again and said, "I was surprised, A.," and I said, "you mean disappointed, don't you?" and she said, "a little maybe, mostly just surprised," and I said, "what surprised you?" and she said, "that you let him talk you into it," and I said, "he didn't talk me into anything—I pulled the trigger, Jane," and she said, "I know, but I still felt sorry for you, A., watching it, because I could see how much you cared for him and how hard you were working to live up to his expectations, and I don't think Cleanth cared for you at all. He just wanted you to prove how great the whole thing was so he could believe in it himself, and if it broke your heart to follow him, I don't think it would have mattered all that much to Cleanth. I was disappointed, A., but not half as much in you as him,'' and I said, ''why's everybody so down on Cleanth all of a sudden? It didn't break my heart, Jane, I liked it, and I think you're wrong, Cleanth does care.'' She gave me a deep look and said, ''he cares about you the same way you cared about that boar, A.—it was like he was hunting you out there today. It made things so much clearer for me,'' and I said, ''how?'' and she said, ''because that's the same way he cares about me. Maybe not a boar, but more like cut flowers—I'm just something he keeps around to look at, to make the room a little nicer for him. I mean, I guess that's what it is, because I know he doesn't love me,'' and I said, ''do you love him?'' and she said, ''he doesn't want my love, A., Cleanth hardly even touches me anymore—he does coke and stays up every night till four a.m., then crashes and wakes up trashed,'' and I said, ''but that wasn't what I asked,'' and she said, ''I can't live that way, A., how can I love a man I don't even trust?''—she sighed and seemed to sink a little—''and it was never about love anyway, A., I don't like that in myself, but it's true. I was flattered, he excited me, I looked up to him—in a way I still do—but, no, not love,'' and because she seemed depressed, I said, ''but it was the same for me with Morgan, Jane, it was the same for all of us—there's nothing wrong with that,'' and she looked at me and said, ''at first I didn't think so, either A.,'' and I said, ''now?'' and she said, ''I don't know, it just feels wrong,'' and sank her head back on her knees.

Thinking how beautiful she was at that moment, I said, ''I'm not sure you should trust me either, Jane,'' and she said, ''why?'' surprised, and I said, ''because I can't blame Cleanth for wanting to look at you.'' She regarded me with doubting vulnerable eyes, and I said, ''I'm sorry, I shouldn't say that,'' and she reached out and took my hand. ''I'm glad you think that, A.,'' she said, ''and it's okay, because the way you look at me is different. I feel safe with you,'' and I said, ''but it's still not okay—it's not okay even to think it, much less say it.'' She held my gaze a long time before she said, very softly, ''it's okay for me, A.,'' and I said, ''is it?'' She nodded without smiling and said, ''but it isn't for you, is it?'' and I said, ''I don't know, I wish it was, but I don't see how it can be,'' and she said, ''that's why I feel safe with you.''

The shimmer was all around us on the dune, streaming off her hair like a solar corona in the wind that blew up from the marsh, streaking with the colors of the sunset, and there was something like a current flowing through me, an unbearable electricity tingling and burning in my nerves. I wanted to touch her so it could come to ground, because I knew that was the only way to ease myself, and Jane said, "what are you thinking?" and I said, almost breathless, "that I'd like to kiss you." She smiled and said, "I can handle it if you can," and I said, returning her smile forcibly, "I can't—I want to, but I can't." "That's okay, too," she said, leaning toward me, putting her cool hand on one cheek as she kissed the other.

Then she stood up, brushing the sand off her seat and said, "we should be getting back now—they're already cooking. That's what I came up here to tell you." She offered me her hand and pulled me up, continuing to hold it as we started down the hill. Halfway down, she said, "I want to go with you to the airport to pick up Cary." I turned to look at her, but she just squeezed my hand, not looking back. I envied her her strength.

As we entered the camp, Cleanth turned from the fire and said, "get yourselves some wine," and I said, "where's Morgan?" as I emptied the bottle into a glass for Jane, noting that it wasn't the first bottle, but the second, and Cleanth said, "I think she went for a walk—she's in an awful funk," and Jane said, "I'll go find her," and when she'd gone Cleanth grinned at me and said, "female solidarity," and I smiled though I thought there was an ugly edge in the remark. "Let's see what you've done," he said, reaching for my pad. I gave it to him, sipping my wine nervously, realizing I cared about his opinion, cared enormously, and for just a moment as he studied it, something in his face—the way it settled in contemplation—reminded me of my father, the good one I remembered and had lost, and despite what Jane had said, I was certain that at the core of it his gift was true. I wanted to believe that almost desperately.

Cleanth raised his eyes from the drawing, about to speak a thought, but when he saw my face, he said, "what's the matter, A.?" and I said, "nothing," feeling myself suddenly, inexplicably on the verge of tears. "This is the best thing I've seen you do all summer," he said, and then he checked himself—"the second best—the first was in the woods today." Our eyes locked over it, a moment of male solidarity, and I wondered if Jane could ever understand it, if any woman could, because I hardly understood it myself, except that there was something deeper there than just the wanton slaughter of an animal, something in the doing of it and in the attitude toward that doing that made a shining rightness out of all the wrongness. "I'll go even further," Cleanth said, "and say I don't believe you could have drawn this before—the kill opened you so you could see," and I said, "Jane doesn't like it, she says it's too unhappy," and he said, "there are some things Jane doesn't know, A.—she's right, it is unhappy, but that's not what matters," and I said, "what does matter, Cleanth?" and he said, "that it's alive," handing me back the pad. I stared at the drawing, then at the tenderloin spitted over the fire on a shaved green stick between two forked branches and said, "unlike the boar," and he said, "don't let the doubleness creep back, A.," and I nodded, struggling with my emotions. At that moment Jane came back to camp with Morgan.

Cleanth gave the meat a last turn, spooning marinade over the hot side. He'd wrapped the slab with thick slices of bacon cut out of the sides and back of the boar with bay leaves strapped under them, all attached with shaved toothpicks of green wood. The driftwood had broken up into large chunks of glowing coal which spat as the fat dropped into it, but didn't flame. Jane and I sat down at the camp table around a Coleman lantern as Cleanth removed the meat and threw more wood on the fire until it crackled and blazed again. It was dark by then, the stars were out, and the sea crashed behind the dune. Morgan looked terrible, the way I'd found her in her hotel room that night she'd acted out her fantasy with me. She was drunk, but it went way beyond that. Her expression seemed bruised, not outwardly, but from within, and I sensed she was at her breaking point, or near. Cleanth carved the meat, apparently oblivious to the trouble that was brewing. Morgan was right—he was the only one who didn't know, and I felt almost sorry for him because he didn't. Jane and I both felt it though—we traded looks.

Early had given us an entire cooler full of shrimp, and Morgan had prepared a chowderlike concoction in a base of fresh milk with tomatoes crushed into it—also Early's contribution, from his garden. There were baked potatoes, cut up with slices of onion between the pieces and pats of Early's butter, wrapped in foil and dropped into the fire. Cleanth kicked them out of the coals and picked them up, bobbling them from hand to hand as he brought them to the table. When we opened them, they steamed, the onions brown and drenched. Morgan sat down, refilling her glass but eating nothing as we had the soup, and then Cleanth served the meat, offering the first slice to me.

"To first blood," he said, raising his glass to me. I felt all their eyes on me, Jane's most of all, as I cut through the brown crust to the pink meat inside. Stabbing it with my fork, I looked at it, then at Cleanth—he smiled and nodded—and I put it in my mouth. The meat had a strange brassy tang, a taste like fear, and I wondered if somehow I could be experiencing what the boar had felt as I tracked her, and its dense texture was something I'd almost forgotten. There were dark savors in it, forest things not present in domesticated meat, and I opened my soul wide, searching for all the innuendoes of an experience that had cost so much, but in the end it was strangely simple, it was eating, the basic gesture of existence, a humble thing which I'd made so complex, my estrangement from it a symptom of my estrangement from myself, yet it felt natural to eat again, the same experience I remembered from before, only heightened from long deprivation.

"How is it, A.?" Cleanth asked, and I said, "it's good," and he said, "bravo, A.," and Morgan said, "oh yes, bravo," and took a vicious swallow from her glass. "Don't destroy it for him, M.," Cleanth said, and she said, "destroy what, Cleanth?" and he said, mildly, "something good," and Morgan laughed and said, "oh yes, so good. It's so good, isn't it, Cleanth—to go into the home of a defenseless animal and shoot it down? You always said so, and I went with you. I shot, too, to try and understand the thing you meant, but I never got it, Cleanth, and it just seems sick to me, sick and gruesome to see you leading Adam into it. He should be painting boars, celebrating the life in them, instead of taking it," and Cleanth said, "do you remember Yeats's line, 'the painter's brush consumes his dreams'?" and Morgan said, "no, I don't," and he said, "I read it to you once," and she sipped again, almost self-protectively, as though warding off a spell.

Cleanth turned to me and said, "do you know it, A.?" and I said, "no," and he said, "but you understand it, don't you?" and I thought about it and said, "doesn't it mean that when you put an image down on paper it dies in your imagination?" He smiled and said, "exactly. The brush kills, too, but what it kills inside the artist goes on to live outside him. It isn't any different with a gun except that it's reversed—what's killed outside comes to live within. Then it's you, you see?"—his eyes flicked from

Morgan to me—"the thing you thought was other, the separate thing, becomes yourself. That's what it means, M., Jane, A., all of you, in eating this"—he pointed to his plate—"the boar we killed becomes alive again in us, it becomes our life, part of our obligation to ourselves in self-love forever. That's what hunting is, and that's why it's not evil—it's a sacrament. And that's why what you did today was a higher work of art than any you'll ever do with paint and brushes, A.," and Morgan said, "don't believe that, Adam, it isn't true. It's all just bullshit, beautiful bullshit, fairy lights. You still took the life of a defenseless thing that didn't want to give it to you," and Cleanth said, "how do you know that, M.? Perhaps the boar comes to the hunter for a reason," and Morgan said, with a disastrous look, "believe me, Cleanth, I just know," and put her face in her hands and wept.

"Excuse us a minute," Cleanth said to Jane and me, "Morgan and I need to talk," and she said, "I don't want to talk, Cleanth, that's all we ever do, all we've done for years," and he said, "that's not entirely true, M.," with mild chastisement, and she said, "you're right, Cleanth. I should have said, you've talked and I've listened, trying to understand what you meant, but I don't think I ever have, not since you came back from Vietnam. Why don't I understand it, Cleanth? why don't I understand you, or us, or them"—the impersonalness of the word stung like a slap—"why don't I understand the Lost Colony, or this weekend, or our lives? what's wrong with me that I don't understand any of it?" and he said, "you've had too much to drink, M., you didn't feel this way yesterday and you won't tomorrow," and she said, "but I will, Cleanth, the drinking doesn't bring it on, I drink to get away from it because it feels that way already, all the time."

"You blame me for that, don't you?" he said, and she said, "no, Cleanth, no—don't you see this isn't about blame?" and he said, "what do you want from me, M.?" and she said, "you know what I want—the one thing you can't give me, the thing you gave me once and took away," and he said, "it wasn't me, M., I didn't give it or take it away—life did. You never accepted that—that's why you're unhappy. I did, and that's why I'm not, not anymore. That's the Big Change, M.," and she said, "the Big Change," in a tone that mingled scorn and wistfulness, "I never understood that either, Cleanth. I kept waiting for it to happen to me, too, to us. I waited and waited, thinking perhaps this summer. But it didn't—you went with Jane and I went with A.''—she put her hand on mine, squeezing hard, but never taking her eyes from Cleanth's—"thinking he'd make me feel young, but it didn't work. It made me feel old instead, so old, when I shouldn't feel old at all. But it wasn't A., it's you that makes me feel that way, Cleanth. That's the only change there's been for me."

"You're wrong," he said, "the change is working, baby, far more than you think. It's working in you even as you doubt. Tonight you can't see it, but tomorrow you will again. This is just a mood, M., it doesn't come from your best self." Morgan sipped her wine contemplatively, having calmed down a little, and said, "no, Cleanth, I think this mood is real and what I've been living with you up to now has been the dream," and Cleanth pursed his lips and said, a little grimly, "then the next move is yours," and Morgan said, "but I've forgotten how to move—that's the only thing I blame you for—you always moved for both of us," and he said, "don't blame me for that. I never tried to take your freedom—I tried to give you more. I still try, M.," and she said, "maybe if you had . . . I wanted you to take it, Cleanth. But you couldn't bear the responsibility of that," and he said, "you may be right, M., but I chose not to. I don't believe in owning someone else that way. I thought you knew. Of all of them, I thought you knew." There was real sadness in his tone when he said that, and in Morgan's as she said, "that's why you loved me, isn't it? All these years you loved me because you thought I understood the change that you'd been through so you didn't have to tell me. But I never did, darling—the beginning was the only part I ever understood, after that it got away from me."

We were quiet then, a somberness in all our faces, but more troubling in Cleanth's because it was so uncharacteristic there. For a moment he seemed just as young as I was, a boy like me who wasn't actually leading it—the night or the event—to a predetermined conclusion in accord with his own selfish aims, which was the thing I'd always suspected and feared in him. He was just as lost in it as I was, as we all were, and for that moment I felt sorry for him, that and a quaver of real love, as though he were my son, and I understood what Morgan had meant by Never-Never Land, because I saw him there, alone in it, and Never-Never Land was not a happy place to be.

Taking out the vial, Cleanth hit off the end of his key, then shoved it to me across the table—I just let it sit—and he said, "I'm not sure I can tell you what the change is, M., but maybe I can tell you how it happens—I can tell you how it happened to me. All my life I'd thought there must be another way to live besides the one I knew, the same way everybody lived around me. I tried painting, I tried sport, academics, I even became a vegetarian, like you, A., and for the same reason, thinking it would change me, change my nature, the things I didn't like about myself—the violence, the selfishness, things I didn't want to be. Nothing worked, and I became dissatisfied. That's where I was when I met you, M., and I thought love might be the key, but you broke my heart—I know you didn't mean to, but you did—so I went to Vietnam.

"That's where it started. I remember stepping off the transport plane—the air smelled different. Everything was different, but the difference was so subtle. It crept up on you. Being in the field was part of it—combat. It wasn't something obvious, like seeing someone blown away. You saw that all the time. If anything, it was seeing that some *didn't* get blown away, and it wasn't random—at first I thought it was, but that was just my ignorance. There was something different in those men, the ones who never never stepped into the booby traps, the ones the bullets didn't touch. It wasn't till near the end of my first tour that I understood that difference, and what made me understand it was very simple—looking in the mirror and realizing I was one of them.

"And suddenly there were others. You might have noticed them before and seen that there was something different in their eyes, but after the change you recognized them and they recognized you. You sought each other out, just like all of us around this table sought each other out. In some of them the change was in progress but not completed yet. You had to try to show them—that was the only duty."

Cleanth looked at me and said, "that's why I took you to the woods today, A., and it was just as I knew it would be. The boar picked you out—it wasn't accidental. There aren't any accidents. In 'Nam it was a secret everybody knew. There were two types of people—the vast majority, and a small group of others who were different, the magic ones who didn't die, who'd found the second way. And it wasn't anything special about them as people, it wasn't some kind of personal accomplishment. It was the opposite of personal, and that was the difference in a nutshell. The magic ones were the ones who didn't take it personally—they took, but never personally. They weren't the gung-ho killer cowboys—those guys died like flies. The magic ones were never eager. They didn't shoot the animals or women. Perhaps they didn't try to stop it, or perhaps they did—it was a judgment call depending on the situation and the moment. Maybe you simply walked away and smoked a cigarette. You heard the cries—it wasn't that you felt numb to it. It was just too big to stop, so you smoked your fag and looked out at the wind waving through the rice. Maybe there was a buffalo grazing in the paddy, no more oblivious than you were, but not taking it personally either, and it was all part of the same thing—the burning vil, the screams, the wind blowing through the rice, the jungle in the distance, the Hueys coming in over the trees, you sitting on your helmet smoking your last Camel, experiencing everything but not holding any of it. That water buffalo in the paddy was different from the ones lowing in the vil, he was out there grazing for a reason while the others died, just like I was sitting there on my helmet smoking and watching him for a reason, and the change was so simple, but it was life and death.

"You see, the first group, the vast majority, couldn't forgive the injustice of the power—it was a personal affront. They posed themselves against it and they either died or went insane. The other, smaller group stopped fighting it—I mean, you fought, but not against the power—they opened themselves to the flow of it and that's what made them magical. Others sensed it the same way I sense it in you. Every one of you is in the change. I'm a little further than you are, M., just like you're a little further than A. or Jane, and there are others much further along than me. That's why I brought you all out here today, to show you the nature of the power so that we could all be bonded in it forever. Maybe you understood it, maybe you didn't, but even if it makes no sense to you you're still in the change, everybody is, even the vast majority who resist. Most of them will keep resisting till it kills them, but it isn't the power that kills you, it's the resistance to it—that's the secret. Because what the power is is life. There's no other word for it. It isn't good or evil, it isn't just or unjust, it isn't beautiful or ugly, it's all of that at once, and you can't choose the parts you want—you have to accept all of it forever without reservation.

"That's what the Big Change is, M.—you were part of it for me just like I was for you. You still are. Because it never stops.

It's being in the change forever that changes you. The only other way is to reject it, but that's the one wrong move. Because you can step out, but you can't go back, the flow just goes one way, and when you try, that's when the unhappiness comes back. That's what you're feeling tonight, M. If it hurts so bad you feel you have to leave me, I won't try to stop you. I couldn't anyway, but it would make me sorry, because you can find it elsewhere, so can I, but it won't ever be like this.''

Cleanth stopped and drained his glass, staring off over our heads. The fire popped and sent sparks raining through the air, and the surf boomed like a shotgun then sighed away, as though regretting its own violence. Even the sea was double, a resounding yes and then a softer no—it was in all of nature, only Cleanth had gone beyond it, or stepped outside it, and I'd gone with him, wholeheartedly, unreservedly, never more so than at that moment, swept away on the flood tide of his words and insights. If he'd asked me to renounce my worldly goods, assuming I'd had any, and follow him barefoot across the world, I would have done it then without the slightest hesitation. What he'd said made me realize I knew absolutely nothing, that the horizon I'd perceived wasn't where it ended—there were people on the other side of it, and Cleanth was one of them. I'd been waiting my whole life for someone to tell me the answer, to show me how to live, and Cleanth had done it—the answer was, ''accept the darkness and be bright,'' the lost key to the lost door. I looked at Jane and knew that it was possible for us, not only possible but right. The last remaining objections were political, not moral, and easily attended to. The morality was us together, and it seemed inevitable, for that brief moment, as inevitable as what had happened in the woods.

Morgan stared at Cleanth, tears running down her face, as moved as I was, obviously, but with something still unanswered in her eyes—I had no idea what it was, or even what it could be—I thought he'd answered everything, and she said, ''you really believe it, don't you, Cleanth—that you're magical and the normal rules don't apply to you?'' and he said, ''we all are, M., or can be—that was my point, it wasn't personal,'' and she said, ''but it is personal, darling, it's so personal, and it isn't about us—not Jane or A. or me—it's about you, don't you know that?'' and he said, ''whatever you've got to say can't diminish what I've already told you, M., all it can do is make it personal and that's so unnecessary,'' and she said, ''I don't believe that,

Cleanth, I did for a long time, but not anymore—I think it is necessary," and he said, "then go ahead, M., tell them what you think the point is," and Morgan nodded to the vial of coke which he was fingering again and said, "that's the point, Cleanth," and he laughed and said, "what? that I do coke? that I do more than you think is good for me?"—he looked at me— "do you think that's the point, A.?"

I didn't answer, feeling something in the air that made my flesh creep, something I couldn't identify, and Morgan said, "not just that, Cleanth, the point is in the cooler Early gave you off the boat this afternoon"—she pointed to it, a white Styrofoam one glimmering in the firelight at the edge of camp—"it's wrapped in plastic underneath the ice." Cleanth's face suddenly darkened, and Morgan said, "the point is, that's why you brought us up here, not so that we could be bonded together forever in some sacramental power, but so that you could pick up two kilos of coke. The point is those little trips A. has been making for you—tell him what was in the briefcase, Cleanth." The shock I felt was violent and physical. I shot a glance at Cleanth, but his eyes were all for Morgan. "You're so wrong, M., so wrong," he said, and she said, "am I, Cleanth?" her eyes hardened, not in cruelty, but conviction, "why don't you just tell the truth?" and he said, "which one, M.?" and she said, "the real one, darling," with deep sympathy for him, and he said, "you mean the literal one, don't you? I already told the real one," and she said, "no, you didn't, Cleanth, but I think you should. I already know it, most of it, and what I didn't know I suspected, but I think you should tell it, not just to me, but all of us. Maybe that will help you," and Cleanth's eyes hardened, too, as he said, "go ahead then, M., I've told my truth, now you tell yours. Let's weigh them in the scales and see which one comes up. A. and Jane can judge."

She held his eyes a long time, then sighed and said, "all right, Cleanth—the truth is that you aren't magical, Vietnam didn't make you that way, it made you human, darling, so very human, but you couldn't accept that, you were ashamed of being human like the rest of us, and you cracked up, you lost your mind. You didn't really shoot that boy like you told A., the way you told me the first time when I believed you, too, not knowing any better, you were on that patrol, you witnessed it, you were wounded, you came out of that ambush with the others, but you didn't shoot that boy, Michael Brighton did, your captain, and he did it because the boy was dying and there was no way you could carry him out of there, to save yourselves, a secret only the five of you knew, and you turned it on yourself because you couldn't handle it, like you'd done it yourself, but you didn't, Cleanth, you didn't shoot Meyer Prosky. Michael did, and he didn't go to prison for it, neither did you, no one did.

"You went into the psychiatric ward at Walter Reed, and it must have been like a prison for you, darling, that's where I came to see you when you told me we'd both changed and it was over. That's where you told me about Meyer Prosky and I believed you because you believed it, and it wasn't till your mother had you moved to Mayfield, after ten months or a year, that Dr. Edwards finally pieced together the whole story and why you'd told it. That's where they diagnosed your psychosis—manic-depression.

"That's the truth, Cleanth, you're manic-depressive, and you need lithium. You started taking it then and it made you functional again. You've been taking it ever since and you don't lose it anymore, but sometimes, once every year or two, always around this time, always summer, it breaks through, not so it's noticeable except to those who know, like I know, now. To everyone else you seem larger than life, and that's why Dr. Edwards told me that you can always tell a manic when they come to the hospital because he's the one who looks like he's having the time of his life and it's the family, the friend, the lover, who look like they should be committed. It's been breaking through slowly now for six months, Cleanth, and I suspected it, but I never really knew till that first night A. came to dinner and told me you'd told him the Meyer Prosky story, which is how it always starts, and my heart just broke, darling, it's breaking now to have to throw this in your face, but you've got to hear it.

"I know you've stopped taking your medication. You've been flushing it down the toilet, or however you've been getting rid of it, and when I've asked you you denied it, and I believed you for a while because I wanted to. It's the feeling of the mania, darling, you're addicted to it, it's beautiful and you're beautiful, too, inside it, I've felt it, we all have here, but it's just a sickness that seems magical, Cleanth, and you take coke to enhance it and then you think you're magical and the rules don't apply to you, not even the law, Cleanth. You start dealing just like you did two years ago in Hilton Head, and you use people, darling, you don't do it out of cruelty, but you do, like you've used A., like you've used all of us in different ways, but it isn't a disaster yet, Cleanth, no one's been destroyed, not even you, there's still time to call it off and get back straight, but you've got to admit it, Cleanth, to me and all of us, but mostly to yourself, otherwise the whole thing's going to crumble down in ruins on your head again, and I can't stand by and watch that happen, darling, not to them, it isn't fair, not without their knowledge.

"You can't expect other people to keep picking up the pieces all your life, Cleanth. If you were insane it would be different, but you're not, you're simply ill, and you can still choose, and if you don't, I'm through with it, I tried to save you once and it doesn't work. I can't deal with it again, Cleanth, however much I love you, and I love you a lot, but every time it comes back, darling, your illness, the weak wounded part of you, the Meyer Prosky part, instead of trying to save it and make it well, which is the really hard part, Cleanth, you shoot it just like Michael shot that boy—you shoot it with the drugs, the binging, the business triumphs, you try to prove it wrong, and it's just like Dr. Edwards said, because you can't face that there's a Meyer Prosky in you, that you have a problem, that you're sick, and that's why you lie—you can't face the fact that you're normal and human just like everybody else, and now A. is as good as your disciple and wants to be just like you, and it's got to stop, darling, it just really does. It's over, Cleanth—it was a good show, one of your best, but it's time to close it down."

I couldn't look at him. I wanted to, I tried, but it was impossible. He looked at me though, at *me*, as though I were the judge, and said, "so, A., you've heard both sides now, it's all been weighed, which truth comes up for you?" and I did look then and said, "it's true?" and he said, "two truths, two ways, two types of people, forever—tragedy and comedy," and Morgan burst out in tears. I wanted to cry, too, and Cleanth said, "what Morgan's truth leaves out is that it's because of my disease, my sickness, whatever you care to call it, that I can see and know the things I do, the things I've tried to share with you. My 'disease' is only that, A., heightened consciousness, and the difference between illness and enlightenment is just one thing—the ability to handle it. I can. I'm handling it now. M. doesn't understand that—I thought you might." To *me*. His handsome face, his golden eyes, his unbroken confidence in the face of Morgan's truth, so clear and sane and vital, only too much so—that was the only clue, even then, when I knew ev-

erything . . . almost everything—it almost drew me down into
the whirlpool, into the mystery of his surpassing brightness. I
wanted to go, that was the truly frightening thing, I wanted to
keep going forever till I reached the bottom of it, of him. My
only other choice was saying "no," my old response, the one
that had never yet brought me a moment's happiness and which,
having once said yes, to him, I knew never would.

When I didn't answer, Cleanth nodded, lit a cigarette, inhaled
and looked away above our heads. Morgan was still crying, Jane
seemed stunned and frightened, and the fire whipped like a sail
the hurricane had shredded. After a moment of agonizing silence, Cleanth sighed out his smoke and said, in an almost
musing tone, "you were asking me about that portrait, A., this
morning in the Jeep. I promised you that story, and I want to
tell it now," and Morgan said, "please, Cleanth," and he shook
his head and said, "no, M., we've started it, let's see it to the
bitter end," and she said, "what I said wasn't meant to hurt
you, Cleanth—I think you know that. Don't hurt me now, because I won't forgive you," and he pursed his lips and said, "no
matter, we're way beyond that, and it's not meant hurtfully anyway."

He inhaled again and said, speaking through his smoke, "less
than six months after my father's death my mother was remar-
ried. I was at home then. I'd just come back from New York
and I was lost, and mother kept the whole thing from me, the
romance, though it's true, it only lasted three weeks. She'd gone
down to Palm Beach on vacation with my grandmother, and I'd
stayed behind at Seven Oaks, our family place, A. and Jane."
Though he addressed himself to us, ostensibly, his eyes never
left Morgan's face, and he said, "one day a limousine arrived
in the driveway. I saw it pull in and Mother climb out, running
up the steps to hug me at the door. Though she was elated, her
face got grave and confidential as she said, 'there's someone I
want you to meet, Cleanth,' and I said, 'who?' and she said,
'look, sweetheart,' and held her finger out to me with a sparkling
rock and said, 'I'm married, Cleanth, your old Mama just went
and got herself married,' and she laughed and laughed, then
threw her arms around my neck and said, 'please don't be angry,
sweetheart. It all happened so fast—I still haven't had time to
catch my breath.'

"Then she pulled away, giving me her best earnest face, and
said, 'I know you're going to like him, Cleanth. Grant rides and

collects art, you'll have all sorts of things to talk about—I picked him especially for you.' I think she meant that as a joke because she laughed, but I thought she'd gone crazy. I didn't laugh, I didn't get a chance to, I never even got a chance to say hello—but that was Mother, full of surprises. 'Now come outside and meet him, Cleanth,' she said, 'and please—please, please, please, please—be nice.' She took my hand and pulled me after her, and in the hallway as she started opening the door, she turned back as though remembering something, an after-thought, and whispered confidentially, 'and, Cleanth, he has a daughter. We met her at the airport on our way—she's just flown in from college. She's as sweet as she can be and absolutely beautiful—long chestnut hair and the most stunning big brown eyes—and I just know you're going to fall in love with her.' Mother rolled her eyes at me naughtily over that, and I was sure by then she'd lost her mind and had no idea what she was say-ing—because it wasn't as though the idea shocked her. In fact, it was almost as though she was granting me a license. In any case, that's where the idea, the unthinkable idea, got planted in my brain.

"Then Mother led me out and introduced me to a tall slim man, attractively bald and elegantly dressed. Grant and I shook hands and I saw a trace of kindness and misgiving in his eyes as though he'd given more intelligent consideration to my feel-ings than Mother had. 'It's a pleasure, Cleanth,' Grant said, 'your mother's told me quite a bit about you, and I know this must be sudden, but I look forward to knowing you.' I liked him actually, leaving everything else aside. Then Mother turned to me, beaming, and said, 'and this is your new sister, Cleanth,' and my new sister stepped from the back seat of the limousine, blinking her eyes in the green summer light, and the moment I looked at her, A. and Jane, the haze of my depression cleared and I went absolutely mad. She was so beautiful, so beautiful and twenty-two. I felt the *oomph* of unmistakeable rightness, the only time—you only get it once."

Morgan's eyes, fixed on Cleanth's as his were on hers, shone with tears—she seemed transformed. I looked at Jane, Jane looked at me, and Cleanth went on, "I held out my hand to her and said, 'I'm glad to know you,' and she said, 'but you don't know me, Mr. Faison'—she was that formal—but her eyes were teasing and she took my hand in spite of it and said, 'I've always wanted a brother, though,' and I said, 'me, too,' and she said, 'sorry to disappoint you,' and I said, 'I mean, a sister,' and she laughed like music, the way a princess in a fairy tale might laugh. Straight off the bat, Grant commissioned me to do a portrait of her, and she resisted nobly, saying it was vain—she was highminded, though, I think, somewhat coyly, and so proper, especially with me—but when she started sitting for me it began to change.

"Mother and Grant went out frequently as she introduced him to her friends, and sometimes we went with them, but many nights we were alone with the run of the whole house. I'd paint her for an hour or two in the library. The whole room was dark except the light on her and on my easel—that's why the background is so dark. She picked out the dress herself, vanity notwithstanding, knowing it flattered her—the hat and veil were my idea, something of Mother's, out of fashion, but that's exactly why I liked it, because she seemed out of fashion, too, or maybe it was timeless, I wanted to make her look that way, an apparition from an age when women still wore hats. It seemed strange to be there in that quiet house with just the ticking of the clock, chimes on the quarter hour—she, my new sister, in a formal cocktail dress and white gloves to the elbow and a small French hat and veil, me still in a coat and tie from dinner. It seemed so civil and refined, and she was used to that, but there was danger, possibility, dangerous possibility, my element, lurking just beneath the surface.

"She'd get tired of sitting, or I would, and we'd pour ourselves a brandy and talk for hours on the sofa. Mostly I'd talk and she'd listen—she liked that then. She didn't have much conversation, but she listened with great point and asked incisive questions which drew me out. I had the sense she distrusted me at first—maybe I talked too much—or maybe it was the fact that I was twenty-six and living in my mother's house, but she was too fine to judge, or perhaps too protected from anything that demanded judgment. But one night she was bold and said, apropos of some remark of mine, 'I think you're a terrible romantic, Cleanth'—we'd reached a first-name basis by that time—and I said, being bold myself, 'is that the same as being terribly romantic?' We'd flirted before—that's almost all we ever did, but never quite that close to the edge—and she said, 'oh, no, I think they're very different,' and I said, 'so that's my problem,' and she said, 'I suppose that isn't news to you,' and I said, 'oh, but you're wrong—I've always considered myself a hard-bitten realist,' and she said, 'you're making fun of me,' pouting, and I said, 'never, wait till you see your portrait,' and she said, 'may I then?' and I said, 'not yet,' and she said, 'I hope it's not too hard-bitten and realistic,' and I said, 'you'll be the judge, but it could only flatter you,' and she smiled at the compliment and said, 'I don't believe you at all. I still think you're a terrible romantic, only you don't see it as a problem, I think you like it while pretending not to, pretending to be hard-bitten and cynical, but it's because you're disillusioned.'

"I loved that, A. and Jane, her studiousness of me and her naive forthrightness—just the proper blend of soft and hard, blunt and subtle, innocence and wisdom. Women only have that once, before life has touched them, and I said, 'what about you, are you a terrible romantic, too?' and she said, 'I don't know what I am, I haven't decided yet—but I'm interested in what you think,' and I said, 'I don't know either, except that you're terribly romantic—beyond that I don't want to know,' and she said, blushing but not losing her composure, 'that's why you're a terrible romantic—because you don't want to know,' and I said, 'but I'm painting you,' and she blinked as that sank in and said, 'yes, that's your way of knowing me, isn't it?' and I said, 'this is only study, it's not knowing,' and she said, 'are they different?' and I said, 'very,' and she said, 'how?' and I said, 'study asks for nothing back, knowing is more intimate,' and she said, becoming very brave, 'do you want to know me?' and I said, 'very much—hold that expression if you can.'

"I stepped back to the canvas and tried to catch the lights and shadows in her eyes, and when I came around the easel for another glance she'd lifted up her veil and there was something in her eyes I hadn't seen before, a new directness, an inquiring, a hint of troubledness, but under that something vast and fateful like the sea—it wasn't a girl's look, or a sister's either. I put down my brush and went to her. We kissed and didn't speak. She got up and took my hand and we walked through the glass doors to the lawn. She stopped to take her shoes off, so did I, and we walked barefoot through the wet grass. There was moonlight quivering on it. It was a night like this—the wind broke through the oaks and I heard my father's horse cantering in the pasture. We went to the stable, up to the loft, and I had her in her plum-colored dress and white gloves—only the hat came off. There was the dusty smell of fresh straw in my nostrils, oiled leather tack, manure, horses, and it was so quiet I could hear them puttering and stamping below, I could hear the muted clacking of their teeth as they ground their oats, and somewhere in the trees outside a bobwhite sang. It was all so soft it simply fused into the stillness that surrounded us when it was over—no peak, no fall into the emptiness—it simply ebbed into an afterglow as sensuous as the sex itself, and I didn't want to raise my head from her neck, or speak, or ever move from that spot, A. and Jane, I wanted to stay there forever, feeling her heart beat under mine through the crumpled satin, smelling the faint perfume on her bare shoulders, watching her flush steal back to paleness. I could have died right there without regret, and many times I wished I had, many times.

"But then I realized she was weeping, and I tried to look at her but she held my face down, clinging, and when we finally separated she turned away from me, her dress all up around her waist and her legs bare and slim with a trickle of my semen running off the bottom one into the straw. I touched her shoulder, but she nudged away, and I stared at her with aching tenderness not knowing what to do for her. Then she stood up abruptly, and as she smoothed her dress down, she said, 'I know it's just revenge for you,' and I said, 'revenge?' and she said, 'against my father,' and her interpretation was so outlandishly wrongheaded I laughed and said, 'is that it? I thought I was in love with you,' and she sat down and wept again, cross-legged in the straw. Then she stared up at me with tortured eyes and said, 'we can't do this,' and I said, 'why not?' and she said, 'because it's incest,' and I said, 'how can it be? I've only known you for three weeks, and besides, we already did,' and she said, 'you don't think it is?' and I said, 'we could look it up but I'm pretty sure it doesn't qualify,' and she said, 'it's not funny, Cleanth—even if we don't think so, they're going to,' and I said, 'I promise I won't tell them, if you won't.'

"We didn't either, around them we behaved with complete propriety, by day, while every night I slept with her and we made love, and when it got light I crept back down the hall and came to breakfast with red eyes. We had one or two close calls—I had to jump from her window once—but Grant never suspected, he never even dreamed. But Mother knew, I'm almost sure of it, though she never confronted me, I don't know why—maybe she preferred not to know, or maybe she felt the guilty justice of that reciprocity. She never told Grant either, but he found out anyway. The portrait was the fatal clue. When I finally showed it to them, even Mother, who bought art to match her upholstery, received it quietly with a darkening face. Grant took one look at it, his face startled, then he turned to Mother and her expression simply gave the farm away. His whole face, even the top of his head, turned red, and Mother said, 'don't you think it's good?' trying to bluster her way out of it, and finally he looked at me—not a trace of hatred, just shock—and he said, 'excuse me,' and walked out of the room.

"Dinner was extremely grim that night, but not another word was said about it, not then or ever. Grant continued to be extremely civil to me—he was until his death, but never more than that. When I came down to breakfast the next morning, trunks were being lugged into the hall. They left immediately afterwards—I only got five minutes with her. We walked out to the stable and she turned to me and said, 'I don't want to go,' and I said, 'then don't, I don't want you to—I love you, M.' " Morgan wept when he finally said her name. I knew it anyway—by then I did, and she said, "you never called me M. back then, you always used my name," and Cleanth said, "yes, the abbreviation crept in later, didn't it?" and there were tears in his eyes, too, as well as Jane's and mine, and he went on with the story, addressing her directly, "you said, 'I love you, too, Cleanth, I always will,' and I knew it was the end, you might just as well have shot me, M. Your eyes were loving and confused and pleading, and you said, 'but maybe it's better this way, don't you think?' and I said, 'no, I don't think,' and you said, 'what choice do we have?' and I said, 'we could go away,' and you said, 'where?' and I said, 'anywhere—New York, London, Paris, Bali—it doesn't matter where,' and you said, 'but I'm enrolled in school,' and I said, 'forget school, Morgan, this is more important, school can wait,' and you said, 'can't this?' and I just stared at you, because I knew it couldn't, even then I knew it moves and you can't hold it still—that was our moment of decision, M.—and you said, 'I think we need some time to think it over, Cleanth—I know I do. I'm so confused,' but I didn't feel I needed time to think about it, A. and Jane, I knew that it was then or never, so I said, 'that's your decision?' and you said, M., with a tender pout, 'do you hate me?' and I smiled and shook my head, saying, 'no, I'll never hate you, M.'—I believe I used the abbreviation then—and you said, 'I'll see you at school, won't I?' and I just gazed into your eyes, and you said, 'you are a terrible romantic, Cleanth, you know that, don't you?' and we embraced and I walked you back and put you in the car.

"Grant was gone for three days, and in the meantime Mother and I talked about it. She offered to send me on a cruise to Greece, and I accepted it and made arrangements. But it never got to that. One morning I went to Angier to get a haircut and post some letters, and on my way home I saw the recruitment office and pulled over to the curb and went inside. I got your letters in Fort Benning, M., I got the ones you sent to me in-country—I read them and kept them all—and when you came to visit me at Walter Reed that time, as I recall—that time is very dim—I thanked you for them, and you said, 'why didn't you write back?' and I said, 'I don't know,' which was the truth, and your eyes took on that melting light I'd seen that first night in the stable, and you said, 'I still love you, Cleanth, I've had a lot of time to think about it, and I know I hurt you—it was a mistake—but I never meant to,' and I said, 'it doesn't matter,' because it really didn't, M., and you said, 'did you think of me?' and I said, 'yes,' and you said, 'but you don't love me anymore,' and I looked at you—it was the strangest thing, M.— because in some way I did, I still loved you and I knew I was never going to love anybody else as much, but 'you' weren't really the young woman sitting by the bed—she just seemed like a kind stranger—it was the girl she used to be, the one I'd painted, that's who I'd loved and needed, M., in the golden spell which is specific to a time and place, a time and place where we no longer were, because you, the woman sitting by the bed, and she, the girl I'd loved, were different in some way, I couldn't fuse the image, so I just said, 'but I did once,' and you got up and left again, and I didn't see you until that night I came to Charleston and met Brent, but I didn't come to meet him, I came to see if, with all the other things that had started to go right, perhaps the image had re-fused—I wanted it to—but it hadn't, and I didn't know how to make it. I still don't, Morgan, I don't know how to bring the two together, but I still want to."

Cleanth rose with shining eyes, bent over Morgan and kissed her lips, then walked away across the dune, and Morgan looked at us and said, "I'm sorry," her face completely young, like the girl's in the portrait—I caught the resemblance then, and also finally understood the weight of the unstated thing that she was

up against—then she looked at me and repeated it, differently—
"I'm sorry"—squeezing my hand hard, before she pushed her
chair back and followed him toward the beach.

Sixteen

A.

Left alone, together, Jane and I stared at one another like two frightened children lost in the woods. I gazed away into the night overwhelmed by a sense of numb floating unreality. "A.?" Jane said, and I just shook my head, got up and stumbled out into the dunes, tripped and lay down where I fell. Jane followed and knelt over me, a black cut-out against the sky with just the glimmering of eyes. "Are you all right?" she asked with deep concern, and I said, "please, Jane, I can't talk about it now," and she said, "do you want to be alone?" and I said, "yes, I think so," and she said, "you're sure?" and I said, "no," and she said, "A.?" and I sat up and put my arms around her.

There was no passion there—if so, it was far far down—but only comfort, a comfort I remembered from a dim time in a world I'd lost. I saw a crystal image of my mother's face, smiling, leaning out of sunlight viscous as a liquid. I felt young and helpless, yet the utter fearless joy of being helped, and at the same time I felt old and strong in the confidence that there was help in me to give, which I'd never truly known until that moment, as I gave it. I wanted to protect Jane, and that impulse lifted me out of the isolation of my suffering, and I knew my suffering was and always had been selfishness, only that. I glimpsed the deeper meaning of Cleanth's lesson—that selfishness, pursued religiously, as a devotion, might open into grace— and its enormous hollowness struck home. The ring which I'd perceived as crystal turned to the thunk of cheap glass as it shattered, and what shattered it was the generosity that blossomed in my heart toward Jane, and suddenly it seemed possible that I, even I, might not be selfish anymore. That moment, a simple embrace in felt love, was a new thing to me, a height I touched and couldn't hold.

Even as Jane went to get the sleeping bags I thought of Cleanth, but his image swam and broke apart. It was like a palimpsest, and through the newer paint as it cracked and blistered, I saw an older scene. The title of the painting was Betrayal. Cleanth's face became my father's as he popped up from the covers in the Sherry Netherland Hotel. I saw the sparkle of that silver bracelet on Eleanor's left wrist, and I was there again. I was that fourteen-year-old boy learning the great lesson of my life, how the dark power of a lie breaks everything, even the brightness of love. It was Cleanth's lie, but it was also mine. I was the man in bed, not with Eleanor, but Jane, the door was swinging open once again, and behind it would be Cary, who loved me in simple trust, as I loved him. That love was the one thing in my life I'd truly earned and never soiled with any taint of falseness or dishonesty. Our friendship had sustained me when I had no other faith, and when the bullshit of cheap pretty words was cleared away, it was the one thing I believed was real, the one thing I held sacred.

The coked-out fog I'd drifted in through those strange days incinerated in a white-hot flash, and I looked down and saw the ledge I'd sleepwalked to the edge of following Cleanth's trail of sugar crumbs, the momentum still unbroken, pushing me to fall. Because I loved Jane, too, who in a single innocent embrace had opened a new sky to me filled with higher stars than any friendship has to give. My love for her, the soft generosity that had lifted me to hope that I was capable of something good, was a knife of killing selfishness aimed straight for Cary's heart, and I knew he would not recover from it, I knew he would die, because the same knife had killed me. And what do you do then? Perhaps a wise man would have known. I simply lay there gutted like the boar, dying with the unbearable intensity of life, holding Jane's small hand and knowing nothing as my soul floated off into the vast limpid darkness of the sky.

I woke up the next morning with Jane beside me on the dune hungover from the emotion I'd expended. I felt drained, but curiously light, like something had been lifted from me. Things looked different. The sand burned a deeper cooler gold. The sky, the seaoats swaying in the wind—everything was vivid. I felt lost in it, but free. I hadn't known I'd lost my freedom till suddenly I found it there again. For the first time in many days I wanted to go running, to run hard and far.

I looked at Jane and she was looking back at me from a different world. Her face was strained with dark emotion, yet beautiful in its reality. There was an intimacy between us that hadn't been there before, and I realized that what flashed hot and bright in me like powder burned in her on a long slow fuse, but it was the same fire. "Hello," I said, and she said, "why are you smiling?" and I said, "I don't know, but you should try it," and she said, "they're in there, A., in the tent, together," and I felt a hand clinch to a fist with my heart in it and then let go. "Are you surprised?" I asked, and she said, "I don't know, I don't know what I am, A., I just feel dirty"—she ran her fingers through the oiled richness of her hair—"I want to take a bath," and I said, "I've got soap, I'll get it."

The second tent, which was to have been mine and Morgan's, stood wide open. On a cot I found a white silk scarf of Morgan's, and when I lifted it I smelled the perfume of her bed, and the memory of the many nights we'd lain there sharing sex and sleep and cigarettes loomed up at me. It was only at that moment that I realized it was over, and I felt a deep throb of loss. I put it down, put the bar of soap in my back pocket, picked up my pad and pastel box, and left.

The flaps on Cleanth's tent were down and the mosquito net was zipped and as I passed it I had the sense that there was something large and frightening inside, not Cleanth and Morgan, but something else which had shown its face to me but which I hadn't truly seen or hadn't recognized to know its name. I felt a child's fear of the dark, and realized there were deeper emotions I had yet to sound. I walked quickly to join Jane, dimly aware, as my early confidence eroded, that it was somehow tied to Jane, that her presence had allowed me to be strong, not with borrowed strength, but with my own, which her need released. My roots were already entwined with hers as I moved in the upper branches thinking I was separate and free. Perhaps there was no choice. Perhaps there never is. I did not believe that then.

As we set out hiking toward the sound Jane was brooding. I wanted to know what she was feeling, but didn't press. In me some trace of lightness lingered, but it had lost its sparkle, clouded with sediment. It was half a mile, around the base of Penny Hill, to the water. There was no marsh there, the trees grew down to the margin of the beach, a narrow strip of grayish sand. I put my things down in a clearing underneath a large live oak tree as Jane waded out into the sound. I followed her, then squatted down and splashed myself in knee-deep water, keeping on my shorts as I washed off the grime and smoke and night sweat, lathering my arms and body. The brackish water didn't get it all, but it was an improvement, and when I looked up, Jane, twenty yards away, was quietly, unostentatiously, taking off her suit, peeling it down over her shoulders, not looking at me.

I looked at her though, through the gauzy shimmer which was thick around her, tapering off across the open spaces, but never entirely. The sheen of it remained, connecting everything—even the water and the sky seemed conscious—and through that connectedness she felt my eyes and turned, naked except for her dark glasses, not shy as she'd been the night before, only covering her breasts with a light but ineffective gesture, and our eyes locked, concealing nothing, stating nothing, acknowledging everything. Jane was not embarrassed, neither was I, but she was still twenty yards away, and she didn't try to close that distance—I didn't either. It only seemed possible to do so—that was the difference.

"Where's the soap?" she said with a blasé factualness that seemed beyond all style, and I said, "are you aware of it?" and she said, "of what?" and I said, "your effect," and she said, "you're a strange boy, A., I mean that from my heart." I laughed and fell back in the water. "You are, aren't you?" I persisted, and she said, "only when I'm naked," and it delighted me that she would not admit it. I cocked my arm to toss the bar of soap to her, and she said, "don't throw it," and I did, grinning. "It's Ivory," I said, "it floats." She smiled and turned away from me and washed. I waded back to shore and lay down in the sun.

Jane came out suited up again and sat beside me. She'd raised her glasses on her head and her eyes were full of doubt, opinion, questions, things I'd temporarily forgotten. And that I could have forgotten them, even temporarily, seemed a testimony to magic. Even then, remembering Cleanth and Morgan, they seemed far away, as though the life I'd lived with them had not been my real one. My real life was here, with Jane, who'd forgotten nothing. That was her strength—it held me down against my tendency to float.

"Tell me how you feel," I said, and she said, "I will," and I said, "when?" and she said, "when I know," and I said, "will you sit for me then?" and she said, "why?" and I said, "because I can see you—I don't know if I can draw it, but I'd like to try," and she said, "only if you promise not to show it to me, ever, not even if I ask," and I said, "why not?" and she said, "because I don't want to remember this, A., I want to forget it ever happened," and I said, "I want to remember it forever," and suddenly she was weeping and I was holding her again. "I'm sorry," she said, "just give me a minute," and I said, "I don't have to draw you now," and she said, "no, I want you to."

We went back to the clearing. Jane balanced on the trunk of a fallen tree and drew her legs up, circling them with her arms and resting her chin on her knees. I flipped through my pad, discovering I had only one clean sheet left. Thinking I'd use it for the drawing, I reversed the pad and began to sketch her on the back of the drawing I'd made the previous night. It felt good to concentrate and work. I did her body in a few quick strokes, then moved on to her face where I slowed down and worked with care. She was still and quiet for ten minutes or a quarter hour, and I began to realize I was doing something different. The likeness came quite easily, but it was more than that, it was like my hands were gloves and my mind had slipped into them. They worked all by themselves. I'd never felt that, and I began to get excited.

I was measuring the distance between her eyes with my green chalk when she said, "they started out like this, A., Cleanth and Morgan, just like us—what happened to them?" and I said, "I don't know," and she said, "what did they do to us, A.? a few weeks ago I was in prep school, I was just eighteen and going to the beach, then I met Cleanth and the whole thing seemed so cool, it seemed so grown-up and exciting . . . now I feel like I'm a hundred, and I know something I don't want to know, something I'm not ready for but have got anyway, and I don't think I'll ever be able to go back." Her face puckered like she was going to cry, then cleared instantly. "I'm angry, A.," she said, "I know I did it to myself, but I'm angry at Cleanth anyway, because I don't think it was fair. He didn't have to love me, but I expected him to care. I did. He was so much older.

They used us, A., they treated us . . ." She put her face in her hands, shaking with silent sobs, and I got up and went to her. "Jane . . ." I said, putting my hand gently on her shoulder. She shook her head and then looked up with hurt wet eyes. "They treated us like dirt," she said, "like we were toys—it's terrible, it's not a little thing. I want to go home, A., I don't want to stay out here another minute—will you take me?" I nodded, and she said, "thank you," and squeezed my arm, and I said, "it's what I want, too—I think we have to face them though, we owe them that," and she said, "why? I don't think we owe them anything, I don't want to see them, A., I don't ever want to see either one of them again," and I said, "I understand, but I do, Jane, I have to do it," and she gazed at me as though uncertain of her decision, and I said, "our stuff is back there anyway, I'll put it in the Jeep and come back for you," and she said, "would you?" like that touched her. I nodded, turned around and started walking back. I'd hardly reached the path when she called, "A." I looked back and she said, "wait for me."

When we reached the camp Cleanth and Morgan were lying together in the hammock in their bathing suits like they'd just come from a swim. Cleanth was on his back with one knee crooked over, kicking off the ground, his arm across his forehead. Morgan's head was on his chest, her left thigh rolled over on his, her eyes open with a vacant dreamy expression, an alertness focused on nothing. When we came around the dune, Morgan raised her head and stared straight at us. I held her eyes a moment, and then Jane said, "I'm going to get my things," and went into the first tent, and I nodded, breaking Morgan's gaze, and went into the second for my own.

While I was collecting them, a hand touched my shoulder lightly and I turned to find Morgan standing there. We didn't speak for a long time, just gazed at one another, and I noticed that the youthfulness I'd seen in her the previous night had deepened. She seemed very clear, not happy, but released, and I found her beautiful, more beautiful in the loss than she'd ever been in the possession. She started to speak, but I said, "you don't have to say anything, Morgan." Tears welled in her eyes, and she said, "I didn't set out to lie to you, Adam. I didn't even set out to care for you, not that first night, but I did care," and I said, "did you?" and she said, "don't you know that?" I didn't answer, and she said, "but however much I cared for you,

I couldn't compromise Cleanth," and I said, "but you did last night," and she said, "only to help. Telling you before wouldn't have helped anything," and I said, "but you might have at least explained your relationship," and she said, "would that have mattered to you?" and I said, "I don't know," and she said, "maybe that's why I didn't. I was afraid you'd judge me and go away," and I said, "would that have hurt so much?" and she said, with great earnestness, "yes, it would have. It's going to hurt me now. I want you to know that, Adam—it's important to me that you leave here knowing that."

I looked at her, trying to judge her sincerity, and said, "I'm not sure I believe you, Morgan," and she said, "if you'd loved me at all, you would believe—you didn't, did you?" and I stared at her and said, "yes, I did," realizing it for the first time, and she smiled and said, "a little bit?" I smiled back in the same fond wistful way, and she said, "I loved you, too, Adam," and I said, "a little bit," elaborating for her, and she said, "enough," and we embraced. After our previous intimacy, I felt shy and awkward holding her—it seemed very strange—but when I tried to kiss her on the cheek she gave me her full mouth, passionately, and that was even stranger. Feeling like I might cry if we prolonged it, I broke it off, and she took one last look at me, like a deep remembering drink, glanced her fingers through my hair, gave me a hurt smile and left the tent. I gathered my last things and took them to the Jeep.

Cleanth was on his knees feeding pieces of kindling into the fire, speaking softly to Jane, who was sitting on a driftwood stump with tears washing down her face from under her dark glasses. I couldn't overhear their conversation and didn't try, just set about the packing, breathing in the wakeful morning smell of coffee on the salty air, a smell that had always seemed to be about hopefulness and fresh beginnings, and still was, but in that moment I became aware of the sadness of the thing you have to leave behind to start over.

After a while, Jane went into the tent and Cleanth stood up, brushing his hands off on his shorts as he walked over. I turned to face him, experiencing an odd breathlessness, realizing, if I hadn't known before, that I'd put far more at stake with him than I'd ever done with Morgan, and for just a moment I felt the keen and searing bitterness of a lost hope, a scent of powder mingling with the coffee and the ocean air.

"Jane told me you're leaving," he said, and I just nodded,

looking at him. His face was grave and his eyes were clear, but there was no apology in them. That was what I'd wanted to know. At that moment I felt I could walk away. "I wish you'd reconsider, A.," he said, and I said, "I don't think so, Cleanth, this feels right." He nodded, but for an instant his eyes flashed hot before he snared what he was feeling in the violence of his smile.

"I believed in you, Cleanth," I said, "I thought you were for real," and he said, "I'm sorry if I hurt you, A., I didn't mean to—I tried to give you something, not take something away," and I said, "then why did you lie to me, man?" and he said, "how did I lie, A.?" and I said, "Jesus Christ, Cleanth, Jesus Christ—don't you even know?" and he said, "what was it, A.? a story I told you in Life Poker the first night I met you? was that it? the drugs?" and I said, "those trips I took—you used me, man," and he said, "where did you think the coke came from, A.? maybe I just waved a magic wand? don't forget, a few thousand dollars went up your nose, too," and I said, "so that makes it right to involve me without my knowledge? and anyway, Cleanth, that isn't even the point. The point isn't the drugs and it isn't Morgan," and he said, "what then, A.?" and I said, "the point is that you told me you were someone you really aren't," and he said, "no, A.," shaking his head, "no, baby, that's the one thing I never did—I told you exactly who I was, and what I didn't tell I showed. No one else, A., just you, and I told you because I thought you could understand. Listen to me, A., Morgan's truth is a net that lets the most important thing slip through. She sprang it on me last night, but I'm not in it—you see?" and even then something in his eyes attracted me, a spark of playful challenge, like, here I am, catch me if you can.

I just stared at him and said, "no, man, all I see is that you sold me something you don't really own. I didn't ask for it, Cleanth. I didn't pick you, you picked me, remember? Sure, I went along, because I always do, and that's my problem, but you said you knew the way, and I believed you—that was your lie—you were the tour guide, man, and you led me to a door you said was paradise and I went in and it was hell, and what I can't forgive you for is that you knew," and he said softly, "but it isn't hell, A., it's my life," and I said, "then live it, Cleanth, enjoy it if you can, but leave me out of it, I want my own," and he said, "good, A., I want that for you, too, carry that away and walk out like a man. Matches come and go, A.—we've had ours and maybe it's time for it to end—but the game is never over, you just stop playing. That's a loser's move. A winner just goes off and plays it somewhere else with someone else.''

He looked down in the passenger seat of the Jeep and picked up the pad with the sketch I'd done of Jane, studying it briefly before he met my eyes again. ''Play it with her, A.,'' he said, ''I think that's what you've wanted all along, only you couldn't let yourself,'' and reading the ink strokes that had bled through the paper and the depressions of the nib, he flipped over to the drawing of the osprey tree, which is when I saw it, too, the curious juxtaposition—Jane's face, full color, on one side, and on the reverse, the osprey tree in black and white, two different things, yet connected, essentially, forever, and he said, ''maybe you can now.'' He stared at it a moment more before he handed it back to me, saying, ''take without regret, A.—that's all I did and all I think you really have to hold against me, because I tried to show you how. You paid dearly for that lesson—don't let it be wasted, A., because it's the taking with regret that spoils. Remember that, especially now,'' and his eyes drifted off across my shoulder to Jane, who was standing there with her things in her arms and a hurt solemn face, waiting for us to finish. I looked at her, then back at him, and Cleanth said, ''good-bye, my friend,'' holding out his hand. I stared at it a moment, hesitating, wondering if I should, and he reached out and clasped both hands behind my head and pulled me to a fierce kiss on the lips. As he drew away his eyes were full of tears, and then he turned and walked away. In spite of everything, I was glad to leave him undefeated.

Jane climbed in beside me and I turned the engine over. As we pulled off, Cleanth was kneeling before the fire again, stoking it with tinder. We rolled away across the dune onto the beach and didn't look back, not either of us, but the shadow followed us. Cleanth was one strong thread in the tangled skein of what occurred, Morgan was another, and the osprey tree, what happened there, was the final twist that bound the rope together, each filament as fine and light as silk, but not to be unraveled.

Seventeen

A.

As we entered Kill Devil Hills, Jane, who'd been quiet on the drive, turned to me and said, "I'm hungry." I stopped at Camelot Pier and we sat on a picnic table in the quiescent amusement park in the shadow of the Ferris wheel, where I watched her eat a hot dog in a slow contemplative fashion. She seemed very dignified, even the way she licked her fingers where it ran. Noticing my scrutiny, she said, "would you like a bite?" I shook my head, and she said, "it's good," offering it to me in the napkin with her free hand cupped under it. I stared at it mournfully, then took a chomp, experiencing a mild disappointed wonder as my vegetarianism lapsed into history. A lot of things were lapsing into history.

Back at the cottage, Pig barked at us like trespassers, then surveyed us with somber reproach as we stepped down off the running boards. Jane went straight to the shower under the porch steps and I got a towel for her, draping it across the door. "Thanks," she said, and I went upstairs and sat down in the rope hammock chair, opening a beer and sipping it as I listened to the water run. I felt bruised and dull. The clairvoyant buoyancy I'd felt when I woke up that morning was long gone. It seemed like a dream. Corolla—everything that had happened there—seemed like a dream. But the house was real, a place where things had consequences.

Breaking off with Cleanth was part of my depression. I didn't question that it was the right thing to do—even if it wasn't, I had to get away from him, because I couldn't live that way. But however he'd used me, he'd given me something, too. I couldn't write it off, it was there inside me, a lump, maybe gold, and maybe lead, but heavy either way. And there were petty things—all the perks, the money, the cars, the job, the scene—I had to walk away from all of it. Suddenly I was just an eighteen-year-old kid again, driving a Jeep the salt air was starting to rust out, making five an hour. My life had shrunk to its real size—it didn't seem like much.

As I went inside for a second beer, I saw the photograph of Cary and the chicken tacked above the phone. Below it was the envelope with his flight number written on it. Oh, yeah, reality. It was splashdown time.

Jane emerged from the shower wrapped in the towel, looking fresh and smiling. The seesaw tilted, and I passed her going down as she went up where I had been that morning. "Did you look through the cracks?" she teased, and I said, "ha ha," smiling wanly, a little frightened of her strength. She seemed so easy with it. It was all still there, I just didn't see how it was going to happen. That was the real root of my depression. Jane didn't seem stumped or frightened in the least. Maybe she just wasn't thinking of me at all. Maybe I had dreamed that, too. This thought was the most depressing one of all, and Jane was more beautiful than ever.

She lifted my beer from the table and took a long strong swallow, saying, "ahhh," in a gruff lusty voice. "There's a couple more in the refrigerator," I told her, and she said, "let's go down on the beach, I feel like walking," and I said, "go ahead, I'm going to sit a while," and she said, "well, Pig will go with me, won't you, Pig?" and he thumped the floorboards with his tail without raising his head from his paws, knowing he was being spoken to. She went in and dressed and on her way back down the steps she said, "you sure?" and I said, "I'll be down in a bit," and she said, "are you okay?" I smiled and nodded and she whistled for Pig who got up, stretching casually before trotting after her. I watched them climb the dune, then went downstairs and showered, sitting down on the board floor and watching the clear water pool in my cupped flushed hands, spilling over. By the time I got down to the beach, they were far to the north, two black antlike figures—a larger human ant and a smaller one, more like a flea, leaping in the air. I spread my towel, lay down and fell asleep.

I woke up with my mouth open, drooling on the towel. My head was pressed into a conforming dent in the sand and my jaw ached. My back felt hot, and pressing my shoulder there was a layer of new red over the nut brown of my older tan. Though the sun was still high, it had slanted in a westerly direction and the quality of the light had changed. I took a dip to cool off and then trudged back to the house. The blue shadows pooling in the sand seemed beautiful to me, and I realized I was no longer depressed. Depression had transformed to sadness, and I felt a spark of life.

The Jeep was gone when I came up and I wondered about that till Jane rolled up the driveway with Pig panting happily in the shotgun seat. She handed me a bag of groceries and said, "I hope you have a grill." I nodded and pointed absently toward the garage and she said, "I bought tuna steaks. We can marinate them in Wishbone Italian and charcoal them—it's great," and I said, "where'd you learn to cook?" and she laughed and said, "I can't. Daddy used to do it, but it can't be all that hard. I also bought some salad things and potatoes for french fries—how does that sound?" and I said, "great," subtly but strongly touched by her initiative, which seemed so simple on the surface, but held complex implications underneath. "Here," she said, handing me a bag of charcoal as she stepped down, "you can start the fire." No more was said, and that seemed right. A new order was unfolding, and it seemed better to wait and listen and feel and not to speak of it too much till it spoke first, announcing its purpose.

It was twilight by the time we ate. Jane had set the table, scaring up cloth napkins and mats from somewhere and lighting the stubs of candles in the pewter holders beneath the hurricane chimneys. The flow was very comfortable and homely, but there were glimmers in it, like gold dust in a miner's pan, and afterwards we washed the dishes—another mystery—and sat out on the screened east porch drinking beer and listening to the ocean till it got dark. Then we went in and turned on the TV—the first time I'd watched it all summer—basking in a vegetative mindlessness, flipping channels till we found Errol Flynn in *Robin Hood*. I sat on the old heavy-stranded wicker couch, Jane in a rocking chair beside me, and at one point she turned to me and said, "you know what this reminds me of?" nodding toward the screen, and I said, "what?" and she said "Killdeer," and I thought I knew what she meant—a distant world from long ago. "You mean Cary, don't you?" I asked, and she frowned, musing on my question, and said, "I don't know, maybe," and got up during a commercial break and made popcorn. Handing me the bowl, she said, "move over, Rover."

I made room for her, and she leaned back in the opposite corner, stretching her legs across my knees and making clawing motions with her hand every time she wanted me to pass the bowl, never taking her eyes from the set. I'd never enjoyed that kind of intimacy with a woman without groping, but there was neither the compulsion nor the invitation. Not even Jane's legs, bare, brown and slightly prickly, across my own, seemed like one, and it was like a new horizon opening. When the movie was over, she stretched, smiling and yawning, and I said, "you want me to take you home now?" and she shook her head with childish exaggeration so that her hair swung side to side. I stared at her, feeling the tingles of a quickening nervousness, and she said, "do I have to go?" with a coy frown, and I said, "aren't you tired?" and she nodded in the same exaggerated way, leaving me at a loss.

"Can't I stay over?" she asked, "I like it here," and her calm happy face undercut the ground of my suspicions. "Sure, okay," I said quickly, trying to sound matter-of-fact about it, "there are sheets on all the beds—choose any room you like," and she said, "do you have something I can wear?" and I said, "like what?" and she said, "pajamas?" and I said, "sorry," blushing, and she said, "don't you wear pajamas, A.?" arching her eyebrows like she was shocked. Her teasing seemed affectionate, but not sexually loaded, and I was mystified again by her knowingness, her confidence and ease. Feeling shy and awkward, I said, "How about a tee shirt?" and she said, "close enough," and I got her one from my dresser, handing it to her on the threshold of the bathroom, where she smiled and closed the door.

I went in my bedroom and undressed quickly, keeping on my underwear against my normal practice and leaving the door cracked—another deviation. I pulled back the sheets and crawled inside, lying there wide awake and nervously expectant. I kept telling myself I was a fool—Jane would go off to bed in another room and that would be the end of it.

I heard the old pipes shudder as she turned the water off, then the click of the latch as she opened the bathroom door. My heart was pounding, and it pounded even harder when I heard her knock. I sat up, switching on the light as she peered around the door whispering, "are you asleep?" I stared at her and she blinked back, then padded in and sat down on the mattress beside me. "What's the matter?" I asked and she regarded me thoughtfully and said, "can I sleep with you?" Before I could respond, she said, "just sleep, A., I promise I won't assault you," and I said, "why?" Her face settled and she sighed and said, "you always have to ask that, don't you? never mind." She started to get up, but I held her arm, saying, "wait a minute, Jane." She regarded me with an expectation of further disappointment in her eyes, and I said, "it's okay," and lifted up the covers. "You're sure you don't mind?" she asked, hesitating, "I don't want you to think I'm being a tease," and I said, "I don't think that," not knowing what I thought, except it wasn't that. She smiled and jumped over me, jogging the mattress, lying there staring at the ceiling a moment before she said, "you know something, A.?" and I said, "what?" and she said, "I feel good, I feel better than I have in a long time." She rolled her head on the pillow and stared at me, saying, "I'm so glad to be out of there. I feel like I'm my own age again." Her expression had an almost childish innocence and gravity and I said, "I know what you mean," though what I felt was neither innocent nor childish. "I like being here with you," she said, and I said, "I'm glad," and she said, "so am I," regarding me with a soft smile before she looked back at the ceiling. "Cary and I used to sleep together sometimes at the lake," she said, "that was the happiest time. I felt safe with him. I wish it had stayed like that," and I said, "why didn't it?" and she said, "you know why," and I said, "no, I don't," and she said, "he wanted to fuck me," and I said, "and you let him," and she said, "yes, I wanted it, too, I guess. But that's what ruined it."

She turned and looked at me and said, "is that what you want, A.?" and I said, "don't play games, Jane," and she said, "I'm not—I don't know, truly. Maybe it's naive, but I keep thinking I can have a friend, a boy, who likes me without wanting me— is that dumb?" and I said, "I don't know, I guess not." She searched my face with a sorrowful expression and said, "is it you, A.? can be we like that?" I wanted to say yes, or maybe, but instead I looked up at the ceiling and said, "I don't think so, Jane." I felt the distance soar between us, and finally I turned to her and said, "I'm sorry." Her eyes were wet and clear in the soft lamp light, fully turned on me, and she said, "I guess I knew that anyway. Maybe I was teasing you." There was nothing teasing in her expression then. I just drank in that look and she said, "I think that's what I wanted you to say," and turned her face back up.

Happiness or sorrow, I didn't know, but only that I wanted to touch her then, very badly, but I was paralyzed by my own tenderness. Something raced inside me as I asked, "do you?" "Do I what?" Jane asked, and I said, "do you ever think of me that way?" and she said, "I try not to think about it at all," not looking at me. I sank back on the pillow feeling a deep ache through my whole being, and then she turned to me and said, "but sometimes I do anyway," and the hope surged back, more painful than the despair that had preceded it.

We lay there casting soulful longing gazes at one another, eighteen years old again, and Jane sought my hand and squeezed it. "I think I could fall in love with you, if things were different," I said, and she studied me deeply before she answered, "but they aren't, A." I took that as an answer in accordance with my expectation—it seemed so hopeless, and so final—and then to my surprise she rolled toward me and blinked into my eyes, her own vulnerable and questioning before she closed them and pressed her lips to mine. I simply watched without responding, and she drew back hurt, and then I put my hand behind her neck and pulled her to me. I tried to kiss her deeply, putting everything I felt into it the way I'd done with Morgan, but Jane was shy and slowed me down to gentle sips.

That guidance was the thing I always remembered about that kiss, our first, not denying me but expressing the terms of its consent. Jane didn't take my tongue or give me hers, though her lips opened to an underlying wetness, and I smelled the toothpaste freshness of her breath and tasted the deeper and more complicated freshness of her mouth beneath it. There was something clean and chaste in her address that made its sexuality more intense, and I discovered with amazement that the practiced voluptuousness of Morgan's kiss was nothing in comparison. Jane's kiss had a purpose in it, something I'd never felt before, controlled and working toward a destination beyond the kiss itself, and there wasn't any hurry in arriving. I grew hard, but without the edge of greedy lust which was the only sauce I'd known. Rather, it was like my soul was filled with something clean and light and sparkling, and by the end of it I was lost and didn't care.

We lay gazing into one another's eyes for a long time, and I said, "why did you do that?" and she smiled and said softly, "somebody had to, and it was obvious it wasn't going to be you," and I said, "are you sure somebody had to?" and she said, "do you work at it, or does it come naturally?" and I said, "what?" and she said, "mental retardation." I laughed without offense and she said, "for someone who's supposed to be so smart, you're so damn slow, A.," and I said, "it was a nice kiss," and she smiled, her eyes shining, and said, "I was there, too—remember?"

"What about Cary?" I said quietly, and she said, "what about him? if you need Cary's permission to kiss me, call him up, or wait till he comes down," and I said, "he'd never give it," and she said, "you never know until you ask," and I said, "I know," pretty certain that I did, and she said, "then I don't know what to tell you, honey," and I said, "what about you? doesn't it bother you?" and she frowned and said, "yes, some, but I can't help it, A. It's none of Cary's business. I love him and I don't want to hurt him, but I do already—I know I do—and he hurts me, but I can't run my life on that. I don't think you can either," and I said, "but he's my friend," and she regarded me sadly and said, "then maybe I should go," and I said, "don't, I don't want you to," and she said, "you're sure?" and I said, "we'll just sleep?" and she laughed and said, "don't get ahead of yourself, A. I told you—I don't do it on the first date," and I said, "so is this a date?" and she made a face and said, "it doesn't feel much like one, does it?" and I said, "what does it feel like?" and she said, "something else," and reached over me turning off the light. Laying her arm across my chest, she snuggled into my shoulder. I thought the beating of my heart would keep her up, but it didn't—in a few minutes she was out. I whispered her name to make sure, and when she didn't answer, I lifted her arm and got up. In the kitchen I opened another beer and went out on the porch.

With Jane beside me it was one thing, but alone it was something else and I felt deeply troubled, wrong with myself, though in another way I was so at ease and happy because I knew I'd wanted it for a long time, since that first night at Jimbo's, perhaps since that first day at the lake when we had tripped. It seemed wrong and dangerous to want her, but the wanting was so much stronger, and it was just a kiss, it was still retrievable—that's what I told myself. This much could be a secret Cary never had to know—I could keep it and still feel right with him. This much just seemed flirting at the edge of a destruction—a trespass, not a sin or a betrayal of the friendship. I knew I was lying to myself, but it was just a white lie, and I consented to it for that moment so I could hold the other thing a little longer, the savor of Jane's kiss which I could still taste on my lips, reawakened by the beer which had her in it. Just for tonight, just until this beer was finished—that seemed permissible. And knowing the decision I would make tomorrow, I felt reassured and strong in my conviction, calm. It was like the hunt, a provisional consent with the determination of rejecting later, then each step as it came, deeper and deeper into the woods, deciding nothing till the decision was made for me.

Eighteen

A.

The next day at work Morgan came down to my stand with a glass of iced tea. As she handed it to me her eyes were full of things that we weren't ever going to broach, much less attempt to settle. "I just got back from driving Cleanth to the airport," she said, "he's going into a clinic in Charleston," and I said, "how is he?" surprised, and she said, "the same," and I said, "he went voluntarily?" and she said, "more or less—I told him I was going to leave if he didn't. He knows he needs it anyway. He's got to break the cycle. Once he gets off the toot and gets his lithium levels adjusted, he'll be fine—that and a little rest," and I said, "how long will he be gone?" and she said, "two or three weeks, probably." I looked at her and said, "how are you, Morgan?" and she shrugged and said, "I don't know," and I said, "you look happier," because she did—or at least relieved—and she said, "I am—for now. We'll see about the rest."

After our chaste night in bed together, I didn't see Jane or speak to her for three days till she showed up on the beach that Thursday afternoon. Putting her flip-flops on the bathhouse seat, she waved and pulled her sundress off over her head and ran down to the water and dove. I watched her slow easy crawl and then she stood up on the bar, waving again, before racing out through the second line of breakers. Back on the beach, she fetched her towel and stepped into her flip-flops, drying off as she walked over.

"You heard Cleanth's in the hospital?" I asked, and Jane said,

"Morgan told me." Her eyes were somber. "You talked to her?" I asked, and Jane nodded and held up her paycheck. "I just quit," she said, "I couldn't stay," and I said, "what are you going to do?" and she said, "I got another job," and I said, "where?" and she said, "guess?" blandly, and I said, "no—the Double Stack?" She allowed herself a grudging smile and said, "I started this morning. I just told Morgan," and I said, "what did she say?" and Jane said, "she was very nice, but she didn't ask me to stay." She shrugged it off.

"How are the tips?" I asked, changing the subject, and Jane said, "not too great, but that's okay. Mr. Vincent is a sweet-heart. He asked me what I'd like to eat this morning and I told him Special K, but he said, no, I needed a balanced breakfast—he fixed me eggs and grits and toast and orange juice. I'll prob-ably get fat," and because she'd livened up I said, "a little more wouldn't hurt you," and she said, "a little more *what*, A.?" I saw a save was in order, but I didn't want to pursue that line of conversation any further so I said, "Cary's coming in tomorrow night—do you still want to go?" and she said, "what time?" and I said, "eight o'clock," and she said, "can you pick me up?" and I said, "I'm leaving straight from here—I'll see you around six," and she said, "bye," draping the towel around her shoulders as she walked off.

It was twilight as we drove. Pig accompanied us, sitting on Jane's lap with his tongue flying out behind him like a pennant. From the observation deck, we watched the plane land and taxi to the gate and met Cary coming up the ramp. He was wearing his red Lacoste and he had a new short haircut that made his ears stand out. His face was pink, a little burned by first expo-sure to the sun, but he looked healthy. A sheen of fond moistness appeared in his eyes when he saw us above a clear frank grin, and the overwhelming impression was one of freshness. That made Cary seem different somehow—not different from him-self, but different from both Jane and me, who'd had the fresh-ness seasoned out of us. I stood outside the scene, outside myself, and saw the contrast—Jane and I like two dark Indians, still and cautious, watchful, meeting the greenhorn white boy at the last outpost of civilization before guiding him into the woods, and I felt sorry for him, and removed from him by my own sympathy.

Struggling against that feeling, I said, "what happened to your hair, man?" and he slicked his hand along the side and said, "it sucks, doesn't it?" and I laughed and said, "don't be modest," and he said, "Daddy's barber did it—he's been coming to the house. I didn't get much say in it," and I said, "I thought I noticed a resemblance—T.O., Jr.," taking great pleasure in riding him, trying to find my way back to the rapport that way, and Jane said, "I think it looks nice, Cary," and he blushed and looked at her for the first time a little diffidently, and I said, "especially the ears, spud—you should try a wad of Double Bubble to hold them down," and he turned to me and said, "it's good to see you, A. hole," and I said, "likewise, Drop," and he held his hand out as I held mine and we slapped them together shaking strongly, warmly, just this side of testing, and I felt him then and was glad.

Dropping his shoulder bag, Cary swept Jane off the ground and swung her around. Her eyes met mine across his shoulder, and her expression seemed a little lost before she closed them, like someone making a hard wish. I knew what that wish was— it was for all of us—that we could get through this and be easy and natural and happy with each other without causing harm, because that was my wish, too.

I picked up Cary's bag and started walking down the concourse ahead of them, and he said, "so tell me, what the hell's been going on?" and the one thing of consequence—Jane's kiss—sprang instantly to mind. I became aware of her thoughts as though a telepathic link had opened, joining us in a guilty complicity from which Cary was excluded, how everything he said would have a double meaning, his light questions and our light answers, joining the three of us in a surface equilibrium, while underneath Jane and I swam in the subtext alone, together. I hadn't anticipated that—that Cary's presence, rather than separating Jane and me, would bring us closer than we'd been before he came.

"Jane and I have something to tell you, spud," I said, walking backwards through the automatic doors. "What?" he said, breaking off with Jane, who flashed me a startled look, and I grinned thinking I was being clever and said, "we've conceived a child." Cary glanced at Jane, and she said, "this is news to me," as a deep flush spread across her cheeks, and I said, "immaculately, of course," hurrying it on, not having anticipated that result and realizing belatedly that the joke, not good to start with, was getting out of hand. I saw something start to dawn in Cary's eyes, and I said, still grinning, but forcing it, "his name is Pig and he's in the Jeep—I wanted you to be prepared." Jane smiled frozenly and Cary stood waiting for the punchline till she took his arm and started walking. "It's a dog," she said, blustering through, exposed but admitting nothing—not to him, and not to me—and Cary said, "you got a dog?" as that vague troubled dawn dispersed, and I said, "yeah, a grade A pound mutt—come on, I'll introduce you," turning around to hide my deep chagrin.

Pig raised his head from his paws, regarding us with mild reproach which changed to milder interest when Cary leaned across the seat to scratch his ears. "I see the family resemblance," Cary said to me, leaving off, and Pig sighed and dropped his head back to the floor as carelessly as though it were a brick. Jane slipped to the inside edge of the passenger seat, glaring at me with astonishment and fury as Cary ducked and slid into the remaining space. My eyes apologized with beggarly profusion but hers refused it coldly, and when Cary lifted her into his lap and said, "let's roll," she looked away without forgiving me.

I pulled off feeling miserable, and Cary said, in a tone of happy chatter, oblivious to the tension between Jane and me, "guess what?" answering before we had a chance to ask, "Cliff's in love," and Jane said, "what else is new?" and I said, "how's your dad?" Cary's expression fell and he punched the lighter as he tapped a Marlboro out of his pack and hung it on his lip. "How's my dad?" he repeated, like the vastness of the subject invited an unhappy wealth of entries. "Shit, y'all," he said with a suddenly earnest face, "let's don't talk about that, okay?" and I said, "sure, spud," and after a brief silence, Cary brought it up himself.

"Know what he did?" he said—I looked over—"the doctors told him he had to quit smoking, right? So about a week after the operation, he gets Ramsey to smuggle in a carton of Kents and a fifth of Seagram's 7. After the nurse turned off his lights Daddy sat there and smoked two packs and got shitfaced. The next morning when they found the butts he had a shit-fit and threw his breakfast tray against the wall. They called Mama and we went out there to try and calm him down."

"Jesus," I said, and Cary said, "you haven't even heard the good part yet, A. I stayed out in the hall at first, and I could hear Daddy yelling and Mama trying to settle him down. I went to the door and leaned against it and I heard Mama say, 'Tommy,

honey, you simply have to stop—that's what Dr. Malone says—
otherwise you're going to kill yourself.' You know what Daddy
said? 'Then I'd just rather die.' " Cary's expression mingled
anger, pain and disbelief. "Mama started crying and told him
not to say it, and he shouted at her, 'goddamnit, woman, I ain't
joking—you can't just change everything and be somebody else
the way they want. If you can't have any decent comfort in your
life and keep on living like you're use to, then, damn it to hell,
it just ain't worth it.' "

Cary's mimicry of T.O.'s rougher idiom was eerily perfect—
even his voice changed. More than the story itself, his vehe-
mence and total absorption were disturbing. "Then I went in to
see him," Cary continued, "and the first thing he said to me
was, 'why ain't you at work, boy?' I told him I'd just dropped
by to see how he was doing and was going right back. Mama
had stepped out of the room, and so help me God, A., I saw
him eyeing the pack of Marlboros in my pocket. 'Gimme a
cigarette, Cary,' he said, and I said, 'I can't, Daddy, you know
you're not supposed to smoke.' Daddy stared off in space with
his eyes all red and teary and said, 'my own damn son won't
even give his daddy one little cigarette. I done a lot for you,
boy,' and I said, 'it's because I love you, Daddy, you know that,'
and he laughed and said, 'shit, what kind of love is that? What
if every time you asked me for something—like that bow and
arrow set, or a car or a boat to haul your butt around—what if I
told you, "no, boy, you might hurt yourself, it's because I love
you," what the hell would you have thought? I'll tell you what,
you'd of thought I didn't love you worth a damn. But I never
did, did I, son? There won't never a time I can remember that
you asked for something that you didn't get it, and all I'm asking
is one cigarette. I ain't a child, son, you can't treat a grown man
like a child, 'specially when it's your daddy asking.' And you
know what I did, A.?"

Cary's eyes were dead on me, not Jane, but me—I kept mine
on the road. "I gave him the goddamned cigarette," Cary said,
"it didn't even shame him, he just said, 'thanks, boy, I know
you love me now,' and struck a match." At that moment the
Jeep lighter popped, and Cary stared at his own cigarette, smiling with bitter amusement. His hands trembled as he lit it.
"That's how T.O. is," he said as he inhaled, "but I don't want
to talk about it." His laugh broke the tension. "Are you all
right?" Jane asked, and he said, "yeah, what the hey. Pull over

there, A." He pointed to a convenience store ahead and said, "let's crack some cold ones. I could use it."

He went in to buy the six-pack, and Jane said, "don't make him talk about it if he doesn't want to," and I said, "I didn't make him, Jane." I looked at her and she was clearly still furious with me. "Did you lose your mind back there, or what?" she asked, and I said, "I meant it as a joke," and she said, "a joke?" and I said, "I know, I'm sorry," and she said, "I didn't appreciate it, A., not at all." She turned away and the light thrown from the store window touched her softly through the windshield. "I almost wish he wasn't here," I whispered, "I wish we were alone." It seemed a terrible betrayal, and I didn't want to be alone in it, but Jane left me there, and I felt the pang of losing something I didn't have and had refused myself permission even to want. But I did want her—permission made no difference. It was like the moment I decided to track the wounded boar, when to stay had seemed the path to nothingness and nowhere, and to go, the path to unknown life.

Cary came back with the beer, and the first thing he said was, "so how's what's-his-face?" as he took a casual sip. The great stillness fell and I backed up, grateful to avert my eyes. I wanted to save Jane, to throw my coat across the puddle and perhaps make it up to her that way, but I had no coat. "Cleanth," Jane said, "I'm not seeing him anymore, Cary," and he said, "you're kidding? what happened?"

Jane told him the story of what had happened in Corolla. She told it quietly, simply and with dignity, though I could hear her pride smarting through her words. It was very brief. She didn't lie about anything, though she left out much. Perhaps those exclusions made it a lie, but it felt honest because she didn't spare herself, or lower herself either. She spared me though. She didn't give me away as I'd done her, unwittingly, before. I was only there as the friendly chauffeur who'd brought her home, a minor role in which I came off almost gallantly, and this consideration of my feelings was also a punishment, by exclusion. Really, I felt the story was for me, and the point was not what was said, but what was omitted, which only she and I knew. My heart ached, listening. She seemed very grown-up.

"So it's over?" Cary said, drawing what was, for him, the main conclusion. Jane answered with a nod. He didn't gloat. He seemed startled, perhaps even a little frightened by the possibilities this opened up. It was so clear what it meant to him.

"So what did you and Cliff do in Charlottesville?" Jane asked, changing the subject, and the moment became something else.

All the way home they chatted, catching up, finally moving on to jokes and easy laughter. I was silent outwardly, but my thoughts echoed like the carom of a bouncing ball on the floor of an empty gym, so loud I was almost sure that they could hear them—Jane, at least, because they were all of her, and for her. When we finally saw the Wright Memorial above the blinking red light on the Kill Devil Hills water tower, Jane said, "I hate to be a poop, but I think you better drop me off at my house, A.," and Cary said, "come on, Jane," and she said, "I have to get up at five, but I'll be off at two. I'll come over tomorrow afternoon and we'll do something fun," and he said, "like what?" pouting, and she said, "we'll think of something," and he grinned and said, "I already did," and she punched him in the arm in protest, though whether at the suggestion itself, or its publicness, I didn't know. They seemed like lovers arranging a rendezvous and I was the odd wheel. I hadn't anticipated being jealous, but I was. Even worse, I hadn't counted on the fact that Jane might still be open to an advance from Cary. The possibility made me sick. I hadn't anticipated any of it.

When I pulled up beside her house, Jane said, "goodnight, A.," in a tone that could have meant anything. She got out and Cary turned to me with an eager face like a sub the coach has nodded to. "Hold on a minute, spud," he said, and went into the game, and I stayed on the bench, grudging him his chance.

I watched them in the rearview mirror, Cary gesturing animatedly while Jane listened with a bland wise face. She shook her head, and he shrugged, his hands thrown wide, and she pointed to the Jeep commandingly and he kissed her on the lips. When he climbed in beside me his face was radiant and beautiful—her shimmer clung to him, or maybe it was Cary's own. He seemed so handsome and innocent and good I didn't see how Jane could help but fall in love with him.

In comparison, I felt like a twisted bitter dwarf. But for just a moment I remembered something from long ago, and it was like the tolling of the bell I'd heard that day in the woods, only a different member of the carillon, a clear ethereal soprano, and for that one moment I wanted him to win. It was one of only two clear emotions I remembered from that whole confusing time, and it made me feel like a human being again, like a man and a good friend who deserved a good friend's love and his esteem. But the other was my love for Jane, two right and joyous things poised against each other and irreconcilable forever. But for that moment and many hours afterward, into the next day, I thought I could give the victory to him—the air tasted clearer— and I was so blind and drunk with my self-sacrificial impulse it never even dawned on me that Cary had already lost, because Jane's choice wasn't mine to give.

The minute we pulled off Cary said, "Jane's free," with a wondering elated face, like he still couldn't quite believe it. Then suddenly he laughed and slapped his thigh, "hot damn," he said, "now's my chance, give me five on that one, spud." I obliged, trying to match his enthusiasm.

Back at the cottage, we put his things in his room and went out on the east porch and opened two fresh beers, sipping them in silence till he said, "it's good to be here, A., I appreciate you asking me," and I said, "you don't even have to say it, spud," and he said, "I know, I just wanted to," and I found that it was possible to be with him without the thought of Jane intruding. That disturbance receded to a whisper like the waves as they ebbed back, a low-grade irritation within a larger spreading comfort, which I'd almost forgotten, a strong good thing whose nature was expressed more in the pauses between words than in the words themselves. I told him about Morgan, whom I'd never mentioned till then, and he listened with a grave expression and tried to be sympathetic. I think he interpreted my casualness about it as stoicism. We moved on to the subject of our friends— he told me who was doing what with whom, who was going to college where, who wasn't. A girl I knew slightly had gotten pregnant, a boy I didn't was going to marry her. We talked a little more about T.O. "He's scared, A.," Cary told me, "he doesn't want to die."

After my voyage in outer space with Cleanth—after the drugs, the cars, the planes, the guns, all the perks of corrupt knowl- edge—it felt good to be back on solid ground, squinching my toes in the dirt of a little hometown gossip. But there was still a thread of sadness—perhaps it was the yellow light that fell on Cary through the window from inside the house. "Killdeer," he said, summing it all up as he pulled the pop-top of a second beer, and I said, "yeah, Killdeer—it's the shithole of the uni- verse, isn't it?" and Cary grinned and said, "you came from it," and I said, "true, but I was screaming all the way," grinning back. Cary laughed easily and we slapped five. "It's not that bad, A.," he said, "it's just like any other town."

Cary was quiet for a while, drinking and staring out into the darkness. Then he said, "this summer has been strange, being home," and I said, "yeah, it's been pretty strange down here, too," and he said, "you remember Bruno, don't you?" and I said, "Bruno Estevez? sure, I remember him." He was one of Cary's kick-ass friends I'd never liked—he'd given me a black eye one time in elementary school. "We've been hanging out some," Cary said, "playing softball, you know. Bruno's been going out with this girl named Tina Blake, who's sewing seams on the line at Dixie Bag. Tina wanted to set me up with this friend of hers, Wanda Brame," and I said, "Wanda Jo?" He nodded, and I said, "hell, Cary, I remember her, she was in sixth grade with us. She had big . . ." I cupped my hands in front of my chest, and Cary said, "you should see them now." I opened my eyes wide, and he laughed a little nervously and sipped his beer. "Well, I wasn't all that interested," he said, "because . . . well, you know why, because of Jane. But Tina kept after Bruno, and Bruno kept after me—he said all she wanted was a good time anyway, but I didn't really believe him, because, Tina, man, all she thinks about is getting married. But, anyway, one weekend they all came to the lake. I was going to grill some chicken, but they'd hardly walked through the door before Bruno was in the back bedroom with Tina, and there I was with Wanda Jo listening to the bedsprings creaking and Tina's moans. It was pretty funny in a horrible sort of way, though you could only appreciate the humor later, but Wanda Jo didn't seem too disturbed by it at all, like this was more or less what you expected when people got together.

"I put on an album to drown them out and got her a beer. 'I think you can tell a lot about a person by the beer they drink,' she said, and I said, 'really?' and she said, 'Miller's distinguished'—that's what I'd handed her—'Bud's red,' and she'd done her hair, A. It was all bouffed up and sprayed, and she had on this really low-cut deal with about four inches of cleavage showing, and as we started talking she moved them around in this way so that I couldn't help but look at them. She brushed them against me as though by accident, but after the second or third time I knew it wasn't. She kept spreading her fingers out and looking at her nails, and finally she saw me watching her and she said, 'do you like this color? it's new,' and she told me all about it, how much it cost, and how the girl at the cosmetic counter at Belk's had recommended it, and how it was worth the extra money to get the best.

"I tried to be nice to her. She wasn't even that bad-looking, but I kept thinking about Jane—Wanda Jo had these big old thighs—and it was like the difference between a hippopotamus and a gazelle, and finally she looked at me and said, 'we can do it if you want to, I won't hold you up to nothing,' and I can't tell you why, A., I didn't even want to, but I took her to the bedroom and we did it. We did it twice, and I liked it. She was really . . . I don't know, she had a lot of spirit, but afterwards I felt like such a heel.

"When we came out, Tina looked at us like the engagement was all planned and said, 'I got to go, hon, but you give him your number,' and Wanda Jo said, 'that's okay,' and Tina stared at her like she was crazy and said, 'no, it ain't okay, girl. You just write it down. He wants it, don't you, Cary?' and Wanda Jo said, 'you don't have to call me, but I'll write it down in case you want to,' and she scrawled it on a pad and handed it to me, and as I walked them out Bruno winked at me and said, 'I told you,' and they drove off and I stood there with that piece of paper in my hand and read it—"Wanda Jo Brame" it said in these big round cursive letters like fourth grade, and underneath the number, a little heart."

Cary stopped and looked away. "It was just a one-night stand," he said, "I didn't force myself on her, but I felt so bad, A., like I'd taken advantage of her, and you know what it was? you know what was wrong with it?" and I said, "what?" and he said, "I looked down on her, A., she was a perfectly nice girl, and I looked down on her. I didn't mean to, but I did." He shook his head. "And the thing about it is, I know exactly how she felt, A., I really do. One of the young guys from the law office across the street will come in the cafeteria to pick up a box lunch. He'll be in a suit, and I'll be standing there in my apron, and he'll look at me, A., and there'll just be this little coolness in his eyes, this thing that just puts you to death," and I said, "fuck 'em, Cary, you're better than any of them," and he said fiercely, "I don't give them jack, A., you know I don't," and I said, "damn straight," and he said, "but the thing about it is, most of them aren't even aware they're doing it. They aren't being intentionally cruel. Even the older guys that know me. They come in and clap me on the back, they're friendly, they want to know how Daddy's doing and when he'll be back, and they ask me for some extra biscuits or another wing, but I'm the chicken man to them, A. I know it's bullshit, but it's out there, it's a real thing, and I never really felt it till this summer,'' and I said, ''I've felt it, too, Cary,'' He gave me a reproachful look, and I said, ''I have, man, when we left Killdeer I saw those looks. I saw it at Keane. Hell, Cary, there were guys up there who thought I was some hick cracker who lived in a shotgun shack and took a shit in a hole in the floor. They thought I wrestled gaters and lynched niggers in my spare time,'' and Cary said quietly, ''but you knew it wasn't true, A.,'' and there was something old and knowing in his eyes which I'd never seen there before.

It took me back, but then I said, ''the other thing, too, spud. There were guys at school that came from real big-time money and big-time names and knew it, and you know something, man, most of them were pussies. Some of them couldn't even run, Cary, they really couldn't—nobody ever taught them. Having it can cripple you, too, spud, just as much as not having it—more. At least not having it gives you something to fight for,'' and he said, ''yeah, I know, A., I didn't mean to piss you off,'' and I said, ''I'm not pissed off,'' only realizing then that I was being defensive and that nothing I could say could assuage the truth of his essential point. ''I just wonder sometimes,'' he said, and I said, ''what?'' brusquely, and he said, ''Jane . . .'' and I said, ''no way, Cary, that's total bullshit, she loves you, man,'' and he said, ''yeah, she loves me, but she's down here and I'm in Killdeer,'' and I said, ''who's fault is that?'' and he said, ''all I'm saying, A., is I don't think I'm a bad person—I may not be great, but I care, and I did it to Wanda Jo. Sometimes I do it to my own father. Good people do it, too, A.,'' and he gave me a deep, resigned and very pointed look, and I said, ''what?'' feeling myself go red in the face, and he shook his head and said, ''forget it,'' and started to turn away, but I sat forward and gripped his arm, pulling him around. ''You piece of shit,'' I said, ''look me in the eyes and tell me I ever judged you,'' and he said, ''no, A., you never did, but you've felt sorry for me, like right now,'' and I said, ''sorry enough to kick your red hairy tail,'' and he laughed and said, ''it's funny though, isn't it? if things had been different, you could have been the suit and I could have been the chicken man to you, we could have been enemies,'' and I said, ''I am your enemy, you fuck, the best goddamn enemy you'll ever have,'' and he smiled and said, ''yeah, I love you, too, spud,'' as the thought of Jane dropped down on me like a ton of bricks.

I almost told him there. I took a heavy swallow, feeling my underarms begin to trickle, but suddenly he turned to me with a big grin and said, ''she's free, fucking A,'' and I collapsed. ''I'm going to turn in, Cary,'' I said, feeling restless and disgruntled, ''I've got to get up early,'' and he smiled and said, ''I don't, I think I'll sit up a while,'' and I said, ''there's more beer in the fridge,'' and he said, ''thanks, spud—it's good to see you,'' and I said, ''yeah, man, same here—I'll be back around five tomorrow. We'll eat here and then go out and catch the fireworks,'' and he said, ''sounds good,'' and I left him and went off to bed.

Fucking A.

Nineteen

Cary's door was closed when I got up, so I made a pot of coffee and left it warming for him and drove to work. The beach was packed, not only with hotel guests but with day-trippers down from Virginia for the Fourth, and I was too busy working to give much thought to other matters. But by one o'clock I'd rented out every umbrella, chair and raft I had and things slowed down. Remembering that Jane was getting off at two, I kept looking at my watch with growing anxiety, and as the hour came something happened to me. I caught the clearest flash of Jane in her mother's Olds with her arm straight out the window resting on the frame, wrist bent, the way she drove, headed toward the cottage. I saw her wheel into the driveway, get out, Cary greeting her, sweeping her off her feet again and swinging her around. I saw the two of them climbing the steps, their arms around each other's waists, I saw them open the screen door and go inside, and then the curtain closed across the stage and the play became invisible to me, but I knew it was still running.

I knew they were alone, together, that they'd been lovers, that Cary wanted her and was attractive and persuasive, most of all I knew he was in need and that Jane loved him and cared for him, and even if she didn't think she wanted him the heart was unpredictable and anything could change—in my experience the worse the end the more likely it would come about—and Jane was none too shy of bedding down and owed me absolutely nothing in that way and Cary even less, and finally, most revealingly, I realized I didn't want it to happen, and the dream of wanting Cary to win dispersed as I woke up. Because in my mind that victory had been like the last act in a comedy, the wedding scene, where it ends, and I hadn't counted on observing the consummation from behind a tapestry in the bedroom in the role of jilted rival. For the rest of the afternoon I sat there feeling green and sick and catching sweaty flickers of the two of them in bed.

When I arrived, Cary was in the driveway basting chicken with a long-handled brush, and Jane was upstairs in the kitchen washing lettuce. Catching her alone, I whispered, though Cary wasn't within hearing, "I'm sorry about last night," and she said, "you should be, A." and I said, "do you hate me?" and she let me squirm a moment before she said, "no, I don't hate you," with a weary smile, and I said, "but?" because I thought her tone implied one, and she said, "I want to trust you, A.," and I said, "don't you?" and she sighed and said, "I feel confused," and my voice trembled as I said, "about Cary?" and she said, "about you—I don't like this feeling, A.," and I said, "I'm confused, too—I thought about you all afternoon. I kept seeing pictures of you with Cary," and she said, "oh, A.," almost with pity, as her eyes melted and went to a new depth. She put the lettuce down and came around the island, putting her hands on my shoulders and staring in my eyes with a pained expression. She said, "I don't want Cary, A.," and I said, "I don't want it either," and her gaze turned quizzical as she said, "what do you want?" and I leaned down and kissed her, circling her waist and drawing her close, which was my answer.

Everything receded and it all seemed simple for a moment—being one place, wanting one thing, there and having it, before she pushed me back and said, "we can't do this, A.," and I said, "so tell me how to stop," and she said, "think about Cary down there cooking dinner," and I just stared at her as though she'd shot me. Her eyes turned pleading as she said, "it isn't right, A.—not like this," and then the screen door slammed and Cary called out, "let's eat," in a jolly voice, and we separated quickly, taking refuge in a frantic busyness.

Dinner was wretched. Cary carried the whole thing—his spirits had risen. He was up, a little tipsy, happy, and completely blind. I tried not to look at Jane, afraid of what might happen. Yet there were still great feasts of loving sorrowful gazing each time he excused himself to get more beers or to go to the bathroom. She was hurting, too, but I couldn't tell if her pain was that of closure or of opening. Afterwards we went to the amusement park at Camelot Pier to see the fireworks. It was still an hour before dark, and we killed the time taking rides and throwing baseballs at a target where the clown sat in a wire cage wearing an orange fright wig and a red rubber nose. Cary knocked him in the water three times and won a large stuffed poodle which he gave to Jane and she lugged it around like Pollyanna in hell.

There was something infernal about it, the whole park an enormous contraption built for fun and pleasure, but no one having it, just some crude unwholesome substitute. All the smiles seemed fabricated, the enthusiasm fake and sinister like the barker's spiels and promises. I was in the sort of mood when the whole thing seems crystal clear, not just a lens you're viewing through in the moment, but the truth, the way it really is, and you just know there's something deeply wrong and fucked up in the world. The Tilt-A-Whirl gave me no thrill at all, it just brought the barbecue sauce back up from dinner on a whiff of beer and gastric acid. Then I stood there with the poodle as Jane and Cary climbed into the little plastic boat, drawing their legs up as they floated down the canal into the smiling mouth of an enormous demented cherub, entering the Tunnel of Love. That just seemed to sum it up—irony didn't even come close to what I felt.

"Who wants cotton candy?" Cary asked, elated as they came out. I shook my head, and Jane said, "I'll have a bite of yours," and he said, "you two go take another ride, I've got to take a whizz, I'll find you," and as he walked off I turned to Jane and said, "how about the Haunted House?" She didn't smile and I said, "don't you think it's appropriate—you and Cary in the Tunnel of Love and me and you in the Haunted House?" and she said, "it just sounds trite, A.—I'm not superstitious," and feeling reckless in my misery, I said, "let's do it then—bring Pierre and let's just go for it."

I bought our tickets and handed her the poodle, climbing in the car beside her. Waiting for the ride to start, she said, "I can't stand this, A.," and I said, "I can't either," and she said, "let's don't take this ride—I am superstitious," her face deeply earnest. I blinked at her and then turned to the guy and yelled, "wait!" He held the lever and we got out, and I was just as glad, because I was superstitious, too. "Don't you want your money back?" the guy asked, and I said, "keep it," as we stepped into the shadows between two trailers, coming together without hesitation or preliminaries in a fierce deep kiss.

When we disengaged, we didn't speak, just gazed deeply into one another's eyes. The fireworks were bursting overhead, bathing us in golden light whose beauty seemed mocking in some terrible fundamental way. I didn't know if I felt happy or destroyed. I started to lead her back, but she held my hand and wet her fingers in her mouth, wiping the lipstick from my cheek.

After the fireworks were over, we dropped Jane off and when we got back to the cottage, Cary said, "can I borrow the keys for a while?" and I said, "what's up?" and he said, "I'm going back to Jane's—I need some time alone with her." I just stared at him and handed them over, and he said, "thanks, spud," and left.

I stayed awake waiting for his return, listening for the granulated crunching of the tires over the loose sand in the driveway. I didn't think about the next step, or the moral repercussions, I just savored the sensation of what was happening, realizing with wonder that at the bottom of it all there was a sense of peace in the surrender, the first I'd felt in many years. There was a deep sadness in me, but an ease also, and I breathed to my lungs' full depth, aware only then that my breath had been constricted since before I could remember, as though I'd worn a leather cinch around my chest, only now the cinch had broken, and I had not expected love to feel like that. I'd thought about it, dreamed of it and tried to reason out its qualities lying on my bed alone at Keane. In my imagination it had always been an elation tinged with joy and happiness, but this was not like that at all—only an enormous fatefulness, a sense of peace, and most of all not wanting it to be any different. I'd only learned one thing, that I loved Jane, but that one thing was enough, forever, and the bell, the rich and mournful one I'd first heard that day in the wood, tolled again, resonating in my head and in my heart, through my whole body, and then I heard the tires and closed my eyes and fell asleep.

The next day when I got off I drove home and Jane and Cary were drinking margaritas on the porch. Jane had put her hat on Pig, and she lay in a reclining hammock chair with one foot up on the frame, laughing, slightly drunk, so languid and at ease, holding her glass on her stomach, the salt half eaten and a lipstick smear along the rim, one arm dangling toward the floor. As she looked at me her eyes were deep and moist and it was all for me, even the slight tremor in her lips, which was her fear I might not yet accept, but I already had.

The shimmer was there, a physical thing, like in a film when gauze is placed across the lens. It was like a haze of magic steam that brought out the freshness in her skin and dark-bright glintings in her churchglass eyes. It made her heart and every thought transparent in her face, like she was part of me and I was part of her. I don't know how Cary missed it.

He poured me a drink and then we piled into the Jeep, leaving Pig behind, and we drove back toward the airport through the long twilight, past fields waist-high with tobacco and cool shadowed glimpses of the sound. There was talk—Cary talked to me and I to him, he spoke to Jane and she replied, but Jane and I never said a word or even looked at one another, though her bare knees weren't three inches from my own, and I was aware of them, and of her unspoken thoughts, and she of mine, and that communication was so loud it drowned out all the rest.

At the gate Cary's eyes teared up a little as he said good-bye, shaking my hand and hugging me, kissing Jane, saying he'd enjoyed it and appreciated it and wouldn't leave at all if he could choose. I felt each thing he said, but it was all at a distance, like something through the wrong end of a telescope. The whole foreground was filled and charged with the buzz of heavy feeling between Jane and me, so that there was no room for him at all, and that gentle swirling buzz of feeling gently swirled him off down the ramp, without harshness or rancor, but with firmness, and then Jane took my hand. We walked outside and sank our fingers in the chain-link fence, still not looking at one another, but watching the lights blink on the wings as the plane taxied out and turned onto the runway. The turbines' roar increased to a shrill pitch and the jet lurched as it released speeding down the runway and then breasting up into the twilight with a slow deceptive grace, growing smaller and smaller until it disappeared.

We turned to one another then with a single impulse, the

feeling so intense we couldn't speak or breathe, and I put my
arms around her back and sank into her mouth, feeling her
press strongly back, the touch a cool delicious shock. We
kissed for twenty minutes, half an hour, I don't know how
long it was, but it was full dark when we finally separated,
trembling and sweating. I was harder than a wooden spline
on a ship's wheel, and I'd long since felt her wetness against
my bare thigh. "The sooner we leave, the sooner we get
home," I said, and she smiled a little shyly and put her arm
around my waist as I put mine around her shoulder, and we
walked back to the Jeep.

We only made it twenty miles. I reached over and slipped my
hand between her thighs which she spread slightly, kicking down
her underwear as she leaned her head back on the seat and held
the taped roll-bar with both hands. She moaned as I slipped my
finger into her. I'd hardly touched her when she came, pressing
my hand down hard with both of hers as it shuddered through
her. I drove with one hand and watched her face with enormous
wonder, the sweet furrow of troubled concentration as she closed
her eyes. Afterwards, she crossed her legs, imprisoning my
hand, and basked in it. Then she knelt down around the gear
stick, carefully unzipping my shorts and sinking her head into
my lap.

Further driving became dangerous. I pulled into the gravel lot
of a small motel, the vintage sort with separate cabins. The neon
sign said Moon-Glo, flashing orange and then blue. I cut the
engine outside the office and sat there, hesitating, until Jane
said, "what's the matter?" and I said, "I can't go in quite yet."
She laughed, and we sat there a few minutes longer, but there
was no improvement, so finally she said, "why don't I do it?"
and I said, "do you mind?" and she kissed me on the cheek
with a merry fondness and climbed out. "Here, take my wallet," I said, sticking it out the window, and she said, "no, I
want to treat." "Jane," I protested, waving it at her, and she
said, "nuh-uh," leaning forward teasingly with her hands behind her back. "Come on," I said, "you've got me at a disadvantage," and she said, "I like you there," and she skipped
backwards toward the office door, barefooted and disheveled as
a nymph.

Through the window I saw her sweeping her hair out of
her eyes as she leaned to sign the register. She was talking
to a heavy country woman who moved with a slow drugged

quality and did not seem quite human, like something in a waxworks. Jane came out and waved the key, shouting, "cabin twenty-one, down at the end," and I started the engine and met her there.

The room was small and poor and dim, but the walls were solid yellow pine and there were real curtains, somewhat yellowed, but tasteful, and they lent the place a quaint antique charm. The box springs creaked as Jane sat down, her hands folded in her lap as she smiled at me, shy and glowing. I slipped her dress off over her head and pushed her gently backwards, standing over her as I unzipped my shorts and let them drop. She lay with one leg propped up, leaning inward in languid self-concealment, but she didn't resist as I set it down.

I stood gazing at her, every inch of her, and she blushed but didn't turn her eyes from my face, following me as I lay down beside her, putting my hand in the small of her back and pulling her against me so that our bodies touched along their length. Feeling her breasts slide smoothly over the skin of my chest, cool and electric, and then press flat, I shuddered and closed my eyes, holding her until I felt her warmth come through. Then I rolled her over on her back, sinking my thigh between the two of hers and pressing my arms straight against the mattress so I could look at her.

Jane's eyes were closed, she almost seemed asleep, and like a somnambulist she slipped her hand between our stomachs, down and down until she found me, when she smiled and opened her eyes, guiding me toward her opening. Putting both hands on my ass, she pulled me into her and I let myself sink, but only head-deep. Her eyes questioned, but I smiled and said, "not yet," remembering Morgan's lesson and glad I'd learned it. Jane put one hand around my back and the other behind my neck, pulling herself up to kiss me, clinging till her weight sank us both, and then I closed my eyes and pushed inside, feeling the walls of her vagina cling with a resistance like dry silk and then slicken, remoistening with her own moisture which I spread behind me as I passed like a roller spreading paint along a wall, a long slow stroke, till I felt her bush crinkle and mat under mine as flesh pressed to flesh and bone to bone. I lay feeling the throb of my own pulse inside her, still pressing down as she pressed up, and when I withdrew it was all one glistening track.

I wanted to amaze her with my energy and prowess, but the

second time I entered her I knew it wasn't going to be that way. Feeling the sweet helpless ache, I closed my eyes and groaned as I felt myself spill, falling stars flaring across the screen of my closed lids, and I lay there as she held me, jetting spurt after spurt, and experiencing a deep chagrin and disappointment. "I'm sorry," I said, burying my head in her neck, not wanting to look at her, and she said, "shhh," and stroked my hair. I started to withdraw, but she said, "don't," and held me tight, and we remained like that for a few minutes.

I sighed and relaxed and breathed the smell of her neck, and I went into a state of dreaming though I never fell asleep. The sense of relaxation became an experience in itself, not passive or even still, but intense and active—my breathing deepened almost to panting—and it went from depth to depth, so that I lost the sense that we were having sex, or that Jane was separate from me, and finally I became unconscious of myself. When I opened my eyes again I felt like I'd awakened from a long sleep, and I was hard inside her. Jane's eyes were soft and happy like she'd known that it would be this way, and we began again. It went on and on, and there was never any sense of satiation or completion, no final stage where the journey was complete, we stopped still wanting one another but unable to go on.

Afterwards I lay there with my head on her chest, listening to her heartbeat, dazed and still, and I remember something golden in the room, some permutation of the shimmer, like falling stardust. "I knew it would be like that," she said softly. I raised my head to look at her—I didn't have to ask her what she meant. She stroked my cheek and I said, "I think I'm in love," wondering at it. Jane just smiled. "Are you?" I asked, and she said, "do you have to ask?" and I said, "yes," and she said, "you're so slow, A.," and kissed my cheek. "It's just so new," she said, lying back and pulling my head down on her chest, and I said, "does it feel new to you? it doesn't to me," and she said, "there's a lot we have to think about," and I said, "I know," and she said, "we have to tell him now, A.," looking at me again, her expression suddenly serious, and I said, "yes, I have to tell him, Jane," and she blinked and said, "yes, you do," and I said, "I don't want to think about that now," and she said, "no, I don't either," and I lay back on the pillows and she nestled her head into my shoulder, draping her arm across my chest.

When she was asleep, I reached over and set the alarm for four, knowing she had to work the breakfast shift, touched that she'd forgotten and pleased I could remember for her. It was just after midnight, a new day.

Twenty

A.

It was still dark when we left the Moon-Glo and the air was chilly. When the sun began to rise it glistened in the dew that drenched the grass and the green crops in the fields. Everything felt fresh and there was a sad sweet pang of autumn in the air. I drove Jane to the Double Stack and we made out for ten minutes in the parking lot until she broke away, saying, "I'll see you tonight?" I grinned and said, "unless you know how to hide pretty well," and she said, "you'll probably have forgotten all about me by then," and I said, "probably," and she said, "try not to?" I smiled and she said, "bye."

That day on the beach, though it was bright and sunny, there was a stiff northeaster blowing, twenty to thirty knots, sending in a heavy swell. I set out the orange flags and the Swimmer's Advisory sign, and almost no one went in off my beach. One young couple started to, but I talked them out of it, telling them about riptides and pointing out the one they were getting ready to step into, the funnel of darker water shooting backwards from the beach carrying an outgoing wave that broke against the incoming breakers. I set out my line of chairs, but no one rented, so I just climbed up in my stand and watched the massive sloppy swells. Whitecaps were breaking over the whole ocean, and they rolled across the bar, not even breaking but just crumbling down like demolished buildings, thundering and shaking the whole beach.

About ten o'clock I saw two guys in vests come down with

their boards. They were pretty far to the north, out of my territory, and normally you didn't have to worry about surfers anyway—they tended to be oceanwise, as a general rule—but no experienced surfer I knew would have gone out on a day like that, not because it was dangerous, though it was, but because there were no rides. It was just a lumbering formless slop. So I stood up and blew my whistle. It was useless—they couldn't even hear it—so I climbed down and started walking toward them, moderately irritated. They were down on their knees waxing their boards, and I guess they saw me coming, because long before I got there they'd velcroed on their leashes and run out, luging their boards over the water and gliding down on top of them as they began to paddle. They were nearing the bar by the time I got there, and I could see it was just two young kids, maybe fourteen or fifteen, one blond, one dark. I blew my whistle again and the dark-haired one looked back and shot me the finger, grinning, and I just stood there watching as they tried to cross the bar and get outside.

The blond kid made it just before the set came in, shooting up the wall of the first wave and disappearing behind it, safe. I saw him paddle out into blue water and sit up, sweeping back his hair. But the other one, the one who'd shot me the finger, got caught inside, and I watched him turtle over again and again, protecting himself with his board as those white oxygenated mountains fell on top of him. I waited till I saw him bob up like a slick black seal in the white foam, and he just stood there on the bar letting his board drift behind him, sinking under each wave, getting driven further and further back toward shore. I blew my whistle a third time and he looked back again, not grinning, and I waved him in, but the set had passed and in the lull he darted out, and I said to hell with it and started back toward my stand.

There was a ferocious southward littoral drift, so that by the time I got back to the Lost Colony they'd been swept down almost straight in front of me. They were getting nothing rides, standing up outside for a few seconds on the windbreak and riding ten or fifteen feet before the swells reswallowed their own foam and drove on toward the bar, which was too murderous to surf. Only the blond kid rode—I never saw the dark-haired one stand up. He'd start to catch one, paddling hard, then pull out every time, sitting up, and I could tell he didn't really want to ride—he was scared and faking it. I knew because I'd been there myself once upon a time, and I remembered what it was like to feel it lift you up and leave you tottering on that liquid mountaintop, then the momentum seizing you like some huge running animal, starting to slide as foam sizzled from your rails. I remembered staring down into the trough a hundred miles below and deciding this wave wasn't really all that great, the next one might be better.

They were starting to get separated though. Every time the dark-haired kid pulled out, his approach brought him a little further in toward shore, while his friend moved laterally, keeping a more constant distance. And when the set came in the dark-haired kid got caught again. I saw it all happen. The first wave reared over him as he pointed toward shore, prepared to paddle. He made two halfhearted strokes before he realized it was too late, and then he sat up, his legs straddling the board— he seemed to be moving backwards at great speed, but it was the wave coming under him, lifting him like the cow catcher on a barreling locomotive. The lip cast its shadow over him and then came down like an avalanche, tipping him forward like an upended hourglass, and as the air turned white around him, the last thing I saw was him diving head first toward the bar, the board still between his legs, still as a statue, as the whole wave came down hard on top of him.

I stood up feeling very lonesome, shading my eyes with my hand as I looked out, waiting for his head to show out of the foam. It didn't. The board just danced up like a wet bean squeezed between two fingers, spinning with a beautiful slow grace until it jerked against the leash and zinged back down, vanishing beneath the still-collapsing rubble.

His friend, the blond, had missed the wipe-out, but he'd turned in, stretching up off his board, searching for his buddy, and when he saw me standing I felt fear shock him across that distance and ricochet back to me, and in the brief lull, even as the second wave began to mount, I saw the dark kid's board again, drifting aimlessly, and the sickening wallow of the wetsuit as it rolled and sank. I leapt down and started sprinting, and before I dove I saw the board spin up again in slow motion as the second wave thundered down.

Once I was in the water I was almost blind. I swam hard for the bar, ducking under the shorebreak, but the current was so strong I felt like I was moving backwards. I went underwater and started pushing off the bottom, making arcing dives like a porpoise, and finally I felt the sand begin to tilt up under my feet and I waded uphill against the current. I saw the board floating skeg-up in front of me and as I struggled toward it a body shot up screaming, "Mikey! Mikey!" but it was the other boy, the blond. He was coughing and shivering and his eyes were wild and scared, and he said, "I can't find him, man, I just saw him but I lost him," and I said, "listen," gripping his shoulders firmly, "go in, you hear me?" and he said, "I can't, he's my brother, man, my kid brother. I got to find him, my dad's going to kill me," and I said, "I'll find him," and he said, "you got to, man," and I said, "I will—now go to the hotel and call the beach service, ask for Mick. If he isn't there, tell them to radio. Tell him to call an ambulance and get down here. It's the Lost Colony, you got that?" and he nodded, his teeth chattering and his lips blue, and then we both looked up as a wave mounted overhead, and we ducked under, embracing, and when we came back up, I said, "now go, and hurry," and he said, "you got to save him, man," almost in tears as he climbed on his board and started paddling.

Standing up in the settling foam, I scanned the water and saw the second board a hundred yards south and started swimming with the current behind me this time. It was inside the bar now in calmer water, just drifting and sliding, but I could see it tugging, too, like a drifting boat pulling its anchor. When I reached it, I took a breath and flipped under, following the leash, which wasn't even a real one, just a piece of nylon rope tied through the skeg hole. I opened my eyes but I could see nothing, just feel the stinging of the salt. The water was no more than eight feet deep, but as I reached the bottom I could feel the pressure in my ears, and it was strangely silent there after the surface din, but then I heard something like a wind, a whoosh with a faint crackling, which was the sand as the current moved across it. I pulled hand over hand until I felt a painful jarring blow across my mouth, which must have been his heel, then his whole body tangled me and I felt him clutch.

Panicking, I pushed him off and shot up to the surface, still holding the rope, hacking out a lungful of water. Clutching the surfboard, I tried to haul him up, desperately aware of the clock ticking toward brain damage. He came up feet first, and I reached down and got my hand into the collar of his vest and tried to pull his head out. He rolled over on his back, his arms spread out, his face ashen and his dark hair swashed across his eyes like kelp. He wasn't breathing and I couldn't find a pulse in his neck, but there was still time. I was sure he wasn't dead. I lugged him up onto the board and pulled myself behind him, kicking and paddling with one arm while I held his head up by the hair with the other. There was blood on the board and I thought it was his until I saw a drop splash and realized it was coming from my mouth.

We were only thirty yards from shore by then, and when we came up in the swash I hoisted him across my hip and dragged him out of the water's reach, dropping him face down in the sand and bearing down hard on his ribs. Water squished out of his mouth and darkened in the sand, and then I rolled him over and worked a finger in his mouth, but he hadn't swallowed his tongue, so I pried his jaws apart and started CPR, holding his nose as I breathed into his mouth, then pressing his chest and listening against his sternum for his heart to kick back in. I was so tired I could feel the muscles burning in my abdomen, but then he groaned as a clear stream of water poured from the corner of his mouth, tinted with my blood. I pressed my lips to his and breathed again. "Wake up, you fucker, wake up," I said to him, but each time I released his head it lolled over sideways, and his eyes were open, staring back out at the ocean, and there was something like a silent scream in them, like he'd left a part of himself out there and was trying to call it back.

Yet he was still alive—I was so sure of it—and I kept blowing into him as the water turned to vomit that was cold but singed my lips like acid. A crowd was gathering, I could see their feet and feel their eyes on me, and I said, "stand back, stand the fuck back," as I heard another gurgling sigh. I breathed and pressed, breathed and pressed till I felt faint, and when the dizziness passed I started over. Each time the sigh grew clearer, and I was sure, so sure that I could bring him back. I must have worked on him for twenty minutes before I saw Mick kneel down and check for pulse, then lift the hair off the back of the boy's neck and press his finger into a dark bruise. He stood up out of my vision and then I felt his hand close firmly on my shoulder, and that's when I began to cry.

"He's still alive," I said, looking up, and Mick gazed at me through narrowed eyes and pressed his lips, shaking his head. "No, man, he is, I'm sure of it," I begged, and Mick leaned down and gripped my elbow and made me walk away. "His neck is broken, A.," he said, "he died instantly," and looking back I saw how his head lay at a funny angle—up close, I hadn't really noticed it—and I said, "but he kicked me in the water, Mick," and he reached out and touched my lip, frowning as he said, "you probably just bumped into him," and I said, "but I could hear him groan, man," and Mick said, "that was just the air you pressed out of him," and I said, "he's just a little kid, Mick, we can't let him die," and he said, "you did all you could, A.," and still not quite believing it, or not accepting it, I started to go back, till Mick pulled me around hard and said, "it's over, son, walk away." I fell down and threw up in the sand, sobbing and sobbing, rocking on my knees and hiding my face in my hands.

When I looked up I saw the surfboard, still tied to his feet, turning on its skeg as the water slid in under it, like a demagnetized compass needle that's been struck by lightning, wandering in a binnacle. I knelt there, my teeth chattering and my flesh pimpled with goose bumps as the swash ran in around my legs. The paramedics came and lifted the dead boy onto a litter, and Mick came over and squatted down beside me, lifting my chin. "Come on, A.," he said, "get out of the water. You're already hypothermic. I want you to go to the clinic and get checked," and I said, "I'm all right, man, he's the one that isn't," and Mick said, "well, I want you to get that lip looked at anyway," and I said, "fuck it, Mick," and he said, "listen, A., we've lost seventeen already this summer, and by Labor Day we'll probably lose another twenty more. I wish it weren't that way, but for every one we lose we save another five or six, and you've done your share. But you don't remember those—I know you don't—it's the ones you lose you remember. You've been with me two years, A., and this is the first one you've lost, and you won't ever forget him, son—I know because it happened to me—but you're a good lifeguard, A., I wouldn't have asked you back if you weren't. A lot of people up there in the crowd saw what you did, and I'm proud of you—you did your job, A., but you've got to put it behind you now, because you didn't send that kid out there, he went himself, and you didn't break his neck, the ocean did that, the goddamned ocean, and what I want you to remember is not that you lost him, but that you tried to save him." He squeezed my arm and said, "come on," picking up the surfboard and untying the rope from the skeg, and I went with him. Mick handed it to a policeman and we watched them go off across the dune, two paramedics in white coats carrying the dead boy on a litter under a green blanket that said Lost Colony Hotel, and the policeman in his uniform and holstered gun, wearing aviator glasses and carrying a green and yellow Vardeman under his arm. The blond kid followed in their wake, crying and carrying his own, his eyes red and snot hanging from his nose—he never even looked at me.

His name was Michael—Mikey Graves, from Suffolk—they told me at the clinic, where they dressed my lip and gave me a mild sedative, telling me to go home and take a hot bath to raise my body temperature. I soaked in the tub an hour and then put on my green terry bathrobe and climbed the dune to the gazebo with a beer, staring out at the water and drinking from the corner of my mouth, because my split lip had started hurting then. Despite what Mick had said, I knew my effort had meant nothing. The only thing that mattered was that I'd lost him—Mikey Graves was dead forever. I couldn't stop thinking about his eyes, that terrible sunken scream in them, like he was crying to his soul to come back from the sea. I tried to feel it out there in the waves, but it was gone. There was nothing human in the ocean—it drove in neither humbled nor chastened, without regret, inhuman as before. Mikey Graves had not affected it—he'd died for nothing, a waste of breath, his soul already disintegrated into cold molecules of hydrogen and oxygen.

I didn't confuse Mikey Graves with Cary. Though dark, he didn't look like Cary—his grin was different, and he shot the finger out of a balled fist. Mikey Graves was a surfer, Cary wasn't—I was the surfer, and maybe that was it. There had been no moment—not when I saw him in the water, not later as I breathed into his mouth—that Mikey Graves's face has fused with Cary's. I knew he wasn't Cary, and I wasn't even really thinking of Cary directly, but I knew it was because of Cary and because of what I'd done that it had happened. "There are no accidents"—the master's words came back to me, and I knew it was a judgment and a warning. Jane seemed far away, like the previous night had happened in the distant past, or was simply a dream.

Then she came. I saw the silver Olds turn in the driveway, and she got out and climbed the hill. "I heard," she said, regarding me with somber eyes, "are you all right?" I shrugged and sipped my beer, staring away across the water, and she sat down and put her arm around my shoulder. "You're freezing, A.," she said, "come inside," and I said, "no, I want to stay here for a while," and she said, "can I stay with you, or do you want to be alone?" and I said, "I am alone, Jane. Whether you stay or whether you leave, I'm still alone, and so are you. So is Cary, so is Mikey Graves—he's the most alone of all," and she said, "I heard what you did, A.—it wasn't your fault," and ignoring that, I said, "I figured something out, Jane," and she said, "what, honey?" and I said, "I don't believe in God or sin, but I believe he judges us for it, and love, which is supposed to be the best part, the reward you get for being good? that's really the sin that brings the harshest punishment," and she said, "but that makes no sense—if there's no God, how can he judge you?" and I said, "that's the point," and sipped my beer, "it makes no sense—the whole thing is a fucked-up joke."

She studied me with concern and said, "do you regret last night?" and I said, "it's a sign, Jane, it has to be," and she said, "of what? that what we did was wrong?" I just looked away, and she said, "I don't believe that, A.," and I said, "what then? what do you believe?" and she said, "I don't think it can be a sin to love someone," and I said, "even if it means betraying someone else you love?" and she said, "that boy didn't die because of what we did, A., and you aren't betraying Cary," and I said, "try telling Cary that," and she said, "you're the one who has to tell him, A.—that's all it takes to make it right," and I said, "nothing's ever going to make it right, Jane, and what am I supposed to say? Sorry, spud, I know I was supposed to watch out for her for you, but while you're there doing time in Killdeer, you can reach us at the Moon-Glo?" I saw the hurt sink in, but she said, "don't fight me, honey, let me comfort you," and I said, "who's going to comfort Cary?" and she said, "you're so selfish, A.—you think you're being noble, but you're just acting like a child," and I said, "then why don't you just leave?" and she said, "is that what you want?" Through the haze of numbness I felt a sudden keen clear ache, and I said, "no, it isn't what I want, but maybe what I want isn't the point," and she said, "then what is?" and I said, "I don't know, Jane, but I'm not sure I can do this," and she said, "then you better make up your mind, A., because I can't take much more of this. I won't do it by myself." Her eyes were wet and hurt and unforgiving, and I watched her walk away, wanting to call her back, but I didn't. I stared back at the ocean thinking it was better that way, but feeling the same scream inside myself that

I'd seen in Mikey Graves's eyes, like Jane was the part of me I'd
left out in the waves.

Finally I went back to the house to try and sleep, and though
it was dark in my bedroom, the afternoon sun slanted through
the south window falling in an elongated rectangle on the floor.
I could see the dust I hadn't swept and the crumpled form of the
shirt I'd worn the night before, and glowing on it, a reddish-
golden thread—Jane's hair. I picked it up and stared at it, and
then I pressed my face into the shirt, inhaling the smell of our
sex, my body odor, a faint hint of Jane's perfume—the ache it
awakened was so intense I thought I couldn't live. I crashed
backwards on the mattress and covered my face with it, like an
anxiety victim breathing into a paper bag, and I lay there hurting
and breathing in the smell of having and of having lost, watching
the light begin to shrink like an evaporating tidal pool, and at
some point I fell asleep.

I dreamed someone was calling me, and I got up and went to
the window. Outside I saw the boar, and I raised the window
and followed her. She led me through a landscape I didn't recognize, but then we came out in the marshes on the hummock
underneath the osprey tree. A great door opened in the trunk,
and she vanished into it. I entered, going down a flight of dark
stone steps into what appeared to be a dungeon. There was a
naked woman with her wrists manacled to the wall. Her body
was young and beautiful, and I wanted to make love to her. I
grew erect, but her face was a demented crone's, and I was
afraid to touch her. She made lewd thrusting gestures with her
pelvis, but I kept my distance and the she squatted and laid an
egg from her vagina, then a second, then a third, each strangely
colored and distinct, like Easter eggs. "Put them in the nest,"
she said, and I picked them up—one was green, one silver, one
gold and heavier than the others. I went through a doorway into
a staircase that spiraled up inside the tree and came out on a
windy precipice with a panorama so vast is seemed to encom-
pass the whole world. The sound spread out in one direction,
the ocean in the other, and I was so high up I could see the
earth's curve. The nest was under me—I had to climb down to
it and the footing was precarious. When I saw the bird, the
osprey, ten times its living size with golden human eyes, stroking toward me through the air—its wings created the great
wind—I panicked and stumbled, dropping the golden egg. It fell
and fell and when it hit the ground the shell burst and something

black and putrid came out of it—the yolk was rotten. I fumbled the other two into the nest and fled, and the bird settled down, brooding them, and looking back from a distance the dead tree was like a crucifix, but there were green shoots sprouting from the top of it.

I woke up feeling strangely peaceful, and though I had no idea what the dream meant, I sensed that it was something precious, and I went over and over it till I had it memorized. I never forgot it either.

who was hurrying, and I didn't think that she was even looking

Twenty-one

A.

The next day on the stand was one of the worst of my whole
life. The wind had come around offshore and the sea had glassed
out and the waves were large and crisp, breaking left with hollow
echoing tubes. There were surfers in the line-up, north and
south, but no one out in front of me, and no bathers on my
beach—the place was haunted—and it seemed ironic that Mikey
Graves had missed that day. He'd died in slop and now the ocean
was precise and lapidary, like a dark cut gem. Strollers stopped
and pointed to the bar, then glanced at me with something wary
in their eyes, like they were scared or maybe thought I was a
jinx—I don't know what they thought.

My mind wasn't on the drowning anyway—not on Cary, and
not on Jane. I just hurt and thought of nothing, my whole body
like an open wound, just hurt and tried to be very still because
movement seemed to make it worse. I felt like I'd lost Jane, and
lost Cary because of Jane and Jane because of Cary—my whole
life was gone, and the old pain I'd felt at Keane after Mama died
came back so that it even hurt to breathe. It seemed like that
was how my life was meant to be, it always came back to that.
That day was simply unbearable, and I thought I'd either split
apart or lose my mind, but I did neither, I just hurt and held
myself as still as possible against the cosmic wind.

At five o'clock Jane appeared in her bathing suit and flip-flops
with a towel thrown across her shoulder, strolling casually,
kneeling down to talk to Ellen. She didn't seem like someone

who was hurting, and I didn't think that she was even going to look at me. It was a deep surprise when she walked over. "Hello, A.," she said, tilting her head and squinting up at me with an expression that seemed both quizzical and settled somehow, and I said, "hi," with a tremor in my voice. "Do you feel any better today?" she asked, and I almost laughed, giving vent to the irony I felt, but she seemed so serious I didn't have the heart for it, so I just said, "I'm all right—how about you?" She pressed her lips in a forced stoic smile and said, "I didn't sleep too well last night. I stayed up thinking about this, about us, and I want you to know I understand," and I said, "I don't, Jane, I don't understand a thing," and she said, "you've got to do what you think is right," and I said, "if I only knew what that was. Maybe it's just a matter of not doing what you know is wrong—don't you think?" and she said, "if you think it's wrong to be with me, then I don't want it," and I said, "how can it be right, Jane? just tell me. I want it to be, but I can't make it scan."

She smiled sadly and said, "I know, honey, that's what I came to say—I understand," and I said, "so that's it?" unable to believe it could be, and tears glistened in her eyes as she said, "I'm going home, A." For a moment I fondly thought she meant back to her house and then it dawned on me. "Back to Kill-deer?" I said, and Jane nodded with a face made for tragedies and sorrows, then said, "good-bye," softly, almost whispering, and turned around. Walking down to the water's edge, she waded out, dipping under a wave, then came up staring out at the horizon like she was saying good-bye to it. Swimming back, she stood up in the swash with the water streaking off her, picked her towel up and went into the bathhouse.

The pipes shuddered as she turned the water on, and deep inside I heard a stopwatch start to tick, the same one I'd heard the day before as I pulled Mikey Graves out of the water, only I was drowning now, and I couldn't move to save myself. I knew that when those pipes jerked again and the water ceased to run it would be too late and I would die, yet I just sat and watched. And then I saw myself, a shining part, an angel or a ghost, leap down and sprint across the sand. People turned to stare, but I didn't care, I didn't even knock, just pushed the door in, panting, and stood there mesmerized by the most precious thing I'd ever seen.

Jane was leaning over in the water, her top already off, slipping down her bottom. Looking back at me across her shoulder,

she continued in one smooth motion and stood up, facing me.
The sunlight from above lit half her face and left the other half
in shadow, and it turned the shower fall to little silver drops.
They seemed to float so slowly, like snow in a glass paperweight
or something in a strobe, and as they touched the concrete floor
they sparked like matches dancing all around her feet in a river
of molten gold.

"You can't leave," I told her, entering and pulling the door
to behind me, and she said, "I never wanted to," and I said,
"then don't, for God's sake, don't," and she said, "I didn't
think I had a choice, A.—you didn't give me one," and I said,
"Jane, I'm dying. I didn't want to love you, but I do and I can't
change it. I tried but it's no use. I don't understand it, but if this
is hell I'm ready to be damned," and she said, "it's not supposed to be about hell, A., it's not about sadness, it's supposed
to make you happy," and I said, "I am happy, but it's sadder
than anything." She stared at me wistfully and said, "happiness
makes you sad, doesn't it, honey?" and I said, "God, Jane, I
don't know," shocked by the thought, "but I don't want it to,"
and she said, "I don't think it has to be that way," and I said,
"then show me how." "I just want you to love me, A.," she
said, "and not resent me for loving you or because of Cary. I
just want you to love me and not to break my heart."

Her face puckered, about to cry, and I walked into the spark-
ing rain and put my arms around her, brushing her hair out of
her eyes and kissing them, and she said, "please don't hurt me,
A., I'm so afraid you will," and I said, "I don't mean to, baby,"
daring the endearment, and she said, "I know you don't. I don't
mean to hurt you either, A., but I know I do," and I said, "I
can stand to hurt like this, it's the other way that's killing me."
She nodded almost diffidently, like a little girl, and I said, "so
you won't leave?" and she said, "not if you don't want me to,"
and I laughed with sudden happiness and said, "do you want
me to beg?" She sniffed and wiped her nose, yawning, and said
with demure wickedness, "only if you want to," and I laughed
again, feeling suddenly reckless and exhilarated, and I got down
on my knees and held her hand, saying up to her as the water
pelted me, "then I'm begging you, Jane."

She stared down at me with something ancient and beyond
me in her face like a madonna in an old religious painting,
something that both frightened me and filled me with the keen-
est hope, and then she said, "get up, honey, I was only kid-

ding,'' and I said, ''no, I want to beg you, I like begging you,''
and she laughed—I laughed, too—and she knelt beside me and
said, ''then I beg you, too,'' and she kissed my mouth and drew
my head against her small wet breasts, and I whispered, ''let's
make love,'' and she said, ''here? there are a million people out
there, honey,'' and I said, ''forget them—right here, right now,''
and she said, ''you must be high,'' and I said, ''I am,'' and she
laughed and said, ''no way, José,'' pushing me off, and I didn't
even care. I just lay there face up in the golden rain and felt it
wash me clean.

That night we pooled our funds and bought champagne, lighting
every candle in the house. While we chilled it, we went to the
porch and Jane sat in my lap. I was quiet, wondering at the
strangeness of it—still so new. I felt no doubleness, and it amazed
me that I didn't. That amazement was so soft. ''What are you
thinking?'' Jane asked, and I said, ''about that first night at
Jimbo's. When you came in Eleanor pointed you out and for a
minute it was like I didn't quite recognize you. When I woke up
at your house I stood in your doorway and watched you sleeping,'' and she said, ''you did?'' I nodded and said, ''the light
from that stained-glass window was all across the sheet, and for
a minute I think I almost knew, but it made me sick to think
about it. Then you started seeing Cleanth—I couldn't believe it
when that happened. I was so mad at you,'' and she said, ''I
noticed,'' and I said, ''I thought it was because of Cary—it
wasn't,'' and she said, ''let's don't talk about it now, honey,''
and I said, ''why not?'' and she said, ''I want you—let's go to
bed.''

I smiled and said, ''not yet—we have to drink the champagne
first,'' confident that I could disappoint her in the short term to
make it better later on, and her eyes deferred to me in trust, and
I said, ''I love you, Jane,'' and she took my face between her
hands and said, ''it makes me very happy to hear you say it,''
and I said, ''you won't get tired of it?'' and she said, ''never,''
and I smiled and lifted her, then stood and kissed her before I
went to get the champagne from the freezer. The cork exploded
like a rocket, bouncing off against the rafters, and I poured and
handed her her glass, kneeling down beside the chair. ''To us,''
I said, clinking glasses with her, ''to you and me,'' and she
said, ''to Jane and A.,'' and we both drank. She said, ''it isn't
wrong, A., I hope you know that,'' her eyes a little doubting,

not of what she said, but of me, and I said, "it doesn't feel wrong, does it? I thought it would."

"It's my turn now," she said, holding up her glass, "to Cary," and it came down on my shoulders like a crushing weight, but I pressed hard and lifted it, standing straight, and I drank that toast with her, not in scorn, but love, because in that moment I discovered I could love them both, and that was a new thought.

Refilling her glass, I spilled it on her blouse and the wet streak turned sheer. I unbuttoned it and spread it on her chest, licking champagne off her skin and lifting the edge of her bra, running my tongue under it for the stray precious drops. Jane leaned back and closed her eyes, her hand lightly behind my neck, and I unfastened the clasp, exposing her breasts and poured my full glass over them, wetting my face and drinking. She startled with the cold, then lifted them up from underneath to feed me, watching with a still and dangerous excitement. I took her flats off and then pulled down her underwear. She was pressed up on her tiptoes, her thighs trembling with unconscious tension, and I gently pushed her feet flat on the floor and lifted her skirt above her waist, gazing at her pussy with frank lust that felt both clean and dark, an ancient thing out of the depths. Dipping between her thighs I tasted her, and she shivered, letting her head fall backwards with a moan.

I stood and pulled her up, lifting her in my arms and carrying her through the house into the bedroom where I threw her on the mattress. As I unzipped my pants, she sat up and traced her finger wonderingly along the large blue vein that pulsed in my erection, twisting around it like a vine around a tree trunk. Her eyes glowed in the candlelight, and I pushed her backwards and she raised her legs around me, reaching down to guide me into her, but it wasn't necessary. I found her first and pressed my head between her lips into a tight warm sleeve, brushing her bangs off her forehead, then cupping her left breast and sliding my same hand along her side until I found her ass which I grasped as I sank down in her, deeper and deeper until I touched her cervix. She shuddered and said, "be gentle," and I searched down with my other hand, cupping her right cheek and pulling her tight against me. With each stroke I felt unknown nerves blink awake along my penis, and a light oil spread between us along our chests and stomachs, mingling our scents.

We started slowly, but Jane nudged up the tempo, and it wasn't like it had been with Morgan, where I felt I had to hold back, fearing her judgment. Jane threw herself into it, challenging me, and I let go, I let myself be lost, pressing down the throttle until my consciousness was swept away in the pure physicality of it—the beautiful race. It was so out of control it was almost scary, and then I heard her start to laugh, and I laughed, too, until she locked her arms around my back, clenching so hard it almost took my wind away. I took a sobbing breath and came as she sobbed, coming, too, and we lay there, gasping, our hearts thundering together like stampeding horses, and I said, "you came, didn't you?" wanting to be sure, and she laughed so hard she almost cried, and so did I.

"A golden spell specific to a time and place"—the master's words to Morgan about their youthful love, but so it was of our time, too, mine and Jane's. Two months, from July the sixth till almost Labor Day. The colors ran again, as they had before with Morgan, only this time the dissolve was happy, like a lump of sugar melting on my tongue. I'd never known a happiness like that, not before, and not in all the years that followed. I'd thought that it might last.

Many mornings I rose with Jane at five and took her to the Double Stack where I met Mr. Vincent and his wife, Pearl. They practically adopted us, as though through us they remembered something they'd had once and felt it stir again—they made sure that we ate breakfast, real ones. Jane sometimes came down to the beach as I was closing up and helped me spread my tarp across the rental chairs and chain them to the stand, and we went to the grocery store for dinner, trekking with a cart between the aisles like grown-up married people. Jane had mastered tracts of esoteric female wisdom that I marveled at. She knew that Heinz—not Hunt's, not Del Monte's—was the best ketchup, but I always mixed the cocktail sauce we dipped our shrimp in, larding it with horseradish, one to one, so that it cleared our sinuses and made us blink our eyes. The simple act of visiting the supermarket and making dinner seemed a mystery as deep as going to the woods after the boar, but nothing had to die for it. Yet there was Cary, but I didn't think of him. I loved him, that was all I knew—my love for Jane did not diminish it—and for a time that seemed enough, though I knew the reckoning would come.

We found a bar, the Croatoan, an old marina perched above the sound with ceiling fans and a wide deck under the stars. We drove there after I got off and watched the sunset. The owner offered Jane a job, but she declined because that would have spoiled it, and he told us what the name meant, that when John White came back to Roanoke, having been detained for three years in England because of the Spanish Armada, he found his people gone and no clue to their whereabouts except that single word—"Croatoan"—carved into a live oak tree, the destination the Lost Colonists had set out to find as they left a place of pestilence and famine to start a new life, walking off the page of history. The Croatoan became our place, who'd also left behind a heavy history and thought that it would never find us.

The days grew shorter, and in the early mornings sometimes you could smell the apple tang of coming fall. The gaillardias began to bloom, red wildflowers tipped with yellow rayed around a soft dark center. I picked a field of them and filled our bed and Jane wore them in her hair. Fleets of white and yellow butterflies appeared from nowhere, sensing the cold weather coming on, hurrying frantically to finish something. The southwest wind blew them across the road and they tumbled helplessly out across the dark blue water. We took long walks on the beach. On one of them Jane found a lightning whelk, a perfect one, in a tidal pool as though the passing storm had left it there just for us. She gave it to me together with her whispered promise. It was silver then. At night we put on sweaters and I lay on the gazebo bench, my head in Jane's lap, and we talked about the coming fall in Chapel Hill, making plans, and then fell silent as the first star fell, and then a second, then scores and hundreds as the Perseid showers broke across the August sky like fireworks. The world was full of signs and wonders, but they all seemed propitious.

Jane and I were happy, and in our happiness my picture of the world reversed, as though through some special condition of my eyes, some derangement, I'd seen the negative instead of the true picture. To me the bright things, love and happiness, had all been suspect—I'd seen the darkness in them—and all the dark things, all the pain and suffering and despair and brinksmanship, had seemed to promise a different, higher brightness to be had only through enduring them. But for that time with Jane my vision became single and things were simply what they were— bright was bright and dark was dark, no tricks and no deceptions. The negative reversed and then it bloomed in living color, and I realized there'd been an earlier time when I'd also seen the world that way. Pain had reversed the picture, hurting me into an odd freakish specialness. I'd thought it was my gift, but I didn't need it anymore because I finally realized that the true specialness was being simple—not an end to darkness, but only seeing the true darkness and not confusing it with what was good.

I knew that there had always been a part of me that had been happy and in love with life, and that self was truer than the other one that always suffered, the self that shivered in the cosmic wind—not so high, perhaps, but truer—and even when I'd lost sight of that true self it had always been there, waiting patiently for me to raise my eyes and see, or, rather, lower them and leave the windswept cosmic place, returning to an altitude where human life was possible. It was so simple it surprised me—I just stood up and left, descending step by step the same way I had climbed. I truly thought that it would last.

Twenty-two

A.

But there was always that dark shadow in the background of the portrait. Jane and I talked of Cary, not constantly, not obsessively, but always to one point—he had to know, I had to tell him. I wanted to, but in the right way—not a phone call, not a letter, but face to face. He was supposed to come the first weekend in August, but T.O. had a minor relapse and went back in the hospital. I left a standing invitation with him, expecting him each weekend, but things came up, one after another. We talked on the phone a lot, and sometimes late at night Cary would call when Jane was there. The phone was by the bed, and she'd sit up against the headboard studying me with solemn eyes as I answered Cary's questions, which were always about her—how she was, where she was, what she was doing and with whom. Mostly I put him off with half truths, but other times I had to lie outright. The guilt I felt over those small lies was eased by my intention to tell the larger truth—they almost seemed means to it, and however distasteful, justified by the end. But I thought about my ethics class at Keane in which we'd read *The Prince*, and I was uneasy, because I'd hated Machiavelli, but in those two months I came to understand him better.

The larger lesson, though, was the master's, the lesson I'd learned in the woods—giving way to impulse, taking the thing you want, the thing life makes you want, not as a desecration, but a sacrament. Sometimes, cornered by my own self-accusation after Cary's calls, I thought of it that way, and though the master was discredited, his teaching lingered, lending point to my experience with Jane and Cary, as highlight needs a shadow and sweetness needs an edge of bitterness to give it savor. I never shared that thought with Jane. Still and all, that time was not about Cary, he was just a footnote to the text. A golden spell specific to a time and place—Cary wasn't part of it, not until he came on Labor Day weekend, reentering the game as a full player only to destroy it.

I hung up the phone after the last and most important of those conversations—the one in which Cary announced that he was finally coming—and turned to Jane. "You got the gist of that?" I asked, and she said, "when?" and I said, "he's driving down on Friday afternoon—this is it," and she said, "are you scared?" and I said, "a little—but I'm ready to get it over with," and she said, "so am I, honey, and I'm glad, A., deep down I am. I know it isn't going to be easy, but it'll be so much better when it's behind us."

She smiled bravely and reached for my hand, and I said, "I wonder how he's going to take it. I know it's stupid, but we're supposed to room together—you know? we already got our assignments," and she said, "don't think about that now," and I said, "you're right, but I can't help it, Jane. I get these awful flashes of us trapped together in that room, not speaking, and every time I leave he'll know exactly where I'm going," and she said, "I've thought about it, too, A., but you know, I think we've got to trust Cary just like we trust each other and give him the benefit of the doubt. He loves us, A., just like we love him, and I know it's going to hurt him—it's going to hurt all the way around—but Cary's not going to hate us, that's not the way he is. If we do it the right way, he'll come around," and I said, "but what if he doesn't?" and she said, "then we'll just have to deal with that—after all, room assignments can be changed," and I said, "yeah, or I can always go to Columbia," laughing because I meant it as a joke, and she said, "I'll kill you if you even think about it," also joking, but with an edge, and I said, "you think I even could?" and she said, "I hope not, honey, because I trust you," and I said, "you should, Jane," pulling her to my shoulder, "because I've made up my mind and it's all settled—I couldn't leave you even if I wanted to." She drew back, reading my eyes, and anticipating her, I said, "and I don't want to."

* * *

I wasn't really expecting Cary to be there when I got off work on Friday, but when I pulled up in the driveway I saw his VW. He was up in the gazebo sitting on the bench back smoking a cigarette. When he saw the Jeep, he took one last drag and threw it in the sand, starting down the hill toward me. As I turned into the garage bay, he stood there watching me, fiddling with a large ring of keys. "Guess what?" he said, giving them a shake as I came out, and I said, "what?" and he said, "I got fired," and I said, "fired?" and he grinned and said, "Daddy fired me," and I said, *"what?"* He nodded, and I said, "when?" Cary looked at his watch and said, "about five hours ago." He held the ring up and said, "I walked off with the keys"—he held out his hand—"I'm free." I slapped it perfunctorily.

"But why?" I asked. Cary shrugged and said, "the same old shit, A. I finished up at noon and went back to the house to pack. On the way out I stopped in Daddy's bedroom to say goodbye. Guess what he said?" Cary nodded. " 'Why ain't you at work? The day ain't over, boy.' " Cary repeated it with an exaggerated boorishness and shook his head. Anger flashed across his face. "Two days left, A., two goddamned days. I just said, 'I'm leaving,' and he said, 'if you do, don't bother coming back.' I slammed the door behind me on my way out, and he yelled after me, 'you're fired, boy!' I was all the way to Roanoke Rapids before I realized I had the master ring—he's going to be pissed tomorrow morning when Ramsey has to call a locksmith, but what's he going to do? fire me?" Cary laughed and I said, "Jesus, spud," and he said, "and you know what?" and I said, "what?" Cary narrowed his eyes and said, "I'm glad, A."—his voice was husky with passion—"I'm so damn glad to be out of it. I'm ready to party—Chapel Hill next week!" We slapped five again, and I said, "yeah, damn straight," glad to see the spark in him, but not quite able to get into it.

"I saw Jane," he said, and I said, "you did?" now sounding casual to myself. He didn't seem to notice. "I went over to her house," he said, "Lucy had a bunch of people over there getting high and doing tequila shooters. I smoked a joint with them and went up to the pancake house. We didn't really get a chance to talk, but I'm going to see her later"—he grinned—"I asked her for a date." "Oh," I said, "well I'd been thinking maybe you and me could go someplace tonight and have a chat." He raised his eyebrows, and I said, "just to catch up," and he said, "sorry, spud, not tonight. We'll have plenty of time to catch up at school. I want to spend tonight catching up with Jane." His grin italicized the phrase. He seemed happy, but I found his mood irritating, or at least frustrating. My own spirits sank as my plans went out the window.

"Listen, A.," he said, studying me. "I probably should have okayed it with you first—I hope you don't mind—but I asked Jane over here. Is that all right?" and I said, "over here?" not casually at all. That time Cary noticed. Seeming startled at my tone, he said, "I mean, we could go to a restaurant or somewhere," and I said, "no, man," shaking my head, "no," as I tried to process it, and he said, "you're sure you don't mind? it'll just be for a few hours. I'll make it up to you," and I said, "don't worry about it," and went off to the shower before I gave it away. I was mad—at him, at myself. I wasn't ready to tell him. While I was in the stall Cary asked me through the door where to buy champagne, and I gave him directions, feeling seedy like I was pimping my own woman.

As soon as I heard him pull out, I turned the shower off and went upstairs to call Jane. "It's me," I said as soon as she picked up, and she said, "where's Cary?" and I said, "he just drove off to get champagne," in a dire tone of voice, and she said, "it's going to be okay, honey—it's probably better that I see him first. Maybe if he understands how I feel it'll make the rest easier," and I said, "you know he's going to ask you if you're seeing someone," and she said, "I know," and I said, "what are you going to say?" and she said, "I don't plan to go into that with him. I'm just going to say I love him and I want to be his friend, but the rest is over. I can handle my part, don't worry." She sounded confident and resolved, and that eased me. "I won't," I told her, "and I'll handle mine. Maybe I'll drive up to Corolla with him tomorrow and do it there," and she said, "whatever you think," and I said, "I love you, Jane, I'll be thinking about you tonight," and she said, "I'll be thinking about you, too," and we hung up. The call relieved me.

I was sitting on the west porch drinking a beer in an Adirondack chair when Cary came back around seven. "You still here?" he asked, and I said, "ha ha," and he said, "look," showing me the bottle of Cordon Rouge he'd bought. "I also got some shrimp," he said, "you'll have to tell me how to cook them," and I said, "Jane knows," and almost croaked at my stupidity. It went right by him. "Have you got an extra house-

key?'' he asked, ''in case we go out later, so I can lock up,''
and I said, ''right inside the door, top of the rack.'' He opened
the screen and got it, starting to thread it on the ring. Then he
reconsidered and took his car key off instead. ''The damn thing
makes me feel like the whole percussion section in a high school
marching band,'' he said, reaching back inside and hanging the
master on the cottage rack, ''Daddy has the locks changed all
the time, and all the old keys are still on it. It takes fives minutes
just to get through the front door in the morning. Don't let me
forget those when I go''—he grinned—''T.O. might re-fire me.''

''Sure, spud,'' I said, ''listen, I was thinking—there's this
place up north I want to show you—Corolla—it's where Jane
and I went camping that time with Cleanth and Morgan. I
thought we might take some sleeping bags and a couple rods
and reels and spend tomorrow night. It's really beautiful,'' and
he said, ''let me see how it goes tonight with Jane okay? I may
need to stick around. Maybe we could go just for the day.''

He went back inside and put his things in the refrigerator,
bringing back a beer. Popping the top, he held it behind his ear
and flicked his fingers, sailing it out into the dusk winking like
a silver fishing spoon. ''The archeologists of the future will love
me,'' he said, grinning as he took a sip, ''they'll be able to
reconstruct my migrations—a trail of pop-tops.'' I smiled oblig-
ingly and took a dark swallow. ''I was just wondering, Cary,''
I said, ''what exactly do you expect to happen tonight?'' Turning
serious, he said, ''I don't really know, A.—something good,''
and I said, ''I wouldn't get my hopes up, man.'' His face fell as
he said, ''what? has she said something?'' and I said, ''it isn't
anything she's said,'' and he said, ''she's not seeing someone
else?'' and I said, ''it's not that either, spud. I'm just going on
what I've seen, and I'm not sure you should expect too much.''

He stared at me as though deciding how to take it, and then
he said, ''I know what you're saying, A., and I appreciate it. I
know how it must look. Jane and I have been apart almost a
year now, and it's been hard, especially this summer. But it's
just like Mama said—'if it's real, time and distance don't make
any difference,' and she was right, A., because it didn't. My
feelings haven't changed. Maybe we'll have to start over in
Chapel Hill, but that's not a bad thing. I just know I love her
and in a few days we'll be together again. The hard part's over.''
He smiled and I looked away with an aching heart, because I
knew the hard part hadn't even started. I sat there feeling deeply

guilty, but there was nowhere else to take it—Jane was right. What she had to say came first.

We were quiet for a while, staring out into the deepening twilight, then Cary said, "do you ever think about the future, A.?" and I said, "not that much," which was true, and he said, "I do," and I said, "what about it?" and he said, "I just wonder what's going to happen," and I said, "it'll be like now only we'll be older and know more—it'll be better," and he said, "you think?" and I said, "yeah—real profound, huh?"

He smiled politely, but his eyes didn't change. "Sometimes I wonder what I'm going to do," he said, and I said, "you'll figure it out, man, give yourself a break—we're only eighteen," and he said, "but you always knew, A.—ever since we were little and you copied those pictures of Jim Brown and Y. A. Tittle out of *Sports Illustrated*. It came naturally to you," and I said, "you'll be a doctor, Cary—that's what I always thought. Daddy said that," and he said, "your daddy said that about me?" I nodded and he said, "why?" and I said, "because you're good with people, and you care," and he said, "I don't think I'm smart enough," and I said, "bullshit, Cary, that's the only stupid thing I've ever heard you say," and he said, "I'm serious, A., you always got straight A's," and I said, "you got good grades, too," and he said, "yeah, two A's, two B's and a C—every damn report card. And I had to work for that. You didn't, A.," and I said, "at Keane I did, and I didn't get straight A's either," and he said, "I envied you for that," and I said, "don't, Cary—Keane was a cold place—and I'll tell you something, I envied you for Jeff Davis," and he said, "why?" and I said, "because they let you be a human being, man—that wasn't the point at Keane. All those high school things—girls, pep rallies, rumbles in the parking lot, going parking back on Braswell Avenue—I missed that, Cary," and he said, "you're better off, A., you're miles ahead," and I said, "in one way, maybe, but in another way I'm miles behind—I don't think I even realized it till this summer," and he said, "how are you behind?" and I said, "just in living, Cary—that's what always came naturally to you, ever since I knew you. Compared to that, drawing's just like having a double-jointed thumb." "Thanks, A.," he said quietly. I could tell that he was touched, and feeling the linkage in our roots I said, "don't let it swell your head, Dropkick," and he grinned and held up his beer, saying, "go for the gusto, right, A.-nuss?" and I laughed and said, "if you can find it," and he said, "that's the thing, spud," with a warm glow in his eyes, "I already have."

He checked his watch and looked at me. "Okay, man," I said, "I can take a hint," getting up to go, and he said, "thanks again, A.—really," and as we shook hands he pulled me into a strong hug.

I went to the Croatoan and sat down at the bar, feeling Jane's presence palpably on the empty stool beside me. Ordering a hamburger and a draft, I ate and watched the people drifting in and out. Knowing some of them, I nodded and they nodded back, or spoke some light joking greeting. Someone asked me where Jane was, and I just shrugged, feeling no compulsion to explain. There was a table of fresh young college girls, getting rowdy and primed for action. They were not bad-looking, and I stared, almost a college man myself. One of them stared back, and I raised my glass to her and looked away, warmed by her attention, appreciating it and her. But I didn't want her—I felt old and married and content. I had the one I wanted, and I was grateful to be wanted back.

I pitied Cary, but I felt better about things. I felt like he could take it. I thought about them at the house, what was going on that minute, what was being said—but it was different from the other time. I still knew Cary loved her and was handsome and persuasive, I knew Jane loved him and wasn't shy of bedding down, but there were no flickers through the parted curtain of their naked sweaty bodies, not even any curtain—I saw it clearly, Jane hurting as she told him and Cary hurting as he listened, and I hurt, too, for both of them, because I loved them and was loved, but there was something sad and high above the hurt, a grace note, which gave the ache a sweetness, and that grace note was the truth. It was time for all of us to wake up from the dream and make it right. Tomorrow my turn would come, and I was nervous, but I didn't doubt myself, and maybe that was why I didn't doubt them either.

The enormous distance I had come that summer soared out behind me, and I thought about all the separate steps that had brought Jane and me together, how in the moment each one had seemed wrong and evil, yet they'd led to something good, and I trusted that the last and hardest one would, too. I felt calm and sat there getting quietly drunk. I stayed till after midnight.

* * *

When I got back to the house, Cary's car was still in the same place and upstairs his bedroom door was closed. They'd left the plate of boiled shrimp on the table, a few shells in a dish. The new candles he'd bought had burned halfway and been blown out. They'd poured two glasses of champagne and they sat there on the table, Jane's lipstick trace on one, still effervescing, though feebly now, beside the bottle whose sides were streaked with rills of condensation which puddled at the base. The misery of an interrupted dinner lingered there, a bottle of champagne they'd lost the heart to drink. I read how it had started, how no one had eaten—it had all been brief—and that misery communicated itself to me. I almost knocked on his door, but instead I just recorked the bottle, put it up and went to bed.

I didn't sleep though. I lay there in a vivid reverie and thought of them, but mostly Cary. I remembered the first time I met him, sixth grade. We'd been thrown together in the same home room, and I was walking home from school one day along a dirt road that cut between the Sherwood Forest section and the Country Club, and Cary stepped out from behind a tree, grinning, with a Marlboro hanging from his lip. I wasn't pleased at all, because I thought I knew the kind of boy that Cary was. He smoked and cursed and hung out with the boys from Journey Street, the mill kids whose daddies' hands had toughened them and given them a canny confidence whose rule was very simple—hurt the other first and win.

"Want a cigarette?" he asked, and I said, "I don't smoke," and he smiled scornfully like he'd expected that. "You ever see the sawdust pile?" he said, pointing through the trees, and I said, "no," and he said, "come on, I'll show you." I followed him past the fork that led to Ruin Creek into a wide clearing overgrown with waist-high broom—shoulder-high back then—where there was a great rusty golden mound. "Put your hand on it," he said, and I complied distrustfully and said, "it's warm," and he nodded soberly and said, "know why?" and I said, "nuh-uh, why?" and he said, "because there's something in it," and I said, "what?" and he said, "a dead man and a woman and their little baby," and I said, "sure," ironically, and he said, "you calling me a liar?" I backed off and said, "how could there be?" and he said, "I'll tell you how. There was a wood crew back here cutting lumber a long time ago. They set up a saw and cut the boards right here and that's what made the pile," and I said, "who told you that?" and he said, "my daddy. And there was this one fellow on the crew named Billy Wild, but the foreman didn't like him, and one day when Billy was running a big tree through the ripsaw and nobody was looking, the foreman pushed him into it and it cut his arm off. Billy bled to death and they threw him in the sawdust pile," and I said, "why didn't they call the police?" and Cary said, "there weren't any. This was way back when. Killdeer wasn't even here."

I had my doubts but kept them to myself, and Cary said, "the next day they went off, and Billy's wife came looking for him. They had a little baby which had just been born, and she called out Billy's name and she heard this voice cry 'help me'—it was coming from the sawdust pile. She climbed up the top carrying her baby, and then that arm—the one that got cut off—reached up out of it and grabbed her ankle and pulled her down. She sank in it like quicksand and nobody ever saw them again, but when it's a full moon that little baby comes out and walks around."

"Sure," I said, "that's so dumb—what does it walk around for?" and he said, "looking for its daddy—that's why it's warm, 'cause they're still in there, and you know what else?" and I said, "what?" and he said, "if you put your ear down next to it you can hear a thumping sound—it's a heart. But you better be careful if you do because that arm'll snap right out at you," and I said, "I'm real scared, Cary, I'm shaking in my boots," not bothering to check it out, and he said, "but I bet you wouldn't sleep up here with a full moon," and I said, "would you?" and he said, "sure, I've done it lots of times—I've seen that baby, too."

I remembered that and how we'd camped out there not long afterwards. Sadie drove us in the Cadillac, packing us a bag of pimento cheese sandwiches and potato chips and Coca-Colas. We took a flashlight and a hatchet and Cary showed me how to build a lean-to out of sticks and evergreen branches. That night we waited for the baby, but it never showed, and Cary said it was because the moon still wasn't full. We lay awake under the stars in the green scent and talked all night with a freedom and a frankness I'd never experienced before. He asked me if I knew what fucking was and if I'd ever heard my parents and I said, "mine don't do it anymore—they're too old." Cary just laughed and punched me in the arm. "You're full of shit, A.," he said, "but I still like you." I was surprised he liked me and even more surprised he wasn't afraid of saying it. We talked about girls and teachers and being grounded and he asked me if I'd ever been in any fights, and I said, "sure," and he said, "with who?" and I said, "lots of times," evasively, because I hadn't, not the kind he meant—the real kind, where people bled and bones got broken—and he said, "I bet I could whip you," and I said, "you could try," hoping he wouldn't take me up on it, and he said, "don't worry, A., I'm not going to. You're my friend, and if anybody tries to mess with you they'll have to come through me."

It had been that simple, that innocent and generous. Cary took me under his wing, and his friendship sheltered me. It never wavered. In my heart I'd always believed that he was stronger than I was in the way that mattered most and that he knew it, too. But he never threw it in my face. He took care of me. Lying on my bed that night, remembering, my eyes filled with tears, because he'd kept his promise all those years, he'd been there for me when the world I knew had turned to shit— Cary had been the ground to me, but now the ground had shifted. I'd tried to keep my promise back to him and failed, and I already knew the truth would not redeem it, but that was all I had left to give him. I didn't know what was going to happen, all I knew was that I loved him and the ground had shifted, and I hoped we could ride it out and end on the same side, as we had started.

The next morning when I went out into the big room the front door was wide open and a gust of west wind greeted me, blowing through it. There were flies everywhere, climbing the candle chimneys, buzzing on the insides of the window screens, especially on the plate of shrimp which had started to smell—ten or fifteen big black ones crawling over the glassy shells with the white and orange meat inside them. I waved them off and dumped the contents in the garbage can, starting to make coffee.

There was something about it—walking out into a house full of flies and the smell of shrimp just starting to go bad—that put things off to a bad start, because I'd had this picture in my mind of how it would be—a clear sunny day with a hint of crystal in the air, football weather. Cary and I would get in the Jeep and make that drive, crossing the high dunes north of Duck, and race along the beach past all the wrecks and gulls and driftwood. We'd fish for blues or croaker and cook them on a driftwood fire with bay leaves down the slitted spines, and after dinner, sitting by the fire, I'd look him in the eyes and say, "I've got something to tell you, Cary. I'm in love with Jane and she's in love with me. I didn't mean for it to happen, I struggled against it the best I knew how, but I couldn't stop it. I don't think love is something you can stop. It wasn't against you, I never meant to hurt you, and I hope you can forgive me because you're the best friend I've got, the best I've ever had, and I don't want to lose you." Maybe he'd get up and walk away and I'd let him go and stir the coals a while before I'd follow him. I'd find him on the beach and say, "I'm sorry, Cary, I know it's not enough, but it's the best I have," and he'd say, "it's okay, A., I understand. It was over between us anyway, and if it has to be anyone, I'm glad it's you," and it would end up being a reconfirmation of our friendship—if not that way, then in some other. But already the day had started differently. The house was full of flies and there was a strong smell of turning shrimp, and when I went outside with my coffee cup there was an overcast, not dark and threatening rain, but just a gray ceiling of low moiling clouds. The weather wasn't right.

From the porch I saw him, up in the gazebo sitting on the bench back exactly as the night before, smoking a cigarette as though he'd never left. He was staring down the beach with a dull, almost vacant expression, as well as I could make it out, but the motions of his hands were tense as he smoked, lighting a new butt off the coal before throwing the old one in the sand. Feeling a queasy flutter in my stomach, I went back inside, procrastinating, and poured a cup of coffee for him, then started up the hill with it. I found that it was hard to breathe and I was glad I had the climb as an excuse.

He watched me walking toward him, his dark eyes strangely vivid within his impassive face—they glittered with a hard knowing light, and I avoided them as though warding off an evil spell, knowing I could not protect myself. But what was in them wasn't evil, it was just despair, a clear pure thing, stripped of human quality, comfortless and past seeking any comfort. That was Cary's truth, the first time I ever saw it, a different thing from mine, not a friend and teacher but an annihilation. Trying to be casual, I handed him his cup, blowing in my own as I said, "how did it go?" Cary swirled the coffee, staring down at it as though it held some trivial interest, then poured it in a steaming puddle in the sand. "It just went," he said, reaching for a bottle of Seagram's 7 on the seat beside him and swigging it. He winced and wiped his mouth and said, "it just fucking went," and he was smiling. The macho of the gesture was so brittle, like thin ice over a dark pool, and I watched with a feeling of sick helplessness as Cary drank again, skating out on it. I felt the hair rise on my neck. I hadn't expected it to be like that.

"What did she say?" I asked, and he said, "she said she loves me," and I said, "and?" and he said, "and she loves me not," grinning like at least there was a joke in it. "She wants to be my friend, A.," he said, like that joke was even better, and I said, "at least that's something, man," and he said, "is it?" and I said, "I think it's a lot," and he said, "yeah, you're right, but it's not enough. I don't want to be Jane's friend, A., I never did. I'm sorry, but that's the way it is. Three years, A."—he narrowed his eyes like he didn't trust that I could comprehend his implication—"three years of my life I've loved her and waited for her. She was it for me. I mean, there was Mama, there was Cliff, there was you—you were my friend, A., but that's what I mean, you see? Because it's not enough, you need something else to get you through, something a friend can't give you, and Jane was it for me. And I thought I'd be it for her— she said she wanted me to be. She must have told me that a hundred times, and I could be, spud, that's the hell of it, because I know her so well—I know where she's good and where she hurts, and I loved every inch of it, I still do, even after what she said, because what the fuck am I supposed to do—just flip a switch and turn it off? How are you supposed to do that? And now when we finally get it to the point where we can be together, she says it's over, she loves me but she doesn't want to try anymore—she can't—that's what she told me, and I just don't get it, A., it makes no sense to me. Why? Why can't she at least give it one last chance?" and not yet ready to give him the answer to his question, I just said, "I'm sorry, Cary, I really am."

He took another shot and said, "why should you be sorry, A.? it's not your fault," and his words set off a demented echo in my mind, bullets fired at random but each one ricocheting back at me. "Take it easy on that stuff," I said, and he said, "don't preach to me, A.," and I said, "I'm not preaching, Cary, I'm just not sure getting drunk right now's a great idea," and he said, "drunk?" like that was funny, too, "do I look drunk to you? Shit, I couldn't get drunk if I tried. It just takes the edge off, and barely that.'' Holding the bottle by the neck, he stared down at the label, and said, ''you know, when I was little I found this pint one time. Daddy had them hidden all over the house like Easter eggs. This one was in the downstairs bathroom, tucked up in the joist braces. I climbed up on the tank and took it down, then brought it straight to Mama. You know what she said?'' and I said, ''what?'' and he said, ''she told me to go put it back. I didn't understand that, I thought it was because she was afraid of him, but it wasn't that. You know what it was?'' I just waited, knowing he was going to tell me. ''It was because she loved him and she knew he needed it,'' Cary said, ''and I never understood it, but I do now. Right now I know exactly why he drinks,'' and I said, ''why?'' and Cary said, ''because he wants to be happy and he can't, and because he can't he drinks to dull the pain. Daddy drinks because he's suffering, A., to try and get away from it, and when it works he passes out, and when it doesn't he gets mad at us because he loves us and he can't help us and because we love him and we can't help him either.''

''Maybe you can't help another person in that way, however much you love him,'' I said, and he said, ''that's it, A., that's the thing, but I never wanted to believe it—there's no help, is there?'' and I said, ''you can help yourself, Cary,'' and he said, ''you always said that,'' and I said, ''it's true,'' and he said, ''maybe for you, A., but I don't think it is for me. I don't think I have that kind of strength, and even if I did, I'm not sure I could stand to live that way, because I know you can love yourself, but you can't love yourself the way another person loves you, not the way I wanted Jane to love me. I can't give myself the thing I needed her to give me, because it's not in me to give,'' and I said, ''but someone else can give it to you, Cary, someone will,'' and he smiled and said, ''like Wanda Jo?'' and I said, ''come on, Cary,'' and he said, ''I know what you're saying, A., and it makes perfect sense, but you're wrong. It won't ever be the same—lightning never strikes the same place twice. There's other kinds of heat and other kinds of love, but lightning is lightning, and whatever it would be with someone else, it won't be that. Jane was it for me.''

''But you knew, Cary,'' I said, ''you must have known,'' and he said, ''maybe I did, spud, deep down, but there was hope, you see? Even last night when I saw where she was going with it I tried to stop her. 'Don't say it, Jane,' I told her, 'at least let

me keep hoping,' and she said, 'I've got to, Cary—don't hope
for me, not anymore, because it isn't going to happen. Hope for
someone else.' But there's no one else to hope for. I don't know
what I'm going to do, A.'' He wasn't crying—it was worse than
that—he said it like another thing of trivial interest, his own life.
He seemed like a husk, a scarecrow, blowing in the wind, and
it began to dawn on me that I wouldn't tell him—not like that. I
didn't think he could stand another blow. Maybe I was lying to
myself—I didn't think so in the moment.

Then he said, ''you were right, A., I should have listened to
you and come down here. I don't know why I didn't. I thought
they needed me at home, but Daddy didn't need me, the whole
thing was a waste. I lugged that goddamned keyring around all
summer thinking it would open something, but it didn't—it just
closed tighter—and I lost Jane because of it. It's not anybody
else's fault, it's mine,'' and I said, ''don't blame yourself, man,''
and he said, ''but I do, A., and I want to tell you something. I
always thought you were wrong when you said sometimes you
have to cut your losses and walk and not look back—that was
the only part of you that bothered me, but I didn't think you
really meant it, not in your heart. I thought I knew something
you didn't and that you'd come around eventually, but now it's
me that has to come around, and I can see how much it must
have cost you to live that way. It hurts, doesn't it? But there's no
choice, you've got to do it anyway. You always could, A., and I
respect your guts. I always did, but I thought it took more to
stay and stick it out. I was wrong and you were right—it's funny,
isn't it?''

''You weren't wrong, Cary,'' I said, ''you were a thousand
times more right than me. It does take more guts to stick it out,
and that's what you've got to do with Jane, you've got to stay
and be her friend and let it change,'' and he said, ''I can't do
that, A., I'll always love her and want what makes her happy,
but I can't be her friend. I can't be around her and make jokes
and small talk because I'd always want her and it would just
remind me,'' and I said, ''give it time, man,'' and he said, ''no,
A., I've got to walk away. But what I still can't quite believe is
that the thing I have to walk away from should be Jane. If anything, I thought she'd be the thing I went to when I left, the new
thing. It's so strange—I really thought she loved me,'' and I
said, ''she does love you, Cary, you know she does.'' He shook
his head and took another drink.

"I believed that for so long, spud," he said, "I told myself it was just the timing or whatever that was off—not for me, but for her. But what Mama said, A., it cuts both ways. If Jane had really loved me the timing wouldn't matter. I don't even know what it was she felt, maybe the whole thing was a dream. Maybe she just kept me hanging on because I loved her and it was something she could fall back on," and I said, "I don't believe that, Cary, I think she was genuinely confused," and he said, "maybe you're right, but she said she loved me, A., she said she wanted it to be me, she told me that so many times—that's why I can't understand last night, because when I asked her if she couldn't try she just said, 'no,' and I said, 'come on, Jane, is that too much to ask?' Her eyes were full of tears, A., she was so damn beautiful, but she just said, 'yes, Cary, it is—I can't try anymore.' I just stared at her, A., I couldn't believe it—it was like she wasn't Jane but somebody else I didn't even know."

Because he seemed a little better, as though the talk had eased him somewhat, I said, "come on, spud, let's take that drive up north. It's beautiful up there and it'll help take your mind off things," and he said, "no, A., I don't think I'm up for it. I probably ought to head on back," and I said, "you just got here, man," and he said, "yeah, I know, but I found out what I came for and I couldn't enjoy myself, spud. I wouldn't be any fun for you or anybody else—I think it's better this way," and I said, "what the hell are you going to do in Killdeer anyway?" and he said, "I've got bags to pack," and I said, "come on, man, just stay tonight—I don't want you to leave," and he said, "my mind's made up, spud—tell her I said good-bye, okay?"

I just stared at him as he stood up. Face to face, he asked me, very quietly, "she's seeing someone, isn't she?" My heart began to pound so loud I was sure that he could hear it, and holding his gaze for dear life, knowing this was it, I said, "yes, man, she is," and he said, "it isn't Faison, is it?" and I said, "no," and he nodded and said, "I didn't think it was. Tell me who it is, A." My mind screamed out, "it's me," but my lips said, "does it make a difference?" and he said, "no, it doesn't, I just want to know." His eyes had the confidence of just and perfect right, a place beyond despair where everything is equal, and thinking I could postpone it just a moment longer—I'd expected it to be so different, I'd expected the initiative to come from me—I said, "did you ask her?" He pursed his lips and nodded.

"She wouldn't tell me," he said, "but I knew that had to be the reason—it was written all over her," and for just a second I was sure he knew, sure that it was written all over me as well, and he said, his voice almost a whisper, "it isn't you, is it, A.?"

Truth stared me in the face—its lidless eyes were terrible and golden like the osprey's in my dream. Feeling the traction of my purpose slipping, my eyes flicked away from that inhuman stare, and even as my mind screamed, "yes!" my lips said, "no," and I was lost that quickly, just like in the woods, the way I shot the boar, and I noticed from the corner of my eye how everything looked dead around me, the glow of life went out of it, out of Cary, too. That was how I killed him, how I killed myself.

Cary's eyes didn't change, he kept them fixed on me with that same gentle but remorseless scrutiny, and I was sure he'd heard my thought, sure he'd seen it screaming in my eyes. Even when he nodded and said, "I knew it wasn't," I was sure. He put his arms around me in a hug, and said, "I'll see you, A.," as he walked down the hill. I watched him go, feeling like a drowning man, wanting to call him back and tell him, about to, but I didn't, I just went down.

Sitting on the bench, I stared out at the waves beneath that moiling overcast and they were gray again like in a negative. A blackfly lighted on my leg and I watched him rub his hands with greedy eagerness and bite and didn't even shoo him. I felt nothing, just the faintest visible surprise at my own cowardice, because I'd thought I'd do it right up till the end. A deathlike numbness stole over me, and I heard the whistling of the west wind in the sea oats, noticing for the first time that they were turning brown.

Twenty-three

ADAM

I don't know how long I stayed there. I heard Cary start his engine and the crunching of his tires as he pulled out—he blew his horn. I didn't stay long after that. I went back in the house and sat down on the bed, staring at the telephone. I wanted to call Jane so badly, for her to comfort me, but it seemed obscene to ask it, as though the victim in a crime should soothe the perpetrator. But I had no self-respect, and right or wrong, I needed her, so I dialed her number anyway.

"Is he there?" she asked, and I said, "he just left—he went back to Killdeer," and she said, "what happened?" and I said, "I fucked up, baby," and she said, "you didn't tell him, did you?" and I said, "no." There was just her silence on the line—that said it all. "Do you want me to come over?" she asked, and I said, "would you?" not daring to say yes outright, and she said, "I'll be there in a minute."

I went out in the big room and stared through the screen door until I saw her car turn in. I listened to her footsteps and then I saw her. She stopped outside the door and we peered at one another through the screen, and then she pressed her hand flat against the wire and I pressed back. She smiled with disappointment and forgiveness, the look a mother gives a refractory child whom she loves anyway, and I couldn't bear it. That look hurt far worse than anything I'd seen in Cary's eyes—not to be a man to her, to have forfeited her respect and admiration, which had been the things that had allowed me to respect and to admire myself. Already in that first look some subtle poison had crept back, and the poison was the old one—the poison was the negative. The small shadow within the larger brightness of her forgiveness and her love was the only thing I saw—the forgiveness seemed irrelevant beside it, mere pity. At that moment Jane started dying, too, and as I opened the screen to her, I noticed that the shimmer, which had grown deeper through those days as with succeeding coats of varnish, had a trace of dullness in it. But it was still there.

"I'm so sorry, Jane," I said, "I thought I could do it, I really did. I was all prepared," and she said, "what happened?" and I said, "he said he knew you were seeing someone and then he asked me point-blank if it was me and I said no." I sank down in the chair and buried my face in my hands. She pulled them off and said, "Listen to me, A., you'll still tell him. You'll just have to do it when we get to Chapel Hill," and I said, "but I really thought I could do it, Jane. He just seemed so depressed—I've never seen him that way," and she frowned and said, "I know, that's how he was last night, too. I'll tell you, A.—I'm not saying this just to make you feel better either—but maybe you were right not to. I'm not sure he could have stood much more," and I said, "but he asked me straight out, Jane," and she just looked at me not trying to assuage it, because that point was unassailable.

"Come lie down with me," she said, taking my hand, "getting all depressed about it isn't going to help. What's done is done." I let her lead me, feeling like a child. "Do you want a beer?" she asked, "I'm going to get one," and I just blinked, too stunned even to make that small decision. She turned away and the flicker of impatience in her eyes scalded me like boiling water. I watched her go, then fell across the mattress, staring at the riddled juniper in the ceiling, seeing eyes and paw prints, sinister omens.

Jane brought back a second can of beer for me and slipped her hand under my head, lifting for me to drink. "Don't baby me," I snapped, jerking away. It spilled across my chest and I sloshed it off angrily. When I looked at her, her eyes were wet with hurt and I said, "I'm sorry, Jane, I'm just so ashamed I let you down." She took my hand and said, "it doesn't matter," and I said, "it does matter, Jane, it matters a lot," and she said, "I want you to know something, A.," wiping her hand across her eyes. "What?" I asked, frightened by her seriousness, and she said, "I couldn't love you any more than I do now no matter what you did. You don't have to do anything." I reached out for her impulsively and clutched her to me with all my strength. We lay like that for the longest time. I don't think I would have ever let her go except that she said, "A.?" in a small voice. I pulled away to look at her, and she said, "you're crushing me, honey," with a tiny cough.

I let go, laughing like a madman—I think I was mad. "I know, I know," I said, "you're very san-sitive," and I cut loose again. Tears ran down my face. Jane smiled like a precocious girl, capitalizing on the success of a joke she hasn't really intended, then sipped her beer. Feeling reckless with release, I said, "for someone who didn't like beer, you've acquired quite a taste for it," and she said softly, "that's the least of the bad habits I've picked up this summer, sweetheart." She ran her hand musingly up under my tee shirt, over my stomach and across my chest. Her eyes deepened and the smoky light in them flowed out into the room—the shimmer peaked and touched my face like mink, and I said, "you know what amazes me?" and she said, "what, honey?" and I said, "I was so depressed when you came over here, now I'm not. I don't know how you do it, but I don't want you to stop, not ever. I love you so much, Jane." She lifted her dress off languidly across her head and shook her hair out, smiling as she sank to kiss my lips. "I won't," she whispered, and we made love for the last time.

We lay there drowsing, her head on my chest, her leg rolled over mine, when I heard the car—the granulated crunching of tires over the loose sand in the driveway. My first thought was that it must be Cary, and my second thought was that it couldn't be. I opened my eyes and sat up, lifting the blind—it was the VW. "Christ," I said, "it's him." Jane looked, too, our eyes met, and then my gaze drifted to the blood on the white sheet. "Guess what?" she said, "my period just started." Her glibness had a note of terrible fatalism, but I still looked at her like she'd gone crazy. She shrugged with resignation and reached for the can of beer. "Not this way, Jane," I said, begging her, and she said, "my car is in the driveway, A., he's already seen it," and I said, "stay here, I'll go out and close the door," and she said, "tell him, A., for God's sake, tell him now—he's going to know it anyway," and I said, "I'll say you came to use the beach." She closed her eyes and leaned back against the headboard. I stumbled across the room, stepping into my pants, then softly closed the door and ran across the floor on tiptoes, kicking Jane's flip-flops underneath a chair. Opening the refrigerator for a beer, I leaned into the cold air and took a deep swallow of it. My hair was sopping wet.

I'd just popped the top and come back to the big room when his form loomed dark against the screen. I looked up from a sip as though surprised to see him and he came in without knocking, regarding me strangely as he reached up to the key rack and took down T.O.'s heavy master ring. "You're back," I said, and he said, "I forgot my keys," in a subdued voice. Something quivered in his face, like a jigsaw puzzle about to burst into its separate fragments, and I said, "you want a beer?" and he said, "no, I really should be going. I was all the way to Elizabeth City when I remembered," and I said, "sorry, I forgot to re-mind you," and he said, "that's okay." The subtext was so heavy, all the dropped hints and double entendres echoing back, only Cary was included in them now. I knew exactly what he was thinking, and I said, "Jane came by to see you. She's on the beach I think. You really ought to say good-bye to her," and he said, "I was just up on the hill—I didn't see her," and I said, "maybe she took a walk," and he said, "I don't think so—maybe you should just tell her for me, A." The bullet ripped my heart out. I put my beer down on the table. "Sit down, man," I said.

He hesitated, then obeyed like someone in a trance, lowering himself onto the edge of the chair. I sat on the chaise lounge across from him, leaning forward with my hands clasped and my elbows on my knees. "I wanted to tell you, Cary," I said, "I was going to today—that's why I wanted to drive up north." His eyes homed on the bedroom door, and he said, "she's in there, isn't she?" like someone who's guessed the answer to a riddle whose interest wasn't trivial at all. I heard the latch snick and turned to look as Jane stepped out in my green bathrobe, her face like death. Cary's eyes followed her as she crossed the room, moving gingerly and quietly, like someone in a church who doesn't want to interrupt the service, or even be noticed at all. She sat down in another chair, completing the triangle, and looked at me before she turned to Cary. I wanted to say something, but there was nothing to be said—that was it, the fact of it, right there.

Cary didn't even look at me, his eyes were all on Jane, filled

with a soft moist love as guileless and unresenting as a dog's.
"I knew," he said, "you looked too good," and she said,
"Cary," with a thousand different meanings in her voice—
gentleness and pity, love, petition, pain—and he said, "I always
wanted to make you look like that," and she said, "don't, honey,
please," as her chin puckered and her lips began to tremble.
The jigsaw finally crumbled. Cary dropped his head toward his
knees and his shoulders started shaking. Covering his face with
both big hands, he wept with the abandon of a child. There were
no words for what I felt.

I sought Jane's eyes, but she got up without looking at me and
knelt beside his chair, resting her hand gently on his shoulder.
He reached up and pressed it, and they didn't speak—she didn't
try to make him stop. When it subsided, she put her hand under
his chin and tried to lift it, but he said, "no, don't make me
look at you," and she said, "please, honey," and he said, "I
can't," then took a great gulp of air and dropped back in the
chair, staring at the ceiling. "I knew," he said, speaking not to
us but up into the air, "I knew all summer—even before you
came down here, but I didn't believe it. I thought it was just
me," and Jane said, "forgive us, Cary, you've got to, honey,"
and he looked at her with sudden tenderness and he said, "I do,
Jane."

Then he raised his eyes to me and his face changed. It grew
dark with blood and twisted up, trembling with suppressed rage,
and then he looked away as though it was too intense to hold,
scorched by his own anger. It struck me like a thunderbolt, and
I said, "don't hate me, man, please don't hate me," and he
said, "I've got to go, I've really got to go," starting to get up,
but Jane grasped his wrist and held him. "It was me as much
as A., Cary," she said in a voice that was still soft but had an
iron core, "I wanted it, too. If you're going to blame A., blame
me, too," and he said, "you didn't lie to me," and she said,
"he was going to tell you," and I said, "I was, man," and he
looked at me again, almost leering, then wrenched his arm away
from Jane and smashed through the screen door, running down
the steps. "Go after him," Jane said, but I was already up.

I caught him in the driveway as he was opening the door. I
held it closed and he stood there with his back to me, shaking.
I was shaking, too. I couldn't even breathe. I half expected him
to turn around and deck me. I wouldn't have tried to stop him.
"Don't let it end like this, man," I said, and he spun around

and said, "I didn't, A., you did this—*you*," and I said, "I'm sorry, man," fighting to hold back tears, and he said, "sorry doesn't cut it, *spud*"—he spat the word—"I knew a lot of things about you, A., but I never thought you were a liar," and I said, "tell me what to say, Cary," and he said, "the only thing you could say is that it isn't true, but that would be another lie," and I said, "I tried, Cary, you may not believe it, but I really did. I tried to fight against the feeling, but I couldn't, and then I tried to tell you," and he said, "and you couldn't do that either," and I just stared at him in total panic, waiting on his judgment, knowing that a word would break me. "I thought you were my friend, A.," he said, and I said, "Jesus Christ, Cary, I am your friend," trying to put my hand out on his shoulder. He slapped it away—the violence of it shocked me—and said, "friends don't do this. I wouldn't have, not ever," and I knew it was true, I knew if we had lived a thousand years he wouldn't have, because there was a solidness in him, a rock nothing could break—in me that place was water. That was where I broke. "You owed me something, A.," he said, "I never asked you, but you did," driving the stake to the last depth, and I said, "I know, Cary," through my sobs, "I know I did. I tried to pay it but I couldn't, I just couldn't do it. Forgive me, man, please, you've got to."

There was a softness in his eyes for just a moment, all the miles that we had traveled, but then he stared down at my hand on the car door, his gaze like a welder's torch, and said, "move it, A." But I didn't, I said, "please don't do this, man, I love you, tell me how to make it up to you." I said it mindlessly, never thinking he'd take me up on it, but he did. His dark eyes burned into me and he said, "you know." It took the breath out of me. "Don't ask me that, Cary," I said, "please don't ask me that," and he said, "I'm not asking anything, A., you already made your choice," and I said, "Cary . . ." and he said, "go to hell," and pushed me back, flinging the door open. I watched him go, backing and then swerving out, flattening the border of gaillardias Jane and I had planted with such care.

Feeling her hand on my arm, I looked down at Jane beside me. She'd slipped her dress back on, and her manner was composed like someone at a funeral. "We can't let him leave like that," she said, "come on, maybe we can catch him," and I said, "he doesn't want me there, Jane," feeling the tears start again, and she said, "he'll cool down on the drive, A., I know he will," and I said, "he won't, Jane, he won't." She took my hand and started toward the car. I went with her a few steps, but everything was swimming out of focus around me. I bucked and shouted, "no, goddamnit, no," and ran away from her up the dune. I heard her call my name, but I kept going and didn't stop till I reached the gazebo. When I turned back I saw her mother's silver Olds pulling down the driveway. I just lost it then. I snapped. I didn't see Jane again for thirteen years.

I plunged into the water and swam toward the horizon. I didn't stop or look back, just stroked on and on through the cold pitching sea feeling the heat steal out of me, out and out, until I'd swum for thirty, forty minutes—I don't know how long it was, except I'd never gone a quarter of that distance into open ocean, not alone, and I knew better, but I didn't care. Nearing exhaustion, I became aware of something following me, lurking under the dark water, and as I turned my head to breathe I saw it, a black fin, now in one place, now another, Perhaps it was the wind chop, blades of water, but fear sang in me like current through a live wire, and I said, "come on, you fucker, here I am, come get me."

When I looked back the shoreline had receded to a pale brushstroke no wider than a ribbon, but against it I could still make out the dark silhouette of a standing figure—a man of sticks. Perhaps it was only in my mind, but I felt like after disappearing for a time that summer he'd come back for me. Taking a deep breath, I flipped and went to touch the bottom, but I never found it, and when I came up I drank water first, and then again, before my head broke surface. Treading water, I realized I was getting sluggish, and it occurred to me that I was going to drown, but I made no move to save myself. Because I could feel it out there all around me and I wanted it to come, I wanted to face it, the dark thing that had trailed me all my life, my fear and misery and pain, and slay it the way I'd slain the boar, or be slain—but just to look it in the face and know the adversary, to recurse the curser and know his name. Finally I started swimming back, the waves jeering all around me with an ugly menace.

Passing the gazebo, I saw the pile of Cary's butts, staining the sand an unhealthy yellow like the soiled cotton in the filters, and beside it a pop-top lay agleam in the late sun. I remembered that day fishing with my father, the way the blues turned in and drove the shoal of minnows on the beach, the glitter of the silver spoon—that pop-top, Cary's, was another one I'd swallowed long ago—the way my line had coiled with nothing on it. There was nothing on it now—not Cary, not Jane, not even myself. I kept going straight into the house and tore my clothes out of the closet, leaving half of everything I owned behind me as I packed. I knew if I stopped to think my mind would shatter, and I held the last shred of it like a climber on a wall of glacial ice with nothing but my broken bleeding fingernails.

Closing the porch shutters, I threw the circuit-breakers, called Pig and scratched out of the driveway, not even knowing where I was going. I just knew it was over. Everything was over. I smelled fall in the air and it had an iron tang. The wind whipped my eyes wet. It was not for Cary, it was not for anyone or anything. I didn't have a plan. There was no reason. It was just against myself. I simply threw my life away and ran.

I went off to Columbia and did not return Jane's phone calls—there were only two—and I became a player and a New York City vampire there. I won, too, for a time—I won until I lost.

That was where I died.

PART III

The Deep, Deep Sea

Jane

"A man who is born falls into a dream
like a swimmer who falls into the sea.
If he tries to climb out into the air
as inexperienced people endeavor to do,
he drowns, *nicht wahr*?
No, I tell you, the way is to the destructive element
submit yourself and by the exertions of your
hands and feet in the water make
the deep deep sea keep you up."

—Joseph Conrad, *Lord Jim*

One

Tap, tap, tap.

"Miss?" the state patrolman said, peering in the window from under the brim of his hat.

Tap, tap, tap. *"Miss?"*

For the first few seconds I could only stare at him and read his lips, like I was in a fishbowl. This is how it comes, I thought, this is how it comes, no, God, please, not like this, as a little voice inside my head whispered, "it's him, it's A., he's dead."

The officer motioned me to roll my window down, and the night air rushed back in on me—men shouting orders on the bridge, the crackling of static on a policeband radio, the hum of idling engines, cicadas out in the dark trees, waves lapping on the riverbank, the smell of brackish water.

"Excuse me, miss," the patrolman said in a suddenly loud voice, leaning in my window well, eyeing me with a look of cool practiced appraisal, like maybe I was a drunk driver, "there's been an accident here, I'll have to ask you to move along."

"I . . ." I tried to talk to him and couldn't find my voice.

I saw a hundred subtle calculations in his eyes, then something human and concerned flashed through the mask of his official-ness. "What is it, ma'am?" he asked, "is something wrong?"

At that note of sympathy I had to fight to keep myself from breaking down. Get a hold, girl, get a hold, I told myself, feeling panic queering through my bloodstream. "I was following

471

someone, officer," I said, "he was very . . . upset." He got it
then, and I looked away from him through the windshield, scan-
ning the long S-curve of the bridge, like a nightmare scene
whose details were just starting to emerge. They seared themselves into my brain like some terrible lesson from grammar
school—yellow was for wrecker, blue was the patrol cars, a
blinking red one on the dark arm of the crane, sitting idle on a
flatbed trailer, and the orange . . . The orange was the ambulance.

"Miss," the officer said, "*miss* . . ." something, something.
I tried to look at him, but couldn't turn my eyes away. Two
paramedics were wheeling a gurney over the broken glass on
the roadbed. They were not hurrying. The back doors of the
ambulance were open in to a brightly lit interior. I watched as
they collapsed the legs and hoisted. A hand fell out from underneath the sheet. I felt the air incinerate around me. "Oh, my
God, my God," I said, covering my mouth with both hands. I
reached for the door handle, but the officer's weight blocked it.
He was saying something, but I couldn't understand what he
was saying. "Please," I begged him, "please, you've got to let
me go."

"Just a minute, ma'am," he said out of a strained whitened
face, "just hold on a minute here—what sort of vehicle was your
party driving?"

My party? My *party*? What did he mean by that—was he
insane? I shoved against his weight and couldn't budge it.

"Try to get a hold on yourself, ma'am," he said, "I want to
help you, but you've got to cooperate. The vehicle, ma'am . . ."

I tried to think—a big English car, old, like a Rolls, not a
Rolls. It was on the tip of my tongue. "A Bentley," I blurted,
as my mind suddenly supplied it.

"A Bentley," he repeated, "you're sure, ma'am?"

I nodded, and he said, "okay, ma'am, now listen. That right
there?" He tilted his head toward the ambulance, the long form
underneath the sheet. "That's a boy out there, seventeen or
eighteen. He was with his girlfriend, driving an '82 Jeep." I
stared where he was pointing and only saw then, in the alley
between the side of the ambulance and the bridge railing, partially blocked from view, the Jeep lying overturned, shoved over
to the side to keep the one lane clear. The vinyl top was crushed
like a paper bag and the windshield was smashed—those were
the splinters glinting on the pavement. And that shoe. That shoe.

For a minute I just couldn't compute it—it was like a time-warp opened, sucking me back thirteen years into the past—because it looked just like the Jeep A. used to drive. And that little voice kept up its evil whisper.

"A Jeep, ma'am," he said, coaching me like a child, "not a Bentley—that's not your party, is it?"

I shook my head and bit my lip, sinking forward against the wheel. Not my party, but I'll cry if I want to, cry if I want to, cry if I want to . . . The words of the old song echoed in my head like madness, and I whispered, "thank God, thank God," squeezing tears out of my eyes. The relief I felt was indescribable. It swept me up like a roaring current and carried me somewhere far far away. Then it dropped me. "Are they . . . ?" I asked, looking back at him.

"Yes, ma'am," he said, "yes, they are," and I said, "both . . . ?" He nodded and said, "they both died instantly, ma'am," and I said, "I'm sorry, how terrible," wiping my eyes, "it's just . . ." "I understand, ma'am," he said, "you don't have to say anything." I tried to smile at him, but he didn't smile back.

"I want you to back up and pull your vehicle over on the shoulder, ma'am," he said, and the continued gravity in his face and tone confused me. I didn't think he'd got it. "But it isn't him," I explained, "it isn't my party," translating into his language.

"Yes, ma'am," he said, "just humor me, miss. Right over there." He pointed behind him to the grassy bank on our side, the near one, where I saw a dark patrol car.

"I can't stop, officer," I told him, "I'm in a terrible hurry. I've got to get to the beach."

"Yes, ma'am," he said, "I understand, but I'm going to have to insist. Park your vehicle and I'll be with you in a minute."

"But . . ." I started to object, and he said forcibly, "in a minute, ma'am," standing up, waiting till I obeyed. He thinks I'm drunk, I told myself as I backed up. He's going to make me walk the line or say the alphabet. Did I have my licence? As I parked and rummaged in my purse for my wallet, I saw him walking toward a group of men out on the bridge.

I stared at my picture on the licence, hating it. I'd been twenty-eight—Robert had given me those pearls for my birthday, in a blue velvet box lined with gray silk. She was someone else, I thought. I looked up as the ambulance splashed orange light into the car. It passed me, heading toward Norfolk, setting fires in the plate glass windows of the few storefronts in the town. The officer approached an older patrolman who seemed to be in charge. The older man was trim and fortyish, military looking. I saw him cut his eyes in my direction, then look away and nod as the younger officer talked. He nodded, too, starting back.

"Come with me a minute, ma'am," he said, opening my door for me. As I climbed out, I said, "I don't understand, officer—what's going on?" and he said, "I'm going to explain it to you, ma'am," opening the passenger door of the patrol car for me.

I sat there as he walked around and climbed in behind the wheel, taking off his hat carefully with both hands. He placed it on the seat between us and switched on the overhead light. Only then did I see how young he was, no more than twenty-five. He had thick close-cropped hair and a beauty mark on his upper lip. I handed him my licence and he took it without looking at it. "This is the situation, ma'am," he said, "there was a second vehicle involved."

I stared at him, feeling suddenly numb and disembodied. "A second vehicle . . ." I said.

He nodded gravely.

"Was it . . . ?" I asked, "it wasn't . . . ?"

He pursed his lips and shook his head. "We don't have an ID on it yet, ma'am," he said.

I blinked at him, not understanding.

"It's in the water, ma'am," he explained quietly, "the divers are looking for it now. They just got here not five minutes ago."

I gazed out toward the smashed railing and saw one drop off backwards, holding his mask. A second was shouldering his tank, breathing through his regulator to test it. Kneeling down, the older state patrolman handed down a large round arclight of some sort to the first diver. It came on and the water boiled a sickly evil white in the infusion of bubbles, then its beam turned downward and in the sheen of the moon I saw a black fin splash and disappear. The little voice said, "I told you so, this is how it comes." I felt like I was going to be sick.

"We'll know in just a few minutes, ma'am," the patrolman was saying—he seemed far away, at the wrong end of a looking glass—"the water's fairly deep, but there's not much current, not enough to move a car. Five minutes, ma'am, ten at most."

An awful picture flashed across my mind—down in the darkness, the pitch-black darkness, A. trapped inside the car, struggling to get out. I closed my eyes and started counting—"one, two, three, four"—but each number was a passing second.

"We're doing everything we can, ma'am," the officer said, and I said, "how long . . . ? when did it happen?" and he said, "we don't know exactly, ma'am," evading me, and I said, "but when did you get here?" and his face froze back into the mask as he said, "approximately half an hour ago, ma'am."

Half an hour, half an hour . . . The wheels of my mind spun, throwing up a host of idle questions, as the little voice played on—how long could a person hold his breath? a minute? five minutes? What if the windows were rolled up? Would there be enough air to last for thirty minutes? Would A. have rolled his windows up? "He used to be a lifeguard," I said, thinking that was hopeful. The officer just looked at me, feeling sorry for me. I crashed crashed crashed, and the little voice said, "it's him, you know it's him," and I said, "not like this," and the voice said, "like this."

"He's dead," I said to the officer, and he said, "you don't know that, ma'am, and neither do I. I know this is hard on you, but let's don't make it worse by jumping to conclusions." I clung to him, his sanity, his calmness, as my own went up in smoke.

"What happened?" I asked, and he said, "as far as we can tell, ma'am, the driver of the Jeep was trying to pass out there in the curve. They'd been drinking, ma'am, the boy and girl had—we found a number of empties. It's a bad curve anyway and he must have been going pretty fast—the best we can figure, he lost control and jerked back into the second vehicle, sent it through the guard rail and then turned himself over as he swung back." His look turned deferential—"your husband, ma'am?"

The unexpected question was like a paper cut across my heart. I felt myself begin to pant, big heaving breaths, and I covered my face with my hands, the tears so close, so close. He put his hand on my arm in a supportive steadying way, taking my re-action as assent. Was it assent? Please, God, I prayed silently, don't let me know it now, let me suffer, but not that suffering, as a terrible light began to dawn in me.

"What was your husband wearing, Miz Pegram?" the officer said, reading off my licence, and the name was like a sobering cold slap. "McCrae," I said, "my name is Jane McCrae, I'm divorced." I threw it up at him, daring his judgment, wanting to be angry at him, at something, but his look was neutral. "A white shirt," I said, "I think it was white."

He nodded. "If you could give me a brief description, Miz McCrae, so I can tell the divers . . . just to speed it up for you." His face seemed apologetic.

Suddenly I couldn't remember A.'s face. "Tall, dark hair, blue eyes," I said, rattling off the list from some vague general idea of him, searching for his face. Then I saw it, underwater, mooning in the window of the car as the diver turned his light on it.

"He was upset, I believe you said," the patrolman said, "as far as you know, ma'am, was he impaired?" "Impaired?" I asked, and he said, "drinking, ma'am, under the influence." I tried to remember. "I don't think . . ." I said, and then I thought about the coke. "Please," I said to the officer, "isn't that enough?"

"I'm sorry, ma'am," he said, "I'm just trying to do my job. Don't put yourself out. I'll be right back." He picked up his hat and started to climb out, then turned back. "Miz McCrae?" he said. I looked at him and the mask had disappeared. "There's a lot of traffic passes on this road, Miz McCrae," he said, "Virginia folks coming down to the beach for the weekend. Lots of 'em drive late at night like this to avoid the tie-ups. Friday night is one of our worst, ma'am. But it could be anybody down there, Miz McCrae, anybody at all. Just going by the plain arithmetic of it, chances are it's not your husband. Try not to worry."

He reached out in the back seat and took out a plaid thermos and a brown paper lunch bag wrinkled soft as chamois. "I've got some soup here, ma'am," he said, "and half a chicken-salad sam'wich. I'm not going to eat it."

He held them out to me and I shook my head, trying to smile for him. "It's homemade," he said, as though maybe that would tempt me, "my wife fixed it up this evening right before I come on the shift."

"Thank you," I told him, "but I don't think I could right now," and he nodded and said, "well, I'll leave it right here on the seat, ma'am, just in case you change your mind. A little something in your stomach always helps." He smiled at me and I saw clearly who he was—a simple country boy, good-natured, honest, proud but without meanness—and how the mask had formed over that human part of him, not all at once, but slowly, built up bit by bit like papier-mâché, each time he'd leaned into the window of some stranger's car, like mine, late at night, tensed to receive the cold shock of their fear or hatred, as a defense against it, until he was trapped inside that armor. Yet at that moment it shone through to me, that human part, he willed it to. I put my hand out on his arm and squeezed it, and he gentled like a colt.

Lifting the flap of his shirt pocket, he took out a pack of Camels, shaking one out, and then on second thought offering one to me. I don't know why I took it, but I did, leaning into his lighter flame. "I haven't had a cigarette in three years," I told him as I exhaled, staring at the coal, and he said, "if I'd have knowed that I wouldn't have give you one," his idiom and accent dropping back a notch as he allowed himself that intimacy. "I been trying to quit myself," he said, "my wife keeps after me—throws 'em out about the time I come in the house with 'em." He shrugged sheepishly as he lit his own, and I said, "you should listen to your wife," and he said, "yes, ma'am, prob'ly should," and I said, "but you don't." He grinned boyishly and said, "I reckon you know how it is, ma'am," and I smiled and closed my eyes in assent. I reckon I did.

"Sit tight now, ma'am," he said, "first minute I know, you'll know." I watched him walk away and stared out across the scene, knowing if it was A., if he was dead, that I would never forget it, that this moment, this picture, would tuck itself away inside the hope chest with all the other broken dreams and promises, and I would climb the stairs into the attic from time to time and take it out and gaze at it like a cursed treasure. I stabbed out my cigarette and tried to put that morbidness away from me like a monster, but the voice kept saying, "this is how it comes, it comes like this," droning on like the cicadas out in the dark trees, like the remorseless lapping of the waves against the pylons, all part of the same thing. But what was that thing? I didn't know its name, but only that it was something old and calm and soulless, indifferent to human life, and against it hope seemed small.

Yet I did hope. I tried to think about the happiness I'd feel when the officer came back and spoke the precious words—"it isn't him"—but hope seemed like a distant country, one you dream of visiting and know you never will. That certainty seemed absolute, like premonition, and it frightened me as much to ignore it as to listen. I closed my eyes and tried to lose myself in prayer, but God's voice was silent. Through the crackling of static on the radio, I heard the dispatcher—a woman—speak some code. What did it mean? Highway fatalities, homicides,

battered wives and children . . . there was a constant stream of
agony occurring all over the world, so insistent and unbearable
we had to keep it secret even from ourselves. I thought about
the terrible headlines—two hundred people here, five hundred
there—my own numb indifference to the things I read. I thought
about the things the paper never told—the families, like Sadie.
I thought about the parents of the two children who had died out
there tonight. Somewhere, even now, a grim-faced stranger, like
the officer, was knocking on a mother's door and she was waking
up, hurrying to answer it, fumbling with the sash of her robe,
gazing out through the crack in the door still fastened with the
night-chain with a sleepy frightened face. He would speak the
words—''your son . . . your daughter''—the lightning flash . . .
He would say, ''your husband, ma'am . . .''

Your husband, ma'am, your husband . . . The officer's words
echoed back, and in my mind's eye I saw him coming back
across the bridge, leaning in the window—I would know just by
his face. He would open the door for me and walk beside me
toward the broken railing. I would watch the divers bring A.'s
limp form up in their arms. They would lay him on a blanket on
the pavement and back away as I knelt and brushed the hair out
of his face. I would close his eyes, remembering the light in
them, the spark of humor. I would gaze at his shoulders and his
arms through the soaked shirt, remembering the way the muscles ridged under the skin as he moved, remembering the feeling
that bloomed all through my body as I'd stood on Mama's porch
studying the shape of his shoulders, the clean line his hair made
against his brow. I would remember how he'd reached out to me
in bed that afternoon and said, ''try not to worry, Jane,'' how
love had been so close. I would remember and remember and
remember. When I was an old woman rocking somewhere in a
chair—after marriage, children, the suffering and happiness of
a full life—I would climb those stairs into the attic of my mind
and take out the haunted photograph, remembering that moment, this moment, out of all the other moments, how I had
seen my hope and love go down in the dark waters of a place
called Deep Cove, without my having known my love, or pos-
sessed the comfort of speaking it to A. For my own heart was
such another code, I had not heard the dispatcher's voice inside
me, and it was only that moment in the patrol car that it broke.
I knew it then. The truth of my own love for A. stabbed me in
the heart, a quiet tender thing of such despair—to learn it there,

under such circumstances, to feel the resounding emptiness of a space that he had filled without my having known that it was full, to see that the questions I had asked—why A. and not Cary—and all the other questions I'd believed would lead me to the truth of my own feeling had only led me further away, blocking what was there already, to finally understand, not in panic but in the sober calm of pure despair, that the thing I wanted in my life, the thing I'd always wanted, had been within my grasp and was slipping away through my fingers even then, as the clock ticked, and that it would never come to me so deep and true again, except through A. . . .

I wanted only to be unconscious, like a stone. But the stone woke up in me, a place deep in the earth where light had never penetrated, a place I'd never even known I was alive. The unforgiving rock of my soul's foundations woke up in that pain, screaming out its accusation to me because I had not known, and I felt mocked, self-mocked, mocked by God. "If you are there," I whispered, addressing Him, "if you are there," and the terrible words thundered down on me—"Thou shalt not tempt the Lord, thy God." I remembered Jesus's agony in the garden—the words came back to me out of my childhood—"O my Father, if it be possible, let this cup pass from me." I tried to say the rest—"nevertheless not as I will, but as thou wilt"—but I couldn't, my heart would not be resigned. "Please, God," I prayed, "grant me this one thing—don't let it be A., let it be someone else." The terrible blackness of that wish seemed blasphemous, but I wished it anyway, for the cup to pass to someone else. God didn't answer, and in that silence I felt he had abandoned me. "If you are there," I said again, as my faith trembled. I had never in my life felt so alone.

My mind reeled out of control, tumbling down a well shaft into memory. Terrible things came back to me. I remembered lying face down on a chaise beside the Country Club pool, listening to the hoarse cawing of a crow in the pines behind the tennis courts, hardly aware of it, as Becky Denton touched my shoulder, how the coldness of her hand made me shiver as I looked up, holding the towel to my bosom because my top had been unfastened. Becky didn't speak, only pointed to the gate, and as I turned I saw a crow light on the gutter of the clubhouse roof, its black feathers full of gleaming oily colors in the sunlight. It was silent. Mama stood there, silent, too, in dark glasses, staring at me across that distance as though afraid to come in. That same awful voice of premonition spoke, and I knew that instant someone was dead. I wrapped myself in the towel and walked around the pool. In the shallow end some little kids were playing, jumping, splashing—their voices seemed far away.

"What is it, Mama?" I asked, but she just shook her head and took my hand, leading me to the parking lot. We both climbed in the car, and she turned in the seat, taking off her glasses. Her eyes were red and had a fever shine, and I said, "Mama?" and she said, "it's Cary, Jane," and I said, "no, Mama." She put her hand gingerly on my arm as though doubting her right to comfort me, and said, "I'm so sorry, honey," and I said, "he's not . . . ?" she just nodded. "They pulled him from the Killdeer River this morning, darling," she said. I stared through the chain-link fence at the kids laughing and shouting in the pool—the crow had gone—and somewhere deep inside I knew I'd been waiting for that moment, for that news, a long time, wondering how it would come, and the voice had said, "it comes like this."

I'd known since the last time I'd seen Cary at his mother's house the year before. It was three months after T.O.'s funeral— I sent flowers but didn't go. I'd put off that visit because the times I'd tried before had seemed so futile. I could always tell Cary was still hurt and that it didn't do him any good to see me. Cary had dropped out of school by then and I'd heard talk— about how he'd taken to sitting at T.O.'s desk, going through the drawers and account books, how people had seen him walking up Advance Avenue in one of his daddy's old felt hats and carrying his key ring. I don't know why I went—I think because I had to know.

I knocked on the glass door and no one answered. But the inside door was open, and I went in. I found Cary in the living room, sitting in his rocking chair in front of the TV watching *Bonanza*, just the picture, not even any sound. He wasn't rocking, just studying it with a dark frown of concentration. Before I could even say hello, he cut his brooding eyes at me, holding up his hand for me to wait as he turned back to the picture. Already frightened, feeling queasy, I sat down and watched with him. Ben Cartwright was saying something to Little Joe. The camera kept cross-cutting between them—Lorne Greene droning on out of a grave wise face, and Little Joe respectful and attentive, worshiping his father. Michael Landon looked so young. "Don't you want to hear what they're saying?" I asked, and Cary said, "I already know"—his face seemed angry. Then Hoss and Adam rode into the courtyard of the Ponderosa and Cary switched the set off, lighting a cigarette. He started rocking, but he didn't look at me.

"I'm sorry about your daddy, Cary," I said, "I know what it's like to lose a father." He gave me a fierce stare like he was deciding whether to give it to me, then he did. "It's a bitch, isn't it?" he said, and the frozen numbness in his face flash-thawed, a wash of tears glistened in his eyes. I felt my own mist up, both for him and remembering my own pain, but the next instant Cary changed the subject. "I guess you heard I dropped out of school," he said, like it still mattered to him what other people said and thought. I nodded and he said, "I've been a little bit confused I guess—that's what they tell me." He grinned like that was funny to him and took a deep drag on his cigarette—that grin had nothing to do with the rest of his face. I sat there feeling heartsick and afraid, out of my depth. "Are you okay, Cary?" I asked, and he said, "I'm getting better," mulling on the statement like he was doubtful of it and weighing it against his feeling.

"I saw A., you know," he said, suddenly looking up, and I said, "no, I didn't." Cary nodded and said, "he came by here a month or so after Daddy died. He'd just got out of school and wanted me to take a road trip with him to Atlanta to see the Allman Brothers." He stopped like he'd lost his train of thought or had forgotten he was speaking to me. "Did you go?" I asked, and he said, "we only got as far as Winston-Salem." I wanted to ask him what had happened, but I didn't, because it seemed like there were landmines everywhere, things that might touch places in Cary I didn't want to touch, so I just said, "I haven't seen or talked to A. in two years, Cary, not since that summer at the beach," and Cary said, "that summer at the beach," with an ironic emphasis, or perhaps just wistfulness.

"That was a long time ago, Cary," I told him, and he said, "do you believe in time?" like he was suddenly eager to escape into abstraction. "I never thought that much about it," I said, and he said, "I have, I think about it all the time," smiling at the clever echo. "Remember when we did those mushrooms?" he asked, and I said, "yes," and he said, "remember how there wasn't any time? how it just seemed to be one moment that went on forever?" "Yes," I said, "it was a little bit like that," and he said, "that's how this is, too." I didn't ask him what because I knew he meant the way he felt. "I read somewhere that time is an illusion based on change," he said, "so if nothing changes there's no time," and because I knew he'd spun that glistening pearl around a seed of pain, I told him softly, "but things do change, Cary." His eyes drifted over my shoulder as he said, "they swirl and make new patterns, but the new ones are the old ones—underneath it's still." He was staring at the van Gogh on the wall—"Starry, Starry Night." "Life isn't like a picture, Cary," I said, and he said, "but pictures are like life and if A equals B, then B equals A—remember that from algebra?" and I said, "vaguely," and he said, "it's funny how it all comes back to you, we know so much, thousands of years, but we still don't know how to change." He'd starting counting on his fingers then, rocking extremely fast, in sync with the inner speed he was traveling at. "But people change, Cary," I told him, "look at us," and he said, "I never did, and neither did you," and I said, "I think you're wrong," and he said, "Jane?" and I said, "yes?" and he grinned and said, "see? you answered— if you'd changed you wouldn't know your name, you'd be a different person," and I said, "that's ridiculous." He gazed at me like he knew more and said, "but you're still Jane, and I'm still Cary, it swirled and swirled but underneath it never changed—I thought it would, but now I know."

He seemed like a sage who'd served a long apprenticeship, but whose only wisdom was despair, but what haunted me most was that he sounded more like A. than like himself, as though having lost his friend he'd re-created him inside. I fought hard to keep from crying as I said, "honey, I think you need to get some help," and he said, "to change?" and I said, "to get better." He came back briefly from that brittle eerie world where you could almost hear the tinkling of ice and said, "I'm getting it." He pointed to a vial of pills on the end table underneath the lamp and said, "know what those are?" and I said, "what?" and he said, "time-producing capsules—they're supposed to change you, but they don't work. It just makes it far away so you can't really feel it, like something in the basement that you can just barely hear through the floor. But it's still down there"— he cupped his hand to his ear—"hear it?" I could tell by his grin that he was baiting me, but I didn't take it up. "But maybe you could talk to someone," I said, and he said, "we do that, too—I've got this shrink at Duke, he's so smart he knows what

I'm going to say before I even say it. We talk and talk, just like I'm talking to you now," and I said, "do you feel it's helping you?" and Cary said, "do you feel this is helping you?" and I said, "at least it's giving me some idea how you feel," and he said, "then what?" and I said, "I don't understand," and he said, "tell me something that will help," and I said, "it's going to get better, Cary, you've got to believe that—it just takes some time," and he said, "but there isn't any time, Jane, you're not listening. The shrink doesn't listen either, that's why it doesn't help," and I said, "there are other people, Cary, you could look for someone else." Cary shook his head and said, "it wouldn't make a difference—whether he listens or whether he doesn't, the truth is still the truth, there's no help for it. The only way would be to change it but you can't, because there isn't any change, and even if there was you couldn't change the truth or else it wouldn't be the truth, not the real one. But when you know the real one, right that second, time stops and you realize it was always an illusion, just a swirling that you took for change, and then you either live with it or you don't, you either close your eyes or you go down in the basement and look at it—I have."

I went up and put my arms around him because there was nothing else to do. "I hate to see you so unhappy, honey," I said. He didn't respond at all except to stop rocking, but when I pulled away I saw the panic far down in his eyes, his utter loneliness, but he just bluffed it out, taking a big hit on his cigarette and stabbing it into the ashtray. "You should have married me when you had the chance, McCrae," he said, and it took me a minute to realize he was joking. I wiped my eyes and smiled. "I guess I missed my big chance, huh?" I said, and he said, "damn straight," and seeing that old mischievous Cary-twinkle in his eyes I caught a clear flash of the boy I remembered who had been my friend and whom I'd loved, still loved, and I said, "you get well, you old shit, and I still might," and Cary smiled and went back underwater.

That's what it had come down to between me and Cary, just a little joke that neither of us believed in anymore, something from the past that we remembered fondly but had no meaning in the present. And for Cary that's all there was, just the past, a timeless state that he was trapped in. He didn't have a present, and what tore me up the most was that he didn't even want one. There'd been death there in that room that day, I'd known it

at the time, it didn't have a taste or smell, but you could feel it
like a wind, thin and cold and clear, so mental, a man-thing. I'd
heard a whisper of the same futility and resignation in A.'s voice,
and it filled me with helpless terror because I didn't understand
it. I only knew they were in love with it, all of them, some way,
A. even more than Cary. I'd thought Cary was different, but it
claimed him in the end. They all liked to flirt with it, to stand
there on that ledge and lean into the wind, feeling it breast into
them, filling their clothes like a sail and toying with the notion
of letting go to see if it would lift them, getting mesmerized if
they stayed long enough till they believed it, and then you didn't
see them anymore. It's the thing that made me think at times
that men aren't fully human, not like women are, they're more
like ghosts that flit about. You had to get them down out of that
wind before they fell in love with it. Once they did it was too
late. That day when I saw Cary he was gone.

I think Sadie knew it, too, by then. As I was walking out the
door that day I met her on the stoop coming in from work. She
looked at me with those sad eyes of hers and said, "he's not the
same, is he?" studying my face as though for a reassurance
she didn't hope to find. "He'll get better, Miz Kinlaw," I
said, "he's still Cary," and she smiled like she appreciated me
for saying it but her eyes remained the same. "But the old slide-
trombone is gone," she said, and I had to run right past her,
holding the sobs till I reached the car and backed out in the road.
Sadie stood there at the top of the steps gazing after me as I
pulled out, like someone in a war who'd lost everything and was
still going to lose more. Her eyes were dry. Sadie had shed all
her tears by then.

I never saw Cary again, just his coffin as they lowered it into
the ground at Laurel Ridge. Cliff tried to read a poem, but broke
up in the middle of the first line. His Uncle Vince had to lead
him back to his chair, and Cliff sat there sobbing into his hands.
I remembered the muted creaking of the motorized winch, and
how my eye had scanned out across the rolling greenness toward the treeline in the distance, where I saw an old man and a
boy, waiting, smoking cigarettes, casting sober glances toward
the tent under which we stood. The handle of a shovel peeked
up from behind a headstone. I dropped a red rose in the grave
and said good-bye to Cary, and then I walked away and left him
there.

It was such a sorrow, such a sorrow. But my sorrow that day

had been for Cary, it had been for Sadie and for Cliff, not for myself. What there was between me and Cary had been finished long before, my pain was clean of need. Now it wasn't. Now in the patrol car on the grassy bank beside a river whose name I didn't know, in a place called Deep Cove, I felt the source and wellspring, the deep nerve of my life, quivering exposed and threatened, and I knew, as I hadn't known till then, that what I'd done, the journey I had taken, had not been primarily for A., but for me, because it was unfinished between us. Whatever the problems—and there were many—they didn't matter, because there was something in my core linked to his, a link that not even thirteen years had severed—deeper than sex, deeper than chemistry, deeper than my admiration for his beautiful attack, deeper than my fear of it. All those things were just the lace around the edges, but the center of my passion and my love for him was a darkness without name, a mystery.

I don't know how long a time had passed—perhaps a minute, perhaps an hour. A commotion on the bridge brought me back to the present. I saw the diver's head break through the moonlit surface of the river, shouting something to the others on the bridge. A man in the glass cabin of the crane tossed a cigarette onto the pavement and the arm began to drop toward the water, lowering a block and tackle. The young officer broke away and started toward me, walking hurriedly. Then he began to trot. I tried to see his face, but it was dark against the lights, as he loomed larger and larger in the windshield. "Please, God," I whispered, "this one thing. Spare him. Give me back my life." I opened the door and got out.

"Miz McCrae," he shouted, ten yards off, "it's a green pickup, Virginia tags." For a moment I simply couldn't comprehend it, then I fell. He caught me in his arms, maneuvering me against the fender. I didn't cry, I couldn't. I must have been in shock. I leaned against the car, still holding my breath, waiting for it to hit me, something, but I just felt empty. I could hear him panting like a boy who'd run a windsprint. He reached for his cigarettes and gave me one. My hands trembled as I took it. "I'm sorry you had to go through that, ma'am," he said, lighting his own in cupped hands, then offering the flame to me, "it's just . . ." "I understand," I said, and he leaned back beside me, sighing his smoke up in the air. I wanted to give him something, but there was nothing left. "Who . . . ?" I asked, and he said, "and old fellow, ma'am, a crabber. The bed was full of pots—probably on his way to set them." That's when I began to cry, quietly, not much. "I've got to go," I said, remembering, and he said, "yes, ma'am," grinding the cigarette underfoot and taking my arm.

As he led me to my car, I noticed that the sky had turned a little lighter. "Thank you," I said as he opened my door for me, and he said, "no need, Miz McCrae, just doing my job," and I said, "it's more than that to me." He just said, "drive careful, ma'am, you've had quite a scare. I wouldn't want you to go have a accident yourself." I smiled and shook my head. "I won't," I said, as I climbed in. "Good-bye, ma'am, take care," he said through the window, and I said, "you, too."

He walked out on the bridge and waved me forward, and as I passed a little spark of life came back in me. "Officer?" I said, leaning out the window, and he said, "ma'am?" I smiled at him and said, "you listen to your wife, hear?" and he said, "yes, ma'am, I'll do that, Miz McCrae," smiling back.

As I left the scene behind me, passing through the cut in a dark wall of trees, suddenly plowed fields opened out ahead of me, miles and miles of them stretching all the way to the horizon. In the east the sky was turning red. Mist was rising from the irrigation ditches running between the furrows, and I pulled over on the shoulder because I couldn't drive. Birds were beginning to sing, and a rooster crowed off at a white farmhouse in the distance, sitting alone in the middle of the fields, dwarfed by an enormous tree. A dog was barking in the yard. The land was waking up.

I climbed out of the car and wandered out among the rows as a light breeze trembled the spaced green shoots. It was tobacco, and as I leaned down to sniff them I remembered Mama's clipping, the one about the girl who'd been killed and buried in a field—the tobacco girl. She came alive right there. My life burst open in those fields, and that buried girl in me, the one who let her heart and not her head decide and always got me in such trouble, came back from the dead, and suddenly I knew, I *knew*, she'd led me there, to that moment and the fullness of my love, and that I should have listened to her all along. I sank down on my knees and wept with full release. I scooped the sparkling crumbly dirt in both hands, inhaling its life scent. I learned to breathe again. A joy as clear and high as my pain and fear had been dark and fathomless sang out in me, because he was alive. There were no questions anymore. "For whether there be prophecies, they shall fail; whether there be tongues, they shall cease; whether there be knowledge, it shall vanish away. For we know in part, and we prophesy in part. But when that which is perfect is come, then that which is in part shall vanish away." It was love, just love. Amazing grace.

I left my doubts and hedgings together with my childhood on the bridge in Deep Cove, and in the abounding happiness of that moment in the fields, I knew I had tested God and he had tested me, and I had failed so miserably. Yet he had not abandoned me, his mercy had uplifted me, and I remembered what I had allowed myself to forget, that it is always then, always in those times and places when you've carried it just as far as you can carry it that the other something kicks in from below and lets you know that there's a force in life, whatever name you choose to call it, that when you let go it supports you, and if it had failed Cary, he was all right now, where he was. Even the terrible decision he'd made hadn't excluded him finally, not even in death, from the consolation of God's power, and I knew that, whatever happened, A. would not be excluded from it either, and neither would I.

My life had never been so clear, so filled as it was then. For the first time I knew who I was and what I wanted in my life. My mind went back to my first day with Dr. Rosenkrantz and the simple question he had asked me—"what is it you want, Jane?" In three years I'd gone through all the answers—a good career, independence, a productive useful life—but they were someone else's answers. My answer only came to me that morning out in those tobacco fields, and it was her answer, the tobacco girl's—she spoke through me and was me. "I want to love again, I want to give my love to A."

To find it was that simple, to know the thing I'd wanted, the thing my life was crying for, was the same thing I'd wanted when I was that fifteen-year-old girl with Deacon; to know, as she had not, that my boy problem hadn't been the boys, but me; to know that what I'd hated them for taking from me was only what I'd given them and that it wasn't really gone, that I could never lose it, that you never can; to know that love itself, even through the possibility of loss and disappointment, was the thing that had restored me to myself and that the door to fullness had been none other than the problem—I praised God and thanked him for the accident, because it was a gift, and my one thought was that I'd be with him soon, with A., and that whatever we had to face, we would have the comfort of facing it together. I knew he wasn't dead. I chose to know it, and my choice was like a prayer I knew God had no power to deny.

As I climbed back in my car, my hands caked with dirt, the awful pictures stopped, there were no more questions. Let A. ask the questions, I didn't need them anymore, because I finally understood what Mama had known all along, just like Sadie did, that it takes more strength and courage *not* to ask the questions than to ask them. Now I knew it, too, and every woman does. And what men know isn't worth lug tobacco compared to it, not worth the dust down in the bottom of the bale. It's *not* asking the questions, holding the doubts in abeyance, knowing they're there and can't be put away, not finally, not ever, but choosing to live beyond them and to trust that life is good—that's what real wisdom is, as any tobacco girl will tell you. I felt wise, so wise, and strong as train smoke or nine rows of onions, maybe even wise and strong enough to knock some sense into a certain party's head—my party, the one that always made me cry, even after all these years—because the boy was seriously confused on that one point, and I was going to set him straight, if I didn't forget the whole thing in the meantime. I was going to give him a piece of my mind that would black his sweet blue eyes.

I set out following my man, knowing it was going to be different this time, and also knowing why—because I was—and for the last hour of that drive, as the sun rose higher, traveling those small roads where people were walking out barefoot to fetch their morning papers, past open-air vegetable stands where country women were setting out their wares, I knew I couldn't get lost if I tried. I felt like Saturday morning, and I was ready to go out to play.

Two

JANE

I saw the Bentley just as soon as I turned up the drive, sitting right there underneath the porch with the door wide open just like Sadie told me Cary's was the day they found it at the dam. I knew he was alive. As I ran up the steps I passed the rusty hooks the hammock used to swing on. I could almost hear it creaking under us as A. kicked off against the wall to swing us and the windchimes tinkling, but all of it was gone, it was dead silent—just the ocean off across the dune.

The front door was open, too, and inside with the shutters closed it was black as pitch. I fumbled at the light switch and hung my nail on it, but it didn't hurt, not then, and when it came on all the furniture was draped with sheets and there was dust on everything. "A.," I called and went straight to the bedroom. His coat, the one he'd had on that first night at Miss Misha's, was lying on the stripped down mattress. I told myself we'd throw that nasty thing away yet, make a bonfire and drop it right on top. But I didn't touch that coat.

Thinking maybe he was in the gazebo, I went back down the stairs. Climbing the dune the morning sun was in my eyes, floating just above the ridge like a big helium balloon. The sea oats off to either side were thicker than I remembered them, green as the new millet on the road to Mama's, rustling all around me in the wind. I thought of Ruth, following the young men in Boaz's fields, but that was not a comfort. The sandy track between the grass was swept down smooth just like the wind had run a broom across it, so different from the way it looked that summer with all our prints in it—there was only one set now. Realizing they were his, I stopped halfway to the top, out of breath but too nervous to breathe, and shaded my eyes against the sun.

A. wasn't there, but as I climbed the steps I saw his old green bathrobe draped across the bench. I stared at it and then my eye caught something on the beach. A.'s long form lay sprawled at the water's edge, face down, and as I stared a wave slid in around his legs. He didn't move. My hands both went right to my mouth. For a moment I was paralyzed. I just looked like some awful magnet was pulling my eyes. Then I ran.

I knelt, almost afraid to touch him. He was naked except for his boxer shorts. "A.?" I said. I shook his shoulder. "A.?" I said again, *"A.,"* screaming it that time, and suddenly he jolted, kicking out and punching the sand, then sat up blinking bleary startled eyes. "Jesus, Jane," he said, "I wish you wouldn't do that—you scared the shit out of me." He picked a grain of sand off the tip of his tongue and stared at it. I just knelt there, panting, and watched him as he said, "I must have fallen asleep. I was dreaming like a mother." He began briskly massaging his scalp with his fingertips, then looked at me with a wide grin, his hair standing straight up on his head. Not even knowing what I was doing I slapped him hard across the mouth and fell back on my seat and burst out crying. A. blinked and touched his cheek, staring at his fingertips like maybe he was bleeding. "Thanks, I needed that," he said, like the man in the shaving cream commercial, and though he didn't laugh I said, "it's all so damn amusing, isn't it, A.,? It's all just one big joke to you, isn't it, you son of a bitch."

A. stared at me for a long time with a mild face and then stood up and brushed off his boxer shorts. Having recovered from the scare I'd given him, he seemed quite calm, and feeling the backwash, I said, "I thought you were dead," and he said, "I'm sorry I disappointed you—maybe you'd prefer to do the job yourself," and I just howled, I don't know why—I must have been hysterical. When I'd recovered, I said, "seriously, A., when I came through Deep Cove there was this terrible accident and I thought it was you," and he said, "I didn't go through Deep Cove, Jane, I came in the back way," and I said, "well, I didn't know that, A., and it was this Jeep like the one you used to drive," and he said, *"what?"* so forcefully it made me blink my eyes. "A boy and girl?" he asked. I nodded, and he said, "I saw them, Jane, Jesus Christ, I saw them . . . the guy tried to run me off the road as I was coming out of Killdeer . . . they stayed with me for five or ten miles, but I lost them when I took the short-cut around Roanoke Rapids—they didn't . . . ?" and I said, "yes, honey," gravely, and he said, "they both died?" I nodded and he spun around and stared over the water, obviously upset.

I left him alone, then stood up and touched his arm. "I see you had your swim," I said softly, and he turned to me with a dazed expression and said, "what?" and I said, "your swim," and it was a surprise when he clutched me to him and dropped his face into my neck. "Thank you for coming," he whispered, "thank you so much, Jane. I was going to drive back. You may not believe it, but I was—this time I was." I melted toward him. He was shivering slightly, and I said, "come on," and took his hand.

We went back to the gazebo, and I said, "put this on," handing him the green bathrobe. Catching my expression, he thumbed the lapel and said, "remember this?" and I said, "how could I forget?" We held each other's eyes a minute with the ambiguous sweetness of that memory between us, and he said, "it's hardly more than a rag now," and I said, "I'm surprised it hasn't self-destructed," which was a slip. A. didn't miss it.

"What happened last night, A.?" I asked, and he looked away over the water and didn't answer for a long time. "I'm not sure if I can explain it, Jane," he said finally. "You asked me a few days ago what all this Cary business was about . . ." He flashed a look at me, and I said softly, "yesterday, honey," and he said, "yesterday?" I nodded, and he shook his head and sighed. "Right," he said, "right, yesterday." He sank into contemplation over it a moment, then stirred himself and said, "last night driving down here the whole thing played back through my mind, Jane, that whole summer—I figured something out," and I said, "what, honey?" and he said, "I lost Cary because I had to. I don't know why life made it necessary, but it did. Maybe if I'd stayed and faced up to what I did I could have salvaged my friendship with him. Maybe not. I'll never know. But you know what? That wasn't even the point. All these years I thought it was. I thought I knew what my big mistake was, that it was betraying Cary—it seemed so obvious—and so help me God, Jane, it wasn't till this morning at dawn when I was

crossing the Wright Memorial Bridge that it finally hit me that
I'd got the whole thing wrong''—he shook his head—''it wasn't
betraying Cary, it was betraying you, betraying our love—that
was where I lost myself. That truth dropped down on me like a
house of bricks, Jane, because in all that time, all the thousand
ways I'd explained it to myself, that one possibility had never so
much as crossed my mind.''

A. wasn't crying, but I'd started to. ''My love for Cary was
a great thing,'' he said, ''but my love for you was greater, Jane,
and losing him was the price I had to pay for you. And the real
hell of it is, I paid. I paid the fucking price, Jane, I just didn't
have the strength or courage to own the thing I bought. No, life
made me lose Cary, but it didn't make me lose you—that choice
was mine. One act, and I've never been right since. That's what
this whole Cary business has been about, Jane. Something inside me, God knows what, has been shouting, 'wake up, A.!
wake up and smell the fucking coffee,' because what's wrong
in my life now, Jane, started then. It all goes straight back to
that summer. That's where I fucked up and betrayed the only
people I really cared about. Just like my father did. I became a
rubber man, too.'' I hurt for him deeply, but in the fierce hon-
esty of that moment I saw all his fineness rise and felt the stir-
rings of a lover's pride. I knew his anger was a necessary and
purifying thing and let him run with it.

''I'll tell you what happened last night, Jane,'' he said, ''I
remembered who I was''—he met my eyes—''remember A.?''
I felt my eyes grow hot and told him, ''very well.'' He nodded
and said, ''I thought I'd lost him, but I just betrayed him. Because that's something else I figured out last night, Jane—as long
as you're alive there's hope. Anything can happen—look at us.
And that's why what Cary did . . .''—suddenly his face puckered—''that's why it's so very fucking sad, Jane, because there
aren't any second chances when you're dead.'' A tear rolled
down his cheek, and he said, ''I still miss him, Jane, I'll miss
him till the day I die, but last night something broke for me.
I've always felt guilty about Cary, like I was responsible for his
death. I don't feel that anymore. You can't be responsible for
that in someone else. Cary has to take that responsibility back.
He has to carry his just like I have to carry mine.'' A. suddenly
looked away over the water and shouted, ''you hear that, spud?
You have to take it back.'' He banged his fist down on the arm
of the bench, then said, ''ouch,'' and looked at me with a weary

sheepish grin, opening and closing his hand. "In case you hadn't noticed," he said, "I'm losing it," and I smiled at him and said, "somehow I don't think so," and I could see how much that touched him.

We sat there for a long time simply gazing into one another's eyes until a crashing in the sea oats startled us. We both turned to look and a dog—a Golden Retriever pup—burst out, bounding up the gazebo steps without the slightest trace of hesitation. He was sopping wet and had a bandanna tied around his neck and a Frisbee in his mouth. He went straight to A., wiggling and writhing in an unembarrassed need for swift attention, his wagging tail a menace. "Hey, boy," A. said, grinning delightedly, dropping his head to touch the dog's and gripping his ears for steering. "Are you lost?" A. said, and the dog dropped the Frisbee at his feet as though responding, then shook, sending sand and water everywhere. "That's what you want," A. said, reaching for the Frisbee, and as he did the dog playfully re-chomped it, tugging as A. tugged back. "Give me that, slobber-puss," A. laughed, wrestling, and when he finally wrenched the Frisbee free the dog got serious. He sat with tensed ears, regarding A. like an honor student studying his professor. When A. moved the Frisbee the dog's head tracked it at exactly the same speed. I laughed and said, "don't tease him, honey," and A. held the Frisbee near my face, his finger pointing to the name. Moon-Glo. I looked at A. He grinned and shrugged. "You want this, Bigfoot?" he said, and the dog whined with eagerness, his tail beating a tattoo on the floorboards. "Go get it then," A. said, dropping his shoulder like a discus thrower and sending it far out toward the ocean as the dog set out barking with wild happiness.

I watched it sail high in the blue air and as it began to curve back toward the beach I heard the sound of music. I looked and not fifty yards south of us a boy in dark glasses—college age by the look of him, probably on spring break—walked onto the dune shouldering a large boom box which was blasting out beach music—Carolina shag. I looked back at the Frisbee and saw that it was headed straight for him. A. saw it, too, and called out, "yo!" The boy looked up and A. pointed, following the Frisbee with his finger. The boy lifted his free hand and casually caught it as the dog skidded on his forepaws like a baserunner sliding home headfirst. The boy leaned over and scratched his ears— the dog was obviously his. Then he stood up and looked at A.

"Thanks!" he called. A. didn't answer, just raised his hand in a tentative wave, staring with a mesmerized expression.

At that moment a girl trotted up beside him, laughing. She leaned over with her hands on her knees to catch her breath, then stood up and said something to the boy. He nodded and tossed the Frisbee down the beach for the dog who set out after it again, barking with unwearied maniacal joy. The boy turned the music up even louder—it was the Tams, "Be Young, Be Foolish, Be Happy"—resettled it on his shoulder, then put his arm around her waist, and they started off, following the retriever south toward Camelot pier.

A. turned to me with wet bright eyes and said, "the boy's okay, Jane," and I nodded, knowing it was true, crying quiet happy tears myself in a world where magic is still possible. A. reached out impulsively for my hand and pulled me up. I thought he was going to kiss me—it seemed about that time—but instead he said, "do something for me," and I said, "what?" and he said, "that little kickstep in the shag—show me how it goes." I thought he was kidding for a moment, but his face was exasperatingly serious. "Now?" I asked, and he said, "now." Feeling a little shy and self-conscious, I went through it for him, and he said, "no, no, break it down for me," with a furrowed brow. I had to think about it a minute, and then I said, "okay, it's like this, A., follow me." I took his hand and led him through it. "Step, back, one-two-three," I said, "kick—that's right—step, back, one-two-three." A. stopped. "One-two-three," he said, hitting his forehead, "that's what it is?" I nodded and said, "it's just all blurred together," and he said, "Jesus, that's why I never got it—is this right?" I watched him and said, "you've got it baby," and he smiled and took my hands, moving me through it, leading.

> "It's the same old story all over the world,
> Girl needs boy, and boy needs girl . . ."

We danced to their music as it faded on the morning air; and when it was gone we danced to silence, until A. pulled me into his embrace. "I forgot to tell you, Jane," he whispered in my ear, "something else I figured out last night," and I said, "what, honey?" trying to pull away to look at him. He held me fast. "I'm not falling in love with you," he whispered, and I stopped breathing, "because you can't fall into something you never got out of in the first place. I *am* in love with you, it never stopped, Jane. There were others, but it was never the same. The light never changed around their faces like it did around yours, like it is right now. Give me another chance, Jane, I'll try harder this time—I'll try so hard.'' I brushed his hair back off his forehead and said softly, "why do you think I came down here, honey?" and he said, "you'll have to tell me, Jane, because I don't know." I just wiped my nose and smiled as I said, "still so slow," with all my love up in my eyes. He put his face down in my neck and I just held him, stroking his hair and understanding for the first time in my life what it is to be a woman and to run the world so quietly without ever letting on.

Drawing a deep sighing breath, A. looked up and said, "I was dreaming when you woke me up," and I said, "what were you dreaming, honey?" and he said, "that you woke me up and I was alive. Let's celebrate," and I said, "let's," and he said "let's go out dancing and stay out all night long," and I said, "I'd rather come home early and shag a little bit in bed," and he smiled and said, "we'll do that before, we've got all day, tonight I want to stay out late"—his eyes took on a darker shine— "I want to stay a little later at the dance than Cary did," and I said, "I do, too, honey." We began to move again, slowly— step, back, one-two-three—and he reached behind my neck and pulled me down to a deep kiss—his lips were salty from the sea, but his mouth was sweet like I remembered it, just like water from the well—and that was the end of it, and the start of something else.

About the Author

David Payne was born in North Carolina and now lives in New York. His first novel, *Confessions of a Taoist on Wall Street*, received the Houghton Mifflin Literary Fellowship Award. He is presently at work on a new story.

The Undisputed Masters of Contemporary Fiction